David Sallon was born in 1938, and has spent the last fifty years inventing, manufacturing, and selling disposables to a global retail, industrial and medical world. Many of these items are now everyday essentials. His experiences have allowed him to negotiate with multinationals and espouse national trends. His eight children have followed in his tracks, often fighting the establishment with new ideas which benefit mankind.

Ever Young has taken four years to write, and exposes the weaknesses of politicians who, tempted to benefit from their given responsibilities, get drawn into a web of criminal activity with disastrous results. Politics and medicine do in reality combine in a delicate cocktail that must be tempered by legislation and exposed by the press. But who should be in control? Without oversight of a non-governmental public health brains trust, there could be unforeseen consequences, when the fiction of *Ever Young* becomes fact.

Previously published: *Pschatts*, 2012

This book would not have been written without the patience and dedication of my darling wife, Susan, who has added and subtracted mountains of commas, spaces and spellings. At one time, I began to believe that I had a hidden secret morse-coded story. I do hope that you enjoy reading it but at least it is now readable. My sincerest thanks to Stephen Lentin who carefully read and commented on the proof, my grandson Noah Lewis and son Jeremy, for their invaluable contributions in the editing stages of this novel.

This book is partly inspired by reflections on the continuing success of IBM despite their wartime activities.

IBM began operations in 1911 in the US. During the 1930s a subsidiary of IBM named *Deutsche Hollerith Maschinen* became the close collaborators of the German government, and by 1939 the company had achieved a monopoly on punch-cards and data-processing in Germany. Their capacities in large-scale data processing aided the war effort and were integral to the execution of the Nazis' murderous domestic policies.

Their activities included the provision of computing equipment and other hardware to the Nazi government, the issuance of punch-cards for government workers and concentration-camp detainees, and the compilation of lists of dissidents and Jewish, gay and disabled people, to be murdered.

IBM were not alone in their collaboration. Many other companies surviving today both as subsidiaries and under their original names worked to enable the Nazis' programme of violence.

David Sallon

EVER YOUNG

AUSTIN MACAULEY PUBLISHERS™

LONDON • CAMBRIDGE • NEW YORK • SHARJAH

A CIP catalogue record for this title is available from the British Library.

ISBN 9781398499829 (Paperback)
ISBN 9781398499836 (ePub e-book)

www.austinmacauley.com

First Published 2023
Austin Macauley Publishers Ltd®
1 Canada Square
Canary Wharf
London
E14 5AA

Chapter 1

Important Government Announcement

FOR THE ATTENTION OF YOUNG MEN AND WOMEN BETWEEN TWENTY-TWO AND THIRTY YEARS OLD.

Ever Young
Do you want to live a life without fear of illness, or the insecurity of losing your job through the pain of ageing? MILLIONS of people today suffer the humiliation of old age, which robs them of the pleasures of living, and often forces them into early retirement and dependence upon others. Imagine playing tennis, discovering new and exciting technology, TRAVELLING THE WORLD AT NINETY or playing boisterously with your great-grandchildren, without any fear of fragility, at NINETY-FIVE.
This is no longer a dream. The new government-backed Ever Young health scheme offers you this guarantee through the Magnum Health Plan. If you are currently without any serious disability and are between twenty-two and thirty years old, please contact your local medical centre for further information. DON'T MISS this opportunity. It is THE PROMISE OF A LIFETIME.

Jack Branson stood in front of the electron board pondering how this claim could be made. It wasn't as if it was placed on the usual advertisement boards sprinkled along sidewalks pushing the latest cosmetics, foods or movies: the Electron board was reserved only for government announcements and for any new laws initiated by the local or national councils.

Jack was thirty-two years old and six feet tall. He was in perfect health and proud of his athletic body upon which he worked meticulously every day. "So, why thirty?" he muttered to himself. "In any event, it would be interesting to see what this is all about," And since his medical centre was only a few blocks away, he decided to make a quick stop on his way to work.

The Autoplug Medical Centre was divided into four departments, each with their distinctive colours. The Green section, for senior citizens, occupied the largest area. These elderly patients would find a cubicle in which to sit.

Placing both hands onto the electronic plate of the Autoplug, a multitude of tiny needles would identify them and verify their medical history. Upon the screen in front of them a message asked that they wait patiently to see a named doctor, who would have already observed their temperature, pulse and an analysis of their current medical condition and all information relevant to the patient's history.

Accident and Emergency, coloured red, was an open area containing electronic frosted plastic sliding doors with large emergency buttons placed on the sides offering immediate nursing. This section was expanded or contracted according to the season. The vacation time was invariably the busiest for overactive children and sports injuries.

The InfeC department specialised in contagious diseases including the flu, and was coloured black. This area was enclosed at the far end of the centre and was fed a continuous stream of Antiviral Dust blowing through giant aluminium pipes. Once again, the patient would sit in their own cube awaiting their doctor or nurse according to their condition.

And finally, the S.R. Autoplug – for general and minor 'self-repair' ailments – coloured yellow. This was the most popular of all the departments, and considered a substantial benefit, not only to the patient but also to the NHS. Jack meandered towards a yellow pod, sat on the plastic seat in front of the screen closed the curtain, placed both hands on the Autoplug and waited for ten seconds. His name emerged and asked him to confirm that a payment of five pounds could be taken from his registered bank account. He immediately pressed a button to confirm. It was still quite early and the centre was relatively empty. He had often visited the centre just to assure himself of his physical condition, but this time he wanted an understanding in greater detail of what he had read on the Electron.

A holographic image of an attractive young woman appeared from the screen in front of him. His credit card was already recorded and automatically placed a minimum of fifteen minutes. He had seen her before and according to a computer evaluation of his present disposition, her image was selected just in order to create in him a feeling of wellbeing. He could see that she had placed various papers in front of her which she casually glanced at, her blond hair slipping over her eyes as she discretely brushed it back, her unbuttoned white jacket suggested a position of friendly authority. A badge with the name 'Dr Jenkins' served to furnish a proper identity for her.
She was wearing heavily framed glasses, which she slowly removed.

Although he had rarely found it necessary to visit the Autoplug, he was in awe of the software that enabled his life records to be so concise and obviously passed from one medical division to the other. Even childhood illnesses and university quirks that he had discussed with the local doctor. It occurred to him that other facts that may be irrelevant to his current medical condition would be included in the files, for the government had by one means or another accumulated every aspect of his life from salary, education, any investments that he might make and even his political leanings, even his DNA, now all available to him to draw upon from the apps which would analyse and advise him if he so required. But these were fanciful thoughts and since he had nothing to hide anyway, he dismissed them as irrelevant. It had even acquired his parents' physical and financial background in order to validate any advice that would enable it to give a cohesive response to any questions that would be asked.

"Good morning, Jack, thank you for popping in, but I can see from your hands and the notations here that you appear to be in perfect health, so I shall assume that you have something else that you'd like to ask."

"Hello, Doctor," replied Jack, always pleased that such an attractive 'Doctor' had been computerised from his hand check. "I was particularly interested to read about the Magnum Health plan; can you expand a little on this project?"

"Of course, Jack," smiled the Doctor, "I assume that you mean The Ever Young project, but you must know that you would not be eligible for the scheme as you're not within the age bracket at this time."

"Nevertheless, it would be interesting to know some details."

"Certainly," she replied. "The Magnum Health plan selected this particular age variance, since detailed medical studies have proven that between twenty-two and thirty the brain and body begin to reach their zenith, and within this health band we can now stabilise both the mental and physical metabolism by injecting a microchip into the brain that anticipates any pathogens or potential imperfections before they materialise. After thirty years, these pathogens will have already established themselves within even the fittest bodies." She spoke slowly and with a degree of intimacy, and Jack experienced and inexplicable feeling of sexuality towards her as she softened her tone. "You may not be aware of the genetic influences that you are carrying until you are in your forties or even fifties, Jack, but by evaluating your biological history Jack and redirecting any possible future anomalies that you have inherited we can now prove that perfect health can be maintained until one is ninety-five years old. What's more, we would be able to keep a close monitor on each individual in the event that something untoward should occur."

"But surely there must be a benefit to those who are as fit as I am but are just over the set limit," he enquired.

"I am afraid not Jack, the Ever Young project is not only evaluated by ones physical condition, it is simply a matter of how their DNA establishes itself within their metabolism, and at this time we cannot bypass its own time clock which is between twenty-two and thirty years old. But you will have the benefit of your good health as long as you continue to look after yourself, and of course you can visit us as often as you like," she smiled.

Jack could see little benefit in pursuing the subject further and was about to close the conversation with his computerised adviser when it occurred to him that if the 'guarantee' was to ninety-five years old, what would stop this healthy individual living on to any age.

"May I ask one final question Doctor?"

"Of course," she replied, almost seductively. "You still have seven minutes."

"If your chosen ones reach ninety-five in perfect health, do they continue with or without the guarantee?"

"That is an excellent question, Jack. First, I would ask you how many ninety-five year-olds do you know that are in perfect health, or even those in their eighties? The likelihood is that they will struggle with all sorts of difficulties by this time. And most of those that reach the magical age of ninety-five are invariably not even aware of who they are. There are of course exceptions but we are considering the average population…If we can bypass all this suffering and humiliation of old age and reach the age of ninety-five in perfect health, are we not giving them a wonderful gift of living life rather than just existing it?" The image of her face became larger as she stared into the screen.

"But you haven't answered my question Doctor, what happens after ninety-five?"

"Quite simple," she smiled. "The Magnum Health plan lease will come to an end and the recipient will have an opportunity to say farewell to their friends and family totally compos mentis before they pass on."

"You mean you would kill them," replied Jack now quite shocked.

"No, no Jack, please reconsider your words before you make an impulsive remark such as that, I can tell by your hands that you are shocked, but you know Jack that nearly twenty percent of your salary is being poured into the health of this country and over half of that maintains the geriatrics in our country alone. Can you appreciate how much can be saved by giving back the elderly their health during these years, and what can be done with these billions of savings, plus the contribution of these fully able senior citizens. This is a win-win scheme but it needs digesting. We must learn to value healthy living more and, even more so, healthy dying. The Ever Young Magnum scheme must be its spear head especially aligned to the Autoplug, every individual that enrols will be monitored throughout their lives. Nevertheless, I have no doubt that you will be amongst those few that will beat the system, and you know Jack that we will support you to do it."

She now looked at him with such compassion that he found himself thanking her for her apparent affection. But the Doctor was after all a simulated and a brilliant facsimile of what was committed to be his mentor.

He left the centre still in shock. The word KILL kept interfering with his logic, and it took a strong coffee for him to settle down before entering his office.

Jack had become an urbanite. He had taken his degrees in History and English at Birmingham University, and gradually emerged into the business world as a journalist. He was now a lead writer with 'The Sporty', a nationally published magazine appealing to the younger sports enthusiasts and he had become a recognised personality. His enthusiasm for the games and exercise equipment had made him popular with a number of leading manufacturers who would readily give him equipment 'to test' and which he found a use for in his trendy apartment in a salubrious block in Chelsea. His friends were many but most of them were passing ships in the night. During the last two years he discovered in himself a need to be with a more permanent partner than the many young women he met through his work and in bars, and whilst he attempted to retain the exuberance of his student days, he was aware that he was no longer classified as a youngster by his work colleagues and that he was his age, and psychologically beginning to cloak himself accordingly.

The meeting today had stunned him into the realisation that the system was in fact moving him into another age group.

It was now Friday and since Jack was relatively up to date with his submissions he decided to visit his parents. It was easy when they had lived in Islington, but after his father retired some 3 years previous, they sold their house and purchased a delightful cottage in Cornwall which was as far away from London as they could get. His dad was now 60 years old and had enjoyed a senior position with a major finance house in the city. However, it became rapidly clear during the last three years that his style of business was being overtaken by modern technology. Many of his old contacts were diminishing and his style of meeting clients in restaurants and offices was becoming defunct. Communication by emails, face books and a myriad of other electronic bric-a-brac and arm's length negotiations were replacing the old pals act, and the larger deals were being negotiated by a younger and hungrier generation. Golf was being replaced with Squash, Theatre or Opera with football teams. He was becoming a Dinosaur. His Retirement would have been a forced resignation had he not accepted the inevitable with a degree of equanimity.

The journey from London to Lands' End was long and arduous, he had thought of flying, but he would then have had to rent a car from the local airport which would still give him a further two hours of driving. There was no easy way to get to Lands' End or near it. After driving for six hours, he at last saw a sign to Falmouth. It would be another half an hour before he would reach Helston, and now exhausted, he decided to stop at an inn to freshen up, have a quick bite and a coffee. As he appeared to be in such a remote part of the country it occurred to Jack that he might be their only customer, but as he walked through the pub door he was astonished to find a packed room, what was even more surprising was that they were mostly young men and women in their early twenties, smartly dressed as if to a party. They had clearly been enjoying each other's company for some time and a number were so inebriated that they were struggling to stand. A pretty young lady approached Jack with a drunken smile.

"I haven't seen you before—where you from?" she giggled.

Before Jack could reply, her partner who was equally inebriated, put his arm around Jack. "What yer having? Give this man a pint!" he spluttered, and a pint glass was thrust at Jack, who had no option but to accept it. "You can wish me a happy birthday too," he shouted, waving his jug in front of him. The pint now in hand, he was immediately pulled into the throng. He needed something to eat, but there was little opportunity to order food; he gave his name to whoever asked and another pint was ordered; he tried to excuse himself to phone his parents but, yet again, he was waylaid; he managed to buy a bag of crisps, but it was becoming difficult to release himself and eventually resigned himself to his newfound friends, buying an occasional round and allowing their reciprocation.

Another two hours passed before the group began to dissipate, and by this time, Jack was aware that he was in no fit state to drive. At last, he made a call. The telephone was answered by his mother.

"Darling, we were so worried about you! Where are you?" He could hear his father in the background.

"Sorry Mum, I've been delayed," was all he could find to say. "I'll be with you in about an hour."

There were still a few of the party left and his mother caught the gabble of them. "Where are you?" she asked.

"I'm just outside Falmouth but had to stop for a break. Be with you both soon." He said his farewells and hung up, then went into the men's room to splash his face. He had had too much to drink and not enough food, and was aware that he was well over the limit. Jack whispered to himself, "I'd better drive carefully if I don't want to get caught; that would be the last thing I need," and walked out into the night air.

The last twenty miles of his journey sapped every ounce of energy from him. He had wiggled off the road and managed to correct his steering only after grazing a tree. By the time he had arrived at his parents' cottage, he could only stagger to the door. It was now midnight. He kissed his parents, found a settee to lie on, and, without any explanation, fell into a deep sleep.

Jack was awoken at 10.00 am the following morning. He had been lifted into the guest bedroom by his parents with some difficulty. They had removed his shoes but left him in his clothes. It was not the best way to have a reunion, and both Jack and his parents were embarrassed by each other's presence that morning. His head was splitting and, as he gulped down a strong black coffee that was duly presented to him, he tried to explain the evening.

"I didn't even know who they were," he admitted, "just a bunch of youngsters, just a bunch of youngsters," he repeated as he held his head.

"You could have killed someone, driving in your condition," croaked his father, "…and yourself!"

The weekend was spent reminiscing about his childhood. Family photos of various holidays recalling their friends that had long ago passed away were rediscovered. But there was no future injected into their lives and Jack could see that they had, without being aware, gone to Cornwall to die. Not immediately, but in preparation. The cottage seemed to be as a large sarcophagus holding their memorabilia ad infinitum. There were no plans to visit him in London, see a show or even to work again, and they seemed quite content to live on memories of bygone years.

It rained continuously during the weekend, which kept them indoors. Jack's Friday had made a deep impression upon him. His meeting at the Medical Centre had simply offered an education, but the pub incident emphasised how different his needs were from the young men and women that he had been with. He had once been just like them. He enjoyed their company but was now from another world, another generation, he had been there, done that. It was history being repeated. It was as if, taken as a trilogy of events, a strange new slant on his life had underlined his mortality. Their futures would soon be their past too he thought in his morning after state of mind.

The following week was to change his life.

Chapter 2

Miriam Bravotti finished her day with some relief and upon arriving home threw off her shoes and went into the kitchen to make herself a fruit juice. It had been a long day, she sat in her favourite swivel chair, her hand went casually to her memo pad to see what messages she might have received. There were a few cold sales calls, and a message from her brother. She was now the grand old age of twenty-eight, and enjoyed simply being, and being herself, she now lived in a delightful apartment that was bought for her by her brothers who had a number of Italian restaurants throughout London. Her grandparents had come from Italy from peasant beginnings to London after the war. After some time, working twelve hours a day they managed to save enough to open their first ice cream parlour in the Edgware Road in London. For them, it was a tremendous adventure but a great gamble, every penny they had went into the business. But with the flamboyance of Southern Italy, even when it snowed they found a way of enticing their customers to spend a little money. They called their first shop 'Sunshine' and projected its warmth with Italian hospitality to anyone who entered. They had three children but it was Frank their second son and Miriam's father and his young wife who carried the business forward and built up a chain of Sunshine Coffee Shops across the country. As the years passed the business was passed onto Miriam's three brothers and sister who expanded the business into restaurants. The oldest was Maria, who had three children but had little interest in the business. Miriam was the baby of the family and her relationship with them was that of uncles and aunts. She had more in common with their children.

Her parents had now retired due to Frank's health but the boys ensured that they were both kept up to date with the day to day affairs of their 'Papa and Mamma's baby.' Miriam loved her parents for what they were, for she had never really known them when they were in full flight and had little knowledge of the joys and challenges that they or her grandparents must have experienced over the years. She allowed herself to imagine that her life would always be as secure as it was now, and found little reason to enquire any more deeply of their trial and tribulations other than through light conversation.

She had taken full advantage of a good education which included a Masters in Maths allowing her to add MSc. to her name. A further two years committed her to acquire PhD on the evolution of computers. Her family nicknamed her

'The little genius', which she thought very amusing as none of her siblings went through the more rigorous educational system. During the holidays, she would occasionally help out in the restaurants which was fun, but had no interest of following her brothers into the business.

She at last left university equipped with as much academia as she felt was necessary, it was time to get a job that would satisfy her and allow her to find a routine but not lose sight of her dedicated subject. One morning whilst having a coffee she noticed and advert in the Times for postgraduates to work with the Spoken Arrow Group. The position advertised required relatively low qualifications and certainly did not justify her degrees, but since she had never had any job of consequence it seemed an opportunity to dip in at the shallow end of employment and find a routine. She replied to a box number and in her naivety she mentioned her qualifications including her Masters and a PhD on the subject of computers at Oxford University. She was rather surprised to receive by return email, a polite rejection for the position applied for but suggesting an interview to discuss other possibilities.

Miriam was delighted, for she was at last faced with a reality of presenting herself to a potential employer, and free of inhibition she would have been happy to accept even a menial position and would at last be able to boast to her parents that she had a job. She replied immediately by email and was given an appointment for the following week with Mr Theodore Jacobs the UK Group General Manager of Sales. Knowing the size of the company with branches throughout the UK she was rather surprised to have a response from one so high in status. Spoken Arrow was considered to be the world leader in computers and known internationally for their research. In fact, Miriam had noted their successes in her studies and felt that it would be interesting to see them in operation at the 'coal face' working incognito. The day before her interview she decided to pop into the Regent St branch, which was buzzing. She was curious to see how the sales staff presented themselves. Feigning ignorance she allowed herself to be given a sales pitch for one of their latest computers, however the young salesgirl knew very little and passed her over to a more senior salesperson. It was surprising how little he knew of the machine's potential but decided to allow them both to babble on for a while. Nevertheless she took their literature and read up on its possibilities ready for her meeting the following day.

She pondered on whether she should dress more formally for the interview after all it would probably be a sales position on the shop floor but decided to present herself in the best light. She had often found her good looks a double-edged sword, just under 5ft 9" and slim with a skin tone that suggested a Mediterranean background, she found serious conversation with men often leaned towards flirtation and women rather more protective than she cared for, nevertheless this was to be a formal interview and so met the challenge with a positive approach. The appointment was to be at the Regent St branch but announcing her name at the reception she was immediately whisked up to the 4th floor.

Theodore Jacobs had in front of him a thick bound thesis titled The Evolution and Future Progression of the Computer and its Global Reliance. Immediately Miriam entered she recognised her work and was taken aback. He noticed her reaction and smiled.

Theodore was in his late thirties, wearing a tee shirt and jeans. "You should not be surprised, Miriam, that I purloined your work. It's not often I have an opportunity to interview a professor. Especially a young one. I was of course wondering why you should even respond to our student advertisement?"

"Well, you should know that I have never actually worked for anyone other than my own family, who have restaurants, so it seemed to me rather unfair to any future employers if I were to impose myself until I found a routine. I'm quite happy, Mr Jacobs, for anything within your organisation. Believe me. I'm not proud."

"Firstly, if anything, it is I who should address you formally, but I'm Theo to everyone here, which I hope might include you, Miriam. We have a position within this particular branch, which is the shop window of our four hundred stores here in the UK to oversee our overseers. The front line of our salespeople are students with a certain nous, they are guided by supervisors, who in turn look towards a more sophisticated explanation of how things work, and what we could stretch our machines to really do. Most of the computers we sell are far more sophisticated than are initially required, and only by showing a captive buyer their full potential can we move forward with them and not leave them behind. The philosophy of Spoken Arrow is not simply to fill a need. We have to create a need and persuade the public's deeper understanding of this amazing invention. Our brain is desperately underused, and the computer is our key to its door."

"I seem to recall writing something like that," she mused. "You have obviously been doing your homework, Theo. What and how might you propose to use me? I shall place myself at your disposal."

They spoke of many things and their minds locked onto a myriad of subjects. She saw a photo of his wife and child, he noted that she had no rings, nothing was said but understood and both recognized and protected their positions.

***

Miriam soon settled into the position of an oracle and mentor to department heads, she acquired an assistant and swiftly became an integral part of the Spoken Arrow's training essentials. She developed a free and easy style to discover a myriad of opportunities that the computers were capable of and translated them into the pragmatics of everyday lives. She had now been with the company for two years, and enjoyed a degree of financial independence that gave her great pleasure.

Her apartment, although relatively small was designed with Italian flourish. Abstract and impressionist paintings and a few small sculptures were displayed amongst a well-stocked bookcase that took over an entire wall and brought the apartment to life. The large windows were dressed with floor to ceiling voile, emphasising her femininity. She had a few friends, both men and women, but was aloof around close relations.

Returning from work she switched on the TV and directed her remote to the news. "What do these people think we are?" she spoke out loud as she watched adverts seemingly targeting idiots, and was about to switch over to one of her favourite soaps when a government announcement caught her attention. "DO YOU WANT TO LIVE A LIFE WITHOUT FEAR OF ILLNESS?" The voice was strong, positive, almost instructive. It reminded her of her father, and she listened to the ad which took rather longer than the usual thirty second spots. She was particularly taken with a GUARANTEE OF GOOD HEALTH UNTIL 95 YEARS OLD. IF YOU ARE BETWEEN 22 AND 30 YEARS OLD, WHY NOT POP INTO YOUR LOCAL HEALTH CENTRE FOR MORE INFORMATION. She froze the announcement, recorded it and transferred it over to her computer. Switching off the TV she heard it again.

It was a strange claim and had it not been a government announcement she would have seen it as yet another vacuous leader line, but such a comment from a bona fide source justified following up. She made herself a snack and decided to visit her local medical centre which was open till 9.00 pm and only a 15minute walk.

There were a number of elderly patients waiting at the green section queueing for a pod, but she went directly to the Autoplug and took a seat in an enclosure. Placing her hands on the Plate in front of her and pressed the interview button. Within seconds, her favourite doctor appeared and brought up a clock in the corner with fifteen minutes recorded and her account diminished by five pounds.

Her doctor appeared smiling. "Hello, Miriam. I haven't seen you for some time – I don't have to ask you if you are well, but you do seem to be a little tired."

Miriam had visited the centre from time to time mostly for advice, and even occasionally to confess her indiscretions, she found it particularly therapeutic to discuss with her charming computerised doctor who was totally non-judgemental and seemed to have an endless knowledge of how she should direct her desires both sexual and pragmatic.

He appeared to be in his late thirties and bore a badge with the name Dr Prado. His Mediterranean manner and disposition gave her a feeling of her roots, which she greatly appreciated. It was better and less inhibiting than her visits to her church or even her flesh and blood doctor, and she spoke with her hologram as a friend, without inhibition, knowing that whatever she told him was solely between her and the machine.

"Hello doctor, yes I've had a busy day but it's good to see you looking so well." She knew that this was a pointless comment but it bonded her to him as a child would talk to her doll. "I saw an advertisement on the TV this evening relating to Magnum Heath Plan, and I'm wondering if you could give me a little more information."

The Doctor smiled showing perfectly white even teeth almost florescent against a light suntan. "It seems to me that you Miriam are an ideal candidate for this plan, but that is only my opinion and you need to consider what I tell you with an independent mind. First I should tell you that Ever Young is owned by Magnum as is the Autoplug so you need not have any fears of indiscretions being revealed. You probably know that only those between twenty-two and thirty are eligible, I am informing you of this knowing that you can be included, but any other person that you have a relationship with should realise that you would have the advantage on them should they not wish or would be unable to be included." He smiled as it was clear that he was referring a previous encounter that she had discussed in some detail and certainly more than she would have done to her priest.

"I am free as a bird at the moment, doctor, but you make it sound very mysterious. I'm all ears!" replied Miriam.

The doctor explained in detail the implications that related to the Ever Young Health Plan, with all its guarantees and assurances relating to unexpected problems such as broken bones etc. "These would of course be incremental and priority treatment is given to those who joined the scheme. The program would ensure that you would be in perfect health until you were ninety-five years old, and at that point we would terminate the agreement."

"This sounds wonderful, doctor, but what's the catch, there must be something more otherwise you could just as well make it compulsory."

"I haven't finished yet," replied the doctor feigning a teacher's annoyance. "First of all let me tell you the benefits to the country, and I'll show you a graph of the current costs and looking at the next 50 years of the bankrupting monies that the economy will have to find to maintain the elderly, it is therefore imperative for us to improve their health whilst they are alive, and the Ever Young plan have found it. We are not advocating that the elderly should live longer, what we are stating with Ever Young is that they will live a healthier and full life until ninety-five before they say farewell to their family and friends in perfect health. You can probably already see how your own family are slowly degenerating, I know this may sound cruel but we are, that is, all humans are, on a wheel of life which must come to an end at some time. We are now in an era that will allow us to control our lives and ultimately our deaths, and unless we take advantage of this amazing technology and temper it to our needs, current statistics show the demise of our world as we know it. I can also confirm that every time you speak with me your intelligence quota is re-evaluated, if that's an added comfort." His charm at this point broke the tension that Miriam was feeling.

"Wow, that is something to digest," said Miriam. "I'm not sure how my priest would take this plan, but I am seriously going to consider it. Do you think I should speak with my parents?"

"Why not, they're progressive thinkers and their thoughts would be a considerable help, so, why not!"

Miriam thanked her doctor said good night and switched off.

Returning to her apartment she tapped in 'Ever Young' into her computer. She scrolled down to discover the finite details of how it could alter her life, and its possible consequences.

**

EVER YOUNG 351 CLINICS. What you can expect when receiving the Ever Young 351.

Under the authorisation of the Health Minister Mr Brendon Tann, Magnum has been offered the facility of all the NHS Teaching hospitals throughout the UK to allocate both a clinical space and operating time plus a six-bed ward to allow a one-night stay if required.

The operation itself will take no more than thirty-five minutes, but each patient will respond differently to the 351 chip installation which would be placed by injection into the hippocampus which is within the frontal portion of the skull. Most patients would be allowed home after the process. In practice, a trained general practitioner would be sufficiently competent to perform the task which would be given by injection. However it is suggested that your doctor recommends to you a neurologist if you have any questions before the procedure.

It is to be expected that the body will react to what is considered an alien element entering the system, it is likened to adjusting a radio program: the end result is much greater clarity but the program has to be adjusted to fit the wavelength. In fact, this will be concurrently controlled by the Magnum Empto Computer which stabilises and balances the body working with the unique wavelength of each individual.

The metabolism and DNA will be fully attuned to your new condition within 48 hours and will immediately begin to resist most of the ailments that you may have inherited from your forebears. There are no side effects other than positive ones.

By registering with the government program you will be given PRIVILEGED tax benefits thanks to anticipated government savings. You would also receive premium health service for your family and reduced insurance contributions. A Magnumite certification also makes better candidates for positions of responsibility.

We work under the auspices of Cambridge University and with the cooperation of three other universities: Edinburgh, University College London and Manchester. Each was charged with selecting 3,000 students between 22 and 23 years old to be given IQ tests prior to acquiring the Ever Young injection and subsequently two years after. At the outset of the test the average IQ of the 9,000 students was 107. Year 2, it was 110; and Year 3, 112. There was a significant improvement in ability to absorb knowledge as a result of Ever Young.

The Ever Young 351 project has been thoroughly tested and is perfectly safe. It will revitalise cells and banish all defective DNA accumulated from countless generations. You should never require medical treatment for inherited malfunctions and your life span will be assured until the age of ninety-five, in good health.

Ever Young and the Autoplug were conceived by Cambridge University and refined and patented by Magnum who are the foremost manufacturers of computers in the world. What better assurance can you have?

EVER YOUNG IS THE MOST PROGRESSIVE MEDICAL DEVELOPMENT EVER TO BE PRESENTED TO THE WORLD.

We wish you many healthy and happy years ahead. MLH – Magnum Loves Humanity

REGISTER TODAY. *We anticipate a substantial demand. Expected waiting time 8 – 12 weeks from application.*

***

What an interesting concept, she thought. *It would be interesting to hear my parents take on it.*

She had planned to meet with both her parents that week anyway, but as she was alone at this time it seemed a good idea to steal a supper with them. Her mother's food would only be criticised by her family at the risk of death, and her traditional menus were treats that one only declined for fear of exploding. Miriam had a been living away from home long enough to appreciate anything that was offered.

Her Papa was out that evening and it was a great pleasure to have her mother's full attention, and although the hair was now grey and she had gained rather more weight than might be healthy, she retained a sparkle in her eye and a joie de vivre that was contagious. They sat by the dining table, their hands entwined across its surface.

"Mamma, I need your advice on an important matter, and before you start worrying, everything is good." Miriam smiled to see her mother relax. "You may not have noticed the government notice recently advertised on the TV called 'Ever Young'."

"No, my darling, I haven't. What is it?"

"It's an offer that is directed at young adults only between twenty-two and thirty. It is a rather bizarre concept so I decided to check it out with my doctor at the medical centre."

"What, you took advice from a computer doctor, it's better that you came to me too, tell me what you want to know Miri."

It was warming to see her mother's Italian ways even though she had been in the UK all of her life, and Miriam wondered if she would inherit them at a certain age. Maybe it was genetic, she thought. She described the scheme in detail, but leaving the conclusion open for her mother to pick up. For she knew that she would.

"Perfect health at ninety-five, so what can be so bad at that, I could certainly get rid of my rheumatism and I'm only sixty-eight," proclaimed her Mamma. "So, what's the catch? Whatcha gonna do with a healthy ninety-five-year-old? Without this guarantee, they'd live forever on the health service I guess," she chuckled.

"That is the nub of the whole plan Mamma, you've hit it on the head," proclaimed Miriam. "In my doctor's words, they would say goodbye to their friends and family with a smile on their faces."

"And POOF – they would give themselves to heaven," her mother concluded. "Listen to me, the idea of a man or a woman's right to extend life seems very reasonable, but it's only God that can take it away, I think that the whole concept is immoral, it's worse than euthanasia. At least euthanasia you're ill when you die. If you were to write to the pope he would say the same, the next thing will be to cook and eat the HEALTHY dead," she stood up and was now waving her arms. "If the government said we could, would that be acceptable too? We have a choice on how to live Miri, and the way we do it will certainly reflect on the way and when we die, so it's in our own hands, and we don't need a chip in our brain to regulate us, it's up to us."

"You would be right Mamma if we did something about our lifestyles, but it's blatantly obvious that our modern society is totally without any self-control or morals, in fact we need a government to tell us what we're doing wrong, and history has not taught us anything other than technology, so what's the alternative?" her words were coming slower than her thoughts and she cogitated before continuing. "If we were to believe that pills, operations and psychoanalysis will help us live longer and happier lives then why is it not working? I know why you have rheumatism, I know why Poppa has a weak heart, and I guess so do you, but I can't see either of you doing exercises or changing your diets, and even knowing the effect on your lives you haven't made any attempt to rectify or alter the actions that cause these things."

Her mother sat now with her hands in her lap contemplating Miriam's response. She knew her mother too well to believe that she had won the argument on round one, and the second round would invariably commence once she had gathered her thoughts.

"Do you want coffee?" And without waiting for an answer poured two cups from the cafetiere and slid a small plate of biscuits over to Miriam. So clever, thought Miri, and so divisive. It was a way that her mother would hold onto the initiative – as she would change her tack the next round would commence.

"You and I have spoken many times over the years on the meaning of life and our purpose here, but the subject can have no meaning unless its placed in context with our belief in an afterlife, and even though we have no understanding of what that really means since our little brains can't begin to understand what happens after we die, and so the modern thinker might say, well if it's not proven it doesn't exist. But I for one am not so clever as to outwit nature. There are powers beyond our comprehension that even scientists of today acknowledge are beyond our understanding. We are born, we live and we die, that's the pattern, but some of our greatest thinkers died in their thirties or forties, Mozart, Shakespeare. Alexander the Great was only twenty-eight when he died yet he had conquered half the known world. It's a recognised fact that we are not as productive when we age, so why extend this non-productivity? It's egotistical to imagine that we should give the world more just because we live longer. Have a biscuit Miri, before I eat them all."

Miriam smiled and kissed her Mamma. Here was a woman whose education was minimal and yet could offer profundities that could compare with Freud. Her arguments did not involve economics or population control, hers were on morality, spirituality and eternity which were difficult to dispute. There was little point in pursuing the subject with her at this stage unless her father was involved, for his opinion might influence, and only might alter her mother's mind.

The evening with her mother made a deep impression on her, but her love for her and her home had a place in her mind of the yesterdays of her life, both grandparents and parents had once been the Alexander's but had passed on the batons to their children. It was a need rather than a choice, and a recognition that they should concede the fast lane to the next generation. She saw how her mother was fighting to retain her energy and vivacity for life which would no doubt slowly diminish. Nevertheless the mind was still razor sharp, and in this respect Miriam took some satisfaction that her mamma had the last word.

Being the youngest of the family presented challenges that became more apparent as she grew older, for she found herself treading the same paths of evolution as her siblings, and it seemed that whatever she did would be in some way a carbon copy of their lives—she would eventually marry, have kids, go on holidays as they did, go to work come home…go to work…and on and on, as if on an escalator, and slowly but surely become the grandparents to their children even before they took the title formally. There had to be more to life than simply existing before time ran out. She considered that any adventure that she might plan would reflect on an existing commitment and would be metered out according to someone else's convenience, either company, partner or children. She needed time, and time to do what she wanted. But what did she want?

***

It would be another busy day. The Regent Street branch of Spoken Arrow was already packed with youngsters looking to update their existing tablets with the latest form of communication and entertainment. Miriam had been given the responsibility of the training department which necessitated overseeing twenty senior trainers across the country, they would in turn guide the young salespeople that were technically orientated but generally students who would be supplementing their frugal allowances. Any enquiries that they could not answer would pass to the trainers who were invariably post grads and eventually be referred to her. She was good at the job and respected by her team, but it was a position that all previous holders of her position lasted no more than six months before throwing in the towel and was without doubt one of the most demanding jobs in the company. The store opened at 8.45 am and as she arrived outside the premises at 8.30 am she stood still, took a deep breath, straightened herself and marched into the fray.

Grabbing a quick coffee from the machine she placed herself in position and switched her Tablet on. Her first message came surprisingly from Head office in the USA. It was most unusual to receive anything directly from LA as the UK head offices generally were the inter-communicators for their four hundred branches. However, this message was sent directly from the International Head of Marketing and Vice president Martin Moran. Addressing her by her first name he informed her that as the company had received such glowing reports of her skills, they considered her to have the ability to assist them in their drive to bring to the global markets innovative products that would continue to improve the world. "We have watched you with great interest for some time Miriam and bearing in mind our own needs, we would like to invite you to LA and to immerse you in our future plans. We believe that you have a great future with us, provided of course you are willing to be involved, may I suggest that you talk with your colleague Julian who will have a very good understanding of our offer to you."

"Your thoughts would be greatly appreciated. Congratulations, Martin Moran."

By the time she had digested the email she already had ten enquiries, without any understanding of the email's content she returned to the floor with a very positive bounce in her walk.

At last, there was a lull and Miriam meandered towards the staff restaurant and reread the message three times and its possible implications.

A sacrosanct ruling in the company demanded that all employees should take a lunch break of at least forty-five minutes. This was to ensure that concentration levels would 'reenergise' the mind and allow them to have a clear understanding of their given workload. To facilitate this demand free vegetarian meals were provided with soft background music. Settees and armchairs with coffee tables or small tables for two were spread out on the 3rd floor. A small meditation room with scattered cushions punctuated the point. Although there were no restrictions on sound levels, the atmosphere was that of a library rather than a restaurant. Whist a few members of the staff might have appeared a little cynical of the company's bohemian approach, the main body of workers appreciated its ambiance and took advantage of a little peace before being swallowed and regurgitated by their eager young customers. From the eighty floor assistants, only one of them was over twenty years old, and it was evident that the entire momentum of the organisation was directed towards the young.

She often used some of her lunch break to talk with her colleague, she would have enjoyed his company on a more personal level but as he was married she thought it advisable to stay at arm's length. The line between flirtation and friendship was a little difficult to judge, but both realised the dangers of any temptations and its consequences.

Miriam had met his young wife and liked her, in fact they bore a close resemblance to one another. Theodore Jacobs had joined Spoken Arrow over seven years ago, it was his first job after leaving college. He had a Mensa IQ but had learned the art of how to pass on his knowledge in a manner that those with lesser abilities would understand. Theo had been given the opportunity to accept a position at the HQ in California but refused on the basis that he had domestic obligations such as his wife's pregnancy. She was only two months gone at that time and no one had been told, not even their parents, however, he had no option but to inform HQ the truth as a lesser excuse to refuse would have seemed unworthy, besides, he enjoyed living in the UK. He greeted Miriam as a friend, her job had evolved beyond that which he had originally envisaged and considered their status as equals.

"Miri, congratulations, I knew all about it as it was me that put your name forward. They knew who you were of course, and it was unnecessary to interview you as they had studied you doing your job."

"But how can that be, I can't recall anyone spying in the branch?"

"Come on, Miri, surely you must be aware of the micro cameras – they're everywhere!" said Theo.

"I've seen them of course, but I assumed that they were simply for internal security."

"This store is totally wired, directly hooked up to our central computers, and can be seen in LA as if we were around the corner… not even round the corner, next to you. They can home in on conversations, look at the dilation of your eyes and even know when you're talking rubbish to a customer. They are virtually in your soul whilst you are in the store…that's how they know who you are," he smiled. "But you don't have to worry in this office, as it's the only spot where we're not bugged. Now I can tell you my little secret: Angie's pregnant again."

"Wow" was all that she could find to say. And after a few seconds opened her arms to hug him. "It seems that this is wonderful news for both of us, but do you think that I should accept, after all I might not be posted back here when I return?"

"If you return," he replied. "But you'd be crazy not to go, but you'll be sorely missed." She smiled and kissed his cheek.

"On another, but possibly related subject Theo, what do you know about The Ever Young Health Scheme."

"Ah, well that is an interesting one, I'm not sure but I believe that Spoken Arrow had an interest in the project. They've been working on the areas of the medical market for some time. I have no idea to what extent, it might well be that the new model will have some health reference classification, but if I hear anything regarding that I'll let you know. When you go there, no doubt they'll give you the total picture and hopefully you will be able to tell me."

"Only, I was thinking of joining the Ever Young scheme, but there are several questions that are worrying me. My doctor explained that they would implant a chip that would modulate any possible imbalances to the metabolism which makes sense, but I would not like to think that there are external controls that might come into play."

"I really don't imagine that anything like that would happen," he replied "And thinking about it, it's a little surprising to me that Spoken Arrow haven't hit the medical scene yet, Magnum's Autoplug have really taken the market, but who knows, we're working for a great company and no doubt they'll surprise us. At any rate we're both on the same page, but promise me that if you decide to take up their offer you'll keep in touch."

"That's a promise," she replied affectionately.

Chapter 3
Brenekov

The Brenekov Brothers had been on the Metropolitan Police lists for a number of years. Both Peter and William were professional gangsters and involved in a wide range of activities from drugs, prostitution, protection rackets and grand scale larceny. They had alternatively done time, each one maintaining continuity of their activities whilst the other served their sentence. It was the risks and dangers involved, and particularly the pleasure of outsmarting the law that motivated them, for they had accumulated sufficient wealth to retire.

Both were married but their different choice of wives influenced their approach to bringing up their children. Pete who was now in his late 50s and the younger had two children, a boy and a girl. Joe, who was now twenty-five and was already known to the courts as his father's son. He had been lucky to avoid a sentence for drug dealing, but was on their books. It was fortunate for him that his father found the right palms to grease. He was in awe of his dad and could not wait to inherit the reigns of the family 'business'. His sister, now a platinum blond and mini skirted, enjoyed the monies splashed around, and intimately knew a few of the Brenekov gang. Neither had been encouraged by their parents to further their education and lived for the moment. Money could buy anything they wanted and their needs seemed unquenchable. A Villa in Spain with a resident staff, various vacations in five-star hotels, casinos, flamboyant sports cars, jewellery and anything that caught their eye.

William, or Bill as he was known, had three daughters and were strongly influenced by their mother who ensured that they had a good education and managed to enrol them into private schools and onto subsequent universities. His oldest daughter studied law and hoped to become a barrister, she registered under a nom de plume of Victoria Blume. Their father thought of her defending or protecting the family's interests gave him some pleasure.

Bill was approaching his sixtieth birthday and was becoming a little tired, Controlled crime was now more technical, and strong-arm tactics were being replaced with sophisticated cyber-based scams which gave massive returns, but it was well above his head and in truth not as satisfying. The irony was that both brothers' intelligence and dynamism would probably have given them a successful career in a legitimate business without the need to place themselves or their families at risk.

They rarely kept their 'staff' for more than a year for obvious reasons, and made sure that the conceptual plans for any job would be kept within a tight family circle. But working for the Brenekovs had a certain status within criminal circles and any man who found himself in jail gained a certain kudos by claiming that they had at some time been part of the Brenekov team, for it was rarely a Brenekov job that brought them to their cell.

It was not unusual for families within a business to have disagreements and often part of its evolution. But this was not a normal business and it was becoming obvious to the family and particularly Joe's father that Joe wanted to replace the more lethargic attitude of his uncle and at least share and ultimately take complete control of the 'business'. Even Joe's mother believed him to be too impetuous and irrational and felt that her boy was not yet equal to his mentors and certainly not ready to take the reins. One mistake would destroy their fragile security which they were prepared to live with, and by meticulous planning each job, and discussing the finite details they had managed to beat the law most of the time. In effect, they were rather more selective with the jobs that they were offered than Joe liked.

Joe's strong cockney accent aligned to a rather overbearing confidence demanded attention from those who met him, His brash manner was compounded by his height and weight. His eating habits were clearly reflected in his waistline for he weighed in at over eighteen stone and was six feet three inches tall. His impeccably tailored three-piece suits, double cuffed shirts and quite visible gold cuff links completed a formidable image and it was obvious that one would not want to disagree with him without consequences. He proved his strength at the gym once a week working on weights which gave him the muscle that he considered a major asset.

Joe visited his medical centre on the first Monday of each month to review his health and today he sat with his 'doctor' who had been imaged to him as an elderly white haired and no nonsense professional and would answer his questions briskly with military authority. Certainly not of the disposition that Joe would have ever experienced at home.

He placed his hands on the Plate and within seconds Doctor Jakofski appeared. The lined face and his Trotskyite beard gave him a degree of authority, and Joe felt comfortable in his computerised presence.

"Good to see you again Joe, how are things with you," the doctor had been given a slight Mid European accent which reminded Joe of his Grandpa who he remembered from when he was five or six. "I can see you haven't lost any weight yet, it's not that important that you should do so as long as you keep burning calories. Your metabolism seems to read OK, Joe, but I suggest that you eat less sugary substances if you want to stay fit. You seem to be heading for an age 70 plus or minus but according to the age barometer, Joe, you will start running into trouble when you're around sixty-four. It could be said that you are a disaster waiting to happen."

"How do you know that, doc?" replied Joe angrily.

"Just look at your own family Joe, you're not doing anything different from their way of life are you, so why should you be other than theirs. You are the sum total of your parents and their parents, and if you abuse your body as they did, what do you expect."

Joe said nothing for a long minute. He was taken aback by the unforgiving comments of his mentor, and was at a loss for words. What particularly concerned him was the intimate knowledge that his Doc appeared to have of his family.

"Have you heard of the Ever Young Scheme," asked the doctor in a more intimate manner. "I could explain it to you now Joe, but I think it would be better for you to read about it yourself and then have a word with me. You will find it most interesting. I am printing it out for you. It's easy to read," he said a little condescendingly, "but it may just be what you are looking for."

"I'm not looking for anything Doc. I'm fine," stated Joe rather belligerently.

"Just read it and let me know your thoughts, it is a serious option and you will benefit from it OK." It was always astonishing to Joe how he could be so persuaded by this computerised man, but whenever he confronted him, on relationships or various inadequacies admitted within the Pod and sometimes in a whisper, he always felt better upon leaving. "OK Doc. And thanks." He switched off and took the notes that were already printed out with a list of vitamins recommended.

***

The Brenekov residences were the last two properties within a cul-de-sac situated in Streatham a once salubrious part of South London. The Brenekov brothers had spent a considerable sum reconstructing the mansions to retain the original Edwardian status but added every modern convenience that their wives insisted upon. The buildings were secured and surrounded by sharply pointed railings and an entry phone. Once past the electronic gate a short drive would lead to a treble garage on the side, and main doors that were framed by a portico supported by two imitation Roman columns. The two buildings had been extensively reconstructed, and each converted into three spacious apartments on the first, second and third floors. The ground floor had various doors but were not allocated to the living quarters, and used as meeting rooms. In the foyer as if laid out as a waiting room were two leather armchairs, a settee and a circular coffee table on which stood a bronze Rodin bust, that is until one touched it to discover that it was resin. A large scenic painting of mountains possibly somewhere in Russia dominated the wall. Peter Brenekov took the first floor and their two children now occupied the other two apartments. A large Crystal chandelier dominated the entire area. It was obvious even to those unaware of the resident's notoriety that the buildings could be well defended against an army of intruders. William's apartment, was rather more sedate than his brother's and designed to his wife's taste, but their close proximity obliged the two women of the family to harmonise their respective interiors where necessary. It was well known that they did not particularly like one another, but for the sake of peace they were prepared to acknowledge each other's idiosyncrasies and values.

Joe parked his Porsche and went straight to his apartment, he would usually call in on his parents, particularly to see his mother and either invite himself to a meal that she was invariably cooking, or raid the fridge. There was hardly a day that passed when he would not clash with his father, but this evening he had found his meeting at the medical centre disturbing. He had imagined himself to be immortal, above fallibility and capable of infinite possibilities, but to be told that his years were to be limited and compromised by deteriorating health, dented his ego. He saw himself as the Superman of the family. The world was his oyster and he would take it and crush it at will. He had once been told that he had psychopathic tendencies, and after looking up its implications and discovered who else had also been labelled, such as Napoleon, Hitler or Stalin he saw it as a compliment. And now to be told that he was 'terminal' waiting to slowly diminish, shattered the illusions of himself.

Pouring himself a large scotch and flopping into an armchair he opened the envelope marked 'EVER YOUNG'.

Joe read the contents twice to absorb its possible implications, it seemed to him that he had nothing to lose, after all none of his family had ever reached the age of ninety-five, certainly his parents didn't look like they would get there, nor his uncle. He looked on the web to see what sort of assurances would be given and how it actually worked.

The Ever Young Health Plan

For the personal attention of Joseph Brenekov. Please read carefully.

Dear Joe,

Welcome to the Ever Young health plan in conjunction with the Magnum medical Laboratories.

***

He was obliged to read the information three times before he mastered its implications.

It concluded:

It has been the dream of civilised societies for centuries to eliminate pain and suffering and prolong life without the fear of living in permanent discomfort, especially during the latter years. You have been advised by your doctor that you will begin to decline in health and be prone to a number of ailments whilst you in your early fifties. The Ever Young Health Plan will, without doubt reverse your present fate.

As a Magnumite you can expect to enjoy your life unencumbered by bad health until you are ninety-five years old when an optional facility will be made available at one of our UK EVER YOUNG locations to gather, in perfect health your loved ones for a farewell parting. Casting his eye over the remaining pages he read with a smile:

The EVER YOUNG HEALTH SCHEME IS DESIGNED TO GIVE YOU THE QUALITY OF LIFE THAT YOU DESERVE. IT IS A WIN-WIN PLAN.

A profound feeling of his mortality overcame him. He poured himself another Scotch and considered his position, he felt that he might be getting another migraine. How he hated this pain. He hoped this may not be on the Ever Young list of disclaimers, and wondered if he should even mention it, would they check his Autoplug doctor?

It was certainly depressing. It was only three weeks ago that in the middle of a truck heist which contained hundreds of fur skins being shipped from Canada and a job that he was to oversee.

He had three good men with him who were supposed to be under his instruction, but the migraine hit him so fast he had to lay down in his car for two hours whilst the men tied the driver up and drove off with the truck, leaving him on the roadside to find his way home. Even worse, the idiots left the man only about fifty metres from his own vehicle. Very embarrassing. As it happened it was a contractual job for the importer of the skins who was based in Sunderland. His clients would make an immediate insurance claim, the Brenekovs would warehouse the skins until the claim was proven. Once the client was paid, Brenekov would return the goods and receive ten percent of the claim. One hundred and fifty thousand pounds' commission, local and easy. This was a regular formula and as the Brenekov operation did not need to hawk the goods about, sometimes the driver was involved too for a small cut. It was easy money. "But what sort of person do I really want to be," he mumbled to himself. "These little jobs are great, but there are bigger fish to fry." He was particularly keen on Protection, but drugs certainly could generate big bucks, he thought. Not enough hours in the day, we need good men who would control the various divisions, this is how the Mafia do it, the boss isn't running around like a blue-arsed fly like we're doing, he thought. "Delegation with targets based on bottom line profits, like a regular business, otherwise I'll end up like my uncle."

"I want power, and I want to control my future, not be at the beck and call of my family forever. And now I'm told that I can become a vegetable before I even reach my peak, or take this chip and be superhuman – I'll make an appointment to do this thing. Ever Young... yes! Yes!"

Chapter 4

Minister of Health Henry Hines

Henry Hines was now the newly appointed Minister of Health. His predecessor Brendon Tann had been Health Minister for the last four years, he retired on health grounds and although Hines was prepped by him, their relationship was quite acrimonious. Nevertheless Hines was the obvious choice for the position.

He had been up all night studying the relevant documents relating to the Ever Young project. He was scheduled to make a presentation to the cabinet today to include the PM and Alex Pickles, the Finance Minister who was chairing the meeting, to justify the extremely high and ever escalating budget costs. He knew Alex well—they had been at Oxford together—and had already forewarned his friend that he was not happy with the inherited Ever Young Scheme, even though it was designed to save the country billions, but certainly not as it stood.

It had been a year since the Magnum's Ever Young project had been introduced by Brendon Tann. Initially launched within the London area and surrounding suburbs, it was now to be rolled out across the nation. The project had also been accepted by the International Health Authority, thanks to the stamp of approval given by Tann which gave it a worldwide status and now a major advertising campaign, which would cost considerably more than he had anticipated, was being planned.

Henry Hines was known to be a man of principle who could work within a team, think on his feet, and capable of handling intricate subjects. He was regarded as a gem in political circles. The Hines family tree extended back to the fifteenth century and were known as kingmakers. Henry was marked to follow his ancestors' footprints. He had acquitted himself in the London courts as a successful barrister, but was now persuaded to enter politics by his friends and family.

The Magnum Program that came under his wing and which encompassed the now well established Autoplug was overwhelmingly complicated, and in particular the Ever Young project which he argued had serious ethical and political implications. He knew that the ministers present would expect more of him than he was currently able to answer and he resolved not to be too drawn into a political quagmire before he himself understood all the aspects of his newly appointed position. Tann and he were daggers drawn and Hines' mistrust of Tann festered.

Both the Magnum's Autoplug and Ever Young projects were the brainchild of Professor George Baylim, a brilliant neurological scientist who with his team at Cambridge University specialised in genetic coding and both he and his team had worked with substantial government funding.

It was well known that Tann negotiated with the German company Magnum for them to buy the concept outright and it was understood at that time that the university and Baylim would receive a royalty.

Baylim and his team managed to complete the research but were unable to see the official results of their work as he suddenly died at the age of fifty-eight. He had no children. Upon his death, his wife (who was also a professor of neurological sciences) took up a position with Magnum in Germany in order to complete the Ever Young project.

As Magnum took control of both the Autoplug and Ever Young Tann shared a great pride in its success, which was now firmly established, and it was generally understood that the Ever Young project would be launched in the UK via the NHS under Magnum's administration and finance. Once established both projects would invariably be accepted by other European countries. Henry Hines was at that time Junior minister of Health and working under Tann. Neither liked each other. He openly accused Tann's relationship with Magnum to be unhealthy and highly suspicious. Heated words passed between the two men on a number of occasions and overheard by their staff.

It was therefore a great surprise when Tann broke the news to the press that he would retire as Minister of Health after four years on the advice of his doctor who had informed him that the pressure of work would substantially exacerbate his heart condition. However, he would be pleased to recommend Hines to replace him. Although it was known that they had had certain disagreements as to policy, he believed that his colleague would be able to continue to pursue the course that he had established and what was now changing the medical profession throughout the world. The Ever Young project would save billions by the elimination of geriatric costs. His claim to fame was already confirmed with the introduction of the amazing Autoplug now under the super-efficient control of Magnum in Germany and would soon include Ever Young.

His sudden resignation registered rumours throughout Parliament, but it was officially posted as ill health that led to his departure. His obvious replacement was of course Henry Hines.

In order to assist her new boss, Henry's secretary had outlined a current summary of the project taken from Tann's notes, and had already passed them on to his cabinet specifically for the presentation. Henry had noted that Tann had worked closely with many of the ministers and their civil servants particularly relating to details required for Ever Young and information required for the Autoplug and he saw himself as a sacrificial lamb as he prepared to deliver his report. Furthermore the financial notes distributed around the table which had already been overseen by Tann showed substantial savings.

Although he had been to Number Ten three or four times, his now elevated position as Health Minister prompted him to feel that he was brushing with history as he passed paintings of the Prime Ministers of the past two hundred years and who, regardless of their political bias, had stamped their marks in the history books. Maybe he too would see himself written into the reference manuals that children would read in school in years to come.

He had already seen some of the more devious political tricks attempted and bore no illusion: he would be attacked if he deviated from his prepared speech by those with suspiciously hidden vested interests.

Following his colleagues into the main conference room Henry found his name neatly typed next to John Berry, Minister of Housing, whom he already knew. An agenda was placed in front of him and he could see that he was to be fifth in line to speak. Although the Prime Minister was attending, this was to be primarily a budget meeting and Pickles took the chair. Various departmental Ministers would state their positions and invariably defend an overspend. Each knowing that whatever was approved by the chancellor, the less there would be available for another.

Transport, Housing, Education and of course Defence each had their moment, and continuous irrelevant and superfluous notes were passed back and forth. Debating points in question would often create tensions and red faces and critics would return insults and a variety of innuendoes, but tenuous conclusions would invariably result and the PM would be left to act as ombudsman.

At last, Henry was called to address his fellow ministers. Pickles gave him a rare smile and introduced him for the first time as Minister of Health. "As you know Henry has very recently taken on the position of Health Minister, we all know what a bright fellow he is but you may have to wait for detailed answers until he gets his feet under the table, nevertheless, we shouldn't be too inhibited by our good natures," he stopped for a chuckle, "to tell him your thoughts. Henry, please." He sat down, leaned back, clasped his hands together, enjoying a few seconds' silence.

Henry had attended Number 10 a few times as an aide to Tann in the past, but as this was his first time as Health Minister he was given a genuinely appreciative clap by his fellow ministers as he stood up to present his speech. To some, it was a relief to have him replace his predecessor, he noted with interest and took mental note of two or three faces showing their displeasure.

Speaking with the confidence of a seasoned barrister, but finding his hand shaking rather more noticeably than he would wish, he had in mind that this first presentation was in some way going down in the annals of history. Clearing his throat, and taking a sip of water, he began,

"It is well known that an agreement has been made between ourselves and Magnum International of Germany who are the current leaders of interactive software and holographic research, and are mass producing the Autoplug which they have now successfully launched Worldwide. I would just like to point out that this project was the result of the brilliant work done by Professor George Baylim and his team based in Cambridge University. There is no doubt that it is an outstanding example of the UK's contribution to world science, and as you are aware the Autoplug is now used extensively in Medical Centres across the UK and abroad. And I might add, a little sad that such a brilliant development should have not been offered to a British manufacturer to produce in this country."

A few confirmed this remark with a "Hear, Hear!"

"As you know the Autoplug holds all relevant medical and social information relating to the entire population and is programmed to give whatever analytical advice and encyclopaedic information that the patient requires by brilliantly simulated and sympathetic holograms, and millions in the UK and abroad have now become accustomed to talk to the face on the screen, as a friend. As a result of the tremendous cooperation from every civil service department the Autoplug will hold even the most miniscule piece of information relating to the individual and align it to mathematical conjunctures that we call common sense and present its information as intimate advisers via holograms imitating doctors. A brilliant achievement."

"There is no doubt of its advantages to the GPs who can now give more time to urgent medical cases. Magnum agreed to install and maintain the Autoplug into Medical Practices throughout the UK free, and the current arrangement agreed between the NHS and Magnum is that each time the Autoplug is used

Magnum retain three pounds fifty of the five pound fee paid by the user for a fifteen minute usage. The remaining pound fifty is retained by the NHS. There has been some debate as to whether the consumer should pay less in the UK and USA. In the US the patient pays seven dollars, taken from a credit card kept on file. Simple prescriptions are recommended by the Autoplug computerised doctor to grade 1 and grade 2 levels of need. This is an amazing innovation which will certainly benefit the country and create a source of income. However this is not the case with the imminently to be launched Ever Young which we know is also to be under the wing of Magnum." A few hands went up, but Pickles, who was chairing the meeting held them back.

Henry continued. "Allow me, please, to explain the anticipated development of the Ever Young project."

"The Ever Young project would seem a natural step towards prevention rather than curing. The Magnum research team are telling us that they are constantly updating the program to include genetics and neurological sciences which incorporates the facility to foresee mental diseases. Using Baylim's research and conceptual ideas giving a healthier life until death to those who are to become the senior citizens of tomorrow."

At this point, Henry placed his notes on the table and noticeably began to improvise.

"After considerable research and investment by our government working with neurologists, brain surgeons, and of course microbiologists, the dream has become a reality. A chip that would subdue the potential causes of physical deterioration by attacking the impaired DNA at their source sounds so logical, it is a feat of genius, and invented once again by our own British scientists. And what could be wrong with that we may ask?"

"We are told that this miraculous microchip named the Neuro351 is only currently available for twenty-two to thirty-year-olds, and we are informed that this limitation is the result of extensive studies that encompass physical and genetic anomalies before they became abnormalities. After the age of thirty, there is clear evidence that the human metabolism resists and attempts to negate changes to DNA, making it impossible to ensure a beneficial difference to the cells."

"With such claims as it can make, it would stand to reason that once governments throughout the world see the financial benefits of such a scheme and the tremendous savings that could be made, the Ever Young project could be celebrated as one of the greatest breakthroughs in medical history."

"National and international health authorities have of course endorsed the project. Our advertising will state that 'It is better to live a life to ninety-five in perfect health, rather than the alternative of a decrepit old age. We could choose to enjoy our great-grandchildren's company in perfect health, years before we say our farewells.' This claim will be seen on TV and magazines continuously over the next twelve months and financed by our government, and no doubt millions will take the chip. However, every individual who is impregnated with this Neuro351 would be registered and monitored by Magnum, and here is the punchline, switched off when they reach the agreed age of ninety-five. This is not advertised, but put into the small print. But my friends, there is another, far more ominous aspect to this Ever Young project. We may consider that ninety-five is an acceptable age to be switched off, but who is doing the switching and by what means. If every individual is being monitored, this implies that this individual is in the hands of a third party by remote control. And this is deeply concerning. Especially as Magnum knows the history of every Autoplug user.

"Furthermore, there are also those groups who will continue to oppose the Ever Young project on moral or religious grounds which requires serious debate. There has already been an announcement from the Pope who considers this irrevocable consent given by thirty-year-olds who would have life terminated by the State at any age, to be worse than abortion. Magnum and others that would have an interest in this project counter with the claim that psychological illnesses alone are losing millions of work hours and billions of pounds to the National Health service.

"Magnum have confirmed that any improvements in the project will be passed on to the recipients automatically by them, via an App whatever it may be, which would be without the recipients' consent."

Henry was now in full-flight, he had now totally deviated from his original notes which had been tabulated by Magnum and Tann. "In my previous role as a barrister I have seen how facts could be distorted, and false claims verified, especially if the client has deep enough pockets which I believe has benefitted a number of our colleagues."

At this comment, there was a sudden uproar. "Please can we have a little respect for the Minister," called Pickles.

He took another sip of water and continued.

"How can we be assured that the button would not be pressed sooner, or, since it can be controlled by remote control that other impulses are submitted changing lifestyles, thought patterns, emotions. We are looking here at a project that allows

40

a foreign entity to control millions of minds and actions; dealing with mind-changing technology by centrally controlled electronic impulses will have serious political and even military implications. I suggest that this be seriously considered as we once again take the Ever Young project into debate."

Hines was now becoming emotional, and his friend gently pulled his sleeve.

He continued in a lower tone, "I believe that my predecessor had taken it upon himself to bring a brilliant but potentially very dangerous project to the market without appreciating some of the consequences."

"You will all know that a hundred and ninety-five billion pounds has already been allocated in order to maintain the health of this country," he saw pens were already scribbling, "you will also be aware how beneficial the introduction of the Autoplug has benefitted the nations' doctors, it is a personal encyclopaedia of every individual's history releasing the surgery from the mundane and allowing them to concentrate on what they were really trained to do. The Autoplug as a stand-alone project justifies any appropriate investment but aligned to Ever Young it can become a treacherous tool for determining the who and how of the population's future. Furthermore, we are certainly going to face a backlash to the Ever Young scheme from those religious bodies who are deeply concerned with the termination clause. It is the core of the government's long-term strategy to offset the projected burgeoning costs of the elderly, but we should consider very carefully before we throw out the baby with the bath water. As you will see from my memo, the Catholic church as well as all the orthodox religious communities are fiercely against the idea that the government would have the right to terminate life."

A mass of hands came up ready to respond. "Let the Health Minister finish his presentation," barked the PM.

"Thank you, Prime Minister." It was noticeable that Henry was stumbling. He had completely deviated from his provided notes and presented himself to his colleagues in far too emotional terms, but he was on a roller coaster.

He repeated, "So, we are now given to understand that the Neuro351 will alleviate all those psychological disorders, from psychopathic tendencies to depression, migraine or even sexual problems. It will be placed in the brain and be self-modulating or controlled by authorised bodies when they considered it necessary...I am deeply concerned, not only for the public's vulnerability, but on the position that we as a government are being drawn towards an irrevocable decision that has monumental implications and would change the very essence of our civilisation and be controlled by extremely powerful and profit orientated foreign companies. The technology of these conglomerates is far beyond this country's ability to replicate, or to find alternatives We are now totally in their hands to control an invasion of our very being, not only in the UK but throughout the world."

This was not what had been expected for him to discuss for he had virtually accused ministers of the government of bribery that could have serious consequences. After all, this meeting had been called specially for the discussion of future finances. He had allowed his heart to rule his head, and there was no doubt that there would be serious repercussions.

First to respond was Judith Bracknell the Minister for Defence. "It seems to me Henry that you have placed us all in a rather compromising position, and it's fortunate that we are without the press to hear your comments. No doubt you will have names that you believe are involved. However your predecessor has already irrevocably committed the Magnum Health care's Auto Plug and the Ever Young project to this country and the concept has been taken up by other countries around the world at great expense, you are now suggesting that we are in serious danger of being controlled by the organisation that has designed our programs, which on your own admission has already saved us billions and is known to have an impeccable record worldwide. It seems to me a rather fanciful conclusion. There is no doubt that many of our departments have been involved in bringing the Autoplug into existence and that it has been of great benefit to the country; now you are accusing us of being in the back pocket of Magnum as if we were criminals!"

Henry paused to take a sip. "I realise that my remarks here today might appear to be bizarre to say the least, and contradicts many of the statements regarding Magnum made and reiterated by my predecessor and those OF YOU," he emphasised, "that he worked with, but my legal training has allowed me the luxury of evaluating situations before making decisions with a degree of clarity that others may not always have. One is not always allowed the benefit of being ahead of an action, and sometimes we are placed in a circumstance that needs to be readjusted before the problem is compounded. In this instance, I can visualise a position whereby the passing of control of our physical and mental stock to mega organisations such as Magnum who can impose their technology upon us, without recourse that would be irreversible and ultimately a disaster. They can and, in my opinion will, determine the way we live and even more important, the way we think. I believe that The Neuro351 will be in a position to invade our minds, surreptitiously and without even us being aware or superimposing information by remote control, changing our actions and desires, in that event we would be glorified zombies. I realise that this might sound outrageous, but if we concede to this invasive technology without the strictest of conditions, the health of our nation will be in the hands of external powers and worse." He hesitated and took a deep breath. "I have always believed that whatever we do in our governmental position should be purely for the benefit of this country, appreciation is always one of these benefits but financial benefits under whatever circumstances amount to bribery which in my book is totally unacceptable."

His last comment brought an angry response and at least ten hands went up, but it was Pickles' turn to take the initiative.

"Your accusations are most disconcerting Henry, to discover a serious loophole in an otherwise agreed project, but I personally can appreciate your dilemma in pursuing, in particular, the Ever Young Neuro351 project without some controls."

Now directing his remarks to the PM. "May I suggest, Prime Minister, that we each put forward by memo an initial response to our Health Minister's presentation before further action is taken."

"Agreed," nodded the PM. "Good. Henry, I would formally advise you to be very careful before you make such strong allegations, and I shall await your detailed study at your earliest opportunity."

Henry was thanked and the meeting continued, albeit with ruffled feathers, on to various other more mundane subjects for another two hours.

***

Three days later the headlines on every TV channel reported:

"Police are investigating the death of Mr Henry Hines, recently appointed Health Minister. It appears that three masked men broke into his home in Holland Park London at approximately 2.00 am and entered his bedroom where he and his wife were sleeping. Mr Hines was shot in the heart and died instantly, as did his wife when the gunman shot her between her eyes. They were discovered by their housekeeper who was awoken by the noise and saw three men escaping. The house was ransacked and it is understood that several works of art and jewellery of considerable value were taken. There appear to be no witnesses."

The Prime Minister being interviewed confirmed that no efforts would be spared to find the murderers, a claim that would be reiterated by the Home Office and the Chief of Police.

Brendon Tann was called back once again to take the position of Health Secretary. He sent an immediate response to the press.

Press release From Mr Brendon Tann Minster of Health:

"It is with great sadness that I have been asked to come out of my retirement and re-join the government as Minister of Health once again.

The death of my friend and colleague, Henry Hines, in such a tragic way, denies the party and indeed the world a tremendous, unmatched ability, and he shall be greatly missed. Under the circumstances I have agreed to step in until a permanent replacement can be found. In the meantime I can assure the government and the people of this country that we will make every effort to continue to maintain the high standards of the National Health Service."

Brendon Tann (Minister of Health).

Chapter 5
Miriam

It was now two months since Miriam had been offered her new post. It took her no longer than a day to accept. This would be her last week in the UK. She was to receive a salary treble to what she had been earning, and which would be commensurate with her new title of Associate Manager for Global Communication. (AMFGC). She had not been told exactly what her responsibilities would be or who her mentor was, she guessed that it was an improvised title but she had sufficient faith in the company to guide her, especially as they apparently knew her so well according to Theodore.

This was to be her first visit to the States and she had difficulty in hiding her excitement. There had been no mention as to how long she might be there, but she assumed that once her training was complete she could, if she wished, return to the UK, and with a new position, but she took some pleasure in not knowing. The company suggested that she travel via New York which would break up the journey, spend a weekend there and continue to Los Angeles on the Monday. They booked her into a five-star hotel and informed her that she would be met by a colleague from the New York Office who would escort her to her hotel.

Having made the rounds of the family and saying her farewells to her friends she packed a few basic needs and thought that she would use her New York time to traipse around a few of the well-known stores.

Upon receiving her ticket, she noticed that she had been booked first class which she thought a little surprising. Once booked in and finding her way to the executive lounge it occurred to her that she might be part of an experiment. In any event, what did she have to lose? She had been used to travelling cheek by jowl on discount flights where anything over your sunglasses was considered extra baggage. As she took her seat and inhaled the aroma of expensive perfume, it was easy to tell the nouveau-riche from the more established well heeled, as those more used to this style of travel wore their old jeans and had nothing to prove.

The journey was lost in sleep and Miriam was gently awoken by a steward to inform her that they had arrived. The queues at passport control neutralised the classes and she fought back the newly acquired feeling of assumed superiority of being a first-class passenger.

As she cleared customs she noticed a young man holding a large board bearing her name.

"Welcome to our fair city Miriam my name is Adrian. The car is a little walk away, we're going to the Plaza which will probably take less than an hour. This is your first visit to New York?" But before she answered, he commented, "It's a great city, it's a shame you're not staying a few days."

"I'm sure I'll have plenty of opportunities to come again," she replied. "But I'll get a feel for it over the weekend," she smiled. They talked a little of the city's many attractions, he informed her that he worked in the New York office in sales. He carried her bags to the reception and bade her farewell. "I'll collect you on Monday morning if that is OK, Miriam." His duty fulfilled, they shook hands and parted.

Her suite was located on the twenty-ninth floor and Miriam took in the luxury, the gold tapped bathroom, the furnishings and all that was to be expected from a five-star hotel in Manhattan. She kicked off her shoes and looked down from the window to see what would appear to be hundreds of ants scampering in all directions. Across the way lay Central Park. She stretched out on the bed and smiled to herself. "This is the life," she whispered.

She had intended to refurbish her wardrobe in line with the LA climate the following day, but could not resist the thought of becoming one of the mass that she saw from her window. She had a spare pair of jeans, she jumped into a shower, put on some lipstick and caught an elevator going down. There was no doubt that they had chosen one of the best hotels in New York as she breezed through the restaurants, the coffee shop and the astonishingly expensive jewellery shop. She took a map from the reception and meandered into Central Park. Like every large city park, on the weekend its vibrancy was contagious.

She visited Bloomingdales, Barneys and Sacks on 5th Ave, and filled an array of bags which was quite pleasurable.

Using a little English charm with the concierge she managed to purchase a ticket in front stalls at the Met who were playing the Marriage of Figaro in Italian which she knew would be a memorable experience. Returning to Bloomingdales she fitted herself out with a dress to suit the occasion, booked a table in the hotel, and for one night celebrated her new life by toasting her parents on her mobile which of course gave them great pleasure.

With the five-hour time difference, she awoke at 5.30 am on Sunday and decided to keep the day for discovery. She threw on a jump suit and sneakers and crossed the road into Central Park and ran. Totally liberated and wondering to herself how she could have anticipated such a different set of events only a few months ago to bring her to this amazing place. By 9.30 am, Central Park was busy. Dog walkers with a gaggle of canine pets of all sizes spread out on leads like a Japanese fan, fellow runners, kids with their parents shouting not to get of out their sight, skate boarders whizzing past.

She left the park at 64th Street, had an American-style breakfast of pancakes smothered in syrup and dropped into the Guggenheim, spent a couple of hours at the Natural History Museum and took a cab to Greenwich Village. What a great city, it was electric, as long as you had money, she thought. That evening she took the subway into Harlem where she was told of a jazz club.

At 7.45 am on Monday, Adrian was waiting at the reception desk. He had already settled the account, and with the customary New York smile took her rather large collection of bags to the car.

The flight from NY to LA would take over five hours, but her first class ticket, Cordon Bleu lunch and a good film took the sting out of the Journey.

Upon her arrival she was met once again, by another young man. He might have been twenty-four or twenty-six years old with a deep suntan and in casual clothes, His remarkably white teeth, seemed almost luminous as he waved his board towards Miriam. They walked towards a white Cadillac and he opened the passenger door for her, but she insisted on sitting in the front. The journey would take no more than half an hour, and through small talk she managed to discover that his name was Pete, his family were from Mexico and he was now an assistant to Martin Moran who was head of executive planning. "There are twenty-five in our team," he stated proudly. She was interested in knowing what that entailed, but other than to say that there were a number of teams Pete became a little more selective in his responses and she felt it better not to anticipate what might be before her.

At last, they arrived at a security gate of an apartment block which was clearly designed to impress. He parked the car and gave a glittering smile. "Welcome to Anderville Lodge, your new home."

There must be a special charm school that these guys go to, to appear so sincere, she thought, and wondered how to identify truisms from the almost plastic smile that purported to be a real appreciation of another human being.

He showed her the various workings of the apartment and with what would have appeared to be a heartfelt desire for her to enjoy her stay. He brought her luggage up and gently placed it in her bedroom, and departed. It was now 8.00 pm. She wandered through the various rooms, opened the fridge to find a few immediate needs, eggs, milk, bread, and musing over to the dining table she found a foolscap envelope with her name handwritten on it.

Dear Miriam,

Welcome to the USA, to LA and in particular to the heart of Spoken Arrow. Knowing you as well as we do, I can understand that you may feel a little surprised or even disconcerted as to the manner by which you have found yourself here. I know that I would, for you have agreed to come here without a clear explanation of what we would have in mind for you. But you may be even more surprised, and possibly initially affronted to know that we have been studying you closely for more than a year, and when I write closely I mean REAL close. When I said I know you well, you will understand why.

The Spoken Arrow organisation directly employs over 150,000 throughout the world, mostly postgraduates, and it has been our practice for some time to look for extraordinary talent from within this pool of thinking young people. Our Central offices and the largest retail outlets globally are carefully monitored, and as Theo intimated to you there are 'IN-DEPTH CAMERAS' placed throughout these locations for the very purpose of evaluating those few who we believe can be groomed for senior executive positions that require a depth of thought, and the ability to put these thoughts into action. Our selected personnel are literally shadowed every moment of the day; the clear majority are deleted after even three months. You will also be surprised or even shocked to know that we also monitor the activities of these 'chosen ones' outside of their store activities as we have access to recording cameras wherever it is required. You can believe me that it is not an easy task to discover these gems from which ever country they belong, and then to evaluate their desire to follow through, with our guidance (not instruction), for whomever we choose will bring their own perception of the job in hand. We do of course interview staff for lesser positions, without going into such detail, but you will appreciate that it really is unnecessary for us to formally interview what we consider the crème de la crème, as we already know them intimately and objectively, sometimes better than they know themselves. We are very conscious that there are laws protecting against the invasion and the imposition of one's privacy, but for our needs we override them. So I suppose we owe you an apology for invading your space!

Spoken Arrow's innovative and creative world requires us to think outside of the box. Our objectives are to improve the world socially, intellectually, morally and still retain a human bias. But to cut through institutional and autocratic barriers which so often suffocates creativity we require free thinkers without inhibitions. The people of our choice will be in a position to alter the lives of millions so you will, I hope, appreciate the difficulty of filling these positions.

At no time during this training period will you be obligated to any commitment and if you should decide to revert to your old position in London, we would accept your decision in good faith. Your return would be by the same manner that you have travelled here. It is most important for you to be as excited with your projects as we are, all we require from you is an open mind and a desire to pursue your role within the company with the same vigour that we have observed during the time you have been with us. A driver will call to collect you tomorrow at 8.30 am to bring you to our offices when I look forward with great pleasure to our meeting.

Yours very sincerely, Martin.

Martin Moran Vice president & Head of Executive Planning. Spoken Arrow International Div.

Miriam read the letter twice, for it was not what it said, but what it did not say that interested her. Ransacking her memories for any possible misdemeanours, and recalling where she might have gone where cameras might have been installed. Clubs, pubs, stores, even streets all had tele-cameras, she had also been to a far-left political meeting, not that she was particularly left or right wing, but was booed down after contesting a particular point on democracy, that would surely have been on record. It was particularly strange to note how the letter had avoided describing her job or training, the mystery became a guessing game to her which brought a wry smile as she conjured up a variety of ridiculous ideas. However, it did occur to her that there may be hidden cameras in the apartment, and out of bravado undressed and danced to the radio music, but no doubt they had seen it all before. She made herself a sandwich switched on the T.V and at last relaxed.

At 7.00 am, she felt ready to take on any challenge thrown at her. She threw on a pair of smart jeans and a blouse both from Sacks, appraised herself in the mirror and waited for her lift into her future.

The driver ignored the parking area and drove directly to the Spoken Arrow main entrance. A glass covered stream had been installed around the perimeter of the building which extended into the foyer of the reception and displayed an array of fish swimming, indifferent as to who was walking above them and giving the impression of walking on water. The vast reception area had settees and coffee tables scattered around with young men and women chatting freely. Looking up Miriam could see at least six floors above to glass balconies of which hung what appeared to be camellias hanging from them. Glass fronted offices could be seen behind them. Nothing was hidden and even the two glass elevator bullets carrying eight or nine passengers, gave the impression that there was nowhere to hide.

As she approached the reception a rather effeminate young man at the counter smiled showing all his gleaming teeth "Martin is expecting you. I shall take you to his office. My name is Doran," he fluttered.

"Good to meet you Doran," she smiled. They took the elevator to the 6th floor and walked along the mezzanine corridor past a number of offices all of which appeared to be vibrantly active.

Martin Moran had been with Spoken Arrow for well over twenty years and had been a quintessential element in the company's growth. He was now in his mid-forties and probably one of the few elders of the higher echelons. A relatively short man, slightly balding, slim but still looking fit with a commanding presence, and an open and honest looking face that engendered confidence.

He put out his hand to shake and covered Miriam's with both of his. "At last we meet our London girl Miriam Bravotti, you are very welcome, come, sit, have you had breakfast, coffee, we have a lot to discuss."

"I'm pleased to be here, I've already had breakfast but coffee would be good," she replied.

"Now according to my notes," he caricatured fumbling through a few papers, "you take it white with two sugars, is that correct?" he chuckled.

She laughed. "Well, just to deny your files of being right, I'll have one sugar, thank you."

"You know Miriam, I have been handpicking teams now for a number of years, we didn't have to dig too deep in the old days, but as we evolved from a marketing and trading operation, to producing of unique and mind-bending products, it became necessary to delve further into the type of people we were to give responsibility to. It's now reached a stage where our standards go far beyond our competitors, and we're so far ahead of the market that there is no one out there that we could tempt away from in the fields we operate, and since we're now able to draw from so many young minds, especially for the middle rank executives whom I would liken to a human library, hence the intense search from within our own people."

He took a sip of coffee and continued. "But looking for the real crème de la crème is a different ball game altogether, but I get a terrific kick from actually meeting that person that we have been so closely studying and, knowing so much about them, and yet it's all an academic exercise until you really see them in the flesh. Of course in the last few years, modern technology has helped us tremendously, but to actually meet them, knowing what we know about them, it's like standing back and looking as if for the first time, at a painting that one has been labouring on for maybe months and looking at it afresh, and a complete masterpiece. When I see them…you understand that I mean You."

"Well, I must admit that you have a substantial advantage over me, Martin, and I'm very flattered that you should compare me to a masterpiece for here I am, in LA, wondering what's in store for me, sitting in front of a senior executive of a multi-billion dollar organisation and wondering why I'm here. It's quite surreal, and I should say exciting, but rather Kafkaesque, so since you already know all about me maybe I could reverse the compliment!"

"OK, Miriam," he smiled. "Let me explain what we are about, and how we see you fitting into our future. You will know of course that we are the leaders in computers, Mobilus, slates and high-tech software and now holographic. There has been no one to touch us in these fields, but you may not be aware that we have been working on our own version of the Autoplug with the intention of entering the medical field. However, we badly misjudged the speed and the marketing capability of Magnum who cooperated with Hitsudi in Japan until recently and have now launched the Autoplug throughout the world, but you obviously know all that."

"In other words, we missed the boat. By the way Miriam, I took the opportunity to read your PhD thesis which I must say was very interesting. The US medical testing systems are, quite rightly, very meticulous and extremely slow in processing claims by manufacturers. We see the medical business as a most important market. Anyone who controls it can lock out the competition. You will already be aware that Magnum have access to all the necessary medical software of every person in the UK and in Europe, provided of course the governments are prepared to cooperate, and can even align their DNA with their parental history. The software distils this information in conjunction with the diagnostic hand monitoring plate and will offer a reasonably accurate diagnosis."

"To complement this, I understand that they have added the WISDOM AI to the system which allows the receiver to ask questions on any subject and will receive an encyclopaedic reply in conversational terms. The personalised hologram will speak to the recipient as if he or she were talking to a friend, and according to the diagnosis the hologrammed doctor will, if requested, offer a prescription to grade 2 level. If the Autoplug feels that a specific medical examination is required, it will arrange an appointment with a human doctor. Are we on the same wavelength Miriam?"

"Absolutely," she nodded. "There's no doubt that the concept is ingenious, in fact I use the Autoplug myself. As you of course know Martin I'm Catholic, and I can admit that I use it as a Confession box, my priest hasn't seen me in months." She giggled a little embarrassed that she had admitted this small personal point. "I hope you haven't any cameras here."

"No, but no doubt Magnum have all that information, but I'm surprised that you have anything to confess," replied Martin a little flirtatiously, and cleared his throat.

"So, to continue. Let's see where this entire project is leading. We are dealing here with a brilliant and I believe devious organisation which has a much larger agenda. Magnum are fully aware that we are interested in the medical world. We believe that the Autoplug regardless of its standalone benefits was, and is only stage one of a series of interrelated projects."

"We know now that stage two is the Ever Young project which is directed at the twenty-two to thirty age group and works on the natural body defences. This is a very plausible scheme as far as the governments of the world and the public are concerned, as it shows substantial savings in social welfare as well as medical. They claim that it does not infringe on the mind's capabilities to make decisions, but offers the participant good health into old age. It has been introduced in the UK and one or two other countries and seems to have been received quite well.

However, as the difference between the age of thirty and ninety-five is sixty-five years, we will only know how financially and even more important, medically beneficial it will be in sixty-five years' time. Nevertheless those participating in this scheme will have committed to terminate their lives according to their agreement."

"I don't think I'm following, what is wrong with the scheme so far?"

"It's not what is wrong with it, Miriam, it's a question of what further implications there are. Magnum claims that when the Neuro351 chip is placed in the hippocampus it will in essence readjust most or all of the vulnerable parts of the body via the brain as it reveals any potential abnormality before it develops. All processes in the brain, generated by the chip. Now added to this, the Neuro351 makes the claim that neurological or mental diseases can also be controlled, with the assistance of a medical software engineer, computerised or otherwise, who will pick up on electronic imbalances of the individual, without that patient knowing. Each individual chip will have its own code and be registered by Magnum."

Martin allowed Miriam to ponder on his words, both considering the possible implications.

Almost in a whisper Miriam spoke first. "It's not a massive step therefore to use this electrode to readjust the recipient's thinking whilst presented to the public as an all-in-one facility. What you're suggesting is that Magnum could use the 351 to control thought patterns. Could there even be political implications, and if so what might be the purpose of such a scheme?"

"There may not be anyone behind it. Conglomerates the size of Magnum would be strong enough to make a global impact on their own. You must appreciate, Miriam, that even operations of our size understand that it's essential to continue expanding, they are beyond making money, even our own company, when you have a worldwide monopoly, those at the head of it can choose whichever direction they want to take it, of course the ideal is to give one's expertise and knowledge for the good of society and the world's population, philanthropy with a bottom line profit, but there are those who would use their power to engineer total control, changing universal truths to their perceived ideas of new truths. Choice is replaced by instruction. Mass and grouped Individuality. Competition would be replaced by directed thought. But now, before we become too depressed, it's time for lunch, I don't know about you but I think much better with food in my tummy."

The eating area was situated on the top floor leading out onto a large roof garden and set out under an array of canopies. She had never seen such a selection of fruits and vegetables so beautifully displayed, there were a number of young men and women, some with their slates in front of them whilst eating, others simply relaxing under the mid-day sun.

They filled their plates with a selection of vegetarian food and found a table in the shade. Martin was sidestepping the question of the main interest to Miriam, not that it was particularly worrying her, for she could see that he had been weaving a pattern that would find its own level. To her delight a butterfly landed audaciously on the side of her plate, and for no particular reason she could think of it made her feel good. She inadvertently thought of Doran and smiled.

"I am of course very interested Martin to know your ideas for diversification, and objectives, especially the medical aspect. I've never thought of Spoken Arrow solely as a money-making machine, its strength has always been in its creativity, so where do we, assuming I'm included that is, go from here? I would be surprised if you were to simply copy Magnum, in any event it would be difficult to displace them from the market without great difficulty, that is unless you have a better product."

"Here's the thing," he put his knife and fork down, "we've had a good look at ourselves. You know Miriam that if you were to find a financial paper of say thirty years ago, most of the companies that you would read about aren't now in business today or have melted into some other organisation, and the same is that of most of today's mega corporations. They become too large, too unwieldly and the original dynamism is replaced with institutional thinking. Maybe some individual will think of a better product, government legislation, cost of labour, a multitude of reasons. Consider how our business expanded into a worldwide operation, and to look at us you would think we're invulnerable. But not so, suddenly we see a Magnum or a Hitsudi, there are dozens of these operations in the making about to catch the imagination of the world and biting at our heels. Ideas that set the world alight only a decade ago are suddenly usurped by an even more revolutionary product or another way of life.

"Most youngsters today have never seen a typewriter, couldn't possibly imagine living without a mobile, emails, social networks etc. Who would have imagined only thirty years ago trying to run a business without a shorthand typist sitting next door and awaiting instructions. And what we have today will be history in only ten years from now.

"What we need is a new level of thinking, of creativity, and if we want to be here in thirty years' time we must consider the next Generation's needs, and that's where you come in."

Miriam suddenly sat up, she had of course given her full attention to Martin's preamble but had not expected such a direct and personal association to his conversation. The butterfly, probably having taken its fill of nectar, left her plate and fluttered into the blue sky.

"I'm all ears, Martin." she smiled.

"I love these English expressions, we have lost so many of these little idioms in our speech, you know I took a Masters in English, it seems like a hundred years ago." Little physical nuances were his way to lighten what would otherwise be heavy statement. Moving his chair closer to Miriam, he dropped his voice to a whisper. "We are seriously thinking of forming a new company solely for the medical market, it will be financed by third parties and no-one other than our inner sanctum will see any association between us."

"But what is the project?"

"You will know when we will know, Miriam." he smiled. "First, let me show you around."

"And my apartment, does it have cameras!"

"Definitely no cameras!"

Chapter 6
Joe

It was not too unusual for Joe to be invited to his uncle's apartment. But there was a sense of urgency in his father's voice. His father was already there with whisky in hand. "Sit down, Joe." He was given a whisky and Joe waited in anticipation. He had executed a number of planned robberies before, and they often worked quite closely with the owner of a property to clear stocks or belongings of any value. The stolen goods would be transported into Brenekov's warehouse until the insurance claims had been agreed. Working on a percentage of the insurance claim, the Brenekovs would return the goods to them when the dust had settled who would invariably start a new business with their old stock. Sometimes they would be asked to tie up the owner and make an anonymous call to the police. It was quite straight forward. However, on this occasion a much more sophisticated hand was required. Very specific instructions were given by the client.

"Listen carefully Joe," said his father rather condescendingly, "I'm going to explain this next job in detail, and I want you to listen real close," he sat forward in his chair and allowed a silence to emphasise the degree of urgency. "OK? We can't afford to mess this one up, it's a very sensitive job and is worth a lot of money to us. OK?"

"OK – I'm not a child, uncle. You know that I can cope with whatever job I'm given," he said disgruntled. "Well, what is it?"

"You've not done anything like this one before. The house in question is in Holland Park. Very expensive area. Well alarmed. The property contains valuable works of art, and I mean highly valuable. I will give you a list of them so that you don't waste time picking up random items. These will be our bunce Joe – it's a great deal but we must be so, so careful not to mess it up. Do you understand?"

"How much are they worth?"

"Millions, Joe. But it's essential that the sale of the works of art of this kind are passed onto the right hands. That's the clever bit."

"What do you mean bunce, that's what we do, isn't it?" queried Joe.

"Not this job Joe, the goods are a cover for the real job."

"I don't get it," said Joe.

"You will but don't interrupt, just listen. We've been given full details of the alarm system and the layout. The instruction we've been given is to bump off the occupant. He would probably be asleep in bed with his wife. It is not important to kill the wife but only if necessary. It must look like a robbery with violence, not simply violence with robbery as an afterthought. For this one night's work, we get one million pounds."

Joe looked concerned. "This is out of our normal league, uncle. Are you sure we should get involved in the rubbing out business?"

"Whoever set this job up has carefully planned it. We are being paid very well to do this and whatever we take is ours. It's a double whammy."

Joe had never killed anyone before. Beating them up was OK but murder was an altogether different deal. Nevertheless the art and jewellery alone would have made it worthwhile. That was a lot of money. Fifty percent had already been paid up front. Joe's uncle would not tell him who was behind this caper, instructions came from a third party, but it was very clear that whoever it was did not want to be known.

"Listen Joe, you have been yelping for over a year that you wanted a big job," said his uncle. "Well, this is your moment. Do this job right and your dad and I will make you a partner. That's what you want isn't it. The job won't need more than four of you, choose the best guys we've got. There are two coppers on the beat in the area, and we've already sorted them. We've done the best to set this up, but now it's up to you. Don't muck it up 'cos if you do you're on your own."

"I can't say that I'm happy with this. Murder has never been on our list. Who's the bloke anyway?"

"I don't know and don't care, I'm not getting personal," replied his uncle, "but I'm sure we'll know the following day," he sneered. "The instructions are coming through a third party."

The instructions demanded that the job must be done specifically in three days' time. It wasn't difficult to organise. The property had an electronic security gate that was alarmed. Details of the alarm and code had already been given to them. The house was inspected by a security company that visited the property every evening. The regular driver that visited the property was an old nag that the Brenekovs knew well. He had been straight for the past seven years, but with a little persuasion plus a nice backhander that would sweeten him up, they could get all the gate codes, and they would be able to drive their truck past the gate to the front door without being seen loading it up. Perfect.

Joe listened intently, gulped down his whisky and helped himself to another. "I hope you know what you're doing," he replied.

"If we follow the plan exactly as instructed it will be the biggest we will have ever done," said his uncle.

"The guard was instructed to stay as far away from the house as possible and make sure to be seen in another street, if the police interrogate him I reminded him that we know where he and his family live. Remember they can't hang you for a smell. I have already told him that the 50 grand he will get must not be spent by him or his family for at least six months," Joe insisted. "If you want to trickle one or two thousand out, but don't make yourself conspicuous, do you understand." His manner and voice made a sufficient impression on the poor man.

The instructions given to Brenekov were meticulous in every respect. Every aspect of the burglary was considered. The bullets used, the gun, van, the gate that had to look like it had been manhandled, the getaway, and in particular the internal alarm, which their client had impressive technical knowledge of. They should ransack the house, and destroy the house alarm to appear that it was necessary to do so, "And do not speak in case your voice is heard or recognised by his wife, and of course no fingerprints. After you have used the gun, wipe it clean and throw it in the Thames, we can't afford to have any association with it that can come back on us. You will drive the van to a warehouse in Kilburn. Upload it into a waiting van and dump the first van. Do you understand?"

"They must think I'm a bloody fool!" thought Joe, but he took careful note of the instructions.

There were several priceless works of art on the list. A Chagall and an Escher were included in the haul, plus two small bronzes of which one was a Giacometti. They would have a job placing these, he thought, but it was certainly a tremendous pull and with a bit of luck could fetch a few million, carefully handled.

The job was planned with military precision. At 1.30 am, Joe collected the three men at Hammersmith Bridge who parked a few houses away. One of the men walked to the house and exactly as instructed found the code to open the gate, he flashed a torch as a signal for the van to drive in. Joe found his way into the bedroom whilst two men ransacked the house the third acting as a watch. They carefully placed the selected works of art into the van. Both husband and wife were fast asleep with arms around each other. Joe looked at them for a few moments, it was a moment of almost spiritual contemplation before he jogged himself back to the purpose of the exercise. He screwed on the silencer and aimed first at the man's heart. The woman immediately awoke and sat up. She was about to scream when he shot her between the eyes.

He was surprised how easy it was to pull the trigger. One minute they were alive and in love, and the next minute they were in heaven. "Quite sweet," he mused. He pulled out a few drawers, and took whatever watches and jewellery he could see, messed the room up as instructed and left with the other two without a word being passed. The property was beautiful and he wondered if one day he could live in such style.

Joe gave both the men each a thick envelope and let them out just before Hammersmith Bridge and took the wheel. There was no need for them to know the whereabouts of the warehouse. They shook hands and he waited until both men were out of sight then took the gun out of its holster to throw it into river, but decided to hold onto it for a while, maybe as a memento. It was strange but he felt no guilt or remorse, but seemed able to detach himself from the killing. The image of the two in embrace was still foremost in his mind as he drove to the warehouse in Dulwich and unloaded the works of art.

As soon as he arrived home he made a quick call to his dad confirming that all went to plan, poured himself a well-earned whisky, smiled to himself in the mirror and slept like a log.

They did not have to wait long to discover who lived in the house. The event missed the early papers but hit the news on the radio and TV. Joe could not help wondering why anyone would wish to kill a Health Minister. It was obvious that it was a political conspiracy of some kind, and he realised that the government would be seriously involved in their attempt to find who was behind it. He would be well advised to lay low until the dust settled.

The following day he came down with a serious migraine, but did not tell his father or uncle, but thanked heaven that it wasn't on the day before.

The papers covered every aspect of the previous night's work. The night watchman was interviewed and said his piece, the alarms examined, and of course the gory details of the murders. A list of various treasures and their value accompanied with a myriad of theories. Henry Hines' background and his family history gave added fodder to the story.

Joe brought the Newspapers into his father's office and slapped them down on his desk "This was a hot potato," he said with obvious concern, "I hope you know what you've got us into dad."

"Don't worry son, provided you did everything you were told, nothing will go wrong. Even we don't know exactly who gave the instruction, you won't believe this but it came via the Russian Mafia."

"But why would the Russian Mafia want to kill a British Minister of Health, that doesn't make any sense."

"Listen Joe, sense doesn't have a place in our business, it's not for us to make sense out of it, as long as we get paid. One thing is for sure, we are not messing with these guys, they are certainly not going to tell us who their clients are. I wouldn't be surprised if they don't know either. Whoever gave the initial instructions will have covered their tracks. Anyway, there's no way they can trace anything back to us. But I do think it might be an idea to take a trip somewhere for a few weeks, you deserve it, only for a few weeks Joe, just in case. We will all have alibis if they come to us. We'll arrange to back date your tickets and hotels wherever you want to go. We need to back date your passport by at least two days."

"And what about the partnership?"

"That's agreed, but when you come back we can sort it out. Anyway, well done son."

It was not difficult to get a back dated stamp on his passport. "Listen Joe, you must not use this passport going out, because you will already have a stamp two days before the job on it. We'll organise a new one with a false name on it which they can stamp, after that you can throw the new one away and when you return, use the old one. Do you understand?"

"I get it," he replied. It was so annoying to be told the obvious. Throwing a few clothes into the boot of his Porsche he drove down to Dover and took the ferry to Calais. His new passport read Joseph Shapero and according to his record this man had travelled the world. From France, he could drive anywhere he wished. His Father had already reserved a room in a boutique hotel in Toulouse, and for a small sum the hotel had back dated his booking and receipt under his real name. It would be the last time he would need to be Shapero unless an interesting opportunity arose, but he considered the novelty of being a 'new man' regardless of who Joe Shapero was as history. He considered his alibi was now waterproof. Once abroad he would have no further need for his false passport, but his new passport would enable him to virtually disappear in a foreign country until he returned, and smiling to himself at the Jekyll and Hyde possibilities.

Immediately Joe booked in the hotel he came down again with a terrible migraine, he threw himself on the bed and slept for twelve hours.

Chapter 7
Jack

It had been over two months since Jack had been to Cornwall – he had no great desire to travel there again in the near future, and settled to speaking with his parents using chat software. However, he took a hard lesson from the trip which confirmed in his mind that he would not allow himself to stagnate the way his parents had.

His normal style of journalism encompassed new innovations and interviews with notable sportsmen or women, and it was rare for him to promote his own opinions on the more political aspects of sport. Of course, the health, wealth and quality of life at the top of the profession would invariably be a topic of interest with the readers, but as his editor had asked him to write an article with a social bias on Ever Young and he was aware that a political slant might be necessary in order to prove its abilities of the latest government sponsored Ever Young project.

Brody Emmitt had been editor of The Tandem Press for over fifteen years. The group covered over thirty titles and like all publications relied on advertising which was becoming ever more difficult to secure. He was in every way the proverbial press man and ate, drank and breathed the papers that he had under his control. A large man desperately overweight and smoking forty a day, he was never seen without a cigarette dangling from his lips, and although every employee was interconnected by phone, he far preferred to use his lungs which invariably found their mark. As Jack's desk was at the other end of the 50-meter room that contained another twenty-five journalists in the open office it took a pair of strong lungs to permeate the cacophony of sound.

"Jack, the Ever Young project seems to be the next big thing, you've got a big following with the young sporty kids in the age group that the government is targeting, and it should be an interesting read, say two thousand or so words."

"Does this mean that you've managed to persuade the government to spend some money with us," replied Jack cynically.

"As it so happens we have, and they're rather keen to give us a six-month contract over as many issues in cooperation with Magnum, so if you can find a positive slant it would be preferable. We've got three weeks to put out the first article. I'll leave it with you Jack, OK?"

Jack had not given too much thought to Ever Young since his initial enquiry, but it was certainly worth investigating in greater detail, and it required some form of continuity over the advertising program.

He told his boss that he would be working from home and immediately directed all his thoughts to the approach required. As soon as he arrived back at his apartment, throwing his coat over a settee, he made a quick coffee and went to his computer. He wrote headers to work from. "Let's start with its conception, then maybe I'll prove its benefits, I might discover a level of opposition and end up with a positive conclusion."

It took some time to absorb all the medical implications written by various neurologists lead by its creator Professor George Baylim, (now deceased), and a myriad of medical articles eventually proving its claims, plus the European and US attitudes towards the project, with a sprinkle of Magnum's promotional sheets during its early development. He could have written an entire article on its conception, but his training had taught him that his readers were end users not scientists, and their understanding of it would be on a basic level. However, it seemed that right from the earliest exposure of the project, both religious and political opposition was apparent. So how would it benefit the individual, and what savings, if any would it offer to the government. Of course he was well aware of Magnum who were one of the largest producers of computers in the world and had launched the Autoplug, agreed by all to be a worldwide success story, and it stood to reason that this Ever Young health plan would somehow complement it.

Jack was not by nature an investigator and was generally happy to take the word of those he interviewed, but his initial reading gave the impression that it had been presented to parliament under the auspices of the then Health Minister Brendon Tann.

Fact: Magnum had acquired The Autoplug from Baylim via Cambridge University and the concept was accepted by the government with great enthusiasm. This was an innovation that, as sophisticated as it was, was an aid. It made no claims or promises to prolong life, there was no doubt that it was a very clever invention using the existing knowledge of the patient taken from all the sources that were available to the various departments of government and capable of arriving at an analytical conclusion. A wonderful and accurate self-healing diagnostic computer aided by holographics. Both the government and the medical profession enjoyed its benefits. Hines did not like Tann, and Tann showed no interest in enlightening Hines as to the relationship he had with Magnum.

Magnum was one of the largest and highly respected computer manufacturers in the world second only to Spoken Arrow. Now this same organisation had added Ever Young. This was a far more serious product that would make promises and demands, yet on the back of the Autoplug would seem part of its natural evolution.

It was only a few weeks ago that the Health Minister Brendon Tann retired, Jack could not remember why and had in fact little interest in the event, but he did recall Henry Hines taking over his job. Hines had been in the papers over the years as it appeared that he was being coaxed up the political ladder, but Jack had not observed anything that would arouse his interest. That is until he read the paper to note that he had been killed.

The press reported the event as a burglary, but a subsequent article in the Times intimated that it was too well organised and might have other implications.

Reading further, he noted that Hines had taken over from Brendon Tann who had recently retired for health reasons. Tann had played a major role in bringing the Autoplug and subsequently Ever Young to the market and, satisfied that all aspects of his project were now in place, passed on all his responsibilities to Hines.

He looked up the various comments on Wikipedia and read again the professional criticisms and promotional claims made by Magnum. Longer, healthier, guaranteed support to ninety-five…and then what…! Life terminated. The benefits to governments' health budgets, and superficially it seemed an exciting plan, all this would be achieved by simply injecting a microchip into the neck of a young man or woman. The Neuro351, he read, will foresee any psychological disorders before they physically emerge. In essence, stabilise humanity's psychosis.

In a world population reaching ten billion within the next forty years and thirty percent over the age of sixty-five, retired and beginning to ail, it would not be difficult to imagine the support needed for nearly a third of the world's decrepit population. If the next generation retained all their faculties into old age, he scribbled, their experience learned over so many years could be an invaluable asset to the world. How bad can that be, especially with the substantial savings to the Health Service, he asked aloud. Nevertheless it disturbed him to note the possible mental intrusion from an outside source such as Magnum. This was only a potential hazard, only where 'psychological readjustment might be required.' But it was possible.

Magnum was in the world's top 10 with assets, greater than most countries, it was worrying to think that such a large organisation could control the minds of millions, but that's science fiction he chuckled to himself.

Jack had to remind himself that he was working for a sports magazine and some reference should be made to the reader's health. Strengthened bones, stronger muscles, long term planning all allowed far more years to enjoy one's sport with a more positive disposition. And with a reasonable concept of the benefits, he began writing.

Hypothesis and reference books would take him so far, but it would be wise to go to the source. Magnum's UK office was not too far away and it would be good to make a call. He began by asking for their public relations officer and was recommended to speak with Julian Ackroyd.

"Why don't we meet over a lunch," suggested Jack. "I'm keen to learn how you plan to take over the healthcare world and to learn of any innovations that might be on the horizon."

Julian's formal function was to get as much publicity as possible, advertising was a necessity but write ups from prominent magazines made a greater impression on the market.

***

They agreed to meet at the Eldorado in Knightsbridge which was noted to be one of the finest steak houses in London. He arrived a little early and found a table where they could not be heard. Julian would identify himself by carrying a briefcase and umbrella, short, slim around forty and it was clear he made no secret that he was gay.

They each introduced themselves and Julian slid into the semi-circular seat as if he was wearing a tight skirt. Jack's good looks did not go un-noticed by him, and it would do no harm to give the impression that there was an essence of effeminacy. He soon discovered that he had a partner who was some years older. Julian's job spec appeared to be quite vague and allowed him to give information freely.

"I understand that the government is to join in the promotion of the Ever Young project, and with that in mind it might be a good idea to write up its pros and cons along with the advertising campaign, naturally we want to bring out the long term benefits and where we can spread across the spectrum of our publications emphasising health, sports and of course for the women's magazines emphasise some of the sexy aspects of the benefits of staying young too."

They ordered a bottle of wine, and even before the main course had arrived they had demolished it and ordered another. Julian was now speaking faster and without inhibition.

"It's an amazing company," smiled Julian. "German companies run like clockwork you know. When I first joined Magnum, they had already planned to take over the NHS, for instance did you know that today more than eighteen percent of all prescriptions are supplied either directly from Germany or by associated companies to Magnum around the world. It's not just the Autoplug, although our wonderful Holographic doctors are programmed to suggest our products."

"So are you saying that Magnum produce all the pills they recommend?"

"Of course not; not all, but some. It's a complete service, but we would be foolish to recommend another company's pills, wouldn't we?" he sniggered.

The second bottle was now half empty and the main course was about to arrive. By the end of the main course, a bottle of red had been introduced to the table. Julian had his top shirt button undone and was now totally inebriated.

"Did you know," slurred Julian, "that our latest Neuro351 can be monitored by our computers to check that it is working efficiently, and through the electrodes we can alter any emotional status. I bet you didn't know that." He giggled.

"No, I didn't know that." Jack replied innocently.

"Yes, it allows cross communication, neurocoding controls mood and ultimately behaviour change. It stands to reason that if you can press a button to terminate!" he shrugged. "Of course nobody is supposed to know that," and suddenly his tone of voice changed and placing his hands together as in prayer he pleaded, "please don't write that in your article will you, I shouldn't have told you that, in fact even I'm not supposed to know that."

"Don't worry Julian my friend, I won't say a word." Jack smiled as effeminately as he could manage, "But how do you know this? Surely this would be a top secret."

Julian blushed. "My partner Frank is a neuroscientist with the company, he was on the research team in Berlin for a short period, but they sent him back to England for some reason." He looked down into his empty glass as if he'd forgotten something. "He doesn't think it will be long before they extend the age limit either," he proudly mused. "We actually met at the company's Christmas do. In three or four years, he estimates that there could be at least fifty or sixty million in Europe alone, maybe more, benefitting from Ever Young," he took another sip of the refilled wine glass, "and he says we'll have the ability to control millions by pressing a computer button." His voice shot up to a squeak as he put his hands to his lips "Oh, my god I shouldn't have said that! Please Jack don't say that I told you this."

Jack put his hand on Julian's arm, poured the last dregs of the wine into his glass. "Don't worry my friend your secret is safe with me."

Julian was now glassy-eyed. "Would you like me to send you the introductory literature that we offer to our Magnumites?" he smiled weakly.

"Excuse me?" exclaimed Jack.

"It's an explanation sheet describing the 351 procedure."

"Yes, absolutely, I'll look forward to receiving it, Julian." They shook hands warmly.

Julian was not in any fit state to return to work. Jack picked up the bill, hailed a taxi to take him home and they parted as if lifelong buddies.

It would have been interesting to speak with Julian's partner, for the information given gave him deep concern. He had poured two and a half bottles of wine down Julian's throat but had learned more than he had expected and wanted to know.

**

There was no doubt that what he had heard from his erstwhile friend was quite disturbing, but it would be irresponsible to print anything that Julian had said until it was factually proven. Jack decided to dig deeper into the driving forces behind Magnum and establish who was running the company. He returned to his office and scoured the files. Tandem Press had in their annals information relating to every notable individual and company throughout the world. He scoured the company files for relevant articles, abstracting official company details, and over the next five hours began to build a picture of the company's origins and evolution.

Summary Historical Information of Magnum GMBH

"Magnum GMBH is a German registered company formed in 1952 by the Heinrich family to produce electronic accounting machines. In the year of 1938 the family of Schickendanz acquired a company called Katalegein and Cohen, that had developed certain mechanisms that catalogued both national and international information. The company under its new name redirected its programs to work with the German government of the time and were contracted to accumulate a manual system capable of storing and cataloguing swathes of names, addresses and details of professions, trades and religions for any specified population in Europe and around the world. After the war, the company was closed and the Heinrich family decided to replace the name Schickendanz. In 1952, Magnum Industrial was formed.

However by the early 60s it became evident that electronic computers and microchips were to be the future and Magnum invested vast sums into their development, initially producing accounting programs. They soon developed machines that were capable of holding other useful client information that could be integrated with accounts...classified as 'intelligent impositions'. Over the next 15 years the company has grown to a global size. In spite of its size, Magnum remains a private company and is owned by the Heinrich Family. Vast sums invested from their own resources have allowed the company an unhindered expansion. Its board now sits in Berlin, Germany and Sao Paulo, Brazil.

The Americas and Asia are controlled from Brazil. There is today hardly a country where Magnum is not represented. It is estimated to employ over 180,000 people at this time.

Magnum have recently expanded into the medical field with the Autoplug, described as a DIY medical mentor for the end user. It is now used globally in clinical settings and is said to substantially increase the efficiency of the medical profession. Magnum is rated one of the most successful companies worldwide."

***

There were a substantial number of articles written recently regarding the Ever Young project, both medical and subjective, and on the Neuro351. Jack wanted to research these before offering his boss a considered opinion, but was finding it increasingly difficult to pursue his investigations without feeling consumed by a strong bias against the company. He could not put his finger as to why but its presentation intimated a relentless efficiency and the feeling of absolute superiority, gave him the impression that nothing in the world would prevent their total domination. All this information would be academic had it not been for Julian's slip of the tongue. His misjudged words kept pounding in his brain: "Neurocoding controls mood and ultimately behaviour change." The Autoplug was the foot in the door. A brilliant concept that offered an intimate friend and medical mentor that titillated the appetite of both the public and governments alike, opening the door to Ever Young. But introducing the Neuro351 was a totally different story.

The speed with which they had managed to launch the Auto Plug was also astonishing. But Jack could not see how Ever Young related to it. He had now accumulated fifteen pages and decided that it was not sufficient to offer them without any personal comments to his boss who would have to draw his own conclusions, but it was obvious that as a substantial government advertising campaign was promised, a series of upbeat articles would be required soon.

He took the remaining papers home with him, grabbed a pizza on the way and munched as he read through a mound of medical reports on the Neuro351 and its ultimate resting place in the hippocampus of the brain.

He continued where he left off.

Summarised Notes on Magnum—Comments from the Neurological Monthly

Magnum offered a categoric guarantee that the Neuro351 would maintain perfect health till ninety-five which meant waiting at least another 65 years for confirmation, although experiments in various countries clearly showed that the Neuro351 would rebalance any weak genetic tendencies during the intermediate years, excluding unforeseen circumstances.

Between the substantial savings of medical costs from the age of 30 to 95, a national figure of medical savings could be calculated to that age of billions per annum.

The ideal age to determine the most acceptable time for the hippocampus to accept the 351 and rebalance any disorders was confirmed by a number of bona fide neurological experts in Austria and Germany and Brazil and of course in the UK assisted by the Magnum medical centre was between 22 and 30 years. Tests had been conducted on patients in mental institutes and prisons in six countries involving 10,000 men and women under 30 years old which have been an ideal proving ground to observe the controlled mood swings that resulted. Behaviour patterns and health was considerably improved of those that had been given Ever Young, suggesting that their sentences could be reduced making further savings.

***

It seemed to Jack in his exhaustion that there were so many medical, social and religious contradictions even within the neurological profession, that any debate would be negated by their opposing opinions.

It was 2.00 am when Jack finally found his bed, and as he lay in the dark his exhausted mind floated into impossible scenarios. He imagined millions of young men and women being directed to feel a need to say or do what they would believe were their own thoughts controlled by an outside source, and he fell into a troubled sleep.

At 8.00 am, the following morning he was awoken by the telephone. "Jack, I do hope I haven't woken you," came the effeminate voice of Julian. "I just wanted to apologise for yesterday, I really shouldn't have drunk so much. But I might have told you one or two things that I should not have, and when I mentioned it to Frank he was quite annoyed, I'd be so grateful if you treated my words as a slip of the tongue." He laughed nervously. "If this information got out, both Frank and I could lose our jobs."

"We're professionals Julian, you and I. Don't worry, I'm sure we'll speak again soon." He thanked him for calling and hung up. In truth, he had little interest in Julian's or Frank's job.

He sat in front of his machine with a black coffee going cold, pondering on how to approach his article and various follow ups that would be required to match the Magnum campaign. He needed to know more, and even more important, to eradicate his fears that some ultimate sinister objectives weren't being concocted. Could it be possible that in these modern times such a plot to control the minds of global masses was possible. If it was a tin pot organisation or an upstart dictator it could be a fantasy, but a global conglomerate in possession of a technical plan of this dimension was a serious consideration.

He decided that he would speak with his boss Brody Emmitt and present to him his findings. After retyping the salient points of his investigations, he telephoned his boss to make a meeting for the afternoon.

Emmitt was in a good mood. He had just put the phone down from the Brent House Advertising agency who were handling the governments promotions and had been given another six magazines to promote the Magnum's Ever Young

69

scheme. "It looks like they are going to be one our best spenders, Jack." It was not often that Jack saw the nicotine teeth of Emmett showing a smile rather than a growl, but in these tough times this was indeed great news.

"I want you to handle the articles for all the magazines relating to this account Jack, you will probably need a couple of assistants and if all goes well, I'll consider pulling you into the executive directorship." He lit another cigarette on the existing one he already had on his lips and directed Jack to a seat. "What is it that you want to discuss Jack, I heard that you were working into the early hours last night."

Jack opened his briefcase and pulled out his notes. "I had an interesting lunch yesterday with the P.R manager of Magnum. I wanted to hear first-hand what they were up to and their future plans. But what he told me prompted me to make my own investigations into the company."

"Sounds good to me," smiled Emmitt, "so what did you discover?"

"I have a problem Brody, and after you've read my summary I'd be grateful for your thoughts." He placed the papers with his comments onto the desk and waited. "Can I get you a coffee whilst I'm waiting?" said Jack.

"Yes and grab yourself one too." He could see the concern on Jack's face and settled into his chair to read what he had been given.

When Jack returned to Emmitt's office, he saw a very different expression facing him. "This is an interesting dilemma," said Emmitt. "There is an immediate decision to be made here, and a long-term investigation before any action can be taken. I've learned the hard way that you need hard evidence, and we've got over a million pounds of advertising on our books with this company and the government. As you know Jack these are tough times. The question is, should we be seen to promote a company that could have a secret agenda that can come back to bite us in the butt? And my executives will say 'what if your guy has totally misread the company's plans?' After all they are a massive organisation with bona fide products on the world market with the government's backing." They both sat contemplating the situation for a full five minutes.

Jack broke the silence. "Let me make some more investigations, I'm as keen as you are, boss, to take full advantage of this account's business, but at least let's be sure of what's behind it, if anything. How much time do I have before the first article is needed?"

"Two weeks. We should speak with their research department and see if they can throw any more light on their plans. Any chance that you could get through the door, speak to this Julian again?"

"If I must," chuckled Jack. "I'll call him this afternoon and see if he will introduce me to his partner. I'll think of an excuse."

As Jack walked out of Emmitt's office he called "he might see you as competition."

Jack had been given his home number but decided to phone the office. "Hello, Jack. This is a pleasant surprise; how can I help you?"

"Well, Julian, I started writing my article and including the salient points that we spoke of, not of course those that you were concerned with, but I'm having trouble with the neurological workings of Ever Young which I would like to explain to the readers, especially with the health and beauty and medical magazines that you are advertising in. I must admit Julian that I'm floundering a little. Are you able to discuss some of the more technical aspects of the project?"

"Not really, Jack," replied Julian, "but if you give me a list of questions you would like answered, what I could do is ask Frank to reply to them."

"That would be great, Julian, if I knew what questions to ask. I wonder if the three of us could arrange a meeting either at your offices or for a drink, in any event it would be nice to see you again and meet Frank," said Jack as he took a deep breath.

"That would be a nice idea, I'll speak with Frank and let you know."

Another meal was arranged for the following evening, this time at Brevotti's, a small Italian restaurant in Kensington that Jack knew. He had taken several women there for intimate dinners, and was well known to the owner Julius. It would be an ideal place to have a quiet conversation. He carefully placed a microphone in his jacket that would record his conversation. His anticipated questions might have answers that he would not completely understand and in any event he wanted to present a case to Emmitt should there be one. If Frank was fobbing him off with gobbledygook, others of greater knowledge would be able to discover it.

During the course of his work had met all manner of characters. He could also play the part of a chameleon. Arriving early he sat at his favourite table near the window. It was always interesting to view the potential customers examining the menu at the front of the restaurant and debating whether to go Italian or the Chinese two doors away. A few minutes late, he noticed Julian walking across the road with his partner. Frank was clearly the dominant of the two, tall and large, he must have weighed over twenty stone, nevertheless he carried himself well for his size. Jack estimated that he was approximately forty-four or five, and substantially overshadowed Julian. They saw Jack through the window and offered uninhibited smiles. After formal introductions, they settled down and drinks were ordered. "I'm so grateful that you agreed to meet me," said Jack, "you will know Julian how hard it is to write about a subject that you are not familiar with, but with an expert in my sights I can blind my readers with science."

"I should tell you Jack," replied Frank, "that I can only explain to you a résumé of information, as you know, much of the specific details are genetically coded and are rather more technical than I could describe in a casual conversation." His voice was impressively deep, which gave gravitas to his remarks.

"What I really need is a quasi-technical approach, something that they will immediately be able to grasp. I mean, the inspiration behind Ever Young is amazing, for example, how do we know that it will actually work or be able to defend any individual against all the ailments that they would otherwise get during their lives or in old age? You must admit that it is an amazing claim."

"Ah, I anticipated that question, that's quite easy," replied Frank. He leaned down to his brief case and took out a detailed drawing which showed the internal workings of the brain, and with a pen pointed to various areas that transmitted neuro-electronic impulses between them. It was a printout that a first-year psychology student might see. "Let me try to explain. There are negative, positive and reversing micro charges that continuously spark off a myriad of reactions according to one's thought patterns. Hundreds of thousands of these impulses are being generated through our brains as we talk, and they generate a mass of knock-on side effects. Of course, I'm talking in metaphors here Jack, but I want you to appreciate how complicated it is and yet how easy it can be to understand the basic principles from thought to action."

Julian looked at Frank with great pride that his very own partner should have such powers of explanation of such a difficult subject.

"So let's say for example that my family suffered from heart problems and it was within my genes to carry this particular ailment, there could be a moment in my childhood where this particular gene might be alerted, maybe a moment of tension, an argument, a degree of stress, whatever. It would not physically affect me now but like a new pair of shoes, it would make its first impression on that gene which would be brought to the fore, and at twenty say I have a fight, a deeper mark, by thirty five the heart is more easily strained and by fifty I'm in trouble with continuous wear over the years it would degrade until it could ultimately result in a heart attack.

"If a forewarning could intercede at the outset of such an incident, it would act as a modulator. The Neuro351 does this and controls those areas which lay in wait within our metabolism that are invariably called upon due to wear and tear of our daily lives. It's designed to moderate all the points in our system, and rebalances them before they find a neurological and ultimately a physical path."

Jack was impressed by this thumb nail explanation, but needed more. "And what happens if there is a glitch in the system, say the chip fails or there is an unforeseen illness, is there any back up? After all you are claiming good health till ninety-five years."

"Yes," he answered enthusiastically. "If the chip is faulty it will be picked up on our own monitors and we would immediately be able to correct it. Our software would immediately read the anomaly, find a norm and modulate the coding. Now if we were to use the code norm created from our original reading and maintain it, that inherited problem would be neutralised. It will also deal with mental interference."

"Please excuse my ignorance Frank, I don't understand what you mean by mental interference?"

"OK," he smiled. "There are two major divisions here: Physical ailments, emanating from the mechanical aspects of the body, they would invariably be picked up by the method already explained, and the mental problems which are generally seeded by circumstance or external emotional disturbances. These can be detected and controlled by electronic impulses generated in our own equipment within the monitors. Migraine for example is a classic case for rebalancing fluids, which would be easily controlled, whereas depression or violent impulses would show up on our monitors as interlopers, and would be rebalanced by adjusting the neurocode of the chip. The result is a perfectly balanced and happy individual."

Jack sat back in his chair. "What an amazing claim. You could eventually control the moods of an entire country by this. Would you therefore be able to readjust, say lifers, murderers, or rapists and the like?"

"Absolutely," Frank proudly confirmed. "In fact, we would campaign to infuse all prisoners. Some countries are very keen to do it immediately, but we have to begin with a degree of caution as legislation may take time to pass in various countries."

"And where are you personally placed in this astonishing breakthrough Frank?"

"Oh, I'm a very small cog within Magnum, Jack. It just so happens that I attended a global conference this year, in fact it was an error on the management's behalf that I was invited," he chuckled. "My invitation should have gone to the director of UK research who passed away last year and it landed on my desk. It was just too good an opportunity to miss and my immediate boss gave me the nod to attend, just a bit of luck," he smirked. "I shouldn't be telling you this, but I guess it will eventually become public knowledge," he shrugged.

It was ten o'clock when they finally left the restaurant, to raised eyebrows from the owner and Jack's rakish reputation was now in question.

"Would you like to join us at our club for a drink maybe?" suggested Julian.

"I have a really heavy day tomorrow, perhaps another time soon," he smiled.

Chapter 8

Immediately he returned to his apartment, he threw off his shoes and spent the next two hours listening to the conversation.

By lunch time, the following day he had summarised the salient points of the dinner date and phoned Emmitt for a meeting.

"We'll munch whilst we speak, pick up some sandwiches on the way in Jack, I'll supply the coffee. I'll have some interesting news for you."

Emmitt was in a boisterous mood, and Jack was still not sure how to approach a series of articles not yet written that could have serious political implications. After all, he was a sportswriter and had never had any inclination to wade into the muddy waters of advanced science. He decided to hear out his boss before parting with the document that contained his more negative thoughts.

"First of all I spoke with our chairman last night and told him of our little coup relating to Magnum. He informed me that on the back of a major advertising program and a few promotional articles in all our magazines, he anticipated the shares of Magnum would increase substantially, and he wants to invest five million pounds in their shares before they jump up. So, your articles will be putting money into the boss's back pocket. You're going to be their blue-eyed boy, Jack; I will promote your articles on the front covers -what do you reckon of that, eh? "STAY EVER YOUNG, SAYS JACK BRANSON." In fact, I am going to do the same. I spoke with my stockbroker this morning and asked him to buy a hundred and fifty grand's worth of their shares."

Jack smiled, "First of all, boss, I'm sorry to tell you that Magnum is a private company and they're not on the stock market. Listen, I want you to read my report and then we can speak about this in greater detail. Can we catch up with one another later this afternoon?"

He left Emmitt's office eating his sandwich and returned to the company's library. His curiosity was now becoming an urgent desire to discover Magnum's roots and the seemingly endless source of money that had predated it.

Where and what were they prior to the 50s? Jack spent time in the library of the War Museum. It was astonishing what facts could be discovered.

It was a well-known fact that the German Reich obtained sophisticated listings of various groups, but who produced them? He dug deep into the machinations of the Nazi regime, the Ministry of Information controlled by Field

Marshall Goring, and at last he found a key. The name of the original company was Katalegein GmbH, then changed to Schickerdanz; its objective was to register all the names in Europe that were seen to be enemies of the State. Millions of Jews were listed. Under Field Marshall Goring, Herr Schickerdanz took control of the company that would employ over two thousand people.

After the war, Schickerdanz changed his surname to Heinrich and the company name to Magnum GMBH. Heavily financed from Brazil, Magnum retained all the listings they made for Goring. However, as the years passed the project became defunct. Nevertheless, Magnum saw the benefits of cataloguing for commercial uses as the systems were already put in place. Substantial finances were injected into the company which supplied various governments with detailed information of targeted groups around the world such as products, contents, locations, affiliations etc. By the late fifties, Herr Heinrich's son took over the operation. Commercial Computers were coming to the fore and the company was in a good position to take advantage of this astonishing development adding advertising research to their agenda.

The development of the microchip substantially expanded the uses of the computer, not only giving it extended memory but giving it access to a plethora of external information. Heinrich's daughter married a Brazilian called Freudenberg with strong German roots and links to the Heinrich family, leaving Albert Heinrich currently President and Steffen, his son, Vice President who now controls the Magnum empire. Only one of the Freudenberg girls took an interest in computers but do not appear on the records.

The Autoplug was the invention of George Baylim and his team. Based at the Cambridge University in the UK, they were at last able to arrive at a final product. He and his team continued to be financed by the university were given substantial government grants over a period of years to develop the Autoplug.

The government were reluctant to invest further substantial monies, however with the assistance of Mr Brendon Tann, Minister of Health, further financial investment was accepted from Magnum, who took control of the product and were able to bring it to market, such that it is now used routinely around the world. It was interesting to note that they also had substantial interests in various German drug companies, manufacturing primarily prescription-class drugs in the UK and throughout Europe. The Autoplug equipment was installed free to the NHS but its use was paid for by the patient's credit card, with the government receiving thirty percent. Other European countries had similar agreements.

Jack was gradually building a historical patchwork of Magnum with a summarised information sheet and returned it to his boss's office. Emmitt had popped out so he delicately took the previous document from his desk and stapled his added information to it. The information, whilst giving a bleak image of the company's history did not incriminate them. There was no positive proof that any hypothetical intentions could be read into their objectives, but their history combined with the imminent possibilities referring to Ever Young caused Jack to feel that he was an instrument of some very distasteful and dangerous plan. The Ever Young project seriously worried him. The ability to alter behaviour patterns by remote control on a grand scale was the stuff for a science fiction novel, but this was a reality.

He awaited the thoughts of Emmitt with trepidation.

Upon Emmitt's return, Jack told him that he had added a few pages to his notes, and Emmitt politely picked them up and read them in silence.

"I can see the problem here Jack and it's something to be concerned about, but since they are not breaking a law nor doing anything that is obviously detrimental to us, we would be courting a massive law suit if we exposed only our theories without justification. Besides which the government is about to give us a massive amount of money for the pleasure of advertising their goodies. The chairman even wanted to buy shares in Magnum and so did I, but you have put the kibosh on that. They've also planned a massive TV campaign in conjunction with the governments blessing and are subsidising the budget."

Jack sat back in his chair looking bleakly at the wall. "So I'm to write for and about a firm that is ready to brainwash millions of the public. The public are totally ignorant of these schemers playing with their minds, but they will be instructed to sing the praises of this Fourth Reich company!"

"Listen Jack, we're committed, and we have no proof to justify being sued, which we would be, I can assure you. I think that we should do what we originally planned until something emerges that might compromise us. They want to promote Ever Young, it's their product not ours." He suddenly found a few more words of defence, "And you must admit it's an astonishing concept."

"Brody, it's one thing to advertise a product – that's their claims, their words, not ours. But once we give our own recognition to their philosophy in editorials it becomes our responsibility too. I think that we are selling our souls. Can I speak with you tomorrow morning? This is something that can just as easily destroy us both whichever way we turn if we're not careful."

"I'll do the same, and I might have a word with the chairman," replied Emmitt. "Until then."

***

Jack's mind was in turmoil and he was becoming depressed. There were not many friends to whom he felt he could unload his heavy heart in confidence. He decided to give his father a call. It was 6.30 pm and they would be sitting down to their evening meal at 7.00 pm prompt.

They got through the usual pleasantries and Jack immediately jumped into the reason for phoning.

"I need your advice, Dad, on a most difficult and secret subject, it is most important that you don't repeat our conversation even to Mum."

"All right, son, but you know she is going to ask why you phoned."

"I must know that you will not say a word to anyone, including Mum, this is a very delicate subject and a word out could cause serious litigation. Your word please."

"You have it Jack, now tell me what this world changing problem is," he joked.

It took Jack over fifteen minutes to describe the quandary he was in. "This series of articles would obligate me and my publishers to a project that could very quickly persuade millions to commit to something that could make them mental slaves to an organisation that had a very dark history."

"If I decided not to do it and am wrong, I would be missing an opportunity of a lifetime and without doubt would be sacked. On the other, if I told the world of my doubts it would bring the house down, especially if I can't prove what they haven't even done anyway."

There was a long silence at the other end of the phone. He could hear his mother calling his father into dinner, but he knew that a thought process was taking place.

At last he spoke "I can see the dilemma and its implications, Jack. You're on the cross roads to hell. It's quite a coincidence as it so happens, I don't know if you read The Times, but in yesterday's editorial there was an article on the health minister who was shot. It seems to have been a well-planned burglary. However, they interviewed Pickles – you know, the chancellor. He was a good friend of

Hines. He informed the reporter that when Henry Hines gave his introductory speech it caused something of a flurry. Apparently he was attacking the concept, the Ever Young project, on moral grounds despite the government's earlier excitement. Maybe you should speak with Pickles personally. Just a thought."

"Well done, Dad. You've given me plenty to chew on."

***

Jack's credentials soon managed to find Pickles' personal secretary. Jane Franklyn had been Alex Pickles' PA for over twenty years; she was now over fifty but retained the efficiency of a head teacher of a private girls school. There were very few secrets that her boss kept from her. She had never married and during the earlier years she had hopes of a possible liaison, but as time went by it was clear that he was committed to his wife and increasing family. They had reached an unspoken understanding but she could not imagine working for anyone but him, and he totally relied on her.

As he gradually worked his way up the ministerial ladder Jane became a reverential part of his office, and even the Prime Minister knew to speak with her before Pickles came to the phone. Jane had now become staunch friends with his wife and the unspoken affection for him by both women settled into a pleasant understanding.

She had seen the notes regarding the meeting with Henry Hines and was sadly aware of the subsequent happenings that had occurred soon after his presentation.

Jack introduced himself and immediately came to the point of his call. "You have probably never heard of me Miss Franklyn but I am the lead writer for the sports section of the Tandem Press, and have been asked to write a series of articles on the Ever Young project. I would have interviewed Mr Hines as to his view of the scheme but as you are aware, he is sadly no longer with us! But I have some very serious thoughts about this project and before I put the proverbial pen to paper, I believe it would be of interest to discuss with the Minister some of the aspects of this scheme. Time is of the essence; do you think that he could spare me a few minutes of his time?"

Jane Franklyn had an aversion to reporters, but there was an urgency in this man's voice that gave him a few more moments on the phone.

"He won't be free at least until the day after tomorrow I'm afraid Mr Branson."

"I would be so grateful for even ten minutes of his time tomorrow; it is important and could have serious implications for the whole country."

There was a long silence. He knew that he was flying a little close to the wind but he needed a life line to give him direction. He wasn't even very sure why he should speak with Pickles, but an understanding of how the higher echelons were thinking would add some colour to the articles if nothing else.

"I assume that you know that Mr Brendon Tann has taken up the reigns again as Minister of health, can you not speak with him?" she enquired.

"No, I'm afraid not."

"Let me have a look at his diary." He could hear her computer clicking away. "3.15 pm tomorrow here at his office. You know where to come. The security will be told, just show some form of identity. He can give you fifteen minutes, that's all." He thanked her profusely and she hung up.

Jack spent the following morning preparing a dossier which included all the salient points that disturbed him relating to Magnum. He was used to interviewing personalities in the public eye, but as this meeting reflected his own future he was uncharacteristically nervous. The meeting was to be at the offices adjoining Downing Street, and where most of the day-to-day work was done by an army of civil servants. He arrived thirty minutes early in anticipation of security checks, but to his surprise, he found that simply mentioning the name of Miss Franklyn, doors immediately opened for him. And by 3.00 pm he was waiting in a small reception outside her office.

Miss Franklyn greeted him with her hand out ready to shake, A surprisingly good-looking woman, slightly greying with no pretentions of hiding her age but slim, smartly dressed and smiling. "Good afternoon, Mr Branson. The minister will see you now. Please try and keep the conversation brief as he has a very busy schedule."

"I'm most grateful that you were able to slot me in." he replied.

Alex Pickles looked up from his desk, sleeves rolled up, spectacles on the end of his nose. He switched his computer off and immediately redirected his attention to Jack.

"Mr Jack Branson, please sit. I've read some of your articles, but I'm afraid I don't have too much time to spare these days for sport. What can I do for you? I understand you're writing about the Ever Young project. I must admit it's becoming something of a thorn in my side, especially with the loss of my good friend Henry Hines. Very upsetting."

"Minister, I have a problem, and I need as much clarification as possible before I begin a series of articles relating to the Ever Young business."

He placed the file on the minister's desk who immediately opened it. "It seems a rather comprehensive study, maybe you could summarise what's bothering you."

"Minister, you will know of the success that Magnum is enjoying with the Autoplug. They have entrenched themselves throughout the NHS. As a result of this tremendous invention it was relatively easy to find a positive response for the Ever Young project from a number of receptive ministers. You may not appreciate that the Neuro351 is capable of remotely accessing the recipient's chip. This is very disturbing for it allows a global company to tamper with the mind set of whole populations, worldwide. Now I don't know how Henry Hines presented this project to your cabinet, but I've no doubt in my mind that there is an ultimate objective planned here, to tempt millions to fall under their control – bearing in mind the history of the company."

"What history?" asked Pickles.

"Were you aware that the story of Magnum began before World War II, and they were working with Goebbels. At that time, they were systematically cataloguing names throughout Europe for the Third Reich under the name of Katalegein controlled by the Schikerdanz Family and had a simple objective, to pick and choose who they wanted in their New World and more important, who they didn't want. You may surmise who these names belonged to. It is all in the file. It is lucky that computers were not invented then, but today they can achieve what they attempted to do especially now that there is an Ever Young backed by the Autoplug."

"Jack, that was over eighty years ago, there were many companies working with Hitler in those days, Volkswagen, Mercedes, I could give you a list of them, beside which we are talking about one of the largest companies in the world."

"I accept that, minister, but supplying goods is a rather different matter than building death camps. You will see that the monies for the relaunch of the company back in 1952 came from a funds in Brazil which continue to fund the company today, passing monies through Switzerland, and I could give a guess where that money came from. It is the same family controlling it who are now into the third and fourth generation who changed their name to Heinrich. Their philosophy does not seem to have changed and substantial monies are still being given by Magnum to far-right wing groups, not only in Germany but in countries throughout the world. I believe that the Ever Young project could be a very sophisticated but diabolical continuation..." A bead of sweat appeared on Jack's forehead and was noticed by Pickles.

"I am now being asked to back up a massive advertising campaign for the Ever Young project, so that millions of our citizens will be given this chip, but I believe that the consequences could be dire if I am right. Therefore I felt the need to speak with you first, rather than Brendon Tann, who I believe is very close to them."

"Do you think that the death of Henry is connected to this theory of yours?" asked Pickles with a noticeable degree of cynicism.

"You must use your own judgement regarding that. I have my own thoughts on the subject, minister, but if I'm right nothing would stop such an organisation – and to them Hines would have been a serious encumbrance."

"My goodness Jack, you either have a dangerous imagination or we are looking at a looming disaster with global effects. I prefer to think of the first option. Listen, you have caught me at a very busy time, but you must leave this with me. I will put our chaps onto this, it would certainly be of interest if you can find a connection to Henry's murder, but I don't want you to do anything untoward until you hear from me – do you agree?"

"When might we speak again, minister?"

"Give me two days, and I shall be able to add significantly to your file by then. Alright. Thank you for coming and please ask Jane to come in on your way out."

Jack left the minister's office with the feeling that he had declared a third world war.

Chapter 9
Tann

Brendon Tann was now sixty-four years old. He had been on the political roundabout for over twenty-five years, gradually working his way up from a provincial MP. He had a grammar school education and came from a good middle-class family. His father was a local solicitor and wanted both of his sons to join him. His brother who was five years older and being rather more academic was happy to follow his father into the legal profession and eventually became a prominent barrister. Brendon passed his legal exams with a very average mark. Nevertheless his father took him into the firm in the hope that he would flower. Sadly, his father died unexpectedly soon after and his practice evaporated, leaving Brendon to find a job with a rather ineffectual legal practice in the East End of London in Hackney. He joined the Conservative party and was soon asked to stand as a candidate for the local seat everyone felt sure he had no chance of winning – it was an old and strong Labour constituency.

But they underestimated Brendon, who did join the council – indeed, became the one Tory councillor in a Labour majority. His efforts were totally wasted as nothing he could suggest would be considered. For the left-wing council, Tory and Conservative were close to swear-words. But Brendon was ambitious and worked hard to become noticed. He sat as a magistrate in the local courts, and whenever and wherever a parliamentary election came up he put his name forward as a potential candidate. He had no chance of winning as an MP in Hackney but at last he found an opening and learned from the experiment. When the Tory MP for West Hertfordshire suddenly passed away, and once again he pushed himself onto the listings, it was generally considered a marginal seat. But the Labour party were in the doldrums at that time, and canvassing furiously with the help of his colleagues, Brendon didn't disappoint and was voted Member of Parliament for the West Hertfordshire constituency.

There was nothing about Brendon Tann that seemed memorable except his persistence. He moved from one post to another by sheer pertinacity. To an outsider, it would have been remarkable for him to reach the heights of ministerial responsibility, but he was considered to be a reliable man who would vote with the powers that be, a safe pair of hands who would do what he was told.

Nevertheless, it should be said during his time as Health Minister with the guidance of his civil service minions not to mention sweeteners given by Magnum he managed to hang on to his position for over four years with relatively little conflict.

***

Although Jack had been advised not to do anything that would interfere with the minister's own investigations, he considered that it would do no harm to interview Tann as he normally would. He would discuss the advantages of healthy living and the benefits of the Ever Young project with him. It was not difficult to make contact with him on the phone, and upon mentioning the Magnum, Tann appeared to become more animated.

"I'm writing a series of articles on Ever Young over a number of weeks and anything that you may note of importance would be very much appreciated. I would of course be happy to quote you." A meeting at his home was agreed for that evening at 6.00 pm.

Tann lived in a beautiful house in Wimbledon. The property was built by Robert Adams somewhere in the 18th century and had been completely renovated to modern standards. It sat in approximately three acres of coiffured gardens and a tennis court. Jack took in the surrounding area and a thousand questions bombarded his brain.

An attractive woman of around thirty answered the door. She was in jeans and a tee shirt and was glowing. She looked as if she had been exercising. She had a relaxed manner and seemed quite comfortable within her surroundings, he thought.

"My father is expecting you, let me take you through to the lounge." She offered him tea or coffee, and left him alone.

It was a large room with high corniced ceilings. Surreal and impressionist paintings allowed the modern to interpose with the traditional character of the room and Jack settled into a deep-seated armchair awaiting his coffee.

At last Tann entered, he was casually dressed and looked relaxed. He had a suntan and had obviously been to some sunny climes. He had probably been quite tall but the years and excess weight had begun to bend him and jutted his head forward. If he had ever had hair thought Jack, it must have been many years ago.

"Pleased to meet you, Jack. You throw what you like at me and I'll be happy to tell you what I know about the Ever Young project." He plunged onto a settee.

"You have a delightful home minister; I don't have a chance to see such large properties in London these days. Did you have a part in designing it?"

"To tell you the truth Jack, you don't mind me calling you Jack do you? Talking privately, you can call me Brendon."

"Thank you, Brendon."

"No, this is my wife's doing, she inherited the house from her grandfather, she was brought up by her grandparents, unfortunately they both passed away a few years ago and we took it over. Big overhead but it's worth it, don't you think?"

"Definitely," replied Jack. There was a moment of silence. "It was terribly sad to hear of your colleague's death."

"A tragedy Jack a total tragedy. Henry and I worked closely together and it was an obvious choice for him to take over my job. I had retired only two or three months previous, I'd been over doing it and was warned to ease off. We have a villa in the south of France and that's where I got my tan." He smiled.

"Starting from the beginning can you tell me about your negotiations with Magnum Brendon, I'm sure the readers would like to know how you brought both the Autoplug and Ever Young to the UK. It must have been a historic moment."

"I wouldn't actually call it a moment. As you probably know the original inventor was Professor George Baylim, and of course his wife, who is also an extremely clever lady, and at that time I was investigating grants. We had given Baylim some considerable sums over the years to create a working model of the Autoplug. Baylim needed to bring his theories into reality. Coordinating medical technology with production is most difficult Jack, and especially the Autoplug. We offered his project to a few British companies, but the cash projection to make it national was too costly and we had no serious bidders. Magnum saw its benefits, had the money and the knowhow, and we went with them."

"Would you be able to tell me who rejected it?"

"No Jack I'm afraid that wouldn't be ethical. But In order to get it off the ground it would cost well over two hundred and fifty million pounds, also bearing in mind that every doctor's surgery would be trained to use it and install it. There were not many companies that would have that much money to invest on a brand-new venture, never mind be capable of doing so, the software alone cost many millions."

"But where would even a company the size of Magnum find so much money to invest on what could be considered as a green field project? I mean it's now global – there must be a billion or more invested in this business by now!"

"Mine is not to reason why," replied Tann. "I can tell you that they are like a well-oiled machine, the efficiency of this company is astonishing."

"I really admire you Brendon for recognising such an amazing invention. You should receive a knighthood. Maybe I should say something to that effect in my articles, of course with your permission."

"I wouldn't go so far as that," he replied with false modesty. "Of course if you happen to mention the idea I won't deny it." He smiled.

"You know, Brendon, it would be good to speak with the man who you negotiated with, his confirmation of the sort of man you are would be a great reference, what do you think?"

"Err," he hesitated. "I'm not sure that the higher echelons are too keen to put themselves in the limelight, but I might be able to recommend you a name in Germany of someone that would give you more information, why don't you speak with a lady called Evelyn Grunsmidt, she's a European director of marketing, she's based in Berlin, just mention my name. I shall send her an email and tell her that I have recommended you to her. I can also suggest you contact the UK MD his name is Paul Shannon. Of course it would be a real coup if you could speak with Frau Freda Gesh; she is the personal assistant to the Vice president of the entire company, if you can make contact with her she will give you all the answers I believe you'll need."

"Thank you, I'll contact her tomorrow," as he wrote down their names.

"Tell me about Ever Young. How did that develop?"

Tann was now more relaxed and getting into his stride. "Ah, now that is indeed a wonderful development, it was originally the work of Baylim and his research team. The man was a genius. We had to sophisticate it quite a bit, and Magnum had over twenty in their team to coordinate their research with the UK chaps in order that it could be imprinted cohesively onto a microchip." He poured himself a Scotch and offered Jack one, but he waved his hand, "thanks but I'm driving," said Jack.

He continued. "The Cambridge team drew on the knowledge of neuroscientists from all over the world to eventually prove the theory of controlling the DNA and involved biochemists, psychiatrists and God knows who else. The sad part of it is that no sooner had Baylim completed his work he died. The government was reluctant to continue subsidising the project without him and Cambridge realised that it would not be completed without a backer. It was fortuitous that Magnum came forward and completed the project in Germany. They are now taking it worldwide, and I must admit I'm very proud that I had a hand in the evolution of it. Eventually the UK team was dismantled and a number of the chaps working in Cambridge were offered positions in Germany."

"So how did you persuade a German company to invest such a considerable sum in the UK? It's an awesome amount. I'm in awe of you Brendon."

Tann blushed. "Don't make too much of it Jack, I was only doing my job and saw its phenomenal potential, one has to seize the moment. My German is quite good and I made a presentation in Berlin that obviously persuaded them to jump on the bandwagon."

"One has a reasonable degree of influence as a minister, but I had to do a great deal of persuasion with numerous ministers and governmental departments here, but the figures worked, and we've saved the country a considerable sum. The Heinrich family are now the third generation behind Magnum and I had the pleasure to meet with the President Albert Heinrich on a number of occasions. But most of my discussions were with his son Steffen. Very charming and shrewd too, you probably know that they are in the top one hundred companies in the world now and still privately owned."

They toasted their newfound friendship, and Jack had no reason to disbelieve that he had met the man who negotiated the sale of the Autoplug to Magnum, its patents and brand names. But it would be interesting to know a little more of Tann's personal history.

With a little investigation, back at the office he checked out Tann's wife. She was from Grimsby and her father was a warehouse manager. Her mother worked in a local dress shop. They paid cash for this delightful property only four years ago, The names of the architects and interior designers he found from the Wimbledon Council planning department, they informed him that it was a three million pound project. Prior to that they lived in a semi in Balham. He proved that Tann was a liar. Moving from mediocracy to wealth in 12 months.

***

Jack was waiting outside Brody Emmitt's office from 8.15 am. At 8.30 am, his boss casually entered with his third cigarette hanging from his mouth and a plastic cup of black coffee in hand.

"It's the early bird that catches the worm," joked Jack as he opened the door for Brody.

"What can be so important that you sleep at my office door, I should make you my pet, except I don't walk in parks."

"Brody I've been working hard on this Ever Young project, and made two visits. The first to the Finance Minister Pickles, and the second to Brendon Tann the ex then retired and now once again Health Minister."

"Ok, tell me about Pickles, and why the chancellor for goodness' sake?"

Jack was beginning to feel he was fighting a lost cause, but he pursued his case. "A leak in a ministerial meeting was reported in the Times stating that Pickles was chairing a meeting, and Hines was invited to speak as the newly appointed Health Minister. He lambasted the Ever Young project as a serious danger to the country, and suggested that the project had ominous implications that had not been given sufficient thought before committing to it. The project was defended by another minister stating that it had already been thoroughly debated."

"There are always going to be disagreements reported, even when they don't exist, as you know Jack," Brody replied, "but I can't see how it would relate to his murder and burglary. In any case it's a bit late in the day to withdraw from the scheme, especially since the government and a number of other countries had already committed to it with, as you know, substantial publicity. Beside the embarrassment of a withdrawal. Any publicity of such an act would place the entire project on ice until it was proven and justified, and would seriously compromise the government.

"In any case, it's unthinkable to imagine that a company the size of Magnum would conspire to brain wash vast swathes of the worlds brains. It's a plot for a second rate film."

Jack leaned forward almost whispering, "Brody, we're dealing here with a reality, this company is openly stating what their scheme will do, I agree with you it's unbelievable, but it's not fiction, it's happening and it's on our plate."

"That's a bit farfetched," replied Emmitt, as he lit another cigarette from the last. "Any way what did Pickles say?"

"I left him my notes, he seemed concerned and he asked me not to do anything before we spoke again, which is tomorrow."

"I must say Jack, I think that you are working on the smell of an oil rag, so you went to speak with Tann! What then?"

"Very interesting. We met at his home, as far as he was concerned it was to be a straightforward interview, and what a beautiful house he lived in. Anyway he explained how he negotiated with Magnum to take over the project after

Baylim died, and he intimated that he negotiated the original deal between Magnum and the government. I asked him who he negotiated with and he gave me the name of a senior executive in the company for me to interview."

"What's more he told me his wife inherited the property he was living in which was worth many millions. So I checked him and her out. Her father was a warehouse manager, and her mother worked in a dress shop. Not that there's anything wrong with these professions, but it won't buy you a four million pound mansion."

"Tann previously lived in a semi in Balham. Suddenly he owns a villa in France and is living like a millionaire. I'm convinced he's in Magnum's back pocket and have a feeling that he is in cahoots with others in the cabinet. What's more I'd be most interested to know how Professor Baylim died so suddenly."

"So, now we have two suspicious deaths. This is turning into a murder mystery. What do you want me to do Jack? I have instructions to smack out the adverts in two weeks and need a thousand-word editorial to go with it, I don't particularly want to wave goodbye to a million pounds' worth of advertising."

"Give me a week Brody. If I'm wrong, I'll work through the night to give you your page I promise. I'm really concerned that there is more to this than meets the eye. Please, if I'm right it could be the biggest story you've ever had and you'll sell ten times the magazines!"

"If!" shrugged Emmitt. "A big if."

***

Jack's mind was still swirling with facts and incidentals when he recalled one point that was mentioned by Frank during their conversation. It was the royalty payment due to Baylim, and he wondered if his wife had received anything after his demise, or even before. In any event, it might be interesting to speak with her and even Baylim's colleagues.

He was still pondering at 11.30 am when he received an email from Miss Jane Franklyn asking him if it would be possible to meet the chancellor at 4.30 pm that afternoon.

Once again he was directed to her office, but this time she escorted him in, asked him if he would like a coffee and buzzed her assistant to bring coffee for three. Pickles stood to shake his hand, he was still in shirtsleeves and his expression as sullen as before, it seemed as if the entire bank of England was on his shoulders.

"I followed up your notes, Jack, your history lesson was easy enough to substantiate, and I was surprised that it hadn't been dug up before. It's most interesting to learn that Magnum is still being run by the same bunch that we beat in '45. However, as we know that's history. If we were to consider how and why dictators are even allowed to exist in today's world, we could eliminate fifty percent of the world's leaders. But I am concerned that the Ever Young project has been allowed to pass us with our eyes open, for the original concept made no mention of a remote control of the Neuro351, especially the facility to adjust the mental state of each individual from a central point, this is disconcerting, especially knowing this company's background."

Whilst Pickles had been talking, Jane Franklyn had been browsing through the notes. "Glancing through some of the recorded meetings that are on the file I managed to read before you came in Jack it seems that all the presentations were made by Tann, but at the point of the eventual approval of the Ever Young project I cannot see any mention of them remotely mentioning the 351 aspect of it, and it must have been added in after it had its certification. The original presentation made no reference to assisted control of mental problems. The termination date would have been negotiated with no mention of a proverbial computer button.

"However, you know as well as I that we are well under way with the launch of Ever Young which in itself seemed a marvellous idea. And would ultimately save the country billions."

There was a silence which no one wanted to break. At last, Pickles quietly muttered, "it would be very hard for us to renege on the project at this stage unless we could find a bona fide reason to do so. You are to be congratulated on bringing the obvious to our attention Jack, but I need your help before we ruffle any feathers here. If we expose our doubts too early, we could be sued by just about everyone including Magnum, and you would be blacklisted, so let us tread carefully." And as an afterthought he added, "…and what's more if it was discovered that Tann and his colleagues were being bribed, it could seriously damage the Party and could even result in a vote of no confidence. The opposition and the public would crucify us."

"I believe, sir, that both Baylim and Hines deaths need to be investigated," Jack blurted out. "There are too many anomalies. Number 1. It's impossible for Tann to live in the style that he does on the income he earns, and during my meeting yesterday it was obvious that he was lying about his sources. Number 2. If we could prove that there was some form of collusion by the manner of their deaths, would that be sufficient to act upon?"

"That would obviously help, but we also need to know much more about their methods of monitoring. I can't understand why the details of the End of Days haven't been set out in greater depth. It would have to be a very sophisticated system to maintain a constant record of many millions. I'm amazed that this question hasn't been asked before, and it's quite possible that he had support from other members of the cabinet," said Pickles.

"Supposing Henry Hines threatened to expose Tann, that might justify the sudden retirement of Tann and Henry's murder," said Jack.

"That could make things rather more difficult Jack. Our Health Minister a murderer. No, I'd rather not pursue that path," smiled Pickles. "However, I would like to hear what Baylim's wife and colleagues have to say regarding the project, and what they received. Clearly there had to be some benefit to them and the university."

"Magnum are taking the lion's share of the income of the Autoplug and that can be multiplied by as many countries around the world," said Pickles, "and have thrown a fortune at it too."

"But it was invented here in the UK, the government also invested millions and so did Cambridge, the question is how was it negotiated by Magnum? I was told by Tann that nobody here could afford the initial investment," said Jack. "But Tann was not able to tell me who else was offered it."

"I would like to see you next week, that's six days from now. You need to do some more foot work Jack, and we will too. I shall also check what we had given as grants, this would give us certain rights to the product. We shall compare notes next week. Please do not tell anyone what we are doing. Not even your boss. Especially not him. He is the Press and in my experience even at the highest level they have verbal diarrhoea."

"With the greatest respect sir…" began Jack.

"Yes, you too," smiled Pickles for the first time. "I'm particularly interested to learn more of the murder of my friend," he said solemnly.

Chapter 10
Joe

Joe had been travelling through France for over two weeks. He meandered to the south staying at small boutique hotels. He phoned his father and asked for him to send some cash and if there was anything he should be worried about, but no further news was reported.

He received a box by registered post containing thirty thousand euros, and a handwritten note stating: "This should keep a smile on your face for a little while, but keep a low profile son, as far as the world can see you have been in France."

Slowly acclimatising himself to the French ways he meandered sluggishly through Nice and into Cannes. He had managed to lose his British pastiness by the time he arrived in Monte Carlo.

He was at first a little taken aback by its wealth and sophistication. Watching the Casino clientele, he bought a white tuxedo and a few clothes befitting a wealthy image and booked into a salubrious hotel that he felt he now deserved. Joe looked and felt good as he entered the Casino de Beaulieu. Although against his father's instructions, he decided to continue using his Nom de plume which gave him a feeling of being reborn. Looking in the mirror he repeated his new name with a Cagney accent, pulling out the revolver and aiming at himself. He felt good.

Joe had been to many casinos over the years playing Blackjack or Roulette, but here in Monte Carlo he was rubbing shoulders with the world's richest. He wanted to be seen as one of them yet his lifelong training in crime gave him some pleasure in how he could relieve them of some of their ill-gotten gains before the casino did. But he squashed the thought, reminding himself why he was there. Tonight, he would be one of them.

He was aware that there were security cameras and a wide variety of hidden electronic gadgets pointing in every direction, but this was not particularly interesting to him, as he was now anonymous. His passport showed a new name, and in any case, he was confident that no one knew him.

He walked to the bar and ordered a whisky. Two men and an attractive woman were arguing only an arm's length away. They were talking very fast and loud in French when suddenly one man took out a knife and stabbed the other who gasped and immediately fell to the ground. The woman screamed and became hysterical as she kneeled next to the dead man. Joe looked on, if not in shock, certainly astonished by the speed of events. He immediately moved back to try to find some anonymity, but within seconds three security guards appeared.

They attempted to speak to the woman but she was almost incoherent and they then turned to Joe. He could not understand what had been said since he could not speak French. They asked him to come to the office where someone there would interview him in English as a witness.

It was not a comfortable situation for Joe as he awaited a police officer, and he could feel another migraine slowly taking route. "I would appreciate a glass of water," he said.

The symptoms were unbearably consistent and he had an urgent need to lie down, there was a settee against the wall which he seconded.

"Migraine," he informed the young officer who joined them as he held his head. He directed Joe to a Settee. "My name is Inspector Simone and I am sorry to disturb you at such an inopportune moment," he stated politely.

Joe was now lying down and in great discomfort, he undid his bow tie, opened the top button of his shirt and kicked off his shoes. He was now sweating profusely. "Let me take your jacket," said Simone. As he removed it from Joe's shoulders he noticed the holster strapped to Joe's hip but said nothing.

"I'm very sorry that you are feeling so poorly sir, but it appears that you are the closest witness to this incident, and the description of what you saw and heard would be most appreciated, maybe if we can leave you for say, a half an hour you would be feeling a little more like talking to us."

"Thank you," replied Joe his eyes now closed. "I have some pills in my jacket, I wonder if you could give me two of them and another drop of water."

"Of course." The inspector felt for the pills that were in the inside pocket of the jacket and noted the name on the bottle and Joe's passport. He discretely removed it and passed it to his colleague. "Take note that the names are not the same," he whispered.

"Let us leave you for a while, we shall come back in say thirty minutes, if that is alright with you, sir."

"Sure," replied Joe. now quietly moaning.

Once outside the room Simone looked more closely at Joe's passport. "Did you notice the holster and the revolver?" He asked his assistant. "Let's just check this fellow out, just for the record."

Joe slept for over an hour, giving Simone an opportunity to delicately remove the gun and take note of its make. By the time Joe awoke Simone had replaced the pills, Passport and revolver, he contacted his headquarters, giving them the name and passport number to verify. They recorded a Joe Shapero from a London address but he had died five years ago at the age of 84. The name of Joseph Brenekov on the pill box, was quickly verified by the MI5. He crept back into the room and noting that Joe was now asleep, slipped out again with his drinking glass to take the finger prints from it. Scotland Yard were most accommodating and quickly reconfirmed Joe's passport Identity. However, as he had done nothing wrong other than travel on two passports showing a Joe Brenekov arriving two days earlier than the Shapero one, it seemed a relatively baseless enquiry.

"It would be difficult to use this guy's statement bearing in mind that he's been dead for a few years," smiled Simone, "but we'll wait and see what he will say. A gun and a false passport suggests that he's up to something, anyway, the Yard had described the Brenekov family records which made interesting reading."

An hour later Joe awoke, the worst had passed but he was still very groggy. He was about to take two more pills but the glass that he had been drinking from had vanished. He was still disorientated when Simone re-entered the room. "Of course he could be here just to gamble," said Simone's assistant, "but it's interesting to note that he used his false passport to travel here under a nom de plume when his actual passport shows he arrived two days earlier."

He had little to say and had no idea who these people were in the casino, and was only able to give a brief description of what he saw. The police officer had taken his details from the passport, his mobile number and the number and type of gun. Joe left the casino to go back to his hotel.

Simone immediately ruled out any association between Joe and the murder. "There is no reason to hold this man, but it would be more interesting to discover if he is up to something, let's keep tabs on him for a while whilst he's in Monte Carlo," said Simone. "A gun and a false passport must have a meaning, and it's worthwhile finding out…" Simone placed a small microchip tracker on the back of Joe's jacket. "We'll keep a tag on him for the next few days."

On his return to the hotel, Joe received an email from his father:

"Hi Joe, hope you are having a good time. We've been looking at the various opportunities to sell off some of the higher value goodies. As you are already on the continent it may be interesting for you to have a few quiet words with one of our friends. He's in Switzerland. As it's not too far away from you, you may like to give him a call. He lives in Geneva and his name is George

De LeClare Tel No. 0041 735457. He is a good man, but a tough negotiator, so don't commit yourself before speaking to me.

I'm enclosing photos, details of the artists and market value. and I suggest that you print them off and then delete them from your memo pad, (for obvious reasons). If we can get 30% of their worth we will be doing well, but be careful. Dad

PS Don't forget to wipe this email."

He looked at the pictures and their valuation, and even with a quick calculation smiled at the bottom line that he could hope for, but as it was now quite late he decided to wait until the following morning before making contact.

It was mid-day before Joe made the call, LeClare answered the phone directly, and it was obvious to Joe that he was expected. "When would you like to visit me, Joe? I would be pleased to see you tomorrow if that is convenient to you."

"Sure, and if you would text me your address in Geneva?" Said Joe.

"No, I will look out for you at the car rental counter at the airport. I will be wearing a black trilby and red scarf. There are cameras everywhere, Joe, and probably trained on that counter too. So when we see one another we will walk out of the airport separately. I will drive to the exit and you will join me there, OK?"

Joe drove to Nice and left his car at the airport there. He landed in Geneva at noon. Concerning the meetup, he understood only too well the delicacy of this meeting with its need for secrecy, and it gave him a degree of comfort that his potential client had taken this into account.

At the car rental counter LeClare briefly touched his hat and walked to the car park. He paid by card and as instructed, Joe casually slipped into his car at the exit.

"I have worked with your father on a few occasions." He spoke with a strong German accent which appeared to have a good sprinkling of American. "But it is unusual to be offered items of art that are so easily identifiable, you can understand Joe that I am placing myself at risk in handling such goods as you are offering." His tone was gentle and had an air of nonchalance. "That is not to say that they cannot be sold, but it will be more difficult and dangerous to do so."

"It's not for me to tell you how to sell them," answered Joe, "but we are sitting on a goldmine for somebody. All we want to do is unload them at a fair price, but we're not giving them away. If necessary we should hang onto them until we find the right customer."

"But first, my friend, we must eat. We can't talk business on an empty stomach." replied LeClare.

It was 4.00 pm when they finally finished their lunch and after a bottle of wine and a good meal both slowly let their guard down. "Show me your photos," smiled LeClare.

Joe produced the file containing the pictures and placed them in front of LeClare.

He stared at them for some time. "Have you transferred these pictures from your mobile Joe? I only ask as they are not too clear and if you could email them to me I would be most grateful. This way I can send them to my client."

Joe hesitated. "I think that it would compromise us Monsieur LeClare it's not a good idea, in fact I was about to delete them."

"I do understand," replied LeClare. "but you will appreciate that if we are to offer them to a client they must see them first. I promise that as soon as they see them I will make it a condition that they must remove the images from their computers."

Joe considered the logic and reluctantly transferred the pictures to LeClare's email. He was about to rub his image off his own pad but considered that he would have no further reference if he might need to show them to another prospective customer.

"The Giacometti is very beautiful, it may be that we can sell this to one of my Russian friends, but the Modigliani painting will take longer to place, you realise of course the danger that I place myself in by offering such works of art, and if you wish me to buy them personally, I may have to hold onto them for years before I can safely find my customer."

"This is for you to decide, sir," replied Joe, "I am sure that you would not have wanted to meet me if you were not interested, so I would like to know what you have in mind. I'm open to offers."

"I suggest a figure around half a million dollars to clear the lot. What do you think?"

"I think that you have a great sense of humour, this consignment is worth over twenty million dollars, and even if you had to wait two or three years it is worth at least seven or eight million."

"Listen Joe," LeClare smiled, "we both know how these pieces came into your possession, they're hot, and the police around the world will know where they came from too. I would strongly advise you to consider my offer, speak to your father and I am sure that he will agree." "Is that your best offer," said Joe.

"I would say so," smiled LeClare.

"OK I'll speak with my father, but I'm sure he won't accept it."

"In the meantime, I will have some discrete conversations, maybe I can find an interested party who will pay a little more."

"Please be discreet Monsieur LeClare, I appreciate that you are most professional but this is very sensitive material, I would be pleased to consider a deal at two million if you would decide now," he improvised.

"I would not offer that Joe but maybe my client will, I will ask him and will phone you on your mobile."

They shook hands and parted, and he returned to Monte Carlo, booked out of his hotel and followed the Mediterranean coastline into Italy.

***

Joe was finding it difficult to relax. He had been travelling around Europe for over two weeks taking in the beauties of the various countries, and upon his father's recommendation drove on to Milan to meet another potential buyer. Signor Alberto Jodi. They met in a hotel near the main station on Jodi's suggestion, and after a brisk introduction Jodi quickly came to the point.

"I know most of the pieces that you are offering, and under different circumstances Mr Brenekov they would have a great value, but they are too famous to sell in Europe, maybe, China, Brazil or even Russia for someone's private collection, it is dangerous to sell them so close to home." He leaned across the table and Joe could smell a pungent perfume as he whispered, "I should mention Senior Brenekov, and I'm sure that you will already know that there have been notices from the British MI5 as to how and where these items were taken, and they are trying to link their disappearance to a murder of a notable politician."

Jodi was a small man, over dressed and giving an image of a gigolo, pencil sharp moustache, slick black hair, winkle picker shoes, yet he had a certain authority.

"I was unaware of that," replied Joe appearing noticeably shocked. "We are simply middlemen in this operation, I know nothing about any murder."

"I understand," said Jodi unconvincingly. "Nevertheless you will appreciate that this will influence any offer made, but I will investigate the market, where can I contact you again?" Joe left his mobile number and informed him that he was staying at the Imperial Hotel.

"Allow me to speak with you tomorrow afternoon," he said.

He left the meeting very concerned, and immediately phoned his father.

"Don't talk about anything again until I tell you, don't worry they won't connect us to it. Don't worry son," he repeated, "everything will be OK, I suggest you come back home, we will deal with it from here."

Joe could hear his father's concern. "I'm worried Dad," he whispered into the phone.

"Don't worry," his father repeated again, "we made enough from the first instruction, we'll just hold on to the goods and wait, there's no hurry. Come home."

***

Inspector Simone had lost track of Joe but was not particularly interested in him anyway as there was nothing to report other than the information passed onto the UK. However, the British police had taken note of the false passport and emailed the information to UK passport control.

To his surprise Joe found pleasure in the continental ways as he moved from one country to another, but it was time to return home. It seemed reasonable to him that since the Brenekov passport showed his exit from the UK, it should also reflect him not returning.

Against his father's instructions he had no problems being Shapero during his travels, and used his Shapero passport without inhibition leaving Calais. However, when reaching the Dover British control the young woman in the passport box looked tired and had no smiles for any of her queue. She took the passport and after a few moments left her box to speak with her superior. They returned together and Joe could see trouble brewing. "Mr Shapero would you please come with me, we need to ask you a few questions."

Her superior was a young man not too much older than Joe, a large rugby type and not to be easily reckoned with.

"We understand, sir, that you are travelling under the name of Shapero, but we have good reason to note your name is Joseph Brenekov, is that so?"

Joe looked at this man as if he could kill him. "What makes you think I'm not Shapero, you can see for yourself that it's my photo on the passport."

"Come on, Mr Brenekov, don't waste both of our time pretending. We know who you are and you might as well save a lot of trouble by coming clean. It's an offense to travel on a false passport, and I would like to know why you have hidden your real identity."

There was little that Joe could say, and after a few moments staring at one another, the officer picked up the phone. Two police officers entered and immediately put handcuffs on him, pushed him into another room, emptied his pockets. They confiscated his car keys, wallet, mobile, his two passports, and checking the car's glove compartment immediately spotted the gun. They left and locked the door behind him. The room was spartan, a glossy white with only a small table and two chairs. It had no windows.

The event had so taken Joe aback that he found it difficult to gather his thoughts. He sat on a chair and held his head, wondering how they knew. He had been so careful, surely LeClare or Jodi had not given his identity away, in any event they were unaware of his nom de plume. He sat for what seemed hours waiting to know his fate. His memo pad was taken away, and he gave some thought to recall if he'd removed his mobile conversation with his father.

At last, the door opened and a man and a woman entered. They were not in uniforms, but had severity written all over them.

The woman took the lead "Mr Joseph Brenekov, we are arresting you for travelling under a false identity, and the illegal possession of a gun. You will have a full opportunity to explain your position in due course, and you can make a phone call to your solicitor on arrival at the station. Do you have his number?" "No but my father has."

A policewoman insisted on standing uncomfortably close to him as he spoke.

"Dad, I don't know what's happened but I've been arrested. It's ridiculous, what shall I do?" It had been years since he had asked for help, but his first port of call was still his father and he was now desperately in need of his assistance.

His father could hear her speak. "You will only be able to discuss your offence with a solicitor. You should ask him to come down straight away or we can find you a local solicitor."

"No. I'd like my own," replied Joe.

"Can we speak with your father?" There was no further negotiation and Joe gave the officer the telephone.

"Your son has been arrested for entering this country on a false identity and a firearm was found in his car. Mr Brenekov. I suggest you find him a lawyer as he's likely to be brought up before the magistrate tomorrow," said the officer.

"A firearm," Brenekov instinctively reacted. But he refrained from expanding on the item in front of the policeman. "I'll get someone there today." he replied.

Brenekov immediately phoned his lawyer Albert Bonham. His practice was in Hammersmith. He was well known in London police circles for he appeared to have a penchant for representing a number of the local mobs, and invariably found a way of unscrambling the mess they regularly found themselves. However, it would take him over four hours to travel to Dover.

Bonham's image belied a wily and rather more creative mind than his profession usually represented. Short, chubby and bald, he could have been a cleric, maybe a vicar, and in court it would have been difficult for a Judge or magistrate to think him a liar.

It was late afternoon before both Bonham and Brenekov eventually arrived at the police station in Dover.

"They won't allow you to be in this interview Mr Brenekov, and anyway Joe will feel less inhibited talking to me alone." "No, I'll stay," barked Brenekov.

"Mr Brenekov, you are not allowed to be here, please leave if you want him to have a reasonable chance, or find another solicitor."

Brenekov was not used to being confronted in this tone but saw that he had no option, and reluctantly left.

Now alone, they sat. Bonham placed his hands on the table as if awaiting a catholic confession rather than criminal.

"What on earth prompted you to travel under another name Joe, and with a gun for goodness' sake. You'd better tell me what you've been up to and where." He was quite prepared to hear a cock and bull story and was expected to believe every word.

"Joe, there are two approaches that you can adopt here, the truth or a fabrication, whatever I am about to hear will be your defence, now I know you're not a fool and if you don't want to go inside for six months you had better give me a damned good explanation.

"Let's start from the beginning. I'm not too concerned about the passport but the gun could be a problem. When did you leave the UK and why?"

Joe thought for a moment before he replied. He was well aware that the first lie would be compounded into a mountain of others, but he could not tell even his own solicitor the reasons why he left England and the actual date he left. He decided to follow the date on his real passport which had given him a waterproof alibi for the Henry Hines murder.

"You know that I work with my dad," he began. "I look after various properties that we own. But I suffer badly from migraine. Well, recently my migraine has been returning nearly every day, so it was decided that I should get away for a while, a change of scenery and generally take a break. There was a property in France that my dad was negotiating to buy and he suggested I look it over for him."

"OK," replied Bonham, "so why did you carry a false passport, surely you of all people must have realised that this was against the law?"

"Look Mr Bonham, you know my dad's reputation, this guy was selling passports and I decided that if I was going into a nightclub or even a casino it was possible they would know my name, I realise it was a stupid act, but I made a mistake, that's all."

"So you went to France, then Switzerland, and then onto Italy all under the false passport. Is that right?"

Bonham's apparent acceptance of Joe's misdemeanours relaxed him and gave some hope that he might sleep at home that night. "Yes," he replied.

"So, Joe," smiled Bonham, "I have no doubt that all these trips can be verified. So why did you take a gun with you, after all you were supposedly on holiday." His gentle tone of voice had not changed but Joe could see that his story would now become more complicated.

"Ah, now that's an interesting situation. I bought the gun after going to a casino in Monte Carlo, looking around the casino I thought I would have a drink and as I came to the bar there were a couple having a terrific argument. They were jabbering away in French when this guy suddenly stabbed the man next to her, right in front of me. The police were already at the casino and asked me to tell them what I saw. Well, after that I felt that I needed some protection…so I bought the gun. I never used it of course. I realise that it was a mistake, but…" He trailed off.

"So, that's your story Joe, well I can go into court tomorrow and tell them that you are a naughty boy who needed to protect yourself, and maybe they will smack your hand, or maybe you'll get six months or a year inside. Does that seem fair."

Joe, was taken aback. "That is not at all fair Mr Bonham, no that would be really bad news. There must be something we can do."

"Well, suppose you tell me a better fairy tale, one that might put the judge to sleep, because this one certainly won't."

"But that's the truth, I swear it, it was just bad judgement by me that's all."

"Listen Joe, if I was the Judge listening to you I would not accept that you hid your identity to protect your father's image, that's ridiculous. I would believe that you are running away from something that you had done and giving yourself an alibi. Now if that is the case take a year in prison and thank heaven that's all. Unless you have a better story for me by tomorrow, I will throw you at the mercy of the British courts. Now we can speak with your father."

Joe's story was related to his father by Bonham with the appropriate cynicism of a prosecutor, but Brenekov had other ideas.

"Who's the Judge?" He asked with a degree of aggression. "I might know him."

"It's a magistrate, all they will do is hear the prosecutor state the facts as they know them, I will make a plea, and they may either take a lenient view and let him go on bail or keep him there and transfer the case to a court hearing, that is if they are half asleep and haven't listened, which is highly unlikely, Joe will probably be held until a date for the next hearing is given or let out on bail if he's very lucky, we don't know. But in my opinion Mr Brenekov he had better find a more convincing story because this one would in my opinion without doubt open a can of worms."

Bonham left Brenekov in the waiting room and returned to Joe.

"How did the passport officer know your passport was false," said Bonham, "was there any time that you left your details with anyone? This is most important, think."

Joe cogitated. "Monte Carlo, when I was in the casino, being questioned, I developed a really bad migraine and they allowed me to rest in their office – maybe it was the shock of seeing this man being stabbed – anyway, I took my jacket off which they hung up for me, and my passport was in it. I remember asking them to get my pills which were still in the jacket, and some water."

"Do you have them with you now, let me see them." Bonham looked at the bottles that had Joe's name on. "That's obviously it, they compared your passport to the labels. Now where did you get the gun? Tell me the truth, Joe, because they will certainly ask you."

"I can't remember," Joe replied. "Oh yes, I bought it in Italy, a rifle shop. I can't remember exactly where."

"If we contacted the police in Monte Carlo would they verify your story?" "I guess so," answered Joe hesitantly.

"I'm going back to my hotel, and will check it out."

"So, what's going to happen now, can I get bail?"

"Your hearing is tomorrow, I shall stay over until then. Your father is here too, but we will have to give them more details before they let you go Joe. Personally, I doubt it. I'll speak with you later."

Brenekov sat quietly pondering on the various implications that could result from this situation, it was a potential disaster, he had told Joe specifically to get rid of the gun, and it was probably the same gun that Joe had used to kill Henry Hines and his wife. But he could only hope that the police would not relate Joe's gun to a murder without relevant evidence.

Brenekov knew that when he told his wife and his brother they would go berserk, he for the security of the business and her for her son.

***

Switzerland is one hour ahead of England, so it was not too surprising to receive a call at 7.30 am. On Brenekov's mobile.

"Bonjour Monsieur Brenekov, this is George LeClare. Your son and I had an interesting meeting you know in Switzerland a few days ago. I have been trying to contact him but fortunately I have found his famous father. How are you, mon ami?"

Brenekov awoke from a heavy sleep and cleared his voice. "George, it's good to speak with you. I hope that Joe made a good impression."

"He's – how do you say? – a chip off the old block," he chuckled. "I have been looking to see where your little gifts could be placed, and I think we could move them to Russia. They will offer you a million dollars to take the lot, less twenty percent for me…I know that you were expecting more, but under the circumstances I think it is a reasonable price. Please accept this offer as I believe you need to move the goods out of your country as soon as possible, what do you say?"

LeClare was right, and even though he was guessing the scenario, current events were now becoming rather precarious it was probably the best deal he could get.

"Supposing I said yes, George. Tell me how you would pay."

"The money would be paid in dollars to an account in the Bahamas which you would open if you do not already have one."

"You must be most careful my friend not to allow anyone to prepare them for transport other than yourselves. As soon as you have packed them you will notify me and the money will be transferred. My clients are prepared to pay before the goods are shipped, for negotiating convenience, but I should tell you, mon ami, that we are not dealing with amateurs here, please do not deviate from any deal that we make. They will not be happy, with me and you, which is not a good idea. Comprendez?"

"I understand," replied Brenekov. "The six main pieces – one million less twenty percent is eight hundred thousand pounds."

"No, monsieur. Dollars."

"It's a ridiculous deal, ridiculous," repeated Brenekov.

"Yes, I agree but I think it's the best under the circumstances, don't you?"

"The parcels should of course be well wrapped and sent from a location in the north of England to an address in Paris which I will give you in due course. I suggest you include a few pieces of bric-a-brac. And send them by air."

Brenekov sat on his bed fuming. "OK it's a deal, I'll telephone you the details of my bank tomorrow."

The sale had become an incidental now and he had to give all his energy to releasing Joe. A meeting with his brother was now essential. The gun which was now impounded by the police was a real problem.

***

Bonham had the morning to prepare his case which had been fixed for first of the afternoon hearings. He used his time on his mobile to discover who the policeman was in the casino. He returned to the police station with Joe's father where Joe had been held.

Although the size of the police force in Monte Carlo was microscopic, it took Bonham over two hours to find Inspector Simonne. Bonham's French did not help, but at last he was given his mobile number and located him having lunch.

Now sitting once again in the interview room with Joe, with his hands in a meditative position Bonham placed his mobile on the table, "I want you to hear my conversation with Inspector Simonne, Joe, and confirm to me that what he said is in fact what happened." He pressed the record button.

"Your client Monsieur Bonham was not who he said he was, and we were particularly interested by his gun and holster. However, although we followed his activities during the time he was in Monte Carlo nothing untoward happened. We simply sent our findings to Scotland yard in the UK and closed our file."

"You saw his gun?"

"He had taken off his jacket and his holster was obvious to us, so whilst he was asleep we inspected it and recorded the number and make, also the name on the pill boxes and his passport which had a different name, but decided not to make an issue of it as he had not done anything very wrong, and we had more pressing matters to deal with. I hope that I have been of some help."

"Thank you, Inspector, you have been of great assistance, au revoir," replied Bonham.

"Our case will be heard this afternoon, Joe, at magistrates' court and I need your instructions to present a defence."

"What should I tell you, I know as much as you," said Joe.

"I'll go with my first presentation, we have no option, but you have said that you bought this gun after the casino incident, however the French Inspector has stated that he saw the gun strapped to you that evening and has reported it to Scotland Yard. It's more than likely that the police will check whether the gun has been used for anything on their file, and if it has, then you are in serious trouble. So I will ask you again: Is there anything you would like to tell me about the use of this gun Joe? Did your father give it to you before you left?"

"No, I obviously picked it up on my travels," Joe replied. "I forgot where I bought it. I made a mistake, my migraine affected my memory."

"Listen Joe, you are facing a jail sentence, but in my opinion you will probably be held in custody until all the checks are finalised by the police. Now once again I want you to take me through your journey and this time tell me the truth."

"My migraine was getting worse and my father suggested I take a holiday. It's true that I had a record but I thought it would be good to change my identity and start again. I found this guy who could give me a new passport, I used my old passport to leave England, but I thought the new passport might come in handy. I know that it was wrong but I made a mistake."

"And the gun?" asked Bonham again, now raising his voice. "Where did you get it?"

"I remember now, I picked it up the day before I left from a bloke in London, and threw it in the back of my car, I just wanted to be free of my past, to start again." He was now sweating and it was clear that he had no defences that would be helpful. "I know a lot of people Mr Bonham, some of them aren't nice. I have never used a gun but it's a reminder to me that not everyone is good and I should protect myself."

"Are you able to tell me who this 'bloke' is that sold you this gun Joe?"

"Just a guy who wanted a few quid. I gave him twenty. It seemed a bargain."

"OK. Joe, I will go to court with that and see what they say. Be humble and apologetic in court and don't answer anything other than the most basic facts, just leave it to me, understand!"

The hearing was scheduled for 2.00 pm. Approximately thirty minutes was allocated for each case.

Bonham used what time he had as best he could to discover the style of the Magistrate. Judge Hawthorn who was on the bench, was well known for her perfunctory approach. There was little room in her day for compromise or excuses that had no relevance to the facts. Her style was short, sharp and to the point.

The prosecutor read the details of the case in a monotone voice that might have been a parking offence. He appeared to have no interest in the detail other than to inform the judge of Joe's misdemeanours, and Bonham hoped against hope that the hearing might just squeeze through with a casual indifference. But it was not to be, for Judge Hawthorn took the lead with the most obvious question.

"Tell us, Mr Brenekov, how you acquired the gun."

Joe was now sweating profusely, he threw a glance at Bonham who looked away. He'd been in court a number of times during his life, but it was obvious to him that the consequences of this case could be disastrous. He was not now scrabbling for factual answers but creative ones that would not trip him up on cross examination and he had to think on his feet.

"Your honour, the day before I left an acquaintance called to see me, and in conversation offered me the gun for twenty pounds, just in case there was trouble. I intended to keep it in the car. However when I was dressing to go to the casino, due to the fact that I could not speak French and am unfamiliar with their way of life I decided that I needed a level of protection. So I strapped it on. The violence in the casino that night justified my doubts."

As he gained confidence he conveniently recalled that three years before in London despite his size he had been beaten up by a gang which psychologically shook him.

Bonham interceded. "Your Honour may I also point out that my client suffers from severe migraine almost weekly."

The judge barely looked up from her notes as she spoke. "And how does that explain how Mr Brenekov was travelling under a false identity?"

Bonham cleared his voice. "Your Honour, there is no accounting for stupidity, my client was given details of a property in France for which his father was negotiating, he was told by his father that if he was in the area, not to mention that he was his son and that it should appear to be an independent enquiry. He thought that it would also be good idea to adopt a nom de plume as well when foolishly acquiring a passport from this man in London who produced these types of documents. He understands now how foolish that was, but he has led an exemplary life since his last offence which was over four years ago and is determined to maintain a correct and honest path. This incident is greatly regretted."

No one spoke as Judge Hawthorn shuffled some of the papers placed in front of her. "You say that it is greatly regretted, but we are also informed that he was carrying the gun, which clearly is not used as an adornment, and invariably carried with intent, would you not agree Mr Bonham."

"Many people have access to guns your honour, but thank goodness they are rarely used," he answered weakly.

Bonham continued to emphasise the painful consistency of Joe's migraine which can be corroborated by his doctor, and in spite of his size is a very insecure young man with a most gentle disposition. To his credit he spoke with such empathy that even Joe began to believe it. "Your honour, there was no intent of any kind, and he has confirmed that it has never been used by him. He felt insecure in a foreign country. I would ask your honour to consider his action as an unfortunate hiccup rather than any malicious or devious purpose in mind. Furthermore, the time that he spent abroad was totally without incident."

It was clear even before the Judge spoke by her cynical expression that his presentation was not convincing.

"Mr Brenekov, I have serious doubts regarding the validity of your reasons for carrying a gun and your false passport, and therefore I am not willing to give you bail. A further court hearing will no doubt reveal your activities in greater detail, when the police will be in a better position to discover any further information on the gun's history and your own activities."

Joe's father left the court with a heavy heart. The next hearing would also be in Dover probably in eight weeks and during that time there was a strong possibility that the police would be able to trace by computer the bullets from Joe's gun to those that killed the Hines. It was in the hands of the gods.

Confronting Brenekov once again Bonham stated the situation as he expected it to unravel. "Your son will be lucky not to receive a six-month sentence even if he has not used the gun.

"If he or you decide to expand on any further information it would greatly help his position Mr Brenekov, I will try my best to put a case forward but you must help me to do so. I'm not a magician. Do you understand?"

"We'll speak soon," answered Brenekov. He saw his world in jeopardy, he blamed his son, for being so stupid, he blamed his lawyer for his apparent indifference and of course the judge for simply being, but mostly he blamed himself for creating the circumstances that brought about this sorry situation. After all, he was his father.

Chapter 11
Miriam

Miriam had now been in LA for four months, she had been introduced to every part of the organisation and in particular the research labs.

Nothing was hidden from her. She had made casual friends with a small group of young men and women who considered themselves to be the Think Tank for innovative possibilities, a science fiction team who could envisage ideas that would change society. Some of their concepts might have seemed kooky or eventually might become accessories to existing products already within the Spoken Arrow range. Other ideas would require a total restructuring of global behaviour which would be considered totally impractical to any other organisation with a strict or bureaucratic ethos.

Most of the team would be considered as boffins by the outside world and in a free thinking environment would bounce a myriad of ideas, some of which would be totally impractical but occasionally would sneak in with a winner. They had left the mundane behind in order to look at what had not yet been invented. At least two of the elite group were experts in genetics and neurosciences. A strange inspirational and magical wonderland of ideas based on futuristic needs, rather than competitive products existing oozed from what seemed to Miriam a micro-utopia.

It was an Aladdin's cave for Miriam. She would muse on this idea or that considering the immediate or long-term need for a product that could change society, but what interested her most was the research into the genetic implants and those concepts that might improve health.

Her regular meetings with Martin enabled her to clarify her direction and she was guided by Martin's concern to find a way into the medical field. He had been investigating his main competitor and it was clear to him that to regain a foothold into the market he would need a system that would entice governments and the public to change to a distinctly superior product.

They sat together in his office sipping fruit teas. Miriam was still without a title, but as she was considered part of the inner sanctum of the executive, she had been given an elevated status by those within the company.

"So, this is how we see it Miriam." Martin was not embarrassed to be contradicted and had the talent to draw people to him rather than adopting a superior stance. "The foot in the door is the Autoplug—the engineering of this computer can easily be copied with sufficient adaptations to duck the patents they have. But the problem is that they are the established product. A lookalike will not cut the ice, we have to have something better. Not revolutionary, they've already broken through and found a need—just better. The holograms were a great idea—it's a face-to-face communication and they accumulate knowledge acquired from all parts the government's departments. Plus, the ability to analyse it—that's a stroke of genius."

"I can tell you, Martin," Miriam replied, "that it's like talking to a friend and the moment I tell my 'Doctor', it is analysed and categorised in its memory banks. The people who created this are genius."

Martin walked around his desk. "You know what? Let's see who brought this to Magnum. I can't believe that they could hide their research without us knowing something. It would have taken years."

"Then they introduce Ever Young—what a brilliant idea! Magnum's Ever Young's approach is based on a concept of a long healthy and active life which is terminated at ninety-five years. The advantages to the government is that they would save considerable monies dealing with the population before they reach an age which may become riddled with disease, and simultaneously keep the population from being overwhelmed with ailing senior citizens. Magnum are now firmly established with the National Health Authorities around the world with their Autoplug in most of the doctor's surgeries, which gives them substantial credibility."

He stood up and looked out of the window. "This Ever Young concept matches well with the Autoplug but it shows no financial advantage, so where's the catch. If the Autoplug holds all an individual's information and Ever Young has access to it, they could in theory use that person's mood patterns to their own ends, prisons, military, sports and goodness knows what else, it's almost a science fiction. Of course the governments would benefit, Magnum would ingratiate themselves to every aspect of life. You might like to share your thoughts with Robert Levine and Jay Harrai."

"Good idea, we need to know what Cambridge were doing before Magnum became involved," replied Miriam. "Why don't I make contact with Theodore in the UK, maybe he can lay out the land for us. Who is now in charge there and if in fact they still have any contact with Magnum."

***

Jay Harrai was one of those rare modulated characters with whom one could never lose their temper. His grandparents had both died in Hiroshima, and both his parents were brought up in an orphanage. It was his sheer ability and determination that eventually elevated his father to one of the best universities in Tokyo. His professorial career began as a junior lecturer in Tokyo. After acquiring a PhD, he accepted a post in California and moved to the US before Jay was born. Jay followed in his father's footsteps achieving distinctions in medicine and went on to study neurology, graduating with honours. He was blessed with a photographic memory and it was not long before he was headhunted by the drug companies and given a position in their research labs. However, as he progressed the job became administrative and less demanding, he was plucked from there by Spoken Arrow five years ago. Now married to a beautiful all American but very traditional Japanese doctor of homeopathy with three children, he felt he had at last arrived. He openly confessed that his early interviews with Spoken Arrow were more excruciating than having a brain operation without an anaesthetic.

Jay's colleague, Robert Levine, had an altogether different history. Born in Brooklyn to Jewish parents. Even as a child they saw that he had an intellect far beyond his playmates. It was said in the family that he inherited his tenacity from his Great Grandfather who was a notable Rabbi in Russia. The story was told that his village was burnt down during a pogrom and he and his wife managed to find a boat that would take him anywhere. He arrived in America without a penny around 1890 and speaking no English. Within three years, he had learned the language, established a trading company in wools. They had two sons. Education was his prime concern and the boys went to University, one to study Mathematics and the other engineering, both settled in New York retaining their orthodoxy and between them had five children. One of them was Robert's father who became a prominent lawyer.

Robert was the youngest and took neuro-electronics as his subject. A Harvard PhD and superior references lead him to work for a government think tank. Bureaucracy and devious politics disgusted him and he was not shy in telling his superiors what to do with their job. He was also discovered by Spoken Arrow, and took a cut in his salary in order to join them. Four years on and now 35 years old, he was head of the research team. In practise, however, that was not his style, there was no visible head, and they operated more as a discussion group.

The three sat on the patio with cold drinks, t-shirts and shorts – any onlooker would assume they were on vacation, but breaking the image were three computers standing to attention on the coffee table awaiting instruction. Three vibrant young adults already at the apex of their careers, each boasting a family tree with roots in other parts of the world.

Miriam opened the conversation "I've been discussing with Martin how we might break into the medical market and compete against Magnum."

"Let's, first, look at the claims that Magnum are making," said Robert. "They've been tremendously successful with the Autoplug which we know saves substantial time for doctors, and money for the government, and the idea that users would pay to use the machine puts substantial sums of money into Magnum's pockets and the government's. It's a coup. Then on the back of the Autoplug they have now introduced Ever Young. Now, that is where they might be vulnerable, but their very selling point to the government is the termination clause of ninety-five years old."

"What attracts the youngsters," replied Jay, "is the guarantee to remain in good health until ninety-five, and the government gain twofold by keeping the geriatric public at arm's length until they die, and secondly the NHS medical costs come dramatically down. Something like thirty percent of all health budgets are spent on sixty-plus year olds. That's thirty-five years off per person of compounding medical expenses especially in the US."

"The problem is more complicated than that," said Miriam. "We might be able to improve on the product in some way, but if we stand against Magnum's policy of termination at ninety-five we would probably not persuade the government to make a U-turn, especially since they have already passed the concept. Populations don't only depend on birth. Every country needs young workers, but if a substantial proportion of the elderly become super elders and live thirty or forty years without any productivity our world population will force bankruptcy. There aren't enough jobs to keep even a healthy fifty year old in employment, and neither do they want to be."

There was a long silence.

"So what is the solution?" mused Jay.

"There is no solution," said Miriam. "Theoretically they're right. To many it seems inhuman but there is no doubt that science is prolonging our longevity, and could even get us to a hundred and twenty years within our own lifetime. If Spoken Arrow wants to compete with Magnum, it would have to be on equal terms, I can't see any alternative. But Martin made a valid point. Where's the profit? There must be a link between the two projects…or we stay with our version of the Auto Plug."

Robert stood up and began pacing. "So if we have to design a package to offer the world market, then we should be looking at improving what they already have. We could reduce the age entry of Ever Young, but I think we should be looking to compete first at improving the Autoplug, after all this is what gave the entry into the health authorities around the world. What do we know about Magnum anyway? For my part it would be interesting to know how they became so dominant. If we are going to cross swords with them, I would like to know who we are dealing with."

"Personally, the whole idea of governmental termination at any age is a little abhorrent," whispered Jay.

"We're faced with an interesting conundrum," replied Miriam. "It's not what we personally feel, and although I'm inclined to agree with you, and so is my mother, who is in her sixties, but we are discussing a worldwide problem here. Older people need help before they begin to deteriorate. I wouldn't think that Magnum are so philanthropic as to invest what will be hundreds of millions worldwide without a profit motive. No company can work for nothing, so there must be a trigger between them. Looking only at Ever Young is a cul-de-sac. There has to be a connection."

Email. Hi Martin. Re: Autoplug and Ever Young.

"Following our conversation, I have had an interesting discussion with both Robert and Jay with regard to the direction we feel Spoken Arrow should go, and we would like to take your guidance on the ethics and viability of the subject before moving in a specific direction.

I am particularly keen to discover how Magnum developed both projects in such a short time and what protection they have regarding patents etc., and it would be particularly interesting to discover what financial gains they expect from adding Ever Young on to their program.

Please give me a time for us to discuss the subject in detail with you.
Thanks,
Miriam."

Email. "Hello Miriam,
Martin has suggested I organise a meeting for next Thursday at 10.00 am.

There are a number of heads of departments that would like to attend and as you have five days before the meeting, any details that you, Robert and Jay can present as a possible agenda would be welcome.

Many thanks,
Carolyn Brosh PA to Martin Moran."

The memo took Miriam a little by surprise, she had imagined another tete a tete, but immediately forwarded the memo to both Jay and Robert.

They agreed to meet that evening at a little Italian restaurant not far away from Miriam's apartment. It was owned by a young couple both of whom had Italian parents. She had not eaten there before and took an immediate liking to it.

"Oh! To speak Italian! What a pleasure to feel at home again," she laughed. Her friends saw her for the first time as if in a natural environment as she came alive. "Let me order for you both," she insisted. "I promise the next time you can reciprocate in Japanese or kosher."

"My idea tonight is primarily to bring together the skeleton of a few concepts, a pathway towards a few objectives that could possibly enter the market with." "Are we talking about the menu?" asked Robert.

She laughed and continued. "And tomorrow each of us would hopefully flesh out an aspect of our chosen direction. Maybe we can compare notes during the day and meet up on Tuesday to formalise a presentation."

Even in this homely restaurant Miriam chose her words carefully for she was aware that she had no formal authority over her colleagues. In spite of the unusually relaxed environment that she worked in here, she understood that as a new girl on the block she was still an unknown appendage.

They studied the menu choosing their familiar dishes, but it was Miriam who oversaw each choice. Garnishes, Garlic, sauces and wine. She would imagine her mother delivering the dishes. Away from home for nearly four months she had not realised how homesick she was.

"I've been giving some thought to this business," said Robert, "I would like to know how Magnum evolved their medical project, I've always known them as computer hardware producers. It seems to me that it was too well coordinated, the soft sell would have been difficult enough with the Autoplug, but then a jaw knocker which went through the UK government mighty quick with Ever Young which is by any standard a highly sophisticated plan. If it was in the States, I would be sure of backhanders, but the UK, no, they're too straightlaced, nevertheless I would like to scratch below the surface a little. The interesting thing is that the concept has now been accepted in so many countries. By the way, this wine you've chosen is really great!"

"It comes from Sicily and cannot be improved, the weather, the soil and a thousand years' experience of producing it make it's unique, I'm so pleased you like it," she smiled. "I was hoping you'd take the path of investigation."

"Jay, I am in great need of education regarding neurochips. How do they work in medical terms? Be as technical as you like and then I can drive you mad with questions. Do you think you could tap out a summary of brain responses and the communication between activator and responder?"

Jay was still eating his lasagne. "How can you torture me like this? Here I am spellbound with this fantastic food and you shoot me down to reality, shame on you. I will need two or three days to understand their claims and get my team to simplify the essence of it for you and then we can chat about what I have written, OK?"

"Wonderful, in the meantime I will try to find a slant on the Autoplug that will allow us a foot in the door."

The ambiance of the restaurant had given her a yearning to phone home, and on returning to the apartment she slung off her shoes and opened chat – she guessed that her parents would probably be eating or watching TV and without knowing or really caring what she should say, she just wanted to hear their voices. Thoughts on the restaurant, the weather, their health, passing thoughts, even silences on the line helped to overcome the physical absence.

It was 2.30 pm the following day when Robert called. "I've been pulling up some interesting information. I'd never really stopped to think how most of these international organisations evolved, but it seems that the company of Magnum GMBH in Germany was a brainchild of an operation called Kataligien originally formed around 1930. The original owners were Jewish, but it appears to have been taken over by the Schickerdanz family who were great friends of the National Socialist Party. During the war the company was instrumental in gathering information on a global scale for Herr Goebbels, don't ask why, you'd be shocked. They were charged to acquire names of every Jewish family in Europe. The organisation was closed down immediately after the war. However, they reformed around the 50s as Magnum with substantial funds which appear to have come from Brazil as an analytical company holding information on every subject you could imagine, presumably servicing the advertising industry etc. When the computer revolution emerged, they jumped on the band wagon with unlimited resources, but the Autoplug evolved only four or five years ago, it seems from nowhere."

"There were a number of companies that supplied the Third Reich which still exist today," answered Jay, "so I'm not surprised to hear that. Take Krupp, Volkswagen, even Hugo Boss, even Ford. Where they raised the money Lord only knows, but we can guess."

"What is rather interesting though is that they still filter their finances from Brazil, and it's the same family running the show today that operated the original company. Don't you find that rather uncomfortable?"

"I would," she replied, "but most of these companies left their Nazi politics behind them, but this one seems to have an agenda. I would love to know," Miriam mused. "How and where they acquired so much wealth in the first place, and what was their original agenda, after all it wasn't as if they were supplying product."

"Well, we know what their original task was and that was to collect names and all relevant details of certain parties throughout Europe. Ultimately for the concentration camps. The common denominator between then and now is the termination button of Ever Young, that's far more efficient than the Gas Chamber don't you think, and there may be the link."

"That is really a terrible comparison," she replied, "but it is a real possibility. Robert, I need to know how this Neurochip really works, I'll speak with Jay and if you can spare the time today we should all meet."

Jay was as usual full of enthusiasm, "Hi Miriam, just finishing a memo to you, I've tried to keep a microchip overview as simple as possible."

She could almost hear him smiling. "Jay, If it's too difficult I'll ask your daughter to explain it to me," she laughed. "There's a lot to discuss, can we all meet up say at 6.00 pm this evening at my apartment."

Welcoming her friends that evening, she had already read Jay's email and took what information from it that she considered necessary, and prepared a few snacks for them. Her mind was buzzing with various scenarios.

"So, let's see," she began. "Historical first." She poured out drinks. "From what you emailed me today Robert, we have here a firm that originated from the dark side of history, we might assume that their original finances were ill gotten gains, but all that tells us is the type of people we are dealing with. No doubt they took some of their personnel from the cream of the crop of their hallowed Nazi party to Brazil which allowed them to keep ahead of the market. We do know that they wasted no time in getting a foothold into computers and this gave them worldwide credibility."

"What I have discovered," said Robert, "through a friend of mine in the UK, it seems that the idea of both the Autoplug and Ever Young actually emanated from a neurological research team based in Cambridge, but I'm waiting for further information as to who they are and how Magnum acquired it. However, the world wide patents are definitely in Magnum's name. But there's no doubt that Magnum have a substantial research team of their own so we don't know at this stage who developed what. I hope to have more information by tomorrow."

Miriam opened her computer and found Jay's notes. Fifteen pages worth. "OK. Jay, I read through some of your essay, and you were right in assuming a simplified translation, but you might have to go even simpler I'm afraid. What is the modus operandi, the directive that drives the Ever Young project?"

Jay's soft and amiable manner masked a brilliant mind, his Japanese upbringing emanated a quietness in him that generated a gravitas in whatever he said.

"Ah. Well, in simple terms Miriam, we know the purpose, of course, is to eliminate inherited weaknesses that are specifically genetic before they establish themselves as permanent entities. Magnum have achieved this by inserting their 351 Neuro microchips which have been programmed into the brain. The result is that a vast proportion of inherited disabilities would be stemmed which would in turn prolong life.

"So it is first necessary to understand how to discover the unique genetic print before programming the necessary algorithm. This is not as difficult as it sounds since we can now read by computers the entire genetic structure of most individuals, but until recently we haven't been able to cure all these potential symptoms before they emerge as positive diseases. Once deleterious genes are found they are controlled and automatically monitored. I assume that Magnum have already devised a system to do this as they would probably be able to automatically realign the subject's metabolism."

Robert had spread himself on a settee with a whisky and was quietly listening, but suddenly as if by an electric shock, he jumped up. "Are you suggesting Jay that Magnum have a constant communication to whoever has this chip embedded in their brain?"

"Of course, how else would it work, I guess that this is how they're terminated at the prescribed age."

"But what else can they be communicated with." "I don't understand," replied Jay.

"He means action, thoughts, controlled direction," said Miriam.

Jay hesitated "Ah, yes, that is possible too I suppose, but not with projected ideas, this is not mental telepathy, but it would be possible to transfer electrical pulses to alter moods, apathy, energy, even aggression I guess."

Robert glared at his friends. "Imagine millions of people all over the world under the spell of this company, my God, it would be a total disaster for the world as we know it, and we have been asked to replicate their demonic plan!"

"Hang on," replied Miriam. "We're making assumptions here that would need to be urgently verified before we condemn them or take any action. If it is true that there could be underlying objectives, we would need to bring them to the attention of all those countries that have taken on the scheme, but we must be sure, because we would be scuppering our own chances of offering an alternative. I think the next step is to discover what long term plans Magnum have and check out the veracity of their claims."

"I think we have enough here to present to our committee," said Miriam as she arose from her chair. "We haven't been very helpful in presenting to them the veracity of their product claims, other than what's on the packet, but we will certainly give them our thoughts on the possible consequences."

"Do you not think," said Robert. "That we should keep it as non-political as possible, that is until we solidify some of our historical facts?" Miriam smiled and agreed.

***

Details of their findings and possible conclusions were quickly printed and given to Carolyn Brosh the day before to allow her yet unknown audience to study them ready for the meeting.

Miriam had not been to a director's meeting before and she found herself rather more nervous than she had anticipated. Both Jay and Robert with a team behind them were quite familiar with most of the board and with the usual Californian familiarity, they gave man hugs and reciprocated to general familiarities with bonhomie. There were thirty in total, seventeen men and thirteen women, most of whom Miriam had not previously met.

Martin waved her over to sit next to him. "Good morning, first I would like to introduce you to our latest Senior executive, Miriam Bravotti, I know that many of you were aware that we were searching for a fresh new mind from within our own worldwide well of talent, and all of you will appreciate how meticulous we are in choosing our team. We were very fortunate to discover Miriam from our London branch who more than fitted the brief. Miriam's task is to take an overview of our activities and think laterally. We need to three-dimensionalise our projects. Her immediate task was to look towards the medical field and take note of our competitors, particularly Magnum."

"We are all very much aware that Magnum has been our number one competitor in the computer, mobile and software markets around the world for a number of years, but it is time to spread our wings, so this morning we are hoping to take a serious step into the unknown. As we've grown, we've fallen into a trap so often experienced by companies of our size, where we have become experts in the improvement of our existing products, but lose the ability to think outside of the box.

"Magnum have already made substantial inroads within the medical field especially with their Autoplug, and now Ever Young. It's up to us now to use our own creativity. We have definitely missed a trick here, the medical market has enormous potential. This is early days but I think you will be interested in Miriam's findings complemented by Jay and Robert who of course you already know…Miriam."

Miriam introduced herself, cleared her throat and took a sip of water. She learned at university to speak without notes and looked directly at her audience. "It's a real pleasure to be here with you, and the last few weeks I have been overawed by the sophisticated inner workings of this amazing organisation. However, the communications and computer business is now moving at such a fast pace and infringes on so many aspects of our lives, that it's imperative that we should not jump into the first obvious opportunity before we do our homework. Sometimes our competitors steal a march on us and establish themselves in green projects, but I believe that we should take note of their own objectives and their mistakes too, which are sometimes hidden.

"You have I hope all received the notes relating to Magnum's Ever Young and Autoplug, and it seems to us that there are several details which need to be clarified before we make positive moves to enter the medical arena. And this is the area that Martin has asked me to evaluate. I've been studying our competition, so to speak, in some detail, the salient points of which are included in my notes, and I would be very pleased to hear your own thoughts."

A few hands raised, and Miriam nodded to an attractive woman in her thirties on her right.

"We have not yet met Miriam but I have of course heard of you," she smiled. "My name is Helen Granzl and I am in charge of PR for Spoken Arrow international." She had what might once have been an eastern European accent but it had been well masked by years in the States.

"Reading between the lines Miriam you seem to suggest that the origins of Magnum might have some significance to their current activities, is this so? I have always seen them as tough but honourable competitors."

"Hello, Helen. No, I'm not condemning them, I'm suggesting that investigating the facts as they emerge will give us an indication of where our competition is going, I'm not in a position to accuse them of anything. We will be better placed to draw conclusions in the next few days, but the history of a company does, in my opinion, give us a good idea of their plans for the future. I don't believe we can ignore any companies background regardless of how it is hidden because it denotes their character and implies a future intent. However, I must admit that their history and their sources of finance does disturb me," she hesitated, "especially with respect to the Ever Young product. From my experience, the apple never falls far from the tree."

A young man who looked no more than in his late twenties raised his hand. Martin acknowledged him and he stood to speak. "Hi Miriam, delighted to have you on board. I'm Josh Volaski, Assistant Director of Sales in the USA. I'm wondering why it seems so important for us to know the history of Magnum and their evolution – after all, we are in charge of our own destiny here at Spoken Arrow. I would imagine that should we decide to enter this area of the market we could outsmart anything they do in Europe."

"Hi, Josh, you have brought up a most important point, the fact is that our competitor is making a claim which we have to validate. They have taken the initiative by bringing a revolutionary concept to the world market namely the Autoplug which we understand was created in the UK. The point is, unless we can take their lead but give the market something noticeably better we will flounder. With regard to Ever Young, we're very keen to discover if they have another agenda. I'm sure that you would not want to find that you're marketing a dream that can't become a reality, and making the claim that a ninety five year old would remain perfectly healthy when in fact at seventy she develops an incurable illness. The entire proposition demands investigation before Spoken Arrow commits to it, don't you think. They are in effect asking the public to sign a death warrant. There is no doubt that if it worked, it would be a massive saving to governments throughout the world. But what happens if they were terminated earlier, selected prisoners, soldiers and others deemed expendable? There are a number of very important aspects of Ever Young that need to be clarified before we can consider it as a reliable project to pursue, both ethically and politically."

A number of hands went up.

Martin intervened. "There are two major products here that we are discussing, the Autoplug, which has been a most successful line for Magnum, and Ever Young.

"It is marketing genius how they have piggybacked Ever Young on the success of the Autoplug, there's no doubt that it's a very contentious project but we would have to agree that the governments around the world would be keen to persuade their populations to join. It would save them billions."

"Miriam, I realise that you have been thrown in the deep water here but I would like to hear your initial thoughts in order that our executive would be able to cogitate on our next moves."

Miriam again rose to her feet. "First, I would like to thank you for placing this project with me, I have also had the opportunity to work with Robert and Jay and will, with their support, continue to rely on their expertise."

"It's too early to be specific regarding our next moves as we're looking very carefully namely at the ultimate objectives of our competition, such as their plans to terminate their clients lives and how they propose to do so." She waited for a ripple of comment before continuing. "Amazingly this does not appear to have been discussed, bearing in mind that it would be in approximately 65 years before the current thirty year olds would reach the end of their contracts. I must say that the Ever Young scheme would be rather less worrying if it were not for the previous history of the company. What we still don't know is how the substantial information that is in the Autoplug can be utilised, or aligned in some way to Ever Young, and if that is so they will have total control of every individual that submits to it."

This last comment caused a ripple of discomfort from within the room, and a few more hands were raised.

Martin pointed to a tall blond man. "Chris, you would like to say something."

"Thank you, Martin, as you know I am a practicing Catholic and to be truthful, I find the Ever Young scheme extremely distasteful. Spoken Arrow have always been at the forefront of improving life and living conditions, not taking it. Do we really think that we should be demeaning our philosophy by even considering such a scheme. To terminate healthy individuals must be a sin in the eyes of any religion or civilised society!"

A few within the room were heard to mumble. "Hear, hear."

Martin stood and was about to reply, but Miriam nodded that she would take question.

"Your thoughts Chris are founded by a solid belief in the respect of life, I am also a Catholic which teaches us to leave our physical and spiritual destiny to God. I am not proposing that Spoken Arrow should or should not be party to this project, but unless we can prove by moral and practical arguments that Magnum should not pursue the Ever Young project, they will continue to persuade governments throughout the world of its financial advantages and the young on the basis of a healthy life before death. We should also take into account the termination would appear to be activated by computer suggesting a control between Magnum and the wearer of the chip. In effect Magnum could control their actions during their lives too.

"Their claim is that the cost of maintaining the healthy elderly will substantially reduce the government budgets, and concurrently an increased ageing population could be controlled both physically and monetarily, and that is a strong argument for any government that has trouble balancing their books. We would like to look towards a more acceptable alternative such as children's health and forgo the termination aspect."

Martin raised his hand, and he stood quietly for a moment before speaking.

"It's clear to me that our first obligation is to study the motives of our competitor. They are worldwide and our number one competition, and if we see that they are going to dominate the market we do have to protect ourselves. I take your point Chris and can see that several of you agree that there are some very distasteful aspects to their scheme, but we are on the threshold of a dramatic reassessment of worldwide moral values, yet faced with the global medical advances to extend life resulting in a major increase in the elderly becoming almost superhuman, but without income and being maintained by the state. It's clear that something must be done to alleviate the obvious problems that will result."

"I've placed this investigation in the hands of Miriam who will report on a weekly basis to me, and I in turn will refer her progress to yourselves. In the meantime, please be free to email me or Miriam with any further thoughts that you may have."

The meeting was monitored by camera and immediately converted to a memo pad marked 'Strictly Confidential' and sent to all those at the meeting.

At last, Miriam had direction and as far as she was concerned the pressure was on. She had been catapulted to the top of one of the most dynamic companies in the world and was painfully aware that she had to justify Martin's faith in her.

Chapter 12
Jack

It was only 11.00 am when Jack left the Minister, he had no desire to go back to his office and returned to his apartment.

The name of Baylim in Cambridge shouldn't be too difficult to find he thought as he opened his computer. He was aware that George Baylim had died but he thought he might find his wife.

He looked through the directory but there was no trace of a Baylim in the area. He spread out his search and even made a national enquiry, but still no trace of the name. He decided to contact the university directly. The receptionist trying find the department that researched Neurological Biology let him hold on for 35 minutes. In total frustration, he hung up, grabbed a quick sandwich, threw on his jacket, locked his door and drove there. It would take him an hour and a half.

Driving to Cambridge was simple, but the university area was a maze. finding the right building lost a further hour.

It was 3.00 pm when he arrived at the reception, and using his press card a charming young woman informed him that there were a number of Neurological departments. "May I suggest you walk over to the Cognition and Brain Sciences unit in Chaucer Road. It's only a short walk, I can print out a map for you," she smiled. She spoke with a hint of a European accent which Jack found quite alluring. "In fact, I am walking over there myself soon, I have a lecture with Dr Ellsworth, have you heard of him?"

"No I'm afraid I haven't," replied Jack. "But I'd be happy for you to guide me there."

She introduced herself as Helga Barworth and said that she was one of his students.

She carefully stacked her papers into a satchel and stood up from her desk. Jack was surprised to discover that she was slightly taller than him and probably over 6 feet with high heels. She had the figure of an athlete. Her fair hair was tied into a long ponytail which went down to her waist, Jack guessed that she was in her early twenties.

"I've finished my work for the day now, I was very lucky to find a part time job especially in the department that I'm studying in. What do you study? I'm sorry I don't know your name."

"Jack, Jack Branson," he replied. "In fact, I don't attend Cambridge, I'm a journalist," he said almost apologetically.

"I'm looking for details of a particular professor who headed a research department for the Autoplug and Ever Young project who worked with Professor Baylim. Have you heard of him?"

"It's funny you should mention his name, his work has been the subject of debate very recently, Dr Ellsworth would know all about the Baylims and the Baylim Effect. You probably know that he died maybe four or five years ago. I'll introduce you to the doctor if you like, I'm sure he will be able to give you more information, but what a coincidence," she laughed.

"Was there not a Mrs Baylim?"

"Yes, of course. They were a husband and wife team and brilliant, both. They were before my time here," she shrugged, and became a touch flirtatious. "But I'm very interested in his work. I'm sure that you'll be impressed with the doctor. He is a marvellous teacher. Are you particularly interested in neurobiology, Jack?"

"I suppose I am," he replied with a smile.

Doctor Ellsworth was between lectures, he was carrying several files and was about to enter a large lecture room which anticipated a substantial turnout. Helga called out as he entered the room.

"Helga, are you coming into my next session?" he replied. He was no more than 5ft 4". She had learned to leave a conservative distance between them as they closed in on one another. Jack smiled at the irony of nature, for this beautiful Amazon of a woman was clearly in awe of him.

"Doctor, this gentleman is a journalist and was enquiring about the Baylims. I told him that you may be able to help him, I hope you don't mind."

Ellsworth turned to Jack, and put out his hand. "Nice to meet you, young man, can't speak to you now, meet me here after my lecture in say 90 minutes, you coming, Helga!"

"You're welcome to listen in too," she casually said as she moved towards the lecture room.

She left Jack standing in the passage but since he had nothing better to do, he slipped in and found a seat next to her.

The lecture referred to a number of preparatory notes on reactions to various drugs affecting the neural pathways of the brain, much of which went over Jack's head, but he found the lecture more interesting than he had expected, and determined to read up on the subject especially as he was already involved in its ultimate future. The room had now filled to capacity and copious notes were being taken by his pupils.

Doctor Ellsworth took questions and answered them with flourish. He remembered many of the student's names and had the talent of relating to the class individually.

It was now nearly 6.00 pm, the lecture had taken longer than anticipated. Helga had been enthralled and clearly fired by Ellsworth's own enthusiasm for the subject. "I hope that you enjoyed it," she said rather coyly. "If you want to see the doctor I think that now is the time."

She looked a little tired and her accent and her exact use of words were proving English was her second language. "Would you like me to join you in your conversation?" she said.

"Why not, you may find it interesting," replied Jack, half regretting his invitation as he said it.

Doctor Ellsworth had several students around him still wishing to pursue a post-mortem of the lecture, but he was aware that they could keep him there all night if he allowed them.

"Thank you my young friends we'll meet next week. If you have any further questions of course, you must send me an email and I promise that I will reply."

Jack walked over to the rostrum with Helga by his side, "Doctor, do you have a moment, sir? My name is Jack Branson and I am a lead journalist for the Tandem Press. I've been given the task of writing a series of articles on the Autoplug and Ever Young project for various national monthlies within the group."

Doctor Ellsworth was still standing on the rostrum and as he stepped down it surprised Jack how short he was as he stood next to Helga.

"What is it you would like to know Jack? I worked closely with the Baylims for a number of years on both products, it was a difficult time for all of us."

"May I ask why?"

"Money my young friend, money and politics. We were desperately short of funding for the research. The government was not very forthcoming with their grants, we had twelve full time neuroscientists but the department had a hard time paying us. There were many problems."

"So what happened?"

"May I ask what is the purpose of your enquiry Jack?"

"Of course, sir. I have been given the task of describing the benefits of the Ever Young scheme to our readers covering a wide selection of magazines. My company has been given a million pound contract to advertise and write up the project and to be truthful I have had some difficulty in aligning its owners with its company. Dare I say that I'm a little worried with regard to Ever Young's objectives. Since my directive is to promote rather than criticise, I decided to begin at the root and its original evolution."

Jack's short explanation made a greater impact on the professor than he anticipated and he held his reply for a full thirty seconds before speaking.

"There is a story here Jack that may entail a little more than you bargained for and I will try to give you some background." He pulled up a seat and Jack reciprocated.

"George and Gilda Baylim were both scientists, they were recently married, she was his second wife. I have never met a man more creative than George Baylim – he was a genius. I have always thought that she was academically cleverer, certainly shrewder than him, but I personally disliked her and I've no doubt that the feeling was mutual. Our research was funded by the university and subsidised by the government. A company was formed with the view of raising external finance. But after she married George she decided to form a separate company naming only her and George, and disregarded the original company that the university had formed that gave George a nominal shareholding and of which he had promised all of us a percentage of profits if they could raise the money from outside the government. It seemed a long shot at the time. Not long after the new company was formed, George contracted a serious bug and died, leaving the future of the new company and its shares to Gilda."

"Do you know what he died from by any chance?"

"An autopsy was unable to discover the exact cause of death. We thought at the time that he may have taken an overdose, since he was very depressed." He hesitated for a full minute. "But what did become clear to all of us was that Gilda had no intention of honouring the previous agreement when she did a deal with Magnum in Germany, and immediately after the funeral she moved to Berlin where their head office is. Her family base was there and in Vienna anyway. All the documentation and research papers were sent over there. What we do know is that she made a fortune from selling her shares to Magnum. One of my colleagues was offered a position there and saw the house she had bought which was apparently magnificent. Interestingly, he decided not to take the job offered and returned here."

"Look doctor, I had intended to return to London this evening, but if you would join me for dinner we could talk around the table and I would stay over, Helga you could join us if you wished."

"I'll phone my wife and see what she's planned. Would you mind if she joined us? She knew the Baylims well."

"No, not at all," said Jack privately thinking that this meeting would turn into a party, nevertheless, there was certainly meat on the bone here and he was determined to take full advantage of his good fortune.

Helga knew of a good restaurant where they could talk without too much noise. She had no inhibitions as a student to ask Jack if he had enough money to pay, and which Jack was happy to accept, smiling at her openness and she phoned a booking for four.

It was now 7.00 pm when Clare joined them at the Restaurant Le Gros in Hills Road. Jack knew that he would have some explaining to do when putting this month's expenses in but threw caution to the wind. He was surprised to find Clare to be a rather elegant lady in her late forties impeccably dressed and seemingly without inhibition. She might have been a model in her younger days. Her high heels gave her height but neither he nor she had any inhibitions as to the height difference.

The waiter took their orders, Jack noted Helga's confidence in ordering her meal. For a young woman, she had an appreciation of quality restaurants, which he found intriguing.

Clare appeared to be keen to speak about their association with the Baylims. "I knew Gilda quite well, of course we were all relatively young when we first met and had few responsibilities. Peter and I had our two children here in Cambridge, George had remarried after his first wife passed away. There were no children."

Ellsworth interposed "Gilda was a senior lecturer of neurological science, and they met here. She'd taken her masters and PhD here in Cambridge and took the position of senior lecturer. There was no doubt that her contribution to both the Autoplug and Ever Young projects were welcomed, but they both had substantial support from all of us. I think her strength leaned towards academia rather than creative or inspirational, which George certainly was. I think it would be fair to say that her Teutonic style of working never went down well with the team, whereas he seemed able to pluck ideas out of the air, and pass them down to us to make them work."

"And who were the others?"

"This is a very sore point because our team were instrumental in the development of these experiments, however we stupidly had nothing on paper of any consequence relating to promised shares or benefits, but when Gilda negotiated a deal with Magnum through, what's his name? The Minister of Health." He suddenly stopped "I must ask you to keep what we are about to tell you in the strictest confidence, do you agree." "You mean Brendon Tann!"

"That's him, but do you agree?" he persisted.

"You realise Peter that I am the press, but for the purpose of this conversation I agree not to repeat this meeting without your permission, you have my word." The naivety of the academic never ceased to astonish Jack.

"Thank you," he hesitated, but it was as if he could not contain himself.

"It was clear that we were to be locked out. Some of the team were offered positions in Germany but most refused. Two of them vanished from the scene completely. If George would have been alive, there is no doubt that he would have honoured his agreement. His death closed the door on everything we had worked for. His cause of death was classified as 'unknown'. We and the hospital requested an autopsy, but that was blocked by his wife." The doctor was now becoming emotional.

"Was it so important that you should know the cause of his death?" Jack was aware that he had asked a leading question.

"Yes, it was, for reasons that I can't discuss with you now." Clare was glaring at her husband and there followed a long silence.

Jack changed the subject. "Dr Ellsworth, could you have raised the finance in the UK?"

"For the Autoplug, no doubt about it," replied Ellsworth. "But the health minister Tann pushed the deal through too quickly, by this time Gilda seemed to be in control of the negotiations, so none of us had a chance to contest it."

"You can call me Peter, after all we're off duty now. But not you, Helga," he smiled.

"Thank you. I'm most interested to know how you were able to prove that the Neuro351 could guarantee perfect health till the age of ninety-five. Were there any recognised tests to prove the claim categorically?"

"Ah there is the rub," he whispered, "our original experiments were based on the concept of fluidly injecting children between the age of five to nine years olds with a microchip neuro501 rather than transplant it into the brain of young adults. By doing this, there was no doubt that we would minimise many inherited negative genetic conditions. There was no intention of killing off healthy geriatrics, our sole purpose was to prolong young and healthy life. George and I had been working in this area for several years, and quite a long time before he met Gilda.

"Although the government had given the project some recognition and offered what they considered to be a reasonable grant, the Autoplug required a substantial number of departments to release explicit details in order that the patient would appreciate any advice given, albeit from a computer and between all these governmental departments the Autoplug would contain everything about each individual. It would be the first time that all this information would be contained in one machine. In other words the computer would know you better than you would know yourself.

"However, substantial finance was required to coordinate this monumental task, and the government demanded a complete and advantageous financial package in order to commit to the project. Needless to say the cost of our research was continuously escalating. Gilda was very insistent that we should transfer our efforts to the brain and calculated that by tempting an older age bracket, a strong argument could be presented to any government based on the termination at a particular age much sooner. With this added presentation our project would appear financially acceptable. George and the rest of us were not at all keen to go down that road, but it was out of our hands. There is another benefit as well: our children's version would have been a one-off and final process leaving the child to its improved health which would save the NHS money but considerably less than the geriatric numbers."

"So where did this new concept emerge?"

Gilda realised that in order to improve our financial position we would have to give the government a reason to do so. Much greater control was required. She and George developed the concept of the 351 which could be controlled by Magnum's app, and quickly dominated the policy of the operation. No doubt her Teutonic upbringing demanded that a far greater degree of sophistication was necessary to sell it to the public, and by placing a chip into the brain of a young adult rather than the metabolism of a child, it could also be monitored externally. Furthermore, it would allow them to readjust the patients mental disposition according to their needs. This added innovation would require a more sophisticated master chip rather than a Nano 501 system originally tested that worked through the body.

George was not at all happy with this method and we spoke at length on the dire consequences of changing the scheme over to include a termination age.

They had horrendous arguments on the subject. Nevertheless she spoke with the Health Minister regarding her ideas on other projects and got the nod to calculate the costs involved, but the investment was still too great, and outside finance would be required.

The Autoplug was an amazing concept. The idea of replacing the local doctor with a computerised replica demanded more sophisticated software and technology than was available in the UK. and we contacted Hitsudi in Japan, and although they were not interested in investing in the project, they were of great assistance.

The Autoplug required the agreement of the NHS to release every piece of medical information that was available on anyone registered in the UK. All government departments were required to pass on details such as education, personal information such as job, sports, size of family, mortgage commitments, income and so on in order to give a complete picture of each individual. This would be a mammoth task, but if we could find an investor, the government would underwrite it. The government have all this information from one department or another. When you think about it, from birth to death, parents even grandparents are on record. However they wouldn't finance it themselves.

"We also received a great deal of help from other technical departments in the Cambridge compound. and under strict confidentiality agreements passed whatever we had onto Hitsudi."

"It took over four years to bring the Autoplug scheme to a level ready for presentation, and we calculated that it would probably need seventy or eighty million pounds to launch only for the UK but up to five hundred million if we were to take the project throughout Europe and globally. But it could be in profit within three or four years. Hitsudi weren't interested in it as a long-term investment, and Magnum paid them a substantial sum thereby taking control of all the software rights. "So, who introduced the Ever Young project to Magnum?" asked Jack.

"Gilda, of course," replied the doctor. "She could negotiate with them in German and took with her all the papers relevant to the newly named Autoplug. She presented her interpretation of Ever Young for young adults twenty-two to thirty years old. The original concept where so much work was done was not mentioned as it had no financial interest to the Health Minister Tann, probably because it had no interest to Magnum. The fact that her scheme was considered by us to be glorified euthanasia was totally ignored. She also had a letter from Brendon Tann, on behalf of the government, who validated the project and expressed his interest in pursuing it, if Magnum was prepared to finance and market the scheme on a global basis.

"It needed the cooperation of a myriad of people within the social services and ministers, I will not say what sort of cooperation was given. You must use your own imagination Jack, but it was astonishing how quickly a deal was agreed and very soon Autoplug doctor's surgeries spread throughout the UK. They are also being introduced throughout Europe and I understand they are now in the USA. And on the back of that they are considering introducing Ever Young, also with Tann's blessing. He is the main key into the market and in particular the ministers whom I believe have been shown appreciation for their efforts, but I can't prove it."

"But the Autoplug works," said Jack. "I use it myself."

"Oh yes, it's a wonderful idea, in fact if Magnum offered a cold potato at this time to the NHS I'm sure that Tann would push it through, he has the ear of the government and they are in his back pocket."

"However, if you think about it the Autoplug gives Magnum information on every person, man, woman and child in the country, and with the new Ever Young they are able to control those individuals who sign up for it…which they would not have been able to do with the original plan."

Ellsworth lowered his voice almost to a whisper "There are some very dangerous aspects of this plan which greatly concern me. You know, I had two meetings with Henry Hines, and he naively presented his doubts to the cabinet. Three days later he was dead. I know that if he would have been alive the Ever Young would never have gotten through, and some heads would roll." "Why

have you not said anything?" exclaimed Jack.

"For obvious reasons, the main reason is Tann and his colleagues. We were very concerned by the sudden death of George, and now Hines. I have no doubt that anyone that interfered with their plans would vanish too. It's clear that he needed further assistance from within the government to push this project through. Clare and I seriously considered our position, but to be honest we're fearful of our own lives."

"So who made the initial contact with Magnum? I was told that Tann did."

"To be honest Jack, I have my suspicions that Gilda knew them from years back, even before she met George, but her close association with Tann was particularly interesting. You will appreciate that there are not too many organisations that would be prepared to invest so much into an unproven project, and I personally believe that she had them in mind from the outset…and of course, you may already know that she is now working with them in Germany and took with her most of the research information that we had spent years accumulating…"

"It's most interesting to discover that George's wife was so involved, because when I spoke with Tann he mentioned nothing regarding Gilda, not a word." Ellsworth simply shrugged.

"You realise Peter that by putting your case forward I would be placing my own head on the chopping block, or worse." "Join the club," replied Ellsworth.

It was now ten o'clock, and Jack realised that he had not booked a hotel room for the night.

"We've been so involved in answering your questions," commented Peter, "that we haven't asked you about yourself. Why are you so interested in this project anyway?"

Jack thought carefully before replying, he felt it unwise to declare his feelings at this stage, but as the doctor had given such a detailed explanation of the project's evolution he considered that he could take them both into his confidence with some reservations. It was easy to lose oneself into an emotional quagmire as Peter and his wife had done, but he had to be careful not to fall into what was obviously a biased point of view.

"You know that I work for Tandem Press and they have many publications. My responsibility is editor of the Sporting magazine, but as you are obviously aware all our magazines depend on advertising. I produce the meat but the advertising is the veg and sauce as it were," he smiled. "As I've already mentioned, Magnum have placed a substantial contract with us to promote the Ever Young project in all our publications over a period of six months backed by the government. That includes health, women's journals, motoring, cooking, sports of course, you name it we cover it. Each issue must have an accompanying article, and it has been placed at my door.

"My boss has given me 14 days to get the first article out. I realised that I knew very little detail and I thought, before I put pen to paper, what better than to go to the source. What you have given me Peter is the history which is of course very important, but most of which I can't actually use. What I have been asked to do is to write a series of articles on the perceived benefits to the person in the street, but the information that you have already given me the magazine would not be happy to print for obvious reasons, beside the possibility of being sued for a fortune until it was proven."

"You know Jack, my heart isn't in this project any more, we feel very sore at the results and very concerned with its implications. I could speak about the Autoplug but I would rather you write about its original concepts and not of a ninety-five year old dying in good health controlled by a foreign company." "I'm inclined to agree," said Clare.

"To be truthful," said Jack, "so do I. I'll tell you what: Allow me to speak with my boss, in the strictest confidence of course, and I will come back to you. If I write what I believe, I'll be sacked and if I don't write anything I will also be sacked. Of course I could write what they want me to but I really will be destroying my raison d'etre for being a journalist and will be writing lies. So my position is rather more vulnerable than yours."

"There's no doubt that we're all in a very precarious position Jack, I don't want to compromise the university either, who I know had a pending court case with Magnum. They were claiming an interest in both the Autoplug and Ever Young. For over seven years, twelve highly paid scientists were paid salaries by the college and had nothing in return. However I haven't heard of any progress and I think it's been dropped. I still have a small research team by the grace of the college's goodwill. We're now working on magnetic combustion."

"I quite understand," replied Jack as he paid the bill. "Maybe we could meet next week, by then I would hope to have more information."

"By all means. Helga, I believe I will see you next week too, don't be late. Needless to say, Helga, what you have heard is strictly confidential!" said the doctor.

Helga nodded her consent. They shook hands and parted leaving Helga with Jack.

She had sat mesmerised by a conversation that took her into another dimension. Both her parents were professionals and were shrouded from the cut and thrust of the commercial world, and observing how the jigsaw of politics, research and commerce intermingled fascinated her.

"I must find a hotel," said Jack.

"I know of a very nice Boutique hotel not too far from here. If you like, we can walk there," she said.

It had been a long and momentous day, and he had a lot of information to absorb. He remembered that he had left his car at the lecture rooms but walking on this balmy evening in Cambridge with a beautiful young woman his thoughts were disrupted. He asked her of her parents, where she was brought up, and what she hoped to do. She enquired about his social life, did he have children, was he in fact married, and had he ever been to Switzerland? Did he ski? He told her that he had just turned thirty-two, she admitted being twenty-two and three quarters. Embarrassingly, squeezing as many months up as possible, they both giggled.

They walked closely together. Both would have liked to hold hands, but felt it a little premature.

They arrived at a charming little hotel near the river. "My parents stayed here," she said casually. He was tempted to invite her in. She would probably have accepted. But he kissed her on her cheek and thanked her for her company. "I'll phone you before I come back next week if you wish."

"Yes, I would like that," she said. They both realised that he was already from another generation and she was untainted by the urban pseudo life in which he had immersed himself.

***

Early the following morning Jack found his car and arrived back in his Holborn office at 9.15 am. Brody Emmitt was already sitting behind his desk.

Jack waved to him through his glass wall "Can you spare a moment?" He mimed. Emmitt waved him in. "What's up Jack? I hope you've got some good news."

"Not exactly, I think that we have a problem Brody, I went to Cambridge yesterday and met George Baylim's associates. We spent the whole evening together and I managed to fill in a number of missing pieces especially regarding the Ever Young project. I have worked virtually through the night to memo it for you, and I need you to study it before we talk."

"Jack I'm completely swamped at this moment, can it wait till tomorrow?"

"Not if you want your articles boss, this could be a serious and international coup. It's not what you want to hear, but it will certainly sell copy."

"OK," he grunted, "grab me a coffee and go and sit in your office until I call you." Forty-five minutes later, he was back in front of a rather sombre editor-in-chief. "You've thrown the book at this company; I don't have to tell you that we've got over a million pounds in advertising from them for the next six months. That'll go out of the window if we go public with what you are saying here, and probably both you and I would follow."

"Not if we can prove our facts," said Jack, "Ever Young has already been launched, I need to prove that Tann is under the thumb of Magnum and I guess there are quite a few within the Ministry that are backing him up too. We need to

135

discover how Magnum are planning to monitor all their applicants and what they propose to do with them. Also where the money is coming from to finance an international launch and the phenomenal amount of money they are spending throughout the world without going public.

"Did you know that they have major holdings in some of the largest pharmaceutical companies and have their Autoplug Holographic doctors recommending their pills. Their ability to control the neuro-electrics that they will put into these young adults can change moods, create inclinations and God knows what else and of course bump them off if they so wished. We have a monumental amount of information that we could prove in court, especially if we show their origins, but if we want the government's support we would have to give them a reason for them to do a turnabout, but it would certainly compromise the government if a substantial proportion of their ministers are accused of being on the make. In fact, Political suicide."

"OK I'm going to let you run with this Jack, but you will have to be able to wrap it up pretty quickly," Emmitt replied.

Jack returned to his office and contemplated his next move. He had accumulated a jigsaw of information. The meeting in Cambridge gave him direction but he had to confirm Dr Ellsworth's version, and somehow discover the cause of Baylim's demise. The next piece of the jigsaw was to discover in which hospital Baylim had died, and on impulse phoned Ellsworth on his mobile. "Hello Peter, I'm sorry to bother you but you gave me a great deal to think about. I need to know where George Baylim was treated, and if you are you able to recall who his doctor was."

"Thank you for last night, I'm so pleased that you have taken this whole business on Jack, of course we'll help you, bear with me a moment, I filed some of his wife's notes."

He heard him speak to his secretary, and rustling papers, "yes, he was taken to Addenbrooke's Hospital. I recall it was on the 14th of August, four years ago. He was quite friendly with his doctor—I can't recall his name but no doubt they will have that information. Let me know if I can be of any further help, Jack."

"By the way, Helga was most impressed with you, just as a throwaway line."

"She's a little young, I think." Jack laughed. "I'll keep you posted."

He knew that the hospital would not be forthcoming with detailed information unless there was a good reason to do so, and decided to bend the truth in the hope of getting to the right source. Reception was easy. "Hello, I wonder if you could help, I'm Inspector Johnson of the Metropolitan Police and

I'm looking for information on a patient who passed away in your hospital a few years back, could you please put me through to the records department."

"Just a moment, inspector, I can put you through to the records retention. Please tell me your name again."

"Inspector Johnson," he repeated. It seemed so easy to pursue a false identity, and Jack waited for a few minutes before the call was taken by a more official voice.

"Hello, Inspector, my name is Francis Western. Sorry to keep you waiting, how can we help?"

"I'm investigating the death of a George Baylim who died in your hospital on August 14th four years ago. Would you still have the files?"

"If they haven't been destroyed, we generally only hold them for approximately four years if there is no reason to keep them, bear with me and we'll check. Maybe I can phone you back in a few minutes."

"By all means," replied Jack, now committed to a false identity. "Ah, can I phone you say in fifteen minutes? I'm just going into a meeting."

"No problem, Inspector," she replied. He breathed a sigh of relief, regretting he was so stupid.

He phoned again fifteen minutes later and apologised for a delay in returning the call.

"No problem," she repeated. "I have the file in front of me what would you like to know, Inspector?"

"Do you have a record of his NHS doctor by any chance."

"Yes, it was Doctor Singh, his telephone number is 01223 345987."

"And what symptoms was he treated for?"

"Reading through the report, he was 58 years old, and had previously been in reasonable health. However he appears to have developed some form of Viral Encephalitis which would not respond to medication."

"He was placed on a defibrillator but didn't respond. Antibiotics didn't appear to help, his body was in shock, the records show that he was put into an induced coma whilst on a respirator. The doctors were unable to bring him back, but the files state that he died of causes unknown. His wife was there on his passing and signed him out. The hospital requested an autopsy, but we were informed that this would not be accepted by his wife on religious grounds. The hospital contested her request, but they were overruled from a higher source, which is most unusual. I'd be happy to forward a copy of the report, Inspector, if you wish."

"That won't be necessary at this stage, but your assistance is most appreciated."

"Always happy to assist the police," she replied.

Jack thanked her, kicked himself, and immediately phoned Doctor Singh.

The receptionist informed him that he was still in surgery, but would phone back when surgery finishes in one hour.

"It is important," said Jack. He thanked her and left his number.

A picture was slowly emerging. "It's time to come above the covers," mumbled Jack to himself. He looked up the number of the UK office of Magnum. He remembered that the UK MD was a Paul Shannon.

After the usual interrogation, the receptionist conceded. "I can put you through to his PA if you wish," said the receptionist. Jack agreed and he was immediately transferred.

"Cockton-Smith here, how can I help you Mr Branson." His baritone voice and rather plummy English accent immediately suggested to Jack a façade of superiority, which seemed a little out of date.

"I'm the editor for the Tandem Press and I would like to interview your MD to discuss the Ever Young project."

"I don't think you would want to speak with Mr Shannon Mr Branson, shall I put you through to our Press department, I'm sure they will be able to help you." Jack visualised the sneer on this man's face.

"No, it IS your Managing Director that I would wish to speak with. Mr Cockton-Smith, your company has placed over a million pounds' worth of advertising with us and we need to give the campaign the credibility that you are paying for. As the campaign is being launched in ten days there is some urgency in meeting Mr Shannon and presenting him as the UK head of the company. In other words Mr Smith, I need to interview him sooner rather than later, I would require approximately 90 minutes with him and our photographer to discuss the company's intentions and the benefits to the British people who we are appealing to. Can I suggest Tuesday or Wednesday of next week?"

"One moment please," he mumbled. "I can see that the next two weeks are going to be rather difficult, may I suggest Friday 26th Mr Branson?"

"My apologies Mr Cockton-Smith, but I'm afraid it must be next week as we go to press soon after. This is most important to your campaign, so next week please. I suggest that you have a word with him and see if you can fit this time in. It would be a shame to go out into 12 magazines without copy."

Jack was aware that he was being overbearing, he remembered that Magnum could, without doubt be their best client, but he had personally already condemned the company. Even before his interview he had psyched himself up with the hope that his magazine would decide not to promote the scheme and he would do everything in his power towards that end, regardless of the consequences.

"I will come back to you shortly," replied Cockton-Smith.

One hour later a young woman called to confirm a meeting for the Wednesday at 11.00 am.

A photographer would not be necessary as they already had stock photos.

***

He sat in his office contemplating every possible permutation, its outcome and its consequences. It was now 6.00 pm when his extension rang. "Doctor Singh here, how can I help you Mr Branson?"

"Doctor, I need your advice relating to a patient of yours who passed away approximately four years ago, his name was George Baylim."

"Yes, I knew him well, in fact I was a great admirer of his work, may I ask what your interest is in this gentleman Mr Branson."

"By all means, I am an editor with the Tandem Press, and we've taken on the Magnum account. You may know that they are marketing the Ever Young project as well as the Autoplug, both of which George and Gilda Baylim were working on."

"I know, in fact we spoke about these projects a number of times, and I like to think that some of my comments were taken on board. In fact, the Autoplug has been most successful in my own surgery." He hesitated, "but in my opinion Ever Young was seriously flawed." "Why so?" asked Jack.

"Look, I'm a doctor, I'm sworn to protect life, there were never conditions added, and regardless of a patient's age or their indisposition, it's my job to assist them in whichever way I can. The idea of terminating a healthy person to me is an anathema. George's original research with children, which would combat inherited detrimental genes was marvellous, but after many arguments with Gilda and discussions with the ministry he obviously conceded. You cannot put financial arguments ahead of maintaining life and in my opinion it broke the very essence of the Hippocratic oath."

"I could not agree with you more doctor, but I have a serious moral problem which I would like to confide in you, can I assume that this conversation is in the strictest confidence!"

"Of course," replied Singh.

"My company has taken a massive advertising contract from Magnum. The brief that I have been given is to write a series of articles extolling the benefits of Ever Young, but I'm beginning to believe that there are serious and extremely dangerous hidden intents aligned to this project. Is there a possibility that Professor Baylim's death was…shall we say, unnatural?"

There was a long silence before he answered. "The problem was that an autopsy was not agreed to and so the cause of death was never confirmed, but I must admit that the thought had more than passed my mind at the time. George and I spoke on several occasions both in my surgery for routine diabetes checks, and at his home, and other than the usual excesses that we all have, he seemed perfectly healthy. It was assumed that he had contracted a bug which immobilised him, he was only in the hospital for four days before he was placed into a coma, and that was it. As a doctor, I am well acquainted with death, but I can tell you that it was deeply upsetting for me personally to lose such a good and brilliant man."

"And what was your relationship with Gilda?"

"To be truthful, I never warmed to her. There was no doubt that she was very clever but her abrasive manner didn't appeal to me." He cleared his throat. "You know that immediately after he died she left for Germany. No, Mr Branson, I didn't like her."

"Would you be prepared to ask for an autopsy if I could find good reason to do so doctor?"

"Yes, I would, but from what I understood at the time, the denial was confirmed from higher sources and agreed by his wife. It should all be on the hospital records." Jack thanked the doctor and they agreed to keep in touch.

Chapter 13

A cloud of depression found Jack sitting in front of his computer once again. All his adult life he had known the direction he wanted to go. His love for words and undiluted ambition placed him squarely into the publishing world. His first serious job with the local paper soon brought him to the attention of the nationals as an assistant reporter. From there on in, he rocketed into positions of consequence, and eventually took on the sporting division within the Tandem organisation. He saw himself heading for junior directorships and knew all the right people. It was rare to be confronted with morals, and whilst facts plus a degree of fantasy could be acceptable, it was, he thought, beyond his remit as a sports writer.

Now, with the biggest break dumped into his lap he was about to jump into a black hole. He looked at his blank screen knowing that it would be impossible to promote Magnum unless they could exonerate themselves in his eyes.

Every piece of information that he had was based on hearsay and his sources were all hypothesis and unsubstantiated comments, and for every accusation there could be a valid explanation. What he desperately needed was proven intent and reason.

He placed his hands on the tabs of his computer as if it was a piano and began to write.

To Jane Franklyn, personal secretary to Mr George Pickles, Finance Minister

Dear Jane,

Following our last meeting in respect to Magnum, I am writing to summarise subsequent information that I have gathered.

I do not propose to detail all my various meetings and by the same token am wary of emailing the minister with, as yet, unsubstantiated information that would be certain to damage Magnum and may result in litigation without proof. However, I am particularly concerned to know how Mr George Baylim died. After speaking with both the hospital and his personal doctor, I discovered that his death is reported as 'unknown causes'. Nevertheless, the autopsy request was denied by "higher sources" which I believe is highly suspicious. I need to reverse this instruction which both the hospital and his doctor would be pleased to underwrite. May I suggest that Brendon Tann is not informed at this stage nor Baylim's wife who is now in Germany.

Your comments would be most appreciated.

Yours most sincerely,

Jack Branson.

He received an instant reply.

Dear Jack,

I have spoken with the minister, he agrees that this request is fraught with problems, and it is a matter of protocol to go through the Minister of Health, which is of course currently Brendon Tann. We should also need to receive confirmation from his wife, wherever she may be. However, this procedure could be side stepped if the police felt that there were suspicious circumstances, but formal confirmation would be required from them.

He suggests therefore that you speak once again to the doctor and he would bring the matter to their attention. We would be able to have further discussions with the police once they are involved.

The minister has asked me to inform him of your progress as a matter of importance.

Sincerely,

Jane Franklyn PA to Finance Minister George Pickles.

***

Jack decided to visit Cambridge again. This time to meet Dr Singh. He considered that it would be more productive to arrange to see Ellsworth at the same time, maybe in his home. He had only a few days before his first article was expected and time was of the essence.

Ellsworth's mobile rang constantly for five minutes but he had his home number. Clare answered.

They exchanged the usual courtesies, and Jack came to the point.

"Clare, you recall that we spoke of George's death. After our meeting, I spoke with Dr Singh and asked his opinion on George's medical condition. He agreed that it was very strange that such a healthy individual should deteriorate so rapidly. I need to persuade him to confirm a 'suspicious death' to the police, in order that they would override the initial instruction and give reason to have an autopsy." He could hear her thinking at the other end.

Jack broke the silence. "Clare, is it possible to invite the doctor and myself to your house so that we can all discuss this matter in greater detail."

"When?"

"Tomorrow if we can persuade Dr Singh to come. Time is of the essence now."

"Let me speak with Peter and I'll phone you back," she replied.

He thanked her and immediately phoned Dr Singh once again.

"Doctor, are you able to come to Professor Ellsworth's house tomorrow evening maybe for supper. I believe that we can find a way to discover the cause of Baylim's death. By the way, I'm told that she is an excellent cook."

"Yes," he immediately answered, "I look forward to seeing you, shall we say 7.30 pm?"

Clare phoned back, "I spoke with Peter and he would be happy to see you again, I can prepare supper, will you be bringing Helga again, she's such a charming young woman?"

"That's a nice thought," he replied, "I'll ask her too."

Helga was delighted to hear from Jack once again and immediately agreed.

At last, there appeared to be a positive direction.

***

USA
Miriam

A substantial file had grown on the Magnum business, but there were still several unanswered questions. The question of origin was uppermost in Miriam's mind. The original patents for the Autoplug appeared to be in the name of George Baylim on behalf of Cambridge University in the UK, suggesting that the university had a claim, but then fresh patents were registered in Germany to include further improvements under the Magnum name. Miriam brought this oddity to the Spoken Arrow patent lawyers who concluded that Germany had not recognised the university's rights, however they had not been disputed, and it seemed that both patents were valid.

In the beginning, Baylim had worked closely with Hitzudi in Japan on the Autoplug, but although the original details were registered under the university of Cambridge, Magnum changed the details of the patent and registered them as their own.

Miriam continued to dig into the details of the Magnum empire. She discovered patents and registered marks on various drugs which were licenced back to prominent drug companies who would distribute them by prescription recommended by the Autoplug 'doctors'. There was no doubt that whoever was behind the company was brilliant and if not crooked, certainly devious. It was now up to her company as to how they would use her findings. Timing was all important, for unless they had a fair alternative to replace either the Autoplug or the Ever Young project it would be a pyrrhic victory.

She decided that it would be an interesting exercise to make contact with Cambridge, if nothing else but to discover if Baylim's colleagues had received any benefits and whatever alternatives they may have been working on. It would also be a good opportunity to visit her family, she had now been away from home for nearly six months. She'd made a number of friends and almost lived in her favourite restaurant, sometimes even going into the kitchen to introduce some of her mother's recipes.

Chapter 14
Martin

Martin was about to embark on a sales campaign in South America, but Miriam needed direction. She emailed Carolyn Brosh to set up an open meeting with Martin and to include Jay Harrai and Robert Levine, to see if their own research could be incorporated within the Baylim engineering. There may have been certain developments that weren't given to Magnum.

A one hour slot was allocated and she immediately contacted her colleagues to inform them.

They met on the patio and took a table overlooking the sea, each one had brought their laptops ready to refer to various ideas that had been catalogued.

"The way I see it Martin, any investigations that we prove might compromise our competitor but would not really benefit us unless we can offer a credible alternative to what they have."

"I agree Miriam but we don't have that alternative," he smiled, "however I guess that you have a proposal, so what is it?"

"I would like to make a visit to Cambridge and see what Baylim's colleagues were doing, and if they had any other plans for their project before it became part of Magnum. If we want to have an alternative product for either the Autoplug or Ever Young, it would need to be similar but obviously not the same. So, if the groundwork has already been done why reinvent the wheel, especially if these chaps are free to work with us."

"Chaps, what's chaps?" asked Robert innocently.

"They're English men I think," laughed Jay.

Jay was scrolling through his 'New Ideas' app. "Do you recall Martin that we had a conversation some two years ago when I discussed with you the possibility of designing a home based medical app. I am wondering if, by using the latest holographic technology we might be able to transpose it onto a Spoken Arrow machine."

"I do recall talking to you about that, but at that time we were having problems with imposing holograms onto our existing models, our latest SA105 model might be able to incorporate it, what do you think Robert?"

"It would need remodelling but I think it's possible, in any event I would certainly like to scratch the brains of the English, they may still be able to teach us something." He laughed.

"We're just waiting our time to take you back into our empire," retorted Miriam.

"I think that it's a good idea for the three of you to make a visit," Martin replied. "But just in case they have an existing arrangement with Magnum, I'll speak with our local 'chaps' to smooth the waves."

"We can ask my good friend and manager Theo Jacobs to make enquiries," said Miriam. "You won't find anyone more diplomatic than him. In fact, it was through him that I heard of my current position."

"OK, give him a call, he's a good chap, I'll leave it to you to contact him Miriam. Give him only outline details, at this stage we simply want to know three things. First, do they have any contacts currently with Magnum? Second, are they allowed to speak with us regarding their Autoplug research? And finally, who is the current driving force, if there is one?" He hesitated, stroked his chin and with a sense of immediacy, he closed his memo pad, stood up and concluded the conversation by capping it. "The sooner the better, but we don't know yet how they are committed to our desire to compete with Magnum, and even if they are, what legal holds do Magnum have on them, if any. Good luck, and Miriam, give my kindest regards to your parents." He shook their hands warmly, and left them to arrange a flight.

Chapter 15
England

The following two weeks were frantic. Arranging and rearranging their diaries as they planned the next fourteen days. Neither Robert nor Jay had ever been to the United Kingdom before, and Miriam was interested to note that they were as excited as when she had first arrived in the USA. Both men were given a long list of goodies that would be added to their Christmas list.

Their plane landed at Heathrow on a particularly cold Mid November with a temperature of 3 degrees. Both men were still wearing their Californian cottons and were totally unprepared for the dank British weather. At last, they were able to claim their bags and walked out into freezing rain shivering and wet. "I warned you guys to dress warm," she laughed.

"How can you people live with this weather, I have discovered the purpose of hibernation," said Robert between chattering teeth.

Miriam loaded them into a London Taxi, instructed the driver to go to the London Hilton, Park Lane. The driver was a talkative fellow, and happily explained how the politics of the world would benefit if they would only listen to him. However, it was all to no avail as both Robert and Jay found it almost impossible to understand a single word. "Is he speaking English?" asked Jay.

"Cockney!" she laughed.

Immediately they found their rooms both men ran hot baths and promised to stay there for the rest of the day.

She immediately telephoned Dr Ellsworth and arranged a meeting for the following morning in Cambridge. This allowed her the afternoon to organise a short shopping spree for her colleagues to combat the elements for the coming week. By the end of the day, armed with woollen sweaters, umbrellas, soft peak hats and Burberry coats they could have been mistaken for locals.

It was natural that Miriam would want to stay with her parents, but this was business and necessary that the three should be together in the same hotel for the short time they would be in the country. Leaving them to discover a little of London her next port of call was to see her family. She had not told anyone that she was returning and decided to surprise them and turn up at the door.

As she pressed the bell, she could hear her father telling her mother to answer the door as he was in the bathroom, she heard her shuffling towards it, looking through the security hole, and seeing Miriam waving on the other side. "Mamma Mia, am I imagining it? Frank it's Miriam," she shouted even before opening it. "Why didn't you phone to say you were coming," she cried. "We might not have been in," speaking as she tightly hugged her daughter. "How wonderful it is to see you." They stood back to look at one another. In the few months that she had been away, Miriam noticed some tell-tale signs that were not there before.

"Are you OK, Mum?" she said.

"Why should I not be! Sure, I'm just so happy to see you." She kissed and hugged her daughter again, this time with Papa trying to muscle in to the cuddles.

She left the evening just for her parents, catching up with local news and telling them of her time away. Was it that she had a fresh eye to see them or were they slowly diminishing. How amazing it would be if we could stop time for people we loved, she thought.

She would determine to see them again before she left and bring her American friends.

Of course, she contacted her good friend Theo, and arranged a breakfast meeting with him. He had been thorough in his investigations and discovered that a Dr Ellsworth had been the head of the research under George Baylim; he had taken over as head of the department after his colleague's death, and was happy to talk with members of the executive of Spoken Arrow on the understanding that a letter of confidentiality would be signed by both parties. Mrs Baylim had returned to Germany. And, with a little cajoling, the doctor confessed that he was already in discussions with a certain Mr Branson who was also most keen to hear their experiences. Theo asked if Mr Branson had any connection to Magnum, he confirmed categorically that he had not and that the doctor also had no contact with Magnum and neither did the university other than a lawsuit that had appeared to have lapsed. He was not prepared to discuss the death of Baylim.

Doctor Ellsworth appeared to be quite open to a meeting and was asked that any contact with Spoken Arrow company should be in absolutely secrecy in the interest of all parties. The conversation concluded with a possible meeting in Cambridge with the three senior executives of Spoken Arrow coming from California and himself. They had a sufficient level of information to pursue a constructive meeting, but "Who is this Branson?" asked Robert. Theo had not been told.

***

From the 23th floor of their hotel overlooking Hyde Park, they could see Buckingham Palace. The flag was flying the Royal Standard indicating that the King was in residence. It was hard to tear them away as Miriam pointed out the various historic points from their vantage point.

She hired a car. It would take just over an hour to get to Cambridge. Neither of the men were prepared to take the wheel as they had never travelled on the 'wrong side' of the road before. Their appointment was for 10.30 am. Miriam thought it wise to phone Dr Ellsworth to confirm once again that they were leaving, and he reiterated that he was looking forward to meeting them.

Each one had their own concept of a possible outcome, with a full understanding of the implications that could result from a domino effect. Each word would be measured and ideas of progression dealt with in a most delicate manner with no firm commitments given and any further progress openly considered and left with various possibilities, as yet unknown.

They were looking for the Hopkins building which they were told housed the Biochemistry department and after numerous stops and enquiries were a few minutes late.

This was the England that they had read about in novels that held the majesty of history within its walls. Robert had checked out on his pad some of the great men who had studied in this very building, Newton, Darwin, Wordsworth, even the King walked through these doors, it was awe inspiring and a little humbling for him and somewhat disappointing that Jay was less interested. "You're too romantic," he sneered, although he clearly enjoyed the moment.

Doctor Ellsworth came to the reception with a broad smile, wearing a vintage tweed jacket with a pipe in top pocket and baggy trousers, caricaturing him as the proverbial absent minded English professor. His pasty complexion would not have been so obvious compared to his Californian guest's tan and open shirts since they could not bring themselves to wear ties.

They were escorted into his office where tea had already been prepared. The room was large with a number of armchairs obviously designed for discussions with students, and with various small tables by their side. They exchanged cards sat in the rather lumpy armchairs. "How do you like tea," asked the doctor congenially.

"Very much, thank you," replied Jay.

"Doctor Ellsworth is not asking if you like tea; he asked if you like milk and sugar?" Miriam gently interposed.

"I can see that I will have to be a little more transatlantic," the doctor conceded.

Miriam opened her case to produce a confidentiality agreement copied from the web, and the doctor reciprocated, both read each other's and signed them. Miriam noticed that the letter she was given was on University headed paper.

"Shall we assume that you are talking on behalf of the university doctor."

"For the purposes of this meeting, let us say so. However, I would not confine our discussions solely to them, let us see what we have in common. I will be as frank as possible with you and no doubt you will reciprocate in kind. But whatever is said in this room is without prejudice to either side. Would you agree to that?" He asked politely.

"Of course," replied Miriam. "May I begin by clarifying a few points with you. Our understanding doctor is that the Autoplug and the Ever Young projects that are marketed by Magnum originated from your laboratories. Is that so?"

"I can say categorically yes to the original projects, but they have been altered by Magnum to suit their particular marketing plan."

"Are you saying therefore that the patents that they are holding do not conflict with your original developments?"

"That is a more difficult question to answer, Miss Bravotti."

"Miriam, please."

"Thank you, Miriam," he continued. "We placed extensive patents on our original research, I really cannot say if our patents were assimilated into theirs or if they have reinvented them. A large conglomerate such as yours would probably be able to define what is exclusively theirs and whether we could lay claim to anything.

"My late colleague George Baylim took the original patents out, but what his wife did afterwards rather complicated matters."

Robert carefully put his cup back onto the saucer supplied. He leaned forward and spoke softly as if others should not be listening "Doctor, it's particularly interesting for us to know as much about your developments in this field as possible. However, I know you'll appreciate how delicate our position would be, and yours, if we were seen, even inadvertently to be plagiarising our competitor. So, what Miriam is intimating in her delicate English manner is, if you should tell us more than we should be hearing, would we all be caught with our pants down especially if we were to go into further technical detail with you for our mutual gain?" He spoke with a typical relaxed Californian style, that it would have been difficult for even the most Teutonic listener to take offence.

"Please call me Robert."

"All right Robert. I fully appreciate both of our positions, in fact we asked ourselves the same question. Not only what are we allowed to tell you, and what are the consequences, but whatever we tell you or work towards will be considered by Magnum as an attack on their privileged knowledge. I hope you don't mind if I light up."

"No not at all," they responded, looking at each other.

"It helps me to concentrate." He spent a few moments puffing away, a smell that could have been horse manure emanating from his pipe. "We spent years researching both the Autoplug and Ever Young and many alternative ideas were considered, which incidentally weren't patented and not even shown the light of day. I can tell you now that the company formed by George Baylim never saw the light of the financial day, but when Gilda Baylim took control she formed a new company and registered new patents which excluded the university and ourselves I should add, from any rights that we were promised in the event that it was successful."

"So, who negotiated with Magnum?" asked Jay. "Did Mrs Baylim pass the existing patents to Magnum, or did they rewrite them in their own name."

"I'm afraid I can't tell you that. I really don't know. Our original ideas on the Autoplug relied to a great extent on the software and programming, and we worked closely with the various government sources towards this end.

"The government was certainly a major factor in its success. After all, there is very little information about us as individuals that is not within the remit of our government offices. So, when one presses their hand on that machine, it will not only know everything about them, because the real genius is that this information can be digested and can be summarised, enabling a logical and unemotional response that the user can rely on. Any question that is out of the computers' medical remit would be called upon from a Cloud and emulsified into their particular circumstance if so required, and what's more its reasoning is compounded every time they speak to it. That was the genius, don't you know?" Ellsworth was now becoming notably excited.

"Don't I know what," replied Robert.

"Just an English turn of phrase," smiled Miriam. "So, this brilliant machine now under the auspices of our erstwhile friends was originally patented by yourselves—does that mean the university or Baylim?"

"To my understanding the university. After all, it was they who were paying our wages."

"Dare I ask you what your original conceptual ideas were for this Autoplug?" asked Jay. "In other words, were there alternative concepts put forward?" asked Jay.

"You may sir, but I don't think we are quite ready to answer that yet."

"You're quite right doctor," butted in Miriam. "The last thing you want is to be passed over again, and it's easy for us to say that we are not a Magnum, but we should prove ourselves to you as well as you to us. However, it seems to me a good beginning if we check who owns what, and what is free on the table to develop either in part or whole.

"We have a division in Spoken Arrow that only deals with our patents, they are as sharp as a needle, and with your permission we would attempt to unravel what we can both do before a possible lawsuit that we might lose. That's not to say that Magnum won't come at us even if we or you had total rights, but we must all know that we are secure in what we do. Would you not agree."

"I must say Miriam," said the doctor, "that for a young woman you certainly have a way of clarifying things…yes I agree, for our part we have nothing to lose, and it would be marvellous to benefit a little from so many years of hard work in this field. I take it that the same will apply to the Ever Young project. I will speak to my board in the strictest confidence of course and ask them to pass over as much information on the patents as is available. I will need a legal understanding from your company that anything that we reveal to you other than that which you have developed will not be used without our permission. Will you agree to that?"

Jay had not said much during this meeting and was happy to allow the meeting to unravel naturally. And with his typical oriental refinement he concluded the conversation. "I should tell you, doctor, that we never work out of house and this will be a first for us. I do not believe that there is another organisation as correct and honourable as Spoken Arrow and I hope that you will soon agree, However, it should be said that Spoken Arrow has already a thick file of researched ideas for future discussions. Therefore I do feel that a degree of trust on both sides will be necessary."

"I agree," replied the doctor.

"Finally, just before we go, doctor," said Robert. "Who is Mr Branson?"

"Ah. That is still for me to know and you to find out, but I can assure you that he is on our side. When are you returning to the States?" he asked. "We can be here for four or five days, or longer if necessary."

"Maybe we could meet the day after tomorrow, it will give me time to talk to my colleagues and maybe formulate some practical ideas!"

"That would be great," she replied. "I'll wait for your confirmation and we will work around your diary."

As Miriam was the last to leave she said, "Doctor, if we find the common denominators that we are both looking for, it would be our pleasure to invite you to LA where I'm sure you would be impressed, and we would hope to build on your foundations."

Robert suggested that Doctor Ellsworth join them for lunch, but he correctly refused. Both had enough information, and anything more would have been excessive at this time.

Chapter 16
Doctor Singh

Peter Ellsworth felt a great weight had been unloaded from him. His meeting with Spoken Arrow gave him new hope. It seemed that time had stood still for the last four years, then suddenly lurched forward beginning with Jack Branson then Spoken Arrow who seemed to have come out of the blue.

Clare had spent the entire day cooking for the dinner that evening. Although Peter had only met Doctor Errol Singh once before at his colleague's funeral, it would be strange bringing his friend to life again, even metaphorically. He found himself in an embarrassing predicament. From the twelve scientists in his Autoplug and the Ever Young project team, eight were given promises by George Baylim of shares. They blamed George's wife for manipulating the company. It was a bitter blow when it was taken to Germany. Nevertheless, they stayed within his group working on various projects and he felt it his duty to update them on his discussions relating to the Magnum business.

But the purpose of this evening's dinner was to discover how his friend died. Once that had been resolved and if his suspicions were proven, he would consider telling his colleagues of his decision to work with Spoken Arrow. Until then all discussions were to be kept strictly confidential.

Doctor Errol Singh was first to arrive exactly on time, to the minute. It was always a wonder to Peter how meticulous some people were. Would they be waiting in their cars or outside the door, maybe for five or ten minutes, possibly in the rain, the thought brought a smile to his face. He was aware that his friend George Baylim had visited Singh on a regular basis to check his diabetes. But he had not met him personally and was slightly ambivalent as to the degree of cooperation he might have. But Jack's request placed a fresh dimension on the evening. "We had a number of conversations over the years," said Singh. "Of course the Auto Plug was in a stage of evolution at that time and I like to think that I contributed something towards its development, but I must admit that I was shocked when he became so ill. I met his wife in hospital two or three times, but I can't say that we saw eye to eye on his condition. In fact, when he suddenly passed away I requested an autopsy but she refused it."

"This is the very point that we need to discuss. I am waiting for my young friend to arrive who has taken a deep interest in George's death, and I think you will be interested in what he has to say."

Ellsworth had taken a liking to Jack. He admired his precocity, and his commitment to a cause no matter the cost, and this evening Jack would also bring Helga, whom he considered a star pupil, but in his heart she reminded him of his lost youth, and he enjoyed her natural persona and in particular her beauty.

Jack and Helga arrived twenty minutes later, they were made comfortable and introduced to Dr Errol Singh.

All parties were keen to discuss the subject in hand, and it was left to Jack to outline the situation. "We believe Doctor that George was murdered, but only an autopsy will prove it. If you are prepared to issue a request to the police that you have your suspicions, they will allow the hospital to release his body."

"I will of course do whatever you think necessary since I'm of the same mind as yourselves," Singh replied. "What would you like me to do?"

"Simply inform the police that you consider that you believe George died under questionable circumstances and that an autopsy is essential to confirm the manner of his death. That will release the restriction imposed by his wife and hopefully answer the question as to whose influence from above she might have managed to persuade. Time is of the essence as the files are often destroyed after four years, and we are very near that time."

Dr Singh agreed to assist in any way, and the evening settled into a normality.

Helga was now totally immersed in the intrigue, and it was not possible to leave her with only part of Jack's involvement, and in truth he took some comfort in telling her his fears and the possible consequences that lay ahead. Her alert mind gave him alternative directions to consider.

Clare had gone to some trouble to show off her culinary skills and by the time desserts arrived the reasons for being there had dissipated into the back of their minds.

As they left Jack whispered to Helga, "I'd love to show you a little of the London that you may not have seen yet, maybe we can find a play or a concert." Despite Jack's worldliness, he found himself fumbling. "Do you think Dr Ellsworth would release you for one or two days." He had developed a feeling for her that he was not capable of explaining. He'd known many women in his work, but Helga had no need to create a pseudo sophisticated image that he was so used to. She had a natural beauty and an honesty that in itself was seductive to Jack, and he felt the need to tell her everything.

"I'm sure the Doctor would understand if I missed one or two of his lectures," she replied slightly blushing. "But I'll ask him anyway."

"I'll call you tomorrow and maybe we can make a plan." He dropped her off at her apartment on the other side of Cambridge. They kissed, said their farewells and he drove back to London in a dream.

Chapter 17
Dr Ellsworth

England in late November is invariably the gloomiest time, and this year was no exception. Both Robert and Jay lay in the warm waters of the Hilton jacuzzi in the certain knowledge that they would soon be entering a cryogenic half-life. They had purchased sweaters, long coms and heavy woollen socks, gloves and scarves, to make the point that California should soon be only a plane journey away. But it was becoming obvious that they would be suffering a little longer.

Miriam had agreed that they would return to Cambridge, and although it was by local standards a normal autumnal day both men reluctantly prepared for what they felt to be the big freeze.

They arrived at the university at noon and were met at the reception by a smiling Ellsworth, still in the same baggy trousers and tweed jacket with pipe in mouth, impervious to the mere five degrees of warmth both outside and inside.

"We are meeting Sir William Hoddington today, but I'm afraid he is in another part of the college. It's only a few minutes' walk, if that's all right with you. He is the vice-chancellor of the university—we can't go higher than him," he chuckled as he relit his pipe.

The Registrar's Office was a humbling experience. The building embodied the best of English traditions in its architecture and on its walls. Paintings of kings, princes, political leaders and icons of the science who had studied or taught here. Busts of Newton, Darwin and Shakespeare were looked down upon by massive ageless oak beams probably from the 16th century.

They walked up three flights of stairs and were directed to Sir William's office. One could imagine that it had retained the same image for centuries. The room was surrounded by hundreds of books. A log fire was burning and a grand and ancient desk of a mammoth size was stacked with files.

Introductions were made, cards passed and the party were directed to seats around an extremely large and highly polished boardroom table. A young lady entered with a pot of tea and coffee. "Thank you for seeing us Sir William," Ellsworth began. There appeared to be a relaxed relationship between the two men which made it easier to fall into a more animated conversation.

Miriam introduced her company. "I'm assuming, Sir William, that Dr Ellsworth has given you a synopsis of the current situation and the reason that we are here. We believe that under the right circumstances a very exciting partnership could be created between our two organisations. However, we both must be extremely careful not to compromise ourselves in doing so. I'm sure that you will forgive me saying that it seems to us the university has had its fingers burnt with regard to your research and development of the Autoplug and Ever Young, and as Spoken Arrow are world leaders in computerised communication, we are keen to see if your efforts could complement our own work or vice versa particularly in the medical field."

"I would certainly admit, Miss Brevotti, that an association with your company could benefit us substantially. For we've worked very hard on both the Autoplug and the Ever Young project and spent considerable sums only to see our efforts passed onto another company without any advantage to ourselves. There's no doubt in retrospect that we should have pursued them but I'm afraid we lost our footing and let the moment pass. However, we now have to untangle who legally can lay claim to what with a degree of confidence."

"What we can't be seen to do," interjected Robert, "is to entangle your original patents from Magnum's and the position becomes too obscure whereby we can't decide what is yours and what is claimed as theirs, but if we can show that their patents are founded on yours, then we have a very interesting situation. We could, with your help, stand toe to toe against them."

"I believe our lawyers are currently looking at all our patents and brands, if Magnum assumed that Mrs Baylim owned them but we can prove that she didn't, then there is a chance we could lay claim to the products and brands and sue them.

"But we can all be sure that however confident we are, Magnum will not allow us to take their market without a fight."

"May I summarise the situation, Sir William, as I see it?" interjected Ellsworth.

"By all means, Peter." he replied.

Removing his pipe he tapped it on the table as if to prepare for a lecture. "There are facts that our friends are not aware of and which may have a substantial bearing on our actions." The three who had been sitting and sipping their tea quite suddenly sat up in unison.

"Mr Jack Branson contacted me recently, he is a lead writer for the Tandem publishing company. They print a plethora of magazines covering all aspects of life. This group have been given an advertising contract worth approximately one million pounds to promote the Ever Young project, and he was asked to write accompanying articles praising its benefits.

"However, when he looked into the company in greater detail and its history, he discovered some disconcerting facts about its origins. The company originated before the second world war as an information bureau and was asked by Field Marshall Goring to formulate listings of Jews throughout Europe for the Nazi party. We know the results and consequences of most of these names. After or during the war, the company Magnum was formed and substantial monies were transferred to Brazil from Switzerland, this is where Magnum was and still is financed from. We have no knowledge of where this bottomless well came from."

"All this could be considered history, even if distasteful, nevertheless history, but for the fact that the claims now made by Magnum have changed from a health improving creation to a termination program, albeit as a guaranteed health promise until the required date. A modern version you could say of the Final Solution. Now to top this our Professor George Baylim whom I worked so closely with as you know, died under mysterious circumstances and at that time his wife refused to give the hospital permission for an autopsy. She is now working with Magnum, but Jack has managed to persuade them to exhume his body and see if there are any suspicious circumstances that caused his death."

Miriam was about to make a point, but Ellsworth raised a finger. "Allow me to finish Miriam—just a moment more." He was now in full flight. "What is most interesting is that the newly appointed Health minister Hines who had contested the Ever Young 351 project on the grounds that Magnum's chip had the ability to control the emotions of those that prescribed to it, was killed with his wife during a burglary. But his demise allowed his predecessor, who had passed the project through the government circles in the first place, to return to office. This man Brendon Tann has over the last four years become extremely wealthy, and we believe he is in the back pocket of Magnum as are a number of ministers who assisted him. All this needs to be corroborated but if it is, a totally new modus operandi emerges."

There was a long moment of silence as the table absorbed Ellsworth's presentation. "Are you saying," said Robert, "that two murders as well as the theft of the business and bribery could be placed at our erstwhile Nazi competitors door who in effect want to control the minds of the world. Doctor. It's better than any John Grisham plot," he smiled showing his gleaming teeth against a Californian suntan.

"Exactly, but three murders including Hines' wife. We'll know the result of the autopsy within two or three days, and I understand that Jack is visiting Magnum tomorrow in order to interview the managing director of the UK company. He of course believes that it is to promote the company and not interrogate them."

Jay had been quietly tapping away on his slate. "You mentioned that the original concept of Ever Young was to save lives doctor, may I ask what you had originally envisaged?"

"Yes, our original research was based on an inoculation program to children, making exactly the same claims to regulate any anomalies of the DNA, but when Mrs Baylim joined the research team she obviously saw substantial benefits in mind control microchips to an older group, and an opportunity to governments around the world that would control the invasion of masses of elderly who would otherwise cost billions to maintain. She was fiercely contested by all of us especially George. There was no doubt that she was and probably still is a very forceful woman. In any event, we had no say in the matter."

"And you know that she is now working for Magnum?" asked Miriam.

"As far as we understand. We'll hopefully know more when Jack contacts me with an update."

"With your permission, I would like to suggest we look carefully into the children's formula and its claims. which certainly seems much more appealing. Is there anything that you can tell us about the Autoplug that could be an improvement on what exists already Doctor?" she continued.

"It's not so much what can be improved but how the costs could be reduced. In my opinion Miriam, they are skimming vast profits off the Autoplug. They don't appear to have changed our original design, but the Hitzudi software is superb. They have cooperated with the government to transfer medical information and social services plus every other factor the government has, which allows every individual to use the Autoplug as a personal mentor. Consequently it knows everything about them and can converse in what the user believes to be the strictest confidence. The more they tell the computer, the more the app absorbs and the greater its understanding of them it compounds."

"You say, 'believes', doctor, are you suggesting that their conversations can be hacked or altered in some way?"

"Of course, Magnum can get into any computer and monitor changing circumstances, such as mortgages, salaries, medical information, children and even divorce. The App can cover every aspect of our lives in one way or another.

It is not so much that they could change factual information, but the algorithms that consolidate the facts are what would influence the user. Come to that so could the government, if they were as efficient. Of course the public see the Autoplug as their friend, as it is, and many are probably aware that this machine holds their lives, but it serves their purpose, and it has become their mentor, and unless the media brought it to their attention they will continue to confide in it and it will become part of their furniture, as it were."

Robert commented "There is a certain irony that every individual has a number but this time it's not on their arm."

"It would be most interesting," Jay replied, "to discover how Ever Young fits in with the Autoplug since the two products in isolation appear to have little in common with one another. Ever Young in isolation would cost a fortune to maintain and has no financial benefit, and even aligned with the Autoplug it offered no added financial value, that is except to Magnums hidden objectives."

"I must admit," said Miriam, "I use the Autoplug just as you describe already. It's remarkable how uninhibited we are when in front of a machine."

"Well," said Sir William a little cheekily, "it's unfortunate that we don't have access to it." He grinned. "But I'm pleased to confirm to you that we are very willing to work with your organisation, on the understanding of course that neither of us is compromised, and we shall instruct our patent lawyers accordingly."

"There is a downside," said Miriam. "By exposing them we place an irrevocable black mark not only on them but on the whole concept, which would be something of a pyric victory."

"All the more reason to play our cards very close to our chest before we can decide to act," replied the Professor.

"May I suggest that under strict confidentiality agreements we should compare what we have in our files that can be used, and a plan of attack should be discussed thereafter. Would you agree to that?" He addressed all three. "Who shall we coordinate with?"

"I shall be happy to follow through the good offices of Peter," replied Miriam, "and it might be interesting to meet with Mr Jack Branson and compare notes, he sounds like an interesting man. Could you organise a meeting Peter in the near future. We really need to return to LA in the next few days, although I'd be happy to pop over here whenever necessary. It might also be a good idea for Doctor Ellsworth to visit us as well in the future. In any event, we need to compare notes in detail. We'd certainly be prepared to send over our team to work closely with you."

"I will probably be speaking with Jack and will try to arrange a meeting with yourselves at a mutually convenient time," said Ellsworth.

Sir William stood up from the table. A noted man of science. "This is very exciting for the college and I hope will help us financially, I must admit that we are in need of a financial boost but even more, direction. It's a rather sad fact that our business acumen is a poor partner to our intelligentsia and a little in short supply."

She replied, "It's a great pleasure meeting you, Sir William. We are all blessed with our particular talents, and I hope that we can learn from one another."

They shook hands and left with a feeling of camaraderie and a much deeper understanding of the task ahead.

Immediately after they left Robert commented to Miriam, "I enjoyed meeting Sir William, but my experience in dealing with academics even in the States is that very little happens unless they are pushed, that's why they've gotten themselves into such a pickle. We'll need to nag them to see their lawyers and discuss their patents, shall we confirm today's meeting and suggest a date."

"Good idea," Miriam replied. "I'll send them a text tonight."

That evening she confirmed all the salient points discussed on behalf of Spoken Arrow to include a formal cooperation between the university and themselves.

Chapter 18

Miriam knew from her own memories at university that her tutors started quite early in the mornings, and to catch Ellsworth before he had his first lecture she phoned him on his home line at 8.00 am. She was about to hang up when a breathless Peter Ellsworth answered.

"I had one foot out of the door, lucky you caught me," he said.

"Peter, I have spoken with our own patent department in the States and we would very much like to discuss the legal status of the Autoplug project in particular with you in greater detail, but if it would be possible to meet a legal representative of the university, it would be appreciated. You can understand that we would consider the university as our potential partners, and the last thing we would want is to find ourselves crossing wires with Cambridge university's legal department."

"I understand, but what would you want from them?"

"Quite simply to know what they consider the legal status is regarding Magnum and yourselves. In other words, do they consider that Cambridge University has any legal claim on the work that Mrs Baylim took to Magnum. If they have ignored your patents, and registered their own then I would guess your original patents are yours to do with what you want. We could in effect sue them."

"I quite understand," he replied. "Let me speak with my principals and I'll call you this afternoon."

They had the morning to enjoy, and it was used to visit some of the tourist spots. This would be a wonderful opportunity for both Robert and Jay to snap away, she thought. The Tower of London, Buckingham Palace, the Changing of the Guards, and roaming around Harrods where both men bought souvenirs for their kids which took them to 2.00 pm without a call from Ellsworth. Leisure time over, she decided to take the initiative and jog the professor along.

"Terribly sorry Miriam but I had a real problem getting to the right person, and eventually managed to relate our position to Sir Henry Porter who is a leading partner of Spilling Mendal and Field who handle the university's more important legal matters. They are based in the City of London. I told him of the urgency and he has agreed to meet at his offices at 4.00 pm this afternoon, is this convenient?"

"Absolutely."

"Their offices are in the Gherkin Building, I suggest you go by taxi. Impossible to park, and give yourselves plenty of time, the traffic is shocking at this time. I am leaving now." he said.

When Miriam informed her friends that their meeting was in the Gherkin, it was another point in their journey to remember in this bizarre country. They immediately grabbed a taxi and returned to the hotel to change into more formal clothes that they had bought.

There was no doubt that the building was architecturally exceptional, and whilst not to be compared with some of the skyscrapers in the USA in height, it was more than compensated by its sophisticated style. The lift took them to the 32nd floor where SM&F had their offices.

Sir Henry Porter was from the old school, now probably in his sixties. He was a big man, over 6ft 3" tall with a large girth which was covered by a double breasted blue striped suit, (probably tailored in Saville Row). Wearing an Etonian tie, and an accent to match. All in all, a suitable representative for such a prestigious University as Cambridge.

Each of the three introduced themselves, their coats taken, cards exchanged, and coffee ordered. The meeting room was as expected, elegantly furnished with rosewood table and chairs. The walls lined with reference books and caricatured pictures of bewigged judges.

Miriam took the lead. "Thank you for seeing us with such short notice Sir Henry. I wouldn't have requested it had it not been that my colleagues and I have to return to the States. But we have a prickly situation and I believe that it is essential to tread very carefully before we move forward."

"Peter has given me an outline of the Magnum situation and I have a good idea of your respective positions." He looked down at the cards momentarily and addressed his remarks to Miriam. "Why don't we begin therefore by colouring in the details!" His voice was deep and resonating, he reminded Robert of his psychologist in LA.

"As you will appreciate Sir Henry," Robert replied, "Magnum is our number one competitor, and until now I believe that we have had a world-wide edge on them, although our methods of business are very different.

"However, one of the areas that we are not strong in is the medical field which has become their domain. In fact, we were a heartbeat away from entering the market with a similar scheme but for the amazing speed that Magnum managed to take the initiative. Producing the right product is one thing but to find your market and get formal confirmation of its claims usually takes years.

"It was common knowledge in the industry that the original concepts of both the Autoplug and Ever Young emanated from Professor Baylim and Dr Ellsworth's team under the umbrella of Cambridge University, but on investigating we found that no benefit seems to have been derived by them or acknowledgement for either project, and we understand that Mrs Baylim had formed her own company on the death of her husband and passed all the patents onto Magnum in Berlin where she is now working."

Sir Henry listened intently. "Whilst Spoken Arrow's philanthropic reputation is well known, I'm assuming that on this occasion your contact with Dr Ellsworth has a business objective in mind," he smiled. "So maybe you would explain what you believe to be the next step in finding common denominators."

Robert took the initiative, he cleared his throat, took a sip of water. He was feeling a little out of his depth, but his mind was on full alert. "Sir Henry, there's no question that neither of us would want litigation unless we are sure of our position. Like many large companies there's always a grey area, but before we would ask Dr Ellsworth to compare his research with ours, it is important that we don't find ourselves copying what Magnum have a right to hold as theirs, and more important what isn't. So, I suppose what we really need now is assurance that what you have is yours, and is patented by you, and what they have is free of your patents, which by the way includes the brand names. If we are both happy with a level of security, we would certainly consider working with your clients to enter the global market with gusto."

"You have made the point very clearly Mr Levine. The problem here is not only who owns the rights to the Autoplug and Ever Young but was Mrs Baylim entitled to pass the patents over without the university giving their permission. The death of Professor Baylim rather exacerbated the situation in as much as Magnum was offered the Autoplug etc. by her before her husband passed away and they could claim therefore that they were part of the research." He walked to the window and cogitated for a full minute.

"The question," he continued, "is when the latest patents were registered. Did they take what was already a Cambridge patent and update it claiming it to be theirs but in fact was legally ours. When this was debated, some four or five years ago it was decided that to try to sue Magnum would cause such bad publicity that it was better to let matters lie. I should mention here that this was against my advice, but the chancellor at the college was not prepared to invest in the legal costs that a multinational giant would certainly amass." He hesitated, "but on the other hand, who was to know how successful it would become."

"The question of litigation was further complicated by Mrs Baylim, whom we understand was also involved in the project whilst as an employee in Cambridge, and leaving to join them, in which case she was the catalyst."

"Supposing, just supposing," mused Jay, "that our organisation was to hold your hand, so to speak. Since you have apparently thrown in the towel you have nothing to lose, and as we are keen to enter this field you could certainly guide us, and we would draw on each other's expertise. Bearing in mind that we are not in the medical field at this time. Let us imagine a new company could be formed. Of which you would have an interest, to be agreed. All manufacturing, marketing and finance would be our responsibility. As you know there is hardly a place in the world that we don't have representation. Research would be a joint cooperation. We would enjoy the added kudos of being associated with you, and continue to cooperate in research."

"Even if we had a better product at a lower price," Miriam interposed, "it would be a battle to replace their product, but with a university of your standing it might give us some added credibility, especially in the UK."

"The Autoplug's presence in the medical market internationally is now worth billions, but we would have to tread very carefully, for there is no doubt that litigation will ensue no matter how sure we are of our patent position."

"I agree," replied Robert. "We wouldn't want to see anything that you have that could be useful to us until you have clarified your legal position Sir Henry, and you are assured that what you have does not belong to Magnum, as that would be considered plagiarism and which they would certainly sue."

Sir Henry returned to his chair and sat stroking his chin, absorbing Jays suggestions. "Peter, can you recall anything that came from Magnum relating to patents, I have had a cursory look but there seems to be nothing on record here at all."

"I will check with the patents department, but I have no reference numbers."

"That's not too surprising for even if there was Mrs Baylim would have erased all the files. We have a record of all the correspondence that is on our computers, but she worked independently and I would be surprised if we could locate anything of hers. But I will contact the patent office, I'm certain that they will have records of the original applications."

"I would like to check the files as to what authority Mrs Baylim had to pass anything on to another company without the permission of the other shareholders. The records I have of the original company showed only George

Baylim and associates with thirty-five percent. The remaining shares were with the university."

"I didn't know anything about associates actually being documented. It would have been before George remarried," said Ellsworth, "and in any case since we didn't have a commercial product at the time of the formation, therefore his word was sufficient for us to believe that maybe, if the Autoplug became a reality, we would enjoy some of the fruits of our labour. But at the time it was a dream."

"Well, it seems to me," replied Sir Henry, "that if she illegally passed on all the information to Magnum, they would be required by English law to pass it back to us or agree a royalty. That is unless they can prove that their new Autoplug and Ever Young are their original ideas, which is unlikely."

Miriam stood and looked out of the window. From this vantage point virtually all of London could be seen, nine million people seen as little ants. "I should mention Sir Henry that the Autoplug is already generating billions in Europe and is now even in the USA, and Magnum will not want to give it up without a fight. And that's even without Ever Young."

"Possibly not," he replied, "but if it does not belong to them that's why we are here." He smiled. "I will get our best chaps onto this immediately and see what we can dig out. When are you three leaving?"

"We had intended to return at the end of this week but I think that we can delay it for another week if necessary."

Jay and Robert looked towards Miriam in shock, which she returned with a smile.

"Just before we leave, might I have a quick word...in private?" Asked Ellsworth.

"Will you excuse us for a few moments?" he asked.

"Of course," they replied.

Sir Henry took Ellsworth into his adjoining office.

"I should also tell you that we are investigating the death of George Baylim, and are requesting a postmortem as to how he died. I personally believe that he was murdered. I don't want to release this information yet because if it proves that he was it would certainly put Brendon Tann in the dock and George's wife. We may also consider the recent death of the Health Minister within the same conspiracy. What is more Sir Henry, if we are right, and it's still a theory, I believe that our own lives could be in danger and I might add it would sorely compromise the government."

This information shocked Sir Henry. "I'll try to clarify the situation as a matter of urgency, and you have my word Peter that what you have just told me will stay within these walls until we can see our position a little clearer. If, and it's a big if, you are right we'll have a very different case to contest Magnum with. Tell me, Peter, do you trust these people?"

"Yes, I do." replied Ellsworth with conviction.

Chapter 19
Joe

Joe had now been incarcerated in Dover prison for over six weeks. He spent a great deal of his time in isolation, allowed out only to exercise and eat, but had little to say to his fellow inmates. However, on the Monday of the seventh week his cell was opened and the guard marched him to the open yard where he was pushed into a police van.

"Where am I going?" he protested.

"All I can tell you mate, is that we're to take you to the Dover police station, you'll find out more when we get there." The police officer had done this countless times before, and had a routine that wasn't to be interrupted.

Upon arrival, he was ushered into an interview room where Bonham was patiently waiting with a plain clothes officer.

"Joe, I have to be present as your legal representative when they charge you," said Bonham. "This gentleman is PC James of the CID who will read you your rights."

The man came forward to face Joe "Joseph Brenekov. You are being accused of the murder of Henry and Sylvia Hines on the night of the 24th of August 2017. Anything you say will be taken down and used in evidence You have a right to appoint a solicitor. Do you understand?"

Joe was taken aback. He knew that he had to contest it but couldn't find the words and simply nodded.

He repeated. "Do you understand?" "Yes,"
replied Joe.

"I believe Mr Bonham has been appointed as your legal representative." "I would like to speak with my client alone please," said Bonham.

PC James left the room. The door had a glass window and the officer could be seen looking at them.

"Joe you've been accused of these murders, and they have proof that your gun fired the bullets that killed these two people on the night of the twenty-four^th of August. Did you do it? Tell me the truth Joe, because whatever you say will be thoroughly checked by the prosecution. This is going to be a high profile case, and I'll need all the help that you can give me here.

"Joe, are you listening?"

He could feel another migraine coming on, and was now holding his head. "I need my pills and a glass of water," was all he could respond.

The policeman was recalled and Bonham requested Joe's pills which had been left in his cell. It would take another 40 minutes before they would arrive.

PC James joined the other officer in the room. "Mr Bonham I suggest we make an arrangement for you to speak with your client tomorrow. We will hold the prisoner in our police cell for the night. There will be a brief court hearing tomorrow probably in the afternoon, so you will have plenty of time to speak to your client."

Bonham had no doubt that Joe was guilty, but regardless of his own thoughts, it was up to Joe to either admit or deny the charges. Joe's dad was the most problematic. Brenekov was a professional and could call upon a myriad of other professionals to do his bidding at a price. Access to the police, judges and politicians were part of a routine formula and back handers were invariably added into the overheads, but there was no way to bribe or coerce anyone on this occasion.

On leaving the police station, Bonham's first port of call was to speak on the phone with Brenekov.

"Mr Brenekov, I have just left Joe. The police have read him his rights, but he's come down with another migraine. I'm meeting with him tomorrow morning. My problem is you Mr Brenekov. The CID will, without doubt want to speak with you. It's most important that you have a good story to tell them that doesn't contradict Joe's. What do you suggest I tell him or will you wait until I tell you what he said?"

"Give me a few hours Bonham, I need to speak with my brother." No sooner had he put down the phone he contacted his brother for a meeting.

"Bill, we've got a situation, I'm coming over."

They discussed all the possibilities, the pros and cons, and whatever they concluded ended badly. It was impossible to deny Joe's gun as the murder weapon, even if he said he bought it he had no proof. Joe had his original passport with the forged back dated stamp on it, but if the police were to check the ferry, which they will undoubtedly do, they will soon discover the actual date registered of his car regardless of his new passport. In any event, the UK had rarely stamped passports for over two years, and recorded all entries onto their computers regardless of whether he was Brenekov or Shapero.

"Pete, your son has got us in a real bloody mess," said Bill, "and there doesn't seem a way out of it. We could all end up inside."

"I told him to throw away that gun, what can I say Bill, I'm sorry. Maybe we should contact the guys that gave us the instructions in the first place. Do you have their number?"

"Making contact with these people is a death sentence, Pete. If they think that we could trace it back to them, we're dead ducks any way."

"Well, I can't think of another alternative," said Pete. "If they can't help us we've had it."

They sat quietly staring into space for a few minutes, musing on the various alternatives and their consequences, both men attempting to draw from their many years of roguery and the many corners that they had wheedled out of when Bill emerged from his trance to ask, "Have we sent the goods to Switzerland yet?"

"Yes, we were paid last week, they were sent by air I told you already," replied his brother. "Not that that is going to make a difference if the police come for us."

"Look, Joe is going down anyway, I can't see how he can be saved, I don't want to sound ruthless Pete but it would be crazy to throw ourselves on the fire as well."

"What are you saying Bill, how can I let my son go down because of me?"

"Pete, we're lost, remember we still have obligations to the rest of the family, it's a very serious decision I know, but if we say that he was the sole organiser of the plan we could have half a chance of not going down."

"I can't do that Bill, I can't," and for the first time in years he broke down and cried.

"I'll tell you what," said Bill, "let's speak with the girls and get their opinions."

Both wives were asked to come into Bill's office. "We have a very important decision to make girls, it effects all of us, you know the situation and there's no doubt that we have bitten off more than we can chew this time." He knew that there would be recriminations as he explained the situation and waited for a response. However, they listened and no doubt had already discussed their prospective positions. Once again there was a long and painful silence.

It was broken this time by Pete. "Joe has really dropped us in it, but whatever we say isn't going to change things, we have to consider what's best for the family. It's my fault for thinking he could do it, I'm to blame I know it, and if I could change places with him I would, but I can't. Bill is now suggesting that we deny any involvement with it and plead ignorance to the whole affair. I need to know your thoughts girls."

"What are the chances of him getting off?"

"Personally, none." Bill replied. "If he pleads guilty he might get a leaner sentence."

"And what will happen to us if we don't do what you are suggesting Bill," said his wife.

"We'll all go down, probably for life," he replied.

"I can't see that we have any option, but Joe has to agree, if he tells it as it is we've had it."

"We need to speak to Bonham and get a message to Joe explaining the situation as soon as possible. This is really bad but I can't see that we have any alternatives," said Bill, "I knew he couldn't handle this job, I knew it, the bloody fool."

"It was you who agreed to do the job in the first place," retorted Bill.

"It's painful enough already," shouted his wife, "without pointing fingers, we're losing our son, so let's see if we can save ourselves without any more accusations, OK."

Pauline had a justified claim to have a higher IQ than her sister in law. She ran her household with a greater degree of authority which clearly showed in the way her children were brought up. Both the Brenekov brothers had learned to watch their mouths in front of her and to some extent looked to her opinion with a degree of respect.

She sat on the settee arms and legs folded in deep contemplation cogitating on the few facts presented. "The problem is the gun," she mused. "We can't deny that it's the gun that was used, but what I think we have to do is prove that Joe was given or bought it from someone else."

"Listen Pauline, there's no one I know that would be so stupid to agree to that without being arrested for murder," replied Bill.

"But supposing that someone bought it, say from the market, say Portobello market, you know enough blokes in the market Pete, find someone that could not have possibly done it and give him a serious amount to say he bought it from a passer-by, it was a bargain and he sold it on to this guy who in turn offered it to Joe. It may not be a guaranteed alibi but we're hanging on to straws. What do you think?"

"Pauline you're a genius, I married a genius." Bill repeated. "I would guess that thirty thousand pounds would find us a so called friend of Joe to say he was in Portobello Market. Pete, we've both unloaded enough stuff in Portobello over the years to find someone who will support the story. Someone who is clearly incapable of doing anything seriously wrong. This anonymous guy of whom there is no record, offers a stall holder the gun for say fifty quid after the date of the murder, he buys it and sells it onto Joe's friend for a hundred, who sells it onto Joe for a hundred and fifty. They would both have to swear affidavits and probably stand up in court, and even if it costs us a few thousand, as long as they are consistent we'd be off the hook. It's absolutely essential," said Pauline pressing the point home, "that he categorically confirms that he only bought it after the murder."

It was agreed that this was to be the policy adopted that would be presented to Bonham. The family allowed Pauline to take control. "What we daren't do is to reveal that we know the market dealer, Pete you can only say that you found Joe's friend who bought the gun. Now search in your book for a market dealer in Portobello. The rest has to be told by him, otherwise they will immediately see it as a fix."

"The hearing is tomorrow, all they will want to know is how Joe pleads," said Pete. "He is going to ask who his friend is and get a statement from him. I'll have to give him some excuse that I don't have his telephone number with me, but I won't be able to hold off with that information for more than a day, because the prosecution will demand it."

"Bill, I suggest that you sort out the contacts as a matter of absolute urgency while you, Pete, tell Bonham you want to meet him tonight. Book a flight to Dover now, before he speaks with Joe. Pete, you find a friend for Joe, but make sure he's not another idiot. Give them whatever he asks for Bill, our lives are in his hands."

***

Peter Brenekov packed an overnight case and managed to catch a 6.00 pm flight from London City Airport to Kent international airport. Bonham agreed to meet him at the homespun terminal where they would find a restaurant and talk over a coffee table.

Bonham was convinced that there would be only bad news to share. Brenekov was particularly aware that he could not compromise his lawyer with imaginary options unless they could be proven, and regardless of how unreasonable his presentation to Bonham was, it had to appear to be a truth.

173

There was no denying that Bonham did not like Brenekov, it was not that he disapproved of the man's morals, after all he made a good living by representing the darker side of the law. It was the man's arrogance, his ego and his seemingly lack of respect for humanity in general that was repulsive to him, but he was a client and his personal feelings were to be put aside, at least for the moment.

"You must imagine," said Bonham, "that I am simply your receptacle, and what you tell me is what will be presented to the court." He looked intensely into Brenekov's eyes, both men appreciating that tomorrow a new reality of events would be submitted to the judge and prosecution.

"Mr Bonham, we have been working hard to prove that my son could not have committed this terrible crime, I know him, it's not in his nature. We have proof that he couldn't have done it, and his friend contacted us yesterday when he heard the news to tell us that he bought the gun from a stall in Portobello Market and sold it to Joe. He can recall who the bloke was, an old fellow who has had a stall there for God knows how many years, and all he has to do is to confirm when he bought it and sold it on. That should prove Joe is innocent, don't you agree."

Bonham considered his question with the gravitas that it deserved. "This depends on how plausible his defence is Mr Brenekov. The first question that I would ask if I was the Prosecution is: Do you personally know these men, in other words, are they in your back pocket?"

"Are you suggesting that I would bribe these men Mr Bonham? Well, the answer is definitely not. We obviously know Joe's friend but that's it."

"I'm afraid you'll not get away easily with such a simple reply Mr Brenekov, the police will definitely push you on that point, and if they discover that your Portobello chappy is a friend or even an associate, you and he will both serve a long stretch. I hope you understand. Are you now instructing me to state to the police categorically what you have just told me that neither Joe nor you had any knowledge of this crime Mr Brenekov?"

His sombre tone had a great effect on Brenekov, but he could only reconfirm his position. Bonham took the opportunity to state his own terms. "Mr Brenekov in view of the work and time that I will be obliged to invest in this defence, in order for me to represent you I will be obliged to charge you a hundred and fifty thousand pounds which will of course involve many weeks work. I would require fifty percent up front and the remainder on the conclusion of the case regardless of its outcome. I would require you to place the second payment in escrow to my account. You will also require a QC who will no doubt charge a similar figure. I am telling this to you now in order that you will not be surprised."

It was the last thing that Brenekov wanted to hear or negotiate at this time, and uncharacteristically was without a response.

"I hope you accept and understand my position. Maybe you can confirm your decision in this matter tomorrow morning before we go to court."

He dropped his client off at a separate hotel and agreed to meet at 9.00 am. Both ate alone.

The following day at 8.30 am Bonham collected his client's father from his hotel. "Before we go to court Mr Brenekov, I would like to know if you accept my terms of employment.

"Just say yes or no."

As if making vows to the devil incarnate, he replied "I do."

"I have to tell you that an Inspector Polton who has been assigned to this case and is very interested in the outcome, no doubt he has been prompted by the higher echelons to solve the Hines murder. I mention this only because it is most important Mr Brenekov that your witnesses are bona fide."

"I can only tell you what I know, Mr Bonham."

Joe was escorted into the crowded court room, placed in the dock and asked, "Do you plead guilty or not guilty?"

"Not guilty," he mumbled.

"Louder if you please," called the judge.

Joe hit his fists on the banister. "Not guilty," he shouted.

***

It was 4.00 pm when Bill took a cab to Portobello market. He hadn't been to the market for a number of years, and although it had changed considerably over that time, the reminder of his youth and the old cut and thrust in his youthful and naive negotiations with some of the stall holders made him smile. They were the good old days, he thought.

It wasn't difficult to find old Tim Brookes, he had the same patch in the market for the last forty-five years. Pete and Bill had known him since they were boys and had taken bits and pieces to him to sell as long as they could remember. He was now a bent seventy five year old, and had seen from his stall how times had changed. The old idea of the drainpipe thief breaking and entry was replaced by drugs, bank fraud and computer scams. Over the years the Brenekov family had gained a formidable reputation, and their name caused shock waves to those that crossed them. But Tim plodded on with his bric-a-brac stall, often watched by the cops but invariably ignored.

"Cor blimey I ain't seen you Pete for years, but I 'eard a lot of what yer up to," He grinned showing a few gaps. They shook hands warmly. "To what do I owe this pleasure Bill, I don't suppose you 'ere for your 'ealth."

"Listen Tim, I have a problem, and need your help." It was interesting how humble the great man was in the company of his childhood mentor.

"I need you to have bought a gun on the 27th August and sold it on the 30th to a young man. You will have bought it for fifty quid and sold it for a hundred."

"Sure, Pete, I can do that easy enough, but what's the story behind it?"

"My Joe is in trouble, Tim, you've probably read about it. He needs to prove that he bought the gun from the guy that you sold it to."

"Pete I'm too old to go inside, and I'd do pretty well anything for you for old time's sake, you know that, but I 'ope you won't get me into trouble… will you?"

"Tim, you're my oldest friend, I really value you. I promise that no harm will come to you – anyway it's worth fifty K – but you must stick to the story, and most important, if you're asked by the police… you don't know me, never met me. And wouldn't touch me with a barge pole. That's very, very important. You get it, Tim?"

He put his arm around him and spoke gently "Remember, Tim, you bought the gun on the 27th August, you remember it because it was a make that you hadn't seen before. That's why you remember that date. OK, Tim. Can you remember that? Now repeat it to me Tim." He reluctantly repeated what he was told and a large packet of twenty pound notes was passed over "… which would help to improve your memory." It was more than he would make in five years.

"I'm going to ask a bloke to speak with you, Tim. He will be the customer that bought it from you, so that you will remember his face and when the police ask you who it was you will be able to recognise him. And it's as simple as that. They will take a statement from you and probably ask you who you bought it from, and you will say you can't remember, but it was a little fella, and hopefully that will be the end of it."

"I don't like it Bill, but if you can promise me that there won't be any problems, I'll do it, for old times."

"I promise," said Bill with conviction. He gave the old man a hug, "remember Tim, you don't know me, OK."

It was necessary that whoever Bill chose as the buyer, they would have to coordinate with Tim, and dovetail their stories. The alibi had to be seamless, he needed someone with a modicum of intelligence and from now on no contact would be made with Tim directly. This was a risky situation and one chink in their armour would bring them down.

Charlie Donn had been at school with Joe, they had met from time to time but now had different agendas. Charlie had a juvenile record but trained as a plumber for British Gas earning a comparatively minimal salary of which he maintained a wife, two children and living in a council flat in Hackney. Joe had approached him once or twice, and he was tempted, but his wife had kept him on the straight and narrow.

However, a telephone call from Mr William Brenekov himself presenting a proposition that might have minimal risk and a possible welcome bit of cash aroused his adrenaline. They agreed to meet at the Starbucks in Bethnal Green.

Charlie was certainly not going to tell his wife that he was to have anything to do with the Brenekovs, she would have had a fit.

"You must be thinking that I'm going to drag you down Charlie into the grimy world of crime," smiled Bill.

"The thought did cross my mind," he replied.

"Well, Charlie, I'm looking for a favour, there's no job, no risk, just a simple favour and one that will earn you fifty thousand pounds."

"No job, no risk, and fifty grand, I'm worried already, Mr Breneko – what's the catch?"

"I know that you haven't seen Joe for a while, and I respect the fact that you are on the straight and narrow, and what I need from you will not get you into trouble. I simply want you to say that you bought a gun from a man in the market for one hundred pounds for no particular reason, but it seemed a bargain, and sold it to Joe, for a hundred and fifty. You would coordinate your exact time that you bought it and sold it, and sign an affidavit to those exact facts. There is no catch but we need to show that Joe did not use the gun, and you will have purchased it after any crime that they claim Joe is accused of. That way everybody is in the clear."

"I heard Joe was in trouble but what he is accused of is going to put everyone in the spotlight Mr B. I don't think I'm interested. I've got a family to protect."

"You cannot be accused of anything, Charlie, it's a no brainer and you will get fifty grand for doing nothing illegal. Charlie this is the best deal you'll ever get."

Brenekov repeated the plan to reassure Charlie how simple his part would be, but he could see that he was dubious.

"OK Charlie," said Brenekov, "I need someone like you who can think things through, and I respect your doubts. But to prove that you are my man I'm going to make it even more interesting. I'm going to give you eighty thousand, forty k as soon as you sign an affidavit, and forty after the heat is off, Joe."

Charlie was struggling, he considered what he could do with that sort of money, maybe open a coffee shop, even start his own plumbing business, put a decent deposit on a nice apartment. It was a painful decision.

"I know I'm going to regret this Mr B.... make it a hundred grand paid when I sign the affidavit and I'll do it. Anything less and it's a no."

Brenekov squirmed, he was not used to negotiating with a comparative nobody. "You're a tough negotiator," he flattered him, "but I agree."

"Do you promise that I won't get into trouble with the cops, Mr B?"

"Definitely, Charlie, as long as you keep to the plan. I will need you to see me tomorrow and we'll go over the plan again in detail, it's very simple. 11.00 am at my home. I'll tell you what, when you come over I'll find you a taster up front – what shall we say, ten thousand?"

***

As soon as Bill left the coffee shop he phoned his brother. "Pete, everything is in order at this end, both are waiting to sign. You can tell Bonham that our boy is innocent, and we can prove it. Tell him that you have a name for him, and he is prepared to sign an affidavit."

"Who is it?" Asked Pete.

"Bonham should confirm to Joe that his friend Charlie Donn is prepared to sign an affidavit. We have to find a way of informing Joe, so tell Bonham that Joe obviously didn't want to give his name to Bonham without Charlie's permission, and now he's got it...do you get it? That was Pauline's idea," said Bill Proudly.

"Got it," replied Pete.

Chapter 20
Jack

Pickles was now deeply ensconced in the preparation of his budget and it was quite understandable that Jack would have difficulty contacting him. He was confident that he had the ear of the minister but was aware that no matter how important he perceived his particular problem to be, the country's economy took precedence. Nevertheless he decided to attempt another meeting and spoke once again with Jane Franklyn.

"Jack, I know that the Minister is most keen to hear how you are progressing, and I'll squeeze you in for twenty minutes tomorrow morning at 9.15 am if that's alright with you, but you'll have to be quick. He has a meeting with the PM at 10.30 am. I suggest you write down the relevant points before the meeting so that he can cogitate on them after your discussion. In passing, I can tell you, in confidence, that he has spoken with the PM regarding this situation, and in the event that your theory is validated, there could be some very serious repercussions. No doubt he will tell you himself."

At 9.15 am prompt, Jack was sitting in Jane's office reception awaiting to be called.

He placed a brown folder containing the updated relevant points on her desk which she promptly opened and read.

"Concise and to the point, as I would expect." She smiled. "I shall just pop them into him ready for your meeting." Ten minutes later he was called in.

"Jack, I can confirm to you that a Joseph Brenekov has now been formally accused of the murder of Henry and his wife. I have no idea what his defence is. This man is part of a notoriously dangerous family but claims that he is innocent. Lord only knows how he can be since the bullets that shot Henry were the same as those that were in the gun. Maybe it's a coincidence that Henry was also involved in a contentious matter, we don't yet know but I'd be most interested to discover what you have."

"That's very interesting Minister, when did you hear?"

"I've just had an email, the Home Office were obviously aware of my interest in this matter, but in confidence I am checking out Brendon Tann's financial situation, that should tell us something."

"I've spoken at some length with Doctor Ellsworth," replied Jack, "who was working closely with Baylim in Cambridge for a number of years, and at the hospital where he was being treated I met with Baylim's doctor. four years since he died, I think we could assume that it's linked to Henry and Sylvia Hines. The question is, can we prove who is behind it?"

"Time is of the essence Jack, it might be a good idea to use my influence here, I'll try to bring this autopsy forward, tell me the name of the hospital and we'll see if we can do it next week. If we have this information whilst Brenekov is being interrogated it might help us find a motive. We could also bring a little pressure on the art dealers around the world, some of their works of art are going to be difficult to place."

Pickles sat back in his chair and cogitated for a few moments. "However, remember Jack that if there is no incriminating evidence and Baylim died of natural causes, all you will have is circumstantial evidence between the two deaths, which in itself will not be enough to hang your hat on without a heavy law suit. That is, unless we can prove a case for bribery."

"I'll be careful minister, but whatever you do, sir, please don't allow Mr Tann to know of our plans."

"I shall try, but I'm afraid the walls have ears here. We think that we have total control of our destinies Jack, but I have to admit that it's an egotistical illusion." He stood up and stared at Jack. "You realise Jack that if Tann is involved in a murder and Magnum is implicated it will place our government in a compromised position, and if the opposition get hold of it, anything could happen, I think that it is most important that this situation should be kept completely under wraps, at least until we can decide how to handle it. Do you agree?"

He nodded and thanked the chancellor for his time and they parted.

***

Jack needed to defuse his situation, He walked along the mall until he found a local coffee shop. Taking The Times from the rack and, sipping a hot chocolate, casually browsed to the opinion page. Specifically an article by a well know catalyst headed "The Ever Young Christmas Present."

***

Leading article in The Times…Gerascophobia and 'The Never' Ever Young:

The advantages of the Ever Young project have been clearly identified. Signs are being posted across the country that Magnum and the government are preparing to spend vast budgets in promoting its benefits to the younger generation and it will particularly appeal to those who have Gerascophobia and all that the twilight years condemn us to.

It is a fact that governments around the world will also substantially benefit from the scheme as over twenty percent of government health costs are invariably spent on the elderly. The services of the NHS hospitals have generously been placed at the disposal of the Ever Young project, but the ongoing medical costs, marketing and all other ancillary costs are being borne by Magnum.

It is stated by Magnum, who have a global presence, that the Ever Young scheme compliments their Autoplug which is now established across the world, and Ever Young is their gift to humanity. If so, we should assume that this is a magnificent gesture. However one must wonder why a company of the size of Magnum would be so magnanimous in what will ultimately cost many millions with no obvious return.

Suspicion is a terrible thing, but commercialism lives and dies on its profitability. Faust sold his soul for another 15 years of pleasure. Magnum are offering 65 years. Autoplug to Ever Young – what's the connection? And where's the catch?
Is there really a Father Christmas in the multi-billion dollar computer world? If so, let's see who else is prepared to offer us something for nothing! A Ferrari would be nice…but for my part I have my doubts.

***

Jack openly laughed as he read the merits of cynicism by his colleagues – little did they realise that their gut instincts were very close to the mark.

Returning to his office his mind was in a quandary. As he pressed the button of the elevator to the fourth floor he knew that it was to be a moment of truth.

Brody Emmitt was his mentor, a man whom he admired, even revered, but he could not deny his own principles, and as he walked towards the glass cage of his boss he felt as if he was a condemned man, condemned by his own conscience.

Emmitt, still puffing away, waved him in. "What's the latest Jack," he boomed, he was clearly on a high and in a business fraught with contradictions, pending lawsuits and time schedules, it was a relief to see his boss not to be on his back foot for a change.

"You seem in a good mood," smiled Jack, "has anything exciting happened?"

"Yes, as it so happens, from your sports clients, we've secured a rolling contract from Jacoby Sports that will bill them over five hundred thousand pounds over the next few months. I should add, Jack, that it's mainly due to your articles on their equipment. The response they say was amazing and reflected their customers readership of our magazines. Now what are we going to do with Magnum?"

"I've a suggestion, boss. You know my opinion regarding this company, and I won't waste your time updating you on the situation, but it's grim. I want you to let me write a series of articles on the Autoplug with no mention of the Ever Young project. Send me to Germany to interview the head of the company directly, I have a meeting with the M.D of the UK branch but they are simply order takers.

"I need another two weeks before I have what I would consider a reliable story to tell. And believe me, Brody, if I'm right we'll have a worldwide exclusive. But if I am right, yet we seriously promote their Ever Young with editorial we will have mud on our faces and totally lose all our credibility. I can arrange to go to Berlin as soon as they will see me."

Emmitt sat smoking in deep thought. "I'll tell you what Jack, I'll speak with the Chief and explain to her the situation, if she agrees we'll book you a ticket to Berlin."

"When?"

He looked at his watch. "Now, I'm having lunch with her and I'll let you know this afternoon."

Jack returned to his office and immediately put in a call to Magnum in Germany. He was quickly put through to a Fräulein Austrich who was the personal assistant to Freda Gesh. She explained that as Herr Heinrich was abroad his PA would be pleased to discuss with him any future plans to expand in the UK. and pass on details to chairman.

"Thank you for your suggestion," replied Jack, "but you will no doubt be aware the British Health service is one of the most influential in the world, and we are not simply promoting your facility, we are presenting to the world the recommendation from the United Kingdom based on the strength of your guarantees. This interview will be placed in front of our Prime Minister. It is essential therefore that we should learn from yourselves what your hopes and aspirations are, the future benefits that you envisage and any problems that could possibly ensue. I would very much like to meet your president personally and ask him to explain his plans of the Autoplug and in particular the Ever Young project. His Majesty's government have instructed me to underline the efficacy of your intentions and to give us these assurances, bearing in mind how important your activities are in respect to our country's future health."

"I quite understand," she replied, "I will speak with Frau Gesh who is the personal assistant to President's son Herr Steffen Heinrich – he is our Vice President – and I will telephone you tomorrow to arrange a meeting if that is acceptable."

He thanked her and mentally planned his visit to Berlin. He fancifully imagined that he had been talking to a robot.

At 2.30 pm, Jack saw his boss returning to his office. The smell of the nicotine had still not cleared from the morning as he continued to add to it.

"Come in Jack, I had a long conversation with His Majesty concerning your investigations, there's no doubt young man that we are skating on thin ice here, but I've persuaded her to take a gamble on you, God help us all if you're wrong. Book the flight as soon as possible, and let's put this thing to bed once and for all," he boomed, still with a cigarette in-between his lips.

"Oh yes," he whispered as Jack was leaving, "don't forget to record it. By the way, I can confirm that we were unable to buy shares in Magnum, they're a private company as you said."

"If events go the way I believe, you'll be pleased you saved your money," Jack replied.

It was only 8.00 am the following morning when he received a call from Fräulein Austrich. "I have spoken with Frau Gesh and she confirmed that Herr Steffen Heinrich would be happy to meet you in Berlin on Thursday the 19th at 12.15 pm and he would also like to invite you to lunch. Please inform us when your flight arrives and we will be happy to meet you and another colleague, if you so wish, at the airport and take you to our offices."

This was a serious breakthrough, an opportunity to find the true motivation behind Magnum's plans. A cocktail of emotions pumped through his entire being. What questions he would ask and what would he like to ask, "Did you kill Hines? Did you kill Baylim? Is Tann being bribed, and how many others? Are you planning to control the minds of millions of young men and women? Where did all your monies come from?" He doubted that he would get confessions from any of these accusations, or even be able to ask, but he had to come away with something.

He immediately contacted the UK office of Magnum to cancel his meeting.

That gave Jack two days to organise his questions and sneakily ask Helga to join him. If questioned, he would say that her German would be useful should it be necessary. He put in his request for two tickets business class.

Upon returning to his office, he was greeted with an email from Doctor Singh informing him that an autopsy had been agreed, and George Baylim's body was to be exhumed and brought to the hospital within the next three days.

***

There was a fresh step in Jack's walk. There was no doubt in his mind that he was balancing on a tightrope. His job was not simply at stake, the path that he was walking would ensure that Tandem press would lose their most valuable client, and a lawsuit would invariably ensue in which he would be the main culprit, yet he fancifully saw himself as the knight in shining armour attempting to slay a dragon.

Helga took a train and arrived at King's Cross Station at 2.00 pm. Although the visit to Berlin would require an overnight stay, she packed for three days. She had not had a boyfriend of any consequence during her entire stay in Cambridge. Not that it mattered too much to her but she found it difficult to become an English style professional student, and whilst she attended and sometimes became involved in the debates and had been invited to parties, she was quite prepared to stand aloof and watch at arm's length watching the world of academia let its hair down.

She wrote home to tell her father that she had been invited to Berlin on a study trip, but she was not going to mention Jack, certainly not at this stage of their relationship. She was excited, and a little scared of her own emotions. Should she suggest her own room, will Jack assume that they should share? Should she resist any deeper emotions? After all, she hardly knew him. But he

184

was such an interesting man, a man not a boy. It was an adventure. Only time would tell.

Jack was waiting at platform 7. The station was buzzing with activity and it seemed to him that the entire country was emigrating. Her carriage must have been one of the last and as she walked towards him he was able to observe her grace and posture. She radiated a natural elegance. He clicked his camera, "just for posterity," he convinced himself.

Their flight out to Berlin was at 9.15 am tomorrow and they would need to be at Heathrow at least 90 minutes earlier. He had in the past no problem in inviting women back to his apartment, sometimes they slept over according to the way of the evening, it was casual and generally without inhibition. However, he had not even been on an official date with Helga. Furthermore she was different from his London cosmopolitan and magazine followers. Heavy makeup, high heels, short skirts showing shapely legs, with a patter to match. He decided to play the gentleman, why not! He was more than interested and wanted her to be different. A beautiful young woman untouched by the blah of modern day society.

She embraced him as a friend would and he took her bag. "The car is only across the road, are you hungry."

"I'll follow you," she smiled, "this is your patch, but I am a little peckish."

"It's still rather early, maybe we'll have a snack and take in a meal a little later. Have you seen much of London, maybe we should drive around a little before we eat."

"That would be great, to be honest Jack I have hardly seen anything of London. Usually I land at Heathrow and go straight to Cambridge. It's quite exciting to see some of the things I've only read about." They popped into a Starbucks and munched sandwiches in the car as they drove through Marble Arch and into Hyde Park. There were people everywhere. "Next stop Buckingham Palace." The King was in residence, he explained. "How do you know?" she asked.

"The Royal Standard Flag, whenever it's flying he is there. Mostly tourists, see that little group over there?" He pointed to two men and a woman, "I bet they're American."

Along the embankment, they drove to the Houses of Parliament. Jack had a press card and whilst parliament was sitting they were able to catch a snippet of what Jack considered a rather boring debate – but not Helga, who was totally entranced. To see the British government at work in such surroundings was like

185

magic. "This is where history is made. I can just imagine Churchill or Mrs Thatcher," she said in awe.

"I've no doubt, Helga, that we'll be discussing the Magnum problem here before too long, and I'm hoping that what we do tomorrow will make this happen. Maybe another sentence will be added to our children's history books."

Travelling past Knightsbridge and Harrods. It seemed to her that Harrods was a national institution. "Would you like to have a look around there?" he asked.

"Of course, I'd love that."

The food section offered a multitude of light snacks from countries throughout the world, and they grabbed a bowl from the Japanese booth. He took great pleasure in Helga's delight.

"Helga, do you have formal clothes for tomorrow's meeting, after all, to all extent and purposes you are my assistant."

She looked a little surprised. "You know Jack I hadn't thought about it," sounding a little embarrassed. "Maybe I should pick up a few bits and pieces. But not here," she quickly added. "Remember I'm only a student."

"Let's not worry about that, we can have a look anyway," he smiled.

One and a half hours later they left the store with three full carrier bags, it was the first time he had bought clothes for a girlfriend, and it gave him as much pleasure as Helga. "I'm embarrassed that you have paid," she blushed.

"I'll put it on my expense account," he fibbed and held her hand tight.

By the time they left the store, it was 7.00 pm and Jack drove directly to his favourite little restaurant.

"I was becoming a little concerned," whispered the manager with a rue smile.

She had not asked him where she would stay, but returning to his apartment, it was 10.45 pm Jack kissed her gently and showed her to her own room. He was only concerned that this should remain a perfect end to the day.

"We have to be up at 6.15 am, and both of us have to be really sharp tomorrow, I hope you enjoyed this afternoon as much as I did, and I'm tempted to tuck you into bed, but I'll just hold the memory of you until tomorrow." She thanked him for a wonderful day, they kissed tenderly and parted.

***

She looked wonderful in her new clothes, in fact a little too elegant to be an assistant. She had bought flat shoes and had chosen to wear a woollen kaftan that floated around her, a loosely tied multi coloured long silk scarf completed a look of nobility. Jack decided to introduce her as Resident Educational psychologist to the Tandem magazines, which she relished and wished she could have such a job for more than a day. He quickly took his mobile out and clicked the moment on his camera. They had a light breakfast and left his apartment as if man and wife.

The journey to Berlin seemed to take minutes in each other's company, but Jack had to concentrate on the matters at hand, and discover how he could find the core of their objectives.

"What do we know about Gilda?" she asked. "I understand that she is working with Magnum here in Germany now."

"That is a very good point, not only did she control the negotiations, but she was there when her husband died."

"Do you think Jack that we might interview her too?"

"You've earned your trip," joked Jack. "We can ask to see their internal workings, with the view of meeting this formidable woman. I am painfully aware that she is a very clever and devious lady, and if we're not very careful could soon trip us up. One of the things we learn very early when interviewing people Helga, is that they must not be allowed to deviate on to safer ground especially when they're cornered."

"That's certainly a point worth noting, but I bet it's not always easy to manipulate. Jack, Doctor Ellsworth reminds me continuously in his lectures to decide what the outcome should be before you begin and attempt to work towards that objective, which I find very difficult, but I guess this is as good an exercise as any to do that, what do you think Jack?" He was ruefully aware that it was the student teaching the teacher. He kissed her hand and took out his memo pad. "Good idea Dr H." He smiled.

By the time they landed, he had listed a loose agenda, and whilst there was every possibility that they would deviate from it, Jack had his objectives lined up. They were ready for battle.

Chapter 21

They were met at the exit by a formally dressed chauffeur who introduced himself as Wolf and took their bags. Wolf was no longer a young man, maybe 60 or 65 years old. He was clearly from the old school. Straight-backed, ultra-polite, practically a caricature of a German. He separated himself quite willingly from those he considered his superiors; and since they were the guests of the Vice President they certainly fell into that category. They sat in the back of a top of the range highly polished Mercedes Benz and were told that the journey would take exactly 37 minutes.

"Our head office is situated at Potsdam, a city having a famous history." began Wolf. He spat out every consonant. "Zere are many beautiful palaces here, and it was ze summer retreat of ze Prussian King Frederick ze Great in ze eighteenth century. In fact Potsdam is considered ze educational centre for politics, science, medical and many other academic studies. We also have our research laboratories at Potsdam," he said proudly.

Clearly Wolf had delivered this speech a number of times, and no doubt if allowed he would have rambled on until they arrived.

Jack, who had waited for a pause in the script, found his moment. "How long have you been with the company, Wolf?"

"Ah, you want to know how long I have been here… *Jawohl*, maybe four years."

"But do you come from Potsdam?"

"*Nein*," he replied. "I was born in Leipzig just after ze war. But I have been in Potsdam for ze last twenty years. My wife works also for Magnum, she comes from Potsdam, going back more than three generations. Even before ze war."

"Very interesting," said Jack. "You mean her parents and grandparents worked for Magnum?"

"*Ja,* but it wasn't called Magnum back then," he chuckled, "it was, how you say, rechristened. They gave it a new name. I cannot remember ze old one now."

"What did they do so many years ago?" Helga interspersed in German.

"*Ah, Sie sprechen Deutch, meine liebe Dame!*" he replied gleefully. "Her family worked there. They were making listings I think. You would have to ask my wife, she might know."

"I am documenting a historical work and studying the conditions in the twenties and thirties in many countries. If she has memory of what her parents and grandparents did, it would be most interesting."

"If you have a mobile, madam, I will ask her to telephone you – she loves to talk about the past."

Helga wrote down her number and passed it onto Wolf. He was noticeably flattered that he had had the opportunity to speak in his own language with such elevated guests, and thanked her for the opportunity to speak about himself.

Thirty-seven minutes exactly they arrived. Jack thanked him, but it was Wolf who appeared to be most appreciative. "*Danke schön,*" he bowed, "I shall speak with my wife tonight and ask her to phone you," he responded in a humble tone.

They were escorted to the reception where they were given tabs to put around their necks. The young woman immediately informed the office that their guests had arrived.

Their coats and overnight bags were taken and placed in another room. The reception area was quite small and Jack had the impression that this was not the central offices of the company.

"Is this building your main office?" he casually asked.

The receptionist laughed. "No, sir, these are our directors' offices. Our main office is approximately two kilometres from here. Those offices are very busy." She waited in expectation of another question.

Jack nodded knowingly, "So Herr Heinrich's office is here. Is Frau Baylim working from this building too?" he asked innocently.

"Herr Heinrich uses these offices occasionally but Frau Baylim is not here, but I shall look her up in my catalogue." She took a thick catalogue from her desk draw and ran her finger down the Bs. "*Ja,* she is in our research building unit number five. Would you like me to make contact with her?"

"*Nein danke,* I was just interested, maybe a little later," he added.

A few moments later a lady clearly in a position of responsibility and in her early forties came down the stairs with her hand out ready to shake Jack's. "Good morning. Mr Jack Branson, I assume? I am Herr Heinrich's Personal Assistant. I must apologise on his account but he has been called to an urgent meeting, and will be a little late. He has asked me to join you in our executive canteen for a light lunch, and hopes to meet you in the early afternoon. I do apologise, this is not a normal practice but," she shrugged, "emergencies happen. My sincere apologies. My name is Freda Gesh."

"Allow me to introduce Helga Barworth our Resident Educational Psychologist." They shook hands and were taken to the canteen restaurant on the first floor.

"We're quite democratic here, many of our senior executives and directors eat here, and I'm pleased to say, liberated from the old class divisions." The restaurant was already beginning to fill up. They found a table near a window and explored the menu on the wall. Whilst she was no doubt correct that the canteen was for all, it was immediately noticeable the fare was decidedly upmarket, aimed at the elite of the business.

"Although Herr Heinrich isn't here, I would be happy to answer any questions that you may have in the meantime."

"Thank you," replied Jack. "It would be very helpful to know the background of the company and where it believes its future is. Our objective today is primarily to give the UK government an assurance that the monies we are investing in your schemes are working in the interest of the population. I am sure that you are aware that Ever Young in particular carries with it a substantial weight of responsibility, and with this in mind we have been asked to take your views on how you see it evolving Frau Gesh."

"Please, I'm Freda, may I call you Jack and Helga? Your name Helga suggests that you are not from the United Kingdom. But your accent seems maybe," she hesitated, "Scottish."

Helga openly laughed, "No, Freda, I'm afraid you're way out. I'm originally from Switzerland, but thank you for the compliment."

"And may I be so curious as to ask what your position entails Helga? it's such an interesting title."

Helga had not considered that she would be asked such an obvious question and hesitated for a moment, and pushing her hair back continued with a degree of confidence that surprised Jack. "Magazines today are fighting for their readership, advertising is also aiming more and more at specific markets, my task is to discover the balance and quality of articles and the type of advertisers that we should be looking for. It is very distressing to find that one has lost readers, invariably because your competition have stolen them. What Jack may write in a sports magazine for instance will be read by a specific category of reader and the advertising should match his articles, whereas a women's magazine will require a totally different approach to the same product and vice versa. You could say that I am the unofficial policeman of the publishing house. Not everyone in the company may be as talented as Jack. As an example, Ever Young will be advertised in a wide variety of magazines and each one will be presented differently according to its readership." She smiled at Jack who could not resist a snigger. "In the course of a week I have often had to smack a number of journalist's hands. The purpose of my visit is to analyse and fragmentise your comments before passing them onto the relevant journals," she added cheekily.

"That is so interesting Helga, Fragmentise, that's an interesting word, I haven't heard that word before, but it's an area that we consumers would take for granted."

"It's an in-house expression," she replied nonchalantly.

She stood up and led them to the counter. Various hors d'oeuvres were beautifully displayed. Liver Pate with cranberry sauce, smoked salmon with asparagus, a variety of cheeses and vegetables, a wide selection of salads and lasagnes for vegetarians. Jack took note to describe the menu to his boss. Half an hour to eat a ham or cheese sandwich was the order of the day back home.

"Let's start at the beginning Freda, the evolution of Magnum. For instance, prior to the computer age. What prompted the company to enter the computer race."

"That's an interesting opening question Jack." She hesitated for a few moments and cleared her throat. "You will obviously have done your homework but for the record let me give you my personal slant on the company's origins. The Second World War was a scar for all Germans and it was a very difficult time after the war for the country, not only to readjust to the new world but also to discover the extent of their sins."

It was clearly difficult for her to discuss this point, but she chose her words carefully and continued. "Whatever knowledge the next generation had was to a great extent inherited from their elders. There was bitterness and a great deal hidden from the next generation as to what happened. My parents for instance were already post war children, but very little was told to them in schools or at home until the 60s. The senior citizens had been brain washed by their leaders and still carried their Third Reich biases, and it was in this atmosphere that the next generation of the Heinrichs started the company in the mid-50s. Who knows where their forefathers had accumulated their monies, or how? No one really wanted to know. But it seems that they found themselves in charge of substantial sums There they were, fighting a battle to justify their existence with a great deal of money to invest. I guess they could have given it back, but to who? Dirty money carries its own conscience. Maybe they did, maybe they didn't. But they began with a sophisticated understanding of inherited information.

"There was still mass unemployment but a new world was opening up and a fresh chance to begin again. Talent of all types was available, mining, electronics sophisticated engineering, plastics, mathematicians etc. etc. were all desperate to offer their services, and many had learned their crafts during or before the war. So from this well of expertise the Heinrich family drew from the best available. In those days, many countries and large organisations such as the car, steel or electronics industries were desperate for information on markets, population breakdowns and a myriad of information and the Heinrich family had the knowhow to acquire, and more important to catalogue it. It was a relatively easy jump to enter the computer world at the ground level. Many of the systems during that time evolved from Magnum or inherited by them, and I believe that they are one of the most dynamic companies in the world probably because they are privately owned and only refer to themselves.

"To be honest Jack I have thought many times how and what I would have done if I was in their position after the war, but my attitude to the business is unimportant. I have only been with this company for five years, and my task is to follow their policies."

She appeared to be slowly letting her guard down which was unexpected, "Much of what you have described is known, as you say Freda, however I doubt that the public today are aware of the details."

"You asked me a question Jack and I have answered you as honestly as I can, I am certainly not making excuses for the company, and I should say that it is not to be stated from me. You should really get this straight from the horse's mouth, as you say."

"You are right and we will, but you must admit that a voice of conscience would suggest that such an ill-gotten fortune that had been acquired from, who knows how many millions of lives lost in the taking, one might think that it could have been put to use in an attempt to rebuild the damage incurred, not only physical damage but the psychological pain that resulted. What are we talking about here maybe billions of dollars that were probably stashed away, where, in Switzerland or Brazil. To be used again for personal gain."

"You are right Jack, but they didn't, instead they built a company that now employs over two hundred thousand people around the world. I suppose that is something to be proud of. Don't you think! In any event, it's history and what has been done is done."

"Let's talk about inventions and revolutionary concepts. Who needs Vice presidents when we have a Freda Gesh," said Jack, lightening up the conversation. "We've seen the computer evolution from the post war, beginning with accounting machines that would cover a building, the information that they held could be accessed today on a kid's mobile, to the evolution of the computer and its amazing path towards todays encyclopaedical information carriers. In particular the memo pads and mobiles, and now of course the Autoplug. The old tickertape replaced by the Fax, Photocopying interplaying with computers machines, books read now on screen. And now health. Where do all these ideas emerge and how can an organisation such as yours find such brilliant concepts. Tell me about the Autoplug."

"Well, as you know the initial idea of this amazing machine emanated from your country. I understand that we first heard of it from Frau Gilda Baylim who conceived it with her husband. He passed away and she took complete control of its early development. She is a brilliant scientist in her own right and I understand that she had the patents for her designs, but only the proto-types and theory of the software. However, she couldn't develop this without finding substantial finance. I do believe that the British government and her university financed the original concept but the monies were insufficient to follow through with the program. Once her husband died, she contacted us to see if we were interested. You may know that we worked closely with Hitzudi in Japan and they were quite prepared to help us. She had already spoken with the British Minister of Health who confirmed that they would be prepared to incorporate all the necessary departments within the British government's domain."

"In Germany too we have everything relating to our lives recorded in various government departments. We don't even think about it, but it's there all the same. So the UK was to be our testing ground and then mirrored here.

"Your Health Minister was a vital point of communication in order to find all the necessary information, and between him and Frau Gilda we began. We bought her patents and re-registered them as we redesigned the machine to suit production."

"I understand that she is now working here. Tell me, Freda, do you know if she had any contact with the company previously?"

"I can't tell you that. Maybe you should ask Herr Heinrich when you meet him."

He could see that he had hit a nerve, but decided not to pursue it at this time. "It is very impressive how well you know this area of the business," commented Helga.

"When we knew you were coming, I anticipated that you would want to learn as much about the company as possible, and burned some midnight oil reading up, to be honest. I was surprised by the amount of information that was new to me," she added. "It's food for thought, don't you think?!"

Her discomfort was becoming quite noticeable, thought Helga.

"May I suggest that we have coffee in my office, and you can continue to interrogate me in slightly more comfort."

"Interrogate you? That's the last thing we would want to do, but you have given us a very good background."

They took an elevator to the next floor. And were now sitting in a large and beautifully furnished office with a framed painting dominating the room looking very much like a Matisse. "Is that a copy of a Matisse?" asked Helga.

She smiled "Herr Heinrich is a great collector and he spreads his collection around the various main offices throughout the world for six or nine months on circuit. Please don't touch it, the entire building will know," she chuckled. "He has an original Picasso in his office. There are unusual and rare paintings throughout the building, perhaps not all so valuable, but wonderful nevertheless."

"I will have to tell my boss to replace his Pirelli calendar when I get back. I hate to think what he would put there instead," he quipped.

Coffee was served, and they began to relax a little.

"When are you planning to return?" she asked.

"We thought tomorrow, it would be most interesting to discuss your research and see how your future plans will reflect on our country's health and of course the government's pocket, if that's possible."

"I think that you should ask Herr Heinrich, I have no doubt that he will be able to enlarge on his program especially the Ever Young project."

"And what is your opinion on Ever Young Freda?" he asked.

"A great deal of work has gone into this project Jack. It has many implications, it is not for me to have an opinion on anything the company does. What is the expression you have. 'Mine is not to reason why, but to do and die.'"

"I get the impression Freda, completely off the record, if I may be so presumptuous, that there are things that you may be a little uncomfortable with, please forgive me if I am mistaken."

She stared at him and then Helga for a full minute. "As you will no doubt appreciate, my position here is one of serious responsibility. There are many things that I am not privy too, but my training is to interpret my employers instructions and pass them down the line. I have to admit to you in confidence that I have been wading through some of the old files, and what I have read is a little disconcerting." She hesitated, "but at this time Jack I should say that I am not at liberty to divulge.

"Of course I realise that your task is to pass back to your superiors what you have learned, but I would be compromising my own values if I…" she stopped. "Let me just say this. It is for you to take away what information you acquire from our Vice president, not from me. I would also suggest that you meet Frau Baylim, and by all means interrogate her if you feel it is appropriate to do so."

Her office phone rang and she was now able to confirm that Herr Heinrich had returned and would be happy to meet them in the board room.

"I really appreciate our conversation Freda, I do think that we should speak again after our meetings. Do you think that you could arrange a conversation for us with Frau Baylim?"

"It would be good to speak in private with you. In any case, I shall try to arrange a meeting with Frau Baylim, and will let you know what time."

"We didn't have the chance to book a hotel Freda, maybe you could ask your secretary to find us two rooms somewhere nearby."

"Of course," she smiled. "I shall personally organise it."

Chapter 22

The boardroom contained two tables one to sit at least twenty. It was a broad oval shape to give the feeling of an open discussion rather than a more dictatorial effect. Once again a few masterpieces were displayed. They recognised a beautiful Klimt that neither of them had ever seen before, a Boccioni abstract and two other surreal artists that were new to them. The cabinets on the wall displayed medals and various cups showing proof of excellence, nevertheless the room showed a thoughtful degree of balance.

Herr Heinrich was already sitting with a thin file that he had been flicking through at a smaller table to seat four near the window. He immediately stood to welcome them. Jack had envisaged, for no particular reason a small bald overweight man with delusions of grandeur, he was surprised therefore to see a man of 6 feet in his early fifties powerfully built, a full head of blond hair going grey, showing a suntan and an engaging smile revealing whiter than white teeth. He seemed at the peak of his manhood and capable of total control of those around him.

"I'm very pleased to meet you, Mr Branson. And looking at her badge, of course you Miss. Barworth. I do apologise for my delay but I understand that you have been well looked after." Jack introduced Helga and summarised her supposed position in the company. "You are welcome to stay, Freda. Just in case I'm attacked by these English!" he laughed.

"Small correction, Herr Heinrich," Helga chirped in, "I'm Swiss, but we're very gentle as you know."

"Quite." he replied. "Now I understand that you have the task of reporting back to the government in the UK of our hopes and dreams relating in particular to Ever Young, is that so?"

"That is so. Bearing in mind the substantial investment that we are making into your two prime products over the next few years Herr Heinrich, I have been asked to clarify, as best one can of course, your views on the progression of Ever Young over the next decade. I appreciate that some of the claims that have been made can only be verified over the coming years and as the scheme progresses, but there are a number of serious criticisms across various groups, not least the religious, but also the medical claims, that you are proclaiming, and which are being made in the advertising program underwritten by the government and carries their stamp of approval."

Heinrich seemed indifferent to Jack's rather aggressive opening comment. "Please excuse my rudeness, will you have a coffee and maybe a schnapps? May I call you Jack and Helga? Steffen, please call me Steffen," he repeated.

"I'm honoured," replied Jack.

Freda immediately phoned through the order. He had interviewed many people over his years as a journalist, and found it strange to include even a personal secretary in a meeting. Nevertheless, he mused, every man to his own, and put it behind his ear.

Jack suddenly felt that he was never going to get his information by pussy footing around asking banal questions that he already knew the answers to, and on impulse decided to go for the jugular.

"Shall we begin by clarifying my understanding of the origins of the Autoplug, sir. In the first instance Magnum, which of course is to say you, claim that both the Autoplug and Ever Young are owned by yourselves and all payments invoiced to the British National Health Services are justifiably owed to yourselves."

"That's a strange comment to make, Jack." he replied innocently. "But why should we deny that they are ours? It has been agreed formally that the NHS should receive a percentage of the income according to our calculations. I don't understand the comment."

"I only ask this question because I have been informed that the original patents were taken out by Cambridge University and substantial British grants were given towards the research of the Autoplug and Ever Young. Maybe you can explain!"

"What is this!" retorted Heinrich, "we have a head on attack here, you surprise me with your arrogance to suggest that we have, what, maybe stolen this business?" Heinrich's face had deepened to a flushed red.

"Herr Heinrich, I am purely a messenger in this respect. It is a point that needs to be clarified, hopefully discreetly — it's not my government's desire to enter into litigation, unless of course there is validity in the argument. Please let us discuss rather than argue this matter. I am saying that it needs to be confronted and clarified."

"All right, I will tell you how we came to this business," he had lost the pleasantness of his tone and would happily have shown them the door.

"Gilda Baylim contacted us some years ago to explain her and her husband's research on the Autoplug. He had passed away and she had inherited his contribution to it. She informed us that the patents were in their joint names which we saw, but in any case, the products were not complete, and she would pass over the research to Magnum if we were prepared to (a) invest the substantial monies needed to complete the development with the software, (b) control the manufacture and (c) market the Autoplug, and when complete, Ever Young. She explained that there were other companies that were interested, but as the concept had global potential and Magnum met all the necessary criteria, she would like to work with us. We agreed, and she came over to us, and between her and our extensive research lab we were able to offer a complete package to the British Health Service. It's as simple as that. Of course, it helped that she was German, and for her it was a homecoming."

"I would agree with you if it were not for the fact that the original patents clearly show that they were registered by the Cambridge University which I understand paid 12 men over a number of years to develop the Autoplug, and they claim that they still have those patents and the brand names. So, the question is Herr Heinrich what patents did Frau Baylim offer you that might be considered belonging to another party? Furthermore, the government grants gave the university many millions too, specifically for this research, but there seems to be no record of them being consulted."

"Your accusations Mr Branson are very serious. Are you claiming that we have no right to manufacture these products after over four years of selling them worldwide and especially in the UK? Without a word from yourselves. I would ask you therefore why you would wait so long before making such a ridiculous claim."

"For the same reason, Herr Heinrich that I am here speaking to you now rather than going through lawyers, Publicity. Bad publicity that would severely hurt us all. There is more. I have just received a text to confirm that Professor Baylim did not die of natural causes."

"What did he die of then?" sneered Heinrich.

"He was poisoned, we conducted an autopsy on him yesterday and the results were conclusive…he was murdered, Herr Heinrich."

"Well, we never murdered him. I understood he died before we even met Frau Baylim and besides which, even if someone did murder the poor man what has that to do with Magnum?" Heinrich picked up his coffee cup and put a cognac into it, his cup was shaking.

"I would suggest that it's to do with whether Frau Baylim actually owned shares or inherited them, or might have formed a new company registering the patents and possibly transferring the rights from one company to another. After all, she was in total charge. May I continue?"

"If you must."

"Mr Brendon Tann, you obviously know him. The British Minister of Health."

"Of course, we know him, he has been most helpful in passing the Autoplug through its relevant channels and organising the many departments that are required to generate the software. He was invaluable."

"A very good man no doubt, in fact I visited Mr Tann recently, he lives in a most salubrious manner and reflects the life of an oil tycoon. To appreciate how invaluable he is we only had to see his lifestyle. But his only source of income is from the government, and we can be pretty certain that his wealth was derived from, shall we say unregistered sources. Bribing a member of the British government is a very serious crime. The fact that who you are and where you are, might give you some protection, but will Mr Tann be so keen to justify his association with you and clarify matters to protect himself?"

"Do you realise where this conversation is going my friend, our resources are limitless, we can sue or countersue you until you are bankrupt, there is no truth in what you say, murder, bribery, theft." His voice built up to a crescendo. "Who do you think you are coming here to threaten me in this way?"

"You are not being threatened, I am merely stating unequivocal facts Herr Heinrich, but we can ratify everything that we say to be true. And you must prove a denial. There are other aspects that I am not at liberty to talk about at this time. However, to bring this to court would be extremely damaging for everyone. We have litigation, criminal and of course parliamentary procedures which in themselves would be damaging and I would be surprised if all these could be avoided. So we have a problem."

Heinrich stood and leaned over his desk, face to face with Jack. "We have invested hundreds of millions into this project, there is no doubt in my mind that our patents are valid. So if Cambridge wish to contest our validity we will, without doubt, countersue for defamation. I am not used to losing, Mr Branson, and unless I receive a letter of apology from your superiors we will cancel our business in the UK. We can live without your animosity, and there are plenty of countries throughout the world that can replace you."

"Maybe it would be an appropriate time to speak with Frau Baylim."

"If I feel it necessary, I shall speak with her, not you."

"For our part Herr Heinrich, we are simply awaiting your response. If you are not willing to confirm your position, you would leave us with no option but to pursue our claim."

There appeared to be nothing more to be said. Heinrich glared at them both and proffered no handshake. The visitors both stood to attention, nodded in true Germanic style and were escorted out by Freda.

She waited until they were once again at the reception before speaking. "I have booked you into a very pleasant hotel, its restaurant is superb. You can try to interview Frau Baylim but I'm not too sure that you will be very welcome at the office. I guess that Herr Heinrich will speak with her first. I doubt very much if she will meet you." She gave a wry smile and with some satisfaction said, "you gave him a real thumping today."

Jack thanked her for the day, but it was not over and she drove them both to a charming boutique hotel only two kilometres from their offices. "I'm a little doubtful as to your meeting tomorrow, and it will be interesting to hear Herr Heinrich's response."

"Would you like to join us for dinner tonight?" offered Jack. "It would be our pleasure."

"I'd like that, say 7.30 pm?"

She bade them farewell and left the porter to show them to their separate rooms, but they both followed him into Jack's room and when the porter left, alone at last, they embraced.

***

It was already 6.00 pm – one hour ahead of UK time. Jack phoned Dr Ellsworth eager to discover the details of the autopsy. There was no doubt that substantial quantities of toxins from a poisonous plant, *Gelsemium elegans*, had been detected in his stomach, and there was some indication that the build-up had been gradual. The report had been passed to the police. There were records of it being used by the Russians in past assassinations. The symptoms were very similar and a note that described green vomiting before he became unconscious seemed definitive.

Jack's second call was to Jane Franklyn.

"The minister is in the commons today, Jack, but we have done a little investigation on Brendon Tann. You must accept the information that I am telling you is strictly confidential at this time, and I mean strictly, do you understand? I can't emphasise this enough. Do I have your word?"

"Of course, but what is it?"

"There is substantial evidence that Tann has been given large sums by a Brazilian financial conglomerate called Pontillo Banken using a Caribbean Bank." "But how do we know that?" he asked.

"By chance we happen to know the bank he is using. One of our friends in the city is on their board of directors. He told us that he knew of the details for some time but as is normal they respected client confidentiality. Bankers make money on money as you know."

"You would be amazed what we can unpick from this office Jack," she chuckled down the phone. "But to have a minister exposed especially by the opposition for bribery and possibly murder could bring us down. It can even lose us the next election."

"I've just had a thumping row with the vice President of Magnum here in Germany, which I'll tell you about when I return, but what is interesting Jane was to discover the results of the autopsy, and I would like to learn of Mrs Baylim's history."

"I will tell the Minister the news, Jack. This is very disturbing indeed. Let me know when you are back in England."

Chapter 23

They lay in his bedroom in silence. A myriad of thoughts whizzed through their minds as they caressed one another. She opened her eyes to look at him and kissed his nose. "I was amazed to see how you changed from interviewer to prosecutor without any warning, Jack. It surprised me but he – it was as if lightning had struck him. What happened?"

"I realised that our entire purpose for being there would be for nothing unless I grasped the nettle, and anyway…" he returned her kiss, "what did we have to lose? But we've opened a can of worms and there's no going back now."

It was nearly 7.00 pm and they quickly dressed, kissed again and went down to the dining area.

Freda was already at the bar. She had obviously been home and changed. She had removed the bun from her hair which was now down to her shoulders and had transformed herself for an evening out. She must have been aware that a meeting with the very people that so humiliated her boss would guarantee her dismissal if she was seen. The point was obvious to both Jack and Helga too.

They greeted each other as friends and were directed towards a corner table.

"I was particularly keen to meet you again," she began. "You will recall that I told you that I spent a considerable amount of time last night wading through files. As you know I have access to most files in the company, the majority are never referred to as they're very old.

"However it occurred to me that it would be interesting to discover for myself when we first made contact with Gilda Baylim. Most of our filing these days is in the cloud, all typed. But meandering through the ancient paperwork I came across three handwritten letters dated twenty years ago. Written by Gilda Schickerdanz. Her address was in Cambridge and she was telling her Uncle Albert that having achieved her degree in neuroscience she had been given a post as a junior lecturer in the college. She was so sorry not to join the company yet but maybe in the future she would bring her studies back to the fold."

"That is most interesting, and what was the next letter?"

"This was a letter from her to Steffen from England. Dated twelve years later. She was commiserating on the loss of her great Uncle Frederick who had been head of the company and although had passed the chairmanship onto his son, Albert, Steffen's father, and I assume he had asked her to return to join the company. Her reply was to decline and informed him that she was still working with her husband on 'the same project I mentioned previously, he is a genius, but he's not one of us and I have taken control of the administration.' She went on to describe their progress of the development of the Autoplug and Ever Young. 'Only time will tell,' she wrote 'but it would be amazing to make it in our country and complete the dream of the Germany we fought for…'"

"Do you have copies of those letters?" asked Helga.

"I didn't have the opportunity to photocopy them and had to return the files, but I can."

"But why would you want to compromise your position, Freda?" asked Jack. "I don't understand."

She looked behind her. Her voice dropped to a whisper. "Because, Jack, I also found old documents dated 1939 to 1940 referring to handwritten notes that the old company had made. Written by Goring himself, congratulating the company for their efficiency, 'which will substantially contribute to helping the Third Reich in its objectives to free ourselves once and for all of these vermin.' They were obviously kept as memorabilia; I had never realised how close I had been to the evil of their past. It was an amazing realisation to me. Here I was in a really responsible position and working in one of the most dynamic companies in the world, and now I was one of them recreating one of the worst crimes in history. And it was staring me in the face and I could not see it. Ever Young. If you had not requested a visit I would have never discovered what they were doing.

"So, I have decided to help you with anything you feel I can. I spoke with my husband this evening before I came. I told him of the meeting today and he agrees. I would have been prepared to accept some second world war activities by them – after all many large organisations here in Germany today were involved in the war and I assumed it was all behind us. But it clearly isn't. I should mention that one of my grandparents was Jewish. I was unaware of this until I was in my teens." She blushed as if it was a punishable confession.

"I'm astonished Freda, I'm not usually speechless but you have taken me aback. I need to digest what you've just told me. You may not even recognise the enormity of this problem yet, and I must warn you and your husband not to say anything to anyone about it until we're ready. Especially for your own sake. What does your husband do for a living?"

"He owns a freight company, in fact we've given him business from time to time, but he's of the same mind as me." "Please be very careful," he whispered.

"OK," she replied graciously.

"What would really help us Freda is to find the raison d'etre of Ever Young. If there is any reference to the time of termination, and control by them on their recipients of the Ever Young 351 chip! We are told that they are now able to alter mood change, as with prisoners, or those suffering with psychological problems, or migraine. But these claims could be a guise. There may be certain political references. It's a long shot, but would be very meaningful."

"I shall try Jack – although I would guess that this would be on Herr Heinrich's personal computer, but I'll check. I feel as if a tonne weight has been removed from me. Shall we eat?"

***

The following morning at 8.15 am Jack received a call from Freda. Her voice had returned to the pleasant authority of her position. "Herr Heinrich would like to meet you again Mr Branson, he has requested that you meet him at his home. He would like to speak with you alone for lunch maybe. If it is convenient for you, we will arrange a car to collect you, shall we say 11.45 am."

Jack accepted the invitation, but only on the proviso that Helga Barnworth would be with him. "She is an integral part of this visit." She asked him to hold, and was left for over five minutes. At last, she confirmed that he would agree.

Over a leisurely breakfast they slowly untangled the various possibilities around the murders of Baylim and Hines and how Freda's information could be relevant.

"I recorded the meeting," said Helga, "but whilst we have on record their previous history. It seems to me that we only have a firm motive for the murder of George Baylim by Gilda. It could be said that she worked in conjunction with Brendon Tann and therefore Magnum, but if that is so we need to prove (a) that he instructed the hospital not to have an autopsy, (b) he was in Magnum's back pocket, which doesn't pin anything on him other than bribery and (c) we have no proof that Magnum organised the death of Henry Hines and his wife, and that is going to be very difficult."

"But equally important is to discover what ultimate objectives Heinrich may have with regard to Ever Young. The matter immediately at hand is the meeting with Heinrich," said Jack. "The most immediate question is: What would he want to tell us after virtually showing us the door?" "Let's hope he's not going to kill us." She laughed.

He picked up the latest news in the UK. The headlines in the Times read. "Accused of Murder. Brenekov Pleads not guilty to the murder of Henry Hines." Each paper had their own bent, inventing, surmising and guessing the outcome. A comment from the police and his lawyer puffed up the case.

The Mercedes arrived for them at exactly the time agreed and once again Wolf escorted them to the car. He spoke in German to Helga. "It is very unusual for the vice President to invite business contacts to his home, You must be very special," he said.

"My mother thinks so," joked Helga, giving Wolf a haughty laugh.

"You will be most impressed with his home, he is a great collector of art and has masterpieces throughout his house. It is wonderful to have so many wonderful treasures, don't you think Fräulein," he chuckled.

"Absolutely," she replied. "Does he live nearby?"

"*Nein*, about thirty kilometres. This is his main residence but there are a number of others, villas, skiing chalets, I've been to most of them in Germany but he has also in France, in America, in Brazil. And he moves art around them and also some of the main offices in Europe. It's a great treat for us to share them with our boss," he said with pride.

"Is his father still active in the business?"

"Oh yes but Herr Steffen is mostly now in control."

Helga translated the essence of the conversation to Jack. They had driven for twenty five minutes when they entered into a forest. It had been raining and the smell of fresh forest rain was intoxicating.

"The master often hunts within his forest, he and his wife are very good riders. We will pass the stables soon."

They continued for a further fifteen minutes. Here and there they spotted deer and various smaller animals darting past. At last, the forest gave way to fields. The grass had been freshly cut. Various paths led to a lake. In the distance, they could see what appeared to be a castle.

"Does this area have a history," asked Helga.

"It has," he answered querulously, "maybe it's not so good to speak about it. But you will agree that it is very beautiful."

To Jack's surprise there were no fences protecting the building it stood proud and surrounded only by flora and ornamental trees. He mentioned this to Helga who referred the question to Wolf. "There are cameras everywhere and it would be a brave man who would try to find his way in. You would not have noticed in the forest a number of small huts. They contain extensive alarm systems and men with dogs. We would not want to mess with them, sir."

Two massive doors opened as they arrived, and a young man wearing a formal black suit welcomed them in. The exterior of the castle was built well over three hundred years ago, but it bore no relationship to the inside. And within the vast space available it had been completely reinvented. There was a strong smell of wet paint. They were directed towards a room at the far end of the hall. It might have once been a ballroom. "I must apologise." said the man. "We have decorators working in our usual reception room. Please excuse the smell of paint and make yourselves comfortable here." It seemed as though furniture here had been temporarily transferred from the main reception. Expansive settees and grand chairs were scattered around liberally and a concert-sized grand piano sat in the far end of the room. Around the walls hung a number of major works by artists of the nineteenth and twentieth centuries. An art gallery would have been jealous of the works on display. A Lautrec, a Cezanne a Modigliani and a Chagall that Jack felt certain had never seen before – but then his suspicious mind became equally certain that these must be clever forgeries. In the corner he noted a sculpture that resembled a Giacometti. "No one could afford originals like these, not even Heinrich. They must be fakes," he whispered to Helga, "or wartime booty." He continued to mutter as he meandered along the walls, noting a Renoir which hung next to a Dali.

"I will tell the master that you are here." the young man said.

The door was closed behind them and they wondered around the room admiring its contents. Jack took out his mobile and snapped a quick photograph. "The man had good taste in art, regardless of his character." he whispered.

Helga meandered over to the grand piano and cautiously sat down and opened the lid. Daring to spread her hands on the keys, she played a few bars of Schumann. Jack smiled at his prize. He quickly took a few shots of her and the surrounding works of art in the room. She delicately closed the lid of the grand and joined him with a gentle kiss.

They sank into two of the settees, saying nothing and consciously overawed by the disorganised splendour surrounding them. After another fifteen minutes, the man in black returned and asked them in broken English if they would be so kind and to follow him.

They took a lift to the second floor. To their surprise, Freda stood waiting for them. Her formal and over polite disposition gave no sign of their previous meeting which they both respected, and she guided them into a rather smaller but beautifully furnished room of a more intimate nature where they were greeted by Heinrich.

He shook their hands. "Firstly, allow me to apologise for my outbreak yesterday. It had no foundation other than my hurt pride. You know when I was a little boy I was bullied terribly at school, but I soon learned to defend myself and responded in kind, and I am afraid that habit has not entirely left me. I do therefore apologise and would like to discuss your comments in greater detail."

"Of course, we accept your apology, Herr Heinrich. I realise that what I stated was harsh — still, may I say, it reflected what we understand to be the present position."

"Please sit, we shall have lunch soon but first you may wish to join me in a small aperitif."

"Why not!"

He took a decanter from a small table and poured out three sherries.

"You are not having one, Frau Gesh?" asked Helga.

"No, I'm a working girl." she smiled.

Heinrich took a sip and sat. "Your comments deeply hurt me, Jack, after all we have invested a great deal of money and a vast amount of manpower in this project. The Autoplug and Ever Young would never have become a reality had we not taken the gamble of investing substantial sums into it."

"You will appreciate Herr Heinrich that we are in an invidious position. On the verge of stating to the world that our health policy has taken a giant step forward, when suddenly we are confronted with a claim that our partners are not what they appear to be…and have devious intentions. It's essential that the matter is clarified before we dig ourselves into a very embarrassing situation."

"I quite understand." Heinrich replied. "After you left, I immediately spoke with Gilda Baylim to confront her, first with the nature of her husband's death. She disputed the point that her husband was denied an autopsy by her. She said that it was a most stressful time for her, her husband was dying, and she had no say in the decision to request an autopsy. It was the doctor and hospital that made that decision. On being told last night that her husband was poisoned, she broke down and cried unconsolably with shock.

"With regard to the matter of the shares, this was more complicated. She explained that due to the reticence of the university to find more monies, the entire project was in dire danger of being closed and something drastic had to be done. This project they had worked on for years was falling to pieces in front of their eyes.

"She therefore formed a new company with her husband and transferred the rights to all the patents and registered names. She said that her husband spoke to the university, before he became ill, who were only too happy to relieve themselves of any further responsibility and openly thanked him for taking it off their backs. It was then that she came to us. We were obliged to make a quick decision.

"After George passed away we bought the company from Gilda Baylim for a peppercorn amount and a promise of some benefits if it was successful and registered new patents, we disregarded the Cambridge claims as they had no value to us, we took over all further responsibility for its future overheads. The university made no call on us to pay them, and why should they? There were no assets, in as much as they had produced nothing but theories. The Autoplug only became a reality when we brought it to our technicians. And the university have obviously seen how successful it is they are clutching at straws to try to make some money. I say if they were so interested in the Baylim's efforts, why did they not try to raise the finance themselves or even offer to join us?"

"The Autoplug is an amazing success, I can fully appreciate the efforts of George and Gilda Baylim, but it would never have happened without our technical input, our money and marketing skills. And now that we have Ever Young, the mass of information that has been generated on the Autoplug of every person in your country allows Ever Young to work even more efficiently. We can not only guide the user in a day to day advisory capacity, we can change their lifestyle to one from which they would substantially benefit."

"Are you suggesting that the personal information that is on the Autoplug can be interlaced with the Ever Young chip?"

"Absolutely, of course with their permission, but we have the ability with our two systems to understand and guide each and every individual to give their lives a perfect harmony, without fear or indecision, the ability to use their minds in perfect health."

"I'm wondering Herr Heinrich," said Helga, "how you are able to evaluate so many millions of the population, the task must be amazingly labour intensive."

"Ahh my dear, you have now hit on the heart of all our hard work. Our algorithm systems are so refined that we only need the most minimum human input. The coding of each individual would automatically monitor and readjust the 351 to direct electrodes in order that the patient or person will rebalance their thought patterns according to their mental state of mind and metabolic disposition if necessary, without them even being aware of it."

Jack and Helga listened intently to his defence; his last comment gave Jack goose pimples. There were so many questions to ask but this was not the place to extend the debate. What he had heard was terrifying and only confirmed in his mind that he had to find a way to curtail or change the dynamics in some way. He could have mentioned the fact that Gilda was related, he could have mentioned the letters, or pursued the poison found in George Baylim, but it was more important to walk away with as much information as possible. Could it be that there was some other explanation? He would show the evidence that had been gathered and it would be a decision for powers beyond his control.

"I would like to ask you about the philosophy behind Ever Young Herr Heinrich. There are implications relating to the claims by Ever Young that have made a number of people within the government rather uneasy." "Let me hear them, I am an open book," he smiled.

"You are claiming," Jack replied. "That at the end of days, so to speak, Magnum will give notice to the recipient that in effect their time is up and provisions should be made accordingly before they are switched off."

"With the greatest of respect, I think that is a rather crass way to describe it, Jack." he said with as much humility as he could muster. "But I understand what you are saying."

"You are also suggesting that prisoners can be mollified and the mentally disturbed could be assisted to alter their aggressions or negative behaviour."

"And what is wrong with that? If we can regulate those who are incapable of regulating themselves, bring them back as normal human beings – surely that must be beneficial to society! Rather than a rapist or murderer, released after some fifteen or twenty years, only to repeat the same offense."

"It depends on one's interpretation of normal. And is it Magnum deciding, or a government? There would have to be a very strict understanding of the type of individual you are reinventing. Or we will have virtual zombies doing the bidding according to instructions."

Heinrich's smile was now starched and it was evident that Jack's questioning was biting into his forced courtesies. "We are not reinventing anybody, Jack, we are placing them in a position where they can cope with the world's challenges. We're not putting words or thoughts in their minds, the Neuro351 will only redirect their fluids to change their mental direction. Levels of energy, aggression, a foggy mind results in indecision. All of these aspects of behaviour can be readjusted to make a complete human, and that must be good, would you not agree. You can appreciate that through the Autoplug we have the most intimate knowledge of them, better than any practitioner. It is better than a loving mother," he laughed.

Jack reflected on Heinrich's comments. "So, allow me to summarise, sir. It seems that Magnum will have the facility to oversee the mental stability of every wearer of the 351 Ever Young chip, remaining unknown to the wearer. Mood changes could be controlled directly, bringing millions under the influence of Magnum. Do you not think that this is something that we should be concerned with, Herr Heinrich?"

"If this was to be controlled by any individual, I would say that it would be worrying, but thankfully it is not so. The strictest controls have been put in place, that would restrict any misdemeanour by ourselves or anyone else. It has been suggested that a committee would first agree how this aspect of the scheme should be conducted."

"And the date of termination, how would that be controlled."

"We have already clearly stated that the date of ninety-five years would already have been agreed at the outset of the agreement. This surely is the golden apple for both the individual and the government."

"I understand Herr Heinrich that you have perfected a system of algorithms for the Autoplug that accumulatively evaluates the input of each individual, can you identify if and how this evaluation would be translated towards Ever Young."

"I can't see what relevance the algorithms have to Ever Young, but it would certainly be interesting to understand say a criminals record of behaviour. The cost of maintaining such an individual to the age of ninety-five does seem unnecessary, but that of course is just my point of view, it would I suppose be up to the government to decide a criminal's fate."

The conversation was moving towards the nub of his ultimate objective sooner than he had anticipated, but Jack needed to manipulate Heinrich's responses in order to find the raison d'etre of the Ever Young project.

He stopped to carefully measure his next words. "So, let us recap Herr Heinrich. We have been told that the concept of the Ever Young project primarily on the basis of prolonged and healthier lives for the elderly, which is clearly understood to save vast sums around the world, the termination program is the cherry on the cake so to speak and can be argued on the grounds of morality."

"However, it appears to me, sir, that Ever Young could have a far more sinister objective, and I was reminded by my colleagues of the policy laid down in Mein Kampf. What are these controls and who is the controller? They have asked: Are you passing on this know-how to the governments that will use the scheme to their own desires? Or maybe Magnum might work with them to mastermind the project. Where does your Ever Young stop, they asked me to relate their insecurities such as! Can you press the termination button on anyone who is not worthy in the eye of Magnum-stroke-government? And now, with the wonderful facilities that are available via the computer, which you are the masters of, one could imagine thought transference and the mental domination of millions. You mention a new Germany, but my imagination looks back to a revisit of the old one. How can my government accept a scheme like this where they are forfeiting the independence of their people?"

A bead of sweat was now appearing on Heinrich's forehead as his voice began to rise again. "Can you imagine a society that has no doubt how their day will be when they awaken each morning, a teacher with only one objective, to teach with a clear mind, doctors who have the concentration to listen to their patients, scientists, academics, even those who have lower aspirations, we would create a society that is pure of mind and follows a clear direction. We are only using a small percentage of our brains, and the 351 will liberate them. With our help, they would be healthy and happy living their lives to the full.

"It is a Utopia, Jack."

"And what of those whose brain will not respond or who can't or won't conform, would the red button be pressed?"

"Of course not, that is ridiculous," Heinrich's face was once again turning red. "In fact, both my father and I have submitted to the Neuro351 and in spite of the age limit, it has certainly improved our physical and mental disposition. We decided not to recommend it to the younger adults at this stage, but it is certainly on the cards once formal confirmation can be presented."

The telephone rang and Freda told Heinrich that lunch was ready. It was a good moment to reduce the pressure, Jack thought. Heinrich's throwaway line certainly needed investigating further, but he decided to allow his host to make further comments.

They moved into an intercommunicating room where the table was now set for four. It was unusual to include a personal assistant such as Freda, and Helga had it in mind to remark on why she was there if an opportunity arose. There was a difficult silence.

She could see that the discussion was gathering a negative momentum and saw an opportunity to change the subject. "I was most impressed with your gallery, sir, and although I'm not an expert, to see such wonderful works of art was a real treat."

To her astonishment Heinrich glared at her and immediately jumped up from the table storming out into the next room where he was heard screaming. The three of them were left only to guess what she had said that could have been so distressing. He was clearly telling someone off on the phone, but the words were not clear enough to catch the drift. The receiver was slammed down and Freda quietly suggested that maybe the conversation should be a little less pugnacious.

"The object of the exercise is to find the truth Freda," Jack whispered. "We're not here to have a free lunch."

Heinrich returned, brushing his hair back and clearing his voice "I am so sorry but it suddenly occurred to me that I had forgotten to deal with an urgent matter. You seem to have seen me twice in this disposition. You must believe me that this is most unusual for me." He cleared his throat again, took a glass of water and rang for the next course.

"Can I get you something, Master?" asked Freda in German.

"*Nein danke*," he replied.

"I am so sorry if I have said something that upset you Herr Heinrich," said Helga.

"Nothing to do with you at all my dear, just an internal hiccup that's all."

The remainder of lunch was completed with small talk, and they returned with their wine in hand to the adjoining room. Coffee was brought and served.

When they were settled once again in their previous seats, Heinrich took control of the conversation.

"My objective today in meeting you here, out of the office, is to explain to you that my intentions and ambitions are totally without any malicious thought. As you will appreciate we are a wealthy family and have built one of the largest private companies in the world. We have proven beyond doubt that we are a force for good, and will continue to do so. I'm very conscious that we bear a heavy responsibility to show the world that the New Germany has no association with the old. But I am continuously dogged with the past. Doesn't the bible say that the sins of the fathers will be upon them to the third generation? Well, I'm the fourth."

Jack had already condemned the man, his company, his past and their intentions and was fighting in his mind to hear this man's plea for a fair hearing. But he saw in himself a judge and jury that had already sentenced him.

Heinrich continued. "These allegations can seriously damage our image, no matter how wrong they may be, and we have to prove them to be false before

212

they become a public matter. I therefore ask you to consider carefully what I have told you both."

"I hear you Herr Heinrich, and it is in all our interests not only to find the truth but to express it in a way that will not be distorted. But what you have just stated is most disconcerting. As an example, our conversation here at this moment, contains very contentious points of opinion, If I were to have your 351 chip it would allow you to change my thought patterns to agree with you even before our meeting."

"And what is wrong with that," he smiled spreading his arms, "I am right and you are…undecided. Positive thinking and singlemindedness create a successful society."

Every word of Heinrich was being recorded by Helga and Jack reminded himself that his sole objective was not to contest him, but draw out his opinions, but he was on a rollercoaster and could not hold back.

He pressed on. "Allow me to bring up the subject of Mr Brendon Tann. It's clear that he had to become ever more involved with the detail of the Autoplug in order that he could coordinate it with the required government information. But it seems that your relationship with him, bearing in mind that he is a Minister of the government, has provided him with a quality of life far beyond his normal income. In other words, he is on your pay roll. Is that so?" now aware that he was goading him. "By the way, sir, it will not be difficult for us to discover it for ourselves without your confirmation."

"Let us understand one another here Jack," he responded without deference to his guest. "Gilda Baylim brought us a proposition, brilliant and innovative as it was, it had no foundation without the systemology behind it. She introduced us to Tann, he brought all the necessary aspects of it together, and without him I can say quite categorically that it would not have happened. Our own German government would not have released the countries personal files willingly. Of course we appreciated it. Once it was proven, the Autoplug spread throughout the world. And today it is worth billions. So why shouldn't we appreciate the man that made it happen."

"But I'm sure that you realise how that compromises the government Herr Heinrich, to have a member of the inner sanctum receiving money, and no doubt a number of ministers of the crown, especially paid from a foreign source, will definitely be seen as a bribe, even if it's done in good faith. The opposition would crucify the government and the company, and probably put Tann behind bars…and may I say, you too. I've no doubt that the British police will want to speak with Gilda Baylim and take a statement from her, or worse. I was going to suggest that I speak with her but I don't think that it would be appropriate at this time. I would like to suggest, sir, that a compromise on the Ever Young project should be considered by yourselves to reflect the dangers of its current claims, otherwise I see serious problems arising."

There was little more that could be said that would benefit the current position, and the conversation ended without a conclusion.

Jack stood and gave Helga a sign to go. "I'll speak with my superiors and try to unravel the situation as best as I can. I am going to suggest that we hold fire with the official launch of Ever Young until we can clarify our position Herr Heinrich, but if you have any further thoughts on the subject that you feel can help, it would be most appreciated. You can phone me at any time of the day or night. Our Prime Minister is very much aware of all the implications, the inevitability and severity of a highly consequential domino effect."

Heinrich put his hand on Jack's shoulder and held him back for a moment. "Jack, I would ask you to tread with great care and caution. One has to study the consequences before they begin a war. We have all learned the hard way that sometimes the casualties may not justify the principle involved."

"I will, sir, but these bones of contention must be resolved first, then there would be no need to go to war in the first place. I am sure we will speak again, and thank you for your hospitality. I will report our meeting to our Prime Minister and allow him to be the final arbiter."

They shook hands as contestants would do. "Maybe there would be some benefit in the two of us speaking privately Jack," he whispered out of earshot of the others.

Jack understood exactly the inferred implication but simply stared eyeball to eyeball but said nothing.

The Chauffeur returned them to their hotel, he mentioned nothing of his wife, and drove in silence. They returned to London that evening.

***

It had been an amazing experience for Helga. She had not only become part of a most exciting intrigue, she had found in Jack a man she would want to be with for ever, the epitome of her expectations. It was ecstasy just being with him. They used the journey home to review the meeting and compare notes.

Arriving back at Jack's apartment, they immediately made love, he with a realisation that he was falling in love but also a fear of losing his long-cherished independence. He had taught himself how to handle loneliness, and found a thousand ways to divert those negative aspects of bachelorhood, yet here he was on the cusp of evaporating into a relationship and nothing would be the same again. And yet he looked at this young goddess and was prepared to throw himself on the sacrificial alter. She had caught him at this most vulnerable time. Yet with all these emotions bubbling he allowed himself simply to fall.

They awoke at 11.00 pm. She threw on her dressing gown and went into the kitchen. She found a pack of smoked salmon and made them both sandwiches and drinks, placing them on a tray which she carried back to bed.

"I can't believe," she mused, "how many works of art were in that one room. I wouldn't be surprised if the castle is full of similar masterpieces." Jack found his mobile and flicked through some of the shots he had taken. He had snapped a few selfies, some of which Helga was not aware of. He was reminded how beautiful she first appeared, walking down the platform to greet him, and again her playing at the piano, she too was a work of art, and he came to the paintings and his favourite the Giacometti, what he would not give to own that wonderful sculpture, its grace in almost caricaturised proportions, and sitting unacknowledged and alone, as if it had lost its soul.

"Helga, I need to rewrite a summary of our meetings," said Jack. They listened once again to Freda and then Heinrich.

"His explanations sounded so convincing," said Helga, "and yet they are in total contradiction to what we have been told. Let's take Gilda first. According to Dr Singh she contested the autopsy and the hospital received instructions from someone above not to proceed with it. We are told by Ellsworth that she virtually hijacked the project from them and George, he was convinced that she killed him.

"Freda found letters confirming that Heinrich and Gilda are related, and that alone is enough to be a reason to bump George off and take the plans back to her homeland, as in effect she says in her letter. On the other hand, Heinrich says that she only made contact with him after her husband died and when she needed money and not before. Yet her letter intimates that she was writing about the Autoplug years before. We haven't yet seen these letters; Freda has told us that she will duplicate them.

"Then of course, Heinrich's dream of the future which is virtually to create a subservient world that will willingly do what they are instructed according to

Magnum. That destroys any faith in the project for me. I was astonished that he was so open about his ideals."

Jack saw the disastrous implications to the government if the wrong slant was placed on the death of George Baylim.

HEADLINE: Health Minister implicated in murder, it would be a disaster for the government, and it wouldn't take too long for the press to associate the death of one minister to another murder. But it was not for him to decide who would carry the responsibility as to how to untangle the lies from the truth and have so many ramifications.

"I think that my first port of call must be Pickles, only he and the Prime Minister can know how to handle the next step. If we could find a tie between Hines and Baylim's death, the position would become much clearer, it may be that there is none."

They managed to get four hours sleep but at 7.00 am. Jack's mobile rang. It was Freda.

"I have emailed copies of the letters Jack, I need to speak with you again, but I daren't talk over the phone. I have this next weekend free and will take a train to Koln, I have an aunt there, I can say that she is not well. I would come to England, but I don't want a record that shows that I have visited you. Can I meet you there on Sunday say 3.00 pm at the Hyatt Hotel in Koln if that is convenient. You are obviously aware that Magnum have ears everywhere I must be very careful not to be recognised. You cannot believe how sharp Steffen Heinrich's claws are."

Cologne! He thought for a moment. "OK, I shall look forward to seeing you there," he replied half-heartedly. She caught his tone and gave a chuckle. "Security, security," she whispered, "but I know you will find it interesting what I will tell you."

As soon as he hung up the phone he opened his computer and saw the letters written to Steffen in German, all signed Gilda.

Chapter 24
Joe

There was no doubt that the police as well as Bonham had serious reservations regarding the statements taken from Charlie and old Tim Brookes, but both played their part well, and the men had met as instructed to corroborate each other's story. Their meeting at the market also allowed Tim to give a description of Charlie, that the police would find useful. The prosecution had no option but to accept their statements and drop the charge of murder.

However Joe remained incarcerated for carrying the gun and having a false passport, regardless of whether he used it – but it was a light sentence, six months, and he would be out in three.

"What a relief, someone is looking after us up there!" stated Pauline. She had now officially elevated herself to the head of the family and persuaded Bill to retire.

"You know, Bill, I wouldn't mind getting out of this country, maybe live in Spain or Italy for a while. We've been playing too near the bone. Joe wants to take over, and good luck to him, but I don't like the idea of relying on Joe. He's going to come a cropper one of these days and he'll drag down whoever stands with him. We've got enough to retire, let's just vanish. What d'you say."

"Not a bad idea, I'll speak with Pete, if he wants to carry on it's up to him, but I've had enough. That lawyer Bonham has sent us a bill for fifty thousand pounds, the bastard, and it didn't even come to court. We'll give him twenty five K. That'll shut him up. This little escapade has cost us a pretty penny, especially Charlie's hundred grand. That was painful."

"But he saved our bacon, Bill – we would have been up the creek without him and Tim."

"The worst part of it is that the family's been put on the headlines," said Bill.

"Listen, it could have been much worse," she replied. "Have you had any contact with the Russian lot? I bet they're watching the case like hawks."

"The only one who can link us to this deal is our Swiss friend, what's his name?"

"LeClare."

"That's right, LeClare – anyway he won't say anything unless he wants to go inside. The goods are probably somewhere in Russia by now. Less than a million, the bastard. That was the bargain of the century."

"Bill," she repeated, "we were lucky to get out with anything."

"Maybe we should even find a hideaway a little further away, what do you think of the Caribbean islands where we can become anonymous. Just you and I."

"I'll check it out," he replied.

Chapter 25
Jack and the Minister

A meeting was arranged with the Minister for Thursday at 10.00 am. It allowed Jack enough time to put his file in order and present a concise report of the German interview. Jane allocated him forty-five minutes which he thought would be sufficient and thanked her. It would have been better if he knew what Freda wanted to tell him but time was of the essence, and Brody had left a number of messages asking how his articles were progressing.

The question Jack asked himself was how important was it to keep the entire business out of the press?

Jack needed no reminder that he earned his living as a journalist, and this was a very big coup. It was therefore with no small degree of trepidation that he waited to be called.

He had already emailed his notes to Jane and hoped that they had been read. The matter immediately at hand would be of Tann's financial benefits. It could not be discussed in isolation and would immediately include Magnum, opening up the entire bag of worms including Baylim's death and probably Hines.

At last, Pickles emerged. He looked exhausted, his sleeves rolled up and hair ruffled, Jack had the impression that he had been there all night.

"I've read your notes Jack, and I must admit that it's a very disturbing situation. I want you to come to a meeting with the Prime Minister. Can we meet tonight at 9.00 pm. Come here first and we will go together, but what we say in the meeting must remain strictly confidential. I trust you Jack even though you're press, so give me your word."

"You have it, Minister."

"There's no more to be said! Until then…next please," he joked to Jane. "See you later, Jack," and immersed himself back to the mass of papers on his desk.

***

Although he had been seen by the security a number of times, and maybe because it was evening, a strict security check delayed Jack by fifteen minutes. Jane was no longer at her desk and a uniformed officer escorted him to Pickles office. He knocked on the door and waited. "Enter. Ah, Jack, I shall be with you in one minute." He vanished into an anteroom and minutes later emerged combed tied and jacketed. "Come with me, I have a side entrance to number ten, it avoids busy eyes, especially the press, barring you of course."

It was a new experience for Jack to be in 10. And to his surprise even at this time of the evening it was thronging with personnel. Pickles knocked and entered, not waiting for an answer.

"George, come in. So this is the trouble maker you were telling me about," He looked down at his notes. "Mr Jack Branson, no less…thank you for coming in. George has updated me on this rather thorny problem Jack, and it places us in a rather precarious position. You understand why of course, to have a Minister of the crown involved in bribery is bad enough, but then associated with questionable deaths, and with a scheme that has already been committed to by us and that has serious implications, could bring the entire government into serious question. In truth, Jack it could be calamitous. So we have to weigh up the effects relating to the various options open to us."

"We appear to have three major protagonists here. First, our Mr Tann, secondly Herr Heinrich who is the Vice President of Magnum, and finally Baylim's wife who appears to be deeply involved. We must acknowledge the fact that Tann's efforts to establish the Autoplug have seriously benefited the country, in fact he could even get a knighthood."

"Nevertheless, we have now seen that he was being given vast sums by Magnum, it would need some explaining but not in itself such a disaster, due to the results of his performance. But then we come to the murder of Baylim, who was the inventor. This is a problem. Furthermore, Cambridge university claim to have patents of both products, yet Magnum have possession of them and no money seems to have been passed over from one party to another. So how can this be justified without a legal battle."

"Tann was working closely with Hines and it is a matter of record that Hines disliked Tann and openly opposed his future plans, especially the Ever Young project. He was murdered immediately after announcing his distaste for the scheme. Now we find that there are other aspects of Ever Young that Heinrich has boasted of that are extremely disconcerting, especially bearing in mind the company's history. Am I missing anything?"

"You seem to have covered all the main aspects, Prime Minister. What I would emphasise are the mind control plans that Heinrich has. They have enormous sums at their disposal and have proven that they can buy their way into anything that they wish. Plus the ongoing influence by Magnum through the

Autoplug that is currently influencing millions every day to buy their drugs and the Ever Young concept."

"Alex, I would not have bothered you with this unless I thought it was sufficiently important," said Pickles, "and looking at the immediate options I know that you agree that the first priority is to keep this away from the press. Once this gets into the papers it will unravel and cause us substantial damage. We have to solve the Baylim murder in secret, Tann's name, regardless of how involved he is, should not be seen anywhere in any documents. The second problem is to stop as soon as possible the termination claim of Ever Young. The fact that they can control the actions of each individual may be a wonderful idea to science fiction fans, but the reality is it's a horrendous twist, that should be totally unacceptable. It is unbelievable that this aspect of the scheme should have been overlooked. There must already be thousands who have agreed to take up their offer. It would be interesting to find out if the chip has yet been implemented…and third, we want to discover if Cambridge have a valid claim on the Autoplug. It would save the country a fortune. Maybe you can check these particular points out, Jack."

"But Magnum aren't going to agree to negotiate their rights." Jack replied.

"It all depends on what we offer. If it can be proven in private that they are responsible for these murders, hopefully we will have a substantial argument to arrive at an agreement of sorts."

Chapter 26
Joe

Although Joe was still held in prison, it was expected that he would be released within a few weeks. He had now been transferred to an open Detention Centre. The rules allowed him to spend more time reading and watching the TV. It happened that the BBC produced a short film called 'The Treasures of the Hines', and theoretically described the meticulous planning that resulted in the gang disconnecting the security alarms in order to enter the Hine's property, kill them and take the art, worth many millions. They interviewed the security guards, some of whom had been fired, and the alarm manufacturers, who described the serious technology required to break the codes without setting off the alarms and showed pictures of the art stolen. They concluded with an interview of Charlie and Tim, who both exonerated themselves.

Joe smiled to himself. In retrospect it was wise to dump it – it was too hot to handle. He used his time to plan how he would reorganise the business when he came back. His dad and uncle had lost the plot. OK he had made a small mistake but… "someone up there is looking after me." He thought aloud. "All these things are a learning curve. Cyber-theft. That's the future. It's much cleaner and leaves no traces. I certainly don't want to see this place again."

The film was picked up by a weekend magazine showing the stolen work in greater detail and giving a little history of the artists and previous owners. A synopsis of some of the master's stolen work was also included suggesting how oligarchs and dictators would buy them, occasionally flaunting their gains to their friends but usually hidden – at least until the heat was off.

Chapter 27

Helga had returned to Cambridge but her mind was immersed in her German adventure and of course Jack. Although it was Sunday, she lay in bed sipping coffee and reading Saturday's papers. She flicked through the supplements and noticed the Hines article and the photos.

Glaring at her were the Modigliani and Giacometti and she immediately recognised them. "My God!" she shouted to herself. She flung herself to the other side of her bed to phone Jack.

"Good morning, my beautiful woman, to what do I owe this call so early on a Sunday."

"Jack, Jack… did you see the Times supplement? Have a look – it's astonishing."

She heard him unzip his computer to look it up. "Fashion tips, lonely hearts. What am I looking for? Oh. The death of Hines article. I've got it."

He threw his eyes over the header and scrolled down to see the pictures. "Wow. Just a minute, Helga, I'm putting you on hold a moment." He checked the photos on his mobile and there were the very pieces, still on the wall of Heinrich's mansion.

"Jack, I bet that was what upset him so much when I mentioned the art in the room. We should never have been in that room in the first place. Why would this man even associate himself with these goods, it's crazy?" She sang down the phone.

"Maybe he didn't think they would be seen by anyone who knew their origins. He might not even have associated these pieces with Hines. Of course he may not have had anything to do with the Hines murder at all. Although I don't believe that."

"If the police became involved the first thing they would ask is "Where and when did you buy these works of art? And from whom?!""

"Thanks for this – well done, my wonderful woman. What would I do without you?"

"Don't worry, it won't happen." she giggled. "I can hear a lot of noise, where are you?"

"I'm at Heathrow and on my way to Cologne." They said their farewells as lovers do and he immediately phoned Pickles on his private line.

"Minister Pickles, we found the missing artwork—you won't believe where!"

"Where?" asked Pickles in astonishment.

"Where do you think? Herr Heinrich's house, of course!"

***

The 8.00 am flight was delayed by one and a half hours, due to a strike in some cursed part of the world, but Jack had given himself plenty of leeway. By the time he arrived in Cologne, other European schedules were causing havoc at the local airports. Hundreds of irate travellers were milling in all directions and passport booths and taxis were overrun. He had tried to phone Freda to inform her that he was delayed but her phone rang through unanswered. Nevertheless, he arrived at the Hyatt at 3.30 pm, only a half hour late. However, there was no sign of her or message left, He waited thinking that she might have also been delayed for the same reason as his. Maybe he had misunderstood the arrangement. He phoned Helga to ask if she had taken note of the meeting. No, the time, date and location were as he had noted.

His return flight was booked for 8.00 pm and without means of contacting Freda, annoyed and disappointed he returned home. He attempted unsuccessfully to make contact by land line and tried again early the following morning. Not wishing to email her, he decided to take a gamble and phone her office, but her assistant informed him that she had not reported for work "…most unusual and out of character."

He thanked her, left no name and hung up. All he could do was to await her call.

Chapter 28
Sir Henry Porter

Sir Henry Porter's reputation as a tiger of the legal profession had been well earned; he had built up his practice by employing only the best lawyers. His advice was given via an army of tough and highly paid young men and women who scoured through law books to prove or disprove disputes. In recent years, he had added a strong and very litigious patents division to his stables. The offices opened their doors at 7.00 am and closed at 10.00 pm. And it was expected that total commitment would include as many hours per day as necessary. Most of his clients were large corporations who defend their names or inventions on a point of principle, which was a wonderful password for SM&F, since they would happily dip into their clients' never-decreasing pockets to do so. They nicknamed it P.O.P.

However, the Cambridge University was an exception, and it gave Sir Henry a feeling of pride to have one of the finest colleges in the world on his books. But the proposition presented to him was a monumental mess, and showed gross incompetence by their board, including his friend Sir William Hoddington. Nothing appeared to have been confirmed, agreed, or contested.

Furthermore, despite its reputation, the university had limited funds and invariably spent far more than then it received. Looking through the papers he could see that this case would involve a substantial number of hours, and he made a decision: he would offer his services for a zero fee but would ask, if not for money, but shares in whatever new company was formed. Also, a tie including Spoken Arrow could only be profitable and would be a very exciting account to have on his books.

He magnanimously presented this proposition to Sir William who greatly appreciated the gesture since at this stage Cambridge had nothing to lose. A formal agreement was quickly signed. Sir Henry suggested that it was too early and unnecessary for their American friends to be informed of the agreement, and on behalf of the university he willingly agreed.

Another week passed and eight or nine of Sir Henry's formidable legal boffins had placed the Magnum/Cambridge and Baylim association under the microscope, and after substantial internal debate had arrived at a conclusion. Plastic-covered dossiers were printed showing all the pros and cons of an anticipated litigation and a further document considering a number of more fluid eventualities that might alter the rigid facts.

Sir Henry primed himself to bring forth another meeting and sent a personal memo to include the Americans and of course Sir William and Co.

Confidential

For the Attention of Sir William Hoddington, Ms Miriam Brevotti, Mr Robert Levinson, Mr Jay Harrai and Dr Peter Ellsworth

After serious consideration and an appreciation that time is of the essence, we believe that we are now able to offer you constructive advice regarding your claims relating to the Autoplug and Ever Young projects. May I suggest a meeting next Wednesday at 2.00 pm at my offices to discuss the matter in detail.

I would be most grateful for your confirmation and the names of those who wish to attend.

With kind regards.

Sir Henry Porter chairman SM&F

What was originally anticipated to be a one-week investigative trip had now turned into three weeks for Robert, Jay and Miriam. They had used the time constructively and had met several of Ellsworth's team and discussed various concepts that had previously been rejected or put on hold over the years. Although a positive rapport had evolved, they were conscious of how their work back home would be stacking up. However, the meeting with Sir Henry would certainly clarify their position and hopefully give them something of consequence to report. One more week and they would be back in sunny California.

As soon as Miriam received her invitation she contacted Peter Ellsworth "You mentioned Peter that your friend Jack was to visit Magnum in Germany. Would you know the outcome of his trip?"

"No, he must have returned by now, I'll give him a call and let you know what happened."

"I'm very keen to meet this Jack Branson," said Miriam. "He might be able to fill in the gaps, especially now we know that George Baylim's death was no accident."

"If you would like to meet up with him tomorrow, I could ask him if he could come to Cambridge again, or we could meet in London."

"London please," she quickly shot back "My friends still have not gotten used to our winters and I'm trying to keep them hibernated where possible. Hilton Hotel Park Lane, you name the time."

"I'll call you back to confirm."

Ellsworth immediately phoned Jack on his office number.

Jack was contemplating the mass of emails from his boss when his phone rang.

"It's been a most interesting few days Peter, but we are entering a black hole. I'm not sure now what to make of it."

"Are you able to meet me and my colleagues from Spoken Arrow tomorrow, Jack?" There was a silence at the other end of the phone. "Why Spoken Arrow?" He asked.

"Spoken Arrow, I'm sure that we've spoken of them before."

"I know who Spoken Arrow is Peter, but when did they get involved? I thought you had taken me into your confidence, this is a surprise."

The Doctor fumbled, "I do apologise but with all things happening I seem to have dropped a clanger, Jack." He expounded on his discussions with them and left Jack with a thousand questions. "Come to this meeting tomorrow and we can update each other. Events are moving so fast it'll be good to pull the various strings together. 'Hilton Hotel, Park Lane, Mayfair, say eleven a.m.'"

***

Miriam received a massage that Ellsworth was unable to make the meeting "but I'm sure that you will be able to manage without me on this occasion."

The three sat in the lounge of the Hotel and cogitated on what they had to do to find some solid ground to take the project forward. "I don't see why we could not work with them," said Robert, "they have the knowhow and we have the resources to do the rest. But we can't do anything until we are sure that the information they're holding belongs to them. It would be the first time that an Spoken Arrow project was not home grown. But if we get the go ahead, working with their team will save us years."

Anyone observing Jay could be forgiven if they assumed that he was oblivious to the outside world or external conversation, but those that knew him would appreciate that he absorbed 360 degrees of his surroundings like blotting paper. "I think we should plan our return journey guys. Can we say Monday or Tuesday of next week." It was clear to the other two that Jay was missing his

227

family and was also a little out of his comfort zone. He had rather less interest in the business aspects of their negotiation than the technical and would have been quite happy to be left alone to study the more intricate technology presented by Ellsworth and his colleagues. "I'm convinced that there could be a synergy with our friends here, but the legal aspects need to be ironed out first, and once we have details of the patents we should be able to present a constructive preposition to the board, would you agree. It's not as if we're taking over a business, it more of a leg up, but either way I can't see us bringing anything to market for at least three or four years."

"You may be right Jay," Robert replied. "But let's wait to see the outcome of the meeting on Wednesday, and I believe that Peter Ellsworth has arranged for us to meet this Jack Branson tomorrow, he'll be able to update us on his German visit. And after that we can go home. Would you agree to that Miriam? That'll give us the rest of the week to arrive at some kind of conclusion before we go. Whatever we decide and even working closely with the Cambridge team, I agree that it could be years before we will get off the ground with an alternative, unless of course we took the entire project from Magnum, and that's highly unlikely."

By way of a reply, Miriam simply shrugged.

***

It was to be a free evening and Miriam decided to treat her friends to a homemade meal at her parents. Although she'd spoken to them each day, there had not been an opportunity to introduce them to her Mamma and Poppa. "You'll love them," she boasted. "If you've never been to Italy, I shall transport you both there."

The evening was full of laughter, and a mutual admiration for each other resulted in a memorable moment in time. "If only I could package them up and take them back with me," she confided.

Peter Ellsworth had given Miriam Jack's number, and she called him to confirm a time for them to meet. She booked a small meeting room in the Hotel that assured them of privacy. Robert drew the short straw to meet their guest and stood by the hotel reception counter to greet Jack. They had jokingly caricatured him as a comic book reporter, New York style in his fifties, overweight possibly with trilby, raincoat and cigarette dripping from his lip, but he hid a smirk as he observed a tall good looking and well suited young man in his early thirties. "Miriam will be surprised," he told himself.

Robert greeted Jack with a broad All American smile and introduced himself as they walked to the elevator. Jack had thought of bringing Helga but as she had returned to Cambridge, he took a mental rain check.

As they entered the meeting room Jack informed Robert that he was totally unaware that Peter Ellsworth had been in contact with Spoken Arrow and he was hesitant to inform them of his part in, what was a quagmire of events, unless an assurance was given by them that he could speak openly and with total confidentiality. "There are aspects of this business that I am bound to secrecy and which could have serious consequences unless handled with the utmost delicacy," he whispered.

"I can tell you Jack that we have signed a secrecy document and have the total confidence of Peter Ellsworth and his colleagues. All three of us specifically came over from LA to clarify our respective positions in respect to the Autoplug and Ever Young. We certainly would be compromised if it was known that we were in touch with Magnum's associates. You should bear in mind that before coming here we had no idea how or if Cambridge University was aligned with anyone." They entered the meeting room and Jack felt an uncharacteristic sense of his own destiny.

"Let us introduce ourselves, Jay Harrari. Spoken Arrow head of Neural Interface Technology. I am Robert Levine and am simply Head of Research, and Miriam Brevotti who will be here in a moment, she's just trying to organise coffee. We need real negotiating powers in this hotel to get what we want. She is in charge of new projects worldwide," he said. "Let us assume Jack that we all have the same interests otherwise we will have a sparring match without any punches."

"I need to know Robert that what we say in this room will not leave without both of us knowing exactly what information will be released. Can I have that understanding from you. You will appreciate why in due course, but it is most important that we keep our meeting here in the strictest confidence." The gravity by which he presented his comments placed an unexpected weight of responsibility within the room.

As Miriam returned Jack was taken aback. He had not expected to confront such a young and attractive woman as part of the trio. "Let me introduce you to Miriam Brevotti. Miriam is another Limey, and she is Head of New developments for the company."

"Miriam," said Robert, "Jack is correctly concerned about security and has asked us that all information learned in this room should remain within it unless agreed between us before we leave. I think we should agree otherwise nothing can be said," he chuckled.

"I'm pleased to meet you Jack, let us agree, we have nothing to gain by gossiping but I would be most interested for you to complete the picture. So whatever you have in mind will be our secret, until you tell us otherwise," she said rather coquettishly. "Unless of course we hear it from somebody else. Your name has been mentioned a number of times and I was most curious to see that you actually existed."

For no obvious reason Jack felt himself sweating, though if it was noticed nobody commented, and pouring a glass of water from the jug on the table he took a seat. "This meeting is unknown territory for me so I would be pleased if you open the conversation," he smiled.

Miriam took the initiative. "So let us first begin by telling you our interest Jack." She placed her hands flat on the table indicating a gesture of honesty, and Jack could not help noticing her long elegant fingers. "You obviously know our company Jack, and I am sure you don't need an explanation as to why we should be interested in the medical market. Our investigations took us to Cambridge where the Autoplug and Ever Young were originally developed. It was essential to confirm that Cambridge had no current association with Magnum who now own it."

"However, what we are very conscious of is the problem of the patents and who owns them. We would soon have a lawsuit on our desks if we were found to be stealing patented inventions, especially from our largest competitor, and so we have been, in conjunction with Dr Ellsworth and his colleagues, trying to find the proof as to whether they own the original rites. However, we have been informed by Peter Ellsworth that you have a serious interest in the machinations of this business and it would be very interesting to hear how you became involved and if your discoveries could assist us in some way."

"Thank you for that," he replied. "I'll try to give you a brief synopsis of the other side of the picture."

"I work for a large publishing house as a journalist and have built up something of a reputation over the period with them especially as a sportswriter. We have one of the widest circulation in the UK covering over forty magazines directed at every level of the population." He felt Miriam staring at him, felt as if he was being x-rayed. Clearing his throat he forced himself to look in the direction of Robert.

"Magnum in their wisdom decided to use our publications to launch their Ever Young project with a substantial advertising campaign. With a six month contract worth over a million pounds and probably repeated. I was asked by my directors to take charge of the editorial side, from women's journals to cooking, health, sports, political and a number of other genres of publication, with a large team of writers under me. A different tilt for each magazine according to their readership, and I generally avoided being too opinionated about our content. But the more I looked into the Ever Young claims, the more distasteful it became.

"Looking at the evolution of the company, I first made contact with Ellsworth and learned of George Baylim's demise – but we now know that he was murdered." The three of them sat up in shock.

"The Health Minister, Mr Brendon Tann, was credited with bringing the project together and was the main negotiator, closely aligned with Magnum; and we have serious suspicions that the death of his successor was also connected to him and Magnum. But it is yet to be categorically proven.

"You may know that I met the Vice President of Magnum. You are probably aware that the company goes back to before the war and has substantial resources in Brazil which fund their business ventures. I can leave it to your imagination as to where that wealth originated. George Baylim's wife is now working in Germany and we have proof that she is in fact related to the family of Magnum. I believe that we could find enough evidence to bring them to trial. But we don't know yet if the patents she brought to them actually belonged to her. If they didn't Cambridge University could still have a claim to them.

"What is most disturbing is the admission of Herr Heinrich of Magnum who during our meeting openly admitted that they would wish to use their 351 chip for means other than repairing genes. I have that on record... and the UK is naively promoting the scheme as healthcare for the elderly, which in itself is questionable. Tann as Health Minister managed to coordinate various government departments' software to make the Autoplug effective, which was no mean feat, and there is no doubt that Magnum generously showed their appreciation to him and a number of his ministerial colleagues. Of course all that is a mere summary of this lengthy and absorbing investigation, which I would be happy to expand on. The problem is that if any of this information is released, the government would probably fall."

"But how?" asked Robert.

"Any government involved in murder and bribery would be committing suicide if it was discovered," Jack replied.

"You've clearly been digging a hole here Jack," said Robert. "Tell me though what you mean by other means?"

"I was interested to discover how the "termination" for the ninety-five-year-olds would work. They claimed that it would be by remote control initiated by the press of a button and allowing time for a formal exit, or a farewell party. I asked them how they anticipated dealing with mental illness. They claim it can be minimised with regular – constant – readings to detect 'anomalies'. When such anomalies arose, they would automatically be adjusted by the control of micro-electrodes. That technology would be most useful in prisons and the armed forces, electrode messages readjusting rogue genes whether for the common good or indeed the mental health of the patient. The program would eventually be spread to children, they suggest.

"They have used the success of the Autoplug to promote Ever Young and will coordinate all the information that is on the Autoplug for subliminal control. It is a brilliant and thoroughly terrifying prospect."

"So where do you anticipate us fitting into this horror story, Jack?" asked Jay. "We could develop something less sinister, but that would not stop them pushing their wares."

"Here's the rub: I've been in close contact with our Prime Minister's office and he has personally informed me that if we were to expose Mr Tann as a crook who would certainly have worked closely with other departments and given them benefits, and could also be implicated in the murders, it would certainly be taken up by the opposition and the press who could and probably would bring down the government. You can imagine what the media would do to them. Therefore I think we need a more sophisticated approach and one that will loosen Magnum's hold on the Autoplug. Ever Young is a problem in its own right, but there is no doubt that the directors of Magnum would be implicated in the skulduggery aligned to the Autoplug."

Miriam would have liked Jack to repeat his last statement. There were many aspects of Jack's comments that needed expanding. "Why?" she mused. "Why would Tann be associated to both or either murders Jack — am I missing something here?"

"Well, I should mention here that after the Autoplug was launched, Tann retired from his position, supposedly on health grounds. His right hand man was Hines, who took over the job, maybe threatened to expose him, who knows? But it was well known that they were in serious disagreement. Hines informed the cabinet in no uncertain terms of the dangers that lay ahead of the country relating to Ever Young, and since the government had already agreed to support the scheme and invested considerable sums it would have severely compromised them. But three days later he was murdered and, very interestingly, major works of art were also stolen and found their way into Heinrich's home. And Tann is recalled to his old position."

"Can you tell us how Baylim was murdered?" asked Robert.

"With regards to Baylim, we now know that he was poisoned, and we also know that Gilda refused to allow an autopsy, which the hospital contested. But the ultimate refusal came from a higher source, which was probably Tann as Minister of Health. We also know that Tann and Gilda Baylim worked very closely together, since, without him the Autoplug would never have succeeded. What we don't yet know categorically is how he was implicated in Hines' death."

"And how did Hines die?" asked Robert.

"Now here is the nail in his coffin. He and his wife were shot during a burglary. He was a very wealthy man and owned several masterpieces. Serious works of art, which of course were taken. Now when we were in Germany we were invited to Heinrich's castle, which by the way was magnificent, and we were ushered into a large antique room, it might have once been a ballroom. They probably transferred the furniture into this room whilst they were redecorating. And to our delight we were confronted with an original Modigliani, a wonderful sculpture that was obviously a Giacometti and one or two other very beautiful pieces. I was so impressed, at first I thought that they were copies, I secretly took a photo of them. We subsequently discovered that their butler had taken us to the wrong room, and when Heinrich discovered this he absolutely lost it. It didn't occur to me at the time that they could be the same pieces that were in Hines' house, but lo and behold in the Times only this morning in an article relating to Hine's unsolved death were pictures of the same pieces. You are one of the first to know."

"The question is how did he get them?" they said in unison.

"I haven't got the foggiest idea, but you can see now how delicate the situation is."

"But there is no doubt that Heinrich can now be directly associated to the murders – what a tremendous blunder! Unless he can prove that they came to him by mistake we've got him. How this can be kept quiet I do not know," said Jack.

"On a lighter note, Jack," said Robert, "I must say I love your accent. I could listen to you all day."

"Hey," said Miriam with false dignity, "what about mine!"

"We're used to yours," they laughed.

"OK, so see where we go from here. We have a meeting tomorrow with Sir Henry Porter of SM&F to discuss patent rights. Maybe you should join us."

"I would if I knew who they are."

"Lawyers representing Cambridge University." said Robert. "Apparently one of the best known legals in the world. I spoke to my colleagues back home and they were impressed. I understand they even have offices in LA. We know they're really good!" he boasted.

"I'll speak with Dr Ellsworth," said Miriam, "and suggest you join us if that's alright Jack."

"I think that we have a very complicated situation here, with serious political implications," Jack replied. He stood up and paced the room. "Let's assume that we could find an arrangement with Magnum that would avoid them being totally exposed. No courts, no litigation, no murder enquiries, all of which would seriously damage, even destroy them, and let's say they passed the entire project over to Spoken Arrow for some undisclosed amount. Especially if we find that the patents belong to Cambridge University, they might not have much choice. The alternative is a strong litigative case that would certainly leave them in a very bad light, perhaps destroy them, and at worst bring down the government. So what do you think?"

Robert leaned back on his chair. "You're suggesting that they pass over a multi-billion dollar operation to us for the sake of avoiding embarrassment, Jack. Is this the thinking that gave you an empire? There's no way they would agree to that."

"You'd be surprised," said Jay. "It's not just embarrassment. Japan conceded only after being destroyed. There are several historical cases that prove that avoidance is better than destruction, but what is disturbing about this hypothesis is the fact that three people have been killed and we know who planned it, and they would be free."

"You're right, of course," replied Robert, "and if they don't a court would condemn them – but the company would probably continue without changing direction. Your doubts about their ethics are well justified. Also add to this, half the British government are on his charity list. I wouldn't be surprised if the Prime Minister himself has put his hand in the honeypot as well."

Jack gave a hearty laugh. "Nothing is impossible, but I would doubt it," he replied, unconvincingly.

"Let's see what transpires tomorrow," said Miriam. "I'll phone Sir Henry now."

They spoke for a further hour, first summarising but eventually moving on to more personal matters – and for no reason that Jack could comprehend he felt suddenly overwhelmed by this meeting, unable formulate a conclusion with his new acquaintances. This woman affected him. Why had he not been told of their involvement before? He thought that maybe the adrenalin rush of his meeting with Heinrich and Helga had suddenly caught up with him.

He felt giddy and the need to sit down. Miriam noticed that he was sweating. "Are you OK, Jack?"

"I'll be alright in a minute – too much going on at the moment. Give me a minute," he repeated.

They invited him for a snack but he politely declined. He needed to clear his mind. He was gravely aware that he was now the bearer of information that would inevitably become a major political bombshell. They agreed to meet again tomorrow at the Gherkin.

Chapter 29

Jack had not yet passed on the information regarding Heinrich's possession of the stolen goods, and he pondered who to tell. It would be too dangerous to tell his boss, who would, without a moment's thought, see it as headline news and optimise the angle to sell every copy he printed, heralding disaster for the government. Yet he owed it to Brody Emmitt who was still paying his wages. The overriding factor was the political aspect. He picked up the phone and spoke to Jane Franklyn.

Jane was only too pleased to arrange a meeting with Pickles as a matter of urgency. "I can find you a slot at 3.00 pm this afternoon, Jack, but you must be prompt – he has a full diary. However I do know he's looking forward to meeting you."

He was early, but on this occasion he was obliged to wait whilst continuous traffic passed through the Minister's door, and at 3.45 was called in.

"What have you discovered my friend, as if I haven't got enough troubles." He gently smiled.

He placed the morning Times in front of Pickles and the photos that he had taken in Germany.

"I saw it in the papers this morning, so what?"

"As you know Minister, I visited Heinrich this week and took these shots at his home. There's no doubt that they are the same pieces of art."

Pickles looked at them again and considered the implications.

"The question here Jack is, how did he get them and from whom? We need to find out, but it will need a great deal of thought as to how, without rocking the boat."

"I can tell you now that I am going to a meeting tomorrow to discuss with Cambridge University's lawyers how valid their patents are in respect to the Autoplug and Ever Young. If we find that they have a claim, we have a strong argument in law to recover their ownership." "Who are they?" asked Pickles.

"I'm meeting Sir Henry Porter of SM&F with Ellsworth and the three representatives of Spoken Arrow apparently they have put an entire team on the case to prove that Cambridge still have grounds to sue if necessary."

"They're pretty good," he smirked. "So, we have Baylim's murder, Hines' murder and Tann with an unknown quantity of his merry men seemingly all knitted into the plot. What else can we throw into the pot before it bubbles over."

"I'm aware, Minister, how terribly sensitive this business is. The question is how can we deal with these killings plus Ever Young without our interventions becoming front page news? I've forwarded to you a summary of our discussions with Heinrich and his intentions regarding Ever Young are very worrying. In my opinion he's a psychopath, and it seems to me that Ever Young in its present form should be withdrawn from the market immediately. What I hadn't been aware of is Spoken Arrow who have taken an interest in the medical market and have been in touch with the Cambridge scientists to investigate whether there is an opportunity for them to work together."

"And how much do they know?"

"They have signed a confidentiality agreement and I am convinced that they will honour it."

"But how much do they know, Jack?" Pickles once again insisted.

"Everything. I had a meeting with them this morning but they had already been updated by Dr Ellsworth who, you recall, worked closely with the Baylims. Both Ellsworth and Spoken Arrow are keen to find a way to pull the rug from under Magnum, and for my part Minister I would be really keen for them to take the business over, but it could take years before it would be formalised."

"OK," he replied. "The problem is quite simple, but the answer certainly is not. If we accuse Tann of anything, it will be opening a tinder box, and if we don't he'll be getting away with murder. We have to seriously consider all the aspects of this problem, I will speak with the Prime Minister this evening. Be on call Jack, I will phone you later, and please do not say anything to anyone until we speak again, especially to your boss."

***

Jack had been trying all day to speak with Freda, and expected her to apologise for their missed rendezvous. Each time he phoned but left no name or contact number and decoded his number in the event that it was traced. At 4.00 pm he tried again; they were one hour ahead and the receptionist was leaving. "I'm very sorry sir," she said, "but Frau Gesh was run down by a truck on Sunday in Cologne and died instantly."

He immediately hung up. He was in shock and without warning found himself crying.

Chapter 30
Heinrich

It was over a week since Steffen Heinrich had met the journalist. He had been deeply upset by the discussions that ensued. His questions exposed the company to accusations of theft, murder and bribery, but most upsetting of all he had allowed himself to be drawn in by this young man, to expound on his intentions regarding Ever Young.

"That stupid Hans had also dropped a massive brick by allowing the guests into the ballroom. He had issued strict instructions *not* to go into that room," he told himself. The man was immediately fired.

Herr Heinrich Sr. was still in Brazil, and although regular contact was being maintained, he now relied heavily on his son to put into effect most of the decisions.

It was Sunday and as Heinrich sat beneath a covered veranda, eating breakfast with his wife, the newspaper lay on the table, still unread. He gazed out onto the gardens and behind them the forest, and drew a deep breath. "The gods are looking on us Hanna," he mused. "How wonderful it will be when we once again can bring to life the dreams that were made."

Hanna put down her coffee cup. "Steffen, you have one of the largest companies in the world, it should be enough, please don't put it all at risk. We thought we could conquer the world before and found that the world was stronger than we were. Let's learn from that lesson, Steffen," she pleaded.

"The cards that we are given, Hanna, must be played to the finish. We're too far into the game to throw our hand in now. It's a miracle that we have acquired both the Autoplug and now Ever Young. It is all part of the mystical plan – you must believe that."

He poured coffee for them both. "I'll miss Freda, I really felt that she would be my shadow for the years ahead, maybe I should have been a little more gentle with her. You know how I struggle with dyslexia, and especially in my position, I sometimes feel that the responsibility of running this business is too much. I hate myself for having this affliction and she had become my transmitter. Whatever was written, whether on computer, mobile or by letter, she was there to pass it on. She was my memory. But what could I do? She turned against me. I don't understand it. I noticed a change in her a few weeks ago, and for some

239

reason she became cold and indifferent, so I had her telephones and mobile tapped. What I heard was disastrous and she had to be stopped. It was not enough just to let her go, she knew too much."

"She was on her way to meet this Englishman, the journalist, and we caught her just before she was going to the station. Nobody would think that her death was anything more than an accident. She was run down by a lorry. We will go to her funeral and will grieve with the family, and ensure their security, and they will thank us."

"Why would you want to kill her, Steffen, she was a really good servant, and I thought a friend to you, maybe you could have spoken with her, persuaded her, you are a master of persuasion, surely there must have been another way."

"Listen, Hanna, if you knew that your closest servant who had intimate knowledge of everything you do, and then aligns themselves to your mortal enemy who is plotting to destroy you, one has to do something about it…and I did. It's a war that has not ended, and when you have an ideal, you must fight the opposition until death."

"You will destroy everything that we have rebuilt, Steffen. Let things be."

"My father and his fathers before him had faith in our future destiny, Hanna. The hand of fate is upon us. Ever Young has been gifted to us. We must seize the moment."

Chapter 31
Prime Minister, Pickles and Jack

It was unusual for Pickles to call directly, but he phoned from his car. "Come to my office at 8.00, Jack, tonight, and we will go together to see the Prime Minister. And bring your files."

They marched through the various passages without a further word, both deep in thought.

Jack had become completely consumed. It seemed to him that there was only one thing to think about, and he always believed one slip would change the path of history. What smallest incident misguided Guy Faulks, or Anthony Eden in Egypt, or Napoleon entering Russia? Had some tiny crumb of information been manipulated, withheld or invented, to change the history of the world? Jack felt that it was all on his shoulders.

They were called in to the office to find the Prime Minister in shirt sleeves, whisky in hand and sitting with an ominous looking gentleman. A gaunt giant of a beanpole in a three piece suit.

"Good evening gentlemen. Jack Branson, this is Derek Horrocks – he is with MI5 and I would like him to listen in. George, I think you already know Derek. Good. I have given Derek a summary of the situation, and it's not necessary to go over old ground, I'm sure he'll catch up, so let's carry this problem forward. Jack, you are at the heart of this dilemma, you already know the damage that it would cause the government and we are here to listen to your thoughts. We may not agree but your opinion is important, so the stage is yours."

It was clear that Jack was now emotionally involved. His hand was shaking as he took a sip of water. "You know that I went to Berlin to see Herr Heinrich and heard his rants regarding the future of Ever Young. What you will not know is that his PA Freda Gesh, after looking through some of his more ancient files, discovered that Mrs Baylim was related to the Heinrich family and as a result of her investigations she decided to help us. She agreed to meet me last Sunday in Cologne, away from the spying eyes of Heinrich where she would give us more information. I was there waiting for her. Of course, she didn't turn up, and I heard today that she was run down by a truck and killed."

"You understand, Jack, that no matter what we assume to be the truth, we either have absolute facts or useless hearsay," said the Prime Minister.

"Well, perhaps we should take the view that this accident compounds these accusations only if it can be proven that she was murdered. But what we have already, is building into a major confrontation with Magnum, and could devastate them and hopefully put Heinrich behind bars. That is if it goes to court.

"Then we have Spoken Arrow. They became involved by choice as they were beaten to the market, especially with the Autoplug, by Magnum, thanks to the strings that Tann was able to pull. Tann sped them along. You should also know, Prime Minister, that the stolen goods seen in his house were the same items taken from Henry Hines' home."

"That really is amazing," said Pickles.

"But knowing the quagmire we are in," answered the PM. "Do you feel we could manage to persuade your Mr Heinrich to hand over the Autoplug in exchange for his freedom?"

"Blackmail, although a real long shot, might well be the ideal solution – but I agree that, since the Autoplug is worth billions, it would require a great deal of persuasion. He could keep his computer business, which is still the main source of their income. I think that we need to find out where he acquired Hines' art collection. Because that will likely associate him and Tann with the Hines' murder. On the other hand maybe Tann himself is in a better position to present the case. He is in serious danger of being implicated in the two murders – Gilda Baylim too. And if they go down so will Heinrich."

"So your idea is that we make Tann the carrot, but what's in it for him?" asked Pickles.

At last Derek spoke. His voice was pure deep bass. "Nothing other than his freedom, and our silence. We can tell him that he can have a long retirement outside jail if he agrees. But if it is opened up to the world he would definitely be the lead actor in this Shakespearian tragedy. He would have the book thrown at him, but in truth none of us would benefit. We would be washing dishes," he concluded.

"So the hero of the day would be Spoken Arrow," replied Pickles, "who would hopefully take over the business, and Cambridge fitting in somewhere if we can corner Heinrich, and the government lives to fight another day. Highly unlikely but remotely possible. And what should happen to Gilda?"

The PM stood. "If Heinrich can't think of what to do with her, I guess we'd pass her over to Derek. There are so many improbables, and if things were to go wrong the consequences could be dire for us."

Derek stood up to the telescopic height of six feet and six inches. "May I make a suggestion, gentlemen, that it might be more appropriate for me to have a word with Tann? I think he will understand the urgency rather more clearly when being interviewed by the MI5, and his powers of persuasion will certainly be sharpened when negotiating with Heinrich. I shall assume that he knows nothing of these investigations to date."

"Correct," replied Pickles.

"Can you lend me your files, Prime Minister, and I shall speak with him tomorrow? I'm assuming that he still has the ear of Heinrich."

"I have the meeting relating to the patents tomorrow. I'll let you know the outcome, Minister," said Jack.

"For the purpose of the exercise I shall assume that the rights to the patents lie with Cambridge," said Derek, "it will add a little grit to the mill. He'll be requested to meet at my office, and we will give him what is generally called the P24 interview. Whatever I tell him, we are hoping he will relate to Heinrich. One way or another."

"We shall leave the matter in your capable hands, Derek – you've never let me down to date but this is rather important as you know."

"You will be pleased, Prime Minister," stated with robotic efficiency, "and thank you for your confidence." He grudgingly smiled.

They shook hands and the interview was over.

Pickles and Jack left together. "What is a P24?" enquired Jack.

"It's a particular type of interrogation," he smiled. "Either way ours is not to reason why, ours is just to do…" He left the quote unfinished.

* * *

Brody Emmitt had not spoken to Jack for the last week and when he at last entered his office, on the door was pinned a notice. "No squatters allowed in here whilst the owner is away."

Jack casually slid his laptop onto his desk and immediately flitted over to Brody's window, mimed to enter and greeted him with an apology.

"What happened to you, O, prodigal son?"

"Brody, you would not believe what we have gotten ourselves into here. You know that I've been to Germany."

"Yes," he replied, "I've had to sign off two business class tickets. Should I ask who the other ticket was for, what's going on?"

"Boss, you know that I have the magazine at heart. I would not do anything that would harm it. You know that, don't you?"

"OK. OK. That's the gravy, now give me the meat."

"Well, that's the problem. At this moment in time, I have been sworn to secrecy, this whole business has become a deeply political problem and I am stuck in the middle of it. Now, before you cut my head off, I promise you that we will have exclusivity for the biggest story of the century to date. I need another week, Brody... Brody," he whispered, "I've already had two meetings with the PM. Trust me. You'll be pleased." He found himself imitating Derek.

"And what do we do with the advertising campaign, due to launch next week?"

"Tell our friends that the campaign should be suspended for another 14 days."

"Jack, I luvs yer, but I hope you come up with the goodies or we'll both be out on the street."

"Don't worry. All will be well in the end."

***

Jay, Robert and Miriam found a seat around the board room table with their computers at the ready alongside Dr Ellsworth, who had hitched a lift in Sir William Hoddington's Rolls Royce. Jack found a place next to the doctor and five partners of SM&F sat opposite. Sir William Porter held court at the top. He began:

"Good afternoon. As some of us have not met Mr Jack Branson or our American friends, may I suggest for the purpose of the exercise, we each introduce ourselves. And it might serve the purpose for my colleagues who have been working so hard over the last few days to know who their clients are, face-to-face as it were."

Notes were taken as introductions were completed, and he continued. "The matter at hand is to prove the validity or rights of Cambridge University's patent for the product named Autoplug and intellectual rights to Ever Young, its technology and brands. We have investigated and evaluated the merits of every piece of information available. But I should mention in passing, Sir Henry, that I hope that the educational systems laid down by yourselves are a little more sophisticated than the methods of filing we discovered. Gerald, maybe you would like to begin with the Autoplug."

"With pleasure, Sir William," replied Gerald in an even plummier accent than his chairman. "The first registration of the name Autoplug was in December 2002. It was registered to Cambridge University in documents signed by Sir Henry Hoddington and Professor George Baylim. All literature relating to it was also formally copyright registered in documents heavily laden with non-disclosure clauses. Nothing happened for four years. However, it appears at that time that a new company was formed under the name Autoplug Developments, whereby Cambridge University took seventy-five percent of a limited corporation and left twenty-five percent to Mr George Baylim. No trading within the company took place, it was just funded by government grants and Cambridge University. In 2007, an extraordinary meeting agreed that thirty percent of Baylim's shares would be passed over to eight named colleagues. However, the company was still not trading and no benefits were given.

"The name Ever Young was added to the registrations in 2007. In 2008, the first international patents for the Autoplug were registered by the second company. It was still not trading but continued to receive government grants. Another long list of technical information was also submitted and patented. We discovered a dictum from the government dated 2007 formally requiring the company to repay the loans should the project be successful in coming to the market. We calculate approximately twenty-seven million pounds was given over the five year period, but that was years ago and it would now be considerably more. And I should mention, Sir William, that Cambridge University are still receiving government grants even though they have no physical interest in Autoplug at this time, which is, we could say, rather naughty."

"Oh dear," commented Sir William.

"Some four years later a new company was formed by Dr Gilda Baylim and Professor George Baylim who between them owned a hundred percent of the new Autoplug Ltd and claimed by a filed letter to have purchased the old shares for one hundred million pounds. A further copy is held by Companies House on Cambridge University headed paper. The company was still not trading but there is no confirmation or acknowledgement of this from the legal department of Cambridge University or in our files, and we believe that this was a fraudulent transaction. It would have been so easy to see had the university been more efficient."

"Nevertheless, grants were still being passed to the old company, and the staff involved were obtaining their salaries through the old company without knowing it. Cambridge University letters on file confirmed that the company, which now included Autoplug, would continue to assist in the project's development for the country's benefit.

"New patents were registered in the new company's name Ever Young but all the costs of registering the patents were charged to Cambridge University and offset by the grants given.

"When Professor Baylim passed away, Dr Gilda Baylim took control of the company and all patents. She then sold the company to Magnum for a thousand pounds. At this stage, it had still not traded."

Dr Ellsworth raised his hand. "In fact, it would have been impossible to trade without the software and that is where Hitzudi formally entered. We had been in constant touch with this company and they were well aware of what was required, but without the British government backing an agreement across the full national spectrum of relevant databases, it would remain an academic exercise. Hitzudi created the code, submitted their invoices which were paid by Cambridge University, and formally withdrew from further involvement. Cambridge then handed the software rights to Magnum."

"That is where Mr Tann became active, and in truth pulled strings from all departments. A few of Tann's ministerial friends actually came to visit us at the time. For a while we continued to work from Cambridge, but as soon as the project was complete it passed over to Magnum in Germany with Dr Gilda Baylim."

Gerald waited for a few moments out of courtesy, and continued with noticeable indifference.

"So, to continue… it appears that Magnum copied the patents with minor adjustments and registered those under their own name. What we were not able to confirm is whether they are substantially different or can be contested."

Robert raised his hand. It felt odd. Back home he would have just jumped right into almost any conversation, but here he was in England, and in the company of two real-life knights.

"Mr Levine, please."

He cleared his throat a little nervously. "It seems to me that our patent department could clarify the technical deviations. Please bear in mind that although we are very keen to find our way into this business, it's as much of concern to us as it is to yourselves that we won't find ourselves in court for stealing knowhow; but if you like we could, by formal agreement of course, help to clarify whose patents belong to whom."

246

Sir Henry had acquired a manner of interposing simply by moving his head. "What we haven't discussed yet are the criminal aspects of this business, which I understand are many and serious. If it can be proven that the individuals in the company were responsible for a number of serious ancillary offences as well, we could justify competing with them but we would certainly have a battle, one that would cost a substantial sum. Although I've no doubt that we can win. But unless we can offer a bona fide replacement for what exists it would be would a Pyrrhic victory. And time-consuming. I imagine three or four years."

Jack had been debating with himself how he could speak without breaking any confidences. However, this appeared to be as good a moment. "Sir Henry, you may be aware that I have been to meet Herr Heinrich, the Vice President of Magnum, and he has a great deal to answer for. To the extent that I have already had two meetings with the Prime Minister."

There was a sudden spring to attention in the room. "It seems to me from what you have said that their patent abuse would be the final nail in their coffin, but as you know Magnum is a multi-billion euro business and all of us standing on its tail will only make it shriek. We need to cut off its head to win this battle."

Jack now gained momentum. "The government has a strong interest in the outcome of this debate, and if it was simply a patent argument they would have left it to the commercial lawyers to fight it out. But it's not. It involves serious crimes including murder, bribery and the ultimate objectives that Herr Heinrich stated on record relating to Ever Young. Without quick intervention it will have disastrous effects that reverberate around the world.

"If Spoken Arrow want to get into this business quickly, and have deep pockets, bearing in mind that the Autoplug business is now well established and turning over well above four billion pounds and growing fast, it should be based on the original Cambridge patents, and not Magnum's."

There was total silence as his words were being absorbed. "In ancient times, before we became inhibited by our victories, our battles would be won when we cut off the opponent's head. And this, as I say, is what we should be aiming for. Metaphorically speaking, of course."

"With the greatest respect," said Robert, "I'm not quite sure of the extent you envisage us to be at the forefront of this Cambridge and Magnum locking horns. I don't doubt that Spoken Arrow would be prepared to be conscripted into the battle – but at this stage I don't feel confident we should be involved in legalities as to your rights."

"If we were to take over this business," reiterated Miriam, "or even an aspect of it, surely Sir Henry would insist it would have to be with a clean slate. Although we have to return to LA next week, as Robert suggests we would certainly be happy to study and consider the technical and financial implications contesting the validity of their ownership. But what you appear to be suggesting Jack is outright war. Are you hypothesising or talking a reality?"

"For the record," Jack replied, "I am suggesting that we cut them down and take the spoils. There is more than enough evidence to put them behind bars."

"However I believe that there is a deal to be made. That is provided everyone is prepared to follow through. May I suggest that we see what transpires over the next week or two?"

"Jack," said Sir Henry, "there is no doubt that you have taken a personal interest in this affair, but I haven't been able to discover why, and I'm wondering if you would like to enlighten us a little."

"With pleasure, sir. You know that I'm a journalist for the Tandem Press and was asked to head a series of articles for a number of their magazines relating to the launch of the huge Ever Young advertising campaign, which I should add is supported by the government. At first I found the concept very appealing, thinking about living to ninety-five in good health and so on, but then as I was investigating the company and its objectives I came to the conclusion that it would have terrible consequences. I cannot say unforeseen since the history of the company is horrific, and their objectives are outright despicable. Subsequent events have proven that nothing has changed as far as their historical ambitions are concerned. Only this week Heinrich's personal assistant was killed. She was a charming lady. I believe they discovered that she was cooperating with me to expose them. There are no lengths that Heinrich will stop at, to achieve his objectives."

"Very disturbing, and more reason why we should reach a solution as soon as possible. Do you personally feel exposed, Jack?"

"Possibly, Sir Henry, but I suspect I'm an implausible target. Killing a journalist working for a national publisher would be a little too brash… unwise, but who knows?" he nervously smiled.

"For our part," replied Sir Henry, "we will meet with the Kings Council to evaluate our chances in court. From what we have discovered so far, I think that we have a strong case. Of course this is provided Spoken Arrow joins us, and that decision only your board can make. However, it is highly unlikely that Magnum would sell their company unless they are placed under serious pressure and especially directly to their major competitor, it is more likely that the British government would step in."

Robert replied. "We're obviously extremely interested in following through and making a partnership, but we must emphasise that it would not be smart for us to become too deeply involved in the political aspects of any takeover. Nevertheless, any agreement that can be agreed that you feel will help clarify the situation, Sir Henry, provided that Spoken Arrow negotiate from an arm's length… yes, absolutely." As he looked at his colleagues who both nodded.

Sir Henry thanked all those present and instructed them that the meeting was held in the strictest confidence and should not be discussed with anyone before a conclusion has been reached.

As they walked out Jay asked Miriam, "What's a Kings Council?"

"It's a top of the drawer lawyer who speaks to the judge and jury in the courtroom. They're the ones who wear the white wigs. They profess to know everything, that is until they lose."

Chapter 32
Tann-Horrocks

Derek Horrocks wasted no time in preparing for his meeting with Tann, and in spite of his gothic disposition, he was capable of formulating sophisticated strategies before facing his opponents with meticulous care.

He decided to send Tann a short but formal letter on the Ministry of Information headed paper and signed by himself. "Derek Horrocks officer of the Law, MI5 requesting a strictly confidential meeting on Thursday at 4:35 pm. At his offices (3rd floor room 358.) A parking space has been allocated on second floor no.526." The letter was sent by special courier, to be signed and acknowledged by Tann. There was no telephone number or email but Tann attempted to discover who this Horrocks was and why he wanted to speak with him. But to no avail. He had no option but to go.

The Ministry of Information (MI5 and MI6) is situated on the south side of Victoria Bridge. A massive beige, concrete fortress acknowledged to be one of the ugliest constructions in London, its visage suggested that only invited guests were welcome, and that any foreigner entering without identification would probably not come out. It should have been a prison.

Indeed as he entered, despite his ministerial position, his identification was demanded. He was tagged and immediately escorted upstairs. The lift was as bleak as the building. The fifth floor passage seemed to vanish into infinity. Not a word was spoken as he was marched unceremoniously to the room 358 by a sombre looking woman dressed in a grey uniform. The escort took a large ring holding countless keys and unlocked the door and ushered him in leaving him alone. The room had four chairs and a table. It was not a small room but institutionally bleak. It's neon lights bounced off the white walls that housed no adornments other than a small picture of the King. The door shut behind him and he was left alone. He was not used to this type of curt treatment and a myriad of reasons as to why he was asked there passed through his mind as he gradually built up a substantial level of resentment. "I'm a Minister of the government, for God's sake." He had no papers with him and sat with his hands on the table. He attempted to make a call but there appeared to be no reception. He opened the door again but only a long corridor with a multiple number of identical doors were noted, and he returned into the room. The smell of a prison loomed around him. It was over fifteen minutes before the door opened again and the long skeletal figure of Derek Horrocks entered. Tann stood up.

"I must say this is pretty…" he began. About to lay into whoever entered.

"Sit," demanded Horrocks. "Sit!" again, as if to a pet dog.

Horrocks sat opposite and glared.

"Why have I been asked to come here, and why I am in this bleak room as if I was a criminal. Who are you anyway?" he ranted. The grim reaper simply stared at him. "You are here because I instructed you to be here. And you are here to confess."

"Confess to what, damn it, who are you anyway to speak to me in this way…"

His voice trailed off as Horrocks stood up again and left the room. Locking it behind him.

"Hey, what do you think you're doing? For God's sake let me out!" he shouted to no avail. There was a small window but it looked out onto adjoining roofs. He shouted and knocked hard on the door again. But nobody came.

Though the temperature outside was a mere five degrees, this room was hot and stuffy. He noted an old iron radiator against the wall on full heat and attempted to adjust it, but it would not move. After a few minutes he removed his coat. After another twenty-five minutes, he undid his tie, and continued spasmodically knocking and shouting, heavily sweating. He took off his jacket. It was over an hour later when Horrocks returned carrying a plastic bottle of water. Closing the door again, this time locking it from the inside, he sat down and waved Tann to do the same, and this time Tann obeyed without a word. Opening the bottle he took a gulp and screwed it up again.

Tann was about to rant again. "Can I have a drink for God's sake." But Horrocks simply raised his hand.

"I want you to imagine that you are at the gates of hell. Tann You're about to be condemned to damnation for eternity when an angel stands before you, I am that angel…"

"What rubbish are you talking, Let me out, I can have you put behind bars, do you realise who I am?" yelled Tann.

"I know Mr Brendon Tann Minister of Health, but if you don't listen to me, the whole world will know who and more important, what you are. You are on the brink of a life sentence, and I am going to tell you how to avoid it, but if you're not interested then we will formally arrest you and throw the book at you. Do you understand. Mr Tann?"

"And what are these charges that I'm supposed to have committed?" He attempted to say sardonically. But his quivering voice lost its intent.

"Murder, bribery, and theft... shall we begin, Mr Tann, with the first, the second or the third? I think the third first – just for fun."

"The Autoplug. We know that you colluded with Gilda Baylim transferring to Magnum patents that belonged to Cambridge University. That's theft and fraud."

"That's a lie!" Tann shouted.

"Don't shout, Mr Tann, remember I have the key to this door. We know that you were involved in the murder of Henry Hines and his wife, then George Baylim."

"That's ridiculous!" he shouted again.

Horrocks waved the key in front of Tann which quietened him.

"You're learning. Good. We can prove categorically that Mr Heinrich has given you substantial sums of money over a long period of time. As a Minister of the crown, that in itself is a Guy Faulks offence. Mr Tann you are a condemned man. Even if you got off lightly with one or even two of these offences, which is highly unlikely, you're doomed to go inside for the rest of your sub-human life. For my part, I would leave it like that.

"Now there are only the two of us in this room and it's my job to discover whether you are prepared to repent or go to hell. I am not asking you if you are guilty, since we know you are, or why, since I couldn't care less. Someone else might have more interest in those questions."

"What is it you want from me? Of course none of these accusations are true, I have given my life to this country, and this is all rubbish you are accusing me of."

"I'm not wasting my time listening to your bleating, Tann. You can bleat in court. Alternatively we could simply kill you. Claim it as suicide, no political embarrassment. That is easy, we could do that now. In fact that is a good idea."

He stood up and walked to the door, unlocked it and took one foot outside, when Tann shouted. "Don't lock me in again. I have claustrophobia. I'm not admitting anything. But I will hear what you have to say."

"That's not good enough, Tann." Horrocks slowly walked over to the seated Tann, stood directly over him and, taking Tann's head in his hands forced him to look up into his nostrils. "You must listen as if – no, because – your life is at stake. Do you understand?" His nostrils flared. "Do you understand, you toad?" he repeated. "Say it: 'Yes, I understand.'"

"Yes, I understand." Tann answered reluctantly.

"Your life is in my hands, Tann. I exercise total control over you. Understand that: one slip and I can have you obliterated, tortured or sent to the moon. I have total power over you. Do you understand, Tann?" he repeated.

"How do I know that? I'm in a government building. Why can't I speak to the Prime Minister? I don't even know who you are."

"The pain that I'm about to inflict upon you is only the beginning if you don't follow my instructions." He stood up and left the room, locking the door before Tann could make a sound. Another painful hour passed. It was now evening. Tann was expecting to be in the commons but had no means to contact either his home or his secretary."

Two hours later Horrocks returned with another bottle of water, from which he took a sip. He had brought a coil of rope with him and pushed Tann back into a chair before proceeding to tie him up.

Tann was now becoming demented. "Give me some water! What do you think you're doing?" he yelled, now soaked in sweat and attempting to stand.

"It's pretty obvious, don't you think?" grinned Horrocks. "Now *sit*," he shouted, and pushed Tann back into his chair.

The ropes were tightly drawn around his ankles and hands. He had obviously done this before, and when he completed it he stood back to admire his handiwork. Tann attempted feebly to loosen the rope. Without warning Horrocks gave him a mighty punch in the face. Tann's blubbering quietened as blood flowed from his lip.

Making the table his desk, Horrocks sat as he produced his mobile phone and made a call. "Hello, Prime Minister, I'm with Minister Tann. He would like to say a few words to you." He activated the loudspeaker and placed the phone on the table.

"Prime Minister, you must help me," Tann shouted, "This lunatic has tied me up and is threatening to kill me – who is this mad man?"

There was a moment's silence, "It's all part of the game, Tann. I'm leaving you in my friend's hands. He has my permission to work closely with you," he lowered his tone and whispered, "or without you. Sorry, I'm just on my way to the commons. Good luck." He hung up.

Tann began to cry. "What do you want me to do, for God's sake? Just untie me. I don't want to die… I've got a bad heart."

"You don't have any heart. I will tell you what I need from you in order that you continue to live, but if you don't succeed in achieving my requests, believe me Tann you certainly will die and so will your family, and they will go in the same way that your colleague and his wife did. Do you understand? Answer." He clearly did and said so. He was but a fly caught in the spider's web.

"You will hear from me tomorrow morning at 10.00 am I will tell you where and when we will meet. Tann you must obey everything that we ask you. There will be no second chances if you don't. If you attempt to escape I will find you, Don't say a single word to anyone, even your wife of what has happened or there will be consequences. Do you agree."

"Yes," he replied. He hit Tann again, and threw the remainder of the water over him leaving him dripping and semi-conscious for a further thirty minutes. Returning with a large pair of scissors. Tann looked at it as it caught the light and burst into tears. But Horrocks took his jacket and coat and methodically cut it into strips. He carefully untied one of his shoes and removed it. He untied him and throwing the ripped clothes back to him instructed him to put the rags back on. Now feeling thoroughly humiliated he opened the door. Tann was unable to hold his water and wet himself. Staggering back to the car park he was barely able to see as he drove back home, humiliated and broken. No explanation was offered to his wife as he threw himself on the bed and sobbed himself to sleep.

***

"He'll do whatever we ask him, how well is anybody's guess, but I need to know exactly what you want him to do Prime Minister."

"Let's meet tomorrow morning at 8.00 am at number ten. I want Jack Branson to be here."

"I'll ask him," Horrocks replied.

***

Jack was surprised to hear from Horrocks. He had never been told what his position was other than his relationship with the powers that be, which seemed to be rather unusual. Then to be invited to number ten compounded the mystery. Of course he agreed, and wearing his best suit arrived at the front of the most famous door in the world, foolishly imagining that he might be photographed. What a childish thought, he admitted to himself.

He was expected, and shown to the office of the Prime Minister. Horrocks was already there.

"Thank you for coming at such short notice," said the Prime Minister. "We have a rather delicate task that I know you will want to assist with, and that we don't think can be left to anyone else."

"I'm most flattered, Prime Minister," Jack replied. "But to what do I owe this honour." They sat in settees and tea was brought in and left for Horrocks to pour.

"My friend here had a meeting with Brendon Tann yesterday to discuss his culpability and its consequences. There are certain problems that your Herr Heinrich has that he may not be aware of yet but would seriously compromise him and his business. We need to explain to him the benefits of forgoing his business, and certainly the medical division for the sake of staying out of jail or worse, considerably worse."

"We want to use Mr Tann as an example of his own indisposition, but we don't believe that he alone would have the powers of persuasion that you could present. Especially as you have already met him."

Horrocks was holding his cup of tea, and placed it carefully down. "Tann has been made to appreciate how valuable his life and family are Mr Branson." The timbre of his voice suggested that something rather sinister had already occurred.

"Dare I ask how persuasive you were Mr Horrocks?" asked Jack.

"You may," he replied, "let us say very, and you are being used as one of my tools Mr Branson. You will certainly be an asset in our next meeting."

Jack now aware that he was being sucked into something far more distasteful than he had bargained for attempted to put up a defence. "Surely someone representing the British government would be more appropriate, and with the greatest of respect Prime Minister, what threats can I impose upon a man who owns one of the largest companies in the world to part with a multi-billion dollar business."

The Prime Minister sat back in his chair, lit a cigar and directed his attention towards Jack. "If the manner by which the Autoplug and Ever Young was acquired and revealed to the world it would seriously damage his business, however if we show him that we have proof that he was implicated in the murders, the stolen patents, the death of Professor Baylim, plus the murder of our Health Minister resulting in the confiscation of all his belongings, and not forgetting of course, his piece-de-resistance, the Ever Young project that would be to him the final solution, the control millions of minds. If we can persuade him that he can be relieved of all these accusations, I do believe he might see the benefits of selling the business for an undisclosed sum to someone such as the British government which is a better alternative to a life sentence or even worse."

"Bear in mind that Cambridge will also sue Magnum for the brand names and patents, and they might very well win, even without the criminal element."

"What do you want me to do?" asked Jack. He felt as if his spine had been removed.

"Our priority is to keep this entire business from the press, certainly until we are ready to tell them, which may be never. If it is discovered that we have such a degree of corruption in our ministry and with all its implications we would be crucified by the media and the opposition. In any event, we don't believe that Tann did this by himself and there's no doubt that other personnel will be implicated, in the government and the civil service. That is our Achilles' Heel."

"You would take all the evidence that we have including your photos and pictures of the original works of art to prove that we know that he is in possession of them, linking him to the Hines murders. The monies passed to Tann implicate not only him but also Mrs Baylim. We can show that she is related to Heinrich and that shares were transferred to his company, implicating him as well."

"All this can be smothered if they are prepared to pass on the business. We could start by asking to acquire the total Magnum computer operation – though I imagine that his father would rather sacrifice his son than give up the business – and as a gesture of good faith compromise on Autoplug and Ever Young. Personally, I wouldn't care who owns the business, but I do care about the principals involved, that reflect the credibility of our government and in particular our party, and I think about our place in history."

"When do you suggest we visit him again, sir?"

"It's Christmas in two weeks, I suggest that we allow the Americans to return home. I understand that they are seriously committed to working with us."

"Let's call Germany today and see how soon we can meet. It's most important that he is unaware of our own vulnerabilities. Heinrich should not be given any opportunity to box out of his problems."

"The likelihood is that he and his family will be away during the holiday. Should we delay it until the new year?"

"Maybe, but let him consider that. I feel we should approach him immediately, see his response. We can be a bit generous, show a little goodwill."

"So, Jack. You've worked very hard in order to reach this point. Are you prepared to follow through? It will probably be the most important event of your life. Take it from what I've said, the government's credibility and quite possibly its continuity rest on your shoulders."

"There would be three of you. Tann, Horrocks and of course yourself. We would need Horrocks to keep Tann in line. Tann has to admit that he has already been seriously exposed to life threatening danger and pressing that home would inevitably result in his incriminating Heinrich – I expect that you could present him with alternatives to make this clear."

"I would have been happier to be at the final killing had you not emphasised so the importance of this meeting. I'm not sure, Prime Minister, that you should throw so much on my shoulders."

"I'm a good judge of character Jack, believe me. I have complete confidence in that there is no one in a better position to confront this man than you. So let's make it easy, I'm instructing you. Is that better?" He smiled.

They stared at one another for a full twenty seconds. "I suppose, sir, that I have no option. But I would be grateful if I can use the offices here to make contact with him. Appearing to be working from number ten will give gravitas to the discussion. It also might not be a bad idea to allow Spoken Arrow into our confidence, especially as they would have to prepare to take over the current Autoplug operation, and would certainly need to cooperate with Magnum," said Jack.

"No, I don't think so at this stage, Jack. Let us first get this meeting under our belts – the slightest leak and the world will fall about us, Jack."

Chapter 33

Contacting the head of any multimillion dollar organisation is extremely difficult, and Heinrich was no exception, especially as Freda had gone. Jack went through a myriad of secretaries in an attempt locate him and was consistently informed that Heinrich was unavailable. But after a half a day of countless reasons why he could not be put through, at last he was given an email address.

> For the personal attention of Herr Heinrich:
> I am currently working at 10 Downing Street, which is the Prime Minister's office in London. It is essential that you personally return my call between 4.00 pm and 5.00 pm UK time as I must report to him at 6.00 pm. If your secretary will reply to my email, I shall be pleased to give her the direct line to the Prime Minister's office. She should then specifically ask for me and I would expect to speak with yourself. In the event that you disregard my request, I shall assume that you wish me to publicly expose you.

At 4.30 pm, the Prime Minister's office received an email. The office replied with a telephone number for her to phone, and at 5.00 pm she made the call and both men were connected.

"After we spoke last I believed that there was nothing more for us to discuss, Mr Branson. What do you want that cannot be discussed with one of my staff?"

"Herr Heinrich, it is essential for your sake that we meet again, I would be coming with Mr Tann and a representative of His Majesty's government. We have a most important message to give you that can only be discussed face to face in absolute privacy. May I suggest that we meet next week at a place of your choice."

"I cannot imagine what can be so important to make a meeting a week before Christmas, I have made plans to travel abroad which cannot be altered. Maybe in the New Year, Mr Branson. I will arrange for one of my staff to forward a time in January."

"I'm afraid not, Herr Heinrich. Any delay and you will be in danger of being seriously compromised by the press and my government. I strongly recommend that we meet next week."

There was a long silence. "Mr Branson, I don't like to be threatened, and I particularly resent your tone. Unless you can be more specific the answer is no. I will not meet you."

"If you force me to be more specific, sir, please understand that this conversation is being recorded."

There was a silence for a few seconds. "Next Tuesday in Berlin at 2.30 pm, we will forward to you the address. I will be accompanied by my lawyers," he snarled.

"I would not advice that, Herr Heinrich. There may be aspects of our conversation that you may not wish them to know."

"Damn you!" Heinrich shouted down the line.

"Till next Tuesday," Jack replied, but Heinrich had already hung up. There was now no doubt in Jack's mind that he would need to be prepared for a bloodbath – the die was cast.

Chapter 34
Miriam's Contact with Martin

Miriam had been in regular contact with Martin by email. He was constantly on the move and working his way with an entourage across the South American continent. Her chosen style was laid out in a diary format, which gave Martin a certain pleasure as if reading a novel, and he used the long evenings in his hotel room sipping a glass of whisky and musing over the possibilities. He particularly enjoyed the aspects of criminal activities which gave her writing the context of a 'Whodunit' story. However, he warned her in his replies not to draw the company into the plot itself. "Stay aloof, at least until we have an opportunity to evaluate our position."

Her reply:

We have agreed to check out the validity of the patents for Cambridge University and their lawyers have concluded that Magnum's claims can be successfully contested. However, the proof of the pudding is in the eating, therefore, we should ensure our own position in relationship to what patents we can safely use without litigation. Jack Branson who appears to be the prime shaker has for some undisclosed reason the ear of the government ministers and they have requested top security at this time to which we agreed. I ought not to be telling you this on record so I would be grateful Martin if you would wait until this business comes out into the open before conferring with anyone."

"We are planning to return to LA next week, by which time we should be in a better position to evaluate a proposal and find a basis of cooperation. We are all very excited, but the boys will be pleased to return home, and I am also missing the sunshine."

We've now been in the United Kingdom for nearly three weeks, and need to reach a reasonable understanding of what could be achieved. There now appears to be three options open to us. (a) to develop our own alternative to the Autoplug using the assistance of Cambridge. This would require new patents, and a totally fresh approach to the manufacture, software, and a means of unseating our competitors. It would probably take us three or four years before we managed to have a product. Or (b) To contest Magnum's right to the patents and registration marks in conjunction with Cambridge, and this all depends on our legal position. (c) If the British government decide to confiscate the business which would be up for grabs, but don't hold your breath. We shall know more once Branson returns from Germany. It's all quite exciting.

I'm told that you are not returning for another few weeks. We shall attempt to refine the project before you return and hopefully be able to present a clarified version by then.

We all look forward to seeing you soon in sunny LA.

With my very best wishes,

Miriam.

He read the note a few times, searching subconsciously for any minute grain of affection hiding between the lines. He had to content himself with only the word 'very', a small but meaningful addition.

Chapter 35
Inspector Polton

For Inspector Ivan Polton of the CID, the task of solving the murder of the Hines was considered a massive opportunity. Not so much in promotion but the kudos that he would gain by succeeding was important to him. There would not be many more cases of this dimension that would give him such exposure. He was due to retire soon and his relationship with the Chief Inspector had seen many ups and downs over the years but had now softened into a professional friendship. He was convinced that he had the killer, but it was essential to discover who was behind such a sophisticated and well planned crime since the Brenekovs were not capable of planning it on their own.

It was 8.00 pm and he sat in the office with the Chief sipping a whisky. Polton accepted his second glass and confided to his boss his quandary. "The witnesses that came forward regarding the Brenekov case were doubtful at their best, but they were correctly accepted by the court unless further evidence could be brought to the prosecutor. The detailed explanations of the method of entry into the house, the alarms, the gate and the fact that the security guards were all away from the house, stank. I've read through the file again and again, and interrogated the security guards, the local police on patrol and the two witness with as much vigour as I was allowed, and even a little more," he smiled "no one broke, so I decided to make a visit to the jail where Joe Brenekov was currently visiting, and with all my many years in the force I had no doubt that he was spinning a bunch of lies, but I couldn't find a twig to hold on to."

"We have to decide if this was a case of a simple burglary that either went wrong," replied his Chief Inspector, "or a more devious plan to get rid of him. Did he have any enemies? After all, he was the Minister of Health, we should follow that up as a matter of urgency. We know that it was Brenekov's gun that killed Hines and his wife. The Brenekovs are a nasty bunch and I don't doubt that they were involved, but what happened to the pieces that were stolen, maybe we should be concentrating on finding them and work backwards."

"But they've not emerged to date, sir, we've put out an international search for them but had no luck so far."

"Let's have another look at young Brenekov's actions. He claimed to have left the UK on the 26th of July which is stamped on his original passport, but his boat ride to France confirmed on the ferry's computer that his vehicle went two days later, which proves that he was in London on the date of the murder, and whilst the car registration would not in itself convict him at least it puts him in the right place. So he used his false passport to leave the country but stupidly returned on it too. Of course he wasn't aware that the French police had picked his pockets. Although his registration at his hotel in France showed the earlier date to match his own passport date. That could have been fixed, I guess, too."

"He would probably have gotten away with that if our friend in Monte Carlo had not seen his passport and recorded it."

"What else did he have on him when he was arrested?"

"What do you mean?" asked Polton.

"Goodness, Polton, you've been in this business long enough to understand. What else did he have on him? Money, trinkets, a mobile, anything that can give us a link."

"Good idea, sir, the mobile. I'll check it out again, although I'm sure our boys must have followed his belongings up as a matter of course."

"Polton you know as well as I that we can't rely on the labs or the local coppers without giving them a kick in the butt."

"You're right, I'll check."

The following morning Polton phoned the Dover jail and told them to prepare all the belongings of Brenekov for inspection. He would personally be with them at 1.00 pm. This would be his second visit.

It was a shabby prison and like most others, soulless and in need of a good coat of paint; he thought, I pity these poor bastards incarcerated here for God knows how long... they will learn to really hate the system... half of them need mental care more than prison... I've put a number of them in here over the years, he confessed to himself, but they'll come out not having learned anything nor repented and will probably do the same again.

"Will you want to see the prisoner, sir?" asked the guard.

"Not at this time officer, thanks."

He signed the form, took the box that was named Brenekov and numbered 748b and went into a small office. There would normally be a witness required at the unsealing of evidence, but he was an Inspector and they did not think of it. Perhaps it would have been an impertinence. A cup of tea and a biscuit were offered to him by an old nag. He opened his briefcase, taking out his file and a note pad, and meticulously placed them on the desk.

The wallet had a few hundred euro and a small number of English notes plus various plastic cards. He copied the numbers to discover what Brenekov might have purchased or paid for. There were various keys, and a mobile phone. The battery had fully drained and Polton returned to the main desk to see about a charger, which they were unable to find. He thought of removing the battery from his own mobile but since he would still need Brenekov's code, which without a court order Brenekov could and certainly would refuse to supply, he decided the alternative was to slip the device into his briefcase for analysis in the lab on his return. He grabbed the nettle.

There was no need to stay any longer. He locked the box and returned it to reception. "Have you removed anything from his belongings, sir?" enquired the officer in charge, rather indifferently.

"No, and thank you officer."

"Pleasure, sir!" he replied with the necessary respect.

Four hours later, he returned to his office in Scotland Yard and immediately gave the mobile to his lab to decode. "Why would this young man decide to drive to France under a false passport with a gun in his possession. There had to be a reason. Who else would he have seen?"

The following morning a brown envelope was delivered to him containing the fully charged mobile and a note with the security code. Most of the messages had been wiped. He browsed through the apps and found the photo gallery, featuring numerous scenes of his trip to France and Italy – and scrolling backwards through them he at last discovered what he had been hoping for. The pictures sent to Brenekov from his father were of Giacomettis, Modiglianis and various other works of art. Polton looked at the Hines file and confirmed these were the same pieces. The shots had been sent onto a Mr LeClare in Switzerland. "We've got him!" he shouted aloud. Without giving any warning he rushed into his chief's office. "Some heads are going to roll, but we've got him, chief!"

Immediate arrangements were made to interrogate Joe and his father. It was irrefutable evidence of the highest order. Brenekov stammered that he had been offered the art and was simply selling them on through Joe.

"Who offered them to you?" asked the detective. But Brenekov could not give an adequate answer. He was immediately cautioned and taken to prison.

"You realise that your son's mobile has photos of the stolen art sent by yourself. You have probably gotten both you and him a life sentence." But Brenekov would not respond.

Bonham was once again called to represent the Brenekovs and, given the latest evidence against them, demanded Peter Brenekov pay his fees upfront.

The discovery was soon passed to Pickles via his colleague, the Minister of Home Affairs and friend, Joanne Parley. She had now read the police file and demanded a detailed report on the cross-examination of father and son.

Chapter 36
Jack in Berlin

Once again the flight was booked as first class, this time paid for by the government. Tann still retained a serious bruise on the side of his face and a black eye that, if anyone asked, would be ascribed to a glass door.

He had been carefully primed by Horrocks whose influence now over Tann was sufficient to justify his joining them in Germany.

They had been given an address and were expecting a taxi but to their surprise a black limousine was waiting for them when they arrived. The new driver suited his vehicle and could have been mistaken for a funeral director. "Are we going to your head office?" asked Jack.

"*Nein*," he replied. "We will be going to our offices in Potsdam. One hour from here."

"Do not speak unless you want to tell a joke," whispered Horrocks, "the car is probably tapped." Tann seemed to have shrunk, he had nothing to add to his situation that would help him, it was as if he had already been tried and convicted.

Exactly one hour later they arrived at a large building clad in black glass. It had the title of Schickerdanz Infinities, which meant nothing to any of them. Jack tried to recall where he had heard the name before, and no doubt it would come back to him, but his thoughts moved to the impending meeting.

Horrocks looked down at down at Tann and mouthed: "Remember your family."

Upon arrival, they were escorted to Herr Heinrich's office. Heinrich was sitting at his desk and without looking up instructed them to sit.

"Good afternoon," said Jack, but still Heinrich did not look up and shuffled his papers.

"You are here to tell me something, well what is it?"

Horrocks stood to his full height and walked to the other side of Heinrich's desk, looking down on him, he pulled up the back of his jacket until he was dangling as if from a hanger.

"Herr Heinrich, if you want respect you have to give it, now let's start again." Heinrich's feet were no longer touching the ground. Horrocks dropped him with a thud.

"Again, Mr Branson, please."

Jack stifled a smile. "Good afternoon, Herr Heinrich," he repeated. Heinrich stared at Horrocks and considered picking up the phone, but Horrocks took another step forward.

"Good afternoon. Take a seat…please," he said begrudgingly.

"That's better," growled Horrocks. "Now, Mr Tann is going to talk to you. It's essential that you hear and understand every word he says… for your own safety, Herr Heinrich. If you cannot understand something, he will repeat it. Go ahead, Mr Tann."

Tann was sweating. He glanced at Horrocks who nodded him on. "Herr Heinrich, you will agree that I have always tried my best for you, but now I am being accused of bribery and, much worse, murder. I will be sent to jail for life, but you must tell these people that I have only done what you have asked of me. The murders, the manipulation of shares, and the money you have given me. Unless you…"

Heinrich suddenly jumped up shouting "I can't hear any more of this rubbish, how dare you accuse me of these crimes? Whatever fantasies you have imagined including me are crazy… I'm going to call the police… the lot of you will be arrested. You are in Germany now, not your country. Do you realise the power of my office? And you dare to come in and threaten me in this manner. Get out, the lot of you."

Jack saw himself in a slapstick comedy: as long as he was protected by his giant friend, his courage persisted. "You are not only involved in these crimes, Herr Heinrich, we can prove that you are the instigator of the murders of Henry Hines, his wife, Professor Baylim and probably your secretary Freda. But equally you have manipulated the shares of Autoplug which belong to Cambridge University and Ever Young, which as you know perfectly well is fraud – without doubt at least a twenty year sentence. Furthermore we believe that you are attempting to resurrect the dream of the Third Reich. An imagined racial purity that you thought would be achieved by transfixing the minds of the world through Ever Young.

"Herr Heinrich, you will be arrested within the next twenty-four hours and probably be jailed for life. That is, unless you agree to our terms." He threw onto the table photographs of the ballroom with the art, and a paper whose front page bore pictures of the same pieces under the headline Theft and Murder. "By the way, Professor Baylim's autopsy strongly suggests that he was poisoned by your cousin, who will no doubt say she worked under your instructions."

"My cousin! What are you talking about?"

"Mrs Baylim, is she not your cousin, Herr Heinrich? We have a copy of a letter she sent you, given to us by Freda."

Heinrich sat back heavily into his chair. "What is it you want?"

"We want you to resign and to pass the business back to Cambridge. We can prove in court that the patents and the brand names still belong to Cambridge University. Your Mrs Baylim was too hasty and virtually stole the brand names and patents for you, but was unable to cut the umbilical cord sufficiently. The patents are still owned by Cambridge and you have lost, Herr Heinrich. Even if we were not to consider your subsequent actions, you would lose Ever Young and the Autoplug. You stole them."

"I won't do it. Do you think you're playing with a mouse, Branson? Our global assets are worth as much as your entire UK. And we would have the backing of Brazil. You would be creating such an international incident that your government would fall. It would be your minister and his cohorts that would be disgraced. 'Murdered by the government'. That's a headline."

"Let's put it to the test," replied Horrocks. "You would have to destroy your own business to win and by doing so would expose not only your own crimes but the fortunes that your ancestors stole. You bankrupted countries and their people to finance your business. There may be pain, but I feel only one of us will be totally destroyed."

"Get out, get out!" he shouted hysterically.

Ignoring this outburst Horrocks stood so close to Heinrich that their bodies were touching.

"I wonder what your grandparents… or Goring, might have done in our position, mein Herr. Maybe they would introduce themselves to your family one by one, burn down their houses. We have a choice, and from a menu that you have created, and for my part it will be exercised with no small degree of pleasure. However, our first step is to inform your government of your behaviour. I am sure that they would not like to be reminded yet again of their past. We have nothing to hide, only you do."

It was now Jack's moment to present the official line. "I have been instructed by the Prime Minister of the United Kingdom to resolve this matter one way or another. We will give you twenty-four hours to consider your position. We want it all. Just sign it over and walk away. Retire to Brazil if you like. If we don't hear from you by tomorrow, 4.00 pm UK time, we will put all our strength behind your destruction." They glared at each other for a full twenty seconds.

Heinrich transferred his glare to Tann, "I'm very disappointed in you, Tann," he hissed "I have reinvented you, given you status and made you rich beyond measure, and you stab me in the back like this. Men like you should be obliterated from this world."

"I will leave Mr Tann in your company. No doubt you will both have a great deal to discuss," sneered Horrocks. His deep base voice reverberating around the room.

Tann stood up as if he had been given an electric shock. "What do you mean? I'm not staying here I'm coming with you," he shouted.

"No Tann it's better for you to stay here for the moment…as security. Oh, by the way I have your passport."

"I don't want him here, I never want to see this man again," spluttered Heinrich.

"I'm not giving you the option Heinrich, I've no doubt that you would look after him better than we. You must consider your position carefully—the contentious aspects of the business can take some time, but the criminal accusations will, without doubt be immediately effective. You will be arrested within days. It's your choice."

"Now, please arrange for your driver to take us back to the airport." Heinrich stared defiantly at Horrocks.

"I have asked you to arrange our return, Heinrich. Do it now." His massive frame overshadowed Heinrich again.

He picked up the phone and did what he was told "Remember, twenty-four hours," as he walked out.

***

The two of them travelled back to the airport in silence. Jack was speechless, he would never have imagined such a scene. His literal mind was already writing an essay on the day's events.

Horrocks sat in the front seat, allowing Jack the legroom he evidently needed. He appeared relaxed as if he was travelling on vacation, and seemingly had nothing to say. To Jack, thought he was awestruck and assessing Horrocks in silence, questions were so many that it was difficult to know where to begin. How does such a person evolve to command such confidence, his height and voice certainly helped, but who would dare to go against such an individual, he thought. He crushed Heinrich, one of the wealthiest men in the world, it was certainly better to have him on my side. Thank God he hasn't an opposite number, he smiled to himself.

"What's going to happen now?" Jack asked.

"He has various options. He can ignore our threats. And wait for us to do something. He's no fool and recognises that we would compromise ourselves by exposing him. He could do a runner and possibly go to Brazil bearing in mind though that he has a massive business to run. Or he could concede to us and pass the business over. It's a matter of who makes the next move. I will have to take advice from the PM. But I have my own ideas."

"Can you elucidate a little?"

"I can to you Jack since you are as deep into this exercise as I."

"So what's next on the agenda?"

"We should eliminate Tann, and possibly one of Heinrich's too, maybe his cousin. He will sit up and take notice then."

"Wow." It took a moment for Jack to digest what he had just heard, and catching his breath: "But Tann is our main prerogative, how can we justify losing two health ministers? There would be pandemonium."

"We would blame it on Heinrich, it would be his problem and consistent with his previous actions. Remember Tann is already in Germany. It wouldn't be difficult to organise his demise, nor come to think of it, Mrs Baylim. Our glorious MI5 has tentacles everywhere Jack. But I need the wink from you know who would be first."

Immediately they landed, Horrocks made his call. "We're going straight to number ten," he told Jack.

"I'm not happy about this," Jack mumbled. "We are degenerating to Heinrich's level."

"We already are, my friend. Who do you think we're protecting?" smiled Horrocks.

"The answer to that says it all."

***

The taxi stopped around the corner of Downing St in the Mall and Jack followed Horrocks to a small inconspicuous door, pressed the bell which opened electronically. Jack looked up to see a small camera. It was clearly not difficult to identify Horrocks. And anyone with him was probably considered an irrelevance.

They walked through a long narrow passage and came to yet another door which opened for them. Jack could now hear the vibrant noise from what seemed to be the power point of the country. The last door opened, and they found themselves in the inner sanctum of number ten.

"The boss is expecting you, go straight through," instructed a rather attractive young woman of only 5ft and compared to Horrocks might have been from Lilliput land.

"We did what we had to do Prime Minister, we left Tann there, Heinrich was not too pleased, but he now understands his position."

"What do you think Jack?"

"To be honest Prime Minister, I was speechless, I have learned a great deal from our friend here, but you are obviously a good many steps ahead of me. Heinrich is not going to go without a fight, I think you already appreciated that, but Tann will be in fear of his life."

"We need to make Heinrich aware that we are serious, sir," said Horrocks "I suggest that Tann should go. This can easily be arranged. It would be blamed on Heinrich."

"I would speak with my friends in Germany to inform them that they have in their midst a mad man for a chairman of Magnum," mused the PM. "We have proof that they are attempting a world domination plot. That will definitely take the onus of responsibility away from us."

"Sir, are you suggesting that Tann should be bumped off? That's a crazy idea, we would be as bad as them. I couldn't be involved in that, definitely not!" Jack shouted.

"Jack, I'm sure that I don't have to say that what we are discussing is absolutely confidential," said the Prime Minister. "These are only ideas."

"And all this is to protect the government's standing," said Jack without even thinking of his words and its consequences. "What would happen, sir, if we simply told the truth. The courts would find that Magnum stole the rights to Autoplug and return it to Cambridge and Spoken Arrow who would no doubt pick up the baton and continue to run with it. Ever Young would be revised. Tann would be scolded for his gratuities, but complimented on the efforts made. No one has to know about Professor Baylim. Is it worth all this devious MI5 business simply to protect our image? Magnum will get its comeuppance if we reveal all the facts that we know about them, without us coming down to their level." He stood with his hands by his side, like a schoolboy in front of his head master. "Prime Minister, I beg of you not to revert to murder."

"You have a point, Jack. Out of the mouths of babes. Not that you're a babe, but…nevertheless. I will speak with a few of my colleagues and arrive at a conclusion."

The following morning an email was sent to the Prime Minister's Office. From the head offices of Magnum, and signed personally by Herr Steffen Heinrich.

Sirs,

It has come to our notice that you are intending to copy our Autoplug. Please be aware that Magnum have extensive patents covering this product, and we will protect them at whatever cost. Furthermore, you have also made serious accusations relating to various deaths supposedly associated to the development of the Autoplug and Ever Young, which are completely erroneous and will be vigorously refuted. We value our reputation and will take immediate action to sue you unless you confirm that these rumours are not true.

Your own Minister of Health Mr Tann will confirm that all our negotiations with yourselves have been without any devious or underhand methods, and there is not a shred of evidence to show otherwise. Our appreciation of the work that Mr Tann has done on behalf of your own country will prove that he has only worked to benefit your own needs which we have respected. It is not within our remit to formally protect Minister Tann, but it should be said that he has acted with perfect honour, and with only your government's interests at heart. You have intimated that he has taken bribes, but we have only shown our appreciation of his work after the Autoplug was completed and proven of benefit to both parties and within the budgets formally agreed between The National Health Service of the UK and ourselves.

I would be obliged to receive formal confirmation that these rumours have no validity, and that the excellent relationship that we have built between us will be maintained.

Yours sincerely,
Steffen Heinrich Vice President Magnum, GMBH

***

The Prime Minister immediately phoned Pickles "You'd better come over George it looks like we have a problem."

"Would you believe it?" said Pickles "The audacity of the man. He's gone on the attack. It could take years to go through the courts, and if we try to stop his antics with Ever Young, he can place an injunction against us. It's possible that he has opened the door to negotiate."

The PM lit another cigarette on the last, "I think we should reply informally at this time, and call his bluff. We haven't directed our attention to Mrs Baylim who plotted the murder of her husband with the intention of passing the Autoplug to Magnum. We can bypass Tann for the moment. We also have proof that Heinrich has possession of the stolen goods belonging to the Hines."

Pickles sat and cogitated on the implications. "We should use Branson to present our case in the first instance."

"But surely by not replying we are passing the buck as it were."

"No, George, let's give him an unofficial warning that his threats will only help to bring him down if the truth is revealed. I'd rather not officially involve government replies at this stage."

"Look Alex," Pickles replied, "would it be so bad if we brought the entire business out into the open. It would prove our integrity and honesty in revealing that we have a bad penny in the camp. If we are attacked by the media we will agree with our attacker. We have three proven murders here and the arrow is pointing squarely at Heinrich. Not us."

"I appreciate your point, young Branson suggested the same action," said the PM. "But I think that we would be committing Harikari if we admitted that one or more of our cabinet was even remotely involved in murder. The Press would soon draw the wrong conclusions and a vote of no confidence would kill us. let's do this then." He continued, "I suggest that Branson replies ignoring his bluff and reaffirming Heinrich's and Tann's misdemeanours, and finally warning him that we will immediately issue arrest proceedings for murder regardless of our own consequences unless he is prepared to concede. We must write a draft and speak with Branson to put it under his own name as soon as possible."

"Leave it to me, I'll send you a copy," Pickles conceded.

***

Email to Heinrich:

Att. Herr Steffen Heinrich,
Herr Heinrich,

I am in receipt of your email which has been shown to our Prime Minister. Your rambling points to justify your actions will have no effect on us. The courts will hear of your cousin's involvement of her husband's murder in order to allow her to freely pass all relevant information onto yourselves. The murder of Minister Hines and his wife can now be associated with yourselves, and as you are aware, we have proof that you are now in possession of their stolen art.

We have the hired murderer in custody with pictures of these pieces on his mobile sent to Switzerland, the police are currently working with the Swiss authorities who will prove that you purchased them from him.

Our net is closing in on you Herr Heinrich and will cause you irreversible damage.

We are now in contact with a major competitor of yours and it our intention to close our business with Magnum. We will also be in contact with all other governments to inform them of our actions. My personal wish is to see that you receive a lifelong sentence, and for my part I would not compromise but to see you behind bars and allow Mr Horrocks (with whom you have already met) to keep his word in respect to everything that you hold dear, regardless of where you are. However, I am told that you are to be given the option of a lifeline.

According to Cambridge University's legal counsel you will owe them in loss of profits alone a considerable amount. They will also demand immediate transfer of all brands stolen from them and which they will prove in court belongs to them. We are giving you the option to concede discreetly.

This note is written on the highest advice but you should know that if you disregard it, it will be out of my hands and immediate action will be taken without further notice. You may consider the protracted battle to follow worth a twenty-five year sentence: it is up to you. *In conclusion, I should mention there is sufficient evidence to justify an immediate warrant for the arrest of Gilda Baylim and yourself.*

I am prepared to meet you one more time to discuss your position in camera. but not in Germany. In such an event, you may wish to have a legal witness with you as we will.

Herr Heinrich, do not waste your words with more ridiculous threats that have no foundation. Your future is sealed.

Sincerely

Jack Branson (Independent Consultant to the government)

***

Jack was called once again to meet with Pickles. The meeting would take place this time at Pickles home in Bayswater.

The house was beautifully positioned directly opposite Hyde Park, but had little in the way of art on show, other than a few photos of their children. Pickles wife opened the door and cheerily directed him to their drawing room where a white grand piano dominated.

He offered Jack a drink and opened the piano top. It had been converted into a cocktail cabinet.

"You have taken a lot upon yourself young man, and I'm afraid that we are going to ask you to jump even deeper into this quagmire." He showed Jack the email Heinrich had sent. After Jack read it, he sat back in his chair and sighed.

"That's what we did when we read it Jack, and the PM and I considered our options very carefully. Option number one put forward was…what would be so terrible if we exposed the situation? We would of course have a great deal of mud on our faces, but we could possibly justify ourselves by openly revealing the entire plan of Magnum, Tann and Gilda Baylim and Heinrich's actions…we would therefore be calling his bluff. Now that's where you come in. Rather than governmentalize the situation at this stage, we thought…put Branson back in the firing line one more time and see if our man bends. It would be a damned inconvenience to put this entire business on the front pages of the press, no doubt quite a few who were probably getting back-handers from Magnum, via Tann, so let's have one more try, we thought…through our Mr Jack Branson." He smiled magnanimously. "We have composed this note from you to him…see what you think and if he decides to meet, for whatever reason, we have him on our hook."

Jack read the email carefully, it was not so much the content that he was considering but his part in it, and the consequences of his actions that would significantly alter history. What would Heinrich's own government say about his ultimate plans to reincarnate Hitler's Superman theory. The murders and so on. The plot was forever thickening. "When would you want to send this reply," he asked. "Now!"

"I have been invited to a meeting at the offices of SM&F tomorrow," Jack replied. "The three representatives of Spoken Arrow and the dean of Cambridge University, plus anyone else associated with the Autoplug, are to discuss their next stage. The legality of the patents, the brand names which they are experts in, but whatever they decide will be a long haul, either to reinvent the project and the legalities that would be fought on before any action to market would be taken."

"Well, my friend," Pickles replied "you could be making their task easy since your demand would be to take the whole damn lot off Heinrich's hands for a penny, so to speak. You would have to persuade him of the benefits he would receive by losing his business. You may arrive at a compromise if he negotiates hard by allowing him to stay in the computer business. But that would be a hard won concession, if you understand."

"I understand but I can't imagine that he will agree, Minister, but it's worth a try."

"So shall we presume that you don't meet with the lawyers but inform them that they adjourn it for another few days, maybe a week, by which time a clearer picture would have emerged, and hopefully to their advantage."

Pickles phoned Jane Franklyn at her home and instructed her accordingly. It was now 11.30 pm. She threw on some clothes, jumped into her car and fifteen minutes later the email was sent from the Prime Minister's office. With Jack's name at the bottom of it.

Email from S. Heinrich to Mr J. Branson:

It is difficult for me to appreciate your naivety. How can you imagine that such unsubstantiated threats reporting imaginary events that bear no relation to reality can stand up in court. They are all fabrications of course which are categorically disputed. Our operation scans the world and has a record of honour and respectability. Do you believe that your accusations will force me to give you one of the largest companies in the world.

However I am prepared to meet you one more time, and without your Mr Horrocks who I understand beat and tortured Mr Tann into a false submission. I will meet you in Paris at the Ritz hotel next Tuesday at 2.00 pm. I shall hire a small meeting room. You will agree that you will not record anything discussed, and only one person will accompany you.

I am agreeing to this meeting only because I have appreciated working with Mr Tann and as a service to him I would wish to protect his name. I have no need to protect my own which I believe is unblemished. I will be joined by my lawyer.

Please confirm agreement to my stipulations.

Sincerely,

Steffen Heinrich Vice President Magnum, GMBH

Jack replied:

I agree.
Signed,
Jack Branson

Chapter 37

Inspector Polton had found a degree of fame. The Hines murders would have been just another unsolved file had it not been for Polton's prescience, all be it jogged along by his boss. It was quietly acknowledged that Joe's mobile should have been an obvious clue to his contacts much sooner but was overlooked and hands were smacked at the local level. Nevertheless, Polton's success was celebrated by the force and overindulged by the press. The world would now know that Joe had emailed the photos sent by his father to a Señor Alberto Jodi in Milan, and Monsieur LeClare in Geneva. One of these men was probably the agent or purchaser, and it had become Polton's quest to discover who. Either way Joe was formally accused once again of the murders of the Hines couple.

It was therefore only a matter of hours before Joe's father had a visit from the CID. and after a short discussion was arrested and taken to prison. With the deaths of the Hines the Brenekov name reverberated around the world. It was still unknown how they had planned the robbery, and as far as robberies went it was a tour de force which was considered by the police force to be far more sophisticated than the style capable of the Brenekovs. Had it not been for the gun discovered and recorded in Monti Carlo purely by chance, it would have been the perfect crime. Polton had a niggling feeling that they had worked in harmony with another party, but cross examination, now in the public domain and rather more formal than he would have liked revealed no new leads.

***

Henry Hines had taken his possessions extremely seriously, and had insured is collection accordingly. The claim in respect to the pieces taken was estimated at over eighteen million pounds which would be paid into a trust.

The Provincial Insurance Company to whom he had given substantial sums each year were understandably most cautious to pay out and only after every stone had been upturned. The method of entry, alarms and their unseen departure was of great interest, and in particular the security guards who were missing on that night, and substantial pressure was placed on the Security company, but to no avail.

It was therefore extremely welcome to hear that the Art Dealers Joe had spoken to in Switzerland and in Italy could be named, and a Mr Ervine McCrow the senior representative of the Provincial was immediately despatched. He would only fly executive and booked a five-star hotel in Milan for himself and his wife as his assistant, and early the following morning, leaving his wife at the breakfast table he left to find Señor Jodi.

Jodi recalled that Mr Joseph Brenekov had made contact with him, but as a respectable art dealer he was soon aware that this young man was not bonafide. He was definitely not interested in any art that was not registered. He claimed that he had not seen any pictures or knew what was being offered.

Mc Crow had travelled the world with his company for over twenty years and had learned early on that very few humans tell the truth when they either make claims or handle stolen goods especially when they see a bargain. But he believed Jodi, not because he thought him honest, but simply because there was no further contact between Brenekov and Jodi he felt that the man was not lying in this instance.

For his second port of call, he decided not to inform M. LeClare that he was coming, he knew that if the man had something to hide he would melt into the ether. And since he had already decided that Jodi was innocent and only two names were on his list, the likelihood that LeClare was his man rose by a hundred percent. The poor man was therefore guilty by default.

His usual practice was to visit either very late, say 11.00 pm when he rather enjoyed finding them often in compromised situations, or early morning, say 7.15 am, often having breakfast or just waking up with a fuzzy mind.

On this occasion, as he had booked into a five-star hotel and decided to enjoy its benefits once again leaving his wife to enjoy the stores in Geneva, he chose early. For a nominal fee and extra authenticity, he enlisted the assistance of a Swiss policeman. Although the majority of Switzerland's population's first language is German, Genevans speak predominantly French. McCrow's French was heavily encrusted with a Scottish brogue, but he enjoyed speaking in another Gallic tongue even though it was barely recognisable to those listening.

M. LeClare was not noted in either the directory nor online, he had found his address from the voting lists available in the local library, and exactly as he had planned he rang the bell of a rather sumptuous villa overlooking the Lake Geneva at exactly at 7.15 am. And waited. He stood outside in minus 7 degrees below zero for approximately ten minutes before concluding that nobody was going to open the door for him. His friendly policeman took upon himself to wonder around the perimeter of the house looking through windows. All was still. The car was in the garage and looking into the kitchen he could see fresh flowers and a fruit bowl on the table. The next window was almost completely curtained, but he was able to peak through to see the naked bodies of a man and woman laying across the bed in a very still position. It was clear from their positions that they could not be sleeping. He wrapped on the window, but there was no response. He ran back to the front. "What's the problem," asked McCrow.

"Monsieur McCrow, it seems that we have an interesting situation. Your friend seems rather dead."

The policeman threw himself at the front door and it flew open. It did not take too much time to observe the blood on the bed and declare that both LeClare and a rather beautiful woman had been shot. Papers were scattered around and whoever murdered the couple was looking for something. There was still jewellery on the dressing table, a Rolex watch and other objects of value.

McCrow's disappointment was obvious – he had a bounty hunters' agreement with his company for two percent which in this case clearly worked out at nothing. There were papers strewn over the floor, but he was unable to understand them as they were in Russian. He picked them up and stuffed them into his brief case along with the Rolex and proceeded his hunt from room to room, but there was no sign of any of the articles on his list. Returning to the UK, he submitted his report and the papers he found, which were dutifully reported to the police but deemed of no relevance to the matter at hand.

***

Inspector Polton's workload was ever increasing. Terrorism in the major cities throughout the United Kingdom required far more men than he had available. He yearned for the old days of a bobby plodding the streets or cycling around his patch. His crooks were now of a bygone age, they were characters and spoke his language. That was now a distant dream. Computer crimes necessitated a language that was beyond his comprehension; software had become too sophisticated; emails now replaced the telephone, even talking to someone next door; and he often found it difficult to understand even his own staff. He sat looking at the screen of his computer, throwing his eyes across a myriad of messages most of which were irrelevant, when his phone rang.

"You have a call Inspector from a Mr Ervin McCrow of the Provincial Insurance. Shall I put him through? He says that it's important."

"OK," he reluctantly conceded.

"Thank you for speaking with me, Inspector. I work with the claims division of the Prudential, and have been investigating the loss of the Hines robberies. I believe that you have some involvement in this case."

"Yes, I do, Mr McCrow. Do you have any information regarding this matter?"

"I followed up a lead in Switzerland to the dealer who was purported to sell on the various works of art, a Mr LeClare, living in Switzerland, but when we arrived at his home we found him and a young lady both dead. They had been murdered. We – that is the Swiss police and I – looked for clues, but other than a batch of scattered papers that had no relevance to the crime there were no obvious leads. We know that he either purchased or acted for a buyer for the works of art from the Brenekovs but we don't know to whom he sold them. I am wondering if you have any information regarding this matter."

"No, I don't, but I'm surprised that this information hasn't been released to us. How did you know of this man LeClare?"

"His name was passed to us by your department, it came from Joe Brenekov's mobile phone, you should have been aware of that, I would have thought," he replied rather too sarcastically.

Deflecting the inference "Two more murders," he mumbled. "It couldn't have been the Brenekovs, and in any event there was no benefit since they were already being charged with murder. When can we meet Mr McCrow. Maybe we can find a route to the killers and the stolen goods too." They fixed a date for the following week, but there was little more that McCrow would probably be able to tell him.

As soon as he put down the phone he drew up the files on his computer. The question still remained as to who gave the Brenekov's instructions. Brenekov Senior said that he received a detailed plan to rob and assassinate Hines from a Russian Mafia. He stated that they contacted him leaving no return numbers and had no point of contact. However if LeClare didn't have the goods he must have forwarded them onto another address. He would not have unpacked them and used a carrier to wherever they were going. We need to find that carrier. Whoever purchased the art would probably have murdered LeClare, and was behind the Hines murders.

The Brenekov trial was due to be heard at the beginning of February, the prosecution had now taken into custody all three Brenekovs for the murders of Hines and the burglary, and it would no doubt hit the headlines again. It would be an ideal opportunity for Polton to retire with glory. He might even write his memoirs. "Real Life crime by the man who solved them, Inspector Polton." He could fill a tome. Anything to release him from this utter boredom of the new age of computers, he thought.

In view of the enormity of their crimes, all the Brenekovs were refused bale. They were now residing in Wandsworth Prison and Polton decided to visit them individually to see if there were any more undiscovered secrets that a lesser investigator would have missed. He would tempt them with the chance of minimising their sentences, even though it was not in his power to do so. There was no doubt in his mind that they were incapable of pulling off such a sophisticated burglary without a superior brain behind them.

If this was a political murder, it would open a possibility that Hines was only the first of many. That would certainly make headlines.

Accompanied by an attractive female officer in plain clothes, he arranged to meet the Brenekovs once again adopting a softer approach. The meeting would take place in the governor's office. Tea and biscuits were offered and they sat in armchairs rather than the hard investigative metal chairs usually available and no one other than the three were present. A camera and recorder were discreetly placed in the corner of the room and Peter Brenekov was brought in.

"Peter, thank you for speaking with me. My name is Harry Polton and I am an Inspector and this is my assistant, Jennifer. You may be wondering why I have requested this meeting."

Brenekov simply shrugged. "What do we have to lose?" He replied.

"We've been studying some of the aspects of the Hines deaths and we're here today to try to see how we can unravel this mess that you and your family have gotten yourselves into. I personally believe that there are other angles that need to be investigated that may help you and your brother, and even Joe. If we can help you, are you prepared to work with us?"

Peter Brenekov had many years of dealing with the police, and was well aware of their techniques, but this was a little more original, he thought. "So, what is it you want to know Inspector?"

"We're talking off the record here, but I personally don't believe that you or your brother should be implicated in the Hines murder, and there is no strong evidence that it was planned by you. That means there would be an argument as to whether you had anything to do with the burglary either."

Jennifer stood up to pour tea for the three of them, "Do you take sugar Mr Brenekov?"

"Two please, Jennifer. So, what do you want me to tell you that will prove your faith in us Inspector Polton?" He replied with more than an essence of cynicism.

Polton could see that he had not yet gained Brenekov's trust, and hadn't expected to. However, he was determined to play the part to the end. "I don't know if you are aware the prosecution is considering involving both of your wives as well, taking into account that you are such a close family and they would have knowledge of your actions. I think that's nonsense, but they want to throw the book at you. What would you be prepared to offer me if I could bring down your sentence to, say, three to five years, and of course your brother's?"

"It all depends what say you want to know, and I'll see if I can oblige. Jennifer, do you think I could have one more lump?"

She stood up, straightened her skirt and passed him the sugar bowl and the biscuits.

"We're not simply dealing with a normal killing here, Peter. This man was a minister in the government, if it was a political Murder, it would change things dramatically. With the greatest of respect, your reputation does not stretch to anything like that, wouldn't you agree."

"You're absolutely correct, I accept that we have a reputation, but by these standards, it's small fry."

"We think there's a lot more to their killing than a botched up burglary. Someone organised this killing and gave you the small change. If it hadn't been for your son's migraine he would have gotten away with it, but it wasn't your style, too out of character. Peter, I need to know who was behind this murder, forget about the bunce, if these people can kill one minister by proxy, anyone in our government is vulnerable, even the Prime Minister. Do you get my point? There's no gain in sticking you chaps behind bars for the rest of your lives when a third party can anonymously assassinate anyone they choose, if not by a Brenekov then a young stooge within another gang. I need your help and we'll give you ours."

"I hear you Inspector, but I really don't know how to help you. Even If I told you that there was another party involved I wouldn't be able to tell you who they were…and if I did know who they were, I and probably my family would be dead ducks within days. You probably know that better than me."

"OK, let's imagine that you knew who they were but had no contact with them. Say they phone you on a particular day, we might be able to discover the number. We could give you and your family protection, change your address and

283

names. What have you got to lose. Your trial comes up soon and without help you'll both get life."

He sat back to watch Brenekov absorb the proposition. Jennifer offered him a cigarette which was refused, and another cup of tea which he accepted. And they sat and waited for his comments.

He took his eyes off Polton and looked at the young policewoman, younger than his daughter and probably quite innocent. What's it all about? he thought. I've brought my family to their knees and for what?

"Can I speak with my brother?"

"Sure. I can call him up now if you like, we would wait outside."

"Will he get a cup of tea and a biscuit too?"

Polton laughed, "Sure, Jennifer will sort him out."

He immediately picked up the phone and asked for William Brenekov to be escorted to the Governor's office.

Fifteen minutes later Bill Brenekov entered with his guard. Peter had not seen him for over four weeks. It was immediately obvious that he was not faring well.

"Bill we've been having a chat and I'd like Peter to tell you what we are considering. Let us leave the two of you to talk, let's say fifteen minutes. We'll wait outside."

"Oh, the tea and biscuits are on the table, help yourselves."

They closed the doors and waited a few moments before switching the camera and speaker on.

The two brothers hugged one another, it was obvious that they had a deep affection for each other, but they stayed together rather longer whispering and clearly aware that they were being viewed from a camera somewhere in the room. They huddled into a corner and spoke too softly for their audience to hear them. After fifteen minutes Polton knocked on the door and entered.

"I'm sorry if we spoke a little too softly for you," he sneered, "but we have given some thought to what you are offering and would be prepared to cooperate. However, if you are so keen for us help you Inspector, we will need something in writing. There's no point in jumping from the frying pan into the fire is there. Are you prepared to give us a written guarantee that you will protect us and our family, and shorten our sentences?"

"That depends on what you have to offer us doesn't it," replied Polton.

"It's a chicken and egg standoff, isn't it? Listen Inspector, we would be daft not to accept an offer, but we're too old and have been on these swings too many times to be fooled. If you say you'll honour your promise, then put something in writing, and we'll tell you whatever we know. It's up to you. Otherwise thanks for the tea and biscuit – sorry, biscuits."

"I'll tell you what gentlemen, if what you tell us helps us get the schemers who gave you instructions, we will honour our deal and will make it so you are shown as reformed characters helping the police, despite the danger you are placing your family in."

"And what if we give you what we think is important information and it comes to nothing?"

"Then my friends, it's nothing. You can't have the cake and eat it."

The two brothers looked at each other and shrugged. They noticed Polton and Jennifer were looking for their coats and the meeting was over. "OK, if we are being recorded I want our agreement to be on it too, OK?"

"You know, Peter, I like you. You may be a rogue but in another time we could have been friends. I'm just sorry you wasted your energy on being bent. But, off the record, I do like you, and if I can help you, I will." He sat, putting his hands on his lap.

"Let's start with telephone calls, like when you first received a call, how did you make a first contact, the sort of thing that could give us a lead. We need to find the source."

"I understand," he replied. "I will need to speak with my wife and see if we can find the information that you want. Can we make a visit to our home? We live next door each other."

"Only if you are under close escort, I'm afraid."

"That's OK."

"Can I see my daughter as well?"

"Only if she's there at the time."

"Can we stay the night?"

"Don't push it."

"Tomorrow," said Polton.

The following morning at 8.00 am both Brenekovs were dressed in the clothes they had arrived in and installed in a police car. Their wives had been informed and had prepared food. They were told it was an official meeting to gather information that might be relevant to the courts. However, their husbands would be under constant surveyance. Polton arrived at their house earlier and introduced himself to the girls. Once again he was joined by Jennifer, who adopted the same relaxed approach, complimenting them on their décor, and soon began a friendly conversation. "There are no holds barred here, Barbara, we need inside information and we will help your men in return," stated Polton.

"We'll tell you whatever we can," they agreed. He waited to ask any further questions until their husbands arrived.

At last the car arrived with the two men plus their escorts.

There were no handcuffs used and the homecoming was with tears as expected. They sat in the lounge where coffee and cakes were set out. An onlooker might have seen them as a Sunday gathering. In such a short time, Bill had lost a considerable amount of weight and the women could only look with tearful eyes.

"OK, so let's begin at the beginning. Tell me how the first seed of this situation emerged. It was so out of your normal style that you're well known for, did you get a call, a face book message, what?"

Barbera looked at her husband. "Go ahead," he replied. "What have we got to lose, tell him."

"A guy named Sam Beaty first contacted us, we knew him from years ago, and asked us if we were interested in doing a special job. It's worth a lot, he said, and if we were interested he would get someone to contact us. We asked who they were and after a bit of persuasion he told us they were Russian. When I asked him to expand on that he just said the Russian mafia or something like that. I passed the message onto Peter and Bill and waited for a call. We didn't think any more about it but after about two weeks we received a call from a man. I think his name was Min something. He had a very heavy accent. Peter spoke with him, and details were given to us in very specific detail, they had checked every aspect of the job, the security guards, alarms, gates, the exact timing, you name it they had checked it."

"Excellent, now can you say exactly when you took this first call and the subsequent calls? And do you have a contact with Sam Beaty? If we can find him he would be a great jumping off point."

"I should tell you this Inspector," said Bill, "these men are corporate contract killers, if there was even a sniff that we are involved in finding them we would be blown away and so would Sam."

Polton leaned forward, and almost whispering "Listen, if we can prove that they are the instigators of the Hines murders and find out who is behind this plot, because of your support we can say that you were told to kill or be killed. It wouldn't exonerate you but it will make a massive difference to your fate. Find me the number of Sam Beaty and the dates, and we can start the ball rolling. You may even need to move home, but we will make sure you're protected."

Barbara went into the office and Polton followed. She took out a large Filofax and Polton could see that she was closely attached to everything the Brenekovs were involved in.

The Filofax index page had a long list of numbered sections and she ran her finger down two pages of headings, probably details of different jobs that they had been involved in. It was run as a business like any other. "I'm surprised that you don't put your details on a computer," he remarked.

"It's not a good idea to put our records on a computer Inspector…for obvious reasons."

"Would you mind if I had a look at your book, just out of curiosity?" he asked rather cheekily.

She looked shocked, "Sorry Inspector, as from now this book doesn't exist," she grinned.

"But I have found a number for you." She tore a piece of paper from the pad and wrote the telephone number of Sam Beaty, quickly closing the fila fax and locked it away.

"That's a great start. Well done. Do you have any record of the telephone dates on record too."

"No, but it was about around February of last year when we had a call from Sam. I think he's from Birmingham. So probably a couple of weeks or so later they called."

Returning to the lounge and having tea and cake with the police was a bazaar experience. Polton casually asked when and how the Brenekovs chose their way of life. The following hour was taken up with an array of adventures during their youth. "We dragged ourselves out of poverty by whichever way we could," said Bill. "It became a way of life. We have tried not to hurt anyone, but looking back I would have preferred to have been a lawyer. In fact, my daughter is studying law." Taking a sip of tea, and in a reminiscing mood and attempting to justify himself. "We've helped a lot of people as well you know. It's tough being on the wrong side of the law. I'm not proud of what we've done, but it's a bit late now to change," he mused.

"I would agree with that," replied Polton.

It was time to leave and the men kissed their wives and left them crying.

Polton considered that he had them in the palm of his hand. "Thank you for tea and your cooperation ladies."

It was late afternoon when Polton returned to his office, it had been a good day. He immediately gave the telephone number of Sam Beaty to his Sargent. "I want you to find the address of this man, and any information, previous convictions and what they were, anything that you can find. It's most important, and don't show this information to anyone else except me. OK."

The Brenekov telephone number was sent to the lab and checked for all incoming calls for the months of February and March of the previous year. "I will want to know the names of every caller, and if possible by tomorrow."

The list was shown to Barbara who identified all the calls which were mostly domestic with the exception of four calls, all from the same caller, and although registered as unlisted, showed a Russian name "Mintov."

On checking him out, it appeared that he worked within the Russian Embassy. The MI5 had records of every diplomat entering the UK. There were very few outgoing calls on his main line to Moscow, but standing out, he noted two incoming calls from Berlin. Polton thanked his Sargent for a good job.

"The Brenekovs didn't make any calls to this number, sir, but we found two calls from Mintov to the Brenekovs. There may have been more but they would have probably been on his mobile."

"We might as well find out who the German calls were. If you can't check by our system, get someone who can speak German to call them and find out who they are."

The following day he received an email to confirm that the call came from a company called Schickerdanz "We have managed to get details of Sam Beaty Inspector, he's got an interesting history this chap, mostly small time burglary, blackmail which he got five years for, and a few other bits and pieces. Do you want us to visit him?"

"No, phone him first, and if he answers, hang up. We'll call on him at 8.00 am tomorrow."

As planned, Polton took the train the evening before, and booked into a local hotel. He was collected at 7.30 am by a local police car and was knocking on Mr Sam Beaty's door on the dot of 8.00 am.

Sam was seen looking out of his window. He cursed his stupidity for being seen and would have had his wife say he was away but now had no option but to open the door.

"Sam Beaty, I'm Inspector Polton. CID," he smiled. "Would you mind if we come in and ask you a few questions?"

"Why," he asked "I ain't done nuffin'."

"Don't worry Sam," consoled Polton "If there is anything we should know about you, I guess you wouldn't tell us, but I'm looking for some information and believe you could help, but what's a cockney doing in Birmingham. Haven't the Brummies got enough clever Dicks already?"

"Blimey, a copper with a sense of 'umour, that's a new one. Anyway my wife's a Brummy. What d'you want?" He looked outside to see if the neighbours were watching. "You didn't 'ave to park right outside my 'ouse did you. I'm goin' straight these days, I'm finished with my old life."

"Good for you Sam, but I'm particularly interested in a contact that you passed on to some old friends of yours. Do you know the Brenekov family?"

"I ain't seen them for years guv'nor. I know they're in trouble but I ain't got nothin' to do with it."

"I know you don't, Sam, but you gave their name to a Russian. Can you remember who it was?"

Sam's face went white. "I don't know what you're talkin' about guv'nor! Anyways I don't know no Russians."

"Listen Sam, we know that these guys are dangerous, but if you can remember their names or a name and won't tell us we could find something to pin on you and put you away for another three years. But if you think you'd be in danger we can protect you."

Sam's wife appeared in her dressing gown, "It's the cops," she blurted, "what've you been up to Sam?" she shouted.

"It's alright, Mrs Beaty, we're just asking your husband if he can remember a particular person we are trying to find. Maybe you can help!"

"She don't know nuffin' and If I told you one single name I would be a goner, boss," answered Sam, "I don't mind doing a little time but I don't fancy being killed, that's for sure."

"Does the name begin with Min?" persisted Polton.

"I don't know nuffin'," he repeated.

"I'll tell you what, Sam," He stopped mid-sentence. "Officers, please wait outside for a minute."

The two policemen looked at one another querulously and left, closing the door behind them.

"OK. You know, Sam, that the Brenekovs are accused of murdering a minister of the government and his wife."

"Sure, it was 'eadlines."

"Well, we don't believe that this was a burglary gone wrong, and we are determined to get the people who organised this job. It's political. Now, you don't have to be mentioned in anything relating to the Brenekov business."

"Well I don't know nuffin' and I ain't ready to be killed."

"We just need to know who instructed them in the first place, and I promise your name won't even be mentioned, but if you can simply confirm to me that the name I have just given you is the bloke you gave to the Brenekovs. It's worth two grand in cash. If it's not and you have another name, I'll add another grand to it. It's that important."

He looked at his wife. "What do you think Betty?"

"If they know the name already they're goin' for 'im, so it seems no harm."

"Mintov, that was 'im and there was another bloke too, Topolski, I 'ad a deal with them a few years ago. Tough bastards, the both of 'em. Anyway he contacted me out of the blue last year and asked me for a name in London that could do a job, he didn't tell me what it was except it was worth a lot to the right person, I asked 'im what was a lot, and he said 'really a lot'…it needed an organised plan and I'm a one man show so I gave Brenekov a call. They said they could be interested so I passed on the name. That was it. I got a thousand for the favour, which was nice. That's it."

"That's two names, Sam. You'll have an envelope in through your letter box tomorrow."

"I don't want no trouble guv'nor."

"Don't worry, you'll be safe as houses."

***

It was relatively easy to find the Mintov address. Alexander Mintov lived in a salubrious apartment in Kensington. However, any contact with Russians is difficult and dangerous, especially if they have diplomatic immunity. They are very tricky, and well connected, but Polton had nothing to lose by making a visit. This time he was accompanied by a plain clothed sergeant. They wore their Sunday best to give the feel of authority, "All the worlds a stage sergeant, we dress for the part."

"What are we trying to discover, boss?" asked the sergeant.

"We want to know who gave them instructions to kill Hines sarge, and why. He is sure as hell not going to tell us unless he gets something out of it, or even better, is going to lose out by not telling us. He's probably making too much money to be bribed, so we'll go for the second option." "What's that?" Asked the sergeant.

"You'll see," winked Polton.

On Sunday at 9.00 am, they arrived at the Riviera Wharf Apartments, a fifteen storey deluxe block off Kensington High Street. The reception phone in the lobby didn't list any occupants but had a button marked administrator, and since Polton had no idea which apartment to call, he was obliged to press that button.

"Can I help you," responded a rather sophisticated female voice.

"I am trying to contact Mr Mintov. Can you please give me his apartment number?"

"Can I have your name please? I shall tell him you're waiting."

"Yes, Inspector Polton from the CID."

"Just a moment, sir." The phone went dead for a few moments. "I'm sorry, sir, but he can't see you today, maybe you could come back tomorrow."

Polton's voice hardened "No, he needs to see me now or I will come back with official authority."

"Just a moment sir," she replied, totally indifferent to his tone, as if he had lost a kitten. "Please go to the 14th floor apartment 1408." He rang the bell and waited. He could hear movement and after a further three minutes with a few more bangs Mintov opened the door. "Mr Mintov, my name is Inspector Polton this is Sergeant Brand. May we come in?"

"What do you want?"

"I could tell you out in the hall here or you might like to know in private."

He was a tall gaunt man in his 50s still wearing his dressing gown. A young woman popped her head out, a good looking redhead maybe in her early thirties, and probably not his wife.

"Come in, what is it you want," he barked.

"Mr Mintov, we don't yet have a warrant for your arrest, but it would not be difficult to get one. However I'm looking for information that you may not believe is more important than you."

"Your arrogant attitude is unnecessary, Polton, I have done nothing to concern myself with your empty threats. So say what you have to say and then you can leave." The woman entered, "Would you like a coffee or tea?" she asked unknowingly.

"They don't want anything," he grunted.

"The subject matter is Brenekov, Mr Mintov. We have evidence that Instructions were given by you last year to murder Minister Hines and his wife.

291

This represents a life sentence, even for a member of the exclusive group with diplomatic immunity."

"This is ridiculous. I know nothing about this business, and unless you leave now I will throw you both out."

"Mr Mintov, you are dealing here with me as the official body of the King's Crown. The next meeting could be with six large policemen with heavy boots and armed. I suggest you listen carefully to what I have to say, and yes, we would love two cups of coffee with sugar please, madam."

Mintov snapped his fingers and his attractive lady turned on her heel.

"We are after bigger fish than you, and I want to know who they are. If you won't tell me you will be locked into the Brenekovs' activities, and don't think you will go back to your country, you would spend a nice twenty year holiday in a British prison. Does the name Schickerdanz mean anything to you."

"If I could help you with your enquiries," he pronounced the words with no small degree of sarcasm "what would I benefit?"

"OK… Mr Mintov at this moment you are being accused as an accomplice to the murders of Mr and Mrs Hines and the robbery of their valued works of art. We have enough evidence to put you away for the rest of your life. However I have given you a lifeline; you can take it or leave it. I need information which you have. If I find that your information leads us to your masters, we will consider how best to support your diplomatic status, which you so much cherish. I will give you until 2.00 pm this afternoon to tell me what you want to do. In the meantime I will place a guard outside your door. And you will not leave these premises."

"That's ridiculous! In any event I would need permission before I told you anything."

"Maybe you'd prefer to come down to the station with us now as an accomplice to murder."

"Should you wish to make a statement and explain in detail your part in this affair we will remove the guard but of course you will not be allowed to leave the country. If you don't want to cooperate with the law of this country we will arrest you, and to hell with your diplomatic immunity. Do you understand. This afternoon we will come with hand cuffs, it's up to you whether we use them."

Mintov was a raging fire and ready to explode, glaring at Polton as if to kill him.

"*Do you understand?*" he suddenly yelled into his face, "Say: 'Yes, I understand, sir.'"

"Yes, I understand" he replied, whilst muttering under his breath in Russian.

Sargent Brand asked for a chair and sat outside the apartment, "I'll find a replacement for you in one hour, sergeant. Under no circumstance should he leave here without my permission."

"Yes sir, where are you going?"

"I'll be back at 2.00 pm," replied Polton, not actually answering. "We'll see what happens this afternoon." He took the car keys from Brand and drove back home to have a prearranged lunch with his wife.

He had surprised himself how the case was beginning to fit together.

***

Sunday lunch was just being put on the table, "Good timing," she commented "You seem very pleased with yourself."

"I am. Francis, I really shouldn't be here, but you are more important and who could resist your beef. This is going to be the best case of my career. I'm going to solve this Hines murder and present it to the boss on a plate. This case will make the headlines," he announced.

He saw this as a celebratory meal, gulping down the last dregs of a glass of wine, kissed his wife, and returned to Kensington.

Sergeant Bland was still sitting outside; his replacement hadn't come. "No activity, boss."

It was exactly 2.00 pm and he rang the bell. There was no reply. He knocked hard on the door, but again there was nothing. "Break the door down, Brand." He attempted a kick but it was constructed too well. "Run down to the porter and see if they have a security key." The sergeant took the lift and five minutes later, returned with the porter. He took a bunch of keys and worked his way through them until he found the correct one. Polton was now sweating. "Is there a fire exit in each apartment?" he asked.

"Only out of the window, but it's a risky ladder to the floor below when you can get into the building via a balcony."

"Damn! Damn! Damn!" he shouted. Polton realised that he had made a cardinal mistake by leaving the apartment without checking the alternative exits. But a fourteenth floor, who would have thought. If this was reported, he would be a laughing stock. "What could I have been thinking?" he said half aloud. They searched the flat, Mintov had left his computer, and had just taken their bare necessities. "I want the place thoroughly searched and a twenty-four hour watch on this apartment," he told the Sargent. "Let's at least take the computer and, if we can, find out the name of the girl."

Not many staff work on Sundays and Polton's offices were no exception. Nevertheless he placed the computer on his desk and plugged it in. It needed a code and nothing would be achieved until the staff returned tomorrow.

"I'll get the bastard!" he shouted.

Chapter 38
Heinrich and Branson Meeting

It was a week before Christmas and the airports were beginning to take the strain of millions escaping the British climate.

The Prime Minister himself had suggested Jack should be accompanied by a top barrister. Mrs Hermione Steinberg was a lady in her fifties, elegantly attired and of a commanding disposition. She was a senior partner in one of the most respected firms in the country and well known for its high profile litigation. He could see immediately that she would not be a silent partner and had read in detail every aspect of the current situation.

They arranged to meet at a coffee shop in terminal two at Heathrow, and it was immediately clear that their relationship would remain formal as they compared their notes on the plane.

Mrs Steinberg generated an air of authority that reminded him of his head master. A blue stocking English accent and years of giving instruction. The flight gave her an opportunity to weigh up not only the task before them, but also Jack whom she was notably evaluating which somewhat diminished Jack's confidence.

They arrived at the Ritz early and were directed by the Concierge to a meeting room on the second floor. Tea and biscuits followed. They had discussed on the plane the modus operandi and the various possibilities that could result. He was notably impressed by her professional style and was happy to watch her dissect the implications as if it was a lesson in anatomy.

It was agreed that the opening presentation should be made by Mrs Steinberg. Smoothing the ground rather than digging up previous arguments. "In my opinion Mr Branson, it was a mistake to bring in Horrocks, I don't believe that any agreement can be made by using violence. Logic and compromise invariably win the day."

"I would normally agree with you Mrs Steinberg but we are dealing with a very powerful and volatile individual here, and in my limited experience one has to follow the mood of the moment which has brought us to this hotel today." "We shall see," she replied unconvinced.

Heinrich arrived at 2.15 pm with an elderly bearded gentleman He was a short bald man well over seventy, but impeccably dressed and holding a silver topped walking stick with a degree of aplomb. They removed their coats and made all necessary introductions. He was introduced as Herr Schreiber and claimed to be a 'legal colleague' of the Heinrich family and probably of a similar status as his opposite number. Heinrich stood silent and clearly defiant.

Coffee was poured and both parties placed papers in front of themselves.

Mrs Steinberg began. "First of all, gentlemen, I would like to lay out the facts as I understand them, if that is acceptable to you."

"By all means," replied Schreiber. "Shall we speak in English, French or in German?" he asked politely.

"For my part, Herr Schreiber, my German is quite fluent, but for the convenience of Mr Branson I believe English would be appropriate. And thank you for your courtesy."

"Let us go back some eight or nine years, before Magnum became formally involved with the Autoplug. Professor George Baylim and his team were working on the Autoplug. They were part of the Cambridge University Neurological department who had agreed to finance their research which they were aware would take a considerable time to perfect. There is confirmation that they were pleased with the progress made. A staff of twelve were permanently placed at the disposal of Baylim whose salaries were paid by Cambridge. Regular reports were submitted to monitor their progress, and approximately two years into the project the government agreed to allocate substantial funds to assist the project to become a reality.

"In order for the Autoplug to be effective, a number of departments within the UK government would be asked to transfer all their software in respect to every individual on their records in order that they would feel assured there was no doubt of the machines totally assimilating the information accurately. A cash flow was calculated of some millions as the project became a reality, Baylim began looking for outside sources of finance on behalf of the university. Substantial grants for the Autoplug were negotiated by the government.

Concurrent to that, the concept behind the Ever Young project was conceived by Baylim and his team. A brilliant DNA breakthrough. Please excuse my lack of technology, Herr Schreiber – I'm a simple lawyer," she smiled.

Schreiber was busy taking notes. "Please continue," he replied.

"Thank you. The original plan was to direct Ever Young towards young children and after considerable tests they could announce that substantial benefits to health and longevity could be achieved by injecting youngsters with a microchip. By this time, patents had been placed on both these projects under the name of Cambridge University."

"Now I would like to come to Mrs Baylim. A brilliant academic lecturing in Cambridge who was formally Miss Schickerdanz. A name that I'm sure you will know Mr Heinrich. We understand she is your cousin. She married Baylim, joined him in his research, and quickly took control due to her demanding personality. She soon formed a new company with her husband and wrote on Cambridge headed paper that they would be prepared to transfer the shares over to the new company.

"She wrote at least two letters to yourselves at Magnum which were filed, and we have copies referring to her progress in bringing the both the projects back to Germany."

"Working closely with the Health Minister Mr Brendon Tann who, because of his position and contacts with many other ministers and civil servants was able to negotiate across government circles to encompass all the necessary details of the population and enter it into the Autoplug software, we understand that Magnum, through the good offices of Tann gave substantial financial encouragement to a number of Ministers which dramatically speeded the project along."

"Bearing in mind that the company was still not trading, it was considered an academic exercise, to give it some minimal value, and she was able to go under the radar of Cambridge. Acting on behalf of Cambridge and unbeknown to them she sold their interest to her newly formed company for a pittance, and then passed the technical specifications of the company over to Magnum. George was extremely saddened that he had lost control and spoke at length to his colleague Dr Ellsworth regarding the situation."

"He suddenly developed a virus and was admitted to hospital, sent into an induced coma and died. An autopsy was requested but rejected by both his wife and Mr Tann from the department of health. However, he was exhumed only a few weeks ago on the request of his doctor and with the permission of the Home Office, and the results proved categorically he was poisoned. We understand his demise was caused by a poisonous plant named *Gelsemium elegans*, on record as used by Russian assassins."

"This is all nonsense," interrupted Heinrich. "I'm not listening to your rubbish but—"

"Let her finish," said Schreiber, as he put his hand on Heinrich's arm.

"Thank you once again Mr Schreiber." She looked down at her notes and turned a page.

"So let us now move over to Mr Tann who was, as we know, Health Minister. His colleague and assistant Minister of Health Mr Henry Hines. Hines was a dynamic young barrister who came from wealthy stock and had recently entered politics. He was marked as a possible leader of a party in time. However, it is recorded that he and Tann had serious disagreements. Tann decided to retire claiming a heart condition and Hines is appointed in his place.

"The Autoplug was now well established and, totally under the Magnum umbrella, generating billions, with Ever Young is to be launched imminently. But it did not suit Magnum to direct its benefits to children and so they redesigned it to be inserted into young adults, and by placing the chip in the cerebral cortex it could be used as a controller – please excuse my broad description. Hines strongly decried Ever Young at a ministerial meeting and three days later, he was killed."

"That has nothing to do with me!" he shouted again.

"Please let me continue. The murderers who shot him and his wife have been caught. They had also stolen very valuable works of art that have been seen and photographed in your house in Germany. We also believe that your PA was so disillusioned with you that she was prepared to tell us of a number of other incidents; but she was conveniently run down by a truck on her way to meet Mr Branson in Cologne. We will of course interview the truck driver."

"Under normal circumstances, the history of your company would have been disregarded, even the source of the vast fortunes that you a appear to be using as your financial base in Brazil. Its origins would also be interesting. But your ultimate objectives have now become clear. Little has been said of the termination of the 'Healthy ninety-five-year-olds' and we now understand by your own recorded words that this final moment is determined by computer which is controlled by yourselves with the press of a button. By the same token, we understand that you can communicate via the 351 microchip to change moods and patterns of behaviour. Millions would be under the control of Magnum. Prisoners, armies, even disabled, and whomever else you chose. It is clearly a Fourth Reich policy of Man and Superman, Magnum being the Superman."

"This was never to be our intention!" Heinrich shouted.

Without slowing her presentation, she continued. "In isolation there can be no doubt that the Autoplug is an outstanding invention and giving great support to the medical profession and public. But aligned to the Ever Young, Magnum could now avail themselves to their ultimate plan of eugenics or at least the minimisation of those individuals or groups that in their eyes are not worthy of existing."

Heinrich's face was now red with anger. It seemed that another word would have him explode. Mr Schreiber was also aware of his boiling point.

"Mrs Steinberg, I am accumulating points that you are accusing Herr Heinrich of, and if they were true I am sure that he would have been jailed long ago."

"Mr Schreiber," she smiled. "You are stating the obvious. There are a number of politicians whom we know have been bribed including Tann in order to promote the Autoplug and especially Ever Young. And whatever I have told you can be corroborated. You will appreciate that I am not in a position to make empty threats, we are one of the most respected firms of Lawyers in the UK of which we also enjoy the patronage of the royal family and I am a senior partner. Your client, shall we say dealt very generously with Mr Tann and his colleagues, which could be considered as bribery, but could be negotiated, but not murder, You must know that that is not acceptable."

Schreiber looked towards Heinrich "Have you completed your presentation Mrs Steinberg."

"For the moment, Mr Schreiber, but by all means I would appreciate your points of view before we arrive at a conclusion, but a conclusion there must be. I believe that you are aware of the terms."

"With your permission, I need to speak with my client in private. I would ask you to leave us for a few minutes. Maybe have a coffee. We will call you no later than thirty minutes."

***

They took their papers and meandered towards the lounge only a few metres away with the meeting room still in sight. Heinrich was heard shouting as they closed the door.

"To say that I am impressed Mrs Steinberg is an understatement. I want to become a disciple."

"Jack, If I was Jesus I would happily include you as one my followers, but you will have to be satisfied with a coffee and croissant rather than twenty thousand fish," she laughed charmingly. "Do you mind if I call you Jack?" "No, not at all."

"You may call me Mrs Steinberg," she laughed.

"In truth this is going to be a bomb shell of a case if it is allowed to hit the media. It will certainly rock the government. I think the PM is very brave taking the gamble."

"I don't think that he has an option. Heinrich can also ill afford to allow the affair to become public, he and his cousin could be put a way for life. You have Spoken Arrow lined up to take over the Autoplug and Ever Young. But Heinrich would fight tooth and nail to hang onto Magnum. It's one of the largest companies in the world. If we push him too hard, we all go down together."

"Let's see what Mr Schreiber has to say. If he asks us what we want to do, we'll throw the ball into his court to pass sentence. But a punishment he must be given."

An hour passed, they had been caffeined out, and both were becoming impatient. At last, the door of the meeting room opened and Mr Schreiber walked towards the lounge. As they stood he saw them and waved for them to join him.

He looked tired as he drew up a chair.

"You have put forward a strong case. Mrs Steinberg, of course we will dispute everything you accuse him of. But we are aware of the implications and I, like you, have a great deal of experience of court cases that can have unexpected results. I have no doubt either that your side would be quite embarrassed too for taking bribes, especially the involvement of your minister's murders. Your opposition would take full advantage of your indiscretions too. So I would ask you what your suggestions are, if we can brush the matter under the carpet ad infinitum, so to speak. A charitable cause of a generous amount maybe. A contribution to Cambridge University. Sixteen or seventeen million!"

"I do appreciate a sense of humour, Mr Schreiber, but we're talking about murder, bribery and fraud. One of our government has been murdered, not some little back street prostitute. If we expose this case, the country and parliament will demand Heinrich's head. There are two cases here. The criminal will certainly take precedence and would have immediate repercussions—the Litigation will follow at its own pace."

"Furthermore If we prove our case, and I'm sure we will, we would gain back the Autoplug, Ever Young and some considerable costs. I agree that a certain amount of inconvenience would result on our part, but the fact that we would have been honest and freely admit that there are some bad apples which we would make example of would go some way to justify our government's integrity. Mr

Schreiber, you're a man of experience, I would ask you again, what would you do?"

Schreiber sat back in his chair. He chose his words with some care "I would prefer to evaluate what my opposition have to lose by going to war. I would of course ask you to consider how much benefit we have given to, not only to your country, but to the world, and whether in fact the Autoplug would have been the success that it has if we had not invested considerable sums into it. Of course I would have to appreciate that black clouds of opportunism would be pointed at us, but the outcome of our efforts have been very positive. Even by your arguments Mrs Steinberg you have to admit that we have achieved what your client was unable to do."

"I would not accept that Mr Schreiber. First of all the product that we are talking about is not yours to develop. Secondly how you acquired it included the murder of its inventor, and then the opposition. I think that you would have to do a little better than that, sir. By the way, I should mention to you that I'm not representing the university, Mr Schreiber."

He leaned forward "Then who are you representing?"

"I am representing the British government. I have been told personally by the Prime Minister that we would withdraw from dealing with Magnum and would inform all our partners around the world of the disastrous situation that we are now in. The fact that every aspect of each person's life is now written into the Autoplug assumedly in confidence and Magnum have that information to do with what they wish though Ever Young is an ultimate killer. No country would want to work with you."

Schreiber was silent for a full minute. "So let me ask you EXACTLY what you want, all I can do is refer it to my client, and it is for him to decide what to do?"

Looking directly at Heinrich but addressing Schreiber. "Your client has a simple decision to make. As it stands now both he and Mrs Baylim are facing a life sentence. They would be obliged to forfeit both the Autoplug and Ever Young business, leaving the remaining business to be not owned but managed by yourselves or sold off. I imagine that you would lose a substantial proportion of main stream Magnum business due to the bad publicity and would probably be forced to sell it. So, once again Herr Schreiber, I would like to know what you would suggest to avoid this drama you describe and keep your clients from the disaster that currently awaits them."

There was an awkward silence. She leaned forward across the coffee table, her eyes became slits. "At worst, we are prepared to suffer some pain but we have resigned ourselves to the inevitable if that is what you want. Their fate is in the balance, but the worst can be avoided. We would want you to formally sell us the Autoplug and Ever Young for an undisclosed sum, which would be one penny. And for that we would hide your client's misdemeanours. There would be no negotiation other than the know-how and an understanding of your current administration. They would not know the value of our negotiations and your client would get on with the business of selling his computers. Since the majority shares of your business are in your own hands, I assume that you won't have to account to external shareholders. His conscience would be for him to wrestle with. I'm sure that you appreciate that this is a very dangerous step for us to take as well, we are allowing two murderers to pursue their business with the full knowledge that they should be jailed for life." Schreiber shuffled uncomfortably.

She continued. "If you don't want to do this, we would not hesitate to pursue you and lay the facts open to the world. I would expect that your clients would be arrested and by the German authorities on our behalf. There is no doubt that our own government will be penalised too, but so be it."

Schreiber stood up and nodded. "This is blackmail, we will of course need to speak with Brazil and will let you know our thoughts in due course," he said.

"Due course is not good enough Herr Schreiber. Tomorrow is our deadline, or our book is closed. Do you wish to meet again here or in the UK? I would be prepared to stay here and since we now understand one another, continue our negotiation until we reach a final conclusion. Any further discussions thereafter would be detail and an appropriate announcement would be made by you, but agreed by us."

"I cannot promise that I would have an answer by tomorrow, I would prefer a week to arrive at our decision."

"With respect, that's not possible, The Prime Minister cannot afford to delay your decision, in the event that you do not accept our proposition we would need to address parliament with an explanation. There are also a number of ancillary ministers and staff who would be asked to account for themselves, including of course Mr Tann.

"I have your mobile, Madame, I will speak to you later today. I suggest that you arrange to stay here the night. I am assuming that you will exclude the computer side of our business." He conceded a small smile but said nothing more.

"That would be a consideration but would have to be agreed with my ministers, however we shall await your confirmation tomorrow."

Jack and Mrs Steinberg gathered their papers, leaving their adversaries at the table. As they closed the door behind then she turned to Jack. "There's nothing for us to do but wait," she said. "If they agree then we shall immediately push the sale through. The government will act as the buyer, and probably transfer it over to Spoken Arrow. In fact, I will dictate and get a letter of understanding, in anticipation of their acceptance, for them to sign."

"Well done, Mrs Steinberg. I'll allow you to treat me to dinner!" Jack replied. "Your expense account is stronger than mine."

Schreiber sat in contemplation. Heinrich had ordered a whisky and was gazing into his empty glass. It was clear from Schreiber's expression that his thoughts were of defeat.

"We have a decision to make, my friend, and to be honest I cannot see how we can avoid conceding. You are being successfully blackmailed, but the alternative doesn't bear thinking of. There may be a chance that we can hold onto our computer business. Have you told your father of this situation?"

"Not yet, but there is no doubt that he will not be happy, and that's an understatement." Both appeared to be lost in thought, each had their own view as to the outcome. Heinrich picked up the phone and ordered a bottle of whisky and another glass. Schreiber took out his electronic note pad more out of habit that intent to put anything on it. "Tell me, Steffen: how much money is in the business? I don't mean spare cash."

"Why do you ask? As far as the business is concerned we work within the finance we require. What are you thinking?"

"How much can you raise outside the Magnum business, and I don't mean lose money?"

"I should say that we have substantial reserves, but they are with our Brazilian bank. What are you thinking?"

"I want you to speak with your father and tell him everything, don't hold back even the smallest piece of information, even better, give him an outline and write in detail the events that have taken place."

Heinrich shifted uncomfortably. "Herr Schreiber I would be grateful if you would do this. You may not know that I lost my personal secretary, and I would not want to relate the events to an outsider."

"So why can't you write it yourself?"

"Because I'm dyslexic, damn it. It's a painful admission and I am usually able to camouflage it."

"OK I will do it, you explain the details to me and I will personally write it out. But I need to know how much you can raise to buy Spoken Arrow. I need to know how much of their company is on the open market, and what it's worth. Can you find this out? But it is essential that your father must be aware of all the facts, he is not a fool, and won't put the remainder of the business at risk without good reason. Even if Spoken Apple get your Autoplug business for nothing they still have to finance it, and there's a strong likelihood that they will have to go to the market to raise cash. If we can acquire only twenty-five percent of the shares we could slowly steal the company."

"You think we could buy ourselves back?" whispered Heinrich.

"If we work anonymously, you may be relinquishing a percentage of your business, but if you have the nerve and the money you could scoop the total pot. Do you understand what I am saying? I need to know how much money is required to finance the purchase of Spoken Arrow on say a three year plan, can your finance department find this out? Also the amount that Spoken Arrow would need to raise in order to continue the business without compromising their own operation."

Schreiber spent the next hour explaining the current situation and listening to Heinrich's version of events. He transmitted Heinrich's words directly onto his laptop without interruption until Freda's demise was described. "I must say Steffen that this seems to me to have been unnecessary."

"Maybe so, but we are fighting here for our lives. And I am afraid she became a liability," Schreiber read back the confessional notes and agreed to forward it onto Heinrich's father, enclosing the consequences as laid out by Madame Steinberg. Steffen Heinrich could almost hear his father's response without a telephone. A request to telephone him was booked in two hours.

Chapter 39

The Pontillo Bank account was now based in Sao PAULO. Its origins only known to a few. It was created in the early 1940s to be overseen by Schickerdanz. As the war proceeded a small group of Nazi elite pooled their ill-gotten gains, banking them initially in Switzerland. Money poured in from all over Europe. As many as two hundred of the highest ranking officers were included to place their booty into the Pontillo bank account with the promise of retrieving their monies at the end of the war. The early years gave them a feeling of confidence that they would be wealthy beyond their dreams. However, the war lost, their very admission to their actions inhibited them from making their claims and they took their secrets to their graves. Under the careful watch of Fritz Schickerdanz The fortunes lay dormant for a few years, and the Schickerdanz family took great care to hide its origins. They changed their name to Heinrich and eventually transferred ownership under the new name. The Pontillo investments now straddle across the financial centres of the world under various nom de plumes, its assets are worth many billions. Pontillo's strength relies in its diversity. It is a black hole hiding behind 12 investment companies which play the markets, each interposing with the other and often appearing to compete with one another to mislead opposing forces.

***

Albert Heinrich was now sixty five years old. There had never been a time in his life when he was not involved in the business, as did his father before him, and his father before him. In 1962 and at the age of twenty-two, Albert was shown his first credible computer. There had been a number of attempts to interpret memory onto machines but at last Albert was facing an Olivetti machine that had a memory and could hold and analyse facts and figures.

Fritz, his father worked closely with the Third Reich cataloguing names and such a machine would have been their Nirvana. The defeat of Germany in 1945 was to him not a surrender but a sad moment in time from which his great country would one day recover, and eventually prove their superiority.

Albert took his degree in electrical communications and working closely with his father. They invested heavily into the research of computers. Using the unlimited finances and the finest technologists they quickly became a worldwide forerunner of Information machines.

Fritz relinquished his presidency after his first heart attack and Albert took control in 1999 grew even greater. However there was never any doubt that these monies would one day reincarnate the original intentions of the party and would follow the manifesto laid down by their idealised leaders of bygone days.

Albert made no secret that he would die with his shoes on. For the last three years, he had passed much of the practical aspects of the business to Steffen but the finances and fiscal policies were still under his control. He had been most concerned with Steffen's approach and his reading disability, but Steffen camouflaged his dyslexia by surrounding himself with confidantes and carefully chosen personnel.

It was therefore very disconcerting for his father to hear about Freda, not because of the manner of her death, but his lack of judgement.

***

The call came at 2.00 am. On the advice of Schreiber, they decided to stay at The Ritz in anticipation of a further meeting. His father's voice maintained a constant stream of abuse, with nothing gained but to vent his spleen at his son, before being passed over to Schreiber.

Every possible alternative was discussed, and all rejected. There were long pauses on both sides, but the result was inevitable and eventually they were obliged to concede to the terms laid down by Steinberg, but a lifeline of credibility was conceded to the Heinrichs to retain the computer business that would allow them an essence of self-respect.

"Our moment will come, mein Herr, but we have lost the first round. Be patient." commented Schreiber.

***

They met again in the same room as before at 12.00 pm the following day. Coffees were ordered. Schreiber slowly poured his own, pacing his opening reply as if on stage. "We have spoken at length to Herr Heinrich Senior in Brazil and we have agreed to accept your proposal under the circumstances, provided that all assurances of confidentiality can be given."

Heinrich closed his eyes and turned away from the table. This was to be the most monumentally disastrous moment in his career, all his plans had been for nothing, he would be considered by his family as a total failure. Under his control the Autoplug had been a worldwide wide success and now simply given away. He would be branded a failure, and his judgement would be forever called into doubt. He allowed Schreiber to take complete control.

Mrs Steinberg lunged forward. "The terms of the agreement must have all the requirements necessary for you to transfer both the Autoplug and the Ever Young projects over to the UK government without any encumbrances and will be free to pass on all or any rights accordingly to whomever they wish."

"Your current knowledge must be transferred for as long as it is necessary for both sides to fully understand the specific nuances of the respective projects, and you must agree not to enter this area of development again. Is that agreed?" said Steinberg.

"We need a time limit; can we say five years?"

"No, if you wish a time limit to re-enter this field, it must be no less than ten years, by which time there will probably be a myriad of new developments. But I would not advise my clients to agree to less. The payment will be kept secret and only those around the table and immediate colleagues will know. Since your company is privately owned and the British government is purchasing the business that should not be a problem. What we do with it thereafter will be our business." She spoke with the efficiency of a headmistress.

Heinrich who appeared to be sulking like a child, suddenly blurted out, "We will require an assurance that you are keeping your word, and I would like to suggest that a deposit of four hundred million euro will be kept in Escrow for this ten year period, not that this would help us but I cannot think of any other form of security unless you have a better suggestion without exposing both of us."

"We will consider it, but I think that will be highly unlikely," she replied. "Bear in mind that it is in both our interests to maintain the raison d'etre of this deal."

"Are you prepared to exonerate Tann, after all if the government will now be controlling the Autoplug etc. he has been the greatest contributor to it."

Jack found this a most interesting point, and one that would possibly elevate Tann and therefore the government from any possible rumours of malpractice. "I like this idea Herr Heinrich, and it might suit both parties if we can turn the project round to be a more generous negotiation between two willing parties."

"We'll certainly consider it," confirmed Steinberg. The atmosphere softened a little and practical points were discussed and allowed to go into the small print of the negotiations.

She adopted a more conciliatory tone and directed her remarks directly to Schreiber, ignoring Heinrich. "I will forward a summary of our discussions, and I hope that you will acknowledge them in order that we can proceed without delay." Her words were like a sword thrust into Heinrich's heart.

Sandwiches were ordered in an attempt to bolster the dejected mood of Heinrich which allowed them to shake hands, all be it reluctantly at the end of the discussions.

***

Both men returned to Heinrich's suite. Not a moment was lost. He immediately phoned his office. His rage had returned and without the inhibition of his adversaries grabbed the phone by his bed and punched in the numbers of his office. Demanding to speak with his accounts director, and not even mentioning who he was, the receptionist took umbrage at the madman at the other end of the line. "Damn you! Put me through immediately!" he yelled.

"Who wishes to speak with him?" she stammered. "Herr Heinrich you idiot!" he shouted. "What's your name?" She knew if she told him it would be her last week in the job, so she put him through.

Boremann answered. "Herr Heinrich here, Boremann I want you to find every financial piece of information on the US company Spoken Arrow. What they are worth, who owns the majority of the shares, which banks they work with what turnover they have. Do you hear me? I want this information on my desk tomorrow morning." his voice was raising again and without waiting even for confirmation he hung up. "Damn. Damn. Damn! How can this be happening to me. Damn."

Schreiber poured two whiskies and sat quietly until Heinrich's rage subsided. "What must be done now, my friend, is to take a moment to contemplate the future. You certainly can't do it by shouting like a wild animal. Our plans must be kept completely secret, and if you want to find a road of recovery, careful and explicit plans must be made. So I suggest that you sit down, drink your whisky and compose yourself. Do you understand? We now know our position and must cooperate with them, for one word out of place will mean a life sentence for you."

It seemed to Jack a Pyrrhic victory. Freedom for a murderer, a convenient coverup for the government, a windfall for Spoken Arrow – a settlement of convenience, and no justice. At least four good people had been murdered and the culprit clearly identified, yet the end game was nothing more than a political bubble. He felt that he was on the wrong side, yet there did not appear a right one. He had the knowledge and the journalistic facility to bring down the government of England and put behind bars a psychopathic billionaire; he could show the world that right is might. The Autoplug alone was worth billions which would be given on a plate to the government by what amounted to blackmail. It seemed wrong. A perfectly honourable minister and his wife killed, a brilliant scientist, and then a woman of the highest calibre who just knew too much. All by the hand of one, still free, man. It was wrong, and the knowledge of knowing it haunted Jack like a dark shadow.

He likened it to a game of chess. He had to know that the benefactors were honourable and that the ultimate outcome would make things right.

There was no doubt in his mind that Magnum needed to be replaced. It had been formed on an evil premise, but what they had established with the Autoplug, even though they had stolen the concept, nobody else would have marketed it as well, and as a result it had substantially benefitted the world. That they were promoting their own medication and building up a massive library of millions of individuals for devious means clearly eliminated them from their right to continue. However the concept was sound and it was correct that it should be placed with another more honourable company.

Jack needed to unload his thoughts, and had no confidante better than his travelling companion. "Let's look at this government of ours," he began. "Ministers and associates within the civil service who were benefitting from bribes. This would not have been so bad if the killings had not mired the waters. Was this anything to do with Tann? Could he have been somehow excluded from the plot to kill either the scientist or his colleague, meaning he is simply a pawn, incidental? Did he in fact deserve to be beaten up and so humiliated?"

But Jack's thoughts kept racing. How would Spoken Arrow handle Ever Young? Maybe it should be left to the government to rationalise, but could they be trusted? And what about other countries who may see benefits of controlling their population through the Ever Young sinister controls? Could the technical wherewithal be sold deviously there?

All these thoughts were thrown towards Mr Steinberg as they flew home. Jack felt that this was the last bastion to bring such pressing questions to a head.

The details were accurately chronicled by Mrs Steinberg without bias. Her written description of events, much of which reflected Jack's meanderings, were forwarded to George Pickles and copied on to Jack and to the Prime Minister's personal secretary. He had just dozed off when he received a call at midnight from Jane Franklyn requesting a meeting at number ten for the following morning at 8.00 am. Every bone in his body ached to release himself from this drama. It was enough to have been a prime instigator but he was in too deep with implications that were far greater than he had anticipated.

He was now becoming a familiar figure and Jane welcomed him as a friend before directing him into a board room. Mrs Steinberg was already chatting with the Prime Minister, coffee was served and instructions were given that no one should enter until instructed.

"I've read the appraisal of your meetings," said the PM, "and must congratulate both of you on the outcome. Of course we have to turn the theory into a reality whilst the iron's hot, but I need to pass the proposal onto my Think Tank and look at the practical implications, and What if's etc. With this in mind, I would appreciate your further thoughts. We would value your opinion Mrs Steinberg, and yours too Jack, any hiccups anticipated, unforeseen situations that would embarrass us?"

"Prime Minister, if you were to ask us for a guarantee I would certainly refuse, but the problem we might have is not necessarily with Heinrich but with Mrs Baylim. This lady has enough information to pass on to anyone interested in Ever Young. I have been thinking of how the project could be totally squashed but it's already out there, like a nuclear bomb. I have no immediate answer to that."

"Are you suggesting," he replied, "that she could join forces with another party or country, like say Russia?"

"I'm not suggesting anything," she replied, "but only as a proposition. I understand that the original concept was to inoculate children which would protect them from negative genes, Magnum altered this claim and the Neuro351 placed in the brain would have very different consequences. However, whilst it can be banned, it would be difficult to stop some country imposing it on their population...or another's. My understanding is that by virtue of the inserted Neuro351 being contactable from an external source, and pressing a button, they can alter mood swings or terminate anyone at any time. Would I be right Jack?"

Jack had not discussed the detail with his colleague but there was no doubt that unless Gilda Baylim was included in the agreement it would be open game for her to work with whomever she wished.

"You're quite correct, she could certainly continue even in Brazil, and there's no doubt that she knows more about Ever Young than anyone else. Even if we work with Spoken Arrow and return to the original programme, with her loose they would certainly have competition."

"Is there anyone else who would also be in a position to pursue the project?" Asked the PM.

"Not with the knowledge that this woman has in my opinion, sir."

"Then we have an interesting problem. I suggest that you speak with Mr Schreiber and state that we must include Mrs Baylim and her associates into this agreement; after all, she carries the weight of responsibility for the death of her husband."

"I shall speak with him today and ask him to include her in the agreement, I can't see why she would refuse, but I can't see how we could stop her passing her know how onto another country even with her confirmation within this agreement."

They left with less of a spring in their step than when they arrived. "My office is only round the corner in the Temple Jack," she said, "Why don't you come back with me and we'll make the call." They walked to the top of Downing Street and Jack found a cab. The taxi whisked them along Embankment. It was strange that although Jack considered himself a dyed in the wool Londoner, he had never had the opportunity to visit this rather elite area where some of the most prestigious barristers held private court. Tucked away between Holborn and Fleet St in buildings as old as the written law, King's Councillors, judges and barristers would meet criminals, business moguls, divorcees, all the while comparing, referring to tomes describing cases of a hundred years ago; all to develop the principles of justice.

He was impressed – it was not that her offices were particularly lavish, but an immediate impact of being around working academia, giving him the feeling that he could present any problem in this environment and in their midst it would be unravelled and solved.

She immediately ordered tea, took her coat off and passed it with a nod to her secretary, and without any further ado phoned Schreiber. "Herr Schreiber, we had a meeting with the Prime Minister this morning and have discussed in principle our negotiations. A point arose that would need to be added to our agreement."

"And what would that be Mrs Steinberg?"

"We would require Madame Baylim and her colleagues to be party to the same terms as Herr Heinrich. Bear in mind that she has a great deal to lose by not being included, for her husband's death is on her shoulders. However, her knowhow relating in particular to Ever Young must not be disclosed to anyone other than through our good offices. I hope that you appreciate the importance of this demand."

"Madam, whilst I fully appreciate your request, I am simply a vessel, and all I can do is pass on your comments to her and Herr Heinrich." She denoted a slight air of sarcasm in her voice which was worrying.

"I should tell you Mr Schreiber that we are taking these discussions most seriously and are quite prepared to revert to our original plan unless our specific terms are accepted. May I suggest that you speak with your clients today and give us an answer no later than tomorrow morning."

"I can assure you Madam that my response was only of what was meant without any undertones that you may have surmised. You can be sure that I will speak with my clients today and inform you of their reply by the morning." She thanked him and hung up.

Turning her attention back to Jack, her style changed to that of a benevolent aunt. "Now Jack, You must be well aware by now that my relationship with his Majesty's government is extremely close. We are involved in many of their confidential discussions with other countries and at home. For this, we are well paid as is expected. With this in mind, I have been given instructions to recompense you for your work to so far, and if you would be kind enough to tell me your bank details I will organise a bank transfer."

It was like a shot of lightning. Jack could not believe his eyes when she passed him a small piece of paper with a figure of a hundred and twenty thousand pounds written on it by hand.

"How do you like your tea?" she smiled.

"I can't take that," he exclaimed, "beside which I'm already employed, if I took this I would be in breach of my contract."

"That's not a problem Jack, did you not say that the government were about to place a major agreement with your company, they will continue with a campaign, which may not be Ever Young, but your principles would be delighted to have us as a client only because of you. In the Prime Minister's own words to me: 'That young man has saved our government single-handedly'."

Jack was speechless. He had a problem attempting to quantify the implications. A painful minute before he could respond. "This is hush money isn't it!"

"No Jack, it's a contribution given in appreciation from friends. Look, you are a successful journalist, no one can sensibly expect you to keep a story like this under wraps for too long—but as a friend we hope that you'll be discreet— a friend."

"It is interesting that our Herr Heinrich intimated the same comments about our ministers, I would certainly compromise myself if I took this money Mrs Steinberg, you know that. I suggest we play this game to its final conclusion and then if you wish you can call me your friend."

Although the room was not particularly warm, he felt himself to be excessively sweating.

"You're right, Jack. I'm simply following my instructions. I would say the same," she smiled benevolently. Had she been younger or he older, she might have kissed him.

"You know Mrs Steinberg that I voted for this government, but I must say that it would not be the end of the world it took a fall."

"I'm not sure what your implication is Jack!"

"Sometimes justice must be seen to be done. In your position, you must be aware of that a hidden inconvenience will invariably come back to bite hard." "My position Jack is to represent my clients, even though I often disagree with them or their philosophies, in this case the government, but you must be the master of your own destiny, you have your job and I have mine. It is to represent the government whether they are lying or not, it is what they tell me, not what I think." She stood up, offering her hand and with a charm honed by years of practice looked into his eyes quoting, "Purity of thought and mind will overcome men's actions of destruction, for their misdemeanours will invariably betray them."

He kissed her hand, put on his coat and departed.

Chapter 40

Jack had never needed a friend as much as he needed one now. He was carrying too much on his shoulders. It was now 2.00 pm and returning to his apartment he immediately poured himself a whisky and phoned Helga.

Her phone rang for a long while. Maybe she was in a lecture, he thought. At last she answered, and even without a hello or asking her how she was he blurted, "Helga, I miss you, I need to see you." She had not heard from him for over two weeks and had begun to believe that their short affair had simply been a moment in time, but his voice felt to her full of pain. "Can you come to me? I need to tell you how much I missed you and all the things that have happened since we last spoke."

"I missed you too, I can be with you in three hours, my darling Jack. Can you meet me at Paddington Station?"

He bought two pizzas and a bottle of wine and they drove directly back to his apartment. She was as beautiful and regal as ever. Their togetherness needed no words as she looked at him with loving eyes.

"I can't get you out of my thoughts," she whispered, "I thought that you may have found some sexy model."

As soon as they closed the front door he took her bag and threw it on the sofa and hugged her so tight that she felt her breath vanish from within. His desire to hold her closed his mind to anything else at that moment, she held onto him and he kissed her lips and eyes and hugged her again.

They could not resist moving to the bedroom and made love.

The pizzas were reheated and wine poured, she threw on a towelling dressing gown and sat awaiting Jack's adventures. "Can you stay over?" he asked.

"You can't get rid of me that easily, but I must return tomorrow. I should catch the 4.00 pm train," she sighed. "Tell me what's happened since we last spoke."

In spite of his promises of secrecy, he spent the next hour describing his various meetings and the conclusions that were arrived at. "That's not to say they will follow what has been agreed, we have a fox in a corner and anything can happen. But what is more important as far as I'm concerned is to battle with my own conscience."

She cogitated before replying. Walking over to the window she could see the traffic down below. It was now 5.30 pm and people were rushing to their trains, buses or simply walking home, what would they know about politics or international affairs, little were they aware how governments directed their lives driven by powerful and often ruthless businesses or even advertising. Innocent masses, pawns hoping to live without fear and trying to avoid poverty.

Returning to her chair she took his hand. "Jack, what does your conscience tell you?"

"I truly believe that this man belongs in jail. Years ago he would have been hanged for murder, but the consequences of revealing this drama would be enormous, it would inevitably bring the government down. The public won't accept the murders and degree of bribery involved, especially the opposition. Whether Tann was directly responsible for any of the murders or not, he was certainly in league with those who were and we don't know how many in the civil service or allies in the government helped him to transmit every individual's life onto the Autoplug for Magnums library. Their devious manipulation to bring the business back to Germany, the ultimate objectives for Ever Young that enabled them to influence every user of the Autoplug, and give prescriptions controlled by Magnum. The country has been hoodwinked and what appeared to be an amazing invention has been soured by their ultimate objectives.

"The fact that Spoken Arrow might take over the Autoplug and cleanse the concept is fine but in the meantime our Heinrich and co. go scot-free, probably to pursue another or the same project around the world."

"And you would be the whistle-blower, the man who brought down a government," she laughed. "If it wasn't so serious, it would be funny that one man – you – can change the history of a country and the lives of countless millions with a simple decision. Do you have the ear of someone that can help you weigh up the pros and cons of this bag of worms, Jack? I know my own limitations, and as much as I have a moral and possibly an intellectual opinion I really don't think I am capable of giving you advice that is worthy of the outcome my darling."

"I could speak with my father, but he's nestled down in Cornwall and really not up to date with what's happening in the world."

"So why not speak with your editor, I remember you telling me that he is a wise old bird. Can you talk to him in the strictest confidence?"

He was looking into her eyes, but for a second, as if by lightning he found himself thinking of Miriam.

His eyes glazed as if he was caught in his own dream world, just for a few seconds.

Helga noticed that instant. "Are you OK?" she asked.

"Yes of course, my boss. Good idea I'll give him a ring."

***

"What in heaven happened to you Jack, we thought you'd left the planet."

"I need to speak with you, boss, but in the strictest confidence – I need your advice and what I tell you will shock you. Can we meet tonight away from your offices."

"OK," he replied "give me your home address and I'll meet you there at say 8.30 pm. Have you got a good whisky?"

"I'll make sure I do. I'll remove the NO Smoking signs. Brody, it's really good to speak with you, and thanks," He replied.

"Do you want to speak with him alone?" Helga asked.

"Definitely not."

***

At 8.30 pm. on the dot the bell rang accompanied by a heavy smoker's cough. Helga opened the door. "This is a nice surprise – I thought Jack was something of a hermit, but you're not his sister are you?" He joked.

"No ,I'm just a friend." She blushed.

Jack came out from the kitchen, "Helga this is my boss, Brody Emmitt, I couldn't wish to work for a nicer chap, although I wouldn't say it to his face."

"I didn't hear that," Brody replied.

"Helga is a good friend. I'm happy for her to listen in," said Jack. "Let's make ourselves comfortable – you won't believe what I have to tell you." He poured Brody and himself a large whisky, and a red wine for Helga and put an ash tray on the coffee table for the exclusive use of Brody. "Dare I ask," said Brody, "Were you the other first-class ticket to Germany?" Helga blushed – and nodded.

The next forty minutes were spent reiterating the happenings until he arrived at the final meeting with Mrs Steinberg.

"So what's your problem Jack, surely it's not your conscience? I'm pleasantly surprised." He lit another cigarette. "The man has killed a few people in order to achieve his objective. But so did Churchill. To him he sees that it's just an extension of the last war, they didn't lose it they took a rain check. God knows how much they squirreled out of Germany during their time, and I would bet that

316

they will have enough to buy their way back. So you are now waiting to discover if Mrs Baylim will refrain from passing her knowledge on. It seems a very loose arrangement for such an important project. Supposing she refuses, what then?"

"They would be forced to reveal the whole story. There would be a massive battle for the government to prove that they knew nothing of the murders, Tann's involvement. The civil servants and various ministers that were involved in pressing through the Autoplug software from all the departments that would be needed to feed their computers with every bit of information relating to each person. I believe that their opponents would push for a cessation of parliament."

"And I assume that would upset the whole apple cart, and a fresh election. And if they agree, what then?"

"If we do a deal, the government will take over both the Autoplug and Ever Young with all the relevant support from Germany and of course Cambridge. They would form a new company between Spoken Arrow, Cambridge and possibly the government holding a small equity. Both Heinrich and Baylim would go free, they'd probably keep their stolen goodies, and the Brenekov's would do time for the murder of the Hines' family. The problem for me Brody is that this man, who is controlling a massive organisation should be free to bump off whomever he wishes, and will not stop there. I have no doubt that he will find a way to take control again by one means or another, when he should be behind bars or more…and we have all the evidence to prove it."

"The pen is mightier than the sword, aye Jack?" quipped Brody. "In any event, I think you should wait to see what Mrs Baylim has to say, you can make your decision then, but it's a bloody good story and since you are at the heart of it you will become a celebrity either way. When will you know. Have you ever met this lady, what sort of woman is she?"

"No, I've never met her," Jack replied. "I don't doubt that she's pretty clever, and probably more sinister than her cousin; anyway, I hope we'll hear by tomorrow."

Emmitt swallowed the second whisky in a gulp and cogitated for a moment. "There is always going to be a bad apple in any government, but if that government has a vested interest to hide a serious misdemeanour, they are as bad as the perpetrator and should be shot. Metaphorically of course," he chuckled. "Of course if they openly hang all those involved out to dry, and throw themselves at the mercy of the country, and are prepared to suffer the consequences, who knows which way the wind blows. That would be the honourable thing to do, even though they would probably be committing

317

Harikarri. You could speak with the Prime Minister and offer him the alternative, let him decide what he wants to do."

"I pretty well know what he'll say, 'Why rock the boat. Let sleeping dogs lie, he's holding all the cards at this moment, but I'll feel him out through George Pickles.'"

Helga had sat on the side listening to the two men weighing up the pros and cons. "You know what I admire about this country—"

She interrupted, "In spite of all the various political and social factions here, it seems to me as a visitor that the British have an ingrained understanding of the right thing to do, we shouldn't accept anything other than what's right. There is no other hand relating to honesty, a government represents the people, and they should be the epitome of what is right and wrong. If the government can't make the right decision and you can, then make it I think the mass of the British people will follow it."

Brody looked at Helga. She had summed up what he himself might have said twenty five years ago. He had often thought that he had left honesty behind as pragmatics became his pass word, but with just a simple sentence she had put him in his place. His mind floated back to his student days when he took his degrees in English Literature and biblical studies. Sitting back in his chair he quoted, "Out of the mouths of babes thou hast ordained strength that thou may still the enemy and the avenger. Psalm 8.2."

"You never cease to amaze me, boss." exclaimed Jack.

Emmitt drained his already empty glass and smiled. "Let me know how you fare tomorrow, OK. Only you Jack can decide, it's pragmatics versus Honour."

He shook both their hands and left. His cigarette smoke and last words lingered.

They used the following morning simply to be in each other's company, Newspapers breakfast, more coffee and love making, and at 1.15 pm they gathered her belongings and returned to Paddington Station. He bought her a sandwich to eat on the journey. "I'll keep you posted and tell you the next exciting instalment." They kissed again and parted.

Jack stood on the platform until the train was out of sight. His emotions were in turmoil and regretted not being on the train with her. Yet his mind kept wondering, almost feeling unfaithful.

He needed to go to his office, but to break the mood he decided to have a bite of lunch.

His favourite restaurant was only a stone's throw away and he prepared himself for a homely welcome and some comfort food.

Chapter 41

Both Robert and Jay returned to LA just in time for Christmas. They had taken countless photos and bought a mass of toys from Hamleys and what they classified as guilt gifts for their wives from Asprey's of Bond St and other ludicrously expensive stores. It was generally agreed that Miriam would stay with her family over the holiday and return on the second week of January.

She shot a quick email to Martin and informed him that the essence of a deal was imminent. She hoped to return with a strong proposition which would allow them to move forward. "With this in mind, can you please give me some idea when you are returning, when we will be able to exchange our experiences on what has been for us a very exciting and earth moving negotiation? Both Robert and Jay have now returned to LA, but I have decided to have Christmas with my family, and also clarify the closing stages of our discussions."

She booked out of the hotel with some trepidation, for although she would be staying with her parents, it had been a number of years since she had slept in her old bedroom and shared a bathroom, waiting for what seemed an interminable age whilst listening to her father singing a selection of Italian arias. She had gotten used to her creature comforts and independence, but for a few days she would forgive them anything. Transfer her luggage to their house, she knew that by the end of fourteen days all her belongings would carry the smell of her mother's cooking, and she hoped that it would stay with her for a few weeks.

It was also a good opportunity to catch up with her brothers and play with their kids. Julius had his restaurant in a small cul-de-sac off Church Street in Kensington and she thought she might surprise him.

The restaurant made a brave attempt to replicate a little of Italy. In the summer, a few umbrellaed tables were strategically placed between outdoor heaters, but now in the depth of a wet and cold London winter only the brave would sit there. However inside one could really feel the warmth of Italian hospitality. Every customer walking through the door was welcomed as if they were family. The waiter was not familiar with his boss's sister but graciously offered her a seat by the window. He spoke English with what attempted to be an Italian accent which amused Miriam, and she responded in Italian. The waiter had no idea what she was saying and responded by admitting that his part of Italy had another dialect, but she continued her banter, and in broken English asked politely to speak with the manager. He scuttled off with a red face. Five minutes passed and Julius appeared ready to take an order. As he walked out of the kitchen he saw her. Throwing his napkin onto the next table he ran up and hugged her. "This is my little sister from LA," he shouted to his customers "Che meravigiosa sorpesa." He sat at the table laughing. "What a delight to see you, you naughty girl embarrassing my nearly Italian staff," he whispered.

They hugged each other again. She told him why she was back in London, apologising profusely for not seeing him sooner, which he took with good grace, but she could see that he was disappointed which embarrassed her even more. He announced with pride that they were expecting another baby. "And what about you, when can we expect a celebration my little sister." "Find me someone and I'll think about it," she joked.

At this very moment, Jack walked in. They both casually looked towards the door and in unison and gasped.

"Miriam, I must introduce you to this man; he is a regular customer and a great guy. Jack!" he called out, "Welcome back! By yourself this time I see," he smiled. "I'm with my sister, she lives in California. Come and join us."

"This really is a strange coincidence, I've had the pleasure of meeting Miriam already."

Miriam could not avoid blushing as she stood to greet Jack. "We're in discussions with the very deal that I have come back for," she told her brother. "What has brought you here, Jack?" she asked.

Julias was effervescent. "This young man is one of my regular customers Miriam. In fact, you are sitting at his table! Come and join us Jack. I can recommend the venison." And with a sweep of his hand pulled another chair to the table.

The conversation was light and without direction whilst her brother was there. Julias saw an opportunity to excuse himself. "I must be in the kitchen for a short while, I'll return soon." He left with a cheeky grin and caught Miriam's stare with a wink.

She could see that he appeared to be absorbed in thought, and her feminine instinct was to empathise rather than the matter of fact approach of measured interest. "How are events developing since we last met? My colleagues returned last week but I thought it would be nice to spend the holiday with my family. It would also give me a chance to discover the outcome of your meetings in Germany." She found it hard to look directly at him for fear of bringing to the surface any physical awareness between them.

"A great deal has happened since we last met, in fact I've found myself in something of a dilemma. You of course want to know how your company can gain by concluding some sort of deal, but I came to this from a journalistic stand. Neither political or technical, more a socialistic stance, but I've now found myself as a main player in a highly political drama.

"Miriam, I appreciate that you need to take back a conclusive overview of this negotiation, I will tell you how we're placed at this moment, but I'm not ready to open the flood gates at this time."

"You're talking in riddles Jack, but what you decide to tell me can be in the strictest confidence if you wish, you have my word." She considered for a moment. "OK what say you tell me whatever you want to and we can rehash whatever you will allow me to tell my bosses back in the States."

"That seems reasonable," he replied. The waiter came to take their orders but was turned away. Julias looked on from his kitchen well pleased with the intensity he noted as more than casual conversation.

Jack spoke for a full twenty minutes. He found himself describing in detail his various encounters, discoveries of stolen treasures and Freda's death. Concluding with his most recent meeting in Paris and the subsequent meeting with the Prime Minister and the awaited response from Mrs Baylim. Finally his own position and moral stand with the probable consequences. He had not intended to be quite so explicit but it was as much an emotional release as a simple update of events.

The waiter returned. This time they ordered, and the mood relaxed. Although Jack was quite familiar with the menu, Miriam guided him with instructions to the kitchen detailing the more minute details that would only be known to those with inside information.

***

She was a good listener but he found himself comparing her manner to Helga. Her responses were that of a mature woman and he found himself more attracted to this woman than he had intended. She was a woman in full flower.

They forcibly distracted themselves from the subject at hand and gave all their attention to the food. She insisted that they have a desert, and had slowly worked their way through a bottle of wine. It was far more than either of them normally ate and Jack had long ago past the comfort food idea that he entered the restaurant with. But for the first time in many days he felt comfortable with himself and his company. It was obvious how attractive Miriam was, more than attractive beautiful, but his sub-conscious told him that this coincidental meeting was an unexpected business meal, and had nothing to do with his personal life.

He had thought Helga had filled that space.

They were sitting in her brother's restaurant and knowing that he was secretly spying on them. His baby sister was now a grown woman in a high powered job, but to him she remained his baby sister, and as he had never seen her before in a professional capacity he found it easier to pick up their relationship as he last knew it when they were all at home and under the wing of their parents. She had come to visit her brother but spent the entire time speaking with this handsome young man whom he saw as a socialite of sorts. He recalled the mixed bag that Jack had brought to his restaurant over the last year. Miriam would be on the lips of all the family by the end of the evening. What they ate, drank and their assumed body language. Did he have any Italian blood, what did he do for a living, and could he be trusted with their baby girl? To Jack's credit, he was a regular, and committed to his Italian food. That had to be a strong point in his favour.

Between them they had almost finished the wine and summarising his position she meandered her opinion as if she was summarising a novel. "It seems to me Jack that there are a number of very different issues here and should be considered separately on their own merit. Looking at the situation from Spoken Arrow's view point it's quite simple. If a package deal could be dropped in their lap, they would save years and a considerable amount of money. I've no idea how much money would be required to jump on this band wagon, but I don't doubt that they could raise it somehow."

"No one has billions of loose cash hanging about, and since the Autoplug is already established in a number of countries, just to maintain it will probably cost billions. Ever Young could be relaunched as a children's product after substantial tests have been done and that will take time."

"What we would be concerned about is the stink that goes with the business and how we could disassociate ourselves from all the politics and murders that have gone before it. We would not figure in these discussions and can only wait until your chaps sort it out."

"If the government want to be shareholders it would have to give undertakings that it would not become a partisan issue."

"In the event that the government changes, it would not be able to have a control on the policy of the company's direction. Any way that's for the lawyers and top echelons to work out. I do agree with you that they should not try to hide what has gone on in order to bring the Autoplug to market. How can we trust a government that hides bribery and murder on this scale. I think they have to swallow the pill and throw themselves at the mercy of the nation…and this Heinrich should be brought down, and so should his company. Tann is simply a pawn, he can be judged on his merits, but it's a big responsibility for you to take this on board. It's a bag of worms."

"However, it seems to me Jack that if you expose them now we wouldn't have the deal you've negotiated, since you would have to go to court to prove any rights that you believe you have until it's battled out in court. You have to prove that you own the patents, they stole the concept and he was involved in the murders. With their deep pockets that could take years."

Jack sat back. "My god you make my life difficult. What would you do?"

She laughed. "If you were to take my advice Jack, you would blame me for bringing the government down, and that I find funny. It would be something I would boast about to my grandchildren, if I ever had them."

"Well, maybe that's why I'm asking you."

"In fact, if you were to tell the world press, it wouldn't matter what happened to Mrs Baylim. She would probably do time. If I was the Mafia, I would agree the deal and bump Tann off, in that order. It's lucky we are in England." Jack's mind clicked to Horrocks and the MI5.

"I agree," he said without conviction.

It was now past 8.00 pm They had been sitting in her brother's restaurant for over three hours almost oblivious of the room filling up around them.

"Thank you for listening to my problems Miriam, I enjoyed your company tremendously."

"It's been a real pleasure speaking with you Jack, I will tell Dr Ellsworth that we met, I'm speaking with him tomorrow."

"I should also call him, but so much has happened that I'm afraid he was rather overlooked. Mind you, He didn't tell me about you guys either. But I'd be grateful if you would keep our conversation secret until I have clarified my thoughts. You'll appreciate how delicate the situation is at this moment and there's a great deal at stake."

"Don't worry Jack, I'll leave it to you to give me the green light, but you'll appreciate that I will eventually have to report on my visit to the board in LA. I'm staying with my parents for the next few days and then returning to the States.

Maybe you could call me to update your position, and of course let me know what you have decided. Follow your heart."

"That's interesting," Jack replied, "my boss said the same thing. Emotions are dangerous barometers and not always reliable."

They shook hands, he reminded himself how attractive she was and became rather more aware than he felt appropriate of what a very charming and intelligent woman he had enjoyed a meal with.

A small voice inside his head reminded him of the net he was about to become entangled in.

As he left the restaurant he glanced down at his mobile to note that Helga had called three times.

***

He spent the evening writing. A long list of emails from various sports companies that had been lambasting him with their latest gadgets. After all, he was still being paid to do the job. At 5.00 am, he was awakened by a text on his mobile. He threw his arm over the bed to feel for his machine and read the message from Mrs Steinberg.

Dear Jack, There has been a serious development. Herr. Schreiber has informed me that Mrs Gilda Baylim took her life yesterday at 10.00 pm. Needless to say she is now eliminated from our agreement. You may like to phone me to discuss this development in greater detail. With kindest wishes, Ada Steinberg.

He switched the mobile off, smiled to himself and went back to sleep.

Chapter 42
Martin

Martin had now visited seven countries. He had covered most of South America over the last six weeks and was not particularly happy to leave his family for so long, but the pressure of keeping ahead of the field was making ever greater demands on his life.

Instant messaging and hologram conversations with his kids exacerbated his homesickness even more. The company was fighting to hold its position in a market that was constantly refining its existing products. He yearned for the old days where invention and innovative ideas rather than often unnecessary sophistication and comparative gimmicks took the world by storm.

The schedule was extended by a further three weeks to include Chile and Peru, and on a sudden impulse he knew that he had to return to base. It was too much, after all it was a self-imposed programme and he could change it to suit his convenience. It occurred to him that a surprise return would delight his family and catch his staff a little unaware. In any event, he was with two colleagues who could complete his presentations, Spoken Arrow had offices in all of these countries. Informing his lieutenants that urgent business necessitated his return and giving them a pep talk to keep up the good work, he booked his return flight.

As exhausted as he was after flying for nine hours, the excitement of surprise gave him a burst of adrenaline as he imagined how his kids would hug him; he imagined how Angela would react, maybe burst into joyful tears as she hung on his neck.

He'd been travelling through the night and it was now 10.30 am LA time. As soon as he cleared the customs he took minutes to freshen up in the first class rest rooms and took a cab home. He now remembered that the kids were at school just as he was, finally, home.

As he opened the door he heard voices, and pulling his bags into the house he was astonished to see a man he didn't know half-dressed and having breakfast. Angela was wearing a negligee. There was a moment of painful silence. The man seemed paralysed in his shorts, holding a mug of coffee. If there was something he should have said, it had frozen in his mouth. Angela broke the bubble, "I can explain, we weren't expecting you today," she spluttered.

"I can see," smiled Martin sardonically. He looked at this anonymous man "You'd better leave. NOW" he suddenly shouted.

The man suddenly became animated and scuttled off like a rabbit to get his clothes.

"You said that you could explain, well explain." To his own surprise, he was not angry, in fact he felt devoid of feeling at that moment. He poured himself a coffee that was still warm on the table and sat where her lover had been. He heard the door slam and wished that she would go with him. She was still the same beautiful woman that he had left and loved, he remembered buying the negligee. There was nothing she could say, the act itself was an explanation. He thought he heard her say she was sorry, but it did not matter to him. He finished his coffee and went to another room. She heard him on the phone to a local hotel, then calling for a taxi. And he took his bags and left.

Leaving the hotel two hours later Martin arrived at his offices. He'd had a shower and shaved. To an onlooker it would appear as if he had no worries in the world but he was emotionally numb, robbed of his greatest possession: his family life. He had not yet seen his children, and still he was going to his office, zombified.

There was a ripple of excitement on his arrival as he passed through the various open offices, which would quickly fade, and then it was to be business as usual. His mind was protecting him from an emotional explosion for now. But as he walked closer to his own suite, the reality hit him.

Carolyn Brosh looked up, surprised and delighted she stood up to welcome him but it was immediately obvious to her that something was not right. She walked beside him "We were not expecting you back for another three weeks. I bet it was because you missed me," she giggled.

"What did you say," he muttered.

"It's great to have you back," she replied, "would you like a coffee or something. Let me know when I can update you Martin, and er," she hesitated "Is everything OK?"

"We'll talk, give me a moment. Yes, coffee would be great. Thanks, and ask Miriam to pop in, OK?"

She had never seen him looking so distressed, "Miriam is still away in the UK." She put his aloofness down to his jet lag and a nine hour journey.

When she returned, she found him sitting on the settee looking out of the window. "Is everything alright?" she ventured again. Carolyn had been Martin's PA for over eight years and considered herself a friend. He had been to her wedding, celebrated the birth of her two children and she had been to his family celebrations on a number of occasions. She considered herself very fortunate to work with him and he appreciated her efficiency and her familiarity without infringing on each other's personal lives. But she had never seen him looking so depressed.

"I have a lot to update you Martin, but is there something you would like me to do."

"Take a seat," he replied. She sat opposite him in silence. He looked up with tears in his eyes. "My wife is having an affair. When I arrived, she was there with her lover in a negligee that I had bought her, with a man. God knows who he was, I didn't wait to find out. He scampered off putting clothes on as he left."

"What did she say?"

"It doesn't matter what she said, but I want my kids and a divorce lawyer. Get me Harold Levison on the line. I'm not standing for this nonsense."

"Don't you think you should have a conversation with her first. Let me call her and see if you can both have a meeting. Not at home, maybe in a coffee shop or hotel… at least give her a chance to explain herself. We both know and probably she does too that she has made a mistake, but there is a great deal at stake here, so at least give her a chance to apologise. You may not want to accept her apology but people make mistakes. We all make mistakes sometimes," she pleaded.

He waited, continuing to look out at the sea beyond the buildings. "It's not as if I treated her badly or was a bad father, I was away for six weeks, goddammit, My Grandfather left his wife in Poland for over a year whilst he found employment and living accommodation here in the US."

"And how do you know that either of them was completely faithful during that time, just because no one caught them! Let me phone her, I will speak with her and arrange a meeting…Martin," she looked at him with pleading eyes, "Think of the kids. Just give her a last chance to explain her side to you. Where have you booked into? What shall we say, 2.00 pm at the Hyatt Hotel?" He said nothing, but nodded.

He arrived a few minutes early and chose a corner alcove where a degree of privacy could be had. His mind was in such turmoil, he had no idea how he would react. The thought that another man had been with her made him sick, and he had an urgent desire to leave before she came. But at 2.00 pm exactly, she arrived, he saw her look around and his first reaction was to get up and wave, but he decided to stay reasonably obscured until she saw him.

Now devoid of embellishments, make up or jewellery, dressed in white, her blond hair loose, she looked as nature would have made her. Standing before him she asked if she could sit down. Her perfume was familiar to him, it was the same as he had bought her from the duty free airport. "I should tell you that this meeting was not my idea, Carolyne persuaded me to meet you. I had put a call into Harold Levison, I can't tell you how disappointed, no, how disgusted I am with you."

"You're right, Martin, I am pretty disgusted with myself." She took a napkin from the table to wipe a tear.

"Don't give me your crying. You're upset because you've been discovered, you're going to tell me that it was a one only slip, you were feeling lonely, or some nonsense. Do the children know? They probably had breakfast with him."

"It wasn't like that at all Martin! of course they didn't, they had no idea that he was there. My car broke down outside the school, he came to my rescue and got it started, but it kept stalling, so he followed me home to make sure I arrived. I thanked him and we had a coffee, and one thing led to another."

"You mean he was one of the parents? Who is this bastard, tell me his name." Martin's voice started to rise when a waiter asked if everything was alright, and would they like to order.

She ordered coffee. "I'm not interested in coffee," he shouted. "How many times has he been having COFFEE with you I wonder. Maybe we should have a key party at the school gates, mix and match parents. I really don't want to carry on this conversation." He stood up to go.

"Just a minute, Martin – you want to know why this has come about? Well, I'll tell you. Do you think that buying a big car, a grand house and throwing all the luxuries you can think of at me makes a happy marriage. Well, it may do to some women, but what makes it really work is to see your partner and children when they go to school, or in the evening to help them with their homework, give them baths, tell them stories. No wonder so many marriages break up. At least poverty keeps families together. You know I love you, but you've become a machine. You tell me of the company's ideals and how pure they are, but a glass of water is pure. A little flavour is what makes it interesting."

He slid back into his seat. "That's not true, I have only worked like this for the family. You can't tell me that you don't like the living standards that you have. I have devoted my life to the family. Had I quit and downsized our house and all our possessions, I don't think for one moment you would be happy."

"You're wrong, Martin. When I married you, we had no idea that you would be so successful. We were both working and we got by. I can't remember being happier. I agree that I have accepted your success but not at the expense of losing you."

"Well, I'm afraid you have, and I can't believe that it was the first or will be the last time you've substituted me for someone else." He could not see where this conversation would end, but to his own surprise he was not quite as vehement as he had first intended and left himself open to reconsider both their positions. "I can't discuss this anymore at the moment, I will speak to you and we will discuss the children and what I want to do in a short while."

He left her sitting, sobbing, at the table. Looking back he saw the waiter come to her once again, who would of course sympathise with her, and tomorrow he would come down to breakfast and would be marked as the villain. So be it.

Returning to the office after being away for so long required a clear head. "This was the last thing I needed." He had convinced himself that all his efforts were for his family, but the reality dawned on him that maybe he enjoyed the success too much, and to a great extent had become addicted to it. "Was she right? Have I thrown out the baby with the bath water? Could it be possible that I should blame myself? What else could I have done? Could I allow my children to be brought up without me? God in heaven, give me strength!"

He had devoted well over twenty years to the company and Jango Price, and had risen to Vice President of Spoken Arrow. He made a serious contribution to its success and it was true, he had become wealthy, but if he had slowed down a little more and been at home would it have made such a difference? Maybe this was a glitch…and for the first time in all those years he decided to ask his friend's advice rather than give it.

He phoned Jango to tell him he was coming up. "Give me fifteen minutes, pal, let me finish what I'm doing." Martin made an attempt to take a few notes with him, but his mind was not on his trip.

Coffee was already on the table and he was welcomed back as an old friend with a hug. "I heard that you decided to come back a little earlier Martin, and I was rather surprised that you had organised such a grand tour in the first place. How did it go?"

"The trip was good, we covered a lot of ground, and I've been continuously updated on the UK discussions. It all looks very exciting." How is your young protégé doing, what's her name?

"Miriam Brevotti, she is really a find, I've been receiving a blow by blow account of her discussions with Cambridge University, especially regarding Magnum. We need time to talk about that, I'm expecting her back in two or three weeks. But Mark, I need to ask your opinion on a personal matter."

"Sure, shall I pour us something a little stronger?"

They sat on the settees opposite each other with two whiskies. "I decided to return a little sooner to have Christmas with the family. I really should have brought my entourage back with me while we still had three or four more countries to complete the tour, but enough was enough." Martin found himself rambling. It was not his style, and was noticed.

"Martin, I know you to well enough to know when you've got something to tell me. Come on, spit it out."

"I came home to find Angela with another man."

"He might have been a plumber or electrician or a handy man," Jango remarked.

"He certainly was the latter, he was in his underpants having breakfast and she was in a negligée that I had bought her."

"What did she say?"

"We met at the Hyatt in their restaurant to discuss the situation, I told her I want a divorce."

"Wow, that is a problem. Has she explained anything to you, who the guy was, was it a regular visit, is there a romance? What did she say?"

"Typical garbage about her car breaking down at school, a good Samaritan helped her and she invited him back. I have no idea if it was a one-off or one of a series of bonking sessions."

Jango moved forward onto the edge of his seat. "Listen Martin, consider very carefully what you want to do. Divorce is a messy business. Think how important your relationship is, your kids, her family, whose side will they take; the house, your home. Where will you live? Seriously consider the consequences before you get involved with lawyers, believe me Martin, it's painful… and expensive."

"I'm feeling very bitter at the moment. I could strangle her, to be honest."

"What you need to discover, my friend, is how often has she's seen this guy. If it really is a one off, OK… slap on the hand and get on with it. But if it's a relationship that's another story."

"Why don't we organise a detective agency to monitor her for a short while, maybe two or three weeks, and in the meantime, play it cool.

"What would I do in the meantime, it's Christmas?"

"Go to England, leave a load of presents for the kids. They'll be upset of course, but I can't think of an alternative. It would be far more constricting for you to be here in the US over the holiday than at home. I'm sure that they could do with a little American bla in the UK."

"Let me organise the agency, we'll start it from tomorrow, school ends at the end of this week, we'll find out who the fellow is as well, and we can tap into her computer if you have her code. Naughty I know but who's better at doing this than us." He smiled.

He gave Martin another hug, "We'll work this out together, OK? We've been through a lot together and this is another problem to be solved."

He left feeling a little more confident that his world had not ended. Carolyn booked him an open first class ticket to London. "Shall I notify the staff there that you are coming?" she asked.

"No not yet. After the vacation if I'm still there we can tell them, but you can let Miriam know, she's one of us, and I can catch up on what's happening there, but don't mention any reason other than my curiosity as to how negotiations are going, OK." She knew him well enough to venture a gentle finger wag. "I understand. I'm not in rebound mode, don't worry."

"Just be careful," she said sweetly.

Chapter 43

Heinrich was a broken man. It seemed that whatever he touched became toxic. With the help of Herr Schreiber, he wrote to his father by hand looking for words of consolation but the reply by email was harsh and unforgiving. And why should he be forgiven? He had failed, and now he was to report to his father as if he were back at school.

What was to be the coup of the century had backfired, and backfired so badly that there was still a danger of him losing his freedom for the rest of his life. Of course, had it not been for his dear cousin Gilda he wouldn't have gotten into this mess, but who was to know. It seemed so perfect, and even his father had rejoiced at the idea that his beloved Germany would be contributing such an amazing gift towards the control of the worlds deserving and less deserving population's minds and emotions. What an amazing combination the Autoplug and Ever Young would have been.

He was sitting in the airport lounge awaiting the Brazil flight and taking stock of his current position. Gilda had already left on an earlier flight under a nom de plume. The name of Gilda Baylim would now be associated with the hereafter, and her funeral would be tomorrow, which he would not be able to attend. Herr Schreiber had now taken control of her transition and given her the name of Alicia Trompe of Brazilian birth. Various certificates would show that she was brought up in New York but had lived in Germany for some time and studied in Leipzig University. It was a brilliant idea of Schreiber to allow Gilda Baylim to vanish, and would hopefully give the Heinrich empire another opportunity to find their way back into the market place that they would rightly claim was theirs. It did not matter by what means it was acquired, the winner can always justify their gains.

His father had already informed him that he would be replaced, certainly for the time being, and he would act as adviser to another of his family. His record would be heralded as a great contribution to the growth of the company but his decision to step down would be on the grounds of health.

He could see no way that he could change the agreement laid out in Paris, and as his father stated, despite Steinberg's promise not to reveal the recent history of events, there would be no guarantees that they would honour the deal although it would certainly be in their interest not to do so. It was necessary that he should keep a low profile as in the event of a leak, or else the reputation of the entire organisation would be undermined.

His first-class flight gave him little comfort. The distance, flying time and his own self-pity placed him in a sad condition to meet his parents who were waiting at the welcome desk in Sao Paulo.

There was little they could say to one another. His mother was all forgiving – if her son was able to fight another day then so what he lost part of the business, it was painful but not the end of the world – she hugged him and saw his pain. Not so his father. To him Stefan was a disgrace, having left a trail behind him that could bring down the whole company and negate everything that his grandfather had planned. Furthermore, his cousin Gilda had married and sacrificed a substantial proportion of her life preparing to pass this wonderful innovation onto their fold, and as it stood now it was all in vain. They would have to find a way of capitalising on this situation. There must be a plan – it just had to be found.

The Autoplug was now in fifty-four countries and substantial income was currently derived not only from the service itself, but also from the medication offered to the public from companies owned by Magnum. There was also the wealth of knowledge accumulated by the software from each user that would be evaluated for further use. Buying habits, voting dispositions, income strains, etc. Even their religious bias. In any conversation with the Autoplug it would dissect and categorise every aspect of an individual's lifestyle, giving a fountain of information to Ever Young, and now this information would be passed onto another company. There had to be a way of recouping their losses. Maybe Schreiber's idea would work, and maybe not all was lost.

***

After driving for nearly two hours, they arrived at his parent's ranch. A mansion the size of a five-star hotel surrounded by over a thousand acres. Even from the air it would have been astonishing. It was built in the middle of a large forest, approximately twenty-five acres were cleared at the expense of thousands of trees, and the road had been drawn as if by an ancient civilisation which connected it to modernity. A substantial extension had been added as offices, and although the official headquarters were in the main city on Sao Paolo, a skyscraper of over forty floors, the home of the Heinrich family was considered the heart of the business, and where his father worked.

"How long do we have you for, Steffen?" asked his mother, but even before he could answer his father brusquely interrupted.

"I am waiting for the accounts of Spoken Arrow. We should waste no time in following up the possibility of buying them, or at least taking a majority shareholding. Do you have any figures?" he asked curtly.

"I was waiting for the figures, father. Maybe we could ask your staff it would be quicker to analyse them from here, but we would need deep pockets." His mother kissed him and parted, leaving him alone with his father in his office.

"I suggest that you ship those works of art over to here. If they are kept in Europe they will be a sore reminder of your stupidity."

"I freely admit that events have gone against us, father, but you were made aware of everything that we did. I'm on the front line but I informed you of everything concerning the demise of Baylim and everything that has transpired since. Gilda would never have been able to bring the Autoplug information to us without his death, employing the Russians who appointed the Brenekovs and LeClare in Switzerland. We, not I, are responsible for this mess, but we have a lifeline. You can decide how to direct our efforts to win it back, but please accept some of the responsibility too."

His father gave a deep sigh. "If it hadn't been for that stupid British guy, Joe Brenekov, and his father, everything else would have fallen into place. The sending of the pictures of the stolen works was virtually admission of the thefts. Absolutely ridiculous." Albert Heinrich poured himself a glass of red wine from a decanter. "I don't understand – why did LeClare offer them to you? How did he even know about you, for goodness' sake?"

"Ah," he replied. "He didn't. LeClare was contacted by Brenekov to buy the art, they had probably done business together in the past. He showed the photos to a Russian Oligarch who had no interest but passed them back to the Mafia, who were of course our own contact and we found ourselves negotiating with LeClare. A third party purchase seemed safe enough, who was to know how it would unravel. The British Insurance company instructed to recover them found LeClare's contact on Brenekov's mobile. I had no option but to deal with him."

Albert flopped into his chair. "So we seem to have very few if any, options open to us. We have apparently now given the Autoplug and Ever Young away for nothing, and that has cost us billions in investment and profits. I understand that If we didn't accept the terms you would, without doubt go to jail for life, and maybe even me. So there are no options open to us in that regard. At least we seem to have recovered our main computer business," he sighed.

Steffen sat silently listening to his father. He had no defences left.

"An announcement will be agreed," he continued, "by the UK and ourselves that the Autoplug and Ever Young are to be purchased by the government for an undisclosed amount as far as the public are concerned, but in reality for nothing. It appears that Spoken Arrow, who are our greatest competitor will join them in some way or another. There must not be the slightest suggestion of any misdemeanour and every assistance must be given to them in order that a smooth transition will take place. We must think of a presentation that shows us in a magnanimous act and that is believable."

He was sitting at his desk, seemingly totally composed, and speaking as if reciting a psalm. "It strikes me that the British government would stand to lose a great deal of face as well if your stupidity is revealed. We should have played our cards better than we did. What we need to do is to start buying the shares of Spoken Arrow as inconspicuously as possible, spread the purchases over a number of companies. Of course it depends what's involved and how much can we raise from Pontillo."

He pressed a button and as if by magic a young woman appeared. "Maria, ask Signor Montello to give me a moment please."

Softening his tone Heinrich poured himself another glass of wine. "Do you want one?" he asked. "How is your family?"

"They're good, Susannah is worried of course, but she is well, thank you." He tried to hold back tears as his father watched him break down. At last, he came over and hugged him as he sobbed.

Montello had been with the organisation for over thirty years and was considered to be Heinrich's most trusted executive. Now Financial Director of the parent company, it was inevitable that he should be taken into their confidence. Nevertheless, it was not necessary for him to know the gory details.

"Alfredo, I need your opinion on Spoken Arrow. You know of Spoken Arrow of course."

Seeing Steffen on the settee with his head in his hands, and having watched him grow into manhood, Alfredo immediately walked over to shake his hand. "Hello Steffen, what a pleasant surprise! I haven't seen you for at least two years. Are you and the family well?" Steffen hesitated. Alfredo could see that all was not as it should be, and quickly returned his attention to his boss.

"Er, yes of course I know them. We've been shadowing them for years. What would you like to know Albert?"

"Their worth, stock ratings, turnover, share distribution. Cash in hand. A broad picture at this stage. They are beating us on some of our products, and we are considering buying in to them. It's a matter of what our exposure is. How quickly can you put something together? For the purpose of the exercise let's get some pencilled figures to begin with. Can you get me an outline by tomorrow?" "No problem. Nice to see you again Steffen." "Same here," he replied, looking up.

It was obvious that something was amiss but he decided that it was not a particularly good moment to ask any further questions, he bade farewell and left.

***

Four hours later, Montello placed a six page document on Albert Heinrich's desk marked <u>Abbreviated Financial Summary of Spoken Arrow.</u>

Worldwide Turnover $95 billion. Profit $7.5 billion. Loan capitol $18 billion. Net value $82 billion. Executive holdings $9 billion. Minimum required to take control approx. $38 billion.

The forward gave him the guide lines he was looking for. Studying the relevant figures, it was clear that they would have a challenge.

"So," said Heinrich, "can we raise thirty-eight billion dollars through Pontillo?"

Alfredo sat as if exhausted. "Not easily, we have assets to cover this amount but are spread over various banks and a multitude of investments as you know, but it would be stretching our finances to a painful point. It's not as if the money is just sitting in the bank, it's working for us in a myriad of industries. We could take out a loan, we would have no problem in borrowing at least thirty percent of the money, but if we could reduce the value of their shares somehow, compromise them in some way. Put a shock through the stock market, that would help a little to reduce our purchasing price, even if only temporarily. I'll give some thought to that."

Heinrich stared at the figures. "If we spread the purchases over nine or ten financial houses around the world, slowly taking parcels of shares under different companies, it wouldn't be too obvious."

"Once we get to twenty percent" Alfredo replied. "We'd have to reveal ourselves. That's where the battle really starts. But if we can get to thirty percent or even twenty-seven percent of the shares we could probably take control, and they're ours. It's a big gamble, Albert, and we're risking our reserves."

337

"But if we win my friend, we would not only have the Autoplug and Ever Young; we would totally dominate the world's computer market, and to hell with the international laws. Fifty percent of all computers around the entire world would be ours. We would have access to billions of users. Now that's power."

***

As soon as Alfredo left, Heinrich went to his computer and tapped in Gilda's number. She immediately answered in German.

"Gilda, Uncle Albert here, welcome home." He smiled as if she was facing him. "I haven't had the chance to speak with you since you arrived, I have Steffen with me, would you like to come over, it would be good to see you after so long." In fact, her uncle had barely spoken to her for the last thirty years, and in truth there was no reason for him to do so, after all, her decision to study in G. Britain as a young woman would isolate her from her family and most of her old friends. She had no immediate reason to return to Berlin.

"Nobody but her mother would have described her as an attractive young woman, and she had little interest in succumbing to the latest fashions. A good book or a historical debate was all that was necessary for her to justify her existence."

Gilda's interest in neural biology was her driving force. It was more than an interest it was an obsession. Not only the study of the brain, but the knowledge of how to control the minds of others, it was her first love. That and the history of Germany from the twelfth century. "If a little more effort would have been given to the manipulation of the mind in the thirties, who knows how Germany would have benefitted. What could human endeavour achieve if the masses were better directed." She was fortunate and brilliant enough to be offered a place in Cambridge university in the UK and committed herself to a Masters, and eventually a PhD at the age of thirty She became a professor. Her presented theses bordered on science fiction.

George Baylim had already completed his research of the Autoplug, and was now attempting with his colleagues to examine the medical implications of controlling genetic inheritance that would eventually become the Ever Young project. Gilda attended a lecture given by him, it was as if he had read her mind. Bombarding him with questions she was obsessed with his intellect, and in the early days of their relationship she became his disciple and eventually lover. It was a meeting of the minds rather than body or emotions that held them together,

George's ability to turn theory into actuality was a talent that she admired most, for whilst her days were still committed to theorems, he was deeply involved in bringing concepts into a reality. Life changing ideas that would make a difference.

Her historical ties to the Fatherland gave her a burning desire to use what she had learned for the benefit of her country, and with this in mind a constant dialogue emerged between her and her cousin Steffen who was slowly emerging as the inheritor of an ever growing computer empire based in Berlin and financed from Brazil. It was always accepted where their wealth had emanated from, but she concluded that it was a rite of passage from a filthy war that should have been won by intellectual superiority, and revelled in the thought that the winner does not always take all.

However it soon became obvious after a short while that George's practical world was in shambles, and the lack of ability to find the finance for his projects, allowed her the opportunity to take the reins. She persuaded Cambridge to continue to commit vast sums to the projects and substantial grants from the government. Their marriage was one of convenience. It was not an unhappy relationship but without any serious affection.

At last, Autoplug was ready to be offered to the world. The University had allowed their team to pursue a dream that would or could change the lifestyle of every human on the planet. Cambridge had paid the salaries of twelve neuroscientists for the last seven years. But even with government grants, research money alone would not launch it. If the Autoplug was to continue to take full advantage of its full potential, it would require the total cooperation of every department within the government and an investment plus at least two hundred million pounds cash flow building up to a billion worldwide to make it a global business.

Every doctors' surgery in Europe and the Americas could eventually change their system to the Autoplug. George Baylim had no idea what to do. He approached a few large corporations who considered the project but after a number of discussions it became clear to them that he would be a difficult man to work with. His presentation to large corporate organisations had no financial, administerial or marketing infrastructure, and regardless of its potential, negotiations failed. All this shadow boxing amounted to nothing for Gilda. It was obvious to her that nothing would come of this amazing invention unless George left the scene. Commercially and financially he was a liability. Ever Young that was concurrently developed, to George was a separate project, but to Gilda and her family it was a perfect match.

This was her moment. Hardly a week would pass when she did not write to Steffen describing how the Autoplug and Ever Young were progressing. Her family had the monies, and she had the brains. She had given George as much rope as he wanted, and she wanted his efforts to fail.

Steffen wrote back instructing her to speak with the Minister of Health, informing him that she had a company that would back the project but only with the cooperation of the government. With the advice given to her by her cousin, she calculated how much the government would save, and earn from each patient that used it, which would eventually earn billions annually. Brendon Tann presented it to the Chancellor of the Exchequer. It soon became clear that the gargantuan task of cooperating with each department would require working closely with the relevant civil servants, and private financial agreements were agreed with a number of departments to maintain their enthusiasm for the project. What did they have to lose? There was no further need of government investment. A long list of government servants substantially benefitted from Tann's generosity via Magnum that enabled the Autoplug to be launched in record time.

Using incentives to bypass the usual governmental bureaucracy was not a business that George condoned but it was an inevitable decision that he had to go with. However, once established and showing a substantial profit for the government, Ever Young would piggyback on its success. By the time of the Autoplug's launch, many millions had been invested with benefits given to various ministers and those working with them.

***

All this was now in vain and, five years on, her passport and travelling documents registered her as Alicia Trompe and any future reference to Gilda would be in that name. Gilda Baylim was deceased and bore no relationship to her new self. May she rest in peace. It was understandable therefore for Heinrich's personal secretary to record that a visitor from Germany by the name of Alicia Troupe would be arriving and to have freedom of the inner sanctum of the Magnum corporation.

But it is not easy to lose a name. Gilda arrived at the reception desk to see the President of a multi-billion dollar organisation claiming that she was expected, and naturally gave the name that had belonged to her for forty-five years. After all, she was coming to see her uncle. Her Spanish was marginally less than basic, but her name and his should be enough to give her at least a visitor's badge.

"I'm sorry Señora but your name is not registered with us," she responded curtly, and before Gilda had a chance to correct herself, the woman pressed a button to call her supervisor.

She spoke quickly and from what Gilda could understand required an answer of explanation. Now feeling cornered she tried to make her understand her German.

Repeating in the language of her birth to explain that Herr Heinrich was expecting her, and realising her error, she now had to justify that her name was not Gilda Baylim. Her explanation only antagonised both ladies even more, and after consulting with one another called the security guard. Gilda decided not to wait for his arrival. She turned on her heal and left.

Once outside the building she phoned Steffen on her mobile. He was not inclined to take calls at that time. She tried again.

The two ladies saw her loitering outside and considered that she may be a security risk.

The scene now became a high point in what would otherwise be a rather boring and quiet day. Within five minutes, a sleek black sedan stopped outside the entrance, and a tall, uniformed woman alighted. Her ancestry may have been Amazonian for she showed power and beauty in the way an advert for Brazilian authority should look.

Both were searching for a common tongue and to Gilda's great relief found her superior female, certainly of physique, and could understand a little English. Gilda showed her new passport without explanation other than she was Alicia Trompe to meet President Heinrich.

Her mood was not improved by this small debacle, and at last, face-to-face with her uncle, she referred her remarks to Steffen who was still in the position of remorse and slouching on the settee.

"All my work has come to nothing. I did whatever you recommended, and now, after all these years, I'm told that I have a new name and personal history, sent to Brazil to live and a language that I can hardly speak. I'm a refugee from justice. Everything I did was for my country, I hoped that you would be able to protect me Steffen."

"How could I do that, we are in the same boat," he replied.

Albert heard her pain, "Listen Gilda, if we had not killed you off the British government would certainly have arrested you for the murder of your husband.

But I don't believe that all is lost. I work on a basic principle in business: If you can't beat them, buy them."

"We will have you back in the saddle again but you must be patient. In the meantime, I would like to suggest that you work with our research department here in Sao Paul. You must hide your name from everyone. From now on, and I mean from now you will answer to Alicia. That is the only sacrifice. We shall have cards printed for you and I will organise accommodation for you, and Spanish lessons and whatever else you need. You cannot of course go back to Europe unless you have plastic surgery, you are one of the family. We'll add the name Trompe to the family tree," Steffen could not help spitting out a laugh.

"Your funeral is tomorrow," he guffawed. "Sorry I won't be able to make it."

"If I had my way it would be yours," she sneered.

"In the meantime, Steffen, you will return to Berlin and conclude this deal with the British and give them all the support they need," interrupted his father. "We shall continue to offer our medication through the Autoplug until they change the software, which will take some time. We shall say that the Autoplug and Ever Young belongs to the UK and that as a gesture of goodwill we are passing the entire operation over to them for an unrevealed sum. The world will know how generous of spirit we are. We shall say that we are directing our efforts in other very exciting areas which we shall disclose in due time. Do you understand?"

Steffen said nothing but nodded.

"…and don't forget to send the art over as quickly as possible."

"But what will I say if they demand it back? They've photographed it."

"Tell them they were mistaken—it must have been somewhere else that the pictures were taken."

"They'll never believe that!" shouted Steffen.

"So what? There's no one alive that can say they sold it to us. We shall simply call them liars. If it's not there, it never existed. Besides, if they did suggest that we have it, it will bring the entire house down." He chuckled.

Chapter 44
USA Martin

Martin had now spent two gruelling weeks in the Hyatt hotel, He could not bear to return to the house, and arranged to meet his children at his hotel. He made no secret to them that he was "having a disagreement with their Mummy," but even though they returned to their home loaded with Christmas presents, it soon became clear to them, even in their childish innocence that they were going to lose their daddy.

Having now decided to take his colleague's advice and remove himself from the domestic scene for a few weeks, he arranged a meeting with Robert and Jay updating himself on the negotiations in the UK relating to Magnum. They informed him that although they had left England without a conclusion, they had worked with their counterparts at Cambridge and were confident of a positive outcome. Miriam had decided to spend the Christmas holiday with her family and also discover how the discussions between Magnum and the government would be resolved.

Carolyn notified Miriam that Martin would be joining her and it would be a good idea to meet him at Heathrow. It was over twenty five years since he had last visited London and even that was only for ten days, passing through from Italy to the States. He was still a G.I. bachelor then and without a care in the world. Once whilst reliving the past he recalled with a rue smile that he had a fleeting relationship with a beautiful young woman that he'd chatted up in a coffee shop in SoHo, and wondered what she might be doing now. Probably a wife with three kids. "The oldest could look like me," he mused. Looking back in time. Life was one big roundabout. "Sometimes it's best not to get off."

Miriam could not deny that she was excited to see her boss on her home territory. She had already organised a meeting with Dr Ellsworth and was rather interested in arranging another meeting for Martin and Jack.

From the story that Jack had described, the final negotiations would be with the British government and it would only be appropriate for Martin to discuss with them both the finances and equity that they would probably want to retain, and certainly a meeting with Sir Henry Porter. He would also wish to visit the UK headquarters.

In spite of Martin's efforts to appear his old self, it was obvious to Miriam even as he walked through the exit door of the airport, that something was wrong. The right words were said with the correct enthusiasm, but he appeared less than straight as if he was carrying a knapsack, but most of all were his eyes, they were dull and glared rather than the sparkle that she had gotten used to.

Carolyn had booked him into a suite at the Hilton, and it seemed appropriate that Miriam should rebook herself there. She was slightly ashamed to have an excuse to leave her parents with a degree of relief. Claustrophobia was slowly overwhelming her, as was her waist line, but she also felt it appropriate to be available to her boss and guide him through the negotiations. They installed themselves in their respective rooms and arranged to meet for lunch.

"I've arranged a number of meetings for you to appreciate the circumstances as they currently are. Whether we like it or not we're going to be involved in a political situation Martin, but I believe that the result will certainly be in our favour." She reiterated the events that she had been told by Jack, explaining that "Magnum would be prepared to transfer ownership of the Autoplug and Ever Young to the government almost as a gift but would retain their computer division."

"This is remarkable," he exclaimed. "The business will be worth billions and they're prepared to give it away!"

"It's the price Heinrich is paying for not going to jail for life."

"But if it is proven that he has no legal right to the Autoplug anyway, why let him off the hook for murder?"

"Ah, there's the rub. Number one. If it's discovered that there was bribery on a massive scale within the government which resulted in the murder of a Minister and his wife, plus the professor that invented it, it would bring the government down. So a compromise has been agreed to keep the muck under the carpet. Secondly, if it went to court, it could take years before a conclusion was arrived at, this way we can walk in and literally take the operation over, and with the cooperation of Magnum. The government and Cambridge will have a small equity and we will take the remainder."

"And what do they believe that equity will be, has it been discussed?"

"No, that's for you to negotiate, but I would say five or ten percent."

They sat in the hotel restaurant finding small talk. "How was your trip to South America? We thought you were not returning for another month. We were a little surprised that you'd originally planned to be away over the Christmas holidays. I bet your wife and kids were delighted to see you." She smiled.

"Didn't Carolyn inform you?"

"Inform me of what? No, she hasn't said anything except that you were visiting the UK. What should I know?"

He knew that the subject would arise, he needed to talk about it. It was waiting to be poured out, even to a comparative stranger, his hurt was overwhelming. And here he was six thousand miles away transporting his grief to this beautiful woman. The words of Carolyn reverberated in his head: "be careful!" Consolation leads to comfort, which is exactly what he needed.

Miriam listened to his plight with complete concentration, but understanding well how her response could compound events. Her own desires must be resisted. I am a wall, an Autoplug she reminded herself. And she listened, showing kindness but withholding her hidden thoughts.

After lunch, she left him to catch up on the nine hours' difference. She arranged as many meetings as she thought would benefit him and justify the trip. Jack was to be the mediator with the government and would be the last of this series once he was fully aware of all the other circumstances relevant to the project.

Sleep came quickly and it was early morning when he arose. He had slept for nine hours and booked in at the Gym, swam, and was at last ready to take on the world.

"I've arranged a meeting with Dr Ellsworth in Cambridge for 1.30 pm today, is that good for you?" Miriam asked.

"Absolutely, shall we meet in the foyer at 10.45 am?"

***

Cambridge was comparatively quiet as the university was now on Christmas leave. Ellsworth took advantage of the break to catch up with his paperwork. His temporary help and one of his favourite pupils being Helga, and as she was so closely involved in this project he allowed her to be present to take notes in the meeting.

The Olde World that he had only seen in Movies was replicated when entering Ellsworth's office. The musty smell gave him the impression of the second-hand bookshop he used to frequent when a student in LA, now no longer existing and replaced by a multi-storied all-singing, all-dancing bookstore with cross-legged students sipping skinny latte coffees. He had a great desire to nuzzle into a history book and release himself from the cut and thrust of the modern world. Miriam observed that Ellsworth was still wearing the same old tweed jacket and corduroy trousers with pipe between teeth. To Martin he was straight out of a 1950 black and white movie.

However, it very soon became clear that the doctor's knowledge of his subject needed an explanation in simpler terms.

Ellsworth discussed with Martin the dynamics of both projects. How the software of the Autoplug was written and transposed from the various government and social sources, then cataloguing to the individual's code number, and whatever information the consumer chose to confide, the Autoplug assessed it and the Hologram responded logically with advice.

The Doctor was told of Gilda's suicide which confirmed her involvement in the demise of his friend. He made no secret of his dislike for her. No one knew better than he what the ultimate objectives of Magnum were, and for the first time he admitted a certain shame for not divulging this information for fear of his own life.

He revisited the files of Ever Young for children which was certainly more appealing than the current 351 scheme that Heinrich was so intent on pursuing. All the relevant children's tests had to be updated and claims verified before launching. The health and mental status of every child injected with the microchip had been catalogued on the Autoplug and monitored annually ad infinitum. It was expected that the cost charged would be covered by the State, and whilst there were no guarantees offered, the health of the child would be substantially improved. There was no doubt that Ever Young would make a massive impact on the health of future generations, but it would be difficult to find a financial benefit from it. Nevertheless, as research scientists the financial aspects of gain were of a lower priority.

As the Marketing Director of one of the largest and most prominent computer companies in the world it was necessary for Martin to understand the complexity of the Autoplug or at least its conceptual workings, and it gave both men considerable pleasure to exchange the minutiae of this amazing development which he was going to take control of. How astonishing that such a happening should fall on his shoulders.

They stopped for lunch at the university's canteen. There were no airs and graces, just four learned individuals sitting around a metal table next to an array of students, lecturers and secretaries. No one knew him, to all intents and purposes he was simply another student. From time to time, a young man or woman would pass by greeting the Doctor or Helga, Martin found himself totally at ease in this academic Shangri-lar.

"We are arranging a meeting with Sir Henry Porter for tomorrow, I think that Jack will also be there. Especially since he's been involved in discussions directly with Heinrich in Germany."

"Yes, he holds the key to all the parties involved," said Helga.

She took Miriam by surprise with her knowledge, not only of the subject matter but also the politics of the Magnum proposition which she appeared to know better than Miriam.

"I'm most impressed by your grasp of the situation Helga." She tried not to sound too condescending but there seemed no other way to ask.

"Yes," she replied with innocent enthusiasm. "I've been assisting Jack, and since my first language is German, I'm Swiss by the way, it was useful for him to know what they were discussing, especially when they thought we didn't understand." She blushed. "And since I'm a student of the Doctor my knowledge of the subject helped considerably." There was an ocean of information given in that blush, it was an unspoken language reserved for women who understand the nuances invariably too subtle for men to catch.

An awkward silence was broken by Martin.

"Well, I would have thought that you were English," commented Martin, "you certainly speak the language better than I do."

"That's understandable," laughed Miriam. "Americans don't speak English, but if you stay here long enough we'll teach you." "I'll think about it," he replied.

The two women smiled with their mouths but their eyes and thoughts were elsewhere.

***

In view of Martin's senior status within the company Sir Henry decided that it would be more appropriate to include as many involved parties who would have a vested interest as possible.

They travelled by taxi to the city and, whilst only three miles in distance, it was a million miles from his memory of a quarter of a century ago. "What on earth has happened to your city?" he proclaimed. "It's transformed from a historic tourist spot to a dynamic multi-cultural and architectural experiment."

"We try our best, but we still hang on to the old ways where we can. When you meet Sir Henry Porter and the Dean of Cambridge, Sir William Hoddington, you will see England at its best."

It was 3.00 pm. Cold, raining and already getting dark. A relative novelty for Martin when they arrived at the Gherkin, and to both their surprise were escorted into a full board room. Martin had not mentally prepared for his welcome. If this meeting had taken place in Los Angeles, he thought, he would have been wearing jeans, sneakers and a t-shirt, as would have been the others; and whilst he appreciated the British degree of correctness, he felt a little out of place with a sports jacket and an open shirt. Nevertheless, his suntan justified his casual attire and gave him the excuse that he was from sunnier climes.

Business cards of each of the main proponents were passed to Martin and Miriam. She was pleased to note that Jack had been included with Ellsworth. Mrs Steinberg sat next to him on behalf of the government. Two juniors had their computers ready to stenograph and analyse all the various comments. Sitting next to Jack was Helga, who was already tabulating the various cards passed around.

The moment Sir Henry stood up it was clear that he intended to give a performance. His double-breasted suit perfectly tailored to cover his substantial size, the points of a pocket handkerchief just visible, and he himself stood slightly inclined forward and with the tips of his fingers gently touching the table, he looked at his audience, took a sip of water, cleared his throat, and began. "It is indeed a pleasure to welcome you to our humble country, Mr Moran. Many great and important personalities from all over the world have come through our doors: academics, politicians, businessmen…and women, I hasten to add, and now to add you to our list of honour gives me great pleasure." There was no doubt that he was playing to his audience, but after all, the Spoken Arrow was one of the most prominent computer innovators in the world, and he had the Vice President sitting in his offices. Martin was in no doubt that there was a play being made for his account, but he enjoyed the pure pomp and plumbiness of the presentation.

"We are discussing two ingenious projects which are the brain children of Cambridge University have been successfully marketed by Magnum. May I first state that whatever is discussed at this meeting must be considered strictly confidential. As we all know, this company competes for world domination with Spoken Arrow. We are claiming that the patents that they hold have been taken by devious means, and following discussions with the government represented here by Mrs Steinberg K.C. of Halter Jones representing the British government, who have agreed to reclaim the business of the Autoplug which is already generating a turnover of over four billion pounds throughout Europe and will probably double during the next four years. Ever Young was to be launched imminently but has been withheld due to a change in its claims.

"Magnum has gracefully accepted that Cambridge University currently own the correct patents and are prepared to avoid litigation by transferring the business over to them and the government who have already invested a considerable sum into its research.

"The amount for the transfer of this specific business is undisclosed as Magnum is privately owned and wish the negotiations to be strictly confidential. However there will not be any return of monies from the government invested by Magnum nor would there be any litigation in respect to any loss of profits by Cambridge.

"Neither the government nor Cambridge University have the facilities or the cash flow which is estimated at approximately five billion pounds to perpetuate this business and therefore it is considered sensible and in all our interests to work with your company Mr Moran to carry the baton as it were. Magnum are prepared to give us whatever information is required to perpetuate the existing operation including the return of the brand names.

"Our initial discussions on behalf of the university and Halter Jones representing the government suggest a new company be formed offering ten percent of the shareholding to Cambridge University and ten percent to the government with the remaining eighty percent to Spoken Arrow, plus a goodwill gesture by yourselves of two-and-a-half billion pounds. Shared between the government and Cambridge University, of which Dr Ellsworth and his team would receive five million pounds. I hope that I have given you a fair overview of the proposition Mr Moran and your thoughts would be most appreciated."

Before Martin was able to reply, Miriam jumped in. "Please excuse my intervention Sir Henry, but you will appreciate that Mr Moran has had little opportunity to consider the ramifications of this acquisition, and as exciting as it is, nothing was mentioned during our initial discussions of a downpayment of two point five billion. We quite appreciate that equity should be offered and naturally a cash flow requirement underwritten. But it is rather surprising to find a further goodwill gesture of such a large sum."

Sir Henry pointed to his head of finance. "John, would you like to answer Miss Brevotti?"

"Certainly, Sir Henry. We have estimated that this business has already a bottom line profit for this year of nearly seven hundred million pounds. We believe that it would probably have lost two billion during the first two years. You would of course be able to avoid the vast majority of this learning curve, and what you will buy is pure profit."

Martin was well aware of Sir Henry's negotiating tactics and decided to respond in kind. "You know, Sir Henry, I haven't been back to the UK for many years and am so impressed by its dynamism and how it seems to have held onto its traditional Englishness. I note in particular the negotiating skills that made it so great, that we in the US sometimes lack. However on this occasion I believe that we are discussing hopes and aspirations since we don't appear to have accurate figures to show how, or even if, profits are being generated at this time, and for all we know they may be losing as much as your assumed profits – that's an uncalculated risk. I rather doubt that Magnum will release their figures, so we have to surmise. Now we are all aware of the benefits of the Autoplug, but from what I understand in spite of its standalone benefits it was to be a tool for Magnum to sell their drugs and also share its information in conjunction with the 351 Ever Young, with what we now understand may have been devious intent."

"Nevertheless," replied Sir Henry, "even if you are correct, your stock holding would jointly give you an immediate profit of a hundred and fifty million pounds."

Martin smiled. "OK. I take your point, Sir Henry. I wonder though if it is possible to find some accurate figures that we can assess the business by, even if they are academically calculated? We are obviously interested in becoming your partners and taking the business forward, but like any business an assessment of its viability is essential before we throw our hat into the ring. Do you have that expression here? After all, we have to report to our shareholders, even if we are getting a bargain," he said light-heartedly.

Using the moment to gather his thoughts, "The important point of this meeting, I believe, Mr Moran, is for us to agree that we have a desire to come to an agreement, and from that point of understanding everything is possible, don't you agree? Mrs Steinberg, would you like to give us your opinion?"

She did not need to stand and Jack noticed that her ability to hold her audience showed in her timing and poise. "Yes. Thank you, Sir Henry. I assume that we are all aware of the circumstances and reasoning that has brought us together. Herr Heinrich has not given his very successful operation away because he likes us. We are protecting him from far worse than the loss of his business. We are dealing here with a murderer, a man who has or had an ultimate objective and means to alter the mind sets of millions. His base in Brazil holds considerable sums and he would have liked to use this ill-gotten fortune especially with the Ever Young project to reincarnate a philosophy which existed before and during the Second World War. We must ensure that he does not find a way to gain a footing into what we believe is a most dangerous concept."

"I have been told by the Prime Minister that even more than any monies made by any party here, it is essential to change the modus operandi of this product, which I hope Mr Moran, on behalf of his company, will agree to. But to expose him openly would create great uncertainty on the world markets and, even at the risk of allowing him a degree of freedom, we believe that would be most unwise."

"However it should be said and obvious to all in this room that we are totally reliant on Spoken Arrow to complete this deal and whilst a certain degree of goodwill be forthcoming, they will without doubt be gaining a substantial asset. I would therefore suggest that a friendly compromise should be found as soon as possible. Sir William, as both of these projects evolved from your university, may we have your thoughts?"

"Thank you, Mrs Steinberg. If we are to assume that the Autoplug and Ever Young still belong to Cambridge, and due to our own ignorance we have allowed it to be completed by another and devious party, I would be happy to place ourselves in the hands of our American friends on the understanding, of course, that we receive some long-term benefits."

"May I say a few words?" asked Jack. "The two projects should not under any circumstance be joined as one. Ever Young is currently designed to terminate those that have signed up for it not by discussion, but by a button or even worse programmed by a computer switching off that life. Furthermore, by using the same technology this automated system would also have the facility to monitor and control mood swings, aggression, excitement, depression and early termination where ever and whomever they wish. Coordinated with the Autoplug which will be able to evaluate the idiosyncrasies of every individual and respond according to its controller's wishes. It becomes a Big Brother. Race, colour, religion, political persuasion and thoughts of millions around the world will be in the controllers' hands. Thumbs up or thumbs down, according to the administrator. Age ninety-five is the shop window, but the devil's in the small print and intent."

"I must confess," Miriam interspersed, as if thinking aloud, "that I have used the Autoplug occasionally, and it became a replacement for a confessional box. I should be quite worried to think that it was monitoring my most confidential admissions, but used in isolation it will without doubt save billions and give great benefits to all that use it."

The men looked at her in surprise, maybe thinking how interesting it might be to have listened in. Helga covered her mouth and smiled but said nothing.

Ellsworth gently raised his hand. and taking control again, Sir Henry replied, "Please, doctor, what would you like to say?"

"It should be noted that Ever Young was originally directed towards children and we have proven conclusively that we can use it repair and improve DNA. Of course there was no external communication attached to the original microchip. The 351 Microchip was never a consideration until Gilda Baylim introduced it. The modus operandi moved from children to the older group and claimed to repair mental problems as well as offering a final termination date. Mrs Baylim was able to prove to the government represented by Mr Tann, the Minister of Health, that substantial savings could be made, and that it would solve geriatric overflow in the healthcare system. Of course, at the time we had no option but to redirect our efforts to the ever-increasing older population, since she took control of our research, however I am very keen to revert to our original program which will prolong millions of children's lives. As you may know she moved over to Magnum and no doubt was their driving force. I'm told that she has committed suicide, so I would be most surprised if they rekindle the operation within the near future."

"That's a most comforting thought, Doctor," offered Mrs Steinberg. "And if that is to be the further direction of this project I would be happy to inform the Prime Minister."

"I should just mention," said Jack, "that the Jack-in-the-box – excuse the pun – is already out and whilst it is absolutely correct to confine our efforts to the children's health but we cannot de-invent what already exists." There was an embarrassing silence.

"Well noted," commented Sir Henry. "Can we at least agree that for our part we can squash conclusively the 351 in favour of the children's inoculation under Ever Young for the moment. I think we all appreciate the problems with the adult version," he said condescendingly.

A number of points were raised on the order of preparation for a first draft agreement which took a further fifty minutes.

"All agreed." He nodded to his secretary who was typing notes, "Please ensure that the approval is in your Minutes Judith, and it is written into a prerequisite within an agreement with Spoken Arrow, if I may be so bold Mr Moran."

Directing his attention towards Martin "I suggest Mr Moran that in the first instance we draw up a draft contract between Magnum, the government and Cambridge, and as soon as you and I have found a mutual understanding, consider a more specific agreement to transfer shares to yourselves. When might we meet again? Can we say the beginning of next week? Will this give you time to discuss your thoughts with your colleagues?"

"I would have thought so. Shall we say next Tuesday?" replied Martin. "I shall pass you details of our UK and LA lawyers and let them haggle over the terminology."

"Excellent. Can we all put Tuesday, 2.00 pm in our diaries, ladies and gentlemen?"

Thanks and handshakes were offered all round and the group parted. Martin noted no back slapping, hugging or typical jokes that he experienced in the States. It was so very English.

As they were leaving, Sir Henry took Mrs Steinberg aside, "that was an inspiration of yours to suggest a two and a half billion pound overrider, Hermione, it rather took Moran aback, but it shouldn't be obvious that we know each other. The irony is that we don't have an alternative firm in the event that Spoken Arrow decide not to go with us. If they decide not to, we're a ship without a rudder."

"I agree, but they will know that. In any case, I don't see why we should give it to them for nothing, but they'll no doubt come up with an alternative offer," she replied. "We'll hold on for one point five billion pounds."

***

Martin left the discussion in deep thought. It had been more intense than expected. Sir Henry had intimated a moral obligation for Spoken Arrow to control the future of the Autoplug and Ever Young. No one would doubt that Spoken Arrow had been run with a moral ethos but had in essence a strong commercial bias. The business that he was now about to add to it was a life changer which imposed a deep ethical responsibility on whomever controlled it. It was not only what he was about to inherit but a serious consideration of the future implications in the wrong hands according to Sir Henry, and like everything else that they had invented would eventually be copied. How many

Germanys were there in the world, Fascist, racist, communist, or simply fanatical dictators that could copy and deflect from its benefits to their own ends. Even now, if the Neuro351 brain chip found its way into the world market it could have devastating implications and his company would be sucked into a political quagmire even if they only ran with the Autoplug.

"You know Miriam, I'm not sure that this is the right path for our company to go down, it's very heavy in content and a big responsibility. We would have to consider our cash flow too. Particularly Ever Young which carries a political stigma and no visible financial return."

"I quite understand," she replied. "But Life isn't simply about making money, you know that, and here we have an opportunity to really help the human race, doing something really good. We fight wars to do that, sacrifice our lives. You are on the threshold of making a decision that can really change the world Martin, and it's been thrown into your lap. And maybe mine too, if I may be so bold. By coordinating the Autoplug with Ever Young, our personal problems pale into insignificance in comparison to the tremendous benefits that we can offer to humanity especially for the kids, but I agree, we should take it stage by stage, let's see how matters resolve themselves and make a decision based on that."

Without any warning, he hugged her in the middle of the street. It was not what she said but the feeling that his very sanity was held in her hands.

***

Mrs Steinberg brought her notes of the meeting to the PM and gently placed them on his desk. "I'm quite satisfied Alex that everything will go to plan, unless of course there's a leak, but that's an unknown. But so far there hasn't been a peep from the media. The acquisition of the Autoplug and Ever Young can be agreed without too much delay.

"We must ensure that all relevant information of the Autoplug's assets, its locations, staff details etc. will be freely transferred to the UK. We will need a specific office to handle all relevant information, and it would be a good idea if we can persuade Dr Ellsworth and his team to work with the Magnum scientists to update their information. Everything of course depends on Spoken Arrow's agreement to buy it from us, it's a mammoth task but I'm confident that they can handle it."

"Very good," he replied. "Agree a date for the official transfer, the quicker we can do this deal the happier I'll be. I don't want it on our books a moment longer than necessary."

"I need to contact Herr Schreiber to clarify the details," she said. "It will be up to Spoken Arrow to decide which of their staff they will take over at home and abroad. I assume that both the Autoplug and Ever Young will obviously operate as a separate division of the business."

Throwing his eye over her file and finding the salient points "If it has generally been agreed that eighty percent will be passed over to Spoken Arrow. Ten percent to Cambridge and ten percent to the government. We will need to form a separate holding company Hermione. Is it going to cost us anything, bearing in mind that we have already poured millions in grants?"

"On the contrary Alex, we have asked Spoken Arrow for two point five billion pounds, after all they would be taking all the hard ware over which must have cost Magnum a considerable sum."

"Two point five billion," he smiled. "My goodness, We'll talk about this formation in a little more detail, don't you know. In truth, we're selling something that we don't even own."

She laughed. "We'll probably agree on a little less, but that will be alright too," she winked. "We'll sort the details out with Sir Henry, he wants the Spoken Arrow account on his books so he might as well do some work for it. And what shall we do with Tann?" she asked.

"Nothing at the moment, let him carry on with what he's doing. Of course he won't get any more backhanders from Magnum, he'll have to work for his money…and there's always Derek," he chuckled. "Is he still in Germany? If so bring him back. I'll speak with him. The important thing is that we're out of the woods, that is of course provided young Jack doesn't spill the beans."

"If there was even a whiff of us being involved with a murder, it would bring all the cards down. Do you think he would take a 'present'?" asked the PM. "A token of our appreciation?"

"No, I already suggested it but he refused it point blank, he's of the mind that everyone involved should get their comeuppance. He's a very straight young man. When the dust settles maybe an OBE, he's too young for a knighthood."

"I'm not too keen on the comeuppance bit," he smiled. Fumbling through some papers he mused, "What do you think of a consultancy which will hold, say, two percent of the ten, and invoice for advice given? We would need to find a non de plume, maybe a trust – my name can't be seen on it of course…and maybe a float of, say, five hundred thousand to cover expenses."

"Of course. Alex, leave it to me," she replied with a smile.

Chapter 45
Spoken Arrow

The UK administration for Spoken Arrow is based in Bracknell on the outskirts of London. It also controls sales throughout Europe, with the exclusion of France and Germany who have similar facilities. In total, there are two thousand seven hundred and fifty employees in the UK, covering software, hardware, stock control and accounts, plus of course the retail outlets. Bracknell services three hundred and fifty Spoken Arrow stores in the UK alone selling computers and mobiles of every size and level of sophistication.

It would have been a flag day if even a general overseer from the USA came to visit, but the Vice President of the worldwide corporation was a unique treat.

Martin had considered simply popping in unannounced. It was typical of him to undersell himself, and Miriam had to forcibly persuade him and explained how excited the staff would be to be in the presence of such an elevated human, an icon of the industry, and a man who invented their jobs from scratch.

He was still very fragile and she was conscious of how much he needed comforting and consolation, she had never met a man with such a strong charisma but the last thing she wanted was to be "the other woman." It was a most difficult situation, she would have loved to become his lover, to be more coquettish, a tease, even his mistress, but she knew that it would rebound on both of them and close the door forever on his marriage.

In anticipation of taking over the Autoplug, it was necessary to find a home for it within the organisation, and with this in mind a meeting was arranged to visit the UK head office. The UK M.D. was a gentleman by the name of Terrence Dole. Carolyn had already supplied Martin with notes on the British operation, which was highly successful, and they decided within reason to take him into their confidence.

Although Miriam had spoken with the UK head office many times, she had never had the need to visit them, and now as it was, they would both be entering the business as a pair, with wagging tongues, wondering, and probably concluding that the business was an accessory to their perceived relationship.

Dole made it known to his staff that the Vice President of Spoken Arrow International was visiting and feathers flew in all directions.

They all gathered in the canteen awaiting his words of wisdom. Every employee was encouraged to believe that they were working for one of the most revolutionary companies in the world, forward thinking, with a constant flow of innovations running through its veins. They wanted to hear that they were special, part of a team that were spearheading a new and dynamic world.

As Martin and Miriam entered the canteen a massive roar exploded, what other organisation would offer such an emotional welcome to a boss. He walked towards a make-shift platform and looked around. The UK Managing Director introduced him with genuine admiration. Most of the staff were under thirty. They loved their work and its ethos, owed their livelihoods to Spoken Arrow and saw Martin as the embodiment of the company. He had covered the globe visiting his offices and lost count of the gatherings around the world he had addressed over the years. But his current emotional state and thousands of miles from home made this moment particularly poignant.

"My dear friends, I had a few words prepared but frankly they were inadequate." He put the speech back in his pocket. "I cannot tell you how much your welcome has affected me. Most of us have some kind of objective that we want to achieve – some of us are into music, art, sport, or committed to inventing a new idea, maybe a plan to make a fortune. We all need a reason to justify our existence, maybe having children in the hope that they will replicate ourselves, or securing a little marker in a history book. But at Spoken Arrow, we are not only driven by a need, we are inspired by the work ethos we have, a cooperative achievement. Bees dedicated to making honey will never individually benefit from the end result, but cannot help producing it for us to enjoy. That's dedication."

"Our objective here is not just to be good at what we do, it's to change the world for the better. To give every man, woman and child, wherever they may live, whether in the outback of Africa or India or the sophisticated confines of the City of London, a window to explore the wonders of our amazing minds, by virtue of the products we make. However nothing happens unless the public knows what we are offering and are taught our ways. In the next few months we will hope to enter the medical world, where our sole objective is to give life and good health to those in greatest need, and to teach those blessed with a little more, to take pleasure in giving."

"You are the teachers and without you here in this wonderful country that has been the back bone of our modern civilisation for the last four hundred years.

whatever we bring to the world would be nothing without the watermark of Great Britain."

"Over the last twenty-five years I have travelled the world and passed our message to over two hundred countries, but my heart is with you here in the UK."

"Now, some of you may have had contact with this young lady on my right, Miriam Bravotti. We recently stole her from our West End Store, and she is now on our main board in LA. Each one of you has that same entitlement. You are our future, and I am personally humbled by the ability that we can see in the UK. I will take a few questions. Please tell me your names." Hands went up.

A young man of around twenty-four raised his hand. "Jeffrey Bronstein. Sir, I wonder if you could expand on the medical products that are about to be in the offering, bearing in mind that Magnum are already deeply committed in the market?"

"At this moment in time, I can only say to you: it's not what you do, it's the way that you do it. You will appreciate my little pun more in the next two or three weeks. We're finalising our negotiations at this time that will profoundly change our position in the market place we are in, but you may be sure that whatever we do will be with the same verve and professionalism that I hope you are accustomed to in Spoken Arrow. However, those of you that have an interest in the medical field may wish to put your names forward."

Questions were rained on him for a further twenty minutes, and copious notes were taken with the intention of following up. At last Martin thrust the microphone at Miriam, who was totally unprepared. Hundreds of eyes awaited a few words that they could savour and take away.

"My friends, this visit is of particular importance to me. I should tell you that I personally have only been with the head office in LA for a few months and was plucked out of my cosy West End branch to help create new and exciting areas by which Spoken Arrow could expand. I can tell you that it is one of the most gratifying experiences to see an idea turn into a reality, from the talking shop to computer graphics, functioning software, and then seeing our baby being born – but more important is for that to be part of a new global concept that will make our world a better place. Each one of you has that opportunity, we are the masters of our destiny, and every individual standing here today makes that happen. In fact, it couldn't happen without you."

"During the last twenty-five years, Spoken Arrow have developed methods of communication that were previously only read about in Science Fiction comics, and thirty years before that who would have guessed what was to be. You represent the next thirty years. The wonders of tomorrow are in our hands, and may they only be for the good of civilisation."

"It has been our privilege to be with you today. Hold your breath for this next critical step into the future."

Martin stepped forward and raised his arms in gratitude, which was matched by a thunderous roar of approval.

***

The following few days required a number of draft agreements sent to Schreiber from Mrs Steinberg. Confirming a date to complete the transfer and details relating to the consumer charges and the Autoplug financial details worldwide.

She requested that stock should be registered of all the Autoplug machines in the UK and throughout Europe. An approximate calculation estimated a hundred and forty-five thousand in the UK alone. And a further two million four hundred thousand throughout the world. The machines were serviced annually by various national computer contractors. The prime cost was for the software that needed to be constantly updated and inspected. Two hundred and forty million men, women and children across the globe were now speaking into the Autoplug approximately once a month, and constantly adding to their history which was being credited to their Persona App.

Spoken Arrow would already have offices in most of these countries and it would be necessary to delegate visits to all of them. Most users of the Autoplug were paying five or six pounds, or seven dollars, for a fifteen minute consultation. From the first of the new year, all payments would be transferred to Spoken Arrow.

Terence Dole was happy to host the new operation for the UK and oversee the European countries which allocated space for a further two hundred new staff, many of which would hopefully come from the offices of Magnum.

Herr Schreiber was asked by Mrs Steinberg to prepare a document informing all the Magnum global managers to cooperate with Spoken Arrow in order to transfer this operation over to them at the earliest opportunity and in good faith and offering whatever cooperation was necessary for a smooth transition.

The Autoplug and Ever Young control systems were based in Berlin and Dr Ellsworth's team would be enlisted to oversee the Magnum system and records.

If Herr Heinrich wishes to save face, he may consider having photographs taken, both parties in a congratulatory handshake. No one should think anything other than a mutually beneficial arrangement had been made.

An immediate and rather curt reply from Herr Schreiber was read to the Prime Minister suggesting that a time limit had not been placed for the negotiation and they would make necessary announcements in due course and at the convenience of the company.

She responded on government headed paper informing him that a trial for the murder of the Hines' was to be held in two weeks. "The direction of this trial could reveal the most embarrassing facts that would certainly negate Herr Heinrich's credibility and bring his misdemeanours to a head with obvious consequences. Photographs would also be available of the stolen goods in his home. (Please do not play games Herr Schreiber, you will not win.)"

"Documents are being drawn up and must be signed within the next 14 days. As you are no doubt aware the court hearings cannot be changed and the prosecution of those in the dock must be prepared. Herr Schreiber, as you may have concluded, my personal desire is to see your client behind bars for life and it would be most tempting to present such a case. I have been asked by my Prime Minister if possible not to embarrass his party and to conclude the situation without making ripples. But he knows our position in law and I am pleased to act upon it if necessary. It is not necessary to reiterate that our own sacrifices are considered more important than your inert claims and we are not blanching from the terms already agreed and the alternatives if deviated from. We therefore demand your total cooperation in order to conclude these negotiations."

"Your confirmation would be appreciated by return."

Schreiber took her to the last hour of the following working day before conceding his confirmation.

***

Martin in the UK

Martin wrote to his friend Jango that "to be in the UK in January is a fate worth than death. Sleet that turned to sludge. Dank weather that hit your joints and intermittent freezing rain that came down as pebbles. God has forgotten this country, it's a winter of greyness and misery. And no one smiles. Including me. Emotions seem to go into hibernation. Negotiations are moving along at a reasonable pace, and we are receiving grudging cooperation from Magnum with the assistance of Mrs Steinberg's office and are filling the gaps by visiting our various branches."

"If we find the time we might visit Paris and then Berlin, Milan and Madrid. Day trips just to show my face. These are long overdue, and looking at their records they vary substantially in efficiency. From a business point of view, it is worthwhile. I suppose I'm looking for an excuse not to return. Miriam is acting as my consiglieri and has proved her worth a thousand times over, her handle on the Magnum deal is invaluable – strictly business. Carolyn is keeping me updated as to what's happening on the home front."

"I mentioned the goodwill gesture to you that the UK government are asking for, two point five billion dollars, which includes all their stocks which is incidentally valued at considerably more, but I'm going to offer one billion dollars and stay firm. However we will need to look at the cash flow, superimposing a multi-billion turnover onto our existing business will have a serious impact on our short term finances. We should speak with our accountants as soon as possible."

"Jango, are you able to tell me the results of the private detective's investigation? I am asking the question with my heart still pounding. I've spoken with my kids but can't bring myself to talk with Janette, I would be interested to know who this bastard is, and of course if she's still seeing him."

Jango replied immediately. "It's great that you're making contact with our European offices, and long overdue. But please be careful, my friend. I'm really excited to get our teeth into the Autoplug, but we will have a great deal to discuss regarding it. Especially cash flow. Maybe we should launch a B share into the market. However I really am a little bemused regarding Ever Young, beside it being a political bomb shell, I can't see where we can possibly benefit from it. Aesthetically it sounds great but it has rather odious implications. Keep me in the picture."

He took a sip of juice and sighed as he continued to type. "I'm sorry to tell you the bad news, Martin. Angela has now met her lover a few times, but not in the house. His name is Brian Fogarty, he's married with two kids, and apparently his wife is now aware of his relationship with Angela and that he's living a double life."

"You must do what your heart tells you, my friend. Let me know if you want me to do anything. We'll speak soon."

***

It was a hammer blow, and even if he was round the corner it would have made no difference, but as much as he hated her he missed her, and especially the kids, and once again a dark cloud of depression came over him. He removed a picture from his wallet, looked at the family photo taken just before he left for South America, and sobbed.

Chapter 46

Mrs Steinberg was now in total command of the transfer of the multitude of assets relating to the Autoplug around the world plus its brand names including Ever Young. Her offices were now in constant contact with Magnum in Berlin. All of which would ultimately be transferred to the British government. Furthermore, an army of her staff were commanded to have in mind that once all headings were agreed a further transfer would be passed over from the UK government to Spoken Arrow. It was now for Martin to pass over his instructions via his Lawyers. After further discussions with Jango, it was agreed that they would ask their legal team to make a visit to the UK in order to speed matters along.

"You know, Martin," said Jango. "Why not let our boys work out the details with their Mrs Steinberg and then come back with them. It will save a lot of time and will kill two birds with one stone. You have to resolve your marriage one way or another anyway. You could probably do with some sunshine too."

"We have another meeting next week to discuss transfers of money," Martin replied.

"Good idea, our guys can join it, and I'll come back with them."

John Spinelli whom he had known for over fifteen years and was now President of Mead and Correl prominent Californian Lawyers had been involved with Spoken Arrow and enjoyed the spectacular growth of Spoken Arrow immediately packed some heavy clothing and with the best of his crop booked three flights to London.

The next morning at 10.30 local time Miriam and Martin were at Heathrow to welcome them. They had arranged a meeting with Sir Henry, the following day at 3.00 pm. This was John's first visit to London and in spite of his worldly disposition and a certain tiredness he was quite excited to meet a knight. "Remember John," said Martin, "You may think that you are in a film set but this is really the way they talk, speak slowly otherwise these Brits won't understand you."

He was given a quick resume of the situation as they booked into the Hilton, and a quick change of clothes.

"All I need from you today John is to take get a grip on the proposition. We will study the notes later and meet with him tomorrow. It's a very exciting deal but has lots of loose ends. Miriam is heading the deal so when you return you will be able to coordinate with her."

She had not had the need to deal with the legal aspects of the business in the US till now, and neither of them had met before, but John was understandably wary of his friend's association with his right hand senior executive. He had visited Martin's home a number of times and considered himself a friend of the family. He was aware of Martin's personal problems but, since he had not been given any instructions, decided to keep his council; but today six thousand miles from home he saw before him a beautiful woman and drew his own conclusions about the perils. He would have liked to say "be careful" to Martin but opted to put the thought behind his ear.

"You'll also meet Victor Straw of our London office, who is meeting us at the hotel. I thought we'd all go to this meeting together."

Like Martin, John imagined London to be as in a black and white movie and was overwhelmed by its buzz. But he was unprepared for his meeting with his British counterpart. Victor arrived wearing a three piece suit and bow tie. He sported a pencil thin moustache, his hair centre parted, and spoke with such a plummy accent that it was difficult to catch his words. John had to refrain from laughing, and the discussion in the taxi was inaudible to both men as Miriam and he prattled on.

***

Sir Henry's presence dominated the room. He had his PA sitting in the corner taking notes, which was slightly unsettling. However coffee and tea was served and an introductory understanding of the way both parties would come together.

Martin was first to confront the money. "We accept, Sir Henry, that a figure should be found for 'goodwill'; however, I do think that the number you've mentioned is higher than justified, bearing in mind that we don't and probably won't know whether the business is making a profit until we jump in at the deep end."

"You realise of course that Magnum have massive stock holdings in a number of countries which will no doubt be of greater value than the amount that we are suggesting, and therefore you are getting the business for nothing." He smiled.

"Not quite," replied Martin. "But I should say that so are you," he grinned. "Since we don't yet have any confirmed figures and therefore could be buying a loss, the specific computers would have no value at all in the event we closed shop. I think that we both appreciate that Magnum intended the Autoplug to play a significant role as a back up to Ever Young which is still an unknown but devious quantity, and of course we have no idea how much they were making on the sale of their drugs which we would have no access to. In other words, to some extent: we're buying a pig in a poke. Is that the right expression?" he asked.

"Absolutely the right expression, Mr Moran, but I don't believe it is used in the right context here, with the greatest respect."

To their surprise Straw, who appeared to be browsing through various notes interjected. "Please excuse me interrupting here Sir Henry. As you may be aware we have been representing Spoken Arrow for some years, and when I glanced through the notes it occurred to me that we are dealing here with two separate entities. The Autoplug which is already well established and is a brilliant concept, very close to my client's line of business. And Ever Young. which I really have difficulty in appreciating. Its marriage to this project has no monetary value. In fact, thinking aloud, Sir Henry, I wonder why it is even in the discussion. After all, whilst it has a certain intrinsic value it bears no relation to Spoken Arrow's current activities and hasn't actually been properly launched yet, and – dare I mention – we are in fact taking over the assets from Magnum, not the UK government."

"Not so," replied Sir Henry, "We are receiving the Autoplug and Ever Young back from Magnum on behalf of Cambridge, and thereafter we would pass it onto your good selves bearing in mind the monies and years invested by us. This would allow Magnum to present themselves to the world as a magnanimous gesture and save face…It is therefore sensible to pass it on to yourselves who have the knowhow required. The monies requested represent our initial costs."

"Is it possible that we might exclude Ever Young from our negotiations and deal with what is currently a commercial and probably viable proposition?" He asked.

"I have been asked by my clients to negotiate both projects, a package deal, don't you know?" replied Sir Henry. "There is no reason why you should not take control of Ever Young and sit on it if you wished."

"Since the government is the first purchaser for both products," muted Miriam, "I believe that it would probably be in their interests to hold onto Ever Young until a policy is agreed don't you think Sir Henry. There's no doubt that it's a hot potato, and unnecessary for our organisation to be straddled with it until we can get better clarification."

366

"You have a point, I'll discuss this with Mrs Steinberg and see where it takes us. Do you have any thoughts on this subject Mr Moran?"

"Yes, I think that it's a very good point you've made Victor, I don't see why we need to be burdened with this project at this time, I do see its potential but we are not the ideal operation to take advantage of its possibilities, and the ethics involved with it." He straightened up in his chair. "Based on the Autoplug's current turnover of four billion dollars, I think that a figure of one billion after you have taken it over from Magnum would be fair, and on this agreed price excluding Ever Young, which must have a value to the right party, we should agree a deal. This would leave you with Ever Young for you to do with what you will."

"I shall put it to my clients, Mr Moran, and see what they say. Would you still be prepared to agree the original equity split as previously discussed?"

"We'd be pleased for you to join us with the eighty percent to ourselves, and the remainder to whomever is mutually agreed. Why not!"

"Shall we speak tomorrow? May I suggest that whatever figures are agreed should be kept between us until such time as it is appropriate."

"Absolutely," replied Martin, not really understanding why.

***

Mrs Steinberg was given instruction to register a newly formed company. 'Government Research' using nominated partners. She had discussed in detail the result of the meeting between Sir Henry and Spoken Arrow, and it was agreed that a deposit of a hundred million dollars would be asked for which would represent a good will gesture to the UK government on their intent to take over the Autoplug excluding the Ever Young operation. This deposit would of course be deducted from the total amount when passing over the billion dollars. She referred it to the Prime Minister who happily conceded to Spoken Arrows offer.

"I'll say that we will require the deposit within fourteen days as a gesture of good will."

"Very good," he answered with more enthusiasm than he intended to reveal.

The following morning Victor Straw received a call from Sir Henry stating that the government had reluctantly agreed to their offer for the Autoplug, but would request a deposit of a hundred million dollars, on the signed understanding.

Martin phoned Jango. "What do you think Jango?"

"It sounds a good deal – provided we get all the necessary assurances from the UK government and all the backup we need, it's a gift. I'll agree, shall I?"

"Sure, we add four billion dollars to our turnover, without the headache of Ever Young. How can it be wrong? Do it Martin, and well done."

"By the way," said Martin, "they want to keep the deal under wraps for the moment and especially the financial aspect, they obviously don't want to reveal why it's been confiscated from Magnum. Too many questions would be asked, and that would put the cat among the pigeons. The Brits want the deposit in fourteen days."

"I'll organise it. Heinrich is putting out an announcement that will be seen as some justification for his selling."

***

Martin's adrenaline was pumping, he had never negotiated such a large deal that had cost so little to buy. It was a challenge but he had the organisation to deal with it. All he had to do was wait for Mrs Steinberg and Sir Henry to sort out all the implications and ownership and he would take it over. There was no doubt that Miriam was the prime mover and he already had in mind that she should head up the Autoplug at least in Europe.

It was really too early to celebrate but Miriam could not resist phoning Jack to inform him of their discussions.

"What price did you eventually agree?" he asked.

"I was asked not to say at this time."

"Miriam, we're in each other's confidence, come on... was it the two billion?"

"No," She conceded "A fair bit less, but what I can tell you is that we've dropped Ever Young which will stay with the government at least for the moment. I'm taking my colleagues to your favourite restaurant. Would you like to join us?" She suggested as casually as she could.

He was going to suggest that Helga might join them, but held back and with a little guilt accepted the invitation for himself.

That evening the four men and Miriam were welcomed by her brother, and for the first time she had managed to bring her two loves together—both her family and her work.

Chapter 47
Brazil

Steffen Heinrich had to return to Germany. He had many pressing appointments and in spite of his father's announcement to replace him as Vice President there had been no appointments yet made.

However, his father was aggressively pursuing his plans, and with Montello's invaluable assistance had realigned the finances of a number of his companies to purchase shares in Spoken Arrow whenever there was an opportunity. It would not be easy to purchase under the shadow of anonymity enough shares to make a meaningful difference, but slowly they would begin.

Montello produced for Albert Heinrich a cash flow chart which showed a twenty-five percent purchase of Spoken Arrow within the region of thirty billion dollars. "That is more than a little uncomfortable for us without damaging our existing operation," cautioned Albert. "I hope you know what you're doing."

"Don't worry, my friend," he replied. "We're going to get them…with the Autoplug and especially our Ever Young, we'll then control the global computer market and the minds of millions around the world."

***

Steffen had been given strict instructions to cooperate with the British government and offer whatever information they required. Technologists were crawling over the Autoplug division, taking notes and interviewing staff in Germany. Lists of all the Autoplugs locations were noted country by country, town by town and street by street, with the names of the appropriate local computer engineers. German efficiency was most impressive, and there were no questions asked whereby exact replies were not answered.

Considerable thought was given to the manner of announcement to the press and industry. Magnum were giving a wonderful business away, and there had to be a reason. It was at last agreed that a half-truth would be the most convincing.

***

Magnum's announcement to the world media was headed:

THE RIGHT THING TO DO

We are saying farewell to the Autoplug and Ever Young.

As a result of our deep connections with Cambridge University over a number of years, Magnum were given a conceptual idea and turned it into a reality that benefits billions of people throughout the world. The combination of Cambridge's research scientists with Magnum's unique technical and worldwide marketing abilities have proven how each party is dependent upon another.

However, we have decided to take the unprecedented step to return the project back to the British government and Cambridge. We have enjoyed developing the Autoplug on their behalf for the last few years, but we feel that it has taken us away from our core business, being one of the largest computer makers in the world.

Experience has taught us that every artist, academic, philosopher and business reaches a moment when they must give back what they have gained in order to devote time to other channels of thought. Magnum have scaled the highest mountains, and as we look at the world we can still see vast opportunities to improve every aspect of society over the coming years. With this in mind, we believe that the return of the Autoplug and Ever Young to its original creators will release us to stretch ourselves once more into what would have once have been considered forbidden territories.

Magnum is without doubt the most dynamic company in the world, we love humanity and are deeply involved in making the world a better place. As we pass on the torch, we hope that the parameters that we have laid down for the future inheritors of the Autoplug will continue to expand it's potential. As Godfathers of the Autoplug we will always be available to assist those who wish to pursue its full potential.

We will continue to look to the future and firmly believe that by giving, we are also receiving.

Signed

Albert Heinrich President.

Steffen Heinrich Vice President.

Magnum International GMBH

The memo was sent to every department within the organisation as well as the press. It became headlines in twenty languages. The die was now cast.

***

Mrs Steinberg was able to inform the Prime Minister that the new company was now formed and payment of the initial deposit could immediately be transferred to 'Government Research UK', of which ten percent would be based in the Bahamas. For a hundred million dollars from Spoken Arrow, a further nine hundred million would be transferred on the completion.

It would take a further month before possession of the Autoplug, Ever Young and all the relevant brands and its assets would formally pass onto the British government. During this hiatus Sir Henry working with Mrs Steinberg was to formalise all relevant documentation which would complete the transaction between Magnum GmbH and the government. Details were then sent to Victor Straw Senior Partner of Coral and Dean working on behalf of Spoken Arrow who would purchase the company from the government with an agreed balance to be paid of nine hundred million dollars. It was agreed that all financial arrangements would be excluded from all formal documents and kept from the press.

***

Martin had been in Europe for three weeks, he had made three one day trips each to France, Italy and Germany to meet his local Managing Directors, and taken the opportunity of priming them on their latest acquisition. Miriam, acting as his consiglieri, filled her time with either the day-to-day operations or the Autoplug.

He was aching to see his children. He spoke with them most days and a verbal diary of his experiences in London became a routine part of their lives, but he needed to be with them, to cuddle them and do what he had so sadly neglected during the last years of his marriage. Did he bring this situation about? Was he fundamentally to blame? Was it too late to forgive and forget? And now he had yet another project to put under his belt. Life was a spider's web that, once caught in, was impossible to untangle.

Then there was Miriam. How long could he resist this woman whom he knew would welcome him into her arms.

He had already decided that he must resolve the situation once and for all when he received a hand-written letter from Jango. Having breakfast with Miriam in the hotel, he used his bread knife and sliced open the envelope. He could not recall ever seeing Jango's writing in the twenty-something years that he had known him and was not surprised to note how bad his friend's scribble was. It was on two pages of foolscap. Miriam was prepared to hear some interesting news. However, as she looked at his expression, it was clear that the news was woefully bad.

From Jango…
Hi Martin,
You'll be surprised to receive a personal note but I was reluctant to put these thoughts onto the machine since, as you well know, nothing is secret these days. But I have had a report from our detective, and I'm sorry to tell you that your wife and her lover are considering moving to Canada with the kids. It appears to have been a sudden decision. He has left his wife with a small degree of security, and it's clear that he hasn't much money, although his family seem reasonably comfortable. I shall assume that he is relying on your wife to supplement his resources. I cannot advise you what to do, but I personally would confront her and find out what the score is. Are there bridges that can be crossed? But you must do what you feel is best. Could you leave the current business negotiations to Miriam and me, and deal with it at arm's length for a short while?

Everything here is fine, we're working out how much we will need to finance the ongoing costs of the Autoplug. We will probably have to go outside to finance it, it won't be a problem. Either way it's an exciting project. Especially without Ever Young which I must admit worried me a little. I might have an interesting idea regarding Autoplug – if you decide to pop back I'll save it until we meet. If not we'll speak…

Use me Martin, I'm here for you.
Fondest wishes
Jango

He folded the note and Miriam saw his eyes well up.

"Bad news?" she asked gently.

"I'm afraid so," he replied.

"Do you want to talk about it?"

He held the note out for her to read. "I'm numb. to be honest. My life is in limbo. Here I am in a foreign land doing what I have been doing for the last twenty-five years, and I can't blame her, really. What use is a husband who is never there? It was my choice, but I never dreamt that my success would rebound on me this way."

"Go to her, Martin. Discover what you're missing, and if she sees that you understand her loneliness and you can find it in your heart to forgive her weakness… maybe there's a chance you could make a new start. What have you got to lose?" She wanted to hug him, but she knew that it would only complicate things further. But as long as there was even a small chance of repairing this marriage, she would suppress what she really wanted to say.

He stretched his arm across the table and placed his hand on hers. "You're right. I'll catch a flight back with John. We'll leave his colleagues here to round things off. Can you hold the fort?"

***

The fourteen-hour flight to Los Angeles allowed him to gather his thoughts, and he spent some time writing up the proceedings relating to their latest acquisition. It was to be a separate activity to the main core of the business and should be a standalone project. It might be a good time for Jango and himself to separate the company altogether. Spoken Arrow would act as guarantors. He had no qualms about its management which could be overseen by a supporting team to include Miriam. She would select whatever talent there was in the existing business. She had proven herself well beyond her brief and he found it hard to separate his admiration from affection and desire.

His brain was now jumping from the sublime to the ridiculous. For goodness' sake, she was still not thirty and he nigh on forty-eight, eighteen years between them. Would he have appealed to her if he was just an engineer? Probably not. He forced his thoughts towards his marriage, or what was left of it, and his children.

Was there any point in returning, if not for an attempted reconciliation, and one that might work?

If this was why he was persuaded to return, there should be some plan. He wouldn't expect any of his men to face a presentation without at least some thought beforehand. NO, he chided himself, this was the problem, it wasn't a business presentation. He had even typed out a format which wasn't too different to a thousand formats that he had told his forces to do.

God, I'm turning into a robot! And he returned to his original notion: guilt, blaming himself for her indiscretions. At last he drifted off, later to be gently awoken by a stewardess. It was 7.00 am in LA, and already a comforting sixty-five degrees. Jango was waiting at the arrival with a big smile. They embraced as only old friends would.

Jango had been married and divorced twice and was now living with one of his old college girl friends of a similar age to himself. "I was fed up with trying to keep up with another generation," he defended himself. It had to be admitted, though, that this woman looked after herself and without any LA plastic retained her vitality with an elegance that only the younger generation aspired to.

"I want you to stay with us for a few days Martin, just until you've caught up with yourself. We think you need a little T.L.C. Anyway, I have an idea which I think you'll like."

Jango and Abby's villa was some thirty miles from the centre of LA, built on stilts over the pacific. A small motorboat was moored to a pier emanating from beneath the villa.

The house was designed for pleasure and although at a glance appeared to be relatively small it contained six bedrooms en suite, over three levels all looking out to sea. A housekeeper had already prepared his room and welcomed him with a freshly squeezed fruit juice. "After three weeks in London, you need plenty of vitamin C!" she cooed in a Spanish accent.

Abby appeared still in her dressing gown to welcome him. He sat in a chair on the veranda and smiled. "You shouldn't stay out here now, wait until it warms up a little," she exclaimed, but to Martin it was heaven.

"You've obviously never been to England," he replied with his eyes closed and absorbing whatever heat he could.

Jango joined them. "Now, my good friend, I want you to carefully consider what you want from the next step you take. Just work out in your mind, first, are you going to phone her, and what would you say? Supposing he answers the phone. We know already that they are together so are you going to argue with her or tell her what is on your mind? Just think about it before you do it – I've been there and I can tell you that these first steps are massive coal mines."

"To be honest, Jango, I really don't know what I want, if there is a degree of remorse in her voice maybe that would help, but if she's already set on going to Canada, should I simply throw my hands up or fight my corner?"

"Only you can answer that, Martin. If you want to mend the marriage you have to offer a reason to do it – just meditate on it for a few moments before speaking to her. I think that it's necessary to make a peace for both of your sakes and of course for the kids in order that you can come to terms with your situations. That's all I'm saying. Listen to the sea and let your mind relax."

They left him to his thoughts. And thirty minutes later he decided to phone on the landline.

His thirteen-year-old answered. "Daddy!" she cried. "Where are you, are you still in London?"

"No darling," he was close to tears, "I've just returned, I'm in LA."

"Mum," she shouted. "Dad's on the Phone."

One of the other children pulled the phone from her hands. "Hello Daddy, where are you, when can we see you?" He was about to answer when Angela came to the phone. "Martin, where are you?" she sounded as excited as the kids. "Where are you, are you in LA?"

"Yes," he replied, "I'm staying with Jango, I've just arrived." There was a silence. "Shall we meet?" He asked tentatively.

"Yes, yes, but please don't attack me Martin, I won't be able to take it."

"I won't, but we have some life changing decisions to make. Can you get to Jango's?"

"I know – yes I can. When?"

"Now?" he blurted more eagerly than he had intended.

"Shall I bring the kids?"

"No, I don't think that is a good idea at this stage, I definitely want to see them though, but not at this time."

"I'll be with you in about one hour."

After hearing him put the line down Jango emerged. "So, what happened?"

"She's coming here in one hour," Martin said guiltily, "I think I'll have a drink, after all it's 5.00 pm in London."

Exactly one hour later Angela rang the bell, and Jango answered. She had been there many times. "Would you like a drink?" he asked.

She nodded as they walked towards the pool where Martin was sitting. And he stood up to greet her, wanting to embrace her but settled for a hand shake. She was still as beautiful as ever, he thought.

"I need to talk first, Martin… please don't interrupt, it will be difficult enough getting my thoughts and emotions together. We have been married for over twenty years, it could be said that it was a good marriage, certainly materially. But I want you to cast your mind back to the early days, especially when we were courting. You were beginning to become seriously involved in the world of computers, I had just gotten my degree in Science, it was a subject that I loved. It wasn't difficult for me to get a job, and I soon saw real opportunities for advancement. But the firm wanted me to go to Boston whilst you were still establishing yourself in LA. So I naturally refused the offer, and found a local job which bore no relation to my degrees."

"At that stage in our marriage, the money was useful too. You continued to expand and were running all over the country, sometimes I wouldn't see you for

375

two or three weeks at a time. I understood but my hopes for any personal progress were sacrificed. This went on for years and when I became pregnant my life outside the domestic world completely died. You deprived us of nothing materially, but I was completely dependent upon you're your success and glories. Your pride became my pride, nothing happened in my life unless it was through you. That's not to say I didn't love you, and I certainly didn't resent you, I was proud of your success, but you made me a prisoner by your success. Even to the extent that I virtually stopped thinking. Afternoon teas, school outfits. Can you imagine if this happened to you. After all, I was once a scientist."

"I had been completely faithful to you for all these years, but this last trip was the breaker, the kettle overboiled."

Martin attempted to interrupt, but was stopped by her hand. "Let me finish," she said.

Her tears were now running down her cheeks. "This chance meeting with John, whom you've never met, awoke in me a real need to be myself, not a glorified housekeeper, his work depends on the labour he puts into it each week, it's not that he's stupid, far from it, but he respects my intelligence, and is prepared to accept my opinion on matters that refer to him, he allows me to enter into his life, which I could never do with you. I feel alive when I'm with him. I couldn't do that with you; it wasn't your fault, it's just the way it worked out."
"Are you saying that you want to stay how you are? If so I can't see the point, why you've come here," he replied almost spitefully.

"Have you not listened to a word I've said, are you so dumb that you have not understood my reasoning at all. You are so wrapped up in yourself you can't hear another voice. Surely it must have occurred to you that a degree of gilt rests with you. Maybe you are the guilty one, it's the cause not the effect that we're talking about."

"I have only done what every man wants to do, and that is to give security to my family."

"If that is your only desire, you might as well give it to charity, there's more to marriage than money Martin, you seem to have forgotten that. That's why so many 'Successful' men fail in their marriages, money does not equate to happiness. I came here to explain and see if you understood that I should count in your life and you should do the same to mine. But I can see that I've failed."

He stood up and walked around the pool, glancing at her sitting on the other side. She was still as beautiful as ever. She had never mentioned her own dissatisfaction with their marriage, he had taken it for granted that this was how it had to be if he was to succeed, and he did. But there was no way that he could get off the escalator now, he was condemned to succeed. "You know, Angela, it's a painful fact that we grow from the seeds we plant. If I had a crystal ball I would not have been able to change our lives from what I saw. If computers and software had not been developed and only mechanical robots ruled the day, I might have been an engineer, but these aren't the cards that we've been dealt. I can't change course now, and it would be crazy to imagine that I could."

Finding his chair he once again sat opposite her. "You seem to have found someone who can make you happy, or certainly happier than I could, and I've no wish to stop you from following your dream. To be honest, however painful it is I can't change direction at my age, I'm too young to retire and too old to start again. What can I say?!" He took her hand and they sat next to each other in silence.

She began a song that she recalled from Mel Torme. "What to do what to do what to do, the outlook was decidedly blue." She stood up and kissed him on the cheek. "I can't tell you how sad I am. For you and for me, Martin. I'll always love you."

"I will love you too," he croaked, not even trying to clear his throat. "Maybe one day I should meet your John."

"That would be nice, but maybe not yet, my darling man. I want you to be happy too."

"We mustn't fight. Let's remember the good things, if you need help let me know," he replied.

"I don't think I will but thanks. Let me know when the kids can visit, as often as you want." Jango looked on as they hugged one another and parted.

"Looking good?" he asked.

"I guess so," Martin replied. He sat back in his chair facing the sun and slept.

Chapter 48
Tann

It had been two months since Tann had been traumatised by Daren Horrocks of the MI5. He had become a shadow of himself and was living in fear of being exposed. No one would believe him, whatever he said, once MI5 passed the information to the press or that Branson man, once he was implicated in the murders of the Hines or, in fact, of George Baylim. However, strange as it would seem no action was being taken. He felt that he was awaiting the executioner. He wanted desperately to retire and just vanish for a while. He attempted many times to arrange a private sitting with the Prime Minister but to no avail. His mentor Steffen Heinrich had now passed the Autoplug to the government but the negotiations were kept from him.

Not that it would make much difference who took over the project, and whilst the kudos of the Autoplug was still attributed to him, in anticipation of a hammer falling he kept a very low profile. He took a leave of absence on grounds of health and allowed his assistant to take control.

Nothing was said regarding Ever Young either, it was remarkable that only two months ago Ever Young was headlines, and now not a word from Magnum nor the government to where it had vanished. Editorials were still being written but all went into a vacuum.

He read over and over the announcement from Magnum, trying to find some link as to what might have been agreed, and attempted daily to speak directly with Steffen Heinrich but was constantly blocked. What sort of deal could have been made to force Heinrich to pass over the entire Autoplug and Ever Young business, it was worth a fortune.

A reporter from the Financial Times had attempted to interview him, and although Tann declined, he picked up the mystery with guesses and summations as to why Magnum decided to offer the Autoplug back to the government and guessed a reasonably accurate value of a few billion pounds. They listed few companies that the government would offer the product to and reported a purchase for 'an undisclosed sum' that was quoted by both parties, could only mean many billions out of the country's budget, but it did not appear to be accounted for in the chancellor's report. Could it really be a gift – it would be unprecedented, even ridiculous if it was – and who would they have in mind to run and fund it? Tann was constantly asked by the press and Television News to give a hint as to the deal, but would not comment and, in fact, could not.

It was therefore a surprise to receive a general memo from the Prime Minister issued to the all the cabinet.

MEMO TO THE MINISTERS CROWN and all relevant parties and Press:

The Chancellor of the Exchequer has now passed the ownership of The Autoplug to Spoken Arrow Computers Inc., who will maintain the same continuity of service as Magnum. Magnum will support all aspects of the administration until Spoken Arrow's systems are in place world-wide. Although the two organisations compete within the computer market, there is total cooperation between these two international giants, and the transfer from one company to the other will run in perfect harmony. The government's departments will continue to update all relevant information which will allow the public to have total confidence in their service. Spoken Arrow are the world wide leaders within the computer market and have given every assurance that total confidentiality of each client using the Autoplug will be maintained ad infinitum. There will be a review of Ever Young, which already is currently being restructured.

Magnum do not consider any conflict of interest in working with their competitor as the Autoplug is a standalone project and both parties believe that it is evolving in a direction more suited to Spoken Arrow than Magnum. The government therefore have acted as a mediator and will retain with Cambridge University a token equity in the company.

10% of shares will be distributed to the government, a further 5% to Government Research, and 5% to Cambridge University. 80% will be offered to Spoken Arrow. Stock will be purchased by Spoken Arrow – to be finalised.

***

Tann read the announcement in the Financial Times. He was livid. He had been sidelined from his own creation and there was nothing that he could do. If he poked his head above the parapet he would be accused of murder and bribery. It was more than he could bear. He carefully placed a headed parliamentary paper on his desk and wrote:

To whom it may concern:

What I have done was for the country, and I believe with all my heart that my efforts will benefit millions. I am innocent of the accusations directed at me, and my actions were only to pursue a better world. I thank all those that have contributed to the success of the Autoplug and Ever Young and especially my dear friends who have supported my endeavours over the years.

Brendon Tann.

He placed the note on his desk, had one last look at his office, closed the door and left.

It was raining as he walked towards the Westminster Bridge, when he reached the middle he looked one last time at the Houses of Parliament where so much of his life had been spent, and jumped.

***

The media gave considerable coverage to his death. He was heralded for his great contribution to the country, various ministers were found to say a few words and like a stone in a pond, the ripples of his memory slowly vanished.

Over the following three weeks Albert Heinrich and Montello gave a great deal of their time to the purchase of Spoken Arrow shares. Autoplug appeared to have integrated well into Spoken Arrow's organisation. However, unbeknown to Spoken Arrow nine of the Pontillo companies now owned twelve percent of the company. It was time to create a degree of discontent on the stock market in an attempt to reduce the share value of Spoken Arrow. At this rate, it could take at least another two or three years to increase their hold. Twenty-five or thirty percent of the company would seriously deplete Magnum's working capital.

"Since our own results are not subject to scrutiny," said Montello, "Why don't we make a statement suggesting that we lost over five billion dollars over the five years we had the Autoplug, and we saw no way of recovering the loss – which would be ongoing. We can publish an article to the world media."

"We admit that we failed. We say the purpose of investing in the Autoplug was to offer the nations of the world an opportunity to allow themselves to see their lives as if a mirror of their own experiences. It was to be a personal encyclopaedia such that each individual could reflect on their personal history and be assess probably consequences of their actions. However, whilst the objective of the exercise seemed bound to succeed, the cost of doing so would have eventually bankrupted us. It was a dream which we thankfully awoke from before it turned into a five billion dollar nightmare.

"If we had continued, it would have cost Magnum many more billions. We sincerely hope that Spoken Arrow will find a formula that clearly eluded us and we wish them luck in making what is a wonderful concept profitable."

Heinrich smiled. "I like it, let's see what this release does for our friends and it becomes a proverbial Broken Arrow."

"Very witty, sir."

"I thought so," smiled Heinrich. "But do we have the funds available to pick up another thirteen percent of the shares?" asked Albert Heinrich.

Montello cogitated on the question. "If the shares drop by, say, fifteen percent even for a short time we might do it, by the time they refute it we have a small window to buy before the shares bump up again. It's a risk and we would be stretching our finances to breaking point. But I'm worried Albert, it's a gamble, it's true we're buying an asset, but we still have a business to run which needs feeding. By giving away the Autoplug, we have lost a fortune in revenue and investment."

"I know that you can do it Alfredo. You're a genius, what would I do without you?"

It was now May and Albert Heinrich and Montello decided to visit their beloved Germany and make their announcement in Berlin. The returning of the Autoplug would be a historic show of humble admission that even the most successful companies sometimes take a wrong turning. As the president of such a prestigious company and a considered elder statesman it was not difficult to arrange an interview with Berlin Television who, no doubt, would be keen to ask why such a brilliant concept as the Autoplug should have been sold to an American competitor. He prepared, and rehearsed methodically, his answers to the anticipated questions.

On hearing the news that Herr Heinrich was visiting Europe, the BBC requested a half hour interview on their HARD TALK program which interviewed major or world-famous personalities 'who were making a difference, good and bad'. They would arrange a tele-interview from the UK to Berlin. France and Italy were also interested to take advantage of the rare visit of such a notable character. "There might be some awkward questions," said Montello.

"Don't worry," he replied, "I'll manage."

Montello's own financial department in Brazil were instructed that on no account must they relate the purchase of Spoken Arrow shares to Magnum or any reference to Pontillo. They were put on a purchase alert, and immediately Herr Heinrich had his interviews, they were to watch the share price fall and buy. "We are looking for at least a fifteen percent discount on the current price," instructed Montello.

***

Albert Heinrich had given many interviews over the years. Not all proceeded as he would have liked and he had learned how easy it was to be tripped up by aggressive reporters. He was collected by a chauffeur from his hotel and taken to the Central Broadcasting Building in the centre of the city. He was escorted directly to an open studio that had a small stage with two arm chairs surrounded by cameras. To his surprise an audience of approximately fifty men and women were already in their places.

As he arrived a sign instructed them to clap. The lights went on and the audience appeared to vanish.

"It's a great pleasure, Herr Heinric,h to welcome you back to Berlin."

The interviewer was polite and his questions at first appeared quite innocuous, but as he progressed in his relaxed manner they required a little more thought. He slowly worked his way into the research and development relating to Magnum. Now leaning forward and almost touching Heinrich. "And to the world's surprise, having brought to the market this wonderful Autoplug, you appear to have sold it to Spoken Arrow. We were astonished that such an amazing facility would be lost from our shores, Herr Heinrich. Maybe you could enlighten us as to why you made that decision."

"Absolutely," he replied. "Actually we didn't sell it to Spoken Arrow, we sold it to the British government and it was their decision to work with Spoken Arrow. Not that it mattered. As you will appreciate, it took a considerable amount of money and time to bring the Autoplug to the market. However what we didn't realise was how terribly expensive the Autoplug is to maintain, I don't only mean the computers themselves, but the software – we lost over five billion euros since we launched it. You will know that there is virtually nothing you can't ask the Autoplug about your health, the weather, the political situation, personal problems, it's your confession box, your friend. Even better than your friend, it is a guiding light for each person to live their lives. But it is also a death warrant for the maker. We created a Colossus and it would have devoured us."

"But why should it cost so much to maintain?" asked the interviewer "So now that you have returned both the Autoplug and Ever Young to the British government, and they have passed it on to Spoken Arrow, what words would you advise your competitor, sir?"

Competition is very important, it sharpens the mind and the pen, and we would hate to see such a company as Spoken Arrow experience what we have suffered, there are not many organisations in the world that could carry this loss, but they have taken up the challenge. We will certainly advise them if they ask us, to help them make it work financially, but I can only wish them luck. I would expect the Autoplug to lose at least one billion dollars per annum, and as they expand the product to more countries, considerably more, the concept is amazing but the world is not ready for it yet.

"And Ever Young, Herr Heinrich. This seemed such a wonderful concept, what are your thoughts regarding this?"

"This was an extension of the Autoplug, it was the monitor of the health of each individual and allowed those who had Ever Young 351 chip to be reviewed within the understanding of their disposition via the Autoplug. Absolutely wonderful marriage. We don't know what Spoken Arrow intend to do with it, it is a service that is monetarily without financial gain to a commercial company but will certainly save vast sums for the government. It might be that the governments around the world will integrate Ever Young into the NHS, but it is now for them to decide."

"I can say though, that now that we are released from this great financial burden, which I am of course saddened, it will allow us to continue to astound the world with products that they can afford and we can produce viably, as we have done for the last 60 years."

"We're proud to have you in our studio today…Herr Heinrich President of Magnum. Thank you, Ladies and Gentlemen."

The Clap sign went on, and the audience did what they were told. "Very good sir," thanked the interviewer.

"No. Thank you," replied Heinrich.

***

The response to the interview was immediate and was given considerable space in the papers and various talk shows, and as anticipated the financial world took immediate note of the potential losses that Spoken Arrow would expect to suffer. Within twenty-four hours, the shares plummeted, losing over thirteen percent of their value. Montello's men quickly responded and made their purchases under the umbrella of nine different finance houses to eight percent of Spoken Arrow. They needed another ten percent to make it meaningful. The demand for the shares soon brought their value back up again but now only two percent under their original price.

"Hold fire," called Montello. "We've done well, but let's wait for the next interview, we'll see if we can do the same again." The BBC was booked in for the following week.

Chapter 49
Spoken Arrow

Seeing their shares suddenly plummet caused great concern in the financial quarters of Spoken Arrow, and Jango Hampton was totally unprepared for his investors, who had previously considered the Spoken Arrow organisation as a blue chip investment. The company had virtually overnight been devalued by eighteen percent, and even before they were able to respond to the drop, a gush of buying pushed the shares back to a nominal value. Someone was playing the market. All because of Heinrich's interview. "Can we find out who the buyers are?"

"They seemed to be scattered around, and it was all because of the interview with old man Heinrich." Neither Jango nor Martin had heard the interview which was in German, but they had read extracts of it which they considered sour grapes rather than actualities. But they never would have anticipated how it would reflect on their company. "I think that there's something brewing here," muted Martin. "They referenced the interview with a translator. It may have been cleverly planned, but the purchasers of their shares appeared to be disassociated to each other."

"We must put out an announcement immediately," said Jango. "There's no way that they lost billions on the Autoplug, they're playing us. We'll write to all our investors informing them that it's nonsense, and our profits will be seven percent up on last year. Even better, we'll place full page adverts announcing that we have acquired the Autoplug which we expect to increase our net value considerably."

Martin immediately spoke to his advertising department and within two days every major paper and financial barometer throughout the civilised world showing a most exciting outlook for the company.

"It could just be a blip, but if so, why would the President of any company let alone that of Magnum tell such blatant lies, unless they had an agenda. The problem is that we can't be sure that it is them. Maybe it was a single blast to make a few million. It happens."

***

Heinrich's next interview was with the BBC.

John Blackmore was known to be one of the last of his kind, his upper class British accent and his meticulous preparation for his meetings tended to pose the question of why anyone regardless of their claim to purity would venture to be subjected to a barrage of often embarrassing questions and the destruction of their defensive answers. Heinrich had met them all over the years and was confident that he could handle them.

The BBC's Hard Talk was shown internationally and had been known over a number of years to carry considerable political punch. Blackmore had no need to travel as the interview was invariably conducted from the BBC London and his victim's own office or home for the interview.

Heinrich chose to use his sons home in Berlin.

Blackmore began, "Herr Heinrich, Magnum is one of the largest companies in the world and is still privately owned by your family. I understand that you are the great grandson of the founder and your son Steffen is now being primed to take over from yourself. There are very few companies in the world of your size today that can boast such a company heritage, is this something that you cherish or do you envisage the company being floated at some time?"

"This is one my greatest pleasures Mr Blackmore, we have been given a mission and unlike nationalised organisations we have been able to maintain the highest degree of quality, ethics and efficiency that I believe would be compromised if run by a nominated board of directors," He replied with some degree of pride "And I could not imagine that we would have reached our current level of success if we had to ask opinions of those that had no history or personal regard for the company."

"Back in the early fifties there were of course no computers and your grandfather's business was essentially an information bureau, which I understand he took over from his father. I can see the synergy of its evolution towards the computer age but would you say that information would have been the motive for his entry or was it more an independent decision?"

It seemed a simple enough question, almost banal, and Heinrich wanted to move onto the present, but was obliged to follow Blackmore's lead. "Yes of course – we were not to know how important the computer age would become at the time, but when you are listing countless names and cataloguing them, the dream was certainly that it could be formatted automatically."

Blackmore might have been warming up. "The evolution of all mega-organisations invariably begins with such a dream, and of course your grandfather would have inherited this concept, which would probably have existed even before the second world war, from his father. Or was the company actually only created in the fifties?"

Heinrich saw himself being goaded into a dark area. "Everything has a pre-beginning before it's beginning, Mr Blackmore. Your own birth emanated from your conception but you are now the result of YOUR beginning." He nervously smiled.

Blackmore was fairly unmoved. "We are not talking, Herr Heinrich, of your beginning, but about the conceptual beginning of your company. What prompted Magnum to be formed – for it seems that it already had a running start even in the fifties. I understand that the name was changed after the war from Katalegein. Can you tell me a little about its prehistory?"

Heinrich: "As you will appreciate these were difficult days for Germany and most of what I understand is hearsay Mr Blackmore, I have been much more concerned to look into the future rather than the past."

Blackmore: "But we are all the sum total of our past, It's true that we can change but from what to what is the key, not from nothing to something, if you follow my trend of thought, sir. Katalegein was already a reasonably large operation before the war, can you enlighten us as to its functions Herr Heinrich?"

"No Mr Blackmore, my memories of working with my father started when I was around 17 years old, we were already involved in the computers by then, this was a revolutionary time when the mud of the second world war was slowly beginning to slip away and a new Germany was emerging. Who would imagine in those years how it has progressed. The Autoplug certainly moved us forward, but too fast."

Blackmore: "If your great grandfather would have seen how Magnum has expanded he would be very proud, but how did he manage to keep the business afloat during the war I wonder, your description of the listings that the company made with the aid of computers must have required a great deal of systemology, in itself a prerequisite of computers, don't you think?"

Heinrich was becoming agitated, "You know Mr Blackmore we are sitting here discussing the history of a company that has evolved into one of the largest and best in what we do, and all you seem to be interested is in our ancient history, I would like to explain to you some of the problems we are experiencing in today's society. Whatever my great grandfather did or did not do is of no interest to me, Ask me about our future and the future of Germany, that is much more important."

"You must appreciate Herr Heinrich that I am interviewing you, and the subject matter is what I believe my audience will want to hear, not necessarily what you want to tell us. I want to understand how you feel your roots have influenced your organisation. A family business by its very nature inherits and carries forward its objectives, and you will agree I am sure, that the roots of your business were closely aligned to the Third Reich and their listings."

"Mr Blackmore, my greatest pride is my German heritage, and everything I do is with the intention of giving the world something that will enhance it and be a jewel in Germany's crown. You would say the same for the UK or the USA, what is wrong in that."

Heinrich's voice began to rise. "If you want to know about the lists, they were made to cleanse the country of those that did not believe in it. We can see the results of the war when we look at the problems that exist today. Nothing was solved. Germany lost the war, but so did the rest of the world. But my dream is to show the world how great our new Deutschland is and will be…We will win…We will, you see, it's in our DNA." The TV camera gave a close up of Heinrich who was now sweating. "The war was lost because Germany could not project its message. The essence of our intellectual superiority. If Magnum had been there then, no doubt the results would have been very different, but we have once again risen from the ashes." Now the cameras honed in to see him sweating. "Deutschland uber alles." He raised his voice again and waved his hand.

This was Blackmore's talent, he had at last revealed the man behind the mask.

It was the end of the interview and Heinrich had not had one opportunity to get his own message across.

"I'm afraid we must end now Herr Heinrich and thank you." The interview was seen by twenty-five million viewers around the world.

The cameras were switched off and Montello approached Heinrich.

"Albert, you allowed this bastard to get under your skin. I must say, the interview certainly was not good for us."

Still sitting, Heinrich shouted, "Who are you to tell me what's good and not good. He needed to know that we are on the way back. You don't even have a drop of German blood so don't you dare tell me what's not good." No further words were spoken, but both men were seething.

Chapter 50

Jango received a call from Mr Saul Penton of the United Investments and one of his largest shareholders who had twelve percent of the company's shares.

"What's this I'm hearing Jango about this Autoplug you've bought, I hear that it's a money burner. I'm wondering if you've bought a pup. According to the President of Magnum, he couldn't wait to dump it, it cost him billions. I had a meeting with my colleagues and they feel that unless you unload it we will feel the need to sell our shareholdings in Spoken Arrow"

Jango was shocked. He was well aware that Magnum's financial figures had not been published, but his own accountants had assessed the proposition and found no problems with its viability. Was he missing a trick? Could this man Heinrich be telling the truth, and if not, what would he benefit from undermining a deal that had already been concluded?

"Please don't do anything Saul until I've had a chance to check the details out, give me ten days."

After cogitating for some time, he decided to bring his board together to discuss all the implications. There was no doubt that if Penton put his shares on the market the price would go through the floor, especially if he gave his reasons.

The Spoken Arrow main board consisted of men and women covering all aspect s of the organisation. Now that Martin had returned and been consulted, he muted that since the Autoplug had been predominantly under Miriam's wing she should be included, and was asked to fly back.

"And see if you can find some figures from Magnum in Germany," instructed Martin, "there must be a whole swathe of people there who are involved in the Autoplug's financial division, and unless they have been given instructions not to say anything we might get some solid facts from them."

Miriam's knowledge of German was very limited, she was not particularly keen to present a degree of doubt to the Spoken Arrow board, after all she had worked hard to bring the Autoplug business to a head, but she had doubts of her abilities to subtly coerce information in German and it occurred to her that Jack's assistant – or whatever she was – could speak German fluently and also had an understanding of the intricate events that had taken place.

She began to dial Jack's number but an unfamiliar feeling of rivalry, for no particular reason, obliged her to put the phone down. *How ridiculous*, she argued to herself, but as she dialled again she recognised in herself an animal attraction that would resist a rival, yet a rival for a man that she had no intention of engaging in a relationship with. To deal with his partner or colleague should simply be 'business as usual'.

Jack was in his office, he took immediate pleasure speaking with her, and it reflected in his voice. He consciously swapped the familiar tone for a more efficient timbre.

"Jack, we have a little problem. I don't know if you had the opportunity to hear Heinrich, but in an interview on Berlin TV the old man Heinrich stated that the Auto Plan is losing vast sums and virtually wished Spoken Arrow good luck to service its losses. And the program was seen worldwide. Spoken Arrow's shares dropped dramatically, for an hour and then bounced back."

"What would you like me to do?" he replied.

"We need to speak with the Head Accountant at Magnum, who is handling the Autoplug in Germany, and find out the true financial position, my problem is that my German is so bad, and I'm wondering if Helga is up to it. I recall that German is her first language."

"What do you mean 'up to it'? What would she have to do, Miriam?"

"We need detailed accounts relating to their viability – that is the Autoplug's viability. If the shareholders of Spoken Arrow feel that their company was about to buy in on a serious loss, there will be a run on the shares. We must refute his comments and state that it has serious potential, and if it has lost money, which I doubt, it is probably through Magnum's inefficiency."

"Shall the three of us meet and discuss exactly what they need?"

"Great," she replied, "I have to return to the States to present the Autoplug's case and need some information within the next two days, why don't we meet tonight if it's possible? Shall we eat at my brother's restaurant?"

Jack immediately phoned Helga who was in a lecture. She whispered that she would take a train immediately after the lecture finished, and would be at the station at 3.00 pm. No questions asked. Jack phoned Miriam to confirm that they would be with her at 6.00 pm.

She was wearing jeans and a sweater and even without make up she could have jumped out of a magazine. It was a surprise to her that Miriam was joining them, but became excited to hear that she was going to be given a task.

"As you know Helga, Magnum have passed the Autoplug to Spoken Arrow via the British government. We urgently need to know the international profitability of the Autoplug."

"A middle management accountant won't really know. We need to speak with someone of authority that understands that it's been taken over, he will assume that we already have figures, so you will have to give the impression that you know them but need a slightly more in depth understanding of them. You could interject that you need country by country profitability. Software costs, mechanical overheads, etc. What we really want of course are the bottom line profits. He should have profit and loss accounts. He shouldn't be too averse to giving them to you since we already own it. But you would have to disarm his natural resentment. If he procrastinates and has been told not to give us the figures, we will smell a rat. Now if I would take a translator they would charge me at least a thousand pounds, but you already know the history of this transaction Helga and I would like to offer you two thousand pounds if that's OK. You would of course have to take a trip there."

It was an exciting task for Helga and she was delighted to be given a responsibility and be paid for it, that was the cherry on the cake. "I would be very happy with that, but my accounting knowledge is not good I will need to have someone with me to discuss the details."

"Don't worry about that Helga we will organise for one of our accounts managers in Germany to accompany you, but as you already have a good understanding of our situation you are in an ideal place to make sure we get the information we require."

Jack saw why Miriam was picked for the job. Her singlemindedness and ability to give direction was superb, he also was aware that she had asserted her authority over Helga.

"Things are moving very fast, and if, and it's a big if, the facts are as bad as Heinrich says, we would need to walk away. I personally think it's a ploy for something devious. Remember that we're not buying the business from Magnum, we're buying from the British government but we'll take on certain staff that are involved with the Autoplug division which would probably include the man you will be meeting, so you are holding the cards. OK."

The three met the following morning at 8.00 in Jacks apartment. It was easy to see that Helga had stayed there and although Jack had gone to some trouble to conceal her night-time presence, little tell-tale signs such as bathroom toiletries gave it away.

Coffee was made and still sipping Jack went to the telephone and dialled the head office of Magnum in Berlin. immediately it rang he passed it to Helga.

She soon discovered from the receptionist who was head of the Autoplug accounts, and within minutes Helga was speaking to Herr Goult's secretary. Passing her was a little more difficult "Please tell me what you wish to talk to him about."

"I would rather speak directly with him please," she replied.

"I'm sorry, he is a very busy man. If you would like to inform me of your reason to speak with him I will pass on the request," she said indifferently.

"Ask her if she speaks English," Jack whispered. She did, and Jack immediately took the phone. "What is your name please?" He asked in a tectonic manner.

"Schmidt," she admitted resentfully.

"Fräulein Schmidt, you will appreciate that Spoken Arrow have recently acquired the Autoplug division from Magnum with all the staff associated within it. Now, if you value your job you will IMMEDIATELY put me through to your boss; if he happens to be on the toilet you will knock on his door. Do you understand?" It was clearly the language she understood.

Herr Goult was informed of his potential executioner and was a little more courteous. Helga was once again replaced Jack and now on loud speaker asked all the appropriate questions that were written down for her. Within minutes, she was given the meaningful figures that were required showing that the project was enjoying a substantial profit. She thanked him and asked if he could prepare a profit and loss accounts.

"It may be necessary for us to meet Herr Goult. Are you available tomorrow to discuss more detailed accounts?"

"Of course," he replied. "I shall be coming from London and will inform you of my arrival time."

They thanked one another and she hung up.

"Well done," said Miriam. "I will arrange to have someone from Spoken Arrow's German accounts department accompany you, so that you'll know what he's talking about. Very good."

"Will you be OK on your own?" asked Jack, "Maybe I should come with you."

She looked towards Miriam and concluded that it was not such a good idea.

Miriam thanked Helga and took her bank details. She phoned Martin and told him the news. "I'll email all the information onto you. But what is Heinrich up to?"

"God only knows," he replied. "But I'm looking forward to meeting you in LA. I'll be waiting at the airport tomorrow."

He referred the news back to Jango, who immediately texted Penton to inform him that we can categorically prove that substantial profits have been achieved during the last twelve months. Heinrich is lying.

Penton immediately replied. "That's really good information, however we agreed here in Texas to spread our investments a little more and tomorrow we are putting half of our shares on the market."

"That's over six percent of the company. Can you wait just a few days?" pleaded Jango.

"Sorry, my friend… we've already voted on it."

The shares were put on the exchange and in no more than five minutes they were gobbled up by a finance house, but as the price had recovered they found that they had to break their promise to themselves and pay the full price.

"Who the hell are they? A company registered in Hamburg purchased a whole batch two weeks ago," said Spoken Arrow's stockbrokers. The second and third organisation to purchase were based in Frankfurt and Munch. Further purchases were bought from holding investment companies in various parts of the country.

***

Jango received a call at 2.00 am. It was Tara Reingold from his stockbrokers in New York, "Someone is trying to take control of your business, Jango. We worked out that it's between eight or nine companies that at first sight appeared to be independent, but they already have over twenty percent. After some digging they all appear to have some association with an organisation called Pontillo. If they were to amalgamate and keep on buying another ten percent, they would be the largest holder of your shares. You may be keeping their seat warm. Do you know Who Pontillo are?"

"No. Tara, that is highly distressing – I need to understand who is behind these companies. Treat this as an emergency."

His wife jumped up, "are we being burgled?" she shouted.

"In a way we are," he replied. "Tara, please look into them as a matter of urgency."

She returned his call two hours later. "It's a conglomerate called Pontillo, primarily a holding company, privately owned, based in Brazil but it has connections with Switzerland; I'm still looking into it, but it seems to have tentacles everywhere. I'm still checking."

Chapter 51

Chief Inspector Polton had been waiting for two weeks for the return of Mintov's computer. He asked the police interpreters to go back six months on their machine. Nevertheless, he was convinced that once he knew who Mintov was dealing with, he would have his man. It was beyond inexcusable that he left for lunch with his wife and lost his man as a result, he would have been a laughing stock by his colleagues and derided by his superiors if they discovered how stupid he was, and he made his sergeant swear that he would say nothing.

At last, he received a call from Scotland Yard's translation department to inform him that the file containing Mintov's notes was now available, and ready to collect. He immediately took them home to study.

Polton could have arrested Mintov on at least a dozen offenses, even within the six month period that he covered. He was a fixer who knew everyone in the underworld. At last, he arrived at the time span suggested by Paula Brenekov. Once again there were a myriad of shady deals being organised, both governmental and private. And there, lo and behold was Schickerdanz. Not just a name casually mentioned, but a file containing details of the Hines address, and specific explanations on the procedure to use the name of the deadly plant sent by him to a Gilda Baylim. With detailed instructions how to use it. He also found information on the running down of Freda Gesh, the train she caught and her arrival at the Cologne station, and which would require a third party to run her over. The name of a Jack Branson was also listed but no plan yet written. And Steffen Heinrich. with a figure of two hundred thousand dollars and the word paid next to his name, and a note from a Mr Heinrich confirming the delivery of works of art that appeared to be with a Monsieur LeClare. He paid two million dollars. That was the name Crow mentioned. So Heinrich had bought the stolen art.

This was worth waiting for. He would certainly be awarded something for cracking this case. It could make the criminal history books.

He would have to concoct a story as to how he managed to get Mintov's computer. He might simply say that he broke into his apartment and found the machine there. Simple.

Polton was well aware of the internal politics in the police force and if there were any points to be gained the Higher echelons would certainly grab them.

This was going to be his swan song. The final case that he would retire with. So what could his boss do if he told the press before him? But the unanswered question was why Heinrich would want to kill the Hines. *We know that the Brenekovs were instructed by Mintov. Who was he, this Heinrich, and what was Schickerdanz?*

He Googled Heinrich. Detailed articles describing the Heinrich family's proprietary stake in Magnum Computers. He was of course familiar with Magnum – who wasn't? – and he read on that they had recently introduced the Autoplug and Ever Young. But there was still in his mind no hint of what the connection could be. His next name was Gilda Baylim. The late George Baylim appeared to be the brain behind the Autoplug, but Mintov had written to Gilda detailing the toxic properties of a plant named *Gelsemium elegans*. So where did Hines figure in this jigsaw puzzle? He made another search: Hines had recently been "Minister for Health, succeeding Brendon Tann in the role. As a result of his sudden death at the hands of Brenekov, Tann was reappointed. Brendon Tann is widely acknowledged as the driving force behind the Autoplug."

At last, he had the complete set. Why would Heinrich want to kill Hines. Why did Gilda need the poison? And how did George Baylim die? Answer: Not for the art, it had to do with the Autoplug or Ever Young. There seemed to be no connection between many of these names. But only time would tell. The main point was that he had laid out the facts, the reasoning would be for others to discover.

Polton immediately phoned his wife. "I've cracked it," he laughed down the phone. "The computer had all the names. I'm going to speak with The Sun."

He was unaware of the many nuances that the story held, and that he was about to open a Pandora's Box.

"Why The Sun," she asked rather incredulously.

"They'll pay us a fortune for this story my love."

***

It was the coup of the century.

EXCLUSIVE TO THE SUN. The front page, and a four-page spread afterwards, including a half-page picture of Polton.

Every detail that Polton had uncovered was reiterated in the paper. Where it lay on the desk of the Prime Minister it seemed to burn into the finely polished wood as he stared at it. He sat with his head in his hands trying to gather his thoughts.

Picking up a call from George Pickles, without explanation he asked him to come round. After shaking hands George immediately went to the drinks cabinet and poured two large whiskeys, "I know that it's only half-nine, but it will help to get us through the day."

"It's going to be a tough one as well," replied the PM. "How did Judith Bracknell allow this stupid copper to publish his findings? She's dropped a real clanger here."

"She probably wasn't even aware of the facts, this man Polton gave it to the highest bidder without being censored," replied Pickles. "We'd better get her over and find out how much Polton knows."

The PM picked up the paper and glanced through it. "From what I see he's got all the pieces, it won't take too long for some bright spark to draw a conclusion." He poured another whisky and called his secretary to get Mrs Bracknell to come to his office immediately.

Whilst waiting Pickles switched on the T.V to hear the news, and there glaring from the screen was Chief Inspector Polton being interviewed. "It's taken many months to bring this sinister affair to its conclusion, I was convinced that the Brenekov gang were incapable of planning such a sophisticated robbery and assassination."

"And what brought you to the conclusion that the head of Magnum, Heinrich was involved?" asked the BBC interviewer.

"It was the Russian's computer we found after breaking into his apartment."

"Fascinating," exclaimed the reporter. "How did you know that this Russian was involved?"

"That, I'm afraid, is classified information and will no doubt be revealed in due course."

"He's damned right!" shouted the PM at the TV. "Now that Tann has gone too maybe it will stop at the murders. I think we'd better have young Jack Branson in, he knows more than is healthy, if we can hide the Baylim death, we could minimise Tann which might hide his involvement."

"It's a long shot since Heinrich used him to push his goodies."

"What does Our Home Office know? If we can keep the facts to a minimum it might help, she'll be here in a minute, we should give her the impression that we are as ignorant as she probably is."

His secretary knocked and came in, "Mrs Bracknell is here, sir."

"You have really caused us a problem Judith, what do you know about this Polton?" asked the PM.

"This is the first time I've heard about his findings Prime Minister. He's turned Maverick. The last record I have is that he interviewed the Brenekov brothers, after that there's nothing on the files."

"What about his superior?"

"He also knew nothing about the case. He'd spoken to Polton regarding the stolen art, but nothing after that. As far as he was aware they had the killers of Hines and that was the end of the case, stolen goods sold, not found. That was that."

"Listen, Judith, and listen carefully: you must not let any further information leave your office without passing it to either myself or George here. If you do you will lose your job, and there's a possibility we will lose ours too, is that clear? I want you to send me all the files and records of interviews relating to this case, and we'll interview Polton personally. Arrange it for tomorrow. Alright? In the meantime, not a word to a soul, not even your husband, alright?"

She noted the desperation in his voice and would have liked to learn some of the darker aspects of this case but decided that her position was tenuous enough already.

She got up to go, still unaware of the problems caused. "Thank you, Judith. We'll speak soon."

Chapter 52

Every morning without fail Brody Emmitt would buy a clutch of national papers and throw his eye over them for interesting news. He was not disappointed upon reading The Sun's headlines and the next four pages. "The little bugger, he's broken his promise." And immediately dialled through to Jack. "Seen the papers today?" he asked sarcastically.

"Have I seen it? I'm absolutely seething, Brody. This flat foot has poked his way independently and has sold his soul to The Sun."

"Are you saying that you had no knowledge of this chap?"

"Absolutely, I've never heard of him and it didn't even occur to me that he would unravel this quagmire by going through the Brenekov murders."

"Come in, Jack, it's our turn to make a killing now."

Immediately he had put his phone back into his pocket, it rang again.

"Hello, Jack, it's Jane Franklyn. You've obviously read today's papers and George wants to meet you with the PM ASAP. Can you come over immediately?"

"To be truthful Jane, this cloak and dagger business is really not good for my image, after all I'm a journalist."

"Listen Jack," she whispered. "I'm inclined to think like you, but we have a serious problem here which you can really help, we're in pain here, think what this is going to sound like to your grandchildren. Come and finish the story… as you say, you're a journalist. We'll expect you in one hour. We love you, Jack." He couldn't see her smile but he felt it. As instructed Jack was ushered into Pickles' office with a cup of tea and biscuit.

Pickles came out whilst putting on his jacket and both marched around the corner to see to his boss and friend.

"There's been a leak here Jack and we know that it had nothing to do with you, but you know more about this situation than anyone. What we didn't expect was our own police messing up what is a most delicate situation."

"I honestly can't see how you are going to hold events from unravelling now Prime Minister – there are too many loopholes and I can tell you that some of the papers are far better at finding the more sordid details than I. Your government will definitely be associated with the murders, and the intentions of Heinrich plus all the details relating to the Baylim killing. Polton had contacted the hospital where Baylim died and has even put on record that they killed him using a poisonous plant, *Gelsemium elegans,* according to the autopsy. It's been used by the Russians in previous killings. What I would like to suggest, if I may be so bold…"

"Go ahead," said Pickles, "don't be shy."

"Reveal Tann's activities sympathetically, how he wanted so much to be remembered for his achievements but became entangled in the deviousness of Heinrich. He was without doubt a weak man, and a stronger one would have resisted the bribes offered. But however we abhor his actions, the Autoplug would probably not have succeeded without his dogged efforts. There is no actual proof that Tann was involved with Baylim's death, so we can say that he simply became caught in the whirlpool of events but did his job well. The fact that our wonderful police managed to open the Jack-in-a-box can only be commendable."

"For my part I will write your government out as best I can, but since all will be revealed, you, in my opinion, should come out of the shadows and reveal yourselves as honest brokers, who have passed the best onto a good company that will continue to develop Baylim's work. The Ever Young project is frozen for the moment, but the history of the Heinrich family and their origins will certainly be revealed, and in particular the monies they are funding their ambitions with and its original sources."

"Our concern Jack is that our opposition will take what we have and if they have half a brain, will lambast us; it's true that the situation is not of our making, and very unfortunate that we have lost two ministers as a result of Heinrich's ambitions. We shall reveal that Ever Young was his ultimate weapon aligned to the Autoplug, to control the minds of the world. It's true that the Heinrich apple didn't fall far from the tree. However we will certainly get some stick."

"Look, sir, it's not for me to tell you about integrity, but the British people voted you in democratically – they might vote you out, but that's democracy, that's our country. It would be such a tragedy if you were to fall into the dictatorial power game. That's not what this country is about."

George Pickles sat back and clapped his young friend. "Well said… you can write my speeches, Jack. A bit left wing but not bad," he smiled.

"All I ask of you now, Prime Minister, is to release me to do what I'm being paid for, I promise to be kind. You have a friend in me. My boss has been very patient, but it's my moment now."

"Do what you have to do Jack, will you send me a draft of what you're writing?"

"No sir, I won't, you'll have to rely on my honesty."

It was as if a ton weight had been removed for his shoulders as he walked into his office.

Seeing Brody in his glass cage puffing away, he knew that this was where he should be, this was truly what he wanted, and this smoking bear of a man was his anchor, his mentor.

"Hey Jack," he bellowed, "what did your mate have to say?"

"I'm sorry to say, boss, that... I'm a free man," he laughed. "I can write whatever I like. and we're going to put this story to bed."

Chapter 53

Albert Heinrich had revealed his message to the world. He had never been shy about voicing his thoughts, even if they were known to be of the old school; he couldn't say the same for his allegiance to the old political party of the second world war – the word Nazi was never used and would be positively unacceptable in modern Germany – although if personally questioned it would not take very long to uncover his rather extreme desire to return to 'the old ways'. His interview with the BBC, however, simply went too far, and resulted in a call from Minister Anton Schmidt, Minister for German Foreign Affairs.

"Herr Heinrich, the chancellor has asked me to speak with you regarding your interview with the British BBC. Our position today in the world market is unique and over the last sixty years thanks to strong leadership we have become one of the wealthiest countries in the world. So in some respects I suppose we have achieved what you would wish for. But you must understand that we are still carrying old scars that are very deep."

"So, minister," replied Heinrich "Whilst I'm flattered that you have contacted me and informed me about our scars, what is it that you want or don't want me to do?"

"Have you read the British papers today Herr Heinrich? If not, I strongly advise you to do so. You and your company are being implicated in murder, and I would not be surprised if they ask us to arrest your son Steffen. The article is in The Sun."

"Just a moment, minister, whilst I pull it up on the computer."

The headline read, "MURDER: German Magnum Boss Implicated In Hines Case." And below that were claims of "incontrovertible evidence" against "the megalith Magnum."

"It's a joke, someone is being ridiculously stupid. Let me come back to you Minister. It's a joke."

"Not a very good one," said the Minister, "I urgently need an explanation. We don't want to be dragged into a historical war waving hysteria and this could happen if we allow your right wing ideas to be aired. Let us speak again this afternoon."

Heinrich excused himself and immediately contacted his son. "Steffen, read the British paper called The Sun and tell me what your thoughts are. These

English bastards have broken their word. I'm waiting. Do it now." He sat looking once again at the details and was horrified to note how many names were involved.

"I'm reading it – my God, this is terrible, father! Someone has leaked it... I need to get back to Brazil with my family immediately. I must get out of Europe. Can you have your office arrange a flight for me? I don't want anyone in my office knowing where I'm headed."

He casually took his coat, telling his secretary that he was not returning today. He could have said: "Or any other day." Drove home as fast as he dared and instructed his wife to pack as quickly as possible, "Just a few things for the kids as well, we'll buy what we need in Brazil."

Speaking to his father again he asked that no details of his itinerary be discussed online. "I don't want to be stopped at the airport."

Montello had now acquired a further two percent of Spoken Arrow. He only needed another eight percent to move for control of the company. The shares were moving up fast, and were now twenty percent higher than their original price. It was clear that someone, probably Spoken Arrow, had become aware that they were being attacked. Montello warned Albert: "We would be seriously stretching our cash reserves by buying at these prices. At this rate we may need a further six or seven percent moving up to thirty percent of the shares. Albert we won't be able to do it unless we borrow, but with this publicity we may have some resistance. With all this publicity, Magnum sales are also being seriously affected."

"Do whatever you can, Montello. If we don't get control we'll only have a foot in our competitor's house and it will defeat the object of the exercise. We must have sufficient power to walk into their offices without being thrown out, and even then we would have a fight."

"I have to tell you, Albert," replied Montello, "that I think this is a terrible idea."

"You may be right but I can't think of any other alternative, Alfredo. If this doesn't work we are lost."

Chapter 54

Miriam was informed by Martin that a mysterious organisation based in Brazil appeared to be behind a group that had been buying heavily into Spoken Arrow.

It was Miriam's daily routine to read the papers each morning with her breakfast. Bearing in mind the US was seven hours behind the UK, most papers were only just picking up on The Sun's big story and she only caught snippets, but went to the source. As she threw her eyes over found The Sun's reporting she was struck by how astonishingly accurate it was, and how suddenly Magnum could become enfeebled. She immediately phoned Jack to get an update.

"Where does that leave us?" she asked.

"You've already legally got the company as far as I'm concerned, you took it just in time. My article will hit Magnum hard, and in my opinion, Miriam, you are already in the driving seat."

She related what information she had on Pontillo "Tell me Jack, what you know of this conglomerate."

"I've never heard of them, but I'll check them out with Mrs Steinberg, there's nothing that she can't find out," he chuckled. Helga came back with all the figures. "The Autoplug will show a net profit this year of seven hundred million euros. Not bad. Considering it cost you comparatively nothing. It shows how Heinrich blatantly lied although for the life of me I can't see why. When are you returning?" he asked not as casually as he intended.

"Soon," she said. "It depends on what Martin has in mind for me to do. I think that he will ask me to run the European side of the Autoplug. The British government is still holding onto Ever Young, not that they particularly want it, but we certainly didn't."

"Why?"

"Because it's a political bomb shell, especially with all the publicity that it's about to get once you have a go at it," she giggled.

"You're right," he gracefully conceded.

Immediately he put the phone down he phoned Hermione Steinberg and within two hours he had his reply.

"Pontillo is a monster," she said. "Based in Switzerland and Brazil it has something above eighty billion of reserves. We don't officially know where these monies originate from, I will have a good indication in the next few days through our banking friends, but we believe it is accumulated booty from the second world war. It is the financing spine of Magnum and controlled by the Heinrich Trusts. It needs an urgent discussion, Jack."

***

Jack's article contained the complete diary of the events that had occurred, commencing from his own first awareness of Ever Young, its mind bending twists and turns and reaching the climax with photos taken at Heinrich's mansion followed by the death of Freda. Copies of the letters from Gilda to Steffen were also published. It was serialised in all the major publications of Tandem.

***

Parliament, The House of Commons

Question Time in the Houses of Parliament is dreaded by all Prime Ministers. It is the one time that the opposition have an opportunity to criticise, insult and aggressively dispute governments policies, if they're particularly persuasive on any subject they would pull onto their side some of the governing parties MPs, invariably making body blows that change the direction of the voting.

Needless to say the subject of Magnum was top of the agenda.

The speaker announced: "Mr Stuart Russell, leader of the Labour party and opposition."

There was a ghostly silence as Russell stood with his notes, ready to lambast his opponent. Both sides of the house knew what was to be his main thrust, he had a look of defiance which was well noted. A self-made Yorkshire man with an accent to match and far more left wing than many thought was healthy for a capitalistic country that Great Britain was known to be.

With his only opening words "The Sun" came a deafening roar from his side. The speaker had difficulty in silencing the members who could, he said, have been compared to football louts. With a wave of the speaker's hand he began again.

"The Sun has exposed what can only be described as a monumental attack by a foreign company, no less than the Magnum Corporation based in Germany who in order to take control of the Autoplug murdered its inventor and killed our Minister of Health and his wife using the services of the Russian mafia. This organisation was to use the Autoplug aligned to Ever Young which has been so

405

heavily promoted with our government finances to encourage young men and women to sign onto a plan to guarantee their health until the age of ninety-five year when they would be terminated in perfect health, in other words killed. Little did they know that Magnum would also have control of their mood swings and their subsequent actions or could be exterminated at any time by pressing a button."

"However we now know that a substantial number of ministers within our current government were on their books in order to accelerate their ghastly plan, many would have been aware of Magnum's ruthless reputation of assassination and who had an active part in the elimination of millions of innocent peopled during the Second World War." Both sides of the chamber went into convulsions. The Shadow Prime Minister was in his element. He continued.

"Here in front of us we have a government that is prepared to sell out our entire nation and to align themselves to the very enemy that we gave our lives to destroy. They would have succeeded with their treacherous plans had they not been thwarted by Mr Jack Branson, a journalist working for Tandem Publishing. We now know that many in this government were paid and benefited in the course of this scheme, and those that vehemently disagreed were murdered, including our Minister of Health Henry Hines and his wife."

The noise was deafening and it took over five minutes for the speaker to take control.

"We now know that Magnum GMBH is owned by the same Heinrich family that controlled Katalegein, an organisation that cooperated with the Third Reich before and during the war to collect millions of Jewish names around Europe for Goebbels – most of whom died as a result of this company's ruthless efficiency. They have intended to inject our population with the Neuro351 on the promise of extending our lives, but what they didn't tell us was that the Neuro351 would also allow them to control us and also terminate those of their choice as and when they wished."

"We can appreciate the benefits of the Autoplug, which is the brainchild of our own British scientists whose leader was also assassinated and ruthlessly acquired by Magnum, but what we did not know is that whilst the Autoplug would be our confession box for the masses, the information it holds is capable of referring to the Ever Young Neuro351 head office in Germany. who would no doubt decide our future to their ends, en-masse."

"It is now known that the newly appointed Health Minister Mr Hine was in conflict with their ambitions, and they saw fit to assassinate him using the

Brenekov family in conjunction with the Russian mafia and the inventor George Baylim. Mr Tann, the Health Minister, who recently committed suicide, was their paid conduit and bribed a number of government ministers to cooperate with them."

"We have here a government that is clearly seen to be collaborating with the same Nazi family, who continue their dastardly work with the assistance of a number of our own ministers of the crown. This government was prepared to sacrifice our country for personal gain. They have made a mockery of this country's standing in the world and allowed a foreign organisation reincarnated from the very enemy that cost millions of lives who died in order to protect us. They pursued their plan only by bribery and murder of those that disagreed with them, even our own minister and scientist."

"I should like to put forward a motion to force the current government to retire and an election offered to our British public in order that we may expunge the ministers that have been prepared to sell our very souls."

The house went wild. Shouts were coming from both sides, it seemed that the opposition were not interested in the Prime Minister's response, but eventually the speaker brought the mob into line. "Mr Alex Winter, the Prime Minister to respond."

For the next twenty minutes, Alex Winter trudged through pages of his governments defences and the deeds that might have kept them in office, but he knew that it was a lost cause.

Finally, he conceded to shouts of "Election! Election! Let the people decide!"

***

The papers loved a scrap. Filling the front pages with fors and against, and other political parties joining in with the single hope of gaining more power and in some cases, any power. Cartoons and interviews abound, and slowly the hysteria spread to neighbouring countries.

Finally with as much confidence as could be mustered Alex Winter conceded to go to the polls. "We will put this to bed once and for all," he told his cabinet but already knowing his fate.

Chapter 55
Martin

Martin was slowly coming to terms with his imposed bachelorhood. The political battles in the UK became academic to him now that Autoplug USA and International were registered as independent companies owned between Jango and himself. Finance guaranteed by SA, it would become a giant in its own right. He would franchise the operation to countries around the world and threw himself back into the business, barely thinking of his private life.

Having now returned to the USA Miriam was asked to oversee the European countries that Magnum had established with the Autoplug. Her function was to find credible franchisees and quickly acquire an 'inner sanctum team' of ten men and women whom she would divide up to oversee the franchisors. Further administrative staff would be enlisted from the Magnum division.

There were a still a number of legal formalities that required attention in the UK and she became sadly aware that until Martin took stock of his personal situation, she would be best advised to steer clear of any personal involvement. It was an affair that never happened, maybe for the best she thought.

Unexpectedly, he called her on the internal phone. "I'd like to take you for a dinner Miriam, are you free tonight," he asked. "Dress up, we'll go somewhere swanky for a change."

"What's the occasion?" she asked.

"It's a Coming of Age party, just you and me, I'm reinventing myself and I want you to be there when I do…before you return to bonny old England."

She left the office early and had her hairdresser go to some trouble, she bought a dress, which was unusual for her. It was years since she last bought an evening dress, his last words told her it was a farewell dinner which saddened her a little, but knowing Martin's precise manner of thinking she knew that he would want to present his farewells as if it was a blessing, a moratorium and she loved him all the more for that.

"Why don't we meet at the Excelsior Hotel, say 8 o'clock and I'll take you to a delightful little place I used to visit some years ago that will keep us out of the way of gossiping tongues." She couldn't put her mind to anything of consequence other than the coming evening. It was a strange experience to celebrate a good-bye, but it carried its own Hollywood style romance. She recalled Casablanca and the beautiful pain of parting.

She had rarely made such an effort to perfect her appearance, usually allowing nature to show her natural beauty, and surprised herself at the result. Was this her, complete, or simply a painted version of her real self. Tonight she decided it was the former.

He wore a white dinner jacket. His bow tie was a little crooked, which suggested that he tied it himself, he too had cut his hair and taken the trouble to cleanse himself of the world of business. He took her hand and kissed it as they left in his car.

Not many words were said during their journey and after about 40 minutes driving along the coast, they turned into a small but very steep side road. Now more than half way up a mountain he stopped the car. Looking along the coast road in the distance twinkled the city, anonymous and just identifying a far off civilisation. It could have been Africa, Italy or any part of the world other than where they were, and behind them was a small but exquisite garden and restaurant.

There were only five tables outside and a similar number inside this delightful hideaway. As they entered the only other couple there turned, they were not young and both in evening dress. Miriam recognised her from somewhere, she was a woman who enjoyed her status, whatever it was, maybe a once well-known actress and he, probably in his sixties had taken care of himself and matched her. They nodded and continued chatting quietly, no doubt wondering who the other guests were.

The owner greeted them both by name and invited them to a table; it was pleasantly warm and they decided to sit outside. The smell of roses permeated the air, and soft music quietly joined it. If he were to propose to her, it could not have been a more ideal setting, but she knew he wouldn't or couldn't and knowing that, she enjoyed the ambiance even more, as there was no pressure of expectation.

"And when is this moment of your reincarnation, my friend?" she smiled nervously.

"Now, Miriam, you have brought me to a new reality, it's not the reality that I want, but to know that someone like you exists in the world that might have some honest feeling for me has given me a strength and a reason to move on to my next chapter, whatever that may be. I made the business my wife, I realise now that I could have been less devoted to it and given more time to my domestic life, but that was not how I evolved. When you're good at something it's difficult to be less good and still achieve another life with the same commitment. And that's why I daren't commit myself again. But that's not to say I should stop loving, even from afar."

"I'm afraid I too have to make an admission Martin," she was blushing and cleared her throat. "I can't tell you how many times, especially when we were in London, that I stopped myself from expressing my feelings, but it had to come from you, and I knew you couldn't say it." She took his hand and squeezed it. "But I don't see this evening as a goodbye, it's a moment in time, how can we say good bye and still have such an evening, we can live all our lives on this evening, and knowing that there can be more."

"You or I may meet someone at some time in the future, that won't change our affection for each other, and why should it. You still love your wife, she's hurt your pride, but you still love her, as I hope you'll do the same for me. But you need to do what you're good at and that's your driving force. Your raison d'etre. I'm not driven in the same way, maybe it's my feminine desire to have children someday, I'm not ready yet but who knows. When I hug my nieces or nephews, I know that one day I'll be hugging my own. Who knows what the future holds. I think not knowing is what's so exciting. So let's not say goodbye. Just enjoy the moment and keep it."

He bent over the table and kissed her. It was nearly midnight when they left the restaurant. He drove her back to her car. And they parted as the lovers that they would always be.

Both arrived at work late the following morning. They had made love without making love.

Miriam returned to England two weeks later with a single agenda: to launch the Autoplug throughout Europe under the banner of Spoken Arrow.

Chapter 56

The police issued a warrant for the arrest of Steffen Heinrich. The Prime Minister was obliged to speak with his counterpart in Germany asking for their assistance to locate him, only to be informed that he and his family had gone to Brazil. A further request to the Brazilian government was rejected.

The Brenekovs were concurrently brought to trial, and in spite of the assistance that the two brothers gave the police and Polton's assurances, they and Joe were all sentenced to life. Their screams that a possible deal was discussed only exacerbated the position of the government.

Chief Inspector Polton retired in the glory that he had personally untangled one of the most audacious crimes this century. He denied that any 'back room' deals had ever been agreed. The court heard that the now deceased Gilda Baylim had poisoned her husband, coerced by Brendon Tann, who was also deceased, and plotted by Steffen Heinrich. A warrant for his arrest for murder was issued but Heinrich had absconded to Brazil.

The government was too compromised to continue. A new, leftwing Labour government under Stuart Russell won a snap election on the premise that his party was honest and without blemish. The UK could still be a citizen's utopia committed to the masses.

***

Montello entered Heinrich's office without knocking. He carried with him a thick file and a heavy frown, and it was obvious that he was a bearer of bad news. "Albert, I now have the latest report of shares and viability. We now have nineteen percent of Spoken Arrow spread over nine separate portfolios. The last six or seven percent have cost us dearly, and we really are struggling with our cash flow. This bad publicity is seriously damaging our main business and of course the income we are losing from the loss of the Autoplug is a body blow, bearing in mind that we had invested so much into the project. Think of all the hardware we have virtually given to SA; it was a ridiculous agreement, a disaster in my opinion," he sulked.

"Listen Alfredo, Steffen is my son, what do you know, you think like a machine, I would have lost him for the rest of my life and probably his if we wouldn't have agreed."

"And now I suppose he's safe," he replied sarcastically. "They'll make some deal with the Brazilian government to extradite him anyway so what have we gained. Nothing. Damn it, I've given my life to you and you simply cut the tree down for the sake of your son. For God's sake, you've been prepared to kill off enough sons of others and with less to gain. Well, what's good for the goose is good for the gander, I say."

"I say!?" shouted Heinrich. "What you say has no value to me, you are nothing more than a trained dog. Just do what I tell you, I'm not interested in your opinion."

"So you won't be interested to know that all your spare capital has gone into this stupid idea, and we have little chance of taking over your competition unless we borrow heavily. Who do you think is going to lend us money with the publicity we are currently getting? And if we dump the shares now the value will drop and we'll lose a fortune. I've had enough of your insults, your bad judgement, and constantly undermining me. You are living in a wonderland. You may think of me as a trained dog, Herr Heinrich, but this dog is not quite as trained as you think... and bites." His mood was close to violence. "I'm quitting. And if you think that you can kill me with my knowledge, I can tell you, my friend, that if something untoward happens to me, all my notes are in a safe deposit box with instructions to be read on my demise."

With these last words, he marched out and slammed the door behind him.

Heinrich immediately picked up the phone and called his son.

Chapter 57
Helga

Helga had never been given a task like this that would allow her to use her own judgment, and her visit to Magnum's headquarters accompanied by an appointed mentor from Spoken Arrow felt like she was walking into unchartered territory. She had a degree in neuropsychology and had studied with Dr Ellsworth for a master's. Nevertheless she was concerned that her lack of experience might not meet the needs of the practical world surrounding her – the world that Jack had introduced her to was a gloves-off boxing match, one she found exciting but scary. Her guide selected by Miriam was a young German called Franz Feltz, a dynamic and enthusiastic accountant working for a company that he loved.

His university education had been sponsored by Spoken Arrow and he had ventured outside his accounting training to understand the company's business philosophy. When his name was put forward to assist Helga to discuss figures with their major competitor, he jumped at the opportunity. He was thoroughly briefed by Miriam on chat to assist Helga and the reality of adding the Autoplug to their agenda was a demanding challenge.

The figures that he was instructed to acquire could have been simply passed on by email, but a deeper understanding of these accounts was asked for and the logics of how they were arrived at omitting drug sales. Helga's perceptive mind would sense any theatrical instructions that might have permeated down from Heinrich, but she was happy to rely on Franz on the accounting aspects of the viability of the Autoplug where she was clearly out of her depth. They spent a week in the Magnum offices, where over two hundred staff were solely devoted to the Autoplug. From the software used, to the stock control, servicing costs, rental charges and locations around the world, the Magnum systems were superb.

It was also made clear that dedicated staff would be transferred from one company to the other in order that a smooth transition could take place.

Time was of the essence in order to justify to the stock market that the acquisition was in fact viable, and this pressure was passed down to Fritz to ensure that he was not being hoodwinked. There was indeed evidence that the figures were manipulated to show a substantial loss in line with Herr Heinrich's TV interview, but as the relationship between their counterparts grew and the hope of being employed by Spoken Arrow, the true figures emerged.

This confirmation would bring the value of the Spoken Arrow shares back to a credible level and the thought that their efforts would be a major factor with such a massive company gave young Feltz a great feeling of pride.

Helga felt very comfortable speaking in her native language and it was pleasant not being placed under the pressure that she had experienced with Jack. Of course it had been exciting, maybe even too exciting, and Fritz was a happy and easy-going young man. They worked well together, ate and laughed together and inevitably slept together, and by the end of the week a strong relationship had taken root.

She returned to London in strong conflict with her feelings. Immediately they landed she phoned Jack but unusually there was no reply. The idea of being a woman with two lovers made her smile, but she knew that she would have to be honest with Jack and tell him of her latest admirer. Would he understand, or should she see Franz as a "holiday romance a delightful memory."

She decided to contact Miriam by email, after all it was from her that she received her instructions.

Miriam replied immediately.

Welcome back Helga, I hope that you enjoyed your first encounter with the enemy, I understand that you worked very well with our guy in Germany, he gave me an excellent report. I shall be returning to London next week but speaking with our PR agency in New York, they believe that it would be most effective if you were to appear on a TV program over here to show the investors in Spoken Arrow that their interest in the company is secure. I believe that your looks, honest disposition and intelligence would make a great impression. Would you like a quick visit for say three days? You will be treated as royalty. If so, I will arrange a flight for tomorrow to New York and meet you there.

(P.S As you are not employed by Spoken Arrow I propose we offer you a further £5,000 for your efforts I shall email your flight details)

Kindest wishes,

Miriam.

She emailed back to say how exciting it would be to extend her travels, and the offer was very generous.

Two hours later her tickets were confirmed first class to New York plus details of a hotel.

Jack returned her call, and she explained that she was meeting Miriam in NY to give her report on Germany… and on TV. She giggled.

The German Ambassador Herr Schmidt

Ambassador Schmidt compiled a five page report of his discussions with Jack Branson to include his opinions relating to Heinrich and in particular Pontillo. Chancellor Brandt carefully read the notes adding his comments, and in turn passed them onto his friend, the Minister of Finance Hans Grieff. With his considered thoughts.

Strictly confidential

Hello Hans,

Re: Pontillo

"Can we investigate this company in the strictest confidence, I'm particularly interested to confirm the origins of this financial conglomerate. We know that they are based in Brazil and have offices in Switzerland. It's one thing to have our thoughts as to its origins but for the record we need facts.

We are going back to 1937/8 to 45. You may need to revert to well-known unsavoury war time names that were later associated with the company and if possible, discover if there are any records of access to large assets during the war. We are talking about considerable sums Hans. Many billions. I should also warn you that certain names of international companies today may know, or might be associated with Pontillo in some way even now, and that could be most embarrassing. We are on very thin ice so be very careful.

Kindest wishes,

Herman"

Three days passed before the chancellor received a reply from his friend.

From Hans Grief:

Hello Herman,

It is astonishing what one finds if they look hard enough. It was quite easy to check out the origins of Pontillo which was formed in 1948. Its original name was Wagner Boranstein Schickerdanz which began to accumulate its monies way back in 37/38. It was formed as a finance House in Switzerland when a select few individuals high up and I mean high up, in the Third Reich circles used it as a bucket. It seems that each name would register their contribution and dumped massive amounts into it. Jewellery, Paintings and even more important, Property all were sold and the proceeds dumped in the bucket of Wagner Boranstein Schickerdanz. The Museum of War Library had letters and accounts ledgers showing substantial sums invested into it. At first, only the big names were there. but as the war progressed less well known characters joined the throng. Each man had his share according to his own contribution. *Massive swathes of land, buildings sold off, even bank accounts transferred, all confiscated, to be reallocated to preferred individuals sub-accounts. When events began to go against Germany, the monies were transferred to Brazil. under another nom de plume which meant that anyone still surviving would not know where it was.*

The reason that it has never been picked up is simply because the money did not seem to exist. Goring and Schickerdanz were now the only ones who knew the name of the new bank. It appears that Schickerdanz was overseeing and now in total control of the funds. Schickerdanz changed his name to his wife's maiden name of Heinrich, and the accounts name to Pontillo, by which time most of those originally on the list were dead. I have not yet been able to discover how much is still in the Pontillo account or who is currently running it, but I'm sure that it's substantial.

I hope this information is useful.
With kind regards,
Hans.

Herman Brandt thanked him and asked, for his own safety, to wipe the information off his computer as he would also do. If the public get to know of this information we will be bombarded with demands from across the world. We should wait until the dust settles. "Come over and share a drink with me this evening," Brandt suggested. "Hans, we've known each other for over thirty years, and I think we can trust one another.

"We have an interesting dilemma here. It's now a matter of finding out how much money is still in the Pontillo account and what assets it has in investments. It was stolen from such a wide collection of countries, we would never know. If we confiscated it, it would end up in our German economy, and since it was stolen by us, all be it in another time, the world would certainly condemn us for keeping it."

"Magnum is the brain child of their wartime information scheme which took on the task of collecting names of millions of people who were then murdered by the Nazis. It is still drawing its finances from the well of Pontillo. Does that mean that we should confiscate all the assets from one of the largest companies in the world?"

"We could leave it where it is until we find a solution," replied Hans with a twinkle in his eye.

"You know better than that Hans. No, we can demand possession of Pontillo and continue to run it and give its profits to someone like UNESCO. Can you imagine, billions, it could almost take poverty out of Africa."

"You must be joking," laughed Hans, "it would go straight into some despot's pocket. Maybe the first step is to confront Heinrich, there's no doubt that if we pursued this it would bankrupt them, his business could still be run by them but it would not belong to him."

"In that case, there's little point in approaching him, we know what his response would be. He'll throw the book at you or worse. Besides, there would not be a chance of him wanting to run a company that has been taken away from him."

"I think," whispered Brandt as if he was in fear of being overheard, "that we must complete our own story and philanthropically announce it to the world. We must first discover the approximate value that is in the pot plus the value of Magnum. Once we see the extent of its worth we should make a grand gesture to the world. Magnum would be state run and the remaining assets would be offered to a world based charity with a historic speech…by me," he grinned.

"So, how do we find this information?" asked Hans.

"Pontillo, we must find out who they have put in charge of that organisation first, and maybe from there we might uncover the rest."

"If it's the Heinrich family they won't tell us, we must find someone within the organisation with a loose tongue, how do we find that?" "God knows," replied the chancellor.

Chapter 58
Brazil

Alfredo Montello was consumed with rage. he sat at his dining table with a glass of wine musing. He had been at the beck and call of the Heinrich family for nearly thirty years. It was true to say that he had become rich from the various dealings that they had negotiated over the years, and whilst he was respected by his team, he was an unsung hero, and at this very critical stage his advice was totally ignored. "Surely Albert Heinrich should have learned by now not to mix his family emotions with the welfare of the business," he bleated to his wife. "His son is incapable of defining a long term strategy, his actions were totally unacceptable and he compromised the entire organisation. It was not unreasonable to expect him to be punished and in fact sacrificed for the sake of the business. Now we've lost a most exciting addition with the Autoplug and Ever Young project."

"The idea that we could buy Spoken Arrow and dominate the entire computer world in order to retrieve the Autoplug and Ever Young was ridiculous. We have used up all Pontillo's reserves," he confided to his wife. "And we still need another twenty-five or thirty billion dollars to buy a controlling share in the company."

"But Pontillo has its investments in a number of other businesses," she said.

"They're intact but it means we can't expand or purchase anything outside our existing assets. We've stretched their cash flow to the maximum. Each company within the Pontillo group have bought the maximum amount of shares that their cash flow will allow."

"OK you know what you do, go back to Heinrich and tell him that he must either sell some of the assets of Pontillo to raise the money from outside sources to take control of your competition. Alternatively, If you are all so determined to conquer the world, go back to Germany and involve them. after all it's for them that you are supposedly doing it. Show your cards."

"You're right Francesca," he said, "you should be running the company not these idiots I'm working for, but you and I both know that my allegiance to Germany was only as strong as my employment with Magnum, which as of now is NIL."

He decided to call Heinrich on his private line rather than walk back as if contrite.

"I thought you said that you quit, spat out Heinrich without giving opportunity for an explanation."

"If you won't listen to advice I will quit. We've been through some difficult times Albert over the years, but have always managed to find a way out, I am telling you that unless we talk this situation through this organisation will irrevocably fail. I'm not a punch ball for you to vent your temper out, but I have an idea that might get us out of this shit we're in." There was a silence at the other end.

"Hello, are you still there?" asked Alfredo.

"Yes I'm still here, OK come over and we'll talk."

***

"Not all is lost, but we've compromised ourselves. If we are to follow the purchase of Spoken Arrow, which isn't a bad idea, we need to raise at least a further twenty-five billion dollars. But the shares have not dropped again and we would need to pay premium prices. If we dump the shares, we will be flooding the market, their value would fall through the floor, and we would lose a fortune."

"So, what do you propose?"

"My understanding is that Ever Young and Autoplug were to be used as an ideal tool to rejuvenate the German spirit, to reincarnate the nation as the dream that we all had."

"I propose we call on the leaders of Germany and ask them to work with us. Show our colours with pride. This could be our moment Albert, if we align ourselves to the mother country, you might be surprised the reaction we could receive especially from the right of the country. Think what Ever Young could do if we only used it in Germany, we would truly have a superior race. And for those that are not so welcome we would program them to our requirements, with or without their knowledge."

"Now you are talking like a true German, Alfredo, it's a shame your blood is not but you can be an honorary nationalist. I'll make contact with Chancellor Brandt, just to have a casual conversation, and see if he is amenable to discussing a proposal in greater detail."

Montello phoned the German embassy, and was put through to the ambassador, whom he had met on numerous occasions. "George, I need to speak with the chancellor on a matter that could be very beneficial to the country. Can you give me his PA's number to organise a direct call? I would arrange for Herr Heinrich to be available at a time of the chancellor's convenience."

"Can you give me some idea what you want to discuss, Alfredo, so that I can at least prepare him for the subject?"

"I would, my friend, but it is a matter of complete secrecy, rather uniquely and with the greatest of respect a one-to-one conversation – but time is of the absolute essence."

"OK I will speak with him and ask, when will you be available?"

"At his earliest convenience. If he would like to phone me that would be good too. In which case maybe you would tell me when."

"Sounds most mysterious, Alfredo. Leave it with me and I will phone you whenever I manage to speak with him. You know that Herr Heinrich met him when he was in Berlin. He never mentioned anything that involved the country specifically."

"We were not ready to discuss this idea then, he rather shocked the country in his interview especially with the British BBC, as you may have noted. Herr Heinrich likes to give an electric shock from time to time. It's all part of the game," Alfredo replied.

Immediately he hung up Montello informed Heinrich of his conversation with the intention of planning a strategy. It would not be easy to persuade a leader of any country, even more so Germany of a plan to dominate the world. But starting with the computer world and nationalising two companies that virtually controlled the market would be a good start. He reiterated a fifty-fifty partnership based on the National Health plan, and only a subtle mention of the Neuro351 communication – anything more would certainly scare him off.

"We need to be positive in our requests and prepared for anything they throw at us. I don't have to tell you, Albert, how important this first conversation is. Please keep cool!"

They calculated that initially they required twenty-five billion dollars up front and a further thirty billion over a period of three of five years for their fifty percent of Magnum to include thirty percent and Spoken Arrow making them the largest shareholders with control of the company, and that would be a bargain. The new company would dominate the entire computer world.

Once a broad base for a positive discussion was laid out, they awaited the chancellor's call.

Montello did not have to wait long. At 9.00 am, Brazil time the following morning he received a call from the chancellor's PA suggesting when it would be a convenient time to chat online with the Herr Brandt.

"Can I suggest in one hour, I would have Herr Heinrich with me for a conference call, but I'd be most grateful if we were able to speak in confidence."

"I quite understand," she replied. "Shall we say one hour on this number?"

"Wunderbar."

Brandt immediately phoned Hans Grieff. "We have a conference call with Heinrich and his henchman in one hour from now, do you want to be included, it's on video so dress well. By the way, he wants to talk in confidence, so I'll have to find an excuse for you being here."

"Of course I'll come. How amazing, it might be just the opportunity we've been looking for."

***

One hour later exactly to the minute the telephone rang.

"Thank you for your prompt response, chancellor."

Chancellor Brandt looked tired, but answered with a genuine interest in his tone "If I cannot look after one of our most important companies I would not be doing my job Herr Montello. I understand that you requested confidentiality, but my Minister of Finance is Herr Hans Grieff works very closely with me as you can appreciate. I can see also Herr Heinrich with you. I hope that you have recovered from your interview Albert… he appeared to rattle you a little. I know the feeling, I can assure you."

Heinrich shook off the comment but it changed his mood, and felt the same anger come over him, but checked himself.

"We are in an interesting situation at this time, chancellor. You will know of course that Spoken Arrow are taking over the Autoplug and Ever Young. Some of the details you may already know. However after considerable thought we looked into this company's activities and it was interesting to see just how much our two companies complimented one another. It might have been easier to speak with them directly about a form of association, but under the circumstances we decided to acquire them through the stock market and absorb them into our own operation."

"That's a very ambitious plan if I may say so, Herr Heinrich, even for a company of your size – my understanding is that they are actually larger than yourselves. May I ask how you would finance such a takeover?"

"You will of course know that we have been established for over eighty years and have substantial reserves to draw from, and I can tell you in confidence that through our subsidiary companies we have already purchased nearly twenty percent of the company, But what I would like to suggest to you is that the German government might like to join us in purchasing their shares in order to take control. This would make us the largest computer company in the world by far, and with the Autoplug and Ever Young we would have the influence that we always craved for, but without war or bloodshed."

"And how much would this takeover cost?" Asked Grieff.

"I would say that to purchase a controlling shareholding of, say, thirty percent of their company, approximately another twenty or thirty billion dollars, and then to purchase fifty percent of Magnum, thirty billion over, perhaps, five or seven years."

"But I don't quite understand," questioned Brandt. "What benefit is there in you bringing us into the business? I understand that you have… what's their name… Pontillo, behind you, can they not support your ambitions?"

"We're happy to separate the two organisations. We currently own one hundred percent of Magnum and Pontillo but if we are to continue to expand in the future we believe that the concepts that we would want to develop would have far greater credibility if the state had some share in it."

Grieff was writing figures and various equations. "You know Herr Heinrich that we have a great regard for the future of our country, and I would like to think that some of your ideas for the nation were not dissimilar to ours. It also depends on how much Pontillo is worth. Let me ask you this Herr Heinrich, suppose we were interested in involving ourselves in a nationalising your operation, we would expect Pontillo to join with us too, let us say making Germany great as you intimated in your interview, and supposing my good friend here was to put aside by some means or another, say thirty or fifty billion dollars – what would you imagine we would benefit?"

"You would of course have fifty percent of its joint profitability," replied Heinrich. "But what would you say Pontillo is worth?" asked Brandt.

"Probably eighty billion dollars," replied Montello. "Maybe a little more."

"That would make an enormous capital base. Suppose we put together a serious plan to involve the monies we have been talking about. Including the

Autoplug and Ever Young and all the assets of Pontillo. We are holding assets of over one hundred and eighty billion dollars, plus Spoken Arrow's value of another sixty billion. based on an equal partnership your contribution would be half. Would that be a reasonable thing to do?"

"Absolutely," replied Brandt "We'll give the idea serious consideration, I suggest that you make contact with us in two or three days with your formal ideas. Maybe a meeting, incognito, might be appropriate."

The conversation concluded amicably, and both sided switched off their computers and poured themselves large whiskeys.

***

Magnum's Computer factories were spread across the world, from China, Eastern Europe and the Americas. The more refined products were produced in Germany and Brazil. In all, over two hundred and eighty thousand workers were employed directly or indirectly where sub-contractors working in China exclusively for Magnum. Brazil, understandably produced the new and experimental designs as the research labs were based in San Paulo.

It was true to say that Steffen Heinrich had been the driving force behind the Autoplug and, in spite of his disastrous current problems, Magnum had benefitted substantially from his foresight over the years.

Regardless of his more recent efforts his father was justified in his anger, but whatever ridiculous agreement that they had been forced to make in Europe, he was confident that his pockets were deep enough for Brazil to protect them— whatever it necessitated.

Albert called Gilda and Steffen to his office. She had not forgiven Steffen and refused to speak with him for destroying her life, a life that she had sacrificed to fulfil a purpose that had been so carefully planned. "If Steffen is coming, I will not," she bleated.

"I'm not asking you Gilda, I'm telling you," He shouted into the phone. "3.00 pm. today." The fourth person included Montello. "Alfredo and I have devised a plan that we think could place us back in the driving seat, and I will be pleased to hear your thoughts too. Firstly you may or may not know that we have been quietly buying up shares of Spoken Arrow over the last few weeks, and we now have approximately twenty-two percent of their shares spread through a number of different companies."

"And what is the reason when we're not allowed to be involved in the Autoplug or Ever Young," enquired Gilda with no small degree of sarcasm.

"The purpose is quite obvious, Gilda. Spoken Arrow have taken the Autoplug, and we will buy Spoken Arrow. It's a checkmate. We intend to take control and by doing so we will have a monopoly on the computer market worldwide and of course we will get back our Autoplug and Ever Young. This will involve and tie up a great deal of money, not only buying the shares but the cash flow to run it."

"You have always had the same dream as mine that we will one day be able to control the purest of societies from our beloved Germany, and to do this we need the support of the government. So, my friend here has spoken with the chancellor and we are to meet him in New York."

"What do you have in mind father? You know that I can't be seen in the USA. Even if they don't arrest me I would be detained and sent back to the UK, and Gilda is by all accounts dead."

"Alfredo and I will go. We will offer fifty percent of Pontillo and Magnum, plus half of the percentage that we have purchased of Spoken Arrow. All we need now is another seven to ten percent to claim control of their business. I am assuming that they will secure to us thirty billion dollars for their fifty percent."

"Can you imagine the control we would have through the computers, Autoplug and ultimately Ever Young, plus the Spoken Arrow, all aligned to the government?" He waited for a response, but both were nonplussed.

"So," he continued. "My understanding is that Ever Young has been put on ice, and we can assume that they don't want it. We, on the other hand, do, and even if they won't deal with us we can take possession of the Autoplug starting in Brazil and South America. We have the facilities, and who knows the products better than us? We would have eventually launched it in South America anyway. We won't allow them to operate here."

"I think you're both crazy," announced Steffen. "Don't you understand that we have signed a formal document. They'd sue us for a fortune."

"Let them try. Listen, we had an agreement on the basis that you would be free. They've broken their side of the agreement, and as far as I'm concerned we have justice on our side. And besides, if we have bought Spoken Arrow who will sue us?" he laughed.

"The British government, that's who!" shouted Steffen.

Ignoring his son's outrage. "If we launch in South America it's equivalent to the population of Europe. We'll market under another name, and change the name of all the Autoplugs. We have better contacts here than they do and we'll block them out of the market."

He could see that they were querulous and depressed and he softened his tone. "I understand that things haven't gone the way they should have, but we're fighters, and we will win this war. Now, if we can do a deal with the Fatherland we'll win our credibility back and have real world domination. With access to nearly every computer and the Autoplug, then of course Ever Young, or whatever we chose to call it, the world will be ours for the taking.

"Coming down to realities," said Montello "I have spoken with the chancellor and am going to suggest that we meet in New York. We'll take a small meeting room at the Ritz and make a presentation to them. If they refuse, we'll pursue our Brazilian plan on our own."

Heinrich now directed his attention towards Gilda "We'll register the new company under your children's names Gilda."

"That's ridiculous, uncle, you know that I don't have children."

"Of course I know that, but Alicia Troupe does. They're both studying Politics in Venezuela. As Alicia you can join us." He smiled proudly showing his gold fillings, and took from his pocket a photo showing two teenagers, Josephine and Stephanie.

She stared at the picture placed in front of her, and she found herself wondering if she could have ever had such lovely young women who would call her mother. "Will I be able to come to the meeting?" Asked Gilda.

"If you have your new passport, why not," he replied. "You'll have to get used to your new family – it's going to keep you out of prison."

"We'll also have to give you a new identity Steffen, A new name and look, I'm not at all sure how we can do that especially with your wife and kids in tow, otherwise it's only matter of time before they expose you, but you must move the works of art from your home as a matter of urgency. Do you hear me Steffen, there must be no sign of those pieces…get rid of them. We've found you a villa in Montevideo. It's a family home, I think you'll be pleased with it. We'll send your pieces there if you wish, nobody will find you there."

"We had already set up medical centres for Ever Young in various parts of Brazil which would serve as an Ever Young operational point, and if Spoken Arrow want to make a claim for their Autoplug operation they will be refused our software facilities and we will exclude them from our factories here too. In other words, we are going on the offensive."

Two days later Gilda received a call from Montello. "Look to see your website Alicia Troupe, you're very photogenic."

There she was standing by a swimming pool with her two daughters smiling away. And her history laid out from birth to university. Studied maths and engineering, husband John Troupe – a lawyer – died ten years ago. Two photos of her and him in front of a suburban house in Chicago. Now in their late twenties. A sub-note read, "Go blonde."

Chapter 59
Germany

On the premise of an unofficial meeting with his ambassador in the USA, Chancellor Brandt and his Finance Minister Hans Grieff arranged a two day trip to meet Herr Heinrich and Señor Montello. The German Newspapers were informed that it was an 'unofficial information Top Up with his ambassador'. They reserved a suite at the Ritz, and officially committed to appointments in order to substantiate the fact. And finding discussions with relevant and irrelevant parties making something out of nothing in order to camouflage the meeting with Magnum.

Heinrich, Montello, and Gilda flew from Brazil in their private jet. Gilda had been given a makeover, she had dyed her hair blond and had been taken to a top departmental store to change her from a rather dowdy middle aged woman to a slightly smarter but still dowdy lady making a brave attempt to look smart.

Both parties booked into the Ritz. The meeting was held early the following morning. Herr Albert Heinrich, introduced Alfredo Montello as Global Director of Administration, and Alicia Troupe, Technical Director. Coffee was poured and Montello placed relevant documents in front of the Chancellor of the Exchequer and Finance Minister.

"Allow me to talk you through our proposal," suggested Montello.

"As you know we are one of the largest producers of computers in the world, the Autoplug was developed by us in conjunction with the British Cambridge University. I don't have to explain the difficulties that have ensued during the last few months which have been most distressing. Nonetheless, our sales worldwide have not been meaningfully affected even though our major competitor has been given the Autoplug, which was in fact generating billions globally."

"There is no excuse for what happened, but I should point out that what we have achieved made a vast difference to people's lives throughout the world. Millions of people have had great benefit from this system which would not have happened without our very substantial input. It simply would not have happened."

"Not wishing to interrupt your flow Herr Montello, but you must know that your reputation has been seriously sullied and is a substantial stumbling block

427

for a government to jump over," commented Brandt. "And your son – Herr Heinrich – is on the wanted list for murder. I won't ask you where he is."

Heinrich was about to reply but Montello held the stage. "We realise that, but you will see that it can be overcome, so I beg your indulgence a little more."

He drank a sip of water and took a few moments to prepare himself for his presentation. "Imagine that we are at war, a silent war that has no name other than a dream, fighting a corrupt civilisation. I am not saying that it has to be ruthless or blood spilling, but a war of the minds."

"Ignorance emanates from lack of education and that invariably stems from parents who have no understanding of their crumbling civilisation. To some extent we, the technological leaders of the world are to blame. We offer the public what their most base desires crave for. T.V and the media in general encourage debauchery, gambling, food that clearly creates obesity and diabetes, licentiousness, not forgetting drugs etc. In other words there are no controls, and government has to pander to the masses for fear of losing votes. The idealist politician soon becomes the pragmatist compromising on any aspirations they hoped to achieve."

"I should have you writing my speeches," chuckled the chancellor.

"Governments are allowing their people to commit crimes that the media compound very day of the week, but what we have in our hearts is a better and purer world, and we can do it."

"So tell us what you have in mind, we're here to listen," commented Hans Grieff.

"It's our intention to acquire Spoken Arrow. We have already purchased approximately twenty percent of their shares without them knowing it through a number of companies that we control. But we need another ten percent to secure the control of the company as we would be the majority shareholder. As you will probably know they have the edge on us in turnover and now they have the Autoplug. At this time, they would have to lean on our past experiences in order for them to support the system technically. If we took control of Spoken Arrow, we would then control eighty percent of the world computers, and with the Autoplug and Ever Young the combination will allow us to influence the world's health and control their desires in every respect. And it would all emanate from Germany."

"I'm not sure how you feel that your control of this market would change world society Herr Montello, but even supposing it did, I'm wondering where we, representing the German government could help," asked Brandt.

428

"Good," Heinrich interspersed. "There are three main aspects here. First. You will agree that nobody can exist in today's society without their computer or mobile. That in itself is a major form of communication. It serves two main functions. It allows the user the facility to communicate, and quite simply gives information. All of which can and is already controlled when necessary."

"However, The Autoplug is more than just a medical informer, it contains every aspect of each individual's life, we are now considering offering a domestic model, even integrating with their normal computers. Their work, home, family, health. They confide in it, take advice from it and every secret they have will be added to the app to give a deeper understanding of that person. And finally, Ever Young. An amazing invention, harmonising the body, repairing defective DNA and ensuring good health until ninety-five years. As you know we were obliged to pass them over to the British government and subsequently to our competitors."

Taking advantage of the short respite in the conversation Montello jumped in, "Herr Brandt, Magnum isn't just a conglomerate company, it has always dreamt of achieving something of consequence for the Fatherland, and that had historically failed because it used physical force against powers who more than matched it. We now have the ability to improve the globe by intellect and a respect for humanity, but the right humanity, that no other country in the world has been able to harness."

"And what would you need to achieve this?" asked Brandt.

Heinrich answered. "If we managed to take control of our erstwhile friends we would need to earmark working capital that would stretch us, but even more important, think what we could do under the umbrella of Germany. Worldwide control of every aspect of society. We would be able to understand and where necessary, direct each of the masses by computer, reduce the ever growing cost of medical attention, prolong the lives of the elderly and save billions, and where necessary control their behaviour…and you would go down in history as the leaders of a new perfect world." Both men sat up in unison on his last words.

Montello had heard this employer's dream for the future of civilisation many times and listened with some degree of satisfaction as Heinrich was slowly burying himself.

Heinrich could not now be held back and continued.

"We would give you fifty percent of both Magnum and Pontillo and of course we would split the Spoken Arrow Corporation shares purchased. With a group turnover of over two hundred billion dollars, probably greater than Germany's total net value. We would ask you to invest forty billion over a two year period and another forty-five billion over the following five years. That would of course include extended working capital which could be borrowed."

"A very interesting proposition Herr Heinrich and one that needs considerable thought," replied Grieff. "You will appreciate that we would have to put this to the Cabinet for such a large sum, they would of course ask what the financial return would be. But I have a few questions for you that will inevitably be asked of me."

"By all means, please ask away," said Heinrich.

"Your son has a warrant out for his arrest, and according to my opposite number in the UK he has vanished. He's been accused of the murders of a British Minister and his wife and others. It's only a matter of time before he reveals himself and is brought to court, how will that effect your position…and I will certainly be asked if you are involved?"

"A very sad situation, he is without doubt a wild flower Herr Brandt. He had his own agenda and one which he definitely did not confide in me. Of course I don't want to lose my son. But we are just as concerned in justice as you are, and if he is brought to face his crimes, then he will receive what anyone else would. I must say that I am personally heart broken. Without his efforts we would not have had either the Autoplug or Ever Young, but his actions were not justified. What more can I say. I am his father and it will grieve me greatly to lose him but…" His eyes welled up and he didn't finish.

"The other question that will undoubtedly be asked is that of Pontillo, its investments and in particular, its origins. Now I have a good idea where its finances originated, but you and I would need to give an explanation that satisfies not only Germany but the rest of the world."

It was the sixty-four thousand dollar question, and Heinrich knew that he would struggle to find a plausible answer that would be acceptable. However he had to respond without appearing to apologise, which would be fatal.

"This question Herr Brandt has been a great worry to me and my father before me. We know that substantial monies were accumulated by the Nazi Party during the war. They had confiscated vast tracts of land and sold them off. From whom and to who we have no record of. My grandfather who was a young man at the time and took control after the war had been left to oversee this vast amount of money. There were no records found of where it came from. It was a pot intended to be shared out after the war by all those that put in their ill-gotten gains, most of whom were killed or executed. And so it sat... of course we could have given it back, but we also had our backs against the wall.

"I suppose he should have revealed it, but he didn't. Nevertheless he promised to put it to good use, and so Magnum was formed. At first, the company really struggled, but when the earliest computers emerged he invested substantial sums on research, and we gradually built a business employing many thousands throughout the world. Without that money the computer technology would have taken considerably longer to develop."

"The Autoplug is and has been a mission of love. We've invested vast sums to bring it to market but look how much good it's done. And by bringing it into the national pot now it is possible combined to Ever Young to exonerate the actions of the Germany of yesterday and prove that the tragedy of war was not in vain for the phenomena that tomorrow's Germany can be."

Brandt considered his response. "You know Herr Heinrich that all hell will be let loose if we reveal this Nazi Germany's gold mine as monies to be reinvested, especially in your own business. I think that if you really want to exonerate the holding of this money for the last eighty or so years, we have to turn it into a gesture. We can then work out a group plan. Let's say that the Pontillo pot was eighty billion dollars. Offer it to the government and we will distribute it to a say UNESCO. That would certainly change the balance of the world's poverty. And then we could look at a takeover and consider all the other plans you've outlined."

Heinrich had shown his hand and could not now reverse his admission, He sat almost dazed by his own stupidity. There was an ugly silence.

Gilda who had not said one word during this meeting suddenly came alive. "Maybe I could ask, Herr Chancellor, what you would be able to do for us if we were to follow your advice. What we have suggested to you is that we would give you half of a substantial business that makes good profits, but would you be able to finance this massive operation. Your opinion of a greater Germany would also be most welcome. I'm sure that you will appreciate that it would be difficult to take eighty billion dollars out of our cash flow, unless the government's guarantee was available to replace it. You should appreciate that the computer business, Autoplug and Ever Young are closely aligned and should be used not just to service a world population, but to improve the society they currently exist in. We are holding the mindset of the world Herr chancellor. Ever Young will influence every aspect of society, prisoners will be mentally realigned, the armed forces more committed, workers wanting to improve society, all controlled by us. You must appreciate the power we are offering you."

There was something about this woman that Brandt disliked intensely, she was grey, grey in all aspects of her being and formidable, and a hardness in her voice, and he was not happy being Pidgeon holed.

"Are you asking that we should return to a Third Reich mentality," Brandt replied. "What you are suggesting Frau Troupe is a society that is politically controlled and no doubt would eliminate those that refuse. My job is to guide our people, not change them as if they were robots. Of course it would be wonderful to be leaders of such a dynamic operation, but if it is seen that Germany is benefitting from this money we would be accused of pursuing a Nazi dream not the aesthetic one that Herr Montello has so eloquently described."

Gilda replied, speaking slowly and with gravitas "I think you will agree, Herr Chancellor, that Magnum have proven themselves as a very positive world force. What we have now is not a deviation from our efforts but an inevitable progression that would not only benefit Germany but would place the country in the forefront of a better world and stop it sliding into chaos."

"I think," said Grieff "that it would be wise to meet again say tomorrow by which time we will have had the chance to look at all the implications relating to your proposal, shall we say 11.00 am here."

Heinrich thanked both men for their time and consideration, and they parted.

***

They returned to their suite and poured two large whiskeys.

"What do you think?" asked Grieff.

"What do I think!" repeated Brandt. "I think that there is something about this Alicia Troupe that makes me shudder. I also think that the public are fickle, look what happened to the British government. They will lose the election on moral grounds, and this could go the same way If we're not careful."

"The interesting thing about this whole exercise Hans is that it is so tempting to take control. If we were to walk away from their conceptual idea, it would end up in the USA. That in itself is not so terrible, but it is so dangerous to jump into the unknown."

"It's raking up old wounds," replied Hans. "But the proposition that would distribute a substantial amount of the Pontillo money and allocate it to charities around the world I believe would actually work, and then we announce that we are taking an interest in the business and the government's purse will enjoy fifty percent of the largest computer business in the world."

"We would insist that Heinrich's son is found and jailed which would prove our desire to rectify matters."

"I think we can do better than that Hans. We should not allow Heinrich to continue to run it, Pontillo would be sold and all assets returned into the pot, but if we were to acquire Spoken Arrow it would all come under the one umbrella."

"That wouldn't work as we would have nobody to run it. What we should do is buy as many shares as we can of Spoken Arrow at whatever price the market is standing, under a government investment company through our unit trusts which will hold their sway and stop Pontillo in their tracks. Then deal with Heinrich from strength."

"Even better, my friend. Let's confiscate their entire operation," replied Brandt, "and we could put that into effect immediately and agree with Spoken Arrow to run it. It's that simple."

"It's not so impossible," smiled Hans. "To be honest, Herman, as much as I like this science fiction scheme, I really despise these guys still living with Hitler's Mein Kampf. The sooner we take control of the company, the better, and if we knew the business we would kick the family into oblivion."

"I agree," Brandt replied. "We'll need some plan of continuity, The business can't just be closed down, there are countless thousands earning their living from it. We'd be thrown out of government in a blink. We would have to make a deal with Spoken Arrow."

Although both parties were guests of the Ritz, Brandt and Grieff took their evening meal in their suite and excluded themselves from view, watching American TV with a bottle of whisky at hand.

***

They emerged the following morning to enjoy the gentle background music of a string quartet whilst at an early breakfast.

Noticing and acknowledging the other party from their respective tables, they departed only to meet again at the meeting room to prepare for the next session. They took their places, exchanged courtesies found their respective places and methodically spread their respective papers out.

"Chancellor Brandt," Montello began, "We would welcome your further thoughts on yesterday's discussion."

"Yes," said Brandt, "Herr Grieff and I spoke late into the night and looked at all the implications that could benefit or damage the country and our own reputation, bearing in mind what happened to the British government…and we have arrived at a conclusion which might satisfy my own parliament and do good at the same time." Heinrich shuffled in his seat already anticipating the worst.

"Shall we begin Herr Montello by calculating the total worth of Pontillo by valuing each of its subsidiaries as accurately as possible for the purpose of these discussions."

"That would be relatively easy," he replied. He dipped down into his briefcase and pulled out the respective file, "Let's say within the region of eighty billion dollars."

"Eighty billion," repeated Brandt. "Let's say we took that money and publicly announced that we are giving this substantial sum to recognised and honest charities around the world. We will say that Magnum has decided to offer up the money which it accumulated through the Third Reich from 1938 to 1945, to give it away to benefit the world. Since Magnum was also financed by Pontillo, it should be given back to the government too, who would negotiate with a third party to manage it and its profits would allow further global employment and extend benefits to needy causes." Heinrich tried to interrupt but Grieff raised his hand.

"We would have to insist that your son should be punished according to European Law, probably in the UK. Herr Heinrich we would strongly recommend that you retire from the business; you would, in effect, be dismissed. Magnum would pass to the government until such arrangements could be made to place it into more practical hands." Montello could not resist smiling and covered his face.

"Regarding Ever Young, it is obviously necessary for the government to have a say in its policy. It is, after all, as a medical exercise, I think that you will agree that it would have serious political implications if in the wrong hands. All this is, of course, hypothetical until we have discussed the proposal in greater detail with my government, and of course the UK."

Heinrich was stunned. Jumping out of his seat, he stuttered "How can you simply take away a lifetime's work, this is ridiculous. We have given the world a most amazing service for over seventy years, and we came here with only good will in our hearts. How can you as head of a government criminalise yourself in such a way."

"Please sit, Herr Heinrich. Let us discuss this matter as gentlemen. Look at it this way, you have built up and lived very comfortably off this business, which you knew had been totally financed by dirty money, for three generation. You compounded the problem by hiding Pontillo's vast reserves. This money was stolen, and masses were killed for its taking. That places you in a most awkward position. The fact that it was your grandfather or great grandfather makes no difference. The sins of your fathers will be punished to the fourth generation. Is that not so. My suggestion to you is to save face, bow out gracefully and let your efforts continue to be developed in a—how shall I say—an evangelical manner, Amen."

Heinrich sat back in his chair speechless. "I came here with the purpose of benefitting our great country, not to destroy what we have built. Can you not realise how much inspiration and creativity has been invested in this business to reach the heights of where we are today. You are cutting the tree down in full bloom."

"Your tree, Herr Heinrich, to use your metaphor, has rotten apples and needs to be pruned rather than cut down, we have every intention to continue its development, but with clean hands, you and your son have even recently shown how you determine what you want by assassination and mind bending. It clearly runs in your 'Aryan blood'," he emphasised with no small degree of sarcasm. "But not ours, thank God."

Montello had not said a word during the discussion and could now see that this was the moment to play his card. "I cannot tell you how pleased I am to hear your summary of events, Herr Chancellor, and your conclusions. For the last thirty years, I had been locked into a business that had one single objective, and that is to rekindle the dreams of the Third Reich. My task was to expand the business keeping our heads down and using the best scientists and technology, and I have tried to stay away from the 'Heinrich dogma' but your decision to homogenise the organisation is to me very satisfying."

"What are you saying?" shouted Heinrich forgetting anyone else in the room, "You're a filthy traitor, after all I've done for you!" He stood up and walked towards where Montello was sitting, but was held back by Gilda.

"Uncle, please calm down!" Her intervention was noted by Grieff but he answered Heinrich regardless.

"I am asking you out of courtesy to accept my plan for Magnum and Pontillo, Herr Heinrich, it gives you an out with some degree of honour. Either way If you choose not to accept my plan it would make little difference, since I will put an injunction on you and your company, announce it to the world and forcibly nationalise these operations. You will end up with nothing and possibly jail with your son. It's your choice and you must make it now."

"We need to talk in private," said Montello. "Can you excuse us for a few minutes?"

"I don't want to talk with you," glared Heinrich.

"Rubbish, give us a few minutes gentlemen please."

The chancellor and his finance minister agreed that they would return in fifteen minutes.

As they rose from their chairs Heinrich pleaded, "Is there not a compromise that we can discuss?"

Brandt smiled. "My dear sir, with the greatest respect, you are not in a position to ask for anything at this moment in time. Do you realise that we could, in a blink of an eye, confiscate your entire wealth including your houses. You would be a pauper. My suggestion to you is to consider our offer as a gift from heaven, your entire business has been built on stolen money. May I suggest that you carefully consider my suggestions, and my advice to you is to bite my hand off."

Immediately Brandt and Grieff left the room, Grieff phoned his assistant in Berlin. "Francene, I want you to immediately speak with the woman who deals with government investments – I've forgotten her name – and tell her to buy, on behalf of the government, all the Spoken Arrow shares she can lay her hands on, even at a record price, and let me know ASAP what they've bought." He put his hand over the speaker "If we don't get the shares, Herman, it's my bet that Heinrich will make a lunge to buy them, that if he can't save his flagship he'll co-opt another, jumping ship to save himself."

Brandt had improvised, he had suddenly seen the light after listening to that woman. "I don't know what it is but I really dislike her – maybe we should check her out – and I have my doubts about Montello."

"Montello will sup with whomever offers him a meal, but I think we'll need him. Did you notice that she called him 'Uncle' Herman. I was just as astonished as they were by your own presentation. Well done, my friend."

The two men returned exactly fifteen minutes later. Gilda acted as spokesperson. "We'll accept our position as you have described it, but we would ask you to phrase your announcements in such a way to show that we are only too willing to give our company back to the State, it would at least allow us a morsel of credibility."

"We will try, but I can't promise that – we don't have control of the press. It's one of the best and worst parts of our democracy."

Chapter 60
Martin and Jango

Martin had now sent a detailed memo to all his staff worldwide that they had acquired the Autoplug. "Every centre will be involved and training given under the auspices of Professor Ellsworth based at Cambridge university by a series of live video lectures. They can be seen via our internal training programs."

Europe and the Far East confirmed immediately. However, for some unknown reason his South American offices complained that there was a distinct lack of cooperation from Magnum in South America. Deliveries of the Software and hardware were being delayed. Alarm bells were ringing. The German Head office of Magnum informed them that there was no reason why there should be such resistance, but in any case South America was controlled by Magnum's Brazil HQ. The difficulty was that Spoken Arrow had no hold on them.

The International media and the courts had now exposed Steffen Heinrich and condemned him of murder in absentia but the problem of dealing with Brazil via the UK, could take years. On that basis, Magnum could continue as competitors unless the Brazilian governments removed their protection.

As soon as Jango heard of the Brazilian problem he called Martin, "Hey, what's going on? We've committed to this Autoplug and passed over a billion dollars and it looks like they're going to compete. Come on over, I'll pull in our legals…and find out where Miriam is."

"She's in New York. I'll set up the chat to include her in this meeting," replied Martin.

Both internal and external lawyers were already there when Martin arrived, they brought with them further confirmation that Magnum were blocking the takeover in Brazil and most of the other South American countries.

Victor Shaw of Coral and Dean opened the meeting. "Here's the rub," he began. "We negotiated this takeover with the British government, not Magnum. We have no exclusivity with Magnum but we do with the UK. I know that they have already put in place an exclusion document, if we are to sue anyone it's the UK government. They have to control the seller, in this case Magnum."

"However, the Political party that negotiated the deal are no longer in power," said Jango.

"We signed our deal with the government, there were no provisos as to who would be in power at any time. If they can't control Magnum, then they are in breach of their agreement."

"So where does that leave us?"

"The first thing is to see if this is a glitch, we need to hear from our divisions exactly what their problem is, what is stopping them receiving information, and taking over the Autoplug administration. Secondly, Miriam may I suggest that you speak with the Lawyers that represented the UK and clarify their responsibility. We don't want to make it too formal in case it's an error, but you should inform them that we certainly will if they can't control Magnum or whoever is behind them."

"By the way, I've noticed during the last two weeks that our shares have begun to jump up, they've gained over fifteen percent. Is there any particular reason?"

"We saw that too, it's probably the boys in Wall Street playing games. Maybe you could check out who is buying."

Miriam was listening with interest. "I'll follow up the UK and let you know the outcome."

"Let's meet tomorrow and compare information," said Jango.

She immediately phoned Jack. New York is six hours behind London and Jack was eating comfort food at her brother's restaurant. He was just sucking up the last of his spaghetti.

"Hi Miriam, I can't seem to escape the Bravotti family, I'm just in the middle of eating my spaghetti. How's New York, I hear you've been with Helga."

Ignoring his question "Listen Jack, I need your opinion on a most important matter. It would seem that Magnum is trying to compete with us in South America. Now our agreement was with the UK government, so I need to take an opinion from them as to what securities they wrote in when they took the business from Heinrich. We don't want to make an international incident out of it if we can avoid it. If it's their plan to ignore the agreement, we have a big problem."

Jack listened intently and mused on the alternatives offered.

"Are you still there, Jack?" she asked.

"Yes, I'm thinking of who best to contact. We could speak with Mrs Steinberg. But I believe that she was a little too close to my old friend Alex Winter."

"She would be close to whoever is in power, her firm would still be representing the new government," she replied.

439

"I'll give her a call. When are you returning?" he asked in a rather less formal way than he would have intended.

"It all depends on how this problem unravels, All the countries in South America are refusing to pass on vital information and are continuing business as usual, it could be a simple blip, although I doubt it knowing the Heinrichs."

"Leave it with me, I'll phone Mrs Steinberg first thing tomorrow morning, shall I wait for a sensible time to call you tomorrow."

"No," she almost shouted, "as soon as you have any more news give me a call." She thanked him profusely.

The last remains of Jack's spaghetti was now cold, but he quietly smiled to himself.

Jack always took pleasure in speaking with Mrs Steinberg, and taking her at her word, although it was now past 8.00 pm he immediately called her from the restaurant.

"How nice to hear from you Jack. It's too late to get any information now but why don't you join me tomorrow for lunch? I'll hopefully be able to find out what's happening by then. Do you know the Wig and Pen, it's opposite the Law courts in Fleet Street, say 12.30. Don't be late or we'll miss the booking. My poison is gin and tonic."

Mrs Steinberg was already there when Jack arrived. Fleet St had been the melting pot for all the national papers for the last hundred years. The Wig and Pen had been the drinking well of the journalist for fifty years and as it was directly opposite the law courts, barristers and lawyers intermingled and swapped their gossip.

"I think that I should update you," he replied. "You'll know that Steffen Heinrich has vanished but was accused in absentia of murder, but we have a problem. Spoken Arrow now find that they are being locked out from every country in South America, and Magnum are refusing to pass on software information, the administration and manufacturing knowledge in South America of the Autoplugs. Of course their claim can't be against Magnum as they weren't involved in the negotiations, and if Magnum to comply Spoken Arrow would have to sue the British government. Worse is to come."

"I'm all ears," she said.

"Magnum are buying up shares in Spoken Arrow and have already acquired about twenty percent." She looked down at her oysters. "I'm always fascinated by this little animal," she smiled.

Jack looked at her as if she might be losing her refined mind.

"They believe themselves to be so well protected, but with the right instruments they're eaten in one gulp, especially with a gin."

"Are we the shell or the instrument?"

"Definitely the instrument Jack."

"The first formality is to write to Herr Schreiber informing him that his client Magnum, appears to have broken the contract. We will therefore consider Herr Heinrich Senior to be included with his son's misdemeanours and issue an Interpol summons for his arrest unless he complies with the agreement. No doubt he will reply in his mordacious manner, disassociating his client from any misdemeanour. Next, we will ask government to issue an Interpol notice against Steffen Heinrich and his father as president of the company, claiming that he was the motivation behind his son. We will of course inform Schreiber of our intentions.

"If he thinks that he can ignore the European laws, we will put a notice out that Magnum are trading on monies stolen by the Third Reich. I'll put this in a separate note to him. We'll cc the memo to the Prime Minister and give Schreiber three days to reply."

"Do you like the oysters?" she asked.

"I'm developing a taste for them," he grinned.

She leaned over the table and looked into his eyes. "It's a shame you're not twenty years older."

"I agree," he replied.

Two hours later with three whiskeys in his system, he sent an email to Miriam detailing his conversation with Mrs Steinberg "She left me with the feeling that we will win the day, but as yet her secret remains with her."

Miriam replied immediately thanking him and informed him that she would pass his note onto Martin, "And, by the way Helga has agreed to join the firm, she'll be working in Berlin for a while."

***

There was no doubt in Schreiber's mind that his clients were continuing to operate in South America. They would make it as difficult as possible to thwart any progress of their largest competitor and decided that he would reply immediately and pass both their and his correspondence onto his client.

As anticipated, with his Teutonic efficiency and sarcasm he replied, stating that he had passed her memo onto his client who informed him that they knew

441

nothing that would impede the transaction between the UK government and themselves, but was aware of local franchisees dissatisfaction for any change. "The Autoplug is franchised in most South American countries and we can only request that your clients transfer their allegiance to another company. If they should decide not to continue with the Autoplug we cannot dissuade them, otherwise it may be that your client should choose to change their distributor base."

"Furthermore I would refer to your aggressive tone which will only inhibit one's desire to cooperate."

***

Returning from New York, Albert Heinrich rehearsed a thousand ways how to tell those closest to him the outcome of his meeting. More important he would have to inform his lawyers that he was conceding the business to the German government.

The return journey was painful. Montello tried to explain to Heinrich that his comments to Brandt would show him that he could be a trusted intermediate that would help both sides in this divorce.

Within an hour of his arrival, Heinrich called a meeting in his office.

Steffen was waiting eagerly to hear the results of their discussions.

Montello had taken a copy of the note from Schreiber and passed it on to Steffen "This man Schreiber is good," said Steffen.

"All he can do is hold the waters back for so long," commented Montello "Spoken Arrow's legal Eagles will soon shoot holes through his defence, anyway I think that your father has to explain the result of our meeting in New York. You won't like it."

They sat waiting for Albert Heinrich to arrive.

It was unlike him to be late. He at last arrived in a dishevelled state, he had been drinking. It had been raining and he was soaked. There were no welcomes, and it was clear that he was a beaten man. "We have been destroyed by our own beloved Germany," he began, "and to be honest I have no solution. All our hopes and aspiration have fallen foul to the very government that could have made history, a world working in perfect harmony, flushed down the toilet." "What are you talking about," asked Steffen.

Gilda proceeded to explain to Steffen in detail of their pending sentence.

"All this, for nothing," he exclaimed. "You've allowed yourself to be tricked, did they need to know about Pontillo? What were you thinking? You tell us to be so careful, then you stick your nose up their arses. You've destroyed us."

"It was Montello's idea originally, not mine and you Gilda had to mention the Ever Young project, I think that was what scared them. We need to transfer as much of the Pontillo monies into another Pot, how quickly can we do it?"

"There's no lose money, we've spent it all on Spoken Arrow's shares," Montello replied. "We must take legal advice before they strip us of the clothes on our back – has Schreiber been told? – and maybe we can get protection from the Brazilian government."

"God, what a mess!" Heinrich shouted.

"In any event you Steffen must take your family, to another part of the world, change your family's name and do it now. There is an Interpol call out for your arrest. Form a new company in, say Argentina, and we will see what we can salvage. They'll have difficulty in suing a totally separate business based in Argentina."

"In my opinion, we should try to conclude the deal with Grieff as soon as possible before he formulates his own version," commented Montello. "I shall speak with Grieff again and see what compromises we can make. There may be a glimmer of light to see by."

"All he's leaving us with is our homes!" cried Heinrich.

For most of his life, Alfred Montello had been under the wing of a virtual dictator who controlled the destiny of a vast financial empire covering the globe. If he didn't do something now, he would also be out on his ear without any benefit. His possible future would only come from Grieff not Heinrich, whom he considered a lost soul. It was now every man for himself.

Gilda had been listening quietly. "I am a scientist; the heart of the business came from people like me. It seems to me that nobody is considering the benefits of marketing it as a financial exercise. Uncle you must transfer a sum now into a new account, say a hundred million dollars. Do it before they see the figures. We must have some reserves."

They all turned to Montello.

Chapter 61

Miriam sent Helga to visit the New York office. "I think you will find it very different to the offices in Germany," she casually remarked. It was a massive understatement. It seemed to her that they were running around in circles and although she was sure that they were speaking English, she barely understood a word. "How does it compare with your experience in Berlin."

Helga laughed. "I refuse to answer that on the grounds that it may incriminate me," She replied.

"I'm very impressed with you Helga," said Miriam. "Do you feel that you would like to join the company, I realise that you are still working for your master's degree, but if it's interesting I could find you a position in Germany. Give it some thought."

Helga's eyes glazed, Miriam hoped that she was thinking of her more emotional experience in Berlin.

"If you want to finish your studies we would leave the position open for you," she quickly added.

"May I think about it? I'll speak with my father, he's my mentor. Thank you, Miriam." She smiled.

***

Martin received a report from his brokers. He could see substantial share movement being invested in the company but had no idea who these investors were. Looking at the existing shareholders a few were being tempted to sell as they increased in value, but the majority were standing their ground regardless of their increased value.

It then hit him like a hammer. He logged onto the internet to check out the identity of the investors' status of each company. It was not difficult to note that between ten companies if linked they would have just under twenty percent of the company. And now another new play was being made picking up a further five percent.

But this time it was under a German government broker.

"My God," he shouted, "They're making a takeover." He immediately contacted Jango.

It was almost a religion. Every morning with a cup of coffee in front of him Jango would go straight to the financial pages to see how his investments were doing, his mood for the day was dictated by the ups and down, He had been doing this for the last twenty years; it was not that he needed the money but it satisfied his gambling instinct. However, he took a special pleasure seeing his company shares float upwards. *We've made seven hundred and fifty grand today!* he'd shout into the kitchen. The following day as it floated down the same routine, but showing a loss always put a smile on his wife's face.

Two months ago the shares dropped to two hundred and ninety-four dollars, but now for some unknown reason they were standing at four hundred and ten. And the demand for buying showed a waiting list.

"Jango, there is a mystery buyer or buyers aiming to take our company over and I know who it is."

"There are ten companies, all with an affiliation to Pontillo who have been steadily buying our stock, and it looks to me that they already have about twenty percent of the shares. And now there appears to be another German government broker wading in.

"We'll send an S.O.S. message to all our stockholders telling them that under no circumstance should they sell their shares, as we believe there is a rogue buyer who has been vacuuming up our shares, and if they acquire enough they will no doubt take control and break it up."

***

URGENT NOTICE TO SHAREHOLDERS

Dear Shareholders,

There is no company more dynamic than us, we have expanded exponentially for the last twenty-five years and will continue to do so. Keep faith with us and we will prove your trust.

Stocks and shares are invariably bought and sold on the turn, and to try to persuade a buyer not to sell when they see a good profit is almost impossible. But you will see that the next two years will show you a much greater return than any profit you might make on the short term.

Spoken Arrow is one of the highest earners on the Stock Market... DON'T SELL YOUR SHARES.

The following morning another two percent was purchased. This time not from the ten but incognito. Theoretically at twenty-four percent someone could walk through the door and take over. In reality they would probably have to reach thirty percent to have any influence. In any event, far beyond either Jango's or Martin's holdings.

"We're getting ourselves into a pickle here, Martin," said Jango, "These guys are like snakes, and with respect you've got to do something about it quickly. If it's Magnum, we should speak with the UK. But where did they find the money? They must have massive hidden resources."

"I was given to understand that they would cooperate with us. We would even have bought their Autoplug computers until we could produce them ourselves. But now I understand that they are not giving us any support. If we hadn't been working with the UK government I would think that we've been scammed."

Martin was without explanation. "I wouldn't be surprised if we have," he replied.

***

The memo landed on the Prime Minister's desk, from Mrs Steinberg of Patton Brown. Prime Minister Russell's PA had already checked her credentials.

A thick file was brought in.

"Why don't we speak with Mrs Steinberg directly?" suggested his PA. "I'll arrange a meeting."

"Get her on the phone and I'll speak with her."

"I was expecting your call, Prime Minister. It's a complicated and serious matter, and as you obviously know it unseated your predecessor. When shall we meet? I'd be happy to explain the current situation."

Russell had been brought up via council estates, grants to university and with only his wit and acumen to help him. It was therefore difficult for him to establish his authority over the obvious blue stocking disposition of Mrs Steinberg who was the absolute master, or mistress of court room persuasion. And here in the Prime Minister's office she felt far more relaxed than he. For many years, he had been sitting opposite what he considered to be the privileged classes, battling what he believed to be the rights of the underprivileged masses. Now faced with autocracy that would stymie both left and right governments he began to understand why so much promised by his opposite numbers were compromised or never done.

She sat in his office with the familiarity of an old friend and slowly wove her web with her charm, describing in detail all the events that she believed would be useful to him.

"Our position would be one of great interest to those of the press but could easily escalate once again whereby any government such as your predecessors could be caught in its web."

Winter listened with growing interest. Reading press reports and watching his old adversaries gradually sink by their own misdemeanours he was aware that he must not simply brush the affair aside or delegate it. "Well, it's clear that we have a responsibility to Spoken Arrow, but how do you anticipate the control of these German buggers, We have a murderer at large, a billion dollar charge to honour and a very nasty global company with a disastrous reputation that refuses to respect its obligations. In any event, I would not like to stumble into a multi-billion dollar lawsuit so early in my reign," he smiled.

"As you've read we have threatened them with everything we can think of, even if they are one of the largest companies in the world and have vast reserves from the Good Old Days," she emphasised, "and we're waiting to see what they have to say."

"Can you imagine," he replied "what the German government would have to say if they knew that this vast amount of blood money was still in the bank waiting to be reinvigorated by a fascist organisation with more reserves than most countries? All hell would break loose. I don't think it would be a bad idea to contact them, let them know that we're sitting on a bombshell. Chancellor Brandt is a committed socialist and I've met him a number of times. It would be most interesting to hear his thoughts. It's astonishing that this hasn't come to light before now. This is a tinderbox."

"I shall speak with Brandt. Maybe you would keep me in the picture. This business concerns me and as we have already discovered has some worrying of implications. It needs to be handled with care. Thanks for coming in Mrs Steinberg, I'm sure we'll meet again." They parted in the knowledge that beside accents they were each other's equals.

***

447

As soon as Mrs Steinberg left. Winter called in his PA.

"I want you to get me Chancellor Brandt on the video chat. If he's not available leave a message for him to contact me on my private line, this evening if possible."

A few minutes later she popped her head around the door. "He can speak with you in one hour."

Russell poured himself a whisky, spread himself on the settee and picked up the file his PA left for him. By the time Brandt called, he had gained a grasp on the problems at hand.

They exchanged pleasantries, Brandt congratulated him on his election win as a fellow socialist. "You obviously know the problems that we have had regarding Magnum, Herman... well, we seem to have inherited a serious situation and I would like to hear your thoughts."

"What is it you want to know?" he replied hesitantly.

"We are on the brink of a major court case with this company, it's common knowledge that we confiscated the Autoplug from Magnum and passed it over to Spoken Arrow, They paid our government a billion dollars for our loss of profits and costs incurred in developing it and now we find that Magnum are barring them from a number of countries especially South America, and we believe they will continue to compete with Spoken Arrow."

"The reason I'm calling is that some of the muck thrown up may land at your front door, and will certainly involve Germany's past history. But you'll recall that our Conservative friends lost the election because of this business. I don't want the same to happen to us...or you."

"There's no knowing which way this business can turn. I know that you have met the Heinrichs, and you must know where their finances emanate from."

"As it happens," replied Brandt, "we have had a very interesting meeting with Heinrich and his colleagues, but tell me what's on your mind and hopefully I'll be able to help you. We're being sucked into a black hole. I need to hear what you know and if I end up with a court case all will be revealed. As a German company you must know something."

Brandt had to laugh, it was a pleasure to speak with Russell even if he wasn't as straight as he claimed. He liked him and his Yorkshire accent gave a feeling of a man of the earth.

"I'm going to talk to you in absolute confidence, Stuart. Heinrich and his right-hand man approached us with the view of semi-nationalising the company to include their finance arm which alone is worth approximately over eighty billion dollars. Their object was to purchase a controlling share of Spoken Arrow. They managed to buy approximately twenty percent but were scrabbling for more. We were particularly interested to know exactly where this money came from. Of course we had a good idea but we needed proof. So Hans Grieff, my Finance Minister, and I arranged a meeting. We agreed to meet in New York to discuss some form of cooperation."

"Heinrich believed that we'd be of the same mind as theirs. A fantasy that we could help them rebuild the Third Reich. They hoped that we would match the vast amount of money they had to form a monopoly, but with the information that we now had we informed them that we intended to confiscate both Magnum and Pontillo and donate the sum total to an international charity. Needless to say we were not the flavour of the month."

"We told them that it was blood money and we would take control of the entire business and finance is future expansion to including the shares of Spoken Arrow. Did you know that that their total net assets are approximately a hundred and fifty billion dollars? Our big problem however is that if we confiscated the business without a deep understanding of it, I would have no doubt that within a short while the entire operation could die, that would be two hundred thousand or more workers out of work, enough for us to become very unpopular. So the idea is to pass Magnum over to Spoken Arrow and let them run the business, they would purchase it over a period of years and the money would be given to a charitable cause. Pontillo would be sold off and all monies distributed. Total, say, approximately a hundred and forty billion. That's real compensation."

"And what would happen to Heinrich?"

"We left him with his houses, but he's out. We would eventually find his son and bring him to justice He has a right hand man, Alfredo Montello who has been with him for over thirty years, and If Spoken Arrow can use him it's up to them."

"The devious bastards have already surreptitiously acquired over twenty percent of Spoken Arrow and were looking to take another five or ten percent with the aim of marching on Spoken Arrow. That would give them a world monopoly of the computer market also control of the Autoplug and Ever Young. In other words, they would use all of Pontillo's cash to take control. The only thing we must now do is put threats into effect before they do anything that requires further action."

"From what I've read so far Herman, Ever Young doesn't make money but shows the government savings. I think there's more to this than meets the eye."

"There's no doubt about it, Ever Young believed that they would complete their dream by the use of mental control over millions. Nevertheless they still have control of their business and we will have to work fast before they beat us to it."

"When did all this happen? Nobody else seems to know. You obviously had some fun with this little debacle."

"We only returned yesterday, so we're just formulating our action plan to present to both Spoken Arrow and all those involved…they're not going anywhere and if they do I wish them luck. So whatever problems you currently have will hopefully dissipate once we move into action."

Stuart took a moment to digest the news. "So in actual fact the German government will own twenty-five percent of Spoken Arrow."

"I suppose we will," replied Herman. "If you have the ear of Spoken Arrow by all means be the first to tell them. Once we take control of Magnum, we will release the shares on the market."

"With the greatest of respect my friend, I think you have overlooked a rather important point," said Stuart.

"What's that?"

"Well, you have made all these plans to circumvent the Heinrichs and pass their business over to their competitors, but from what you have told me Spoken Arrow haven't been asked if they want it, which is a rather important point, don't you think."

There was an uncomfortable silence before he replied, "you're quite right."

He laughed. "Thank you and I'll keep you posted."

Brandt took a deep breath before asking his secretary to find the President of Spoken Arrow Jango Hampton. It was only 6.00 am in California but Brandt couldn't wait. At last, his secretary found his home number.

"Mr Hampden, we have not spoken before but we have negotiated the most amazing deal on your behalf." The conversation describing the deal in detail would go down in history. It was fortunate that it was not on Video chat as Jango's habit in the morning was to swim in the nude. "We will need your lawyers to discuss the details and we'll speak in greater detail very soon I hope…and that is of course presuming you want it. Sorry to wake you." Jango immediately phoned Martin who contacted Miriam in London.

Chapter 62
Brazil

For the first time in his life, Albert Heinrich was a ship without a rudder. He had no idea how to offset the imminent disaster of losing everything he had built.

He called Gilda and Steffen into his office.

"Can it be possible that we are so easily shown the door, kicked out from our own business? I'm at a loss to know how to defend ourselves, and none of our friends have said a word or even made the slightest attempt to help us."

Steffen poured himself a drink. "There are a few of our group that would sympathise with us but in truth I think that they would want to keep themselves in the shadows for fear that the same could happen to them. Where did all this come from?" he asked.

"That English Journalist Jack Branson," answered Steffen, "he told me that he was writing a series of articles on Ever Young, I should have gotten rid of him right at the beginning."

"It's not too late, not that it would make any difference now but it would give me some pleasure," said Gilda. "What have we got to lose, I'm supposed to be dead and you, Steffen, are on the wanted list for murder."

"I think we should put some names together," said Steffen. "Branson, Ellsworth – I never liked him – and Branson's assistant or girlfriend… Helga something She took photos of the art work we acquired. That was a serious mistake. Let's do it. We'll get their movements through an agency, and choose our moment. We can use our Russian friends to organise it."

***

UK

It was 6.00 pm when Mrs Steinberg received a call from number ten asking if she would meet the Prime Minister there at 7.00 pm. She'd planned to be at the first night of La Bohème at the Opera House in Covent Garden and had two rather expensive tickets for a box. However there was no way that she could refuse. Dressed for the evening she now sat opposite the PM open shirted, unjacketed, and braces showing.

Thank you for coming over so quickly, only I'm travelling to Scotland tomorrow. "I have some news for you Mrs Steinberg that will I hope make your job a little easier."

As if it was of no consequence she told him it was a pleasure to be called anytime.

Without further ado he informed her of the terms that the German government had laid down with Heinrich. "According to what he told me," said the PM in a broad Yorkshire accent, "in fact it wasn't so much an agreement as a demand. All the assets of Magnum and their associate companies will be transferred to the German government, and my understanding is that Spoken Arrow should run it."

She put her drink on the desk. "That's astonishing," she replied. "Of course it depends on whether Spoken Arrow wish to and what benefits they would get for doing so, but what is happening with Ever Young?"

"I suppose we would revert to the original plans. If Heinrich doesn't cooperate we'll stick him and his father in jail, in any event Ever Young is still under the ownership of our government. My understanding is that Spoken Arrow didn't want it."

"We can't just put a billionaire in jail, we'd have to prepare a case against him, the fact that he's built a business for over eighty years on stolen money won't stand in a court of law in the UK without considerable preparation that is unless we can show that he gave instruction to his son relating to the murders."

"Mrs Steinberg you're a woman of the world, we'll find something." He grinned.

***

It was too late to phone Sir Henry or Spoken Arrow's lawyer. But not, she thought, too late to pass the information onto Jack, as he had the ear of Spoken Arrow.

"I thought that we had passed the point of no return with this affair, are you saying that Magnum is now going to the German government. What are they going to do with it?"

"I understand that Brandt and Grieff met them in New York, and that's where they confirmed that Pontillo was to be confiscated. They're giving Pontillo's to charity, the Magnum will be under the wing of whoever can handle it and its purchase price will also go to charity too over an agreed time. They're rightly concerned that whatever they do with the money will be under microscopic investigation, and they will certainly take some credit for its recovery and their magnanimous behaviour. It will probably be worth around a hundred and fifty billion dollars."

"I would have loved to have been a fly on the wall at that meeting," joked Jack.

"I'm dressed to the nines Jack and had planned to go to the opera tonight which I have now missed, so if you would care to join me at the Savoy I would treat you to a snack. Suit and tie would do. Say 9.30 pm. Just friends."

"Fine, at the Savoy I would definitely be your guest on my wages."

He was still at his office, and immediately dialled Miriam. She was now having her lunch in LA.

"All is settled," he said. And explained to her exactly what he had been told.

It took her a few moments to absorb the apparent turnaround of events. "So where does this leave us? I seem to be having difficulty in keeping the thread here," she chuckled.

Jack reiterated the current situation. "The general idea discussed is that Spoken Arrow would purchase the Magnum business over years and the money they bought it for would go to world charities. There was no suggestion that Spoken Arrow would need to invest anything of any consequence up front except working capital."

"So now you have the Autoplug, with a four billion dollar turnover, Magnum eighty billion and Spoken Arrow one hundred billion, plus of course Ever Young which is still in the hands of the British government and is in limbo. And there you are, Miriam, sitting at the top of the pyramid."

"Why is it," she replied "that every time I speak with you, you dump another bombshell on me, I'm going to have to go to my bosses with this astonishing piece of information just when we were about to bang in a lawsuit to Magnum. When does all this come into effect Jack?"

"As far as I understand immediately, or as soon as the paperwork is ready."

"I'm planning to return to London on Tuesday. I guess this will be another discussion to resolve."

"Maybe we should get together when you return. How about Thursday. You'll have settled back in the UK by that time. Shall we meet at your brother's restaurant, say 7.00 pm. I think that the only reason you want to eat there 'cos you know I'll get a discount."

"Darn it, you've got me!" he quipped.

To Jango in California the latest turn of events was riddled with problems to the point of being almost farcical. He sat back "This whole thing is well beyond me," he sighed "Who would run the company? Did they really need the headache? Of course they did. Working capital. Maybe the German government could channel some of the Magnum reserves over to them as a loan."

"We'll get our lawyers over there next week, and certainly the preliminary discussions can be organised by Miriam before the heavies' takeover. She was planning to leave for London tomorrow anyway," said Martin.

There was a decided adrenaline rush and an exciting challenge that they had not experienced for years. Miriam was despatched back to the UK post-haste.

Chapter 63
London

It was true that both Miriam and Jack would want to compare their current state of play, but Miriam found herself looking forward to seeing him again and the intermittent days were mentally crossed off for their meeting.

Miriam had already arrived and had an apron on when Jack entered. It was a quiet night and she took pleasure helping in the kitchen. Welcoming him as if he was her guest she showed him to a discreet corner, took off her apron and poured two glasses of wine.

"Are you enjoying what you do?" he asked.

"What, waiting at your table?" she laughed. "Very much, yes, very much, both jobs. My life couldn't be better. It's true that I came at the most dynamic time in the history of the company, but I love it. What about you?"

"I could say the same, but the last few weeks I've hardly been doing my job, it's been a difficult time. I've had more than my share of a learning curve, and it would be good to get back to normal."

Rolling the glass in her hands "My job is pretty departmentalised. It's the team of people that make it happen, and as long as one recognises their function as part of the machine we're like a concertina, someone is puffing it in and out and someone pressing the buttons, no music can be heard unless we have both the buttons and the wind together."

"A little corny but I like the analogy," he smiled.

"I hope you're not too upset that Helga is going to Germany, she'll only be an hour flying time away, but she was very excited to be in the team."

"I heard that she had a great time," he replied wistfully. "I must admit that I am a little sad but in truth…well, in truth, what can I say. Everything ends up for the best, I heard that she found a nice little German lad, we had some wonderful moments, but it became a little too political for her, maybe these things happen for the best."

"Not always…but often." She smiled sweetly.

"Maybe this is one of those 'best moments'," he ventured to add.

"Maybe," she blushed.

As she finished her sentence a motorbike skidded to a halt outside the restaurant and threw what looked like a parcel at the window, first breaking the glass and shortly exploding in a powerful blast that set the entire building alight. Of the ten customers sitting inside, including Miriam and Jack, six were thrown to the floor and the other four died instantly.

***

Steffen Heinrich had made it his business to record the movements of his considered mortal enemies. It would be relatively easy to monitor Ellsworth. His journey to the university and return home were all meticulously recorded. Gilda had worked with him over the years and knew his habits. His pipe, his choice of tobacco and where he bought it that smelled of horse manure, his clothes. His place of lectures and easily discovered times. Her husband's demise had been far more complicated. To all extent and purposes, for Ellsworth it would be simply a matter of how and when within the parameters of his routines.

With regard to Helga, Steffen had met her and was quite impressed at their first meeting. Tall and elegant, she had mentioned that she was Swiss, clearly well educated, and probably twenty-four years old but his agency had checked with the Tandem Group and found no record of her working there, she clearly was not who she claimed. She had been a major factor in his downfall even unknowingly, there was no doubt now in his mind that she was a plant and possibly his mistress. In any event, she found what she was looking for – how dare she photograph his home? – and these pictures were the prime reason for his demise. She must have known what she was looking for… she had to be on his list. To hell with her.

Heinrich used his usual Russian agency who would check out Jack's routines. They learned he worked from the offices of Tandem. They also found his home address. He frequented a small Italian restaurant in Notting Hill Gate. They would gather notes and images on his movements, and be it in his home, office or social haunts if there was evidence of them together, there would be satisfaction.

***

The British press was rather more vague than he would have liked in reporting the explosion at a London restaurant. However, his own investigators noted that Branson and a lady were there and ambulances had taken away a number of the restaurant's customers. Surely no one in the restaurant would have survived intact.

There was a question as to who was the woman with him, however as there was no trace of Helga to be found, Heinrich was prepared to accept that it was her in the restaurant with Branson. He read, "The owner of the premises and his kitchen staff were shielded from the main explosion as they were in the kitchen but have been retained in hospital with cuts and burns. A number of the customers in the restaurant have still not been named. Police are investigating their histories and any leads to a targeted plot."

Heinrich guessed that it would not take too long for them to associate his name with Branson, but they could accuse him as much as they liked as long as he stayed incognito.

He now planned his escape to Uruguay where he had friends in Montevideo. His father had now received a formal letter from the Foreign Minister demanding that Steffen be made available for questioning. Simultaneously another handwritten letter from the President of Brazil informed Herr Albert Heinrich that he had been instructed by the German Foreign minister to the effect that Magnum and Pontillo Investments were to be nationalised by the German government. A detailed explanation was given, which would leave the President with no option but to cooperate with them.

"In view of the substantial support that the Heinrich family had given the country over many years, he requested that a meeting would be appropriate to discuss this most delicate matter at the earliest opportunity."

"There's no way that I will give myself up," contested Steffen. Under the cloak of complete secrecy he informed his wife that she was to pack only the most essential belongings and with their children they would take a private plane from Sau Paulo, she would not know the ultimate destination until they were in the air. "I will travel separately. When you arrive you will be met by friends. Do not worry. All will be well."

His father's friendship with Davila Majuca went back many years and although their political views differed somewhat, the President of Brazil had acquired his position and subsequent wealth with considerable help from his friend. It was therefore with no small degree of regret that he was placed in the embarrassing position of watching him being defrocked. To deny the European world of their discovered lost monies and announcing publicly its origins would be politically cataclysmic.

"What can I do to soften the blow, Albert?" he asked.

"I have a request that will also make you famous, Davila. Nobody knows better than you my credentials and ability. Everything I have done was to improve what I believed would improve society."

"Of course," nodded the President.

"I've no option but to give up Magnum, although it breaks my heart, but I am not going to give back the Autoplug and Ever Young to them, they don't want it anyway. I intend to launch it here in Brazil, and also keep the Autoplug. You may not realise what this Ever Young can achieve. We will make this country so powerful no one will stand against it commercially, creatively and intellectually."

"So what is the plan my friend? Who could deny themselves of such benefits?" he grinned rather too light-heartedly.

"I'm serious, Davila. We already have the Autoplug in surgeries throughout Brazil. And the infrastructure set up for Ever Young in hospitals across Brazil, all we need to do is promote the project. We had intended to heavily market the scheme first in the UK and then Europe followed by the Americas. That was not to say we would not activate the scheme anywhere else. But we can now seriously promote Brazil with the health plan promoting the ninety-five-year option here, and it will save the Brazilian economy billions in health care."

"What's the downside?" he replied.

"There is no downside from the government or Ever Young's point of view. There will probably be some comment from the UK and Spoken Arrow but they don't matter. You may already know that Spoken Arrow are now running the Autoplug in Europe, but they don't have Ever Young. What's more we can still record all input from the Autoplug through our San Paolo Auto board which means that you can exclude Spoken Arrow from Brazil and we'll maintain it."

"How sure are you, Albert? I really don't want to get into litigation with a country like the UK plus one of the largest companies in the world. I don't need that aggravation."

"Believe me I would not let you down, Davila, and of course we can have our own arrangement. I will make you richer than you have ever imagined."

"So what do you want me to do?"

"Nothing, we will launch Ever Young on the TV, radio, newspapers, social media, everywhere, and I believe the response will be amazing. Especially with the seal of approval from yourself. With a fifteen percent uptake among twenty-two to thirty-year-olds, your health bills will drop through the floor. Just you wait and see. And you, my friend, will receive twenty-five percent of its profits."

Chapter 64

Montello had been busy separating the Pontillo businesses. He had very little time to set aside Heinrich's request of a billion dollars of Pontillo's assets into another country and decided to simply take one complete company and transfer its ownership. It was quite easy to name himself as a director and nominate fifty percent of the shares to himself. The remainder he put into Albert's name with a codicil that on his demise his shares would pass to Montello.

On reporting to Heinrich, he informed him that the company San Remo Investments, holding approximately one point two three billion dollars in property and stock assets, had now been registered in Argentina. "If you want to see all the relevant documents I can pass them onto you."

However on the spur of the moment he transferred all the shares under his own name.

Heinrich rarely looked at the details of documents and left them to Montello to deal with. "You know what to do," he said. He was so blasé regarding the detail, Montello wondered why he had not thought of taking a cut years ago. He had been ridiculously honest and received nothing but insults in return.

"What do you want me to do with the Ever Young business?" he asked.

"Transfer its name and patents. Put it with the new company, it can be financed by us."

Heinrich immediately called in Gilda and told her of his discussions with President Majica. "We can run with the Autoplug and Ever Young here in Brazil immediately Gilda, we'll also change the name since we haven't launched it yet. SEMPRE JOVEM. It means Ever Young in Portuguese. We will keep the Autoplug name as it's too complicated to change. I'm putting you in charge of its launch.

"What we need now are promotional staff to launch Ever Young into Brazil and secure our position with the Autoplug, we still have the admin and sales but we'll have to move fast before Spoken Arrow claim them as their own. If you find a hiccup, speak to me.

"Remember you are Alice Trompe. May I suggest, Alice, that you re-dye your hair, change your image and smarten up; you don't have to look like a frump - your last attempt was a dismal failure. You'll be looked on as the boss. If you are photographed I don't want them coming down on you again."

"How come you can be so generous and so insulting at the same time?" she replied. "But thank you. What are we doing for finance?"

"Don't worry, Alfredo is dealing with that."

***

Brandt instructed his administration to send a formal notice to The Bank of Switzerland and the Banco de Brazilia informing them that "The government of Germany is confiscating all Magnum's assets and those of Pontillo, a holding conglomerate, and are herewith freezing their accounts. Any continuation of their businesses will be under the strict control of German government officials or those appointed by them. The Swiss government should be informed and asked to cooperate."

Detailed explanations that supported the action were sent to the press, and the news immediately hit the headlines across the world.

***

Press announcement:

MAGNUM IS SIEZED BY THE GERMAN GOVERNMENT

PONTILLO, a hidden company that controls the worldwide Magnum Computer group and a wide dossier of companies around the world and is valued at approximately a hundred and twenty billion dollars has been seconded by the government. It has now been revealed that the source of its wealth emanated from the Third Reich and was blood money stolen between 1938 to 1945. Chancellor Brandt stated that this money will be distributed to world charities. Our country can only apologise to the world for this blot in our history and hope that the discovery of this money and assets will in some small way compensate for the pain that was endured by so many during this disastrous period in Germany's history.

Magnum which is one of the largest computer companies in the world had known the source of these monies which were accumulated during the second world war and used these illegal fortunes to finance their business for the last 80 years.

The Heinrich family who own the company have been dismissed. And the government has taken control of the international operation. Negotiations are currently taking place to pass the Magnum administration onto an alternative company and it is anticipated that the company's profits will also service various international charities under the strict control of the government.

Chancellor Brandt has taken upon himself a massive challenge. Whilst the organisation had to be seen to be cleansed, its continuity is essential. With factories and administration scattered across the world it was not easy, but it was essential to cut off its head.

There will be no redundancies during the interim period. The government is in negotiations with Spoken Arrow at this time.

***

Chancellor Brandt asked his PA to arrange a meeting at the earliest opportunity, and was put through once again to Mr Jango Hampton.

"It seems," said Jango, "that we are purported to own Magnum even before we knew it. Events are overtaking the theories, chancellor. Anyway what can I do to help?"

"I suppose it's more a case of what I can do for you Mr Hampden, you are obviously aware that we need someone to run this giant, and thought, what could be better than to have another giant to do it. Can we meet up?"

"Sure."

"If I can get to New York, it's halfway to California – can you meet me there? Say in forty-eight hours? I think that it could be your lucky day," said Brandt.

"Since you were here only a few days ago, we'll have to give you an honorary US Passport."

"My European one gives me enough of a headache already my friend."

"We'll arrange a rendezvous through our respective PAs. I shall be bringing my vice president and possibly another, probably our lawyer."

As he put the phone down Jango received a call from Martin to inform him that Miriam had been in a restaurant in London that was bombed. "She's in a coma," Martin stammered, clearly holding back tears. "I think she was with Jack Branson. It all stinks of Heinrich… this man is seriously dangerous."

"My God," Jango reacted with a similar sense of shock. "The quicker they get this man the better."

Chapter 65

The scale of the transfer meant a vast amount of paperwork by both parties, but as time was of the essence listing of all assets were to be passed on to the German exchequer, checked, sorted and eventually agreed with Spoken Arrow.

The deal was relatively simple. Spoken Arrow would be given Magnum without payment, they would control the entire business. It would be given a value and over say ten years they would purchase it. All monies would be paid to a deposit account in the government's name and they would distribute it to their nominated international charities. However twenty percent of the profits for a period of the first five years would also be returned to the German government towards agreed causes.

Every factory, office, and sales outlet was to send a listing of their in-house assets. Cars, computers, buildings… nothing was left to guesswork and serious penalties would apply if information was proven to be legally questionable.

Spoken Arrow having swallowed up their largest competitor would be competing with themselves. It was therefore agreed that they would continue to work independently.

Jango urgently needed to find honest management that would carry the business on a day-to-day basis. He was given the name of Alfredo Montello by Brandt.

"He will know every little knot of Magnum and was for many years and maybe still is the right hand man to Heinrich. He's based in Brazil, but be careful my friend, he is very clever and, in my opinion, just as devious." commented Brandt.

Jango considered that he would at least speak with him. No one would know the operation better than him but he knew not to trust someone who had all his bosses sins in his back pocket. On an impulse, he picked up his phone and asked his secretary to put him through to Senor Montello of Magnum in Brazil.

***

"Señor Montello, you obviously know who I am and why I'm phoning you. You must have your hands full at this moment in time."

"I have, Mr Hampton, in fact I was expecting your call."

"How so?" asked Jango.

"Because that is what I would do if I inherited a large business riddled with politics."

"Well, maybe you would like to answer the question that I have not yet asked," suggested Jango.

"Shall I say maybe, and play safe? You would like to know if I would be interested in running Magnum, Mr Hampton, but as you know I have been with Herr Heinrich for many years and it would be very discourteous to jump ship at this difficult time."

"May I suggest Señor Montello that you would not be jumping ship, I would rather describe the analogy as a man overboard."

Montello laughed. "I am in New York next week. Maybe we can meet there if that is convenient."

"Very good, I realise that you have a number of many headed snakes to control at this time, but I've been given to understand that by the time we meet many of your problems will hopefully be resolved, am I correct?"

"Only time will tell, sir. I look forward to meeting you Mr Hampton."

"I usually stay at the InterContinental on fifth Ave. Shall we say next Wednesday at 8.30 am? I shall book a breakfast for us in a meeting room."

Even after such a short telephone conversation both men had sized one another up. Jango understood that Montello had no need to be in New York other than to meet him, but both men knew the signs and Jango took the initiative as Montello had expected.

Alfredo had three days to organise his trip. He also had to ensure that Heinrich would not know. In Heinrich's mind, it would naturally be assumed that if the ship was sinking they would all go down together, but Alfredo Montello had lost his allegiance to his master, what his wife called a Teutonic dictator. Nevertheless, he would do nothing before consulting with his wife.

"You're going to meet the largest computer boss in the world, you have to dress the part."

"But we're the second largest," he bantered.

"Second is not the first. Let's treat ourselves to some New York style clothes."

Like a school boy he bleated that he didn't need to look like a Spanish waiter but, as always, she had her way.

Two new pure wool navy suits, three ties, even though he rarely, if ever, wore a tie and his suits were usually linen. Two pairs of shoes, a raincoat and a trilby.

"Ridiculous!" he shouted. He had bantered with presidents, billionaires and autocrats around the world but he was used to losing battles with his wife.

"Stand your ground," she said and kissed him gently on his cheek.

Both men arrived the evening before the meeting, but they made no attempt to speak to each other sooner than arranged.

Jango had little regard for formalities and especially clothes. He was identified by his charisma but certainly not the way he dressed. In fact it was rare indeed that he wore anything other than jeans, and the meeting with Montello was no exception.

Alfredo Montello arrived a few moments earlier than his counterpart, and was musing over the breakfast layout when Jango arrived. Thinking that the waiter was still arranging the breakfast, Jango began to place his order, "I could do with a quick coffee," and was smiling as Montello looked up.

"With pleasure. I did tell my wife, who dresses me – would you believe? – that this makes me look like a waiter. I might apply for the job while I'm dressed the part," he replied, "I'm Alfredo Montello at your service, señor." He smiled back, to the embarrassment of Jango.

"I do apologise," Jango blushed, "let's say the first round goes to you, I'm Jango Hampton. Let me pour."

It was a good beginning but with regard to important matters Alfredo broke the ice.

"Let me explain my position, Mr Hampton. I have worked for the Heinrichs for thirty years – man and boy, you could say. It would not be an understatement to claim that next to Albert Heinrich I am the force to be reckoned with. Sounds a little hierarchical but that is it. However, unless one truly is another Heinrich, or the like, there is a cavernous drop in stature and respect between the boss and second in command. Anyway, having said that, our organisation is meticulously run and, as you know, is a worthy competitor to yourselves and the rest of the world."

"The trouble is not in the internal workings of the organisation, it's the raison d'etre of the company. Unless I'm mistaken I do not believe that your Spoken Arrow wishes to change the world. It produces innovative products that will enhance civilisation but follows its needs rather than dictating them. However, Magnum has far darker ambitions which I dislike intensely. I follow the rule book because I work for the man who wrote it – but I don't agree with it."

"And what is that?" asked Jango.

"You will know of the history of the company and its financial sources fed by Pontillo and, unlike most companies, finance has never been a problem. That is until now. You should also know that the Autoplug and Ever Young were the products that the Heinrichs dreamt about. With their financial resources and Neuro351 mind-bending facilities, they could dominate the future of the world. After Steffen Heinrich's antics, we have been pushed against the wall in fact, through it…and our meeting with Herr Brandt in Germany virtually sealed our, or should I say their fate. We tried to persuade the German Chancellor to come on board to recreate the Third Reich's dream. It was ridiculous, and they exercised their options and simply confiscated the lot. I was present when Heinrich made his presentation and was dumbstruck by his audacity. I realised that I was the mouthpiece for his sins."

"For my part, I have made a great deal of money within the company, and I understand every aspect of it. I don't need to work, or even work with yourselves, but I see myself as responsible for the jobs of many thousands of workers around the world, and for that reason alone I would make myself available if so required. I should also say that I am strictly controlled by a very domineering wife who won't allow me to veer off the path, although I've been tempted to on many occasions, especially since as I have already mentioned there is little love lost between the Heinrichs and myself."

Their coffees had gone cold and this time Montello poured them a second cup.

Jango listened to Montello's confession with ever increasing interest. He said nothing for a full thirty seconds and drank his cold coffee before replying. "You know Alfredo there is something that I can't comprehend, we come from such different worlds, it is like a fish trying to understand the life of a gorilla. Your ability to stay with an organisation that you obviously despise yet function in such a successful manner within it is beyond my understanding, and can only be commended. And I ask myself, was there any time in your thirty years that you related to their philosophy without making it part of you?"

"No is the answer. Maybe we should compare the situation to a Roman general who has worked his way up from slavery, he has a job to do and morality has no place in his life, until he snaps. I have snapped. You must understand that my position was to make and sell computers, the wealth of the company made it easier to do that but was already there. Mine was not to reason why!"

"And how would you imagine you might reinvent yourself within my organisation, for I demand a similar commitment of regimentality, but without shadows of any kind. Equality and an understanding of the human needs, I am not interested in reinventing the human psyche. But am desperately interested in saving what is good in the world, and God knows there's plenty to save."

"Jango, do you mind me calling you Jango?"

"Not at all."

"Superficially you need me at this time more than I need you. But under the microscope we see a very different picture. Magnum is riddled with objectives which I have had no party in creating but have maintained. I have learned from them systemology and an acute business sense. Which side-steps their ultimate objectives, and now we are seeing their ultimate ambitions materialising, and our paths have crossed. I need to cleanse myself and the company of its objectives and bring it into the light. At Nuremberg I would probably have been hanged, not for creating anything but for being complicit in its actions and funding its associations."

"I think that you are being too harsh on yourself, Alfredo. You know what I suggest. Two things, first, that you should come to LA to meet my partner, see our setup, and secondly that I meet your wife. Then, if you like what you see, we would see your set up in Brazil."

"I'm for that," Alfredo replied. "When?"

"Why not now?" Jango replied.

"And I can get out of these stupid clothes."

Chapter 66

Miriam lay in a coma for two weeks at the Royal Free Hospital in Hampstead. Her hair and clothes were burnt but she miraculously escaped any flesh wounds. She had suffered a serious blow to the head from flying furniture. Her family took turns to stay with her in the hope that she would be aware of who they were. They read to her, talked of family matters imagining that she quietly absorbed their prattle. The doctor informed them that it was difficult to assess the degree of damage to her head until she regained consciousness. Martin constantly sent emails to the hospital enquiring after her progress.

Jack had not lost any long term consciousness but the explosion tore his left leg off at the knee. He too was in the same hospital, but in great pain and on morphine. The cuts on his face would mend but leave scars, but the loss of his leg greatly depressed him. He had already concluded that the bomb was intended for him and placed the blame squarely on Heinrich.

A bitterness wracked his emotions and a determination to destroy the man that did this. The memory of Freda returned and he wondered how her husband must be feeling too.

As soon as he was able he was wheeled onto Miriam's wing and met her family. Looking at this beautiful young woman, he had brought this on her, it was his fault that she lay here. He found himself sobbing uncontrollably, quietly telling himself that he loved her.

Brody Emmitt visited regularly, they were relatively short visits, depending on how long he could be without a cigarette, but full of the latest news, both social and political. The explosion made headlines, and as usual the press soon related the restaurant bombing to the string of events associated to it, which soon became known as The Magnum Effect. Reporters lined up to interview Jack but were flitted away. He sent a message stating that "When the time is right the story will come from my pen."

The police had no hints or information relating to the bomb. Forensics found little to align the type of bomb to its source. Inspector Polton was once again interviewed but as much as he enjoyed the limelight, he too had no constructive leads other than the computer listing that included Jack Branson's name, but as there was no trace of Mintov whose computer it belonged, he was unable to help.

A twenty-four-hour police guard was stationed outside Jack's door, they also served to protect him from the press. Only his parents, Brody Emmitt, and of course Mrs Hermione Steinberg were admitted.

He tried to keep his spirits up but found it very difficult. The pain was still intense, and morphine seemed the only panacea and friend. But slowly and with the encouragement of his select visitors who forced him to view the outside world again he began to re-emerge.

"I have to tell you Jack," growled Brody. "We have taken on somebody to do the sports section, we told him that he is filling some big shoes, but when he heard that you only needed one shoe now he felt a little more comfortable."

"You mean I'm fired!"

"Not exactly," he smiled. "We thought you might like to come on the main board, help us run this bloody company, I suppose it's a bit of a promotion. We won't talk about salary now, but I don't think you'd be unhappy. After all, there's not quite as much of you to support as there was."

"You're a real cruel bugger, Brody. I'm not sure that I'm ready for your humour," and for the first time he grinned.

***

After four weeks, Miriam regained consciousness. She awoke to see her parents, smiled, said a sweet hello and fell asleep. She had no memory of the explosion, except that she had been with Jack. A further two weeks brought her back to some form of normality.

She had been bombarded with neurological tests, x-rays and psychological interviews all of which confirmed that she had returned to her normal disposition. While she was regaining her strength she had taken to visiting Jack on a daily basis. He had been transferred to his own specialised prosthetics ward in the Physiotherapy wing of the hospital.

"I received a letter from Helga last week, she had heard of our injuries and wanted to visit us, but I told her that it wouldn't be a pretty sight and her fondest wishes would suffice until I'm able to visit her in Germany. She tells me that she's really enjoying the job, thanks to you. It was meant to be. I felt maybe she should be grateful to you for another reason."

"And what's that?" asked Miriam.

"That it could have been her."

Chapter 67

It had been nearly six months since Freda had been Killed. Rolf Gesh had worshiped her. He still wore a black band around his arm in her memory. Those close to him saw the band as unnecessary, for his grief could be seen in his face and manner. His speciality freight business gave him a small degree of distraction from his mourning, but his staff mostly held the reins and hoped that he would eventually accept his future without her.

His company specialised in packing and transporting valuable items around the world, and in fact Magnum had used his services on a number of occasions rotating artworks between various offices, occasionally even setting up exhibitions. He had a list of the company's locations and was familiar enough with it that when his instructions specified offices referenced by internal abbreviations or even a string of numbers, he wouldn't have to double-check.

It was therefore a little unusual for the company to receive an instruction from Magnum specifically to remove certain pieces of art from a new, private address and deliver them to a construction company. The pieces would anyway first be brought to his warehouse for packing, and sent onwards to Montevideo Construction in Uruguay. He might have been unaware of this particular instruction – his staff would print out all relevant purchase orders and despatch notes as they came in and input them into the company database unseen by him – but as it happens his secretary included it in a batch of invoices for his approval, and it immediately drew his attention. He had no previous knowledge of Montevideo Construction, and it seemed rather unusual for valuables from a private address to be brought in then despatched to a construction company without a further forwarding address. The driver was to be identified as "Jay5", and Rolf had no idea what this meant. He checked the booklet showing all the Magnum offices but this forwarding address was new to him. The consignment was to be air freighted and booked in for the fifteenth of June, which was seven days away.

Looking at the collection address again he realised that the art emanated from the home of Steffen Heinrich. Every sinew in his body seemed to come alive. Of course he had been following the events surrounding Heinrich, but in his state of mourning he had left justice to find its own way to punish this man. There was a warrant out for his arrest; it was said that he was in Brazil but he had disappeared. But now, literally in his lap, was the answer, the way for him to take his revenge.

"This swine was taking his stolen booty to his new home and only I know where it is." It was an amazing stroke of fate.

But why a construction company? He checked them out – it was simply a docking station. The goods would require immediate collection and couldn't stay where they were. Someone of authority would need to be there. He decided to find out.

He instructed his manager to email Magnum and ask Montevideo Construction who Jay5 was, 'for insurance purposes', before they released the consignment. This was a normal request bearing in mind that the final address should be displayed on the delivery note He received a reply the following morning informing him that they would be collected by an exhibition organiser giving a code number of 3798B who had authority to sign on behalf of Magnum. The driver would identify himself as Jay5. Export documents confirmed their place of origin and the country of destination was declared as Uruguay.

This was not the information Gesh wanted, and even if he had discovered the address, would it be Heinrich's residence? He wanted revenge, but what sort of revenge? This man had killed his beautiful Freda, his whole reason to live – could he actually take revenge by killing him or his family? How? He needed to do something that would balance the scales, and more. Even at the risk of his own life – what did that matter? – but Uruguay was thousands of miles away.

Rolf Gesh was normally a tidy thinker and was suited to tight and meticulous planning. However he recognised that he was out of his comfort zone and, overriding his emotions, he sat in front of his computer and contemplated his next move

Assuming that these works of art were going to Heinrich's home, only Jay5 would know it. He could find no record of Jay5 in Germany, nor in Uruguay, but whoever they were would arrive at the warehouse very soon after the consignment and make contact with Montevideo Construction whilst there.

He concluded that whoever was driving the vehicle would not want to give the address, and therefore would need to be followed. Then, even if all the previous facts fitted together and it was confirmed who was at the address that it was the correct party… what then? He had come full circle and could not imagine himself following a van in a foreign country and "taking his revenge." "Shooting, stabbing. Blowing the place up, God knows what to do, but I certainly don't," he smiled cynically to himself.

He recalled how all this came about and looked in Freda's address book to find the number of Jack Branson.

***

It was 10.00 pm when Jack received the call from Rolf Gesh. He was watching TV, still on morphine. He was slow in making the connection between Rolf and Freda, and had to be reminded that this was Freda's husband.

"Mr Branson, please excuse me phoning you at this hour, but something of great importance has occurred that could be of interest to you and certainly to me"

"Anything I can do to help you, Mr Gesh," he replied. "I bear some of the responsibility for your wife's death and I'm ashamed that I haven't thought to contact you sooner."

"No, no, no, we have one common enemy Mr Branson and this is why I'm phoning you."

He explained in detail the situation and how fortuitous it was that Magnum chose to use my company to take these works of art. "I have thought how I can find a way to destroy this man, but I just can't seem to formulate a plan, and wouldn't know what to do if I had one anyway."

"I should tell you, Mr Gesh, that I also have a desire to destroy Heinrich. He tried to kill me too, and very nearly succeeded. But it seems to me that we need to discover if these works of art are the ones stolen. I think that there are ways that we can pin point these goods. First of all I would like you to photograph and send me the pictures of the pieces. If they're not the ones we are looking for we could be on the wrong track. Email the photos to confirm that they are the real thing, and we'll speak tomorrow."

As promised the photos confirmed that they were the same six pieces that Jack saw with Helga. He immediately phoned Miriam to share the problem.

"You know what Jack… is Gesh packing them for despatch? If he is, don't send them. Pack six bits of rubbish and let the freighter take them. It'll be interesting to hear the response from whoever receives them."

"Have you read this story already?" Jack laughed. "I'll contact Gesh straight away."

Gesh was delighted and did exactly as instructed. He immediately went to a junk shop in Berlin and purchased the worst paintings he could find and a cast iron statue of Mephistopheles that he thought particularly appropriate for the occasion. He instructed his staff to take meticulous care in packing them. Wrapped and documented, the three pallets had 'fragile' labels stuck on each side, and Gesh took great pleasure in waving it off. Upon returning to his office, he gave instructions to pack the originals identically but for the labels on the pallets. He transferred them to a small warehouse, that would never normally be visited, and for the first time in many months sat at his desk and laughed. Phoning Jack once again he confirmed having done exactly what was suggested.

"That's good work," came the reply, "I need you to send me your contact's address, Rolf."

"Why do you want it?" asked Rolf.

"Because we will need to follow them from the airport that they will arrive," Jack replied.

"When this rubbish is discovered, there will definitely be hell to play. He'll realise his staff's error in giving this consignment to you and I bet that you will be his next target. So at least for the next two weeks you will need a bodyguard. A private detective who knows how to handle a gun. You know that this man is dangerous, you've lost your wife and I have lost a leg because of Heinrich. You are taking a big risk here. my friend, so be very careful."

"Thank you," he replied. "I will."

Chapter 68
Montevideo

Exactly according to paperwork three pallets were duly loaded onto the scheduled airline for Montevideo and seen off with particular attention by Rolf Gesh. The plane was going to Montevideo and would land in 14 hours. Miriam carefully monitored their collection by a black van which drove five miles to a small derelict storage building, unloaded them and drove off. Miriam's plan had failed.

"We'll keep a monitor on the building for the next two days and see who collects them, and failing that we would have to wait for Heinrich's response," she said. "He won't be a happy man when he sees what he has received and you can be sure that you'll have a visit. I'm going to organise some protection OK Ralph."

The reality of the situation suddenly hit him. "No don't do that... I will sort something out," he pleaded. But Jack insisted.

He immediately phoned Miriam who organised a private detective agency in Berlin.

It was not easy to find an agency that could take on the task of defending him against a murderer, and one that could blend in with his staff. But at last he interviewed two ex-policewomen who were registered as a detective agency.

Gesh informed them that the same man that killed his wife was determined to assassinate him, they would need to blend into his staff for probably two or three weeks. His manager was taken into his confidence and told to welcome the extra help, "They're here to protect me Joel, I can't tell you yet but be prepared for anything that happens." Both men were surprised to find two rather muscular ladies, both taller than six feet, join the team. It was obvious that they were there for a reason.

***

Albert Heinrich was already immersed in plans to launch Ever Young in Brazil. He needed the expertise of Gilda. Using his own mansion he had organised a small army to insulate the Brazilian operation from the rest of the world, to include computer sales, Autoplug rentals, and of course Ever Young.

Sitting in his office he called through to Montello but his secretary informed him that he was away for the week.

"He hasn't mentioned that to me," he commented. "Was this planned? Where is he?"

"I believe he's involved with the Pontillo business," she replied as instructed.

"Well, ask him to contact me as soon as he returns."

He needed him by his side now more than ever. He couldn't depend on Steffen.

A number of the staff had already received notice that they would soon be under the employment of Spoken Arrow. "All instructions relating to future policy will be given from the German government until the new administration is organised. There will be no redundancies unless it is seen that there are devious or secret plans that interfere with current negotiations."

Heinrich immediately sent a notice to all the staff working in Brazil that "Magnum Brazil would exclude foreign invaders from attempting to steal the business from the company, and that Magnum Brazil would be protected from foreign competition. Magnum Brazil will continue to flourish and expand and their jobs and future are secure."

Current turnover in Brazil alone represented two hundred and fifty million dollars, and there was every possibility that other South American countries would soon join, according to their government's desire to cross swords with the USA and Great Britain. The total Brazilian organisation would require at least five thousand staff to be retained. And under Montello were over a hundred senior executives delegating instructions to smaller cogs.

Gilda was given a personal assistant who could speak fluent German and English. Her responsibility would be the Ever Young project. Over two hundred hospitals were now listed. And a further notice went to all the medical centres informing them that the EVER YOUNG IS NOW TO BE LAUNCHED, SO PLEASE PREPARE TO MEET THE DEMAND.

TV adverts, magazines and newspaper campaigns which had already been designed to launch some months later were reincarnated and all Heinrich needed was confirmation that there were monies available.

Chapter 69

Alfredo Montello was taken through the world of Spoken Arrow without inhibitions, even knowing that he still was in effect a core member of their competition at least until Spoken Arrow were holding the reigns. The relaxed style of administration, research think tanks, and general ambiance of an operation, the size of Spoken Arrow impressed him greatly. It had grace, their systems were brought together in alignment with one another, not clunked together under pressure as in the way he had inherited, but nevertheless succeeded. He appreciated how hard it was by pushing his staff with a cudgel in one hand and following a rule book in the other.

After two days, he returned to his offices in San Paulo. He was immediately aware of the state of tension that existed, and marching into his department he called his secretary in to update him. She immediately placed the notice on his desk from the German government to all the staff instructing them of the change of ownership, and beside it the message from President Heinrich instructing them to ignore it and introducing Magnum Brazil which would disregard any takeover by foreign competition. "They should be considered as our mortal enemies. We own South America," stated the document in large print.

"Seignior Heinrich has been asking for you, sir. He appeared rather upset. I did inform him that you were negotiating with Pontillo, as you instructed, but he was not very happy," she smiled nervously.

"I'll give him a call immediately. Don't worry, Phillipa, everything will be good, your job is secure. Tell the girls that they will be OK too." He had discovered in himself a sense of unity with her and those under his control, it had been buried for so many years and it gave him a feeling of oneness with his team.

Heinrich's barking voice jarred on his ears. "Alfredo, I'm putting together the New MAGNUM BRAZIL. They're not going to beat us. We will stop them from entering Brazil and then we'll hit them with the rest of South America. By the time we're finished, they won't be able to sell even a hand mobile in our neck of the woods, you'll see. I need to know Alfredo if you've managed to secure the billion dollars from one of the Pontillo divisions we discussed. I know it's holding fixed assets but if it is placed with the bank as collateral we can do what we have to do to keep what we have in Brazil."

"You've already signed a switch of assets before I left, Albert. I'll speak with the bank first thing tomorrow to confirm our facilities." replied Alfredo.

"Good, let's see if we can launch Ever Young this month, Gilda is in charge of Ever Young, she will certainly guide us with the technical aspects but her Spanish and Portuguese is shocking.

"We need to separate our administration from the rest of world sales and production. If our Brazilian production of the Autoplugs is geared for the world market, we will either cut it or offer the machines to Spoken Arrow with conditions that they will not enter South America."

Alfredo listened to Heinrich for another hour, but exhaustion and bitterness suddenly overwhelmed him and he excused himself and went home.

***

His adventure into the world of Spoken Arrow had made a great impression on him but he now found himself riding two horses.

There was no reason why he should have any further allegiance to Magnum under Heinrich. But to totally desert him after thirty years was an excruciating dilemma. He knew the man so well and in some ways had become a slave to his beckoning calls.

In any event, his call to the bank was in his own interest since he had written Heinrich out of the Pontillo division and replaced his name as sole director. It was the one dishonest act in his career, but he had no conscience since he considered the money was in no-man's land.

His wife knew him too well and noticed that he was troubled.

"Tell me what's bothering you, Alfredo. You know I'll find out eventually, so spit it out."

He attempted to explain to his wife how he felt, to relieve a guilt that was now hanging over him.

"I have just stolen a billion dollars," he spluttered.

She sat him down with a glass of wine. "Listen to your heart, Alfredo. If this Spoken Arrow is what you say and will give you the opportunity to protect all those thousands who are working at Magnum, you can ask yourself if they would be protected if you walked away and left it to them. If the answer is no and they would be in danger of losing their jobs, you should consider yourself their defender."

"There is no doubt that Heinrich has had it — you and I know it. He can try to save his glorious Ever Young, but to what end? To brainwash millions and turn them into Brazilian Nazis? It's a crazy idea from a crazy man whose son is a murderer and is just as nuts as he is. The money you are taking doesn't belong to Magnum, but on the other hand you are intending to take what is, after all is said and done, blood money. That can only bring us bad luck."

"Are you saying that I should refuse to take this money. Nobody other than you and I even would know that it was taken."

"Just because nobody knows doesn't make it right. Alfredo, you are an honest man and what you have achieved for the Heinrich family has all been worthwhile, for all that wealth that you helped them make is going to charity. They may have lived off it but that was all, it's going to where it belongs, to make a better world. You have done this. My husband who I'm so proud of. By all means, take the money and tell your new friend at Spoken Arrow that you are giving it away too. That would really be a great thing to do… in my opinion anyway."

He stood up and looked down on her. "You know that you're not always right, I looked a complete idiot in New York wearing those clothes." He took her in his arms and hugged her. "What would I do without you, you terrible woman? You've kept me on the straight and narrow all these years and I suppose it's too late to get off it now." He went to the phone and dialled directly to Jango.

"Jango, if you want me to run Magnum I'll do it, for the sake of my wife. I would like you to come here and I will take you on the same route that you gave me, and which I am rather proud of too."

"You've got it!" cheered Jango. "I'll clear my diary and be with you next week," he said excitedly.

"…and I'll wear a suit."

Chapter 70

Steffen Heinrich had now settled his family in Uruguay in the town of Montevideo. He had adopted a new name of Mandella and versed his family to state that they had returned from a diplomatic post in Austria and he had now temporarily retired from the service.

There were so many loose ends of various negotiations that he had left in the balance. He had good reason to be concerned, he must face the reality that his life with Magnum was over. He had failed miserably. Was he in fact the biblical fourth generation? What would he pass onto his children except disgrace? Notwithstanding all these disasters, life had to go on. Who knows what might happen. After all, he was hidden away and under the umbrella of his friend whom he had financially helped to retain his position as President of Uruguay, at least for the moment until the dust settled.

His father had set up a new account number on his computer in order that they could communicate without the fear of hackers. And in spite of his natural resistance to his father's wishes he had taken every precaution to remove the works of art in his Berlin House. Nothing was left to chance, even his forwarding address was hidden. His new address was also registered as a Box number. And so it was when he received an envelope with the keys to the small and inconspicuous warehouse that was situated two miles from his new home.

The goods had now been there for three days. Long enough for any possible spy to have followed or discover its whereabouts. He rented a small truck and instructed his servant to drive there and wait before entering into an adjoining warehouse. He would collect six large bags of sand. From there, he should phone back to confirm with that he was not followed. He was then to load the sand and as instructed waited, for what he did not know.

From around the other side of the building appeared a black limousine two men got out showing police badges an asked him to open his van. Upon seeing the sand, they apologised and left. Heinrich had outwitted them. To Heinrich, it was just a game of chess.

On Sunday morning driving a large Mercedes he went alone, wearing jeans and taking all the necessary equipment to unpack the three pallets. He was unusually excited, he remembered as a nine-year-old taking his Christmas present to a secret place before opening it. Warehouse 105. What could be more exciting than secretly to own some of the most valuable pieces of art in the world?

He was not used to physical work and had some trouble removing, first the steel straps then jemmying the top of each wooden crate. He was sweating by the time he came to the bubble wrap probably covering the Modigliani painting.

At last, he pulled it out of the case, and carefully unwound the wrapping, but what he saw was something that a child of seven would not be proud of. He scrabbled into the crate to see if there was another painting. But nothing. Fear, and hatred welled up and he immediately attacked the next case. There must be a mistake, the real works must be in the other two pallets, he thought. And with fresh vigour he attacked the next pallet. Carefully pulling the bronze which was to be the Giacometti out of the case. Even whilst it was so carefully wrapped in bubble wrap he could see that it was as bad a statue as the previous painting, and what he received was an ugly replica of Mephistopheles made in cast iron. He reluctantly tackled the third pallet. There was supposed to be here a Chagall painting, which he had taken a particular liking to. But he now knew in advance that it would be some rubbish. The contents met his expectations. He'd been wrestling with these pallets for nearly three hours and this slap in the face was the final straw. "Who would do this to me?" He sat on the empty case and cried.

Leaving the pieces where they were he shut the door, left the key in the lock and returned to his vehicle. *These goods must have been swapped either at my house, at the freight company in Berlin, or here in Montevideo,* he thought, *but how would I find out without revealing my identity?*

He'd taken so much care to cover his tracks and now he would have to reverse the actions.

He returned home and immediately called his father. "Someone's playing a game with me sending me this junk, and there are only three points where it was possible."

"My advice to you son is to let it rest for the moment, they will have to reveal themselves in time, even if it is just to sell the pieces. Don't be rash – wait your time, Steffen. It's too dangerous to pursue."

"We can't just accept the loss of art worth millions, father, without making some attempt."

"I'll tell you what I'll do," his father replied. "I will check who handled the pieces from your house, and we can also check who packed the goods, but it has to be done very discreetly, remember you are claiming that you didn't have them in the first place. Were they packed professionally, or did they appear recently repacked?"

"What do you mean?"

"Had someone tampered with them?"

"No," Steffen replied. "It took me hours to unpack them."

"Then it's likely they were switched at the packers in Berlin, not at your home. Now, we must find out who they were. I'll find out, but don't do anything – do you hear? Don't do anything that will expose you!"

It was not too difficult to discover where the works of art were sent for packing. The transporting of art from various departments was a perk of the job and paintings were often taken off walls around the world and replaced by another work of consequence. So the name Gesh Speciality Transport soon emerged. The trick here would be not to seem too interested before accusing them of stealing.

Heinrich emailed his son to inform him that the packing firm was Gesh Speciality Freight, GMBH. Steffen stared at the reply hypnotised by the name. "My God, how many things can go wrong? That's Freda's husband! Of all the firms, we had to use him. I should have killed him at the same time, the swine. He's after me. It would be ironic if he was trying to get his revenge… I know his plan! He is trying to discover where I am. Well, I'll get there before him."

From old messages on his computer he found the man he was looking for. Yuri Mintov.

They exchanged greetings as if they were best of friends although neither of them had met.

"I have a little job for you, Yuri. A man in Berlin needs to meet his maker sooner than he expected. It's a simple job and worth fifty grand."

"Your jobs are never simple, Mr Steffen." he replied.

"I'm going to give you his address, but it is most important that you leave no tracks. The last job caused all sorts of problems."

Ignoring the last remark. "My fee is a hundred and fifty thousand, Mr Steffen, up front this time. You have too many problems on your head for me to wait for my money. But I can get someone to do this for you very quickly, you would pay him directly, he's a good man and knows Germany well."

"Why can't I pay you?"

"Because I'm in Argentina at this time."

"I don't want to pay a stranger in advance for obvious reasons."

"If you make it a quarter of a million I will do the job personally and collect from you after it's done. After all, we know each other, don't we?"

"You're a robber, Yuri, but I'll agree: we will arrange to meet when you return."

"No, my friend. If I am to murder on credit I must know where you live otherwise I have no security."

Steffen hesitated. He had to get rid of Gesh before he discovered where he lived. *It's only a matter of time. He already knows that I'm in Montevideo… if I kill Gesh I may never find the art, but at least he'd be out of the way.*

He gave Mintov his home address and arranged to meet him there with the money in Montevideo within four days. There was no chance that he would tell the police. *After all, he is a wanted man too,* he reasoned. All was agreed. "Contact me when the job is done."

Chapter 71

Mintov's journey from Buenos Aires to Berlin took over ten hours. It was a tedious amount of wasted time. It was not that he calculated his costs by the hour but with time changes that required him to be particularly alert in his line of work, he calculated that he would lose at least two days before he was ready to face his challenge. For this reason he always travelled first class and stayed in five-star hotels.

No detail was too small. He gathered maps of the local terrain and local buildings, details of the building he planned to enter and exit from google. Every aspect was catalogued, for there was no room for error.

He arrived in Berlin in the late afternoon and rented a car under a false name that matched a driving licence and passport. Booking into his hotel he relaxed for the rest of the evening. He had a picture of Gesh from a convenient web site of his company showing a photo of him behind his desk. The following morning was Wednesday. Leaving his car at the hotel, he rented a white van and changed into worker dungarees whose pocket displayed the logo of a major electric company, WE Einfach. He needed to see the layout of the Gesh warehouse and the position of Gesh's office. It was one thing to shoot someone but it had to be done with an escape route in mind.

Parking the van on the opposite corner of the road with a false moustache and soft worker's hat he walked to the main entrance and approached the secretary in the role of engineer. "According to our report you appear to be using far more electricity than last year. Is it possible to check your meters?" he asked the receptionist. She looked at his badge and small bag, that also bore the logo, and saw no reason to deny his request.

"By all means," she agreed.

"Where do you keep the meter?" he asked casually.

"I'll ask the manager."

She left him for a few moments. "It's in the back of the building, I'll take you there."

As he passed the main office he saw Gesh sitting with his back to the window, various staff were on the main floor pushing consignments into line for despatch. It was a small business and looked well run.

"Can I leave you to it?" she asked.

He played around with it for a few minutes then shut the meter door. "If it's convenient I would like to come back tomorrow morning to adjust it, the meter seems to be running too fast. If I speak with your boss, I will probably be able to halve your costs, will he be here in the morning?"

"Yes, I'm sure he will," she said innocently.

"Good, I'll bring the forms with me." He thanked her and left, and she saw him drive off in the white van.

The detective noticed something a little odd. He was wearing snakeskin shoes that must have cost at least seven hundred euros. "That's not an electrician," she whispered to her colleague. "Did he say he would return tomorrow?"

"Yes, how did you know?"

"Was his van labelled?" she asked.

"No, it was white."

"When you see him tomorrow, driving up on the external camera, tell me. Don't forget. It's very important."

The young amazon informed Gesh that his business had just been scanned, perhaps by his future assassin. "Tomorrow is the day. In the morning I'm bringing in a bullet proof jacket for you. Unless he drives here in a tank to shoot you, you'll be safe."

"Why didn't we arrest him?" he asked.

"Herr Gesh, you can't hang a man for a smell. Caught in the act means…doing it, and you are IT. It's up to you. You will literally be in the firing line but we will protect you."

"If you wish we can hide you and simply catch him with his gun, but he will live to fight another day. Or we can deal with him, if you know what I mean. It's your decision. If we were still in the police force we would have to hide you. How much do you want to get rid of this problem?"

"Let's just do it," he sighed.

**

Gesh and the two young women arrived early the next morning. They brought with them a waistcoat and asked him to put his jacket on over it. "The trouble with this type of situation is that we can never be sure where the shooter is aiming – ninety percent of the time it's to the chest but sometimes it's your arms or even your face. This man will be an expert, and will almost certainly aim for your heart."

"And what happens," replied Gesh, "if he aims for the head?"

"That's bad shooting," smiled the young woman.

At 10.45 am the following morning the receptionist could see from her TV as the van turned into the road outside, and quickly warned the young woman, who informed Gesh to remain seated behind his desk. There should be no one else with him. The rest of the staff were not informed of the expected drama, but it was clear that there was some excitement at the top, that something unusual was about to take place. Maybe a photoshoot. A cup of coffee was on his desk and he lifted to his lips but his hand was shaking so much it spilt.

Mintov stopped at the top of the road, He was putting on his moustache and preparing himself for the moment at hand. He removed his revolver and screwed on a silencer. After five minutes he drove to the other side of the road, turned his car round, and leaving his engine running he entered the premises.

"Guten morgen." He smiled.

"Guten morgen," she replied.

"May I go to the meter?" he asked. She nodded.

The two young women were stationed at the ready behind a stack of pallets. As Mintov was about to pass Gesh's office he quickly darted in, took his revolver out and was about to shoot when the ladies in unloaded their firepower in unison, hitting him at least six times. Mintov's gun sent a bullet into the heart of Gesh's vest. Gesh fainted and Mintov fell on the desk, coating it with blood.

Gesh soon came too but was in shock. His manager rushed over to him, traumatised. With the dead man on the desk – it had happened so quickly – and seeing his boss in a bullet proof suit, he realised that explanations would be forthcoming, but he couldn't contain his distress.

"How could you allow this man to be a bait for an assassin?" he yelled.

"We work to instruction and Herr Gesh wanted to goad this man to him. It was our job to deal with the situation accordingly, and we did. He was a professional but as you could see, so are we. Dealt with accordingly."

"But my friend could have been killed."

"He certainly would have been, left to his own devices. Once we understood how this man was going to handle the killing we had to take the initiative. This guy might have chosen to catch Herr Gesh as he came to work or at his home but we were lucky that he came as the electrician on this occasion. He probably used this ploy in the past. We saved Herr Gesh's life but of course there was a risk… as it happens we won and he very clearly lost, sir. Now let's see who he is, or was, before the police come."

They rummaged through his pockets but found very little of significance, and went to the van. His regular clothes were on the passenger's seat, and there they found his wallet and false passport, but his credit cards bore the name Mintov. There was also a piece of paper with an address... Heinrich's address! But the prize find was his mobile. Gesh quickly snatched both and put them in his pocket. He'd found out what he wanted to know.

The police were told that Rolf Gesh's wife had been murdered by contract and clearly he was on the list to follow her. The instruction came from Heinrich and this dead man was his contractor. Nothing was said relating to the consignments.

***

There was no point informing the police where Heinrich and his family lived. He had protection, but there was now an ever-growing list of those who wanted him dead or alive.

Gesh was in no state to work and was given a lift home by the two young women. It had been a most dramatic morning, and now that he was in possession of Heinrich's address he wondered what to do with it. He phoned Jack and told him what had happened, and that he had Heinrich's address and a mobile with some relevant emails.

"Well, we can assume that Heinrich would be expecting a report from Mintov to tell him that you have been bumped off. We don't want to email him that good news in case you get some awkward publicity in the papers as a result of today. So let's email him on Mintov's phone saying that I have had to delay the 'activity' due to local circumstances, and will let him know my progress in due course."

"If we are to bring Heinrich to court we need to get him to meet us where he has no political influence, but no fears about travelling.

"The chancellor is most keen to clarify the situation too. Let me speak with him. I'll tell him that we have the address in Montevideo but we're reluctant to call the police there as he's probably under their protection."

"According to his emails it seems that the assassin, Mintov, was going there to collect two hundred and fifty K," said Rolf. "I'm flattered to be worth so much."

Chapter 72
Germany

Chancellor Brandt phoned his friend Hans Grieff to see how the purchase of Spoken Arrow shares was progressing.

"You know of course that Magnum still have approximately twenty percent of the shares. They will come over to us when we sort out all the paperwork. We have managed to acquire eight percent of the company, if we were to join both purchases we have a total of thirty percent. Not that we can do much with the purchase at this time but at least we appear to have delayed them from getting it."

Brandt cogitated on his country's latest acquisition. "We have to conclude a deal with Jango Hampton and legalise the purchase soon, we don't need their shares. But they will help us persuade Hampton to work with us, and for his own good. We'd sell them back to him if he wanted over a period of time and even at a loss.

"We have an election in a few months, it would be fantastic if we can announce our agreement. If he decided he didn't want it we'd be in the shit, without a force to run it. I recommended Alfredo Montello to him but the ball's in his court. We would virtually change the poverty line throughout the world if we released that money. Think, Hans, what we could build. Hospitals, schools. Dams, power plants... eradicate poverty. There's no limit if we control it, and it's up to us. We need to show the world how to treat people like Heinrich. It's a package deal. By the way, where is he?"

"Last I heard, both father and son were in Brazil," said Hans.

"Without Heinrich under lock and key we only have half a story. I think we should place some pressure on our friends in Brazil and see if they'll cooperate. I know Davila Majuca in Brazil well enough to talk straight. The odds are that he has been well looked after by Heinrich and will need some persuasion to cooperate with us. Let's get him on the line." He instructed his PA to see when it would be convenient to set up a video meeting.

She returned ten minutes later. "In two hours. Is that all right, sir?"

They passed the formalities quite quickly, and Brandt came to the point. Listen, Davila, we have a problem. You know all about us confiscating Magnum, and Pontillo, which is worth countless billions, and we are giving its fortunes to worldwide charities."

"I know that, Herman, but what do you want from me in this regard?"

"We have an election coming up very soon and it would do us the world of good if we were able to announce the release of these monies. but to do this we need to find Steffen Heinrich, in other words we need your help. You know that we have a warrant for his arrest. Can you please help us?"

"To be honest, Herman, I haven't the faintest idea where he is. If I knew I would obviously tell you."

"Look, Davila, I know that you're good friends and all that, but we could do so much with this money if we put our minds to it. There's a lot riding on this, and if you can help us, I would consider that we would owe you a big favour."

"What favour?" he asked pensively.

"You name it: back door, front door, political or otherwise."

"German production in Brazil – Mercedes, can you fix that? And a spare one if possible!"

"The second part definitely, and I can certainly see what I can negotiate on your first half. With pleasure."

"Or a firm of similar calibre. We need quality factories, and it would help my standing too. See what you can do, and so will I, but time is of the essence, OK? Tomorrow maybe?"

"I'll see what I can do," he repeated. "But I'm looking forward to hear how you do too." Brandt immediately phoned the President of Mercedes.

"Henrique, I need a favour from you. I know that you're thinking of building a plant in Venezuela, but have you considered Brazil?"

"Herman, I wouldn't touch them with a barge pole, the place is riddled with corruption."

"I agree, but for the purpose of the exercise, an announcement that you may be considering building a plant in Brazil… without commitment at this stage, of course… would be very useful. You only have to consider the possibility, that's all. It would help me tremendously and, if I may say, ultimately you too. I can't say more but it would really help me and…I would appreciate it."

He heard a chuckle at the other end of the phone. "You're the total politician Herman. OK leave it to me. When for?"

"This week!"

"Mein Gott!" he laughed and hung up.

"Two days later the financial columns reported a statement from the president of Mercedes suggesting that Brazil, having a substantial population of middle to higher earners, would benefit from a local production plant in Brazil. A team would consider financial implications of Brazilian production of the latest electric cars that could possibly serve the South American market."

As soon as Brandt read the paper he phoned Davila. "I'm a man of my word, my friend. How are you doing?"

"All I can tell you, Herman, is that they have moved to Uruguay."

"Well, that's a start, and thank you for that, but it's not worth a production unit… a small car, maybe. Can you find out a little bit more?"

"I'll see what I can do, but my friend in Uruguay should be able to help. I'll tell you what, I'll give him a call. I want that Mercedes. And the production of course. You might have to open your goodies bag for him too. I will call him now and tell him that you want to speak with him as a matter of urgency. I'll call you back."

Twenty minutes later as promised he was able to tell Brandt that Fernando was waiting for his call. "I've softened him up for you. Remember production and Mercedes."

***

The two men had barely ever spoken to one another, even at international conferences. But they both led their countries with a degree of gravitas, and would leave a respectable legacy for the region if they weren't first assassinated. Nonetheless it was well known that that any president of a South American country would invariably exit their position considerably wealthier than when they entered.

"I have a good idea what you are wanting, Herman, but it's not the same here as it is in Europe; politicians scratch each other's backs here, and if it's not a scratch it's a dagger. Steffen Heinrich has been very helpful to me. The least I can do is reciprocate now that I have a chance."

"That's very commendable, Fernando, but the reality is that one way or another Steffen Heinrich has had it: The King is Dead, Long Live the King. This is a chance to do something important that will be appreciated… I mean really appreciated. Our election depends on it, and you are holding the ace here. Give your country something they really need. Go, make a wish. You never know!"

"I can't just destroy someone like that, Herman, I would not be able to live with myself."

"There is an international search out for him. He's had it, He has blood on his hands. He daren't raise his head above the parapet. Fernando I am asking you to save a government and you're trying to save a dead man. If we find him will you allow your police to arrest him and bring him back to Germany. You don't have to tell us exactly where he is, only the area. And for this I promise you a brand new two hundred bed hospital that you can tell your people that it's donated through your efforts, which we will confirm."

"When would you contribute this money for a hospital."

"No, we would design it and build it for you, and put it in your name. How's that."

He hesitated, wondering if he could have asked for a more before squeezing out his agreement.

"OK, if you find him you will have my permission to arrest him. but don't mention that I 've helped."

"I'm relying on you not to hide him or give him any hint that we are on his tail, is that fair."

"That's fair," Fernando conceded. "Two hundred beds plus a research lab!"

As Brandt finished his call his secretary informed him that Jack Branson was on the line with some very important news. "Put him through."

"We've found him."

"Well done," he replied. "If you had phoned me ten minutes earlier you would have saved me a two hundred bed hospital and a Mercedes," he chuckled.

***

Two days later four black sedans drove up to the Heinrich villa at 7.00 am. The door was answered by his wife in her dressing gown, but without explanation they marched into the bedroom where Steffen was still sleeping. They gave him a few moments to go into his bathroom leaving the door open, and the courtesy of dressing. They were instructed to hand cuff him and bundle him into the sedan that would take him directly to the airport accompanied with an officer and return to Berlin where they would await further instructions.

The international press was informed of his arrival and came out in droves. There was little that his father could do or say that had any influence on the reporters' imaginative accounts according to their publications. Chancellor Brandt was delighted that he was now able to conclude his takeover of Magnum and Pontillo complete with the criminal now incarcerated. He would tell the world that through him Germany could eradicate poverty and at last should be forgiven.

Chapter 73

Albert Heinrich sat alone in his office with head in his hands. He was a beaten man.

Through his great grandparents he had inherited a vast fortune and a business that, under his control became a Colossus. It was always accepted that the gods had ordained its destiny.

He picked up the phone to speak with Gilda and asked her to come over. It was still only 10.00 am but Heinrich had already gulped down two whiskies.

"I guess that you've heard the news about Steffen." She nodded.

"How could Brandt deny his country?" he confided "We are the forbearers of The Fatherland that had sacrificed so much, and to throw away the opportunity to reign supremely over the world. How could they misunderstand what civilisation is by simply pandering to the masses? We were offering a state of order. There is no plan to their lives other than transient and foolish pleasures. We could have brought about a unity of thought that would eliminate those that were genetically or rebelliously uncontrollable. Through the Autoplug we know every aspect of each individual, understanding their strengths, and their weaknesses, and passing this information onto Ever Young to identify and manipulate their talents."

"I blame you Uncle," Gilda replied. "It was ridiculous to give so much responsibility to Steffen, he was incapable of handling it. He threw it away."

"What else could I do, he is my only son, who else could I pass it onto, not you, a woman. How could you have controlled it? Any way it was you that decided to poison George Baylim, we could have taken control without killing the man."

"You can't blame me," she insisted, but she saw little point in debating it, "So, what will happen now?" she asked.

"I have organised to transfer one billion in assets from Pontillo, Alfredo has transferred it over to a new business before it could be frozen by the Nazis. And with the help of my friend President Majuca we are going to isolate South America from Spoken Arrow."

"Have we any other reserves?" she asked with more cynicism than Heinrich liked.

"No, but it should be sufficient to underpin the computer business and the Autoplug in Brazil. Ever Young doesn't need too much money as the Hospitals are all organised and prepared to take it into their programs. I have asked our Advertising Department to prepare a launch as soon as possible."

"And what about staff, will they stay with us, I understand that all staff will be paid by the German government until Spoken Arrow take over officially.

"We will get rid of all those that are working in the European department, but any staff related to the Brazilian market we will obviously keep."

"Spoken Arrow may try to take over the Autoplug locations here in Brazil. But without the servicing facilities they will be unable to maintain the business, we won't allow them into our business. Our cash flow will be covered by the Pontillo division organised by Alfredo."

"So we are going to fight the German and British governments plus Spoken Arrow. Uncle, I think you're mad. You have no chance, and all you'll do is squander the money on administration and advertising for them to pick up."

"What else is there to do?" he asked innocently. "We can secure our position with the help of most of the South American governments. The rest of the world can rattle their sabres as much as they like, but provided my friends are in my pocket they will back me."

"Uncle you are beaten. Sink into obscurity, vanish, you'll be lucky if they don't find something to drag you into the murders. Or do what the Fuhrer did."

"What's that?"

She simply shrugged, and he understood.

"I seem to recall that Steffen and you both had the Neuro351 injected into you before it was decided that we should direct it to the twenty-two to thirties."

"We did, we knew that it wouldn't do us any harm, you must admit that it was a rather clever marketing ploy to appeal to the youngsters, and it worked."

He picked up the phone once again. "Is Señor Montello back yet?" he asked his secretary.

"No, sir," she answered.

Gilda saw little reason to stay, and Heinrich filled his glass again.

492

Chapter 74

Alfredo Montello arrived back in Sao Paulo a man reborn. He had been totally converted by Jango and Martin Moran's ideals and was determined to start with a clean slate. No devious bank accounts, no hidden companies or plots to unravel the opposition. It was therefore a self-imposed decision for him to break his word with Heinrich and leave the one isolated Pontillo company to melt into the remaining group. "This money belonged to the world's poor and deprived." His wife's words rang in his ear. As one of the smallest of the Pontillo group, it values approximately two billion dollars and would have been quite easy to separate from the others, and anyway, he had sufficient to live a comfortable life, it was sheer vanity to accumulate monies that he did not need.

His more onerous task was to tell Heinrich that he was now working for Spoken Arrow. He rehearsed in his mind how he should present this fait accompli. Heinrich would have no future in Magnum or Pontillo as all assets would be passed back to the German government. He would advise Heinrich that he should leave with grace before he was forcibly removed.

Montello had not thought to mention Gilda, now Alicia, to his new employers and saw little reason to include her in the future plans of the company since she was formally dead.

Entering his office it seemed to be business as usual. Nothing had stopped and the fire that raged above the surface had not been reflected at the coal face of the operation.

His secretary informed him that Señor Heinrich had been phoning him twice an hour and was very keen to speak with him. She phoned Heinrich's secretary to inform her that Señor Montello would be there in fifteen minutes.

Heinrich immediately phoned Gilda and asked her to come to his office to hear what Alfredo had to say.

Having worked with Heinrich or under him for nearly thirty years Montello was not looking forward to the response he would receive. The Pharisaic manner by which he was controlled had become deeply ingrained. He had no problem in contradicting his superior but knew the final word would invariably be with Heinrich. In fact, he could not recall a time when he was given the last word. Even ideas originating from him were reiterated by his boss as if they were his own. But their relationship had now reached an impasse and for the first time he could dictate his own future.

He knocked and entered without waiting for an answer. He had no files nor his memo pad with him which had been part of his uniform but was a little surprised to note that Gilda was there.

Heinrich barely looked up. "I was expecting you to see me four days ago. What have you to tell me Alfredo, have you organised the Pontillo finance? We've formed the Brazilian company for the Autoplug and everything is now in position to advertise Ever Young. Talk to me."

Heinrich's discourteous acknowledgement only exacerbated Montello's response. "You know Albert, don't you think it would be nice, especially knowing that I am holding your future in my hands, to ask me how I am, where did I go? Did I have a good trip? Was it successful? Even dare I say an apology, maybe even a dash of humility for having thrown your problems at me."

"Why should I apologise, I'm paying you a fortune to look after the business, you work for me because I want you to, where else could you have so much kudos and responsibility? You love it. It's for you to bend a knee in respect. But this is no time to talk of peripherals, tell me what finances have we managed to secure."

"OK. I shall tell you your situation in three words Herr Heinrich. You are broke. You're broke," he sneered. "The last Pontillo company has been passed over to Germany with the others, I have not left you with a penny, If you have personal money I suggest that you hide it because I would like to believe that would be taken from you too. For my part, I am no longer working for Magnum and as of this moment I am an employee of Spoken Arrow."

Gilda had been sitting on the settee listening to both men attempting to draw each other's blood. She stood up and slowly walked over to Heinrich's side. "I suggest Uncle that you have Señor Alfredo Montello arrested for stealing and fraud. Do you have the telephone number of the Chief of Police." Heinrich looked at her in amazement. "Why?" he asked.

"Do it...NOW, for God's sake," she shouted.

Heinrich immediately picked up the phone and asked his secretary to get the Chief of Police. "Tell him to send to senior officers over to my office immediately," he said. And hung up.

"Do you honestly think that you will scare me with such nonsense," Montello chuckled.

"You are on the wrong side of the fence Alfredo," Gilda shouted. "We will concoct any number of claims against you until your name is used as a swear word, do you really believe that you can take over my uncle's empire simply by associating yourself with the competition. We will fight you with everything we can lay our hands on, and if you value the lives of your family I really think you should think again."

"Are you threatening me," he retorted. "My family…you have the gall to threaten my family, is this how you are going to conquer the world, how many do you think you will have to kill before you achieve your objectives?" He moved towards her as Heinrich opened his desk and removed a revolver, and aiming at Montello he pressed the trigger.

Montello fell to the floor, blood pouring from his shoulder.

Hearing the noise his secretary entered to see Heinrich with a Lugar P08 gun in his hand standing behind his desk. She immediately ran over to where Montello was lying. Without another word she went to Heinrich's phone and called for an ambulance.

Montello was still conscious but unable to raise himself from the floor.

"He was about to attack Alicia," Heinrich bumbled.

"With what?" she asked looking around for an implement. "He has to go to a hospital, he's losing too much blood."

Two police entered, and seeing a man bleeding on the floor, asked what had happened.

Gilda immediately told the policeman that he had tried to attack her and fortunately the President managed to forestall him.

"It seems a little dramatic, was he armed?" he asked.

"We didn't know if he was, but he could have been," she replied unconvincingly.

The policeman directed his words to the secretary, "Did you see what happened?"

"No, officer, I heard the shot and immediately ran into Señor Heinrich's office where I saw him with the gun in his hand and Señor Montello on the floor bleeding. I called for an ambulance. I hope that it will be here soon."

Heinrich was still holding the gun, and the officer took it from him and wrapped it in a cloth. "I'm afraid I must ask you to come to the station with me, Señor Heinrich"

"Are you arresting me?" he asked as if surprised that such a man as he would be treated as a commoner. "Do you realise who I am, I'm the President of this company and know your commissioner. You're making a big mistake."

"Sir, you have just shot a man and seriously wounded him, even you must realise that's against the law."

His colleague immediately handcuffed him and marched him out. The secretary followed. As they passed the outer offices the staff looked on in amazement. In the other direction arrived the Ambulance men.

Gilda was left in the office alone. If it was her initial intention to humiliate Alfredo Montello, her plans to do so were now in ruins. She went to Her Uncle's computer, logged her code into it and looked for Albert Heinrich's Ever Young code. It did not take too long before she found his file. She saw that he had been side tracked on a heart complaint and Diabetes. He was sixty-five years old. She meticulously entered the decease code.

Albert Heinrich was dead before they arrived at the station. Ever Young had claimed its first death.

She then looked for Steffen Heinrich's code, and was about to repeat her action, but decided to let him suffer a little longer.

She sat once again on the settee and considered her position. She clearly could not expose herself to the world, In fact since her new identity now had little value in either Europe or the Americas she would certainly be exposed in a trial relating to the shooting…unless she vanished. She was not short of funds for Steffen had paid her well for her shares in the formation of the Autoplug, and most important she held the secret of Ever Young. She returned to her apartment packed her belongings and booked a flight to Austria under her new name where she would find her old friends.

On examination of the gun, it was noted that it was an antique and had been kept in its leather holster in meticulous condition. Its inscription read: *From Field Marshal Hermann Goring to my friend and colleague Schultz Schickerdanz with sincere thanks for your amazing contribution towards our ultimate goal. 15th June 1940. HEIL HITLER.*

Heinrich's death and the surrounding incident made immediate headlines. His funeral drew admirers from around the world. Montello had no reason to attend but thirty years of 'slavery' drew him back. Maybe it was his way of ensuring that he was finally gone. It was fortunate that the shot was only a flesh wound and he took a certain pleasure from the injury. The press had made him a hero. It was officially announced that under the Spoken Arrow organisation he would be appointed by Spoken Arrow as chairman of Magnum.

Chapter 75

Chancellor Brandt decided to place the Spoken Arrow shares that he had inherited back on the stock market, and by virtue of the amalgamation of Magnum into Spoken Arrow, the shares increased by thirty percent which added a further twenty billion to the pot.

He would take full political advantage of the eighty billion dollars from Pontillo, plus a further sixty billion to be paid By Spoken Arrow over ten years for the purchase of Magnum. Such a bulk sum had never been allocated to charity before and the media justifiably named it Conscience Money. He decided to form a committee comprising of twelve countries that would advise where it could be best put to use. He was aware that many of the country's most in-need were controlled by despots. However, hospitals, educational facilities, climate control, and of course abject poverty around the world were all listed and the spending of it would be overseen strictly by an international committee.

Brandt considered where he might make his official announcement, and after careful consideration with his ministers it was decided that he would officially present what would be a groundbreaking statement to introduce an international committee in Israel which seemed the right place to apologise for its history.

Heads of governments and religions from across the world were invited. Jack received a formal invitation from Brandt to speak on the presentation stage. Dr Peter Ellsworth, Mr Jango Hampton, Señor Alfredo Montello. Miriam, Martin and Mrs Steinberg were also to attend as honoured guests.

Chapter 76
Epilogue

As all stocks and materials were passed over to Spoken Arrow, and as Miriam gained her strength she was given the task of the transition and found herself valuing the vast collection of art that had been acquired by the Heinrich family who had spread them in various offices around the world. Heinrich's desire to bring art to his employees would seem at first glance to be out of character, but it was a desperate need to prove their superiority not only by the precision of their business but to emphasise their 'Arian' intellectual status. Jango continued the company tradition but included his own offices into the system and passed the ownership onto the Guggenheim Museum.

Rolf still had the three unmarked pallets relating to the Hines collection. He called Jack to ask him what he should do with them.

It was not difficult to discover the insurance company that had put a figure of half a million dollars for their recovery.

It was inevitable that Jack would marry Miriam and they had three children. Martin found a common spirit with Mrs Steinberg who eventually retired from her firm and spent six months of the year in California.

***

History has proven time and time again that we will never eradicate evil, but we must fight for our right to overcome it by whatever means we have. Our ultimate heroes were without doubt Jack and finally Chancellor Brandt who cleansed the world of one of the most dangerous and destructive schemes of our civilisation without any personal gain.

***

The Autoplug was a great success with Spoken Arrow and within the four years that followed it generated a turnover per annum of over twenty billion dollars throughout the western world and provided an annual bonus for the Cambridge University of over forty million pounds.

Neither Miriam nor Jack confided in the Auto Plug ever again or took advantage of its intermate knowledge of them.

Sadly, Peter Ellsworth passed away. It was said that he had cancer of the lungs. It was generally considered to be as a result of his smoking, but Jack had his doubts. A statue of both Ellsworth and Baylim working together was placed in the Cambridge grounds as the inventers of the Autoplug. Nothing was mentioned of Ever Young.

Two years later a certain Madam Alicia Teretski was photographed in the leading Russian national paper Pravda introducing Khoroshaya Zhizn (Good Life) into health centres throughout Russia. It was picked up by Brandt's PA and passed to him as a matter of interest. She translated the article that described the equivalent of the Autoplug. Madame Teretski was also now heading the launch of the Kogdalibo Molidoy (for Ever Young). It read: *Do you want to live a life without fear of illness to the age of 95 years without sickness?*

Less than one year later similar announcements were displayed on Chinese billboards across the land, followed by North Korea.

Martin spent the rest of his years being happily dominated by Hermione Steinberg who retired from her practice but retained her position as consultant to the British government and spent six months of the year in LA.

Over thirty thousand Magnumites were registered in Brazil. They were placed on the Russian info listings and constant communications encouraged them to lean towards Russian sympathies. Many found a great need to learn Russian and were noted to be closely marked as sympathisers by their respective governments. Ever Young was tested for children in the UK but good diet and healthy living proved equal to the Ever Young claims.

The rights to Ever Young were retained by the British government.

The End

***

List of Main Characters

George Baylim (neuroscientist)

Gilda Baylim (aka Alicia Troupe. Wife of George)

Bonham (Solicitor of Joe)

Judith Bracknell (Secretary to Pickles)

Herman Brandt (German Chancellor)

Jack Branson (journalist)

Barbara Brenekov (daughter of Bill)

Bill Brenekov (Joe's father)

Joe Brenekov (Bill's son)

Pauline Brenekov (wife of Bill)

Peter Brenekov (Joe's uncle)

Julius Brevotti (Miriam's brother)

Miriam Brevotti (Spoken Arrow)

Terrance Dole (MD. UK Spoken Arrow)

Charlie Donn (Friend of Joe)

Peter Ellsworth (Doctor, Cambridge University)

Brody Emmitt (Editor)

Jane Franklyn (Prime Minister's secretary)

Helga Franz (Swiss student)

Freda Gesh (personal Secretary to Herr Heinrich)

Rolf Gesh (Husband of Freda)

Hans Grieff (Minister of Economy Germany)

Jango Hampton (President Spoken Arrow)

Jay Harrari (Head of Neural Interface for Spoken Arrow)

Albert Heinrich (President of Magnum)

Steffen Heinrich (Vice President of Magnum)

Henry Hines (Health Minister)

Sir William Hoddington (Dean and chancellor of Cambridge)

Derek Horrocks (MI5)

Fernando Inodoro (President of Uruguay)

LeClare (Swiss dealer)

Robert Levinson (Neuroscientist Spoken Arrow)

Davila Majuca (President of Brazil)

McCrow (Insurance)

Alfredo Montello (Financial Adviser to Heinrich)

Angela Moran (Wife of Martin)

Martin Moran (Vice president and Marketing Director of Spoken Arrow)

Mintov (Professional Assassin)

George Pickles (Chancellor of Exchequer) PA Jane Franklyn

Pontillo Investments (Ex. Freudenberg)

Sir Henry Porter (Solicitor. Spilling Mandel)

Stuart Russell (Labour leader)

Schickerdanz (Previous family name of Heinrich)

Herr Schmidt (German Ambassador)

Herr Schreiber (Lawyer to Heinrich)

Paul Shannon (M.D.) UK Magnum)

Victor Shaw (Senior Partner Coal Dean Lawyers)

John Spinetti (Head of Legal Spoken Arrow)

Hermione Steinberg (Barrister)

Brendon Tann (Health Minister)

Alex Winter (Conservative Prime Minister)